I0749261

Rend

Rend

A Novel

Annette I. Smith

This book is a work of fiction. Names characters, places, events and incidents either are the product of the author's imagination or are used fictitiously and are not to be construed as real. Any resemblance to actual persons, living or dead, or actual events is entirely coincidental.

Cataloging-in-Publication Data is on file with the Library of Congress

Published in the United States by Ione Publishing

First Edition: December, 2012

ISBN 978-0-98304262-4

IP

Ione Publishing
P. O. Box 21357
Brooklyn, NY 11202
Visit our Website at www.annetteismith.net

Dedicated with pride and honor to:

My Ancestors, Ancestral Guides, and Griots

All who came, whispered in my ears, guided, and

Are still guiding me through

This beautiful labyrinth called Rend

Ashe! Ashe!

Richard Anthony Smith

My son beloved, and child of my heart,

The very best "Collector" of his

Gran Gran Irene Margaret Smith's

**gold nothings*

And

Phenix Ezekiel Cohen – grandson

The Keeper of his Gran Gran Annette's heart

Ashe! Ashe!

*My mother's way of getting Richard to do her bidding—she promised him that at the completion of each 'task', she'd give him a gold nothing. It took Richard 'till he was about ten years old to figure out that there was nothing for him to get. After that, he would say to her, "I know, Gran-Gran, you're going to give me a gold nothing."

Contents

Acknowledgements

Baba Collin Leroy Carter (*Last Boy*) — I'm thankful for many wonderful and amazing gifts in my life, but there are some gifts I feel truly inadequate to fully express thanks for. The gift of your friendship is one of them. The way you shared your passionate spirit, attitude, and approach to life, the myriad ways you taught me how to truly live one moment at a time, your endless passion, vision, and quest when it comes to the liberation of our people, and the way you shared your knowledge of our history are but a few of the gifts you've so unselfishly given to me, and for them I'm eternally grateful.

Thank you for every life challenge you presented to me and your refusal to let me back down from any of them. I understood and clearly that challenges were for you those things you took by the horn and didn't turn loose until they resolved. Having your spiritual as well as physical presence on this leg of my journey has been a blessing. My heart rejoices in knowing you. Ashe!

Richard Anthony Smith — My First Edition, One-of-a-kind, Leather-bound, Hard Cover, Pulitzer-Prize-Winning "book". Chapter 1, first paragraph: "Bold and brazen, he lifts her skirts and pursing his lips he blows a bitter and biting breeze against her sandaled and naked thigh. She shudders. Unable to move, she stands still as he wraps his cold hands tighter around her and the rest of the city. It's January 4, 1979 and winter, cold, unfeeling and with a heart of ice, has decided that the grand lady with her torch and the city she watches over should be chilled to the core. He blows his hardest but she doesn't flinch; inside there's a warm glow in her heart because she knows that across town in Bedford/Stuyvesant, Brooklyn, one of her adopted daughters, a child of the Diaspora (Barbados), has just been blessed with a son beloved; you.

Thank you for always being encouraging, supportive, and believing that I could do this: write. Thank you for constantly saying, "Mom, I had a great childhood, thank you." That touches me to my core and it says to me that somehow without a Parenting Handbook, I'd figured out and gotten some things correct. Thank you for being accepting and understanding that I was doing the best I could to give you the best I could. Your amazing sense of humor made the journey a lot easier and the empathy you showed when your beloved Smokey passed on November 21, 2012 touched me deeply. Your text messages to me that day said, "I'm thankful for the time I had with her. A stray cat that found a home in my heart," showed me the depth of your character and your ability to love…yes…even a stray cat named Smokey (RIP Smokey)

Zenoebia Asia Washington-Cohen—my daughter beloved, and child of my heart. If there was a way to love you more, I would. If there was another way to say daughter and always have your image manifest before my eyes, I would say it. If there was another way to say you are the epitome of what a daughter should be and is, I would say it but since there is no other way to say all these things, I'll say it the way I've been saying it all these years, "Noebie." Thank you and Tony for the beautiful gift of 'my baby, my baby, my baby – Phenix Ezekiel Cohen.' I will never forget the joy of holding him for the first time.

Isaiah Leo Smith — my youngest nephew and so far my mother's 'last' grandchild, your presence in my life is such a heartfelt joy. Each time you 'struggled' when you were learning to talk to say "Auntie Annette" touched me deeply. Those two words gave you 'hell' to say together, but you were determined to say them so you never gave up. I'm smiling now as I remember your first trip (age 2) to Sesame Place and your joy and excitement as you 'told' me about it. I have to confess now that all I ever understood was "Elmo"; after that I was lost. God bless your mom (Chris "Angela" Smith) for being so well versed in *Isaiah* she could 'interpret' for me all that you were saying.

James Lovell – My friend, thank you for your bravery to travel through a thousand lifetimes so you can be my guide on my journey to knowing who I am. Thank you for your willingness to teach me about my lost heritage. (Garifuna*) Numada, seremein niyan bun lau bubafu lun bafayahan aban milu ibagari lun guaran lan biabi lun badundehanina lun nasubudiragun nunguwa. Seremein niyan bun lun bidaragunina lun barufudahani luragate nirasan nu.*

Vida McWhite (Lil' Sis) — For every time you listened, made me laugh, shared your amazing poetry, cared for, and loved August as if she were your own dog, and demonstrated what a true kindred spirit is, I am deeply touched. Thank you for being a beautiful little sister and for being obedient to your spirit. Keep your head always in the celestial, your heart in the spiritual, and your feet firmly planted on the Ancestral.

The Honorable Lennox Price, Consul General of the Barbados Consulate New York, Linda Watson-Lorde & Team Barbados – For your generosity and professionalism as you hosted the launch/reception for my debut novel ***Etched***. Your continued kindness is forever Etched in my heart.

Michael Thompson – Thank you for your continued unconditional love and support. I don't know if there's anyone who can love me any more than you do. I love you back unconditionally and appreciate every day and time you listened over the years and into today. Thank you for sharing ***Etched*** with all those that you love and hold dear.

Emir Pehilj – From the first day we met, you opened your heart and made a very comfortable space in it for me. You are an amazing man with warmth, compassion, and a deep love and I'm so glad that you've allowed me to share in it. I love you back.

Kemit Imani (Josie Carter) and all the powerful women of **PowerSis** – thank you for being the first European Book Club to select my first novel ***Etched*** as your book club read. You were also my first Skype book read. I truly enjoyed reading and sharing with all of you. Kemit what an amazing pleasure it was to finally meet you when you visited New York in October, 2012.

Richard D. Piggott – You listened when I needed a friend. Cared when the entire world felt like it was falling in, and when it did fall in and down, you came and found me in the rubble. Though my life has been no fairytale, you've been my own Sir Lancelot. Your presence in my life is appreciated.

Rudolph Carter – an amazing Griot. Your storytelling ability is spell-binding and your sense of humor, unmatched. I'm so very glad to know you.

Theresa Carter – Many months ago while I was in Barbados, you shared a beautiful story with me about the leaf from the *wonder of the world* plant. I can tell you now you were right. I tried it; the leaf grew.

All my English teachers at **Parkinson Secondary School**, Barbados, who instilled in me a passion and love for writing that, to date, is still unquenchable.

Foreword – Baba Collin Leroy Carter

I first met Annette I. Smith shortly after she published her first book *Etched.* In reading *Etched,* I was convinced that it was non-fiction; it read so realistically. I often had the feeling as if I were an observer to history. *Etched* spoke of the women of Greenwood and the inhumane treatment the whites imposed on the enslaved; not only of Greenwood but throughout the Diaspora.

Rend continues the rollercoaster and gut-wrenching ride from where *Etched* ended. It reveals how slavery impacted the thinking of the enslaved whereby affecting their deeper image of themselves. Readers of both *Etched* and *Rend,* like the black women in the former, should understand the need to make sacrifices, to dream, and not give up until those dreams are realized.

Rend forces the reader to stop and ponder many poignant questions. For me it was, "What happens when you control a person's thinking by slavery, brutality, and the breaking down of the family unit?" The answer was simple; you won't have to worry about that person because you've enslaved their mind and broken their spirit. That individual will find their proper place based on the oppressor's expectations of him or her. That phenomenon is most adequately expressed in Milkweed's undying love for her slave master Fields.

Today we can clearly see that the legacy of slavery, which was so brilliantly captured in the pages of *Rend* continues. When read with deep thought, Rend, even though horrifying yet at times comical, touches the integral parts of most conscious Black persons. It reminds us that after 400 years of oppression, the African's deeply engrained spirit of survival is alive despite the attempted annihilation of our language, culture, and belief in our self.

Since reading *Etched,* I've embarked on a quest to rediscover the lost part of my history; the Barbadian/Carolina connection. This has given me the continued drive to reconnect with the broken segment of the

African history and heritage which we have lost as a result of white domination.

Both *Etched* and *Rend* will form part of a cumulative body of work that tells *'OUR STORY' and* constantly reminds us that to lack our cultural, historical, and knowledge of self is the first step to the destruction of our people. I'm truly proud and highly honored that Annette I. Smith asked me to write the foreword for *Rend.*

Baba Collin L. Carter
London, England

Rend

To tear something apart: to pull something apart violently, or be pulled apart violently.

To tear or pull clothes or hair, out of rage, frustration, or grief.

To take somebody or something away forcibly.

To tear or wrest something or somebody away.

To shatter something: to disturb the silence or pierce the air with a loud sound, or

To distress somebody: to cause pain or distress to the heart or emotions.

Ecclesiastes 3:7

A time to ***rend***, and a time to sew
A time to keep silence and a time to speak (KJV)

Prologue

The best place for blame, I've always heard, is at the feet of the person it belongs to. This is where I am in my life. Looking for the feet and not just any feet, but the right feet to put the curse that has, for almost one hundred years, followed the women of my family and is now, because I'm female and part of this family, following me. I don't want it behind me. I want it where it belongs; at the feet of its owner.

Who is the owner? Was it my great-great-great-great-great-grandmother Milkweed; yes, that's her real birth name, with her mixed-up head over a white man; her master and father of her eleven or was it twelve children who birthed it into our family? Does this mean because she'd given birth so many times, that she birthed the curse into the family? Can we then place it at her feet for that reason? All these questions have gone unanswered forever. Why? Fear and our refusal to accept some unchangeable truths about life and love: as long as you are living, you yearn for love.

These truths started that life-changing night before President Abraham Lincoln signed the Emancipation Proclamation Bill and continued to unveil itself the morning after. For a long time, we, the Daughters of Greenwood, believed that she was the one who actually caused the curse to come into our lives. The truth, real truth, one we could finally accept and live with would come years later, but by the time we figured out who was truly responsible for the curse, it was too late; the curse had already claimed many of the women in this family.

It's true that when the sun rose that morning, Milkweed, my six or seven times removed grandmother, was unaware that she would do something other than what she'd always done: go to the cookhouse and make her master and father of all but one of her children his breakfast. She had no idea that before the sun rose fully in the sky, she would break the promise she'd made so long ago to her mother, and by doing so, start the germination process of the curse.

The promise was this: she would remember what they'd endured and she would let nothing come before freedom and book learning. Nothing was ever to come before those two. She'd promised faithfully, but then she didn't know that a white man named Everett Fields was on a head-on collision with her life. This collision would bring with it death, destruction, and the seed to the curse.

At some point during the night of December 31, 1862, she would accepted that she no longer saw Everett Michael Poole Fields as her master but as the man she loved and had far longer than she was willing to admit. At this realization, she forgave him his many sins, and God knows they were many. She also looked past his wickedness, which exceeded his sins. She surrendered her mind, body, and soul totally to him. As he caressed and entered her body, she freed her heart of a hatred that should never have been unbound.

It was right there, in that split-second, as the vibrations of his name was screamed so guttural that it shattered the exhausted silence of the plantation and reverberated in her belly, that she knew. As the last syllable of his name came to rest on the edge of her lips, bruised by his hungry and ardent kisses, the hate she'd felt for him dissipated. The intensity of what she felt scared her. She knew but didn't want to admit what it was. Looking at him, she saw the same intense love looking back at her as he smiled with the knowledge that she loved him too. As he softly and lovingly caressed her, she languidly drifted off to sleep. Her questioning mind wondered where her hatred could be, but she didn't dwell on it or allow her mind to linger because all she knew now was that a great and truly deep love stood in its place.

Unbeknownst to her, it was this shattering love that by the dawn of the first day of 1863 would make her cry. It was these tears she would use to fill the proverbial line she drew in the sand. This line was so deep, it would become a ravine separating faith and fear, hope and helplessness, sorrow and joy, and most of all, freedom and bondage. It would take the Daughters of Greenwood almost ten generations to fill this ravine back in and seal it shut once and for all.

As she stood on her side of the yet uncreated ravine, other deep guttural and throaty sounds reached her ears. The sounds weren't coming from either of their throats. This time these groans of passion were coming from the throats of slaves. A different kind of pleasure was its impetus. It comes to her ears as alive, real, and as raw as the cries that emanated from their throats the night before, reminding her of how they had joined in a scream of total and intense surrendering of emotions and passion. The difference between their earth-shattering screams and the screams they were hearing was that slave after slave was singing their freedom song. The same song she'd sung when hatred for him had fueled a hope eternal in her heart and had kept her alive. The slave in her responded to the pulsing rhythm. A yearning to answer; to join in this unified pulsing coursed through her entire being.

She moved towards the call…she was after all a slave and a call to freedom this pure demanded a response. She made it to the threshold of her cabin where she watched, listened and felt the excitement. She felt a welling up in her belly again, but this time it wasn't passion stirred by him. It was fear and uncertainty…what should she do? One step in either direction would mean certain changes in her life. One step outside meant freedom, wrought with fear and uncertainty but it would be the fulfillment of a promise made to her mother so many years ago. A step back inside her cabin meant emotional bondage. As she stood contemplating her next move, slaves were rejoicing and rushing around and past him as he too stood and watched. He was on the brink of a different threshold.

As they listened, an understanding for all the chaos mixed with rejoicing fell from the air and revealed itself: President Abraham Lincoln had done what he'd promised. He had signed the Emancipation Proclamation Bill, setting all the slaves in the Union free. She, like all slaves on all plantations, would be free if she could only make that step. She stood in her hurriedly thrown on dress, with one bare foot firmly planted on the dirt outside her cabin, where she'd stepped to see the reason for all the commotion. Her other foot, because she hadn't completed her step, was lightly resting in a "waiting and ready" stance on the floor of her cabin. She had to make a decision: in which direction should she complete that one step?

Should she take her lightly-resting foot from the floor of her cabin and bring it to join her firmly-planted foot in the dirt outside her cabin; the one pointed towards freedom, and move like all the other slaves towards this newly granted freedom? Or she should she take that firmly planted foot, the one pointed towards freedom, up from the dry dirt outside her cabin and bring it to rest beside her now slightly trembling, lightly-resting foot inside her cabin?

She contemplated her moves: the step back inside would mean just that: back into emotional slavery. If she took her slightly trembling, lightly-resting foot off the floor of the cabin and brought it to rest outside the cabin, she would be able to join the now-free slaves, including her one true friend, Neala, as they headed toward the great unknown called freedom.

She stood still, straddling the threshold of her future, paralyzed with fear and uncertainty. It was a step she knew she could and had to make and yet deep in her heart, she was momentarily unable to make it. He was watching her. He knew, before she made the slightest move, which foot was going to move and where it would bring her. He waited.

Her body started trembling. She wanted to but she couldn't make that step because she'd allowed her heart to do the unimaginable. She thought what her friend Neala would say. She knows. Neala was going to tell her that she'd done the worse thing a nigger woman could ever do. She had allowed mixed up feelings over a white man, but not just any white man: a slave owner and her master, to come before her promise to her mother.

Uncertain which side of the threshold to step towards, she looked at the other slaves as they giddily prepared to walk behind the soldiers towards freedom. She closed her eyes for a moment. When she opened them, she fixed them on him and with her eyes focused firmly on him and only him, she moved her foot. Standing every so temporarily on one leg, she trembled as the full weight of what she was doing made her light-headed, slightly dizzy and even more mixed up. Her foot moved quickly, but to her heart beating so rapidly that it was making her feel more than slightly dizzy, it felt as if it was taking a thousand years to complete the journey. The foot came to rest. She had made her decision.

Her heart continued to beat rapidly, her legs were unsteady. An unexpected coldness enveloped her as she heard a sound unlike any she'd ever heard before. It was coming from near and around her feet. Taking her eyes away from him, she looked at her feet and saw the source of the sound. It was the shattered fragments of a broken promise mingled with a mother's disappointment. The fragments of that shattered promise spread and filled the cabin like moss on a river rock. She looked and she saw it as it spread and covered everything in the cabin. It had made its way to the wrinkled and damp heap of bed clothes on the bed where they'd spent the night intertwined and wrapped so deeply physically and emotionally into each other that they had indeed become one. The hearth was quickly covered; there would never be warmth from that again; the coldness covered the table, her one chair, and all that was in the cabin.

The fragments of that shattered promise and dreams huddled together, coagulating and becoming dark and sinister. The thick dark mass came to rest at her feet. It moved silently and stealthy up and into the very place where he had entered and his children had exited. Coming to rest in her womb, it attached itself to the seedling root of the family tree where it would follow her and us, her future generations for years. It would follow and stay until a woman in this family fulfilled her mother's dream of education, which she knew would finally bring about true freedom for the women in her family.

For this reason if for no other, it would seem fair that this curse was Milkweed's and yet it couldn't be named after her. It had to be named after the one that had come barreling into her life with an unnamed yet insatiable evil and sinister hunger: Everett Michael Poole Fields. It was he, plantation owner and as much as this family didn't want to admit, our great-great-great-great-great-grandfather, who was responsible for turning this curse loose on us.

You would think that the women in this family who knew they were under the tarnished glow of a cursed halo would, knowing better, do better. None of them did, and so, though not intending to, I didn't either. I did like all the other women in my family. I saw the tarnished glow of the halo, heard the music that summoned me, and through the haze of the tarnished glow, a dance partner invited me to dance. Believing him to be some kind of guide towards a fairytale future, I followed him onto the proverbial dance floor of life.

The smell of sulfur trailed behind him as he walked away following our passionate and, to me, fire-fueled tango. Had I not been so caught up in his stallion-like walk or the way his mane-like hair hung down his back when he approached me, I would have recognized him. When he said his name was H. A. Des, I should have caught on, recognized him, and at first chance, with one clean blow chopped his god-damned split hoof off the minute he'd extended it towards me.

As he stood momentarily shocked, I would have then ever so casually sauntered slowly away and back to the wall, where I and all the other wallflowers were leaning, dancing, and pretending that we didn't care no one was asking us to dance until he'd approached me and made me an instant celebrity in our non-descript, mostly-ignored group by asking me to dance. With my back once again safely against the wall, I would have continued the slow sultry grind I was doing before he showed up and interrupted it and me. I really wouldn't care who in the room might be watching me, knowing what I'd just done.

From there, I would've watched him when, in shocked panic, he tried with his other equally split hoof to pick up his other appendage, now on the floor pouring out his royal blood. I also would know that for him, it wouldn't be as impossible a task as the one he'd handed to the women of my family so long ago. We'd tried, and most times unsuccessfully, to pick up the charred remains of our sulfur-and-brimstone-burnt lives; the results of dancing one too many dances with him. I would also know that once he picked up his severed limb and re-attached it, thereby staunching the flow of the sulfuric blood burning holes into the dance floor, there would be no forgiveness in his heart for me. That's if he had a heart.

For just about one hundred years now, the women of my family have been trying to avoid dancing with him. We dodged, bobbed, and weaved, but ultimately we all did the same thing. We stretched out our hands and accepted the same reincarnate, split-hooved dance partner: Hades, Beelzebub, Belial, Lucifer…none of the names he'd used over the years mattered. It all came down to the same thing: none of us had yet learned how to refuse his dances.

This dancing had torn us. None had escaped and now, like most, if not all the women in my family, I was holding onto his split hoof. I was dancing and I was torn. I wasn't torn like my great-great-great-great-great-great grandmother Cornbread. She was torn between freedom and finding her daughter, who was trapped in the very bowels of slavery. She chose freedom.

I wasn't torn, like my great-great-great-great-great-grandmother Milkweed, Cornbread's daughter. She was torn between the love of her master and freedom. She chose her master.

Nor was I torn like my great-great-great-great-great grandmother Charlotte, Milkweed's daughter. She was torn between being bound to life on a plantation with her mother or the hope of being the mistress of a plantation owner on a neighboring plantation. She chose hope and lost everything.

Nor was I like my great-great-great-grandmother Neala, Charlotte's daughter. She was torn between being a free spirit and leaving not just Fields' plantation but South Carolina altogether or staying and seeing 'bout her great-grandmother's sister, her Auntie Beccah, as everyone that her Auntie Beccah loved was either dead or gone. She chose being bound to her Auntie Beccah.

Nor was I like great-grandmother Etta Pearl, Neala's daughter. She was torn between her daughter and a chance at a Happy-Ever-After. She chose Happy-Ever-After; the "Ever-After" part didn't happen. She was happy, but more than a few years short of Ever-After.

Nor was I like grandmother Gina Pearl, Etta Pearl's daughter. She was torn between trying to find a new love and a thin slice of happiness she'd heard other people talk about, and working hard and then a little harder than that to carve out a future for her daughter. She chose hard work and carving out that future for her daughter.

Nor was I like my mother, Lilly, Gina Pearl's daughter. She was torn between living with us (my brother, Daddy, and I) and our love for her, or dying because she couldn't live without her momma and her momma's love. She chose dying, leaving us to live with our love for her but without her.

The way I was torn was more like a physical tearing. I'd just given birth. Love didn't create this baby and so love didn't help me push her out into the world. As I went through the throes of labor, I understood a little better what had happened to the women of my family. Pain would do that; clear your mind. As my pain-filled mind cleared I understood that I had some of the pieces, but not all. I had no idea where those missing pieces would come from. Ignorance, blissful or otherwise, can do that to you. In my blissful state I didn't spend a lot of time thinking about it.

A few days however after I came home from the hospital with the baby who had torn me, and I was having the most difficult time thinking of as my child far less as a daughter my life changed. Those missing pieces of my family's life came to me; you could say to my doorstep. As I listened, the word torn faded from my mind and was replaced by a different word. It meant basically the same thing, but the impact was much different. By the time the telling of the story ended, the word would be Rend.

Rend took me back. Back to my bible, well, Nana's bible. It took me back to Field's plantation, to Breckenshaw's plantation, to Greenwood, South Carolina, and most importantly, it took me back to myself. It was there, with this child that I would start my forward journey to understanding what it meant to be a daughter of Greenwood, a descendent of a Seminole Indian and a Mandinka warrior.

Book One

Andrea Matti Hirsh Greenwood

A Time to Rend

Chapter 1

Torn

Andrea Matti Hirsh Greenwood

The dance was over and with a child in my hand, I was trying to figure out what I'd fallen into. It was the ravine created the day my great-great-great-great-great-grandmother Milkweed cried her heart out before she stepped back into her cabin because she knew the step she would take before she took it. After having cried her eyes out, she took her foot and drew a line in the sand when she decided to give up her chances at following freedom to follow love instead. Had she not felt so tied to him and had simply kept her promise to her mother, I wouldn't be trying to dig myself out of some un-nameable hole as I braced myself for an unenviable climb up the side of this blasted, ragged, rugged mountain called hard life with a child tethered to me. A child that even though right now is quiet, not asleep, just quiet, I can feel isn't going to make one step of this journey easy for me.

As much as I didn't want to, I had to remember that just like me and all Greenwood women, she had his blood and because of that, the curse was still hanging over our heads waiting for a woman with that Fields blood coursing through her veins to break it. His blood brought it in and his blood must take it out.

As I stood at the banks of this tear-filled ravine surrounding the mountain, I heard a song in my head. It wasn't the freedom song heard by Milkweed, nor was it a collective symphony of excited voices exiting the hated and horrible conditions of slavery. The music I was hearing was erratic. It sounded like something only the devil and his henchmen—minus or actually it might be plus one, named Hamilton, could play and dance to. It was similar to the music I'd heard the day of my labor, which was intense and as it reached a feverish crescendo, I'd pushed out a baby that was proving that not all babies have faces that even if no one else loved, they could be assured of their mother's.

My baby had taken the hope of every ugly baby and dashed it to the ground. I was having difficulty that couldn't even be explained to find the place where I could see me lovingly caressing and caring for that face. As I looked at the slivers and fragments of my now-shattered dream of a bright and carefree future scattered all around her, I shuddered. Where did this ugly baby come from? Surely not from me? No sooner had I asked the questions than I knew the source of her ugliness. She was making gushing and cooing sounds at my baby; Mrs. Trindle. By giving her weak, hateful son Hamilton her ugly-gorilla genes, he had, with all his hate and insecurities, pushed this baby into me.

I heard a faint cry. I opened my eyes. I wasn't in my room. Daddy and Mrs. Trindle were still sitting on the couch and in their midst was the little gorilla-child that had fought me every inch of the way to be born. She was crying a demanding cry and the more she cried, the more I realized that Cornbread's dream had to be realized. A woman in this family must enter somebody's college and walk out with the fulfillment of dream: an education.

I watched as Daddy and Mrs. Trindle sat with her and, succumbing to the blindness of love, sunk deeper and deeper into their state of blissful denial about the true ugliness of my baby. As I looked at them, I wondered what would become of my life with a baby that I had to prepare myself to defend when I didn't know how to defend myself. This wasn't what life was supposed to be like for me. I was supposed to be on the threshold of fulfilling the dream of a slave who was willing to sacrifice everything for book learning.

The deeper Daddy and Mrs. Trindle sunk into their murky abyss of grandparent-hood, the more my hatred for Hamilton grew. At the very thought of him, a searing pain of anger and resentment shot through me. This baby, his child, would stand as a constant reminder that he, with one cruel, hate-filled act, had snatched me from the path of my destined joy-filled journey and placed me at the tail-end of time. I determined in my heart, and with the same tenacity of this child that had struggled against me to be born, that I would find a way to get back to the place where I would break this generational curse that had derailed the dreams of every woman of this lineage.

There was a way back. I had to find it even if it meant searching on my hands and knees with this child strapped to my back. Either way, come hell or high water, I was finding it. I had to. A lot of people, including this mirror of Hamilton and his mother, were depending on me. I closed my eyes and prayed. Even after I was done praying, I kept them closed for a long time. I was hoping that when I opened them again, I would be in my room the day before I tried to make Hamilton happy.

Chapter 2

Rend – Two Sides to Every Story

I got up reluctantly and walked over to where Daddy and Mrs. Trindle were seated and as I extended my hands to Daddy to take Leela from him I wished there was a void, unseen but present, to suck both her and me away. There wasn't one. Daddy placed her in my outstretched arms. I took her and as I looked into her tiny, wrinkled, Trindle face I tried to find the map that would take me back to the path I was on before Hamilton and, God knows, before her. Her little newborn baby eyes struggled but finally opened the ways that baby's eyes do, as if the lids were heavy and, unaccustomed to being lifted, they opened half way and crooked. That was enough for me to look and see the little jet-black opening to the void I was looking for.

I looked in those almost-opened eyes and in them I saw something that made me want to drop her: a fire. They weren't little flames burning the way they do on a stove turned down low, but it was a fire like the one people imagine is burning in hell. The fire in the eyes of this child, less than a week old, was an all-consuming fire. Bright as it was, it was dark. It had a very sinister look to it. It shouldn't be there; nothing should be there because she was, after all, a tiny thing, newborn for that matter. So what was a fire, and a dark sinister one at that, doing burning in her eyes?

I stared hard into the tiny openings because I knew that as far as a newborn baby's eyes go, they don't stay open very long. I had to get all my looking in before those portals to the void I was trying to figure out how to climb into with her closed. As I stared, I could have sworn that if I didn't know better, my baby was staring back into my eyes with those fire-burning, tiny jet-black pools. In that look, I understood what I was seeing in her eyes: a fiery determination. It burned back at me with an intensity that was more than slightly scary.

I wasn't sure what one so little could be determining about or why I should feel scared looking into her eyes, but something in that gaze told me that once she grew to match whatever was going on in her eyes, I and anyone else she felt was in her way would have hell to pay. I looked away. I would have to find the path back to my destiny somewhere else. It was going to be with this child, but God knows I wasn't looking forward to her company; not for a split-second.

If what Nana said about the eyes being the windows to the soul was true, then what I'd just seen told me that I'd either just given birth to a soul-less creature or the windows to her soul were closed to me. I took a deep breath and accepted that her jet-black pools weren't the void I was looking for; I would have to find another way to get to my daughter's heart and soul on my own. Something told me that even if she knew, she wasn't about to tell me. I felt a strange thing stirring in me. I wanted to hand her back to Daddy or put her on the sofa, the floor, anywhere and just walk away from her and whatever was burning in her. I badly wanted to but I didn't.

I'm not sure why, but a part of me said that if I'd handed her back to Daddy or put her down, I would never take her back or pick her up again. Against all I was feeling, most of it not good, I brought her closer to me. Holding her as if my life, not hers, depended on the closeness, I made my way to Auntie Noreen's chair to sit with her in my arms. As I made the very short trip, I silently asked the Lord to help me. I was going to need it with this child, I could tell. I took a deep breath and as I exhaled, I thought, 'Lord when you said, "Suffer the little children to come unto me and refuse them not," did you mean Leela as well?' I waited for an answer. Nana had taught me that it would come in His time. I hoped that it would come in one of those twinkling of His eyes that Nana always talked about.

Leela didn't give the Lord time to twinkle His eye or to answer. She opened her mouth, framed by the lips that were too big for her tiny baby face, and let out a wail. Even that was a little too loud for one so tiny. It snatched me back to my present reality: her. The road back was going to be a long one. A very, very long one indeed but I, with my Mandinka, Seminole, and Jewish blood, was going to make it back, and Leela, with her Mandinka, Seminole, Jewish and that additional gorilla-Trindle blood, was coming along with me. From the way she was carrying on right now, it would be kicking and screaming.

I was OK with that because the only thing that mattered was that I found the road back. I sat down and, with a degree of dread that hinged on pure fear, I started to breastfeed her. I didn't want to put my breast or any part of it near her mouth. A thought crossed my mind. 'Didn't gorillas have teeth when they were born?' I knew I didn't see any in Leela's mouth when she was first born, but she was approaching a week now, what if that gorilla blood had caused her to teethed early? As she latched on, I closed my eyes preparing for the snap and squirting of my life's blood as she bit my nipple off, but none came. She pulled as if she hoped to suck me into her void. I planted my feet firmly on the ground, prepared to drop her if the choice came down to her or me. As she nursed, she relaxed. I took a deep breath and let her get her little belly full; after all, she was going to need something in her stomach for this journey. It didn't make sense starting out with her hungry.

After I burped her, I took this child with Everett Michael Poole Fields' blood, which had brought this curse upon us and now, sadly, her, and I vowed that his blood was going to take the curse out. I had to get across this ravine of Milkweed's tears before I could start my climb up life's mountain. I gathered Leela more tightly into my arms and, placing one foot on the banks of the ravine surrounding the base of the mountain, I slipped my toes in. As I stepped in, Leela spat up. It landed in the water and, maybe because I was tired, I thought I saw the water where her spit-up had landed start to bubble. Not molten-lava bubble but faint tiny bubbles surrounded my feet, rose, and popped. Perhaps I would have dismissed that as my feet disturbing the ravine bed but then the faint smell of sulphur rose from each popping bubble surrounding my feet. I couldn't ignore that. A faint fear rose in my gut. Who or what was this child I had in my arms? There wasn't any time to ponder this thought as the water rose and lapped at my legs. And so, ignoring my fears, I moved toward the base of life's mountain and started my climb.

Chapter 3

A Disappointment So Deep

It's a strange thing about life and the way it can make you see things differently. While I was pregnant and before Leela was born, I had two ways of looking at my life. When I tilted my head to the left, I saw it one way: a mess. When I tilted it to the right, I saw it another way: mixed up but redeemable because the pregnancy, like all pregnancies, had to come to an end. It did. Leela's birth forced me to look at my life quite differently.

I now understood what had happened to us and it wasn't as I had first thought. I thought we'd been torn, but days after Leela's birth I could truly say the best word to describe what happened to us was *rend.* Now, I know that this isn't a common word but common or not, it best describes what happened to this family. On one side, if you look **rend** up in the dictionary, it's defined as a verb that means: To **tear something apart**: to pull something apart violently, or be pulled apart violently. To **tear or pull clothes or hair**, out of rage, frustration, or grief. To **take somebody or something away forcibly:** to tear or wrest something or somebody away. To **shatter something**: to disturb the silence or pierce the air with a loud sound **or to distress somebody**: to cause pain or distress to the heart or emotions.

Then one night, and thank God it was one when Leela kept her eyes and mouth closed for more than fifteen minutes, my brain had time to relax and it saw the other side of the word rend, and not just as a word to describe what had happened to the women of my family, but also as a word to describe what had happened to all of us: a race of strong, intelligent, beautiful people that more often than not still tear at each other to the satisfaction of some and the shame of others.

However, after my mountain-top experience with Leela and having time to process all the pieces of my life, I can truly say I have a better definition of **rend**: To tear something apart when you take somebody or something away forcibly and it shatters that something or someone, which causes distress to that somebody or something.

Rend; an uncommon word, true; but not so uncommon if you are the one looking at the fragments of your family scattered all around you and holding a screaming child, an unwilling partner, in your arms.

Rend, not so uncommon after all.

Leela Phoebe Hirsh Greenwood had, just by virtue of being born, put a new shine on the curse. I felt an extra weight as I struggled up the mountain. I didn't have to look back to see if the curse was attached, it was and it was coming up the hill with me. I hoped that by the time I came down from the mountain, and I pleaded with God to not let it take me forty years, that it would somehow be magically, mystically, but not momentarily be broken. We would finally be free from it.

I wanted freedom from the curse and I wanted it now. I wanted to get back to the place where I was: on the road to college. Nothing else other than me getting back on that road mattered. I had to get into college. Not just in but graduate. I wouldn't care if, or when, I walked boldly and proudly out of somebody's college I had a degree in one hand and a child walking beside me holding the other. If she didn't want to walk, I would drag her; I had no problem thinking or doing it. She was coming; I didn't care how. The curse had to stop with me. I had to be the one to break it once and for all. It had hung around and over our heads like some twisted tarnished halo far too long.

I, like the others, knew about the curse and I'd fallen, but that would be the last fall 'cause times were changing. We had more book learning but with getting that book learning, common sense always seemed to evade us. If we wanted to, we could think things through and make our own decisions. It's true I'd made a decision, a bad one, that got me here, but I was also making another one. This one would have far-reaching consequences. It would reach back to all the women that had come before me and it would tell them that we'd overcome the curse.

A daughter of Greenwood, a daughter with Fields' blood had done it. It was time that this curse was over. I was going to break it or it was going to break me, and breaking me wasn't an option. I had no intention of breaking. The curse would be broken. I was going to see to it. We, the women of this family, kept getting closer and closer yet further and further away from breaking the curse. It was time.

I, the one Daddy, Auntie Noreen, and Uncle Neal had hoped would escape the dreaded Promise Land, Greenwood curse hadn't. I'd fallen victim and had given Daddy, Auntie Noreen, and Uncle Neal such a deep disappointment gash I felt they would never heal or recover from. I was the only one holding the bandage that would heal them. I had to get to college. I had to fulfill the dream that had managed to elude every woman of this family.

I tried hard not to see the journey before me as miles and miles of frustration and uncertainty, but as a journey from an immature woman-child into full maturity, womanhood, and freedom. I accepted that with my personal detour and unwilling companion, Leela, attached to my hip, my climb was going to be hard. Leela's unwillingness was the one common thread that bound us. She didn't want to come anymore than I wanted her along. Each step with her reminded me of that day when I allowed my heart and, as Auntie Noreen called it, too much feeling sorry for someone who didn't deserve it, to get me where I was: with a child. In my case, it was for a man so weak, he'd just gone off and left me with it growing in my belly.

There were days I watched my belly swelling with his child growing inside and I couldn't admit to anyone how sick the sight of it made me. I was also overcome with such an intense anger that I couldn't even if pressed describe how I was truly feeling. I mostly wished that Hamilton was dead and not just in one place but scattered over many places. I imagined the many ways he could have arrived in that state and none of them gave me pleasure because I would have missed it. I wanted him dead so badly for what he'd done to me that if I could have, I would have killed him myself and worried about the consequences later.

Leela started crying. The unexpected and unsurprisingly irritating sound started to grate on my nerves. I looked at the mountain ahead of us and wished I were already at the top. Not so I could look back and relish having accomplished all the dreams in my heart, but so from there, I could let her go; pretend I'd slipped and, unable to grab onto her, my not–so-precious or treasured cargo had slipped, dropped, fallen, or somehow gotten out of my hand. Of course, I would do the requisite hollering and wailing. That would only be for show. Deep in my heart where it mattered, I would feel no remorse or sorrow. No, not one solitary second would I be sorry; not one.

No sooner had the image of Leela wrapped in swaddling clothes bumping down the side of life's mountain entered my head than I wanted it gone. I was sorry. Not mournfully sorry but the kind of sorry you are when you see a puppy caught in a cold downpour with nowhere to go for shelter. I didn't feel sad in my heart because that was all the sympathy I could muster for her; I didn't know her long enough to feel true sadness if something bad was to happen to her. I accepted that at this point in my life, all I could feel for her was the same as if I'd seen that cold wet puppy, but that was a start.

I must truly be going through something because even that thought bothered me. This was not even remotely what I'd considered when I'd envisioned motherhood. My journey to motherhood was supposed to be different than all who had come before me. Daddy had worked hard on getting me the best road map. On Daddy's roadmap to my future, there was Spellman College. He had called on everyone he knew to pull out every stop that might have been in my way to prevent me from getting in.

All the strings that needed to be pulled were pulled, if a hand needed greasing, Daddy saw to it that a good plop of grease went in. One of Daddy's friend's wife, Tory or Miss Victoria as I had to call her, used her connections to Spellman. She knew every place that had to be touched. Daddy did just as she'd said and before we knew it, I was in. All I had to do was apply myself, graduate, and perhaps get a job at Daddy's law firm. I would work there long enough to meet a young handsome lawyer. After a few months of a carefully orchestrated courtship, I would marry this nice man who would be able to give me the kind of life Daddy had gotten me accustomed to, and then…and only then would I become a mommy. But now, instead of being on my way there, I had an angry and, though apparently only to my eyes, gorilla-looking baby tethered to me by an unbreakable bond; a string called motherhood: damn that string.

Leela hollered again and this time she, knowing about the string, grabbed it with both of her hairy gorilla paws and pulled so hard, I almost fell backwards. Without looking at her, I grabbed my end and pulled back equally hard. My tug sent her airborne and she flew over my head and landed with a thud in front of me. Momentarily stunned, she shuts up but not before she gave me a look that frightened me. I didn't have time to react. The end of the rope in my hand was on fire. I wanted to drop it but I knew if I did, she would know that she had won so I held on. There was a scorching feeling. With her tiny gorilla realization that she had lost this battle, she glared at me. I walked over to where she landed and, picking her up, I dusted her off. I knew that my pats were just a little harder than they should be, but I didn't care how hard I was hitting her. After all, she had just tried to burn me.

She started a fresh wailing. I stopped. There was another tugging. This time it felt different; it was at my heart. Shit. I was feeling sorry for her; genuinely sorry. I looked at the child in my arms and I was sorry for all the thoughts I'd just had of letting her fall down the mountainside, of her having a demon seed growing in her heart and a certain unnamable evil glowing in her eyes, of watching her sail through the air and landing anywhere in a broken baby bunting heap. My heart begged me to see her as she really was: an innocent little baby. That was all she really was: an innocent.

Innocents were just that and they weren't responsible for anything. If anyone was responsible, it was me. I was responsible for everything. I wanted to tell her that I was sorry, that I knew she wasn't responsible, then I felt something warm. A warmth was reaching my still-soft belly, right underneath where her butt was resting. I didn't have to look; her plastic panties had split when she'd hit the ground and now the pee was soaking both of us. The warmth of the pee snapped me back to my reality. I was a mother and responsible for a child that had a face this mother was finding very hard to like, far less love. As I looked at her face and realized with a deep and unreal sadness that I might never learn to love her face or her, I became grateful for Daddy and Mrs. Trindle and the fact that all they saw was a little girl worthy of their love.

I looked around for a flat rock or something, anything, to change her on. I put her on the first flat rock I saw. A part of my brain, the part that was going to keep the fire of hate burning for Hamilton said, 'Leave her. Walk away. A vulture will come along in a day or two. She'll be a small snack, leave her.' As much as I was thinking and feeling it, I knew that leaving her was something I couldn't do. Daddy, Auntie Noreen, and Uncle Neal were waiting for me on the other side of the mountain with a plan, a mapped out, thought-out future for me and this little she-gorilla, so with the realization that it would be easier than the lie I'd have to tell about losing her, I changed her diaper.

Leela sighed almost as if she were relieved. I wasn't sure if it was because she was now dry and comfortable or if she somehow knew, with her gorilla survival instincts, that I'd had more than fleetingly thought about letting her go bump, bump down the rough side of the mountain. She was too young to really know that so I let the thought go. I gathered her bunting closer and, reaching up, I dug the fingers of my left hand into a crevice slightly above my head. With strength I didn't know I possessed, I began my climb up Life's Arduous Mountain. I pulled myself up with one hand and, with the other holding onto my baby, I inched my way up.

'My baby.' I let my brain say and savor that thought again. 'My baby.' She was my baby. Whether I liked it or not, she was my baby. Something moved deeply in my soul. It made me wrap my arm tighter; protectively around her. No sooner did my spirit connect to the thought of 'my baby' than I felt a grinding at my heart. I became very sad. I could see the wheels of sadness, hope, despair, and self-loathing clogging, grinding, and turning like the little wheels inside a watch. I smiled for a fleeting moment as I remembered how many of Daddy's watches Andre had taken apart, shown me, and then, unable to put them back together, he'd just put the back on and put the watch back.

The wheels moved on in my heart. Time moved on. My pain mounted. My heart ached. I started to cry. I looked around for a sign, any sign that would point the way off the mountain and bring me down on the side where the door to a college waited and I could, with this child, step through it. There was nothing. I decided to sit still. I didn't know what to do and even if I'd come up with some kind of idea, I wasn't sure I would know how to start. Doing nothing seemed like the best thing to do. At least for now.

Chapter 4

Going Backward to Come Forward Again

I'd only been up my mountain of motherhood about a week and still doing nothing about changing my life when the doorbell rang one day. Yes, my mountain was only at the top of the stairs. As Auntie Noreen was outside in the yard hanging out some clothes, I went to the door. I opened it and standing there was an old-ish looking woman. I'd seen her before and as I stared at her trying to remember where, she said, "I'm looking for a Mrs. Noreen Peters. I was over on Chauncey Street and I was told I would find her and you here."

I wanted to ask this old lady why she was looking for Auntie Noreen, but I knew better. Auntie Noreen would never have tolerated me asking a grown-up why she was looking for her so I replied, "Auntie Noreen is out back. Would you like to come in while I go and tell her that you are here? Miss, who should I tell her is asking for her?"

When I said that, she looked at me as if I'd lost my mind. "Drea, I know you ain't standing there looking at me and asking me that foolish question. You really don't know who I am? Well, if you don't know who I am, go and tell your Mrs. Peters that it's Mrs. Phillip Fillmore and since you don't know who I am, I'll answer you before you ask again, no, I don't want to come in."

I looked at the old lady and shame rose all over me. "Mrs. Phillip Fillmore? Mrs. Fillmore…Oh my God, is that you, Auntie Thea?"

She neither said yes nor no. All she said was, "Now go on, child. I'm an old woman and I've picked up impatience and all its kin in my old age."

"Auntie Thea, I can't leave you standing here. When Auntie Noreen comes, she's goin' to wonder why you're still outside. Please, Auntie Thea, you must come in."

"Child, just go on and get your Auntie Noreen, as you call her, and know that I don't have to do anything. Especially when my own kin don't know who I am."

"Auntie Thea, please. Are you sure you won't come in?"

"I'm sure."

I started to close the door and just as suddenly realized that I would be closing the door in her face. I couldn't do that so with urgency coursing through me, I stepped back from the door, leaving it open and hurried to the back of the house. I called through the open window in the spare bedroom. "Auntie Noreen, there's a lady here out front on the stoop, come to see you. She says her name is Mrs. Phillip Fillmore but its Auntie Thea. She won't come in even though I asked her. Can you come and see her and get her to come in?"

"Who?"

"She keep on saying Mrs. Phillip Fillmore, but I'm sure it's Auntie Thea, who moved down to Virginia with Uncle Phillip, Bernard, and all the rest of her children. I'm sure that's who it is. Come, Auntie Noreen, and see."

When I said Mrs. Phillip Fillmore, Auntie Noreen's face changed. "Fillmore? You sure the woman said her name was Fillmore? Then if she's your auntie, why she ain't coming in?"

I replied, "I don't know, but yes, she said Mrs. Phillip Fillmore. That's her married name. She never used it when I was growing up but that's got to be who it is."

"Go quickly and tell her to come in. Tell her I'm coming."

Auntie Noreen's voice took on an edge like she was a little nervous. She left the little vest she was getting ready to hang swinging on one arm as she dropped the pins and started wiping her hands on her apron. She looked and saw I was still in the window. "Now! Drea, now. Go and let that lady, Auntie or no Auntie, in by the time I get inside."

The edge in Auntie Noreen's voice made me anxious, as I turned around to head back to the door, saying the lady's name again. I'd moved without even noticing it. I was at the door. I stepped to the open door and said, "Mrs. Fillmore…I'm sorry, Auntie Thea, Auntie Noreen said she's coming and to ask you to come in…please."

The old woman looked at me and smiled a shy smile that said, 'I know you know who I am, but I'm going to let you keep on guessing.' She rested one hand on the frame of the door for support, before hoisting herself up and onto the threshold. I stared past her to what must have been a mountain for her: the steps leading to where she was now standing. I realized then that it must have been quite a herculean effort for her to make it to where she was.

I stepped out of the way, allowing her more room to get through the door. She stepped in and as she stood next to me, I could see that even though she was slightly bent from age, it was clear that in her younger days she must have been really tall, big-boned, and really good-looking. She wasn't really that big now, but she had that 'used-to-be-fat' look, a little soft, a little jiggly, and body parts that moved just a little extra slowly. What was showing of her hair from under her beautiful hat was gathered together and held in place by a hairnet. The amount of hair in the hairnet let you know that if she were to free it from the hairnet, it would be down her back; if it didn't make it to her waist then it would stop below her shoulders.

The hat almost looked like a tiered cake. It sat a little fashionably crocked, which made me smile just a little because she was an old lady wearing the latest style hat. It was cream with a beautiful soft pinkish feather sitting high on the front. The feather seemed to be pointing the way to heaven. There was a darker pink wide satin or silk band that went around the middle, stopping at the place where the feather was attached to the hatband. There were pearls, like the ones found on hat pins, and sequins all mixed together. The hat was beautiful. It made me think of and miss Nana.

As Mrs. Fillmore, "Auntie Thea", passed the big hat and coat rack, she stopped and gave herself a quick check in the mirror. She smoothed her skirt. Her dress looked like one you would see on rich white women. The brown and pink jacket had about a dozen square, medium-sized buttons down the front. It had sleeves that stopped somewhere between her elbow and wrist, with a smart split cuff that had a button sitting in the middle of the split. At her neck where the jacket had a double collar was a soft rose-colored, very neatly tied bow sitting softly on her chest. The jacket extended over her still-big hips with what looked like two frills or two small skirts. These skirts didn't go on very far. They stopped just over her hips and from underneath this her real skirt extended downward almost to her ankles, where it just stopped. The gloves, which I never noticed until she'd taken them off, were now being held in the same hand as her brown purse and cane.

The purse had a bow on the flap that covered the opening. Again, my mind went to Nana and I started to really miss her. I looked at her feet as she stood looking at herself. I noticed that her shoes, which didn't have much of a heel, also had the same stylish bow on the top. She stood before the mirror long enough to satisfy herself that she was all smoothed out. She took the few steps to the door leading to the parlor or up the stairs to the bedrooms just as Auntie Noreen made it to the basement steps and stepped into the hallway. Auntie Noreen hurried to meet her as if she were her long-lost family member, extending both her hands to the woman. Using one hand for support on the cane, the visitor extended her free hand and said, "So glad to meet you. I'm Thea Fillmore."

I smiled. I was right. It was Auntie Thea. I wanted to run and hug her, but there was something about the way both Auntie Noreen and Mrs. Fillmore stood looking at each other as if they were waiting on someone else, or they were trying to decide what to say next that made me wait. I'm not sure what I was waiting on or for, but since both of them seemed to be waiting, I decided to wait along with them. There was no one else in the house beside us. Uncle Neal wasn't home; he never was on Thursdays; it was the day when you could find him on Clermont Avenue at the Lodge Hall. If he wasn't at a Lodge meeting, he was with his old-time friend, Boysie Cox.

There weren't many things that mattered to Uncle Neal except Auntie Noreen, me, Andre, Daddy, Lodge meetings, Uncle Boysie, Colroy, politics – just the kind that had to do with Negroes, or as he called it Civil Rights or Negro People's Rights, Leela, and Auntie Noreen's specially prepared dishes; those were the things he lived for. Auntie Noreen knew this and each day she made sure that a comingling of special treats came out of her kitchen for him and anyone lucky enough to be present when she was done. Thursday, his Lodge meeting and time with Uncle Boysie never changed. That also meant that dinner would either be yellow split peas and rice served with fricassee salt fish, or Auntie Noreen's special fried liver: beef, pork, or chicken; it didn't matter which to Uncle Neal as long as it was liver.

I watched Auntie Noreen and Mrs. Fillmore, who I knew now for sure was Auntie Thea, watching each other and waiting, for only they knew what, I knew that dinner was either going to be late or not at all. I couldn't imagine not at all. It simply wouldn't happen; not in Auntie

Noreen's house. Auntie Noreen prided herself on many things: her always spotless house, her care, love, devotion, and daily dedication to those of us who lived with her, and most importantly and at the very top of this list was Uncle Neal and all his needs – whether mentioned, expressed, or even just thought of.

Out of an old Bajan habit, Uncle Neal didn't like what he called 'left-back food' so therefore Auntie Noreen saw to it that Uncle Neal never had to think about eating 'left-back food'. She never one day fussed or complained. Her Neal didn't want 'left-back food' and she was going to see to it that he didn't eat it in her home. Since he didn't eat other people's food, she never had to worry about him being displeased like that somewhere else.

I remembered one of Auntie Noreen's friends coming to visit on a particularly hot summer's day and Auntie Noreen was in the kitchen cooking. The friend wasn't helping but just doing what Auntie Noreen always said people who visited while you had work to do did: "Stopping people from doing their work." So, knowing this woman was stopping Auntie Noreen from doing her work, I was surprised when she said, "Noreen, why you still goin' on with all this cooking foolishness on what must be the hottest day of the year?"

Before Auntie Noreen could answer her, she went on, "Noreen girl, tell Neal that he in America now and all that old time Bajan foolishness 'bout hot food every day goin' stop. You don't see no American woman rushing 'bout making all this hot food every day. You in America now, girl. Ain't you nor Neal hear that when you in Rome, you do what the Romans do? This ain't Rome, but it's America so do like the rest of we and let Neal get use to hot over food."

Auntie Noreen, in her quiet way, looked at this woman who was stopping her from doing her work and said, "And maybe that's why you, after all these years in this Rome, still going from pillar to post looking for a man that like left-over food. You ever stop to think that maybe, just maybe, if you find an old Bajan man and cook him hot and fresh food on a regular basis, you might be able to get one who would want to stay with you from night to morning or from breakfast back to another breakfast?"

That woman, whose name I don't remember now, didn't say another word. I'm guessing it was something she didn't expect Auntie Noreen to say and what Auntie Noreen said a few minutes later surprised the woman even further. "I know it's almost time for you to be going 'cause you have to find a pillar or post that you ain't touch 'pon yet and me, well, I got to be starting up my pot 'cause my Neal goin' be coming in looking for something fresh and hot to eat. So, I goin' let you go on home now so you can get fresh and go look for that different pillar or post you ain't spread yourself under yet. I goin' stay right here in my kitchen and do what keeps my husband satisfied and coming back where I see him every night: home. You see, unlike you who don't cook for no man, and as you said, 'ain't washing no dirty draws.' I got a man to sleep with every night that I done know before night fall. So you go on. You go look for your next pillar or post man and I goin' cook my Neal his fresh and hot food."

I think it took that woman a full minute to realize that not only had Auntie Noreen put her in her place, but she had also put her out her house. She didn't stay but a half minute longer after that and when she did leave, she went really quiet. She never came back and Auntie Noreen, not appearing to miss her one bit, went on with the things she loved doing: cooking us hot meals, which was always some remembered Bajan favorite. It didn't matter what the meal was; it was lovingly prepared and served with the utmost care. It was what made us a real family. I loved my family.

To watch the way Auntie Noreen served us meals, you would think we were the white people she used to work for. Uncle Neal's meals were never on the same plate, never. Auntie Noreen would set his plate, knife, fork, and glass on a place mat then she would put every part of the meal in separate dishes so Uncle Neal could take as much as he wanted. She never wavered from this. Daddy got the same treatment when he ate with us. Only Andre and I got our plates fixed in the kitchen. Sundays, Thanksgiving, Christmas, and our birthdays were the exceptions. Then we ate as family because those were special days.

"Andrea! Andrea!" It was Auntie Noreen's voice. "Child, you day dreaming or what? You ain't hear me talking to you; calling your name?"

Looking at Auntie Noreen, who was now standing in front of the sofa opposite Mrs. Fillmore, who was also still standing, I answered her. "I'm sorry, Auntie Noreen."

"I said that this here lady is Mrs. Thea Fillmore and, as you guessed, your Auntie Thea. Come, say a proper hello."

The woman was smiling. I stepped closer to where she was and as I got ready to extend my hand to her, she said, "That won't do. Now how

I can that do? Shake my family's hand. Child, when I first met your Aunt Bess, she didn't shake my hand, and I won't have her or Gina Pearl looking down and watch me shaking your hand."

I watched as Auntie Thea worked herself into a stronger standing position. She leaned a little on her cane and then, smiling, she told me, "Child, now don't just stand there after I've worked myself into this strong standing position. Come and give me a hug; a great big ole hug. You do remember how to give your ole auntie a real hug, don't you?"

Smiling, I stepped forward and into her one-armed embrace as she was using her other arm to support herself on her cane. The hug, even with one arm and her being old and all was strong, warm, loving, and filled with memories of all other loving hugs: Mommy's, Nana's, Daddy's, Auntie Noreen's, and Uncle Neal's. I started to feel as if I would cry. I also wanted to stay in her embrace. A lot of what was familiar and missing was there, buried deeply in that hug. I took a deep breath and hugged her harder. I allowed her smell of jasmine and lavender to fill my nostrils. Everything about her said, 'Stay, settle in, and hold her a little longer.'

As the thoughts filled my head, I started to feel my body wanting to relax and, just as the tenseness started to leave the first muscle, she let me go and stepped back a little. I wanted to ask her to hold me just a little while longer, not forever but just a little while longer. She didn't motion for me to return so I stepped back. I hung my head a little because I didn't want her to see that I was hungry for her hug.

"Child, ain't no reason for you to hang your head. Ain't no shame in wanting to hold onto somebody. That day, when I held onto Aunt Bess, it was the safest I'd felt in months; almost years."

I raised my head and smiled a little.

She surprised me when she added, "Child, you sure remind me of myself. A few years ago, no it was more than a few, it was many actually. Yes, many years ago, I stood in a bus depot and I felt just like you are feeling now. The only difference is that it was me wishing that Aunt Bess would never let me go. It was the most comfort I'd held onto for a long time and I didn't want to be put away from her. So, believe me, I know how you feel. I don't know your reason as to why you hungry for this kind of hug but, child, when I stood there in that bus station, you should have seen me and my scared hungry-for-a-hug-self. I wanted to hold onto her like she was my Alpha and Omega. But she let me go and just like you I hung my head too, but she looked at me and something in the way she looked at me said she understood. I had some real bad circumstances leading up to that day. She turned me out of her hug, but she never turned me away from her 'till I was standing on my own two feet."

Both Auntie Noreen and I stayed looking at Auntie Thea who seemed to have slipped back to a place that only she knew the way to and back from. We waited as Auntie Noreen had taught me—patiently. I could tell from the expression on Auntie Noreen's face that she was waiting to welcome her back. I waited with her. The welcome, even though she'd just met Auntie Noreen, would be a warm one; they always were.

Returned from where she'd gone, Auntie Thea made her way to one of the two wing chairs in the parlor or as Uncle Neal insisted on calling it: the Drawing Room despite the fact that no drawing ever occurred there. I remember the first time I said that to Uncle Neal, who still spoke little and seldom unless it was about the Lodge, the way Negros were being treated, or making things better for the Negro race. He said, "We may not draw in there in the true sense of drawing like artists, but it be a drawing room for us 'cause it's where we draw them that we love, friends and family alike close, so for that reason it's our drawing room." I never questioned it again.

Auntie Thea said, "Andrea, sit for a minute, please."

I sat down in the chair nearest to the door where I could hear Leela if she cried. I also had a feeling of expectancy. I was waiting. I wasn't sure what I was waiting for, but common sense told me to be still. I looked at Auntie Noreen and her face didn't really have an expression; she didn't really look concerned but she wasn't exactly grinning from ear to ear either. I waited. Auntie Thea took one more of those deep breaths that people usually take when they have something hard to say. I started to imagine all of what she would have to say that could be so hard, but since Mommy and Nana were both gone and she didn't really know Daddy, I didn't let my heart jump all over the place, and besides, Auntie Noreen was right here next to me.

Auntie Thea leaned a little forward. She smoothed her skirt and then she finally spoke. "I came special to talk to you, Andrea. I owe it to you. I should have come a long time ago, when your nana was alive. I should have but sometimes we make decisions that, at the time, the reasoning seems sound but as time passes, that sound reasoning is like a waffle; full of dents and ridges and you losing everything; like syrup in the ridges and stuff. I can't tell you enough how sorry I am that I didn't come…you know, make peace with Gina Pearl."

I wanted to ask her what she was rambling on and on about, but I got the feeling that Auntie Noreen was staring at me. I turned my head to look at her and I was right. Her face had that look of, 'I know you're not thinking of asking some foolish question.' I turned my head away quickly and the foolish question faded.

"I don't mean to make it all seem so mysterious and serious or more serious and mysterious than it really is, but before I talk to you, I need to talk to your Auntie Noreen for a few more minutes and after, you and I goin' talk."

I got up and as I walked across the drawing room floor, I knew where I was headed; first to check on Leela and then the kitchen. I'd just made it to the open half of the parlor door when Auntie Thea spoke again. "I should have gotten here before but sometimes getting to do the right thing or set things right can take a long time. I promise you though that by the time I leave here, I hope to leave you with a lot of answers. Aunt Bess and Gina Pearl finally goin' turn me loose and me, well, my conscience goin' be clear, crystal."

Unsure what to say, I replied, "Ok. Excuse me then, please. Auntie Noreen, I'm goin' in the kitchen."

Auntie Noreen said nothing but looked from Auntie Thea to me and then back again. Just as I got ready to step out into the hallway, Auntie Thea asked, "You've taught her to cook?"

Chapter 5

Edge Teeth and a Lamb Basting

I stopped dead in my tracks and turned to look at Auntie Noreen to hear what she was going to say. I turned in time to catch the expression on Auntie Noreen's face. Auntie Noreen doesn't, as she calls it, get vex quick or often, but certain things or people could make her vex. She was looking at Auntie Thea like she was a two-headed goat, or worse. I saw that quick look, the one that usually crossed her face when she was vexed. Auntie Noreen was vexed now and as Uncle Neal in one of his funny moments called it, Auntie Thea was about to get 'a lamb-basting', which God knows had nothing to do with lamb and basting of anything other than the person who was about to get one of Auntie Noreen's infrequent 'dressing-downs'.

I watched as Auntie Noreen let the look go away, but when she spoke there was an edge to her words like she'd sucked on too much tamarind; both she and Uncle Neal had told me about getting 'edge teeth'. She said, "Teach she to cook? What Bajan woman goin' have a young impressionable girl living in she house and ain't goin' teach she to cook. And not just cook, mind you, but wash, starch, and iron. My Drea can clean, fix up she self, and cook 'most good as any Barbadian; here, in America, Barbados, or any place else that Barbadians living."

The pride with which Auntie Noreen said that made me feel good. I smiled. Auntie Thea didn't flinch. She simply said, "I lived with Aunt Bess. Now that was a lady that had some fire in her spirit. The only difference with what you just said and Aunt Bess would have been some cussing. Yes, Lord, Christian as she was, Aunt Bess could sure cuss when she got ready and she would have given me such a taking down just now; I would have to think two or three times what made me open my mouth and ask her such foolishness. So you're right to put me in my place. You should have even asked me who the hell I thought I was with my

Johnny-Come-Lately-self walking into your house and asking you how you raising this girl. Please forgive me, Mrs. Peters."

The stiffness came out of Auntie Noreen's back and I could almost feel the edge coming off her teeth. Auntie Thea then, with a big smile on her face added, "Very well then, Miss Barbadian Cook, go and get to cooking while I talk to your Auntie Noreen. You can come back once the pot don't need you anymore."

I looked at Auntie Noreen to find out if she was OK with me going out the room. Turning, I answered, "Yes ma'am, I'll hurry."

When I said I'd hurry, Auntie Noreen gave me one of her looks. Then she said, "Now, Drea, you know how we Bajans, well, the two that live in this house feel 'bout food, cooking, and the word hurry being in the same sentence; so you go on and take your time with that food."

Auntie Thea looked from Auntie Noreen to me and added, "Now, Ms. Noreen, you know that you don't just up and say something like that and not fully say what you mean."

Auntie Noreen replied, "It don't have a whole of meaning and may mean less to some modern people now who can get someone to fix them their food, but for people like me and Neal, we don't eat what we call 'hurry food.' Hurry food is food that the person cooking didn't have time to make properly. It was just cooked up in a hurry and…"

She stopped talking as Auntie Thea interrupted her with her sudden laughter. It was a full laugh. You could tell that it came from a far-away part of her soul and it was attached to some distant memory. Auntie Noreen just looked at her. Auntie Thea was lost in her memory-filled laughter. I watched and listened as the sound of the laugh filled all the open and available spaces in the room. My aching empty part, which was almost closed off to the feeling she was stirring up, opened and a sliver of hope that was keeping it open brightened.

Her laughter filled me up and, like a tiny bead of mercury from a broken thermometer, it slid into my heart. Each echoing sound of laughter melted and merged with the one before. A smile crossed my face. Her laughter had reached that part of my heart where the flame of anger and hatred for Hamilton had been raging out of control. Her laughter didn't put out the flame, but it touched on a good memory of Nana that I'd almost buried with the hatred and woke it up.

As the memory came alive in my heart, I suddenly wanted to talk to Nana; to hear her voice, and tell her that I loved, missed, and needed her.

I also wanted to tell her so badly that I was sorry I'd gone and had a baby and not made it into college. Then just as quickly as Auntie Thea's laughter had started, it died. She looked over at Auntie Noreen, who was giving her another one of her looks. This one said, 'Oh Lord. I done let a mad woman in my house.'

Auntie Noreen, even though she looked concerned, told me, "Drea, you were on your way to the kitchen. Go on, child, and get started. Your Uncle Neal is going be looking for something hot when he comes back from over at Boysie's."

I walked out and headed directly to the kitchen, where I found everything for the evening dinner laid out. Auntie Noreen always did that. She'd said that she'd picked it up from one of the white women she worked for before she and Uncle Neal worked for Daddy's mommy; my grandmother Mrs. Esther Hirsch. Grandmother? Strange how I hadn't thought about Daddy's mother since the first and only time I'd seen her. She was the only memory of that day, Mommy's funeral, that wasn't a constant thing with me. Even now, all I could recall about here were her wrinkles, a withered-looking white hand burdened, almost weighted down with bangles and things, and her raspy scratchy voice. I let the image of her fade; it wasn't hard to do.

My thoughts returned to the items on the counter before me: salted cod fish, yellow split peas, rice, green and red bell peppers, onions, tomatoes from the garden; one fully ripe and the other— a little green with carelessly thrown splashes of yellow in various shades; Mother Nature the artist. Uncle Neal loved these tomatoes in everything and so Auntie Noreen put them in everything; she was like that. If you let her know that something was important to you, it didn't matter what it was, then that thing became important to her.

There was also Auntie Noreen's famous secret frying flour; she called it that because she and only she knew what went into that flour she used to fry the things that we liked. Today, I didn't have to guess. It was Thursday which meant it would be liver but the salt-fish was out as well. Was Auntie Noreen planning on cooking both? Had today been Tuesday, then it would have been chicken wings. How Auntie Noreen had worked this routine out was beyond me, but somehow she got the meals and days to work and Uncle Neal always ate as if each day and combination was something new. Even Daddy had days and things he looked forward to. For Daddy, it was beef soup. She made it just the way he liked it with what he called, 'all that stuff.' Potatoes, celery, carrots, green bananas, yams, and split peas. No soup in Auntie Noreen's house ever got made without split peas.

I knew my way around the kitchen so I did just as Auntie Noreen had taught me. I got a medium-sized pot and filled it half-way with water and put the salt-fish on to boil, I'd have to remember to change that water at least two more times to get the salt out. I started to slice the onions, peppers, and tomatoes to make the gravy. I would let the split peas wait as they could sometimes be tricky. Splits peas were definitely not dried green peas. Dried green peas, you could boil for a week and they still wouldn't be cooked, but split peas; you could blink and some of them would be soup and some, well some would just up and made you believe you were boiling a pot with some small pebbles in it. Hard split peas were always a problem. I took the liver out the fridge and rinsed the lime and salt off. Auntie Noreen limed and salted everything including liver, though the salt watered it down, it didn't escape the lime and salt. Rinsed properly I seasoned it and placed it back in the fridge until it was time to fry it.

I was deeply into trying to recreate the food just as Auntie Noreen had taught me and Uncle Neal would be expecting when I heard a faint cry. At first, it sounded like a mouse but then I realized it wasn't a mouse. The baby, my baby, was crying. I didn't, as I thought I would have, drop the knife I was slicing the tomatoes with and charge up the stairs; I placed the knife down, turned the tomato on its flat side on the chopping board so that it wouldn't roll to the floor, washed and dried my hands, and then and only then did I start up the stairs. I wasn't in a hurry and I couldn't, not even with Auntie Thea in the house, pretend I was.

The sound stopped as I neared her room. My mind said, 'Just go back downstairs and leave her.' Another voice said, 'Check. She's your child.' I continued up. I peeked from outside the room and I could see that she was still asleep. She'd just cried out in her sleep, the way babies, even those that look like gorillas, do sometimes. Thank God that's all it was. I looked in the crib anyway and I could see that her little legs were uncovered. I guess she'd just cried out a little because she'd become cold, poor thing. I stepped to the crib and pulled the soft pink blanket over her legs. I smoothed the blanket and, as she was still asleep, I turned to walk away.

I hadn't so much as put my foot down to make the first step when I heard a movement in the crib. I didn't have to look. I knew even without looking that she'd found a way to reject me yet again. I didn't want to look but I did; she'd kicked the blanket off. I looked at her exposed legs and, shrugging my shoulders, I just turned away. A voice sounding like my own said, 'If she wants her blasted legs outside of the blanket, that's just what she's going get.'

I left her as she was and turned away. A part of me said I should care and another part asked why I should. I didn't respond to either part. I left her with my thoughts just hanging in the room, and intending to walk back downstairs, I turned away from the crib. I was indifferent to what my thoughts about her were, negative or otherwise. She was a child I'd given birth to but she still wasn't my baby yet, not in the true sense of the word. We hadn't formed a bond yet and I had a strange feeling that none would be formed, well not today.

Letting my mind wander over the thoughts that even when asleep, Leela could crawl under my skin and start gnawing at my sore spot, I rubbed the skin over where my heart sat beating a slow mournful dirge. Why did things have to be this way? Why couldn't I get my heart to move past the hurt imposed on it by Hamilton and his mother and just love my child unconditionally the way I, as her mother, was supposed to?

The minute I had that thought, Leela jumped in her sleep. I turned in time to see her arms flay and reach out. I stepped back closer to the crib. Why I don't know, maybe it was instinct or something, but I reached in and placed my hand on her back in an attempt to soothe her troubled spirit. The minute my hand touched her back, her legs kicked out and she whimpered as if she'd been hurt. The cry sounded like a puppy that had been kicked. I pulled my hand back and out the crib and she immediately settled, turned her head, struggled to open her eyes and, although they weren't focused on me or anything for that matter, she looked in the direction where I stood and fixed her sleepy glare at me. It defied me, daring me to touch her again. I stepped back feeling hurt. I felt like crying. My baby of just eight days old hated me.

I stepped out of the range of her glare, even though I knew that she couldn't really see me. Somehow assured in her spirit that I wasn't going to come close to her crib again, she closed her eyes. My heart swelled and I walked out the room. As I reached the door, a soft sigh, a sound she shouldn't know how to make came from the crib. A tear of regret slid down my face. I wiped it away and headed down the stairs.

Chapter 6

In the Stranger's Place Stood a New Friend

As I came down the stairs, I could hear them talking. It sounded friendly enough; not like old friends, but as if a friendship could develop given time. Auntie Noreen was like that; people liked being her friend and as she liked making friends, no one was a stranger for long. I made it to the bottom of the stairs but I was unsure what to do. Should I go back inside and sit with them or walk past the parlor and go back into the kitchen? A part of me wanted to go in and hear what she had to say and I would have been happy just leaning behind the closed half of the parlor door and listening from there, but even as the thought made it in and through my head, I knew I wouldn't do it. I knew better.

Nana, if she were around, would have lost her mind at the idea of me eavesdropping. Nana would never have stood for that kind of behavior, nor would Daddy and God knows that Auntie Noreen would be the most disappointed. Though she'd been gone from Barbados almost fifty years, she still had a lot of the ways she grew up with. I could hear her voice in my head as clearly as if she was standing in front of me if she'd caught me eavesdropping. She would be sucking her teeth and saying, "Drea Matti Hirsch Greenwood, what foolishness you carrying on with? Why you maliciousing in people's business? I didn't know I raised you to be gypsy."

Then she would have sucked her teeth one more time and, with the harshest voice she could muster would have shooed me away. Her voice echoed in my ears and, not wanting to hear it for real, I started to head to the kitchen. I had just started to drain the salt fish when I heard Auntie Noreen calling me. Knowing better than to answer her from the kitchen, I set the pot down in the sink and walked back to where she was.

"Yes, Auntie Noreen, you calling me?"

Auntie Noreen had an excited edge to her voice. I became excited at the tone in her voice but because it had an edge to it, I also became nervous. "Come, Drea. Me and Mrs. Fillmore was talking when you went to the kitchen and this is so exciting. Mrs. Fillmore has come to tell you some news. It's not really news, but it's about your family when they were slaves and even before that. I don't know what was before that, but from what Mrs. Fillmore has told me, she'd asked a lot of questions and has, over the time since your nana passed, been getting bits and pieces here and there and today, or however long it takes, she's goin' to tell you."

Before Auntie Noreen could say anything else, the words from Auntie Thea came again. "I should have come before. I should have. God knows I've had some real sleepless nights because of my stubbornness, but all that done pass and I got to do this thing for Aunt Bess so she can finally rest in peace."

The walls of my brain echoed with her words. A fireworks-type explosion went off in my head. I got an instant flash of something Nana had said about when she lived at Aunt Bess'. I looked at Auntie Thea and I instantly had a feeling that Nana was going to come right in the room and hug her. I stood there looking at this smartly dressed woman that was now saying to me she held the key to my family's history and I wasn't sure what, if anything I should say.

Auntie Thea added, "I've been getting here forever like I said earlier, but before I got here, I had a lot of things to do. I've done those things and now I'm here to see you." Stopping like something had just dawned on her she said, "Drea, tell me, how is Andre?"

"He's fine. He's away at school."

"I didn't expect to see you home. I thought you would be at school. What school, I mean college are you attending?"

I lowered my head and suddenly I felt very ashamed. I didn't know how to answer. Auntie Noreen answered for me. "Drea's not in school now. She had a baby a few days ago. She'll be going back soon as the baby is a little stronger."

To my surprise, Auntie Thea said, "I'm sorry, Andrea. I really am."

As I looked at her trying to figure out what she was sorry about, she added, "I don't mean that I'm sorry you had a baby. Babies are beautiful and precious gifts from God, but Fields women or any woman with some Fields blood seem to be able to just make babies. I got married and for the first six or seven years of my marriage, all I did was make babies. Aunt Bess even asked me if I intended to do like Milkweed – your grandmother four or five times removed – and just make babies. If only Aunt Bess had lived, she would have known that after Bernard, I didn't make another baby. With her goin' the same day Bernard was born, it did something to me; I just ain't make another baby. I didn't do one blessed thing to stop them from coming; they just stopped.

Truth be told, I was tired and I was missing Aunt Bess something fierce so I was really glad when no more came." She smiled and then continued, "Phillip, he was really sorry when no more babies came, but I wasn't. I was glad. I started being glad to see my feet again. It also felt good to have ankles that were regular-looking." At that, she just burst right out laughing. It was such a full laugh that both Auntie Noreen and I laughed with her.

When the laughter died down, Auntie Noreen told me, "Drea, look at this, now you got somebody who's goin' fill in all those missing pieces for you; your own family."

I smiled a genuine smile because there was something about Auntie Thea that reminded me of Nana. She was older than I remember Nana being, but that didn't matter I had someone to call family. I liked that idea. I didn't know what to do so I just stood there. It was Auntie Noreen who said, "Mrs. Fillmore I know you've come a long way just to tell Drea this thing that's been pressing on your heart, but you also got to eat so can I invite you to stay and have supper with us?

"I wasn't planning on supper. Actually, I wasn't sure what my plan was. I just knew I had to find Gina Pearl's grandbaby. It's been resting on my mind for so long and now that I'm here, I'm not sure I know where to start."

Auntie Noreen said, "I hear that the beginning is always the best place."

"In this case, this beginning has already been told and if nothing had happened to Aunt Bess, the rest would have been told and I wouldn't be here today. But life being as it is, Aunt Bess got called on to be with the Lord before she could tell the rest. I knew some but not all, and so I had to go back and get the rest. I still don't have it all, but I got enough over these years since me and Phillip left that I know there'll be no rest for me 'till I've told you what I done found out."

Auntie Noreen looked at Auntie Thea as if she wasn't sure if she'd said she'd stay for supper of if she wouldn't so she asked her. "Miss Thea…that mean you staying to eat with us?"

"I can stay, but I'll have to let them over at the house know that I'm still here. Phillip Junior is at the house. You know we own those twin houses on MacDonough Street?"

"Which ones? There are two or three big house over there, but I don't know of no twin houses."

"We own the two big ones that are side by side. Phillip Junior is there. He came up with me. We goin' be up this way for a few weeks. Phillip, my husband, suddenly decided that he wanted to be in New York. We've been gone almost twenty-five years, of course, with the exception of a few visits here and there, and suddenly he wants to be in his house…it's the dotage. He still thinks he's in the funeral business. Every now and again, his mind wanders and the only place it can wander to is when he used to be the only one that all the Negro people came to when they had their dead to put to rest. Most times, we can get him to let go the idea of wanting to come but this time he couldn't be dissuaded, so Phillip Junior, always one to dote on his father, came up. He brought his wife and children. I think he and them are planning to stay on in one of the houses once me and Phillip go back. So yes, if you would please let me use your phone, I'll tell them to come and get me later. Thank you so much for asking me to eat with you."

"The phone is over here, come."

Auntie Thea raised her large frame up and walked slowly over to the small table where the phone was. As she dialed, Auntie Noreen spoke to me. "Drea, you stay here. Let me go in the kitchen and push this food further along. Neal goin' come home and if there isn't any food, he'll wonder what I was doing all day." Auntie Noreen made her way to the kitchen and I waited for Auntie Thea to finish her phone call.

I looked at Auntie Thea and I couldn't help but wonder why she was here now. A lot of questions started to float around in my head so I left her talking on the phone and followed after Auntie Noreen, who was already in the kitchen. She was turning around in the kitchen as if Auntie Thea wasn't here. She was slicing the liver. I watched the way Auntie Noreen had that knife going through the liver like a hot knife going through butter. She was busy getting ready to flour and fry the liver just the way I'd seen her do it a thousand times, and had she not called me a few minutes ago, I would have done it myself.

"Drea, why did you boil salt-fish and also season the liver?"

"'Cause I saw the salt-fish on the cupboard so I figured you were going to do something with it. So I boiled it. I was going to come out and ask you."

"I wasn't really planning on it, but since we have company, I'll go on and give your Uncle Neal a special treat."

"You want me to help you?"

"No, somebody has to be out there with your auntie and since she came to see you, then you are the best one to be out there. You go back. I can manage."

"Auntie Noreen, before I go out, can I ask you a question?"

"Now, Drea, why you got to ask me if you can ask me something…since when you can't ask me what's on your mind?"

"I know, but it's 'bout Auntie Thea."

"What 'bout her got you troubled?"

"Auntie Noreen, why didn't she come when Nana was sick or when Momma was sick? Why she didn't come when Momma died and Andre and I had no family. Something in my belly is starting to get nervous."

No sooner had I said I had the nervous feeling, when I heard Nana's voice in my head. It was so clear. "Everything has a time."

I was about to tell Auntie Noreen what I'd just heard when she said, "This is God's appointed time for you. When your nana and I worked together and on those few times when she talked, and she never said much, but she would say, 'In God's time. Everything has its time.' That was always it for her. If Mrs. Hirsch was acting up, your Nana would say, of course under her breath, 'In God's time. Everything has its time.' So it's my feeling that this is God's time for you to get the missing pieces 'bout your family.

"Those pieces that not even your nana could tell you 'cause she didn't have them to give to you. So you see how God works. He's picked the time and He has sent someone to tell you 'bout your kin, your history, and hopefully help you better understand why some of the things that keep happening to your family be happening. I'm glad she's here. I am, Drea. I know 'bout my family going back so far that it almost don't even make sense. I think my family can almost put themselves back on the slave ship and tell you what song them was singing coming over." Auntie Noreen smiled. "That last part I made up. I don't know 'bout my own family no further back than my grandmother, and I'm not even sure if I can tell you her real name. So you go and get the bits and pieces that goin' make you able to tell Leela 'bout her whole family line."

I looked at Auntie Noreen and I knew she was telling me the truth as she felt it. She smiled at me as if to reassure me and, feeling reassured, I walked out the kitchen and made it to Auntie Thea just as she was finishing her call.

She turned to me and said, "Drea, I am really glad I came. You've been on my mind for a long time. I started to feel if I didn't come, I was getting in the way of Aunt Bess getting her wings and settling down in heaven. I don't know if it's true what they say about some people can keep people that want to go on into heaven rooted here on Earth or not, but just in case it's true, I don't want to be the one keeping Gina Pearl or Aunt Bess' spirit here on Earth any longer. They were both good to me and if I'm the one keeping their spirits here on Earth, I promise you that by the time I leave here, them going be flying 'round free, free up in heaven."

Chapter 7

The Beginning… Always the Best Place to Start

"Come. Sit. I have so much to tell you and as I said to Miss Noreen, I'm not sure where to start but as she said, the beginning is always the best place."

Auntie Thea walked back into the drawing room and as if she'd decided that the chair she was sitting in was her comfortable spot, she settled herself back in the same chair. The way she sat made the chair seem new, as if I'd never seen it before or as a matter of fact, as if I'd never even been in the room before. That wasn't true because Auntie Noreen always said she believes in 'living in her whole house.' By that, she meant if she had something, she was using it; nothing was too good for us. We used everything, but of course, some things were only used on holidays and birthdays, but we used the drawing room a lot. It was Uncle Neal's favorite room and after that, for him, it was the dining room, the corner of the kitchen where we ate most meals, and then his bedroom. Uncle Neal could just lie down for a whole day. Said he'd worked hard enough as a young man that he could lie down a whole day if he felt like it.

Auntie Thea smoothed her skirt again. She leaned her cane by the corner of the chair. And then raising her head, she looked at me. I looked at and past her at the same time. Something in the mirror above her head caught the light and my eye at the same time. I guess it was the sun bouncing off something outside that reflected and then bounced off the glass. It put a little extra light in the room and then as it started to go away, it looked like a ray of golden light in the shape of two sets of slowly flapping wings. I blinked my eyes and held them shut for a split-second. When I opened them again, the shapes were leaving. It looked like angels riding on a sunbeam. I watched until it faded away. The room went back to normal as if nothing had happened, but something inside of me said that something important had just happened and what I was about to hear was going to make that vision make sense.

"This is a very nice room. It's almost like the one that Aunt Bess had on Chauncey Street. That was a beautiful room."

I smiled, remembering how beautiful it was the day Daddy had taken us all over there when he'd gotten the house back from the man who had tried to steal it from Nana and Momma.

"So what is it you are smiling about, Drea?"

"Nothing much. When you mentioned Chauncey Street, I just remembered Nana and Momma and the time when we'd moved in, me and Andre for the first time, and Nana and Momma moved back in after Daddy had gotten the house back for Nana."

"Back?"

"Yes. For a long time, Nana believed that the house didn't belong to Aunt Bess."

"Child, what foolishness you talking about? That house was always Aunt Bess'. Why would your nana ever stop and think that that house didn't belong to Aunt Bess?"

"A man, I believe his name was Mr. Cooper, had come when Aunt Bess died and said that the house didn't belong to Nana anymore and so she would have to take Momma and move."

"Yes. Yes. I remember that time. Bernard was still a baby and Gina Pearl refused the offer to move into the house with me and Phillip. At the time, I didn't understand why Gina Pearl didn't want to come when we had so much room, but over the years I understood."

"Why didn't Nana want to live in your house?"

"It was Bernard."

"Cousin Bernard who did her funeral."

"Yes. Your nana always felt it was because of your cousin Bernard that Aunt Bess got hit by the milk truck that night. But it wasn't Bernard's fault. If Gina Pearl had listened to Aunt Bess all the years we lived with her, she would have known that Aunt Bess wouldn't have been mad at Bernard. She wouldn't have kept him in her mind for as long as Gina Pearl did. I think your nana died and never forgave Bernard. It's not that he needed forgiving because all he did was get born on the same night that the Irish policemen had killed and tried to kill over and over again one Negro man. I know you can't kill someone that's already dead, but those Irish policemen was so mad at…what was his name? What was his name? Phillip had told me, but it slips my mind now. It's not that important to the telling of this part, but it was because of Rawlins Fitzgerald, yeah, that was his name…Rawlins Fitzgerald…"

"Who was that? Was he family to us?"

"No, child. This Rawlins Fitzgerald was a Negro who was stupid enough to get drunk and take a swing at a white Irish policeman. Them Irish policemen was so mad at him that they just kept killing and killing him long after he was dead. It was all that mess with the police that made it so Phillip couldn't get home and take me to Women's Hospital. When I realized that the baby was acting like it was in some kind of rush, I called Aunt Bess. It's true she was rushing to be with me but it was Naum Glassberg and his goat eye that hit and killed her. It was his fault she died."

"I'm sorry. I didn't know that Nana felt that way about Bernard."

"I know you didn't know. It's not something we ever talked about, but Bernard knew. He knew that his cousin Gina didn't favor him. I knew, or I should say once I figured out that she didn't right favor him, I brought him 'round to see her less and less. Gina never asked me for Bernard. So I just stopped bringing him. I would leave him with Phillip on those evenings Phillip didn't have a wake, a funeral, Lodge, or something."

I could see that Auntie Thea was sad so again, I said, "I'm sorry. I'm sure Nana liked him."

"She didn't. She never learned to forgive him. I think, not that I ever heard her call him that, but I think in her heart he was a Bitter Breeze…"

"A what?"

"A Bitter Breeze. That expression comes from slave times."

"What does it mean?"

"A Bitter Breeze was never a good thing or a person. You know how wind blows everywhere it feels like? Well, a Bitter Breeze in slave times would take all the slave business back to the master."

"Somebody would do that?"

"And worse. So that's why it would hurt me so deep to think Gina Pearl thought that way 'bout my Bernard."

"You never asked Nana about it?"

"No, but I should have talked to her and then that night when she asked me to tell her what I knew 'bout our history, I could have told her what I knew. I didn't know all you know. I didn't know as much as Aunt Bess, but I knew some. I could have told her what I knew."

"Nana asked you?"

"Yes. You see, Aunt Bess wanted us to know what had happened to the women in our family; she made it her business to tell us. She was nearing the part 'bout what happened when Milkweed and Fields' sons went back to Brekenshaw's plantation, and Milkweed's inheritance when the accident happened so when your nana asked me if I knew any more, I told her no. I told her no because she didn't like my Bernard. I was his mother and my boy hadn't done her nothing. She didn't have a right to hate my boy and so I didn't tell her any more."

"Did you know any more?"

"Not as much as I know now, but it would have been enough to show your Nana that I was telling the truth."

I could feel excitement rising up in me. I wanted to know more. Auntie Thea continued. "Did your nana talk to you about the women in our family?"

"She'd told me a little, but had always said when I got older she was going to tell me the full story, but then by the time I'd gotten to where she could tell me, she was sick."

"I'm so sorry. I'm sorry about so much, but I plan to fix it before I leave here."

"You can tell it all in one evening?"

"I wish I could. How I wish I could, but I can't. It's a lot."

"So how am I going to know?"

"Don't worry. I came here to tell you and I'm going to tell you. I owe it to Aunt Bess, your nana, and your momma. I was wrong and all these years it has rested on my shoulders; heavy and weighing me down almost as it's weighing, I guess, Aunt Bess, your nana, and maybe even your momma, but I plan to get that weight off my shoulders and free everybody so they can fly, either off to heaven or around heaven just the way Bernard did."

"Bernard?"

"Yes. He forgave her. He forgave her the day he heard she'd died. He came to me and said, 'Momma, I know that if Daddy was able to, he would go to New York and take care of Cousin Gina. I'm going down to New York and I'm going to take care of her funeral." I looked at him and wondered why he was going. Why he wasn't letting your daddy take care of things. We'd heard he had money, so we knew he could afford to send Gina Pearl off nicely. It was as if Bernard was reading my mind, and he said, 'Momma, it's time to put it to rest. It's time for me to let it go. Cousin Gina can't love me now so I have to love her enough to forgive her for never forgiving me. I know I didn't do her anything wrong, but I knew she always had it in her heart that it was my fault Aunt Bess got killed. None of that matters now, Momma; none of it. I'm her cousin and Daddy can't go, he's too sick.'

"When Bernard came back from New York, he said to me, 'Momma, I put Cousin Gina down today. I did it, Momma. I couldn't take away her hatred for me, but I made sure before I laid her down to rest that I told her I'd forgiven her. I told her as we dressed her. I told her as we put her in the casket, when I folded her arms, when I smoothed her dress to make sure she looked just right, and I told her over and over when I drove her to the church. Momma, I even told her as her casket was being lowered into the ground. Momma, I said it as I heard the casket hit the bottom of the grave. I said it until I walked away.' Then he said to me, 'You know something, Momma? Cousin Lilly didn't even know it was me. She saw me but I don't think she really saw me, and I know for sure even if she'd gotten her eyes to focus on me, she wouldn't have recognized me. You should go to her, Momma, she's taking it real hard.' He mentioned you but I don't remember him mentioning your little brother.

"Bernard was right. I should have come. Once he'd come back to Virginia, he and his brothers and sisters could have looked after Phillip for a while, but I didn't come. I refused to let my heart care more for Gina Pearl's baby than she cared for mine. I'm sorry. You all were so little and your momma could have used the help, support and love of her kin. I left her alone even though I knew she didn't have anyone else. Aunt Bess would have been so disappointed in me. I don't know why I fixed it in my heart to be so unforgiving. I made your mother carry that heavy burden of losing her momma all by herself and I could have come. I could have and I would have been able to help her understand her grief. I could have told her about the women in our family and how they'd had to handle situations like hers. I could have told her what to do with a heart that was broken like hers. I could have come."

Auntie Thea held her head down and then she took a shallow breath.

I heard it as it went into her nostrils and I heard it as she let it out slowly. As she let it out, her shoulders lowered as if the air was holding them up. I felt sad all over again because she was talking about Momma and it was making me remember Momma just giving up on life and choosing to die. I wanted to feel something bad in my heart towards Auntie Thea for not coming and perhaps helping Momma to want to live. I wanted to be angry, but just as I was fixing it in my heart to go wherever you go when you want to become hateful, my mind suddenly remembered the dancing ray of sun I'd seen when Auntie Thea and I first walked back into this room and just as the anger or whatever that feeling was had started to raise up in me, it went back down. I just looked at Auntie Thea and I felt sorry for her. She seemed to have a major burden to deal with.

Auntie Thea raised her head to look at me and when she did, her eyes looked wet. She wasn't outright crying, but it was clear she was misting up. She took another deep breath and when she let it out, she said, "Even if all the children wanted to come, we could have brought Phillip with us. I had no excuse; none whatsoever. That's a lot to live with. Bernard set his soul free by forgiving Gina Pearl. I knew then that I had to do the same thing and make things right. I had to not only tell you what I knew, but I had to get the rest of the story so I could tell you the whole thing, and I'm going to set it all right before I leave here. It's time. It's time."

As soon as Auntie Thea said it was time, I heard a faint cry come from upstairs. Auntie Thea looked at me and said, "My goodness, if that little one didn't cry, I would have gone on talking; I'd forgotten about her. She was so quiet."

I got up."Excuse me. I'll be back as soon as I see about the baby."

Going to see about Leela was the last thing I wanted to do. I would have traded places with anyone rather than go see about her, but judging from the smells coming from the kitchen, Auntie Noreen was very busy. I went up the stairs slowly. When I reached the crib, I could see that she was getting ready to really cry. I didn't want her to so I picked her up. I almost expected her to go rigid in my hand, but she didn't. She stayed baby soft. I changed her diaper and sat on the edge of the bed to feed her. When she'd taken as much milk as she wanted, I burped her and was getting ready to put her back down when I suddenly felt guilty. A part of my brain said, 'You don't hold her enough. Hold her. Take her downstairs with you.

I looked at her and the part of me that had grown weary of being her mother in one week said, 'Just put her back down. Let her get used to her own company. Walk away before she looks at you with her little gorilla eyes and rejects you again.'

I'd made it to her crib when I heard Nana's voice in my head saying, 'You are her mother. You aren't going to get a second chance at knitting her close to you. Pick her up. She's a little innocent thing. Show her a mother's love and she'll love you back, you'll see. Drea, don't put her down; don't.'

The voice was so clear, I almost expected to see Nana in the room. I tightened my hold on her, wrapped her a little tighter in her blanket and headed down the stairs. To my surprise, Leela was still. She felt as if she'd settled closer to my chest. I walked into the drawing room and Auntie Noreen was talking to Auntie Thea about dinner. "The food is far enough along where it doesn't need me. I can sit with you and all for a minute."

"Drea, may I hold her?"Auntie Thea asked me. I was afraid to walk the short distance over to where she sat. I didn't want to see her expression when she saw Leela. Auntie Thea saw my hesitation and she added, "I won't drop her. I've birthed quite a few of my own and I even have great-grands at this point."

I handed Leela over to her. Auntie Thea took her and as she looked, I watched the expression on her face. When she didn't look as if she was going to just drop Leela and run away screaming, but instead was looking at Leela and appeared to be seeing her just as Daddy and Mrs. Trindle had, I breathed a sigh of relief. Auntie Thea started cooing and saying how beautiful Leela was. I watched Auntie Thea, who was now lost in her seemingly unfettered adoration of Leela. Looking at her, I deeply wondered what she saw to make her coo as she was. Not having the gall to ask, I sat down.

"Drea, while you were gone, I was talking to your Auntie Noreen about the best way to work out telling you this story."

I smiled and answered for her. "You could just stay here until you are done."

Auntie Thea replied, "I can see that Miss Noreen is really schooling you well. Would you believe she also suggested the same thing? But great as that idea is, I don't want to be gone so long or make you all wish you'd not invited me. I think the best thing would be to come by in the evenings and visit. This way, I would know that Phillip is fine and I can get on with my storytelling. It would make me feel just like when Aunt Bess was telling the story to me and your nana."

Auntie Noreen added, "Trust me, Miss Thea, it won't be any problem if you wanted to stay. These days, Neal is busy down at the Lodge and he's also got himself involved with as he calls it, 'the liberation of the race' and once he's on that soap box, there's no getting him down nor is there any getting him to notice anything that's going on that doesn't have to do with setting the record right and straight for Negroes. Come on, Miss Thea, say you'll stay, at least for a few days."

Auntie Thea, with Leela still in her arms, looked from Auntie Noreen to me and then she finally answered. "I'll tell you what…after a few days or maybe by the third or fourth week, after we've gotten to know each other a little better, I may stay over one night and in the morning treat you all to some good old-fashioned, down home Southern food. Now what do you say about that?"

I smiled. I would like that. It had been a while since I'd had some Southern food. Auntie Noreen was an amazing cook, but she didn't quite care for Southern food so she didn't cook it much.

Auntie Thea went on. "Don't think I don't see that smile on your face. You just can't wait to sink your teeth in that food. You better pay real attention to what your Auntie Thea does in that kitchen so that when she leaves here, you know how to make some of that food for yourself."

Auntie Thea smiled and said, "Then I guess we are all good about how we going do this story telling." Both Auntie Noreen and I nodded. Auntie Thea then continued, "I think and I'm sure you'll agree that we've got a lot of getting to know each other done tonight. I better be getting home and see 'bout my Phillip. Don't want to leave him alone too long and the next thing I know, some hussy done steal my sweet man from right under me and my nose. I'm too old now to be lifting buckets.' Laughing a little, she patted her bag and added, "That's why I now carry a gun. I'll shoot and ask questions after."

I looked, not sure what she meant by too old now to be lifting buckets or if to laugh as I wasn't sure if she was serious or not about having a gun in her purse. Auntie Thea saw me looking and explained, "One of these days, when you find the right man and he loves you as hard as Phillip loves me, you'll understand what it feels like to not want to lose him. You have to get there first. The part about the bucket goin' take a little longer to explain but I've called Phillip Junior and he's going to come and get me shortly. When he rings the bell, can you get it for me? We won't be staying too long as sometimes Phillip Senior fixes it in his head to want to walk off.

"Yes. He doesn't remember much. His mind comes and goes. Sometimes he remembers and sometimes he doesn't. With his remembering me, I accept how that works, but somehow he always remembers all his children. He doesn't see them as grown as they are, but he knows them all. Phillip Junior is great with him. Did I say that he's a doctor? He's the finest Negro doctor in Virginia. His wife, she's a fine nurse. Phillip Senior can't be in finer hands."

Auntie Noreen spoke up. "That's good, so on the night you are sure your husband will be fine, you know you would be more than welcome to stay as long as you like, and beside if we were on the other side of the street, we would probably be sharing back yards."

That made Auntie Thea laugh. It wasn't as full a laugh as the one earlier, but it was still a good laugh. A few minutes passed and then the door bell was ringing. I went to the door and a fine-looking gentleman was standing outside. I knew right away who it was. I opened the door and greeted him. "Good evening. You must be Phillip Junior?"

He smiled and replied, "I am and you are?"

"Andrea. I'm Andrea. Would you like to come in?"

He said, "Just long enough to say a quick hello and then Mother and I must be on our way…Daddy, you know."

He stepped in. I closed the door and walked him down to the parlor. Auntie Thea was smiling when we stepped in. She made the introductions. "Noreen, this is Phillip. This is Mrs. Noreen Peters, Drea's guardian."

Philip crossed the space between him and Auntie Noreen and shook her hand. He stepped over to Auntie Thea, kissed her on the cheek and turning to Auntie Noreen, he smiled and said, "Thank you so much for letting Mother stay. She said she had a very nice visit. It was nice for her to get a break from the care of Dad; a mini-vacation of sorts."

Auntie Thea smiled as well. It was a good feeling. I hadn't spent much time with her, but I tell I was going to like having her around. She gave Leela back to me. Holding her hand, Auntie Thea's son turned and headed towards the door. When he was in the hallway, he turned and spoke to Auntie Noreen. "Your house reminds me of Aunt Bess'.

"It's true, I was just a little boy when she was on Chauncey, but every time you stepped in the smell always greeted you; just like now." Smiling, he took the few steps that would bring him to the door. Auntie Noreen and I walked with them to the door and only after the car drove off did we close the door. We walked back into the living room and sat down. We'd only sat down a minute when I heard Uncle Neal's keys.

He called from the door, "Good evening."

Auntie Noreen called, "Neal, we're in here. We had company. You just missed her; it was Drea's Auntie Thea from Virginia."

Uncle Neal stepped into the drawing room. He stood for a minute looking at Auntie Noreen and I could tell he was trying to figure out where he knew the name from. As if reading his mind, Auntie Noreen added, "You don't know her, Neal. She's Drea's kin come from down south to pay her a visit."

Auntie Noreen filled Uncle Neal in about most of what Auntie Thea had talked about then we all went into the kitchen as we'd done since I started living here. We had dinner and then Uncle Neal got up and went into the drawing room to watch the *Outer Limits.* Auntie Noreen and I always laughed at the fact that for one hour, Uncle Neal, the same man that said in one breath that he was his own man and no one could tell him what to do, always sat there and let 'them' control his mind as the voice at the opening of the show said, '…for the next hour…'

Neither Auntie Noreen nor I bothered Uncle Neal. He stayed in the *Outer Limits* and we went on with the business of putting away the food, not that there was ever that much to put away as Auntie Noreen knew Uncle Neal wasn't going to eat it the next day. That was for our lunch; hers and mine. We would clean the kitchen and after Uncle Neal returned from the *Outer Limits*, Auntie Noreen would have a big cup of tea and something sweet for him to eat. We all liked something 'sweet' with our tea.

"I looked forward to that, but with Leela in my hand, it was beginning to feel as if she was intruding on the special time I had with Uncle Neal and Auntie Noreen. Neither of them saw it that way, but I felt that way; I couldn't help it.

Book Two

Thea Fillmore (Cousin/Auntie Thea)

A Time to Sew

Chapter 8

Stepping Back into History… One Word at a Time

The next evening as promised, Auntie Thea came, dressed as smartly as she was on her first visit. Today she was wearing a shade of blue that would be suited for a brand new baby boy. Though she was no boy and was as far removed from being a baby as anyone could be, it suited her. The hat, which looked as if it was a firm kind of cloth rather than felt, sat smartly on the side of her head. I was starting to think that it was Auntie Thea's style. The suits, the shoes, bag, and hat matched the gloves, which she never seemed to have on. Today, there was a beautiful pin on the jacket front. Her earrings and necklace matched the bracelet she was wearing. The beads in the necklace were different sizes with the biggest one in the middle. Auntie Thea was one smart dressing woman.

As luck would have it, Uncle Neal was getting ready to go upstairs but he stepped back in the drawing room to meet her. Auntie Noreen said, "Neal, this is Drea's Auntie Thea; Mrs. Fillmore. Remember I said yesterday that she'd stopped by and would be coming by for the next couple of weeks?"

Uncle Neal was formal in his reply. "Good evening, Mrs. Fillmore, a pleasure to make your 'quaintance."

Auntie Thea replied, "Likewise; the same."

Knowing it wouldn't be a problem, Auntie Noreen added, "Mrs. Fillmore is staying to supper this evening and, if I can convince her, for a few days at some point down the road."

Uncle Neal, always a man of few words, answered, "That would be good. It would be good to have company; when you are ready."

That was it. He'd said as much as he was going to say. It's not that he didn't like her; it was just Uncle Neal. He left the talking, as he said, to me and Auntie Noreen.

Uncle Neal walked to the door and from there, he called, "Mrs. Fillmore, if you'll excuse me." Uncle Neal walked out. I knew he was headed to the small room next to his and Auntie Noreen's room that he'd fixed up and was now filling up with books. These weren't story books or the novels that Auntie Noreen liked to read when she got a minute. These books were about Negro people and by Negro people. This was his evening for, as he called it, learning as much as he could about Negro people all over the world. I didn't know anyone that read as many books as Uncle Neal.

Uncle Neal read as much as he did 'cause as he said, "Drea, I have to make up for all those years I was blind to what was happening to our race. When I was in Barbados, things were just the way they were. You went along. You accepted and you just did. Didn't even know for sure that there was something really, really wrong with the way things were. Now it's not that you couldn't see, but back then when I was a youngster like you, it didn't come in my mind to think there was anything I could do. Shoot, the most I would think about, child, was stealing some sweet potatoes to roast or breaking some cane to suck. Girl, those were some days. You risked getting some white man setting a dog on you for some sweet potatoes or something.

Uncle Neal laughed."Can you imagine, Drea, we even had a time for all those times. We had "stealing sea egg time" or "stealing yam time". Yes, Drea, there really was a time for everything."

I was so deep in thought, I jumped when Auntie Noreen called me."Wake up, Drea. Why you got to stop right in the doorway like you dreaming." Laughing slightly, Auntie Noreen continued, "I think too much of Neal is rubbing off on you, child."

I smiled and stepped out the way. Auntie Noreen walked with Auntie Thea into the drawing room. I followed. We weren't inside a good few minutes before Auntie Thea spoke up. "Miss Noreen, I don't mean to inconvenience you, but I would like to use your bathroom. Lord, I tell you. I just went before I left home and it ain't like I drove for an hour. I've only come from just around the corner and here I am having to go again." And getting up, she added, "Quickly to boot."

Auntie Noreen who had been sitting with Leela got up with her. "Drea, take Leela and let me show Thea where she can freshen up."

I walked over to Auntie Thea and took Leela. Auntie Thea laughed as she told Auntie Noreen, "Lord, Miss Noreen, I sure hope I don't have no mountain of stairs."

Auntie Noreen also laughed as she replied, "Not a one, not a one. Just a few steps and there's a bedroom. Neal had it built, he said for our old age."

Both Auntie Noreen and Auntie Thea laughed. It was good to hear Auntie Noreen laughing. The house had started to take on a holiday feeling. I felt the steady rhythm of Leela's breathing and I knew she'd fallen asleep. As Auntie Noreen and Auntie Thea walked down the hall, I went upstairs to put Leela down. Uncle Neal was in his reading room where he would stay until I came and called him for supper. That was Uncle Neal. He didn't say much but you could feel his love and devotion to us.

I peeked in the door and told him, "In a few minutes, Uncle Neal. In a few minutes."

He said, "You go and take your time. I'm fine. Your Auntie Noreen finally got some talking company." He smiled when he said that. He knew I understood. For him, that meant he could escape Auntie Noreen trying, failing, and then giving up on trying to get him to tell her what went on at the Lodge meetings. It was always the same. Every evening that Uncle Neal went to Lodge meetings, Auntie Noreen would say the same thing. "Neal Peters, did they tell you yet that it's OK to tell your wife what you all be doing in that big old drafty building; did they, Neal Peters?"

Uncle Neal would laugh and Auntie Noreen would add, "One of these days, Neal Peters, one of these days you goin' tell me and I goin' march right in there and tell them that you give 'way their secrets."

Tonight, even with Auntie Thea here, if it were a Lodge night, it would be no different. It wasn't a Lodge night so Auntie Thea would have to wait for another night to see it. None of us ever got tired of it. When I reached downstairs, Auntie Noreen was setting the table. I helped her to put the food on the dishes and put them on the table in the dining room. Ordinarily, we ate in the kitchen but we had company tonight. Everything was brought up to company level. When all the food was on the table, I went upstairs to call Uncle Neal and Auntie Noreen went into the drawing room to get Auntie Thea. Auntie Noreen and I made it back to the table before either Auntie Thea or Uncle Neal, but they joined us a few minutes later. Auntie Noreen said grace.

Conversations at the table was kept to the delicious food and compliments to Auntie Noreen.

With dinner over, Auntie Noreen and I cleared the table and took the dishes out to the kitchen. Auntie Noreen went into the drawing room to sit with Auntie Thea and Uncle Neal went back upstairs to sit and read and, as usually happened most evenings, eventually drift off. In between reading and dozing, he would write letters home. Uncle Neal still had friends and family in Barbados and he still wrote to let them know what was going on in his life. Sometimes he fell into a deep sleep and Auntie Noreen would wake him from his chair to go to bed. Uncle Neal loved that chair. On the days he didn't feel like reading or writing, he would sit at the window and watch the seasons and people go by.

I joined Auntie Noreen and Auntie Thea in the drawing room. Auntie Thea was still going on about the food. Auntie Noreen was promising to show her how to make the liver and salt-fish. As I walked in, Auntie Thea said, "I have no doubt that I'm where I'm supposed to be. I feel very comfortable. Thank you both for accepting me and, Miss Noreen, thank you so much for saying I was welcome to come, visit, and even stay with you. I appreciate that."

"Her face got a bit somber as she continued. "You know, when I stayed with Aunt Bess, this was just how she told us about the women in our family. We would eat dinner and then we would sit around and she would talk. Aunt Bess didn't just tell you the story, she made you live it. Now I don't know if I'm going to be able to tell it clear like her so you will see it and feel as if you living it, but I'm going to do my best.

"Yup. I'm going to do all I can to do the best job I can. Yup. The best job I can."

Chapter 9

A Promise Is a Promise Is a Promise

When we were all back in the drawing room, Auntie Thea started as she said she would. There wasn't a lot of fanfare or anything. Auntie Noreen and I were waiting and once Auntie Thea had picked a good place to start, she began."The beginning of this started for me when I had to leave Promise Land. My leaving Promise Land was different to how your nana left. She was sent and I, well, I had to just get away from that place and in a hurry to boot. Once I got out of Promise Land, I made a promise that I was never going to set foot in the place again."

Auntie Noreen, forgetting what Auntie Thea had said about interrupting her, asked, "Did you keep that promise; I mean 'bout never going back?"

Hesitating, Auntie Thea looked at Auntie Noreen as if by answering the question, her composure would crack and her true self would fall out and be exposed. Lowering her head, she answered, "Yes. I went back. But why you asking?"

"No special reason. I was just wondering."

"The fact that you could ask me if I went back and ask it like that tells me you don't know or haven't heard 'bout me and Crawford."

"Crawford? Who is or was Crawford?"

Auntie Thea smiled and adjusted herself in the chair. She took a deep breath and held it for a minute, closing her eyes, before easing the breath out very slowly. It took so long that in my mind it felt like someone was pulling a stuck inch worm out of some wet mud. Satisfied she'd emptied her lungs completely, she stated, "I didn't think I would ever be repeating this story ever again in my lifetime but since the purpose of my visiting is to give Andrea the part of the story I kept from

Gina Pearl plus what I've picked up these past twenty something years, then the story bears repeating. Who knows, perhaps if I'd told Gina Pearl the part I knew, it might have changed the path or direction that not only her life, but Lilly and now yours have taken, and who knows, it might even have broken the curse."

"Broken it? How?"

"You're starting to remind me of your grandmother with your questions."

"How?"

"Right there… how? Gina Pearl would ask a question, right dead smack in the middle of Aunt Bess' telling us 'bout Fields, Milkweed, Cornbread, or Molasses. Aunt Bess didn't take much to being interrupted but she would answer Gina Pearl. So for that reason, I'll answer you. Now I ain't goin' tell you all the fine, fine details 'bout me and Crawford, but enough for you to know why goin' back to Promise Land was so hard for me. I had to go back for Gina Pearl and for my baby Lilly."

When Auntie Thea said Lilly, her eyes got misty again and she added, "Why he had to do what he did? I mean, bury that girl without her kin. Me, Phillip Senior, Bernard, Phillip Junior and his wife, we would have come if word had gotten to us sooner. Bernard heard from one of his undertaker friends that she'd passed and 'fore he could come and claim her as kin, we get word that he, what was his name again?"

Auntie Noreen sat up a little straighter in her chair and she looked at me and then at Auntie Thea before she answered, "Matthew. Matthew Hirsch is his name."

"Hirsch? He's Jewish…a white man?"

Auntie Noreen replied, "Yes. Yes. Yes and why you asking 'bout something that you already know and you not only asking, but you making it sound like you surprised. Now don't tell me that for all the years you done come around Miss Gina Pearl and Lilly that you missed out on the fact that these children's father be a white man. Tell me that you asking me what you asking me 'cause age done made you forget."

From the way Auntie Noreen answered Auntie Thea, I could tell she was either vexed or was getting vexed. Auntie Noreen didn't take to anyone saying anything bad about Daddy and I could tell she was feeling that Auntie Thea was getting ready to say something bad about Daddy. I also started to get that feeling too. Auntie Noreen started to talk and I was right; she was vexed.

"Miss Thea, not meaning you no disrespect, but Mr. Hirsch did proper by Miss Lilly. Right proper. He even sat Shiva."

"Shiva? What in God's good name is a Negro Baptist girl doing getting one of them Jew things for? He probably done gone and have her soul lost over there wherever them Jews go to wait and see if Jesus goin' forgive them for not believing in Him and let them in His Heaven. Now what it going to take for Jesus to see that Lilly only in that Jewish part by accident?"

Auntie Thea started to lament. "Lord, Lord, Lord, he done gone and lost Gina Pearl's baby. Got she stock off in some part of heaven where no Negro ain't got no business being."

Auntie Thea started to rock like it was too much for her to even think about. I could tell that Auntie Noreen was two steps away from forgetting her good manners and was getting ready to un-invite Auntie Thea from coming by when she spoke in a voice so calm is was unnerving, "Miss Thea, it don't call for all that. She ain't lost. 'Cause the God I believe in knows every part of His Earth and all of what between all the way up to heaven. I don't doubt that He knows where everybody: Jew, Baptist, AME, Negro, white, and even them don't right know yet what they believe in belong.

"He done put her in the right part of heaven. If you remember right, it be white people that started goin' up to heaven first 'fore them start telling Negroes 'bout heaven, so you can best bet that them done put a big ole' sign up in God's heaven that say, "Colored this way," or Colored? Over here." They ain't going be no mix-up in heaven 'long as white people up there. Believe me, she with her Momma and all them other colored folks."

As if that was something that Auntie Thea never thought about before, she stopped her rocking, looked at Auntie Noreen, and burst out in the loudest, fullest laugh I'd ever heard in this house. She was laughing so hard that before I knew it, both me and Auntie Noreen were laughing with her. I wasn't so sure what we were laughing at, but the more Auntie Thea laughed, the harder Auntie Noreen and I laughed.

Suddenly, she stopped laughing and with a big smile on her face, she answered."I reckon so, I reckon so. Can't say I ever thought of it like that…Colored Folk This Way. Ain't God something else? He can go 'bout His heaven and if He sees somebody out of place like a poor Negro Baptist girl angel over by them rich Jewish angels, He can take her by the hand and lead her back to where she 'pose to be. That's what He did for me. He led me back to and from that hell. I had to go back so I could come forward.

"It was so I could come forward and beyond that I had to go back to Promise Land, Crawford, Fields' Plantation, Brekenshaw's Plantation, and now here. All of this so I can go forward in peace."

Auntie Noreen had stopped from being vexed when Auntie Thea started laughing. She answered, "Miss Thea, what going forward in peace you talking 'bout?"

In the most somber tone that she'd used since she came in, Auntie Thea replied, "To meet my Maker."

She said it just the way you would say, "How much for a pint of milk?" It was like she didn't even think for a moment that we hadn't seen her for a long time and this sudden bad news might disturb us. Forgetting that she was just vexed with her, Auntie Noreen asked, "You making it sound like you dying; you ain't dying or nothing like that, are you?"

With a face showing less emotion than when she was concerned that Momma's soul was lost on the Jewish side of heaven, Auntie Thea retorted, "Ain't we all? It's just that I got a definite time on my dying schedule. About a month ago they said six months; some kind of woman tumor, but my body don't feel like it got five months left of living in it so that's why I taking this time to right my wrongs; you know, just in case my not-feeling-poorly-body just up one day and start to feel poorly and then stop from feeling altogether."

Auntie Thea smiled a funny kind of smile and continued, "It's hard, real hard to have a husband who was in the business of sending people home to meet their Maker and, you know, sometimes he would come home and tell me 'bout his day. It's not that I always wanted to hear, but I was his wife and I knew better than anybody else that he didn't have no ordinary day; never could have an ordinary day in that kind of business. The good Lord knows there was nothing ordinary 'bout his days. So if telling me meant he was goin' sleep better that night, then I listened even if when he was done telling me only one of us got sleep. That's how much I loved and still love my Philip. But I'm getting off why I started this bit of talking. Anyway, he would say that sometimes when he was dressing them, he wondered how they done lived their life. You know, if they been good to people; friends, family, and strangers alike. If they lived a good enough life to make it all the way up to and through the Pearly Gates.

"Now, here I am on this short schedule to the Pearly Gates and I find myself wondering when my turn comes and somebody is dressing me, fixing me up to send me to meet my Maker, if they goin' be wondering where I goin' end up. I'm here to make sure that don't happen. I don't want anybody over me wondering if they working so hard to make me look my best only to know that their hard work goin' be for nothing 'cause when I get to the Pearly Gates, the angel Gabriel goin' look at me and tell me I can't come in; that I got to go back and into that eternal fire 'cause of this one thing."

As if the full realization of what Thea was saying had just hit her, Auntie Noreen gasped. "Miss Thea, you really serious? They really said that you ain't got much time?"

"Truth is I don't know if they hadn't told me that if I would be here today. Sometimes, it's sad that we let our hearts and our minds dwell on something so long that we can't see the wrong in it. I'm glad that my heart didn't reach that point."

Auntie Thea looked from Auntie Noreen to me as if she was already halfway expecting one of us to say something. I was feeling bad for her but not bad enough to cry. I guess that was 'cause I hadn't seen her for so long. I started to feel a little guilty 'bout not feeling really bad, but before either of us could say anything, Auntie Thea continued, "I'm here to put things right and to make sure that neither Peter, Gabriel, or none of them who make up the heavenly host goin' have no reason to turn me back. When I get to the Pearly Gates, I putting my hands on them and I pushing real hard and I going through, you hear me? I goin' through. Praise the Lord! Thank you, sweet Jesus."

Auntie Noreen looked at Auntie Thea and she said, "I've been knowing the Lord since I was a little girl and I can tell you He won't hold this one thing 'gainst you if you done a whole world of good. He's like that. He makes room for forgiveness and He understands humans; after all, he made us. So, Miss Thea, even if you didn't come here to tell Drea what you come to tell her, I think just by being a wife to your husband and doing what you just said you did; listening to him tell you 'bout his day even if it meant when he was done you, for whatever reason, couldn't sleep. The Lord would look at that and He'll let you in."

I was expecting Auntie Thea to take what Auntie Noreen had said to heart or even be a little sad, but I didn't expect her to do what she did. She burst right out laughing. Auntie Noreen looked at her as if she'd lost her mind. Auntie Thea laughed a little bit more before finally speaking. "I know you all thinking that a few of my lighter marbles done float way, but I'm laughing at myself. I say at myself 'cause I never, for one day, thought I could have earned my way through the Pearly Gates by having been Philip's wife all these years. The way you just said that, Miss Noreen, is why I'm laughing. If only you knew what it took for me to be where I was the one that Philip could come home to and unload all them dark stories on. Lord Jesus, I didn't want to hear the first one, but there I was; his wife, making all them babies for him and I guess after all of that, listening was the least I could do."

Auntie's Noreen's face had a real puzzled look and she asked, "Miss Thea, you mean this wasn't something that you did easily; out of love?"

"I loved Philip alright, but getting to where I am took a lot." Auntie Thea started to laugh again and then she added, "You have no idea what it took out of me to become convinced at the end of the day that one of them didn't follow him home. Auntie Thea didn't answer but just as she was getting ready to she started to laugh Miss Noreen, you don't know what frightened is 'till your brain tells you in the midst of one of your special moments that the hand rubbing your thigh and making you feel so sweet done dress a dead earlier in the day. That thought right there is enough to make you get up and run like the same dead is behind you."

"So how you got past it?"

"A dream!"

"How a dream make you get past that kind of fear?" Auntie Noreen asked.

"Let me tell you how. It was like this. You see, when I first saw Philip, I didn't think a handsome Negro man like him would even take notice of me."

"Why would you say that, Miss Thea?"

"Well as you can see, I still carry some weight on me and back then, I was carrying more and there were more women around with less weight on them than me. I also wasn't dressing as fancy as them, nor was I trying to push myself up to him."

"Women were doing that?"

Smiling, Auntie Thea replied, "Doing that? It seemed that every woman that could smell herself was trying; even them that you could smell… you know, they had that moth ball, slightly old woman smell…"

Auntie Noreen started laughing. "Old woman smell. Miss Thea, what you talking 'bout? There ain't no such thing as old woman smell 'cause if there was, I would have it and I ain't got no particular or different smell."

"Trust me. Old women or women that past doing woman and man business got a smell and even them was trying to get Philip to see them 'cause they figured that he was a fine upstanding man and they wanted to be Mrs. Philip Fillmore. I wasn't joining in that fracas."

"So how you got him to see you?"

"I didn't do anything. Well, I went to a funeral and since he was the only Negro undertaker around, he was the one doing it. Lord, he looked so handsome standing there and telling the people what to do. I don't particularly go and look at dead people but, Lord, I wanted to get a closer look at him so I got brave and the next thing I know, I passing right by him. I don't think I even looked in the coffin at Sister Ethel for one minute. It could've been empty for all I know."

Both Auntie Noreen and I started to laugh.

"Laugh all you want, but you all never saw Philip in his young days."

"But how did you get to where he was thinking to ask you to marry him?"

"Would you believe he remembered me and asked somebody who was at Sister Ethel's funeral if they knew who I was!"

Auntie Noreen replied, "I would believe it. Men get like that when they see somebody they want."

"Anyway, he found where I lived and he was bold enough to come by one evening and ask Aunt Bess if I lived there and could he speak with me. Lord, Lord, Aunt Bess didn't take to his boldness at first, but when she realized who he was, she softened. He made his intentions known to her that day and asked if he could talk to me and that's how me and Philip got to start our courting. I tried, at first, to get past the idea of what he did, but then one evening he went to hold my hand and I almost jumped from my seat. He looked at me and asked me what was wrong. I couldn't hide it so I just up and told him that I couldn't think of him touching me and being a real man to me 'cause when I looked at him, I saw him with the dead people. Philip said he understood but didn't think I would get past my fear 'till I saw what he did and realized that dead people couldn't really do anything to me."

"And how was Philip planning on making you realize that?"

"By me going down to the funeral home with him."

"By you doing what? You went?"

"Not at first but one night when Philip came to take me out, he said to me, 'Thea, I'm planning on making you my wife and I want when I ask for your hand in marriage that you ain't scared to put your hand in mine. I got to know that you goin' be comfortable with me doing what I do and still be a full man to you. I don't plan on stopping what I do 'cause Negro people need somebody who going care 'bout them and their loved ones that pass on. So will you trust me and come down to the funeral home and see what I do?'"

"At night time? He wanted you to go down there at night?"

"No, he was talking to me at night time. Don't think I didn't think he meant that same time 'cause 'fore he could get done, my mouth opened and I heard me say, 'Mr. Fillmore, I ain't goin' to no funeral home no night time. I may get up enough nerve in the day but, Lord, don't be asking me to go now.' Philip smiled a real smile and he said to me, 'Is that all you heard?'

"I looked at him and said, 'I heard you. You said you plan on making me your wife. That's all well and good, but you also said that you ain't planning to stop dealing with dead people. So I think it left up to me to decide if them two things can go together.'"

"What two things, Miss Thea?" Auntie Noreen asked.

"Me being his wife and him being an undertaker."

"So my guess is that you went and seen him work as you and he been married so long?"

"I went but it ain't as easy as you making it sound."

"How you do it?"

"Well, I kept waiting on Philip to ask me to marry him or bring up talk 'bout us getting married again, but since the night he first said he was thinking on asking me to marry him, no more talk 'bout marriage came up and he went on doing his funerals and undertaking business. The only thing that was different was the amount of time he was spending with me. Philip started seeing me less and less and when he did come by, he didn't try to touch my hand or anything. I started to miss his touches; not that he was ever rude or anything, but you know sometimes when we went out, he would hold my hand or when he took me to the picture show, he would let his hand touch my shoulder. Now he was keeping his distance and his hands to himself. I didn't like that so when I realized that he might be getting away, I picked myself up and I went down to the funeral home."

"Oh my God. You just up and went?"

"Yes Ma'am. I just up and went. I didn't want my man to get away from me. You see, by then I knew how much I loved Philip and I didn't want some woman who was braver than me to come along and take him."

"So how did you know he was going to have a duppie down there that day?"

"A duppie?"

"That's what we call dead people in Barbados."

"Lord Jesus, what a name; that sound far scarier that just plain dead."

"Ok, not a duppie then but, Miss Thea, how you know that there was going be a dead there that day?"

"Philip was the only Negro undertaker in all of Brooklyn, I think, so every Negro was using him so there would be somebody. When I got there, I was told that he was busy and I would have to wait or come back. The woman didn't know who I was as I'd never been anywhere near there and Philip was a very private man. I made myself known to her and asked her to show me where he was."

"Lord have mercy."

"Don't think I wasn't calling on the Lord in my heart. The woman didn't even bat an eye. She just got up from her desk and started to walk down a short hallway. Not knowing if I was following her or not, she stopped and was about to turn to make sure. I was following so close behind her I almost knocked her down. She said nothing. She just turned back around and when she got to door that said, 'EMPLOYEES ONLY' she turned to me and said, 'You sure you want to go in there? He's fixing up Headley Lessman and he in but long start. If in you never been close to a dead man, this might make you a might nervous if not outright scared.'

"I took a deep breath and said, 'Can you let him know I'm out here and I want to come in?' She didn't say one more word to me. She knocked on the door and said, 'Mr. Fillmore, it's me, Dorthea. There be a Miss Thea here; she wants to see you.'

"From inside the room, I heard, 'You said Thea?' She said, 'Yes, Mr.

Fillmore. She can come in?'"

"Oh my Lord, Miss Thea, you stand there while them be talking back and forth like that?"

"Yes. It be less than a minute when I heard him say, 'Yes.' That was it. Dorthea turned to me and I don't know if she didn't think I heard 'cause she said, 'He say you can go on in.' It was like I blinked and she was gone. She was gone so fast, I started to wonder if she might be a spook. I put my hand on the door and I turned the knob. I think if I'd looked, I'd see my heart right outside my chest I was so frighten. I pushed the door and I went in."

"Lord have mercy. I would have dropped down dead right there," Auntie Noreen gasped.

"I thought I would have too, but Philip, knowing how scared I was, had pulled a sheet right over the person."

"Thank you, Jesus."

"I stood at the door and Philip stayed where he was. He said, 'What made you come, Thea?'

"'You. I don't want to lose you, Philip, and since this is what you goin' be doing, I got to get used to it if I'm going be your wife.' Philip smiled a half-smile and staying right where he was he said, 'I know how much this is taking from you, so you go on back out and if you want, you can come back this evening when I'm done and you can see. Over there,' and he pointed to a hook with a hanger that had some clothes on it, 'are his clothes and I don't want you to really see this. No sense you getting all of this in your mind.'"

"That was it?"

"No."

"No?"

"I did just like Philip said. Later that evening, I went back. Mr. Lessman was all dressed and in his coffin. I didn't see him as a dead man, but as a dead man my man had dressed and put in a coffin so his family could come and say goodbye."

"And that's how you got over being afraid of dead people?"

"No."

"No?"

"It was the dream I had that night that not only helped me get over my fear of dead people, but pushed me right into Philip's arms. I was so frightened. I didn't want another night by myself ever."

"A dream? What kind of dream could make you do that?"

"One where a dead man sits up and talks."

"Sweet Lord Jesus, you had that kind of dream?"

"The same night I called myself being brave enough to go down by the funeral home, I dreamed that Philip and I were driving in the country and he says to me, 'Thea, I got to stop by a friend of mine over in Clover County, would you like to come with me?' So in the dream I say, 'Of course. I like Clover County.' Phillip drives and drives, and it like we never going get to Clover County but anyway, we reach it. Philip turns into this long country road and something 'bout the road make my heart start to beat real fast. The place got trees on both sides of the drive and it's dark. We reach the end of the drive and I see a building and at the same time I see a sign. The sign says 'Country Road Funeral Home and Chapel. Enter through these gates to the Pearly Gates.' Lord Jesus, my heart start to beat real fast and I turn to Philip and I say, 'Why you didn't tell me your friend is an undertaker?'

"Philip looks at me shyly and says, 'You wouldn't have come if I'd told you and I wanted your company here and on the way back. I won't be long. I'm just goin' to drop this package off to him and I'll be out right quick. Wait here for me.' I start to breathe a little easier and then the door to the place opens and a tall, skinny Negro is standing there. He starts to smile and more than a few of his teeth are missing, but that don't stop his smile from being a nice friendly one. He calls out to Philip, 'I'm sure glad you here. I got a Negro in here giving me a hard blasted time.'

"Philip says to him, 'It's your place. You don't have to put up with nobody giving you a hard time in your own place. Just tell him to get out. That's all there is to it.'

"The man starts to laugh and then he says, 'It's not that easy. This one can't go nowhere by himself. It's me bring him in here and it goin' be me taking him out and over to Rolling Hills Cemetery tomorrow.'

"Philip says, 'Oh. I see.' When Philip said that, my heart starts beating even harder. He turns to me and says, 'I ain't goin' be long. I goin' help him quick fast and we going be on our way back home. Wait here.'

"I'm fixed to stay right there when the man says, 'Let her come. It gets dark out here quick and sudden like.'

"Philip looks at me and seeing the fear in my eyes, he says, 'What you want to do, Thea?' I look at him and hear my lips say, 'Come with you.'

Philip says, 'You sure?' I says, 'You promise me that I'm goin' be safe.'

"'Promise. I promise you nothing goin' to happen. It probably ain't no more than he need me to help him lift the guy or something and that don't take much.'

"I follow Philip inside and just like that, we step right into the room where the dead man was. I'm fixing to run when the tall Negro closes the door. I rush over to the little window and, keeping my back to them, I stare out the window. Lord Jesus, my heart's beating harder than it ever beat before. I swear each time my heart beat I hear a rib crack. I start to worry 'cause I know it won't be long 'fore my chest goin' bust wide open and my heart goin' fall out.

"I hear Philip and the man talking. Philip says to him, 'Jesus, man. You do some real sloppy work. You see his toe nails?'

"The man says, 'Yeah I seen them but ain't nobody goin' see his feet."

"'None of that matters, man. It comes down to how you feel 'bout your work. Give me a file.'"

"I hear Philip filing the dead man's toes and Lord when he's done, he says, "Look, Thea, look.'

"I'm scared but Philip is asking me to look so a part of my brain says he won't ask me to look if it wasn't ok to look. I turn my head slowly and I look at the man's toe nails. They were filed neat and looked nice. I look away quickly. As I look out the window, night comes just as the man says it would. One minute it's getting dark, and the next minute it stopped getting and is pitch. My heart starts to beat wildly again. As my heart is beating, I can hear Philip and the man busy behind me. Then they stop. Philip says, 'Look, Thea. We done.'

I turn my head even slower than before and look; they are done. He, the dead man, is dressed. He looks neat. Shirt tucked tight into his pants. His belly is cardboard flat and he has shoes and socks on. Then something says to me, 'There's something strange 'bout this man.' I can't figure it out and then I notice…he doesn't have a head. The man doesn't have a head and that's the problem the other man is having. It isn't dressing him, it's what to do with a man whose head is sitting off some place other than his shoulders.

"As I turn, almost frozen, the tall man turns to Philip with the dead man's head in his hand and says, 'This is the problem I'm having.'

"Philip says, 'What problem you having with that?'

"'Man, it's the strangest thing. He stays dead as long as it isn't on his shoulders?'

"'Man, what shit you talking 'bout? Look at him; he can't be any more dead than he is.'

"'I tell you, man, I ain't lying; it's really like that. Yesterday when I tried to dress him, I put his head on first and I had nothing but talk and trouble from him.'

"'Man, you in this business too long. If you want my help sewing his head on, just put the head on, give me the needle and thread, and let me do this thing for you so I can get my woman out of here. I didn't plan on being here this long.'

"The tall Negro says to Philip, 'Just watch and see.' He puts the dead man's head on his shoulder and just as Philip was getting ready to stitch it, I think I heard movement more than Philip and the Negro. It sounds to me like it's coming from the table. As I look, the tall Negro reaches for a straight razor to shave the dead man and, Lord Jesus, the dead man sits up and says, "I don't want you shaving me with that piece of shit. Shave me with something proper.'

"When he said that, I want to run but the door is closed. So they can work properly in the small space, Philip and the tall man pull the table with the dead man on it out into the middle of the floor. There's no way for me to get out. The dead man and the tall man start to argue 'bout the kind of razor he was going to get shaved with and my heart is getting ready to stop when I hear Philip say, 'I don't believe this shit; the two of you arguing over a razor; what difference it going make, man; you dead already?'

"'Look at that rusty ass nasty razor. I don't know how many Negroes he done used that shit on. I don't want that piece of shit on my face. I want an Erase razor!'

"The tall skinny Negro says, 'Living get Erase; dead people get whatever I can put my hands on. You lucky I didn't break a bottle to shave your dead ass.'

"'A bottle? What if you miss and cut my head to fuck off?'

"'Then you won't be here talking and giving me such a hard time. So just shut your fucking mouth and let me clean you up. You keeping my friend here from taking his woman home.'

"The dead man slowly turns to me and he has that look in his eyes."

"What look, Miss Thea?" Auntie Noreen asked, her eyes bulging as if they would pop right out her head.

"The one a man gets when he's feeling to… you know."

"Oh my good Lord."

"That man starts to ease himself off the table like he was coming towards me. I start to holler and thinking how to get past them and out when I hear Philip say, "Man, you make one fucking step towards her and your dead ass goin' get to experience dying all over again. I would suggest you bring your dead ass back on this table.'

"The dead man says, 'I may be dead but I know a good piece of…'

"I don't know what else he was going say 'cause, child, I heard some rumbling and scuffling and all the while I'm screaming.

"I forced myself awake when the dead man's head rolls and stops at my feet. His eyes are open and one of them winks at me. That was the last bit of sleep I got that night. I turned on the light, got my bible, a cross, and everything that looked religious and brought it next to me. I prayed to God, Jesus, Mary, Joseph, the Disciples, Saint Anthony and even to Bethlehem."

"And you married him after that?"

"Yes. It was either marry him or spend the rest of my life wondering 'bout him and whichever woman was brave enough to get past him being an undertaker and marry him."

"I think I would have passed on him after that. He could stay right there with all his duppies. I don't think there's enough love in the world to get me to walk down the aisle with him knowing that he spent so much time dressing, boxing, and pushing people up and down aisles and then putting them in the ground. I was going without a husband," Auntie Noreen stated, still looking a little shocked from the story.

"That's why the Lord put me in Philip's path. There's a right kind of woman for every man. You got your husband and I got mine; duppies, as you call them, and all." Auntie Thea started to laugh. She looked at me and added, "When I told Philip 'bout my dream with the man with no head, he laughed and he said, 'Thea, that man only didn't have a head 'cause when you came by I was working with Mr. Lessman. It was Headly Lessman, not Mr. Headlessman. Your brain only did that to you 'cause he was covered over. Do you remember I told you it was in a small funeral home down a lonely country road where I got my start? I also told you that to me, it felt like night came there first and then spread to the rest of the country. All those things in your dreams were small parts of things I've told you. So, Miss Thea, are you ready to take these hands in marriage?'

"I took those hands and all the rest of him in marriage and I ain't ever had one day of regret. I love, truly love my Philip; duppie hands and all."

We all laughed and then Auntie Thea started talking again. "Lord Jesus, I took so long telling that story I 'most forgot why I'm here. It's knowing that I'm on my way to meet my maker and it don't look like Phillip going be here long either. He may even go 'fore me, but nonetheless, it's hard. Not the dying part but leaving unfinished business behind that's hard."

Auntie Noreen's face got all sad. "Miss Thea, don't be talking like that. Only the good Lord knows when our time goin' be up so you stop all this Pearly Gates talk."

Auntie Noreen was getting ready to say something else when Auntie Thea replied, "It's not foolish talk. It's the truth. The doctor told me and Phillip Junior last month. You see, I hadn't been feeling well in my woman parts for some time and then when I start to have a flow again after all this time, I knew in my heart that something was really wrong. I finally got up enough courage to talk to Phillip Junior's wife and she and him took me to see a doctor. The Negro doctor didn't have an answer that satisfied Phillip Junior so he drove me to Fairfax and got a white doctor there to see me.

"Them doctors may hate Negroes, but if a Negro got enough money they can forget your color for a little while. This one was able to forget 'bout my color long enough to run some test and when them tests come back he, 'fraid that he won't get all his money when he give us the bad news, ask that we give him his money first. Phillip Junior was mad but he gave him the money anyway. With the money in his hand, he told Phillip Junior and me what his tests said. I don't know if he was looking for me to holler or what but I didn't do none of that. I just thanked him and we left.

"Death ain't nothing new to me and Lord knows how much of it I've lived with from the day I met Phillip Fillmore and decided I was woman enough not only to love him, but to up and marry him. Philip is as kind and loving a man to me as any soul you could ever want. The way he was with me after that dream; I mean kind and sweet. His kindness took the fear right out of me. I don't just mean the fear of dead, or anything to do with dead people, or dying. I was afraid to live too, you know. I was so full of fear: Crawford, the police, white people, being so poor, and Lord knows I was even 'fraid of some colored people. Anyhow, so now that it's getting close to where it's goin' be my time, I don't have the least bit of fear. Phillip loved all the fears I had right out of me."

Auntie Noreen was real quiet for a while. I could tell she was feeling just as sad for Auntie Thea as I was. But Auntie Noreen didn't let none of that show in her voice when she spoke. "Now, Miss Thea, it's getting late. You go and rest and when you come tomorrow, if you want to talk some more 'bout all this, then we goin' listen. But you stop all this talk 'bout going to meet your maker. You look mighty strong to me." Smiling, Auntie Noreen added, "Besides you dressing so smart and all, it take some good years off you, even put some spring back in you. You don't look a day over fifty. Shoot you even looking younger than me and I born back in '98."

"Which '98?"

"Now you know I don't mean 1798."

"Which month in 1898; 'cause I born in 1898 too."

"No! Ain't that something? Both me and you born the same year. I was born in May and you?"

November."

"You born the same month as my Neal."

I watched as Auntie Noreen and Auntie Thea forgot about what Auntie Thea just said about her dying and instead, started talking about birthdays. Auntie Thea got really excited when Auntie Noreen said that Uncle Neal was also born in November and she exclaimed, "I was born the twenty-first of November 1898."

Auntie Noreen shook her head from side to side. "Ain't this something? Neal born the 1st of November 1895 and I born on May 5th 1898."

"Ain't that something? Now we got more than just Gina Pearl's grandbaby in common. You and me we got the same birth year; and me and your Neal, we got the same birth month." I'm glad I came and you right, I'm feeling a bit tired but not that tired that I can't tell Drea here something 'bout her people. I got all dressed up and came over to talk so I don't have time for all this resting. I'm going to have plenty of time soon to rest, so I won't be going and rest to come back tomorrow. I goin' tell you all what I learn on all them trips back to Greenwood starting with Crawford."

Auntie Noreen settled herself in to talk. She told us, "The first thing I want to share with you before I get into the real meat and potatoes of your history is this small part 'bout your nana: Gina Pearl Fields, that is before she started calling herself Promise Greenwood. She never forgot Greenwood. It flowed in her veins. The good times, the bad times, even the in-between times; everything, all of what made her a Daughter of Greenwood flowed right along with her blood. Everything in Gina Pearl, expressed or not, intertwined with her very being to make her who she was; a strong, proud, and determining woman. She wasn't Aunt-Bess-strong, but she was strong enough.

"Back in 1929 when she and I were on that bus headed to New York, we didn't really know or fully understand what was going on around us. Rich white people, and a lot of them that used to be rich were falling. They weren't fainting or nothing like that. They were falling out the sky. Even that ain't the right or best way to say it 'cause that will get you to thinking that they were falling from heaven like rain. They weren't. They were jumping from buildings, bridges, and anything high enough with some sort of ledge or window; anything they felt that when they jumped, they would make the kind of splash they weren't able to make in the market."

"The market?"

"Not market the way we understand market. The market that had all them white people throwing 'way their lives was the stock market. That's where they had all their money tied up, and they never figured they would do anything but have their money make more money, but that's not what was happening. During the last week of October, 1929, instead of making money they was losing more money than I think some of them could count; their beloved stock market crashed. None of them rich white people who was jumping was the least bit of Gina Pearl's concern. Not enough of them could jump to get her to care. I shouldn't say that because she cared. She cared that none of them jumped and landed on her with her belly rising up. All she was concerned about was finding enough of them living to keep Aunt Bess working, 'cause it was now me and she depending on Aunt Bess for everything.

"But as the market got worse, those white people got better; they got better at jumping and dying. One evening, Gina Pearl asked, 'You think that anybody ever told them white people 'bout Jesus? It seem to me from the way they just jumping out of anything high enough to either kill them or at least break their whole body up for life, nobody told them 'bout Him or they would know that where there's life, there's hope. You know, long as you have breath, even a little bit, you can still hope. I don't think there's one Negro who don't know this. How come we know and they don't?'

"Before I could answer her, she added, 'You know what I done figured out 'bout white people, their money, and why so many of them jumping?'

"I looked at her and by now I knew that she wasn't waiting on me to answer; she was going to tell me and just as I expected, she did. She said, 'Those white people always had plenty of everything including money. They had so much of it they never had to put their all in Jesus, faith, or hope. After Jesus and faith, hope was all that Negroes had cause we didn't have the money.'

"That was Gina Pearl. She would think and most times when she told you what she was thinking or had thought about, it made sense. But even knowing that, I couldn't accept what she'd thought or was thinking about my Bernard. He was my baby and he was innocent of all those things she was thinking he was responsible for; he wasn't. He really wasn't. He was just a baby trying to get born and Bess was just an aunt doing what aunts do; they come when you need them. I needed her and she was coming to me; that was all. We were family."

As Auntie Thea talked, I saw myself on my mountain. I wasn't alone and a lot of the fear was leaving me. I was feeling the most at peace I'd felt since discovering I was pregnant. As I sat at the top of my mountain, I had a feeling that my life was going to change. I wasn't sure how or why, but it was just a strange feeling I had inside of me. After Auntie Thea said what she did about Nana and was just getting ready to talk about something else when the phone rang; it was Philip Junior calling for her. It seemed that this evening was one of the evenings that Philip was remembering her and had been asking where she was. Philip Junior felt she should come back rather than have him as upset as he was that he was calling out for her and she was neither answering nor coming.

When Auntie Thea hung up the phone, she announced, "Tonight is a good night and a bad night. Phillip Senior is not remembering Philip's wife so he doesn't want her to do anything for him. Philip Junior is coming to get me."

Auntie Noreen told her, "Go and do what you have to do and when you can; you come back. We ain't going nowhere."

Auntie Thea replied, "I'll come in the morning. Philip usually sleeps late in the morning and when he wakes, he usually doesn't want anything more than a cup of coffee. Philip Junior can give him that. He'll take it from him; he always remembers Philip Junior. I'll come early and by the time he's ready for his lunch, I'll be back to give it to him. OK. I promise I'll come in the morning."

Auntie Thea no sooner said, 'morning,' before the doorbell was ringing. It was Philip Junior. We walked Auntie Thea to the door and as we did the night before, we watched the car drive away.

Auntie Noreen and I sat downstairs for a few more minutes and then Leela's faint cry reached me. Auntie Noreen told me, "You best go see 'bout her."

I got up and as I headed to the stairs, I told her, "Good night, Auntie Noreen."

As my feet started up the stairs, I heard, "Good night, Drea. Sleep good, you and that baby."

I walked the rest of the stairs quickly as Leela's cry was starting to pick up steam.

Chapter 10

A Morning Like None Other

I woke that morning the most excited I'd woken up since I could remember. I don't know if excitement was in the air, or if it was just how I was feeling, but either way I hurried with Leela. I fed, burped, washed, and dressed her so quickly, the whole thing felt like one motion. Either way, one motion or ten, I had her back in her crib in a flash while I went to get a bath myself. When I came out the bath, she had fallen asleep. The sight of a sleeping Leela thrilled me. I was beyond happy. Now she was sleeping, I had time to brush my hair properly and instead of just slapping some Ponds on my face, I actually had time to give my skin the same care I was now giving hers. I took my time and got myself dressed a little slower than normal; it felt good.

Once I was done, I decided to take her downstairs with me. I felt as if this morning was as much hers as it was mine. I wasn't sure what Auntie Thea was going to tell us, but whatever it was, I wanted the sound of the words to go into her ears. I knew she would have no idea what she was hearing, but I wanted her to hear it nonetheless.

When I got downstairs, I heard Uncle Neal, Auntie Noreen, and Auntie Thea, to my surprise. She was already here. I hurried my steps. When I walked into the kitchen, she smiled. "And a bright good morning to you and before you asks, Miss Gina-Pearl-Andrea, for all the questions you ask, yes you did see me go home last night, but I was up so early that I called your Auntie Noreen. I remembered she said she woke early. So that's how I was able to beat you to the breakfast table."

I smiled back at her and greeted them. "Good morning, Auntie Noreen, Uncle Neal, and Auntie Thea."

Auntie Thea had a cup sitting in front of her. I didn't have to guess what was in the cup. I could smell the bay leaf in the air. Auntie Noreen had made her famous cocoa. I started to wonder if she was going to treat Auntie Thea to her sweet bakes when the toaster popped up. I was disappointed.

Uncle Neal looked at my disappointed face and commented, "Good morning, Drea, so glad to see you've brought the baby down this morning. Give her to me. I've already had my tea."

I almost laughed out loud when Auntie Thea asked, "But didn't you just have a cup of cocoa from the same pot as me?"

Auntie Noreen answered, "It's an old habit from Barbados. There, we call every hot beverage tea whether it's tea or not."

All Auntie Thea said was, "OK then, I'll call it tea too while I'm here and whatever you put in my cup is going to be fine with me."

We all laughed. Auntie Noreen finished making the breakfast and put it on the table. She'd made her scramble eggs with tomatoes and scallions, toast – which Uncle Neal liked buttered – and a few thick slices of sharp cheddar cheese, a pitcher of orange juice, and a mountain of bacon; Uncle Neal loved bacon so Auntie Noreen gave him bacon often, except of course on those rare mornings when Daddy joined us for breakfast.

Like last night's supper and as was custom, breakfast was eaten in relative silence. When it was over, I cleaned up, as usual. Auntie Thea, Uncle Neal still holding Leela, and Auntie Noreen went out of the kitchen to the drawing room. I hurried to finish. I wanted to hear all of what Auntie Thea had to say. When I got to the drawing room, only Auntie Thea and Auntie Noreen were there. I didn't have to ask where Uncle Neal had gone. I knew. He had gone off to sit out back in the yard with Leela so she could get some morning sun and air, as he called it. He would be out there with her until she started to fuss for something to eat and then he would bring her to me to feed.

When I walked in, Auntie Thea said, "Child, somehow I feel like Aunt Bess. The only difference is that she used to tell us about our history in the evening. Then we had a lot of time. Your nana was pregnant with your momma and we would talk and make clothes for your momma. Those were some good times. Anyway, I didn't come to tell you 'bout those times 'cause I'm sure your nana done told you all about that, but what I'm here to tell you is what I know she couldn't tell you. I discovered it for myself, 'cause as I've already told you, Aunt Bess didn't live long enough to tell it.

"I had to go back to Promise Land and try to find somebody, anybody that would be old enough to know. Finding that somebody wasn't as hard as I thought it was going to be, but it was getting up enough nerve to go back. That was the hard part. Remember I started to tell you all last night 'bout Crawford?"

We both nodded.

Auntie Thea continued, "Well, it was him I feared and had for one year and three weeks before meeting Aunt Bess, and then it was a few more months 'till I met my sweet Phillip. After that, I didn't fear Crawford. I never forgot him, but I didn't fear him 'cause I knew as long as I had Phillip, I didn't have to worry 'bout Crawford coming and doing me anything. I had every faith in my Phillip's ability to take care of me."

Auntie Thea paused as if she was expecting either me or Auntie Noreen to say something. Neither one of us did. I guess curiosity was sitting on the top of our tongues and holding them in place. Realizing that we weren't going to say anything, Auntie Thea continued with her story. "With Gina Pearl gone, then her Lilly, guilt, and Aunt Bess' Earth-bound spirit walking beside me every day and talking to me, I couldn't take it anymore. I made up in my mind to go back and face Crawford. I told Phillip what I had to do. He was sick and couldn't come with me, but he sent Bernard and Willie; he's my second son, and Bernard is my last boy as you know.

"Having Bernard and Willie with me gave me courage. On the ride to Promise Land, I told them why I was so fearful. You should see how my sons got all tall and puffed out their chests. They were going to protect their momma come what may. I was glad yet a little fearful. We got to Promise Land in a few hours and then I wasn't sure what to do or where to start once I got there. I knew that the first thing I had to do was face Crawford. But before I can tell you that, let me just say this. Me and Crawford was like husband and wife. We were happy. He was a blues singer like you never heard a blues singer. He could also blow that saxophone like no one else ever blew one. It was the saxophone that caught me; that and his smile."

Auntie Thea smiled a little here at the memory. The smile didn't last long.

"Me and Crawford set up house and was doing really good 'till I took in a distant cousin. She visited us often, but behind my back, she and Crawford took up. When I found out, it broke my heart. I guess I didn't realize Crawford had feelings for her 'till he started to treat me really bad and then, to make matters worse, he asked her to come live with us. She came. They carried on right in front of my face. Back then, I had a different spirit. I found her and Crawford together one day and I went to fight her. I shouldn't have gone to fight her. I was near ready to deliver my baby.

"Crawford, as he'd been doing for a while, beat me. This beating was the worst. I lost my baby. It died. Crawford killed my baby. He didn't kill it outright, but all the shoving and kicking on me that he was doing made the baby fall out. He just kicked it out of me and it died. It was a boy."

Auntie Thea took a deep deep breath like the memory was more than she wanted to remember. Auntie Noreen told her, "Miss Thea, you don't have to tell that part if it's too painful for you."

Auntie Thea replied, "I've had a lot of years to live with losing my baby. Anyway, just before I ran from Greenwood, I scalded him and the cousin. I hid for three weeks. I moved around a lot in those three weeks. It was fear that moved and yet kept me. I was like the children of Israel. I hid by day and at night when I felt no one could see me, I moved; always trying to find a place that would be safe. You know; where no one could find me. Sometimes I crawled in a cellar, on a back porch, or even, if you can believe it, in somebody's house if I tried and they'd left the door open; back then folk didn't worry 'bout somebody coming in their house and taking what they had. Most of us didn't have nothing to take so doors, more often than not, were just left alone.

"I'm shame, but not quite, to admit that I even stole food. I wasn't particular you know; hot, cold, fresh, or not so fresh. I had to stay alive. So I ate what I could to make sure that I did just that: stay alive. I remember now how I would sweat. Do you know how bad fear stinks? It not only smells but it's also a robber. It robs you of sleep, yes, child, sleep was the first thing it took. Then it eats away at your mind. Night after night, as I lived like a rat, hiding and scurrying through the dark, and as you can tell I was always a big woman so scurrying wasn't that easy for me. I had to learn a hard thing too. I had to make my eyes adjust to places and surroundings I would never have seen if that nasty woman hadn't come 'tween me and Crawford. I used to think on her and hate her; you know, how could a woman do that to another woman and in her own house?

"I used to listen real hard. The slightest sound would send my heart racing. Sometimes it would be morning 'fore I could get it to settle down. I was mostly listening for Crawford's voice. I listened for the police too as I inched my way closer and closer to the bus station. I wasn't sure what I was going to do once I got to the bus station, but I felt in my heart that if I could just make it to the bus station, I would be able to get away; I had to get away from Crawford."

"My cousin, the one I met when I first ran from Crawford's house, the day I threw the lye on him."

A high-pitched voice responded, "I thought you said you scalded him?" It was Auntie Noreen's voice. It didn't really sound like her but since I knew I hadn't asked anything; high-pitched or otherwise, it had to be Auntie Noreen.

Auntie Thea went on in the same tone she was describing her days of running, "I scalded him with a mixture of water, oil, grits, and yes; lye."

Auntie Noreen's eyes opened wide, wide. She formed a giant "O" with her mouth and then as if she were yawning, she covered the big 'O" with her hand before speaking. "Oh my great God. Water, oil, grits, and lye? That poor man."

Auntie Thea looked at Auntie Noreen and with tight lips and a firm set to her jaw, she retorted, "It had nothing to do with God and he wasn't no poor man. He was a nasty stinking cheating dog and she was just a female version of him."

And then like Auntie Noreen hadn't interrupted her and as if she hadn't stopped mid-sentence to answer her host, she continued, "I don't rot or quite get to smelling like rot, not long enough without washing to, but I'm a woman and so I start to smell, you know, like fronts that ain't been washed." Auntie Thea stopped and just laughed out real loud. "Me, Thea Fillmore, going unwashed and living like some wild animal. Oh the hate that kept my company those nights. It was a lot of hate. I'm not sure now which one of them I hated the most; the cousin or Crawford."

Auntie Thea was looking at Auntie Noreen, who was shaking her head from side to side, and then shrugging her shoulders as if what she was hearing was all unreal to her and didn't make any sense.

"Now, 'fore you ask me 'bout my family and why I didn't go to none of them for help, let me explain 'bout this thing called fear. Fear can either root you or it can free you. I'd experienced the rooting part of fear while I was living with Crawford and he was treating me so bad because of that cousin, and now fear was behind me pushing me to freedom. I couldn't get caught; didn't want to take any chances, and I didn't want a soul saying they saw me with anybody, so I stayed 'way from my family.

"I was mostly related to everyone in Promise Land. Ma was still there but I couldn't go near her 'cause I knew that would be the first place they would come looking for me. I think it was 'bout the third day when I double-backed to that cousin I'd seen the first day when I was first running. It must have been God himself told me to go 'round and in the back. He, my cousin, just happened to be out on his back porch; you know the way country folk do. No real purpose or if they have a purpose, then it's to thank God for His grace.

I called my cousin's name, soft like but loud enough for him to hear. The way he jumped, I think he thought that God done answered him and if it ain't God, then spooks fixing on riding him.

"I saw Law; his name was Lawrence but everybody called him Law. His momma, my cousin more times removed than I could remember – truth is it wasn't that many times but you know she was never a close-close cousin – but anyway she'd married this man named Wallace. She named her baby Lawrence Alonzo Wallace and so everybody just called him Law, since that's what the first three letters to his name spell out. So I said, "Law, it's me; over here by the willow.'

"Promise Land full with willow trees. Every house got one. Some got two or more. He stood up and I can see his tall thin frame; child, he so thin that when he turns sideways, he gone like magic and all you can see in the place where he was standing is a long thin black line like somebody getting ready to measure something and going use a string for it."

"Auntie Thea started to laugh again. I guessed she was seeing him turned sideways and disappearing.

"Cousin Law made to step to me and I said, 'Don't come. I just wants you to know I be fine. I right hungry though.' He said, 'I be right back.'

Auntie Thea lowered her head and she started to shake it from side to side, and real soft like, she added, "You don't know what some love from family can feel like when you lonesome. I was right lonesome for love and family."

When Auntie Thea raised her head from her bosom, her eyes were wet with tears and I could see where the escaped tears had run down her cheek and dripped to the front of her dress. She looked sad. She closed her eyes and continued to shake her head from side to side. A firmness came to her mouth and that was soon replaced by a strange kind of grin. It wasn't a happy grin because she had pursed her lips firmly over her teeth. Her wrinkled lips looked like a drawstring purse. The only difference was the part that would have the string running through it she had pulled firmly back to her teeth.

She didn't stop from shaking her head, but she tilted it to the side and looked at Auntie Noreen. The look on her face was so sad, I could feel tears coming to my eyes. I wanted to go to her and hug her, but I didn't. She stopped shaking her head but the tears were freely flowing now. She said, "Noreen, you're a woman. You know love and kindness so you know what I'm talking 'bout. I'm talking 'bout going from one kind of love to that person not loving you at all. Then you come face to face with a different kind of feeling that makes you don't care if you kill somebody or not, but you don't stop from being human. You're still human and that means you want a little bit of kindness. That's what's making me cry now. That cousin, Law, when he said, 'I be right back,' was saying to me, 'I here for you. I love you. I goin' show you kindness.' It was the first time in more than a year somebody was goin' see 'bout me."

Auntie Thea started shaking her head again, and this time she took her left hand and tucking in her thumb she made a fist, turned it sideways, and pressed the fist firmly against her lips. It almost looked like she was sucking her thumb. She then took her right hand and gently patted her forehead. I couldn't take any more. I started to cry and as she sat there in her remembered pain, I excused myself and was just about to go and check on Uncle Neal and Leela when he came in with a fidgeting Leela. He was headed out to Uncle Boysie's and would be back in time for dinner.

I, for some strange reason, was happy to see him. I took Leela from him and, excusing myself, walked slowly up the stairs to my room. As I climbed the stairs, I was thinking of what Auntie Thea had said about Crawford and that made me think about Hamilton and the hate that was growing in my heart for him. Was it enough to make me want to kill him, and if it was, did that mean that I once loved him. I answered my own thought. No. He'd never allowed me to get where I could be in love with him. I was relieved. He would live and I would continue to hate him.

I put Leela in her crib and checked her diaper. She was wet so I changed her. Once she was dry, I sat down to feed her. She wasn't pulling as if she was hungry and, ordinarily, I would be in a hurry for her to get done, but what Auntie Thea had said was going through my head and I needed some time to absorb it. Today, I appreciated Leela drawing slowly. After what seemed like forever, Leela was done. I wiped her off. She let me hold her and I did so until she fell asleep. I knew that it would be at least another two hours before she fussed for something more to eat. I put her in her crib and she stirred but she didn't wake. I gently covered her legs and before I went downstairs, I made sure that the door was fully ajar so I could hear her when she woke. I hoped the fully belly and dry diaper would keep her asleep just a little longer than normal.

I went back downstairs and Auntie Noreen was alone. I asked, "Where's Auntie Thea?"

"She went to the bathroom. I think all that remembering was too much for her. She's been through a lot. It just goes to show you. You can see a person going about his or her business and you'd never know what that person's carrying around inside. That's why I tell you, Drea, when you are out there to treat that next person you are going to come in contact with as if he or she is on their last nerve; they just might be."

Auntie Thea came back into the drawing room and Auntie Noreen, as she did with everyone who ever leaves her, welcomed her back. Auntie Thea made it to the chair she was sitting in and said, "Sorry 'bout that. I didn't think all this remembering was going be like that. It's just that right there and then, that minute just when you got up to go check on your baby, I was back there; back there hungry and scared. It was just like when Aunt Bess used to tell us 'bout all them slaves and how badly they used to be treated, but I came to get you to where you can fully understand how we got to be Fields, Beaufords, Breckenshaws, and now me a Fillmore and you…a Greenwood-Hirsh, or is it Hirsch-Greenwood?"

"It's Hirsh-Greenwood."

"Ain't that something? Gina Pearl's grand-baby is half-Jewish…ain't that something? We done come full circle, but 'fore I forget why I here, let me go on. My heart almost bled all over my chest when Law comes back. He must have piled everything his ma cooked in that skillet, the same skillet I had on the bus when I was finally able to run free. I still, after all these years, got it. Never letting go of that. It stays to remind me of how far I've come and why I started out on that journey.

"Anyway, that's how I got food. Every two nights or when my spirit told me it was safe, I went to that willow tree and every time, there was something for me. The night before the morning I got on that raggedy tin can, there was something else in the bucket. A note. It said, 'Tomorrow. Bus station. Bus to New York.' The note also had Mrs. Winter's name and address and it also said, 'Bessy Fields' goin' be waiting for you.' My heart got so happy. I ate some and saved some. I took the few pennies and got myself to the bus station. I waited 'till most every Negro was on the bus and then I hurried on. I tried to get as far in the back as I could. I seen this woman, younger than me but just as sad looking, so I picked the empty seat next to her. That was your nana. Didn't know it then, but we were both on our way to her: Aunt Bess."

Auntie Noreen had tears in her eyes. We were both looking at Auntie Thea with wonder. Auntie Thea noticed how we were looking at her and she explained, "Bess was my rod when I needed to cross my Red Sea. She, with her love and kindness, parted my Red Sea of fear and in that one amazing hug right there in the bus station, she'd crossed me through and over. From that day on, whenever I would look back to see if my Egyptian army, Crawford, was coming, Bess would let me know that the sea had been closed up. All I had to do was get on with the business of living and that's what I did.

"Years later, I let my vision get clouded by focusing on the fact that Gina Pearl held my innocent Bernard responsible for Aunt Bess getting killed; I put all of you, her children, and grandchildren, and now great-grandchild, back where the sea was closed. I promise you though that when I leave here, I'll be leaving you all, as Bess would say, 'In the best part of Promise's opened field.' I'm going to tell it all; all of what I know and learned so that the women of this family can finally stand firm on a solid rock and enter their Canaan, our long-promised garden of Eden; there is one. It's been promised to us…really a promise; as he said, 'one to hold—'cause you asked for it.'"

I looked at Auntie Thea and there was no doubt in my mind that she was out in an open field alright. One that had only insane people like her running around; only stopping when they ran head-first into one of the many trees in the field.

As if reading my mind, Auntie Thea scolded me, "It's time the two of you stop giving me those occasional looks like I done lost my mind. I haven't. Love has brought me here and only when my spirit is light 'cause I finally done what I should have done so long ago will I go back to Virginia. This time, my travels will be easier. It's goin' be easier 'cause I know that Aunt Bess, Gina Pearl, and your momma can finally fly 'round heaven free and loose. In my telling, I would have un-tethered them from this Earth where I'd been keeping them, 'gainst their own will, bound here because of my selfishness."

Looking at me, Auntie Thea continued, "Child, the only thing worse in this world than selfishness is hate. This family done known a lot of hate and it pains me, even now, to know that I let what I was feeling 'gainst Gina Pearl almost make its way up the ladder to hate. That's not right. Gina Pearl had a right to feel what she was feeling. I don't think she really hated Bernard; she just didn't learn or try to love him since she... well you already know that part. What part you don't know is what I plan to tell you. Now I don't plan on staying here forever 'cause I got to go and see 'bout my Phillip. You don't have a husband yet but, child, there are some things that only a wife can do just right for her husband."

When Auntie Thea said this Auntie Noreen smiled to herself. Auntie Thea saw her smile and turned to face her. "Miss Noreen, I don't mean that; me and Phillip too old for that and you and Neal should be too."

Smiling even wider, Auntie Noreen replied, "Talk 'bout yourself, but Neal Peters fought hard to win me and my love and ain't nobody going tell us what we too old for. So you go on and speak for yourself."

Chapter 11

Speaking for Herself and How

"I ain't saying that he didn't, but there comes a time when you stop fooling yourself and admit or accept that you too old for some things; even that. These old bones, hips, and back done past bending and moving like that. The only thing moving these bones these days is will power and old age, and you know old age never in no hurry, never mind what will power be thinking. What you talking 'bout takes more time and energy than my old bones able to get up to, and even if I think I could get up to it, then it's convincing Phillip that he up to it."

Both Auntie Noreen and Auntie Thea suddenly started a strange loud laugh, it was as if they were sharing a secret.

"Miss Thea, let me tell you something 'bout that quiet man you seen this morning. He isn't always as quiet; well truth is, he was always quiet, but I found out in my young days that that quiet-looking kitten could become a lion and roar something fierce and now that he's getting on in age, he's taking on the whole white race and he roaring again."

"What you talking 'bout? Your husband? The man I met? That quiet-looking man don't look like he could get anything 'bove a whisper out his mouth; you sayin' he can roar and what you mean, taking on the whole white race?" Smiling her big infectious smile, Auntie Thea added, "Miss Noreen, I know that I done come here to fill in the missing bits and pieces of this family, but every now and again you hab to be willing to step back from the journey you on and let somebody talk a spell. You want to tell me what got you smiling so broad?"

Auntie Noreen smiled and then she looked at me as if she was about to say something that she wasn't sure she wanted me to hear so I told her, "Auntie Noreen, if this is something you don't want me to hear, I can go upstairs with Leela."

"Auntie Noreen looked at me and answered, "Child, history is history. You done been knowing your Uncle Neal now a few years and you know that unless he's with Boysie, he's just your quiet Uncle Neal, but every now and again something changes and you get to know or ought to know some more of the history 'bout the person or people you living 'round. Your Auntie Thea here done come to tell you them bits and pieces that goin' give you a better understanding of what life was like for your family 'fore you come along and so I can give you a bit of his-story or our-story. Me and your Uncle Neal had a story 'fore we started to work for Mrs. Hirsch you know.

"We had a life in Barbados. It wasn't much compared to the life we found when we got here back in 1916, but it was back there in Barbados that Neal let me know he had a voice. Me and Neal started talking from little children. Not that we knew we were talking back then 'cause all children in our village played and talked together, but me and Neal was different. Neal moved into my village when I was 'bout seven. He, his mother, father, three brothers, and two sisters came from town to the country. His grandfather had died and left his mother a house spot so they moved to it. Neal was the quietest of his brothers and sisters and I don't quite know what made we start to talk, but I think it had something to do with gooseberries, that's a fruit, or something like that but if my life depended on telling you exactly what it was, I would lose my life.

"Anyway, I was every place that he went and he was every place that I went. We weren't that far out of slavery that we didn't know our place; well our place 'round white people and so that was what people in the village did. We stayed together and only when life and hardship made us we was 'round the white people, but never like friends or nothing. Most everybody worked for the white people in one way or another.

"But me and Neal wasn't concerned with that, we were… well growing up just the way everybody was growing up in Barbados back then. There was no time to be young. If you could stand, bend your back, and wrap your hands round some cus-cus or pond grass, you pulled it, weeded the ground, or helped to clean up garden beds. Everybody worked. You had to work. There was no time for idleness. Life and living was hard and everybody was doing their best to eke out a living. It didn't have to be great; just better than slavery. Then when I was fifteen and Neal was eighteen or nineteen, a boy, 'bout Neal's age came to visit some people who lived down the road from us. He came from St. Vincent and it was the way he sounded funny had me getting a giddy head. Not one person could tell me anything. My ma, who could tell that Neal was sweet on me, told me to stay away from the foreigner. She said she heard that the foreigner was a cannibal and that he does eat people and if I didn't stay away he was goin' eat me. I looked at Ma as just an old woman and figured what did she know 'bout a sweet-talking foreigner. So, of course, I didn't listen. Every free minute I could get, I was somewhere near the house where he was staying so I could hear him talk."

When Auntie Noreen said that, she looked at me like she was sorry she was making me remember. I was remembering alright. It was the same thing Auntie Noreen and Uncle Neal had told me about that dog Hamilton. I didn't think Auntie Noreen was old or anything like that, but for a minute I was sweet on Hamilton and his accent did sound different. Auntie Noreen looked at me long enough as if to say, 'I'm not bringing this up to hurt your feelings. This story is my story, not yours. It's mine.'

I felt like I wanted to take a deep breath; this day had already been filled with deep breaths so what was another one. I took it, held it, and when I felt as if I couldn't hold it any longer, I let it out. Auntie Noreen, realizing that I was as good as I was going to get with her story, continued.

"You would think that with Barbados filled up with strong, strapping young men willing-to-work themselves to death for you, I would look at my own and pick from one of them. No, sir I didn't. I was woman enough to walk right past Neal Peters and let some foreigner catch my eye. I let him and then I let Neal know that my eyes had catch hold of the foreigner. Now, it's not that I didn't see Neal looking at me and even telling some people, well people our age, that he was my boyfriend. At first I felt real smart with Neal Peters picking me over all the other girls in the village but, girl, that foreigner with his smooth black skin, and he had some thick lips that when he parted them to smile looked like the top lip took its time and did like one of them Hawaiian dances as it worked its way over the top of his teeth, real slow and ended up in a crooked smile. It was the crooked smile that did me in. His smile seemed to come from the bottom of his heart and by the time it made it to his eyes, well, they just light up like he'd reached up to the heavens, snatched a few stars, and was now using them for eyes.

"And when he talked! Lord, when he talked, I just wanted to talk to him even if it wasn't nothing real important. Just hearing it coming out of his mouth made it important sounding. I just loved the way he said my name. He made it sound like it had nothing but rows and rows of Rs in it and then he rolled the second R round his tongue and when my name finally made its way out his mouth, it seemed to just slide right off his tongue, through his parted lips, and kicked the doors of my heart wide open.

"It was Nor-RRRRRRRR-EeeeNnnnn. Then when he was done, you know when he reached the N, it was like he stopped sudden and remembered me. He would look at me with that N hanging there; waiting for me to smile and become his Nor-RRRRRRRR-EeeeNnnnn. I did. I smiled, you know. I just stood there smiling at that foreigner like God had done something real special there in St. Vincent. Like he had made a special man just for me."

Since I'd never heard the story, Auntie Noreen had my full attention. She looked at Auntie Thea and continued, "In all this telling, like you I have to tell the truth. It wasn't all sweet. I have to admit that this foreigner didn't let on all the way what he was really looking for. He almost got the best of me if it wasn't for Neal and his pursuing, knowing what he wanted in his heart ways. This part of my story don't have no fairytale parts in it. That's the part that got me to say I hope they close the doors of Barbados to foreigners forever. There I was, smiling every time I would see him and happy that I was his Noreen with all the Rs in my name, and then one day he made Neal have to come and be my knight in crocus bag."

Auntie Noreen started to laugh a little here and then she added, "It wasn't really as bad as I making it sound now and, truth be told, I didn't really need Neal Peters to rescue me 'cause truth is I wasn't in harm's way; well not in that true true sense of the word. You don't know, Miss Thea, 'bout people in Barbados, but like every place else there's always somebody minding your business. Barbados was no different. Back then and maybe even now, everybody in Barbados does mind everybody's business. So it was somebody minding my business that made Neal Peters get in his head that he had to come and act out one of them stupid fairytales and do the knight in shining armor or crocus bag part and come and get me 'fore that foreigner had me on some boat headed back to St. Vincent with him."

I looked at Auntie Noreen and wished that Uncle Neal was sitting here with us today. I was trying to imagine Uncle Neal as a love-crazed teenager. Auntie Noreen put her left hand up to her mouth and with a big twinkle in her eyes, she chuckled and added, "That fool Neal Peters get all vexed and stupid like because somebody, who should have been minding their business and not mine, had gone and told him that they'd seen me going in the house where the foreigner was staying. They even told Neal that the people that owned the house wasn't home and it was me and the foreigner alone in the house. Jealousy climbed all over Neal Peters and so much so it had him standing in the middle of the road and not caring who was looking or hearing him as he shouted, 'Noreen Stoute, you come out here now or I coming in that house for you. I mean business. You better come out here now!'

"You should have seen it. Neal Peters out in the road, right in front the people's house, in the middle of the day calling my name at the top of his now-man voice. And then he shouted, 'Noreen Stoute, you raise better than this! What self-respecting man goin' have another man's woman in his house, and what self-respecting woman goin' find she self alone in some man's house and he ain't even from Barbados? That's what wrong, Noreen Stoute. He's a foreigner! Foreigners ain't got no sense 'bout how we do things here in Barbados. Noreen, I ain't telling you again; come out of that house! He ain't know how to treat no Bajan woman! Come out here now, Noreen! Don't make me have to come in there and bring you out! You is my woman. I ain't mekking no sport wid you! Come out now like shite or I gine come in there and burst he ras and as vexed as I is, I can't promise you, Noreen Stoute, that I may not drop a few hot ones in you for not having no better sense than this. This is the last rass-hole time I saying this.'"

When Auntie Noreen said that last part, she burst out laughing so hard that me and Auntie Thea started laughing too. We laughed like that for a few minutes and then Auntie Noreen went on with her story. "Wuh-Lord you should have seen Neal Peters standing in the road carrying on like he woke up that morning and somebody said to him, 'Neal Peters, this morning you are a man now, go out and act like a fool.' You should have seen him. Standing there in his first pair of long pants like having them on gave him some special kind of courage."

Auntie Thea interrupted. "But if you could see the man in the street making his love known for you, why didn't you come out the house and stop him from making a fool of himself?"

"Miss Thea, he didn't give me or anybody else a chance or time to stop him. The next thing I know, Neal Peters was bending down and when he raised up, he got a big rock in his hand and then he said, I ain't mekking no sport!" He let a shower of rock rain down on the people's house. He had obviously had a plan before he started calling me out. He had the biggest pile of rocks I'd ever seen. Miss Thea, it looked like he'd been gathering rocks since and before Moses' mother put him in that basket. He was really letting them fly. You see, Miss Thea, Neal Peters might have lost a lot of his mind or was acting like if he had, but there's only so much mad a person can act before somebody come out and stop them. Neal Peters had reached that level of mad."

"But, Miss Noreen, why was he so mad?"

Auntie Noreen started to laugh as she replied, "He was so mad because he thought I'd lost my mind and was letting that foreigner foop me."

Auntie Thea laughed and asked, "Foop? What is foop and why would that make him so mad?"

"Auntie Noreen suddenly started laughing again. It was the kind of laughter that made you join in even if you didn't know what the person was laughing about. When she was able to control the laughter, she explained, "Foop is the way people back home talk about what men and women do in private."

Auntie Noreen said, "You mean the same thing that got us started on this conversation? That same thing that you feel you and your Mr. Neal still young enough to do?"

"Auntie Noreen laughed again as she answered, "Drea, cover your ears. I don't want you to hear your Auntie Noreen talking like this."

Smiling, I covered my ears and Auntie Thea looked at me, laughing as she spoke."I think I've seen Miss Drea with a baby, yes? So I don't see why she should be covering her ears. Isn't it a little late for all that?"

Auntie Noreen replied, "I guess you right. So yes, it's that same thing that Neal and I don't think but know we still young enough for. Miss Thea, if a man thought another man was fooping his woman, he would kill; just like here in America."

Auntie Noreen smiled and shook her head from side to side as she answered. "Lord have mercy. I've never heard such words; foop and fooping…that's funny. Foop. Well I tell you; you live and learn every day—foop. But, Miss Noreen, didn't he think you would have more pride and sense than that?"

"When a man is in love, he doesn't think about you and your pride. All he thinks about is his pride, how wounded it would be if his friends found out his woman let another man foop she."

"But didn't he think about all those rocks he was throwing and whether or not he was going to be breaking the people's windows?"

"He didn't have to worry 'bout hitting no glass 'cause ain't not one house in the village had any glass anywhere."

"No?"

"Miss Thea, it wasn't any different to those share croppers' houses down south. No glass to worry about."

"Oh. But, Miss Noreen, what did you do then? How did you get out the house?"

"Get out?" Auntie Noreen started to laugh even harder. "Out? I didn't have to get out. I wasn't even in the house. Some stupid lying friend of his had gone and get Neal from the factory with that stupid story and he neither waited nor stayed 'fore he'd come down by the people's house making all kind of racket. Miss Thea and Drea, it was some kind of funny. There was Neal Peters carrying on and pelting rocks at the people's place and I come down the road and I watch him for a few minutes 'cause I couldn't believe my eyes but when he started letting the rocks go and with such force and frequency I shouted out, 'Neal Peters, what you doing pelting rocks at somebody's house and calling out my name like that for?'

"You should have seen his face, but poor Neal didn't have time to think or make sense out of the fact that I was standing behind him and there was no way for me to get out that house if I was really in it, with everybody who was watching seeing me come down the road. Then that stupid-as-Neal foreigner, stay right in the house and let lose two big rocks at Neal. They fly past Neal's head and almost knock it right off his shoulder."

Laughing, Auntie Thea asked, "What did he do?"

"That fool Neal Peters marched right up to that door, yanked it open, and would you believe he stepped in, bold as day, and pulled the man out of the house. Yes. He pulled him out the house and back then, Neal Peters used to use a few bad words. He let him have all the bad words he knew and I think Neal was so shamed and mad at the same time he even made up a few. I don't cuss none so I ain't gine disrespect you, Drea, or my home by repeating all of them that he said then. I can tell you this though, he called him a tall, lanky big funny-shape-headed fool. Then he said, 'No foreigner, in coming to Barbados, try to steal my woman, pelt rocks at me to try and knock off my head, ruin my reputation, and get to stand 'bout here. You leffing Barbados and 'fore you leff here, I goin' give you two stiff kicks in your rass and send you back to that so-called spice pit you come from smelling like the pig shite that on my shoes, 'cause I gine leave my footprint in your rass.'

"Girl, that man was so frightened by the idea of a man coming in the house where he was staying, dragging him out, and putting his foot to his behind that he forgot that it was Neal Peters who was wrong. But Bajans are Bajans, and not one man told Neal Peters that he was wrong 'cause the woman that was hiding inside the man's bedroom was another man's woman. Thing that was funny was the same man who had gone and told Neal that he'd seen me slip in the man's house had missed the fact that the woman slipping in the house was his woman in my good town dress. Me and she was friends, and it was my dress she had on. Back then, we used to lend we one another clothes.

"Anyway, soon as he could, that foreigner was on his way out of Barbados on the very next boat and he did put people to talk, but they didn't talk 'bout me and Neal. Them talk 'bout Neal's friend who had started the whole thing. His woman, the one that was in the house, was on that boat when it sailed with that man. She never came back, you know.

"When the whole thing had settled down, or as settled down as people would let things in a small village settle, I put Neal Peters in his place. I asked him how he could ever think that I would even set foot in the house. How he could even think that I didn't know better than that? Girl, once if I'd ever set foot in that house, my good reputation was goin' be gone. I was poor and my reputation was all this poor girl had. You didn't just up and throw that away. No, you treasured that."

"So, my dear, what happened after the man stole Neal's friend's woman and went back to his spice island?"

Auntie Noreen started to laugh again and then she said, "He left and we got married but, Miss Thea, I here forgetting myself. You didn't come all this way to hear some old woman's story. You here for Drea so forgive me all this blabbering and let me let you get on with your telling."

"I don't know if that means that nobody else gets to talk, Miss

Noreen. Sometimes you'll be surprised what comes out in the telling of a story. I know I come here for Drea, but who knows what else the rest of us might learn from all this talking and sharing. So if you want to take this time and tell me 'bout your Mr. Man who had all the Rs in the world rolling off his tongue, you just go on and tell it, but from the way I see you busy with your Mr. Neal's food, I don't know how much more they can be in the telling of this story." Smiling, Auntie Thea asked, "Is there a lot more in the telling, Miss Noreen?"

Auntie Noreen smiled back and answered, "You right. Ain't no sense in bring up all that old talk. I real happy with my Neal and I ain't one day truly wonder what happened to that man. I really never wondered, you know."

Auntie Thea asked, "Never? Never ever, Miss Noreen? You got to be real good never to have thought about him, but here you are talking 'bout him now. You sure you ain't never once thought about that foreigner as you call him?"

Auntie Noreen burst out laughing again as she'd been doing most of the time telling this story and then she replied, "You know, truth and real truth; I bring him up from time to time just to be sure that Neal still feel the same way 'bout me now as he did back then. You know, no you don't know, but let me tell you this bit. I sailed on a ship with Neal Peters all the way from Barbados to New York City's Ellis Island. Now that was something else. Neal Peters hears that we can travel on a boat and he fix it in his head that we should leave Barbados and try our luck someplace else. He picks America to be that someplace else."

Looking directly at me, she added, "You know, Drea, all this time I ain't once ever thought to tell you that part or how me and your Uncle Neal came here on a boat called *The Raphael.* I was so scared of all that water just lapping at the boat all day and night; God, nights was the blackest you could see a night. But Neal was good. He was seeing 'bout me. I was his wife, after all. I didn't know at first after the incident that he had marriage on his mind, but it wasn't too long after he stood in that street and made a fool of himself and put my name in people's mouth that he figured since he done mix my name up in foolishness, that he best do the right thing by me and it was his idea for us to get married and leave everybody and everything and come try our luck here.

"Me and Neal got married real quite like. It wasn't a big wedding the way people get married these days. My mother killed one of her goats and a black-bellied sheep. Neal's mother killed a pig and a few chickens. Women in the village that knew me since I was a little girl baked up all the flour they could put their hands on. Everybody chipped in to make it a nice wedding. I didn't have any fancy wedding dress, but at the end of the day, I was Mrs. Neal Peters: a wife.

"We moved into a little shed-size house that wasn't no bigger than the small bedroom at the top of the stairs, but that didn't matter to me nor Neal. We had plans. We were going to leave Barbados; come to America and turn our life around. It took Neal and me a little while to come up with the passage money, but once we had that and our minds made up, we left. We didn't go back for a long time, but while we waited to go back, we never forgot Barbados.

"While Neal's mother was living, we would send back what we could to her. She was something else, you know. All the time Neal was sacrificing to send her a few dollars, she was sacrificing too. We didn't know 'till long after she was dead that she never spent one penny Neal sent to her. Told people she was getting by 'fore Neal went to America and she could get by just the same so she saved the money and bought a piece of land. That's the piece of land that Neal had a little place built for that day when we couldn't stand the cold no more, but now that goin' wait a bit. We got to see Drea settled and after that; well me and Neal goin' talk 'bout goin' back. We not goin' take no boat back. We goin' do like everybody these days and get on that Pan Am."

"You not 'fraid to get on one of them things, Miss Noreen?"

"Afraid don't have nothing to do with it. I goin' approach it just the same way I approach that big ship we come here on. I ain't never been on a boat before, but it was the only way I could get here if I wanted to be here so I walk that creaky gang plank, all the while begging the good Lord not to let me fall in the Careenage since I couldn't swim.

"Would you believe, Miss Thea, that when we got off that boat at Ellis Island, they said that me and Neal was Africans; Africans. Can you believe that? We leave Barbados one thing and when we get to America…we be Africans…right back where we started. We was African when they stole us and brought us to Barbados. In Barbados, we was slaves and when we stop being slaves and come to America on we own; we back to what we started out in the first place: Africans. We felt proud to be Africans, but neither the pride nor being called African lasted long.

"We went from Africans at Ellis Island to niggers time night came and now we are Negroes and only God knows what they going end up calling us soon. Ain't it funny though 'bout white people? Them the only ones that don't get called nothing else. From day one, Adam and Eve, them be white but Boysie and Colroy say that Adam and Eve couldn't be white people since the Garden of Eden was in Africa. But true or not, them white but we, they keep trying to find a name that goin' fit us better than king or queen. They can never think of us as ever being kings or queens back in Africa so whatever name they call us goin' always be what is best for them. Something to make you think right away of some dark and evil thing; a name that always goin' make them feel better and more important over we. I tell you, Miss Thea, only God knows what we goin' be by the time them done trying to give us the worst names them can come up with; only God knows."

Chapter 12

Things Keep on A-Changing

Auntie reached the part of her remembering, or as far as she wanted to go now and turning to Auntie Thea, she said, "Life sure can be funny. One minute you think you know the path you goin' be goin' down and then something falls in the middle of that path and you got to find another way to get where you plan to go. That was what that foreigner was for me. If not for Neal thinking I was in his house, he never would have come and throw big rocks at the people's house and finding himself too shamed to stay 'bout the place after that 'cause everybody talking 'bout how Neal Peters near mash up the people's house looking for a woman that wasn't even inside. One of the men that used to sing songs for a penny started singing every time Neal went by. The song wasn't funny when I was with Neal but, girl, when Neal wasn't near round, I even used to join in and sing it. You should see we when we was singing ***Raining Down Rocks***; that was the name of the song."

Auntie Noreen stood up and, putting one hand on her hip, she started shaking her shoulders from side to side, then she started pointing a warning finger and shaking that from side to side too. Then Auntie Noreen started to sing. She was smiling as she sung.

"Pam puh lam, Pam puh lam,
Neal Peter where you gine?
Neal Peters, Neal Peters you looking vex man.
Man you in got no reason to look so vex
'cause de foreigner didn't steal your woman.

Rocks coming through the air,
Rocks breaking down your door,

Bruh down, bruh down look out, look out
Neal Peters got rocks raining down,

Neal Peters got a good right and
He even got a good left – but none of them ain't his fist.
It be one of them big sea rocks he gine throw at ya house.
It ain't God's judgment raining down but it's Neal Peters
and his pile of sea rocks.
You better duck or Neal Peters gine hit you wid a rock
and if it ain't your hip then it gine be your back he gine brek up.

Rocks coming through the air,
Rocks breaking down your door,
Bruh down, bruh down, look out, look out
Neal Peters got rocks raining down.

Bruh down, Bruh down it raining rocks.
Bruh down, Bruh down de rock coming through de air
'cause Neal Peters think de foreigner
gine tek he woman all the way to de land of de spices.
Bruh down, bruh down it raining down rocks.

Rock coming through the air,
Rocks breaking down your door,
Bruh down, bruh down, look out, look out
Neal Peters got rocks raining down."

When Auntie Noreen finished singing the song, she almost collapsed in a fit of laughter. She then said, "Your Uncle Neal couldn't take it. People singing the song and making real monkey sport at him where ever he went. Some people even went so far as to say when they seen him, 'Neal Peters, Neal Peters, where's the foreigner? Did he get back to his land of spice or you done chop open he head and bury him under a pile of rocks down by the sea?' It start getting more than Neal can stand and I think it was that, more than anything, that make Neal start looking for a way for us to leave."

Auntie Noreen caught herself when she stopped talking and I could see she felt badly 'bout just going on and on so she said, "Drea, why you didn't stop me from making mock sport at your Uncle Neal? You know he won't like to think that I told you 'bout that calypso they make up 'bout him just before we left Barbados. Miss Noreen, please forgive me and my old woman ramblings and go on and tell us 'bout you going back to Greenwood. That got to be more interesting than some old woman talking 'bout her remembered time."

"I told you, Miss Noreen, that we talking and telling to help Drea. You don't know which little piece might save her life someday, but like you said, I come to tell Drea. But only if you done telling, then I will get back to how I finally got out of Greenwood."

When Auntie Thea said this it brought us to a different place. Suddenly we realized that it was late. We'd be talking forever or so it seemed. I left the drawing room to attend to Leela.

Auntie Thea and Auntie Noreen weren't in the drawing room when I came back. They were in the kitchen making sandwiches. We'd talked right up to lunch time. Auntie Noreen opened a can of corn beef, added finely chopped onion, mayonnaise, ketchup, and grated cheddar cheese to this. Making a paste, Auntie Noreen piled it onto thick slices of bread she'd baked over the week-end.

I reached for the mauby bitters that Auntie Noreen kept in the fridge. I knew better than to get lemons or anything with acid in it, as Auntie Noreen called it. Neither she nor Uncle Neal drank anything with any acid as long as anything they were eating came from a can.

We ate our sandwiches and mauby in the kitchen and took slices of Auntie Noreen's pudding with us. When Auntie Noreen asked Auntie Thea if she would like some pudding, I'm sure Auntie Thea wasn't looking to get big fat slices of pound cake. Auntie Noreen made the best pudding in all of Brooklyn.

As we ate the cake, Auntie Thea picked up from where she'd left off in her story telling. "It was that cousin, Law, and his momma who helped me to get out of Greenwood. I got that chance to run to New York and I took it and never went back well until after your momma died."

When Auntie Noreen asked the question I was afraid to ask, I knew she was back from her remembering of the fellow and times that made her and Uncle Neal leave Barbados. "Did you see him, Crawford, when you went back?"

Auntie Thea answered with one word. "Yes."

"What happened?"

"You sure are reminding me of Gina Pearl. I promise I'll tell you all of what happened but you goin' have to give me chance to tell it 'fore I forget. Remember, I'm getting old now."

"Hush with that old talk. Remember, we the same age."

Auntie Thea smiled. It was like she and Auntie Noreen were old friends.

"When me and my boys got to Promise Land, we went first to the house of the cousin, Law, who had put food on his back porch and fed me during the three weeks 'till I could get away. He was older but he remembered me. It didn't take him long to tell me what happened to Crawford during the three weeks I was hiding. You see, right after I told him what I'd done and while I went into hiding, his momma, the nasty cousin's momma, an old lady who knew about herbs and roots, and two other people went to the house I used to live in with Crawford. They said that when they got there, they could hear Crawford and the cousin screaming. The men broke down the bedroom door I'd locked behind me when I ran, and went in to help Crawford and the cousin.

"They said that Crawford was a sorry sight but as fate would have it, his face, a good portion of his back, as well as his arms were unmarred. He was scalded from slightly above his navel down to just above his knee, but not on both legs. They said it was funny how he was scalded; it was like he just turned right into what was thrown at him. As for the cousin, they said it was like he had used his body to protect her from whatever had come through the door at them.

"He told me that they told Crawford they would help him, but he would first have to promise a few things. They said he was in so much pain, he was willing to sacrifice his two unmarked arms just to get an ease from the burning that was still going on in his body. As for the cousin, when they saw that she didn't have much on her body but some slight splotches compared to what Crawford had, they said her momma beat her naked as she was right in front of them. After Crawford saw the way her mother beat her, he was willing to promise everything; he did, and then her mother made her help clean him up.

"All that cooked skin had to come off. If the two men weren't with them, laughing a little, Law said that the women, the nasty cousin's mother included, would have left his man-business to fall off. But the men said they shouldn't do that to him. They said that Crawford was still a young man after all and despite the fact that they doubted that he would ever make any babies with it the way it looked, he could still think of himself as a man if when he looked down there, he still had something that said he was a man and not a woman.

"Anyway, they made her scrape off that cooked skin, even with Crawford calling on a God he had forgotten when the two of them was mistreating me. The two other people with them were men. They knew they would need men to hold him down otherwise they were never going to be able to treat him."

"They didn't take him to the hospital?"

"Child, it was 1929 and he was a big scaled up Negro. What hospital was they goin' take him to? Even if they'd taken him to the hospital, and just by some miracle the hospital had treated him, they was going to call the police. They didn't want the police involved. They'd only planned on treating him right there in his own house that's why the roots woman was with them."

"My God. That poor man. In all that pain," Auntie Noreen lamented.

Auntie Thea retorted, "He asked for it."

"I know but still…all that pain."

"Do you want me to continue?"

"Yes, by all means. You can't stop now. I want to know what happened."

"Well, they stayed with him while she scraped or tried to scrape off the cooked skin. Nobody paid her any mind when she tried to start. I say tried 'cause the minute she got the first little bit scraped off, she vomited. When she was done vomiting, they made her go back at it. He said she vomited until she was doing dry heaves, but they wouldn't let her stop 'till she'd properly scraped off all that cooked skin. Crawford, by then or by the time they reached the real burned parts, was almost out his mind. He had vomited too and if they didn't have the two strong men holding him down, he would have fought them and possibly killed them just to get away from the pain."

"My God." Auntie Noreen cried again. This time Auntie Thea didn't stop.

"When they had all that cooked skin off him, the old roots woman put a salve on him to help cool his raw and exposed skin. She then gave him something to drink that would make him fall asleep. Then they made that cousin go out back and bury all that cooked skin. It wasn't 'till she was done that they tended to her. Her momma, my other cousin, and one of the men stayed with them all night. They knew when Crawford woke; he was going be out of his mind from the pain.

"Each time Crawford woke, they gave him a little something to eat; not a belly full cause he didn't want nothing to eat, but enough to hold the roots tea that was going make him go back to sleep.

"The healing was slow but it happened. The cousin left his house as soon as she could get away from tending to Crawford. Her momma didn't let her come back to her house and when word got out that she'd scalded up Crawford in a jealous rage and had tried to kill me 'cause he wouldn't leave me and that's why I had to run from Promise Land, no man wanted her, and no woman wanted to be her friend. They said she tried to stay in Promise Land but with nobody wanting to be her friend, she boarded at a rooming house on the edge of town and close to nowhere for a while.

"It wasn't long after she was there that a tall, half-good-looking, too-white Negro stranger came into town. My cousin said that that Negro was so white that folk didn't think he was a Negro at all. Wasn't one thing 'bout that man made him a Negro, but he said he was a Negro so folk took him at his word, 'sides he came into town flashing more than a few dollars. It's funny what a few dollars can make people see. All that green made that too-white-to-be-a-Negro man a Negro if that's what he wanted to be.

"She, still a dirt-poor, man-hungry, money-grabbing whore, locked her eyes on his money. He, not knowing 'bout her, fell for her smiles, sweet talk, and then, not knowing how often and wide her legs could swing open for any man with a few dollars, fell between her swing-wide-open legs. A few times between those swing-wide-for-anybody-legs the poor fool got himself caught on the hinge of her swing-gate-legs and liking the feel, took up with her. Soon after, she was pregnant. She started not caring what folk whispered behind her back as she paraded around town with her almost-white Negro and her belly rising high to the heavens.

"Then 'cause he was doing all that he could to make her happy, she said she didn't want to have her baby in Greenwood and so, with a few weeks left 'fore her baby was to be born, she got real excited when he said he had kin in Florida. Anxious to be gone from Greenwood and her past, she, packed up and left with him. It broke her momma's heart 'cause her momma wanted to see her grandbaby. That nasty cousin didn't care 'bout her momma 'cause she'd never forgiven her for making her clean off all that cooked skin off Crawford. She left without even so much as a goodbye to her momma. Anger and mixed-up emotions; especially a pregnant woman's, or a woman who is pregnant for a white man and knows deep down in her heart that he's not a Negro but, for whatever reason, didn't want to be a white man, well in Greenwood anyway made her do that; just up and leave her momma without a hug or a, "Take care of yourself Momma."

"They were gone almost a month when word got back to her momma that as they tried to make their way to Gainesville in Florida, they met with the Klan. They lynched the no longer-almost-white Negro man and set fire to him as he was hanging there 'cause they knew he was a white man that was a nigger lover. She, well, they had their way with her. They kicked her in her belly and when the baby was almost out of her, they torched her and her almost-out baby. I was sorry to hear that. She was wicked, but that was no way for somebody to go…all that fear. When I heard that part, I begged the Lord to have mercy on her soul. I forgave her then.

"As for Crawford, 'cause his hands and face were spared, he could still play his saxophone. He stayed in Promise Land, in our house, and from time to time he went to the Sugar Spot, that's the place where I met him, and played. People were sorry for him. They were sorry for him because he went along with the story that the cousin had been trying to come between him and me. He also told them he told that nasty cousin that he wasn't that kind of man, reminded her that he loved me, and that we were expecting our first child. She left and came back. I wasn't home. I was visiting my momma. She waited 'till he'd fallen asleep and then she scalded him."

"Oh good Lord Jesus, you all let him go on with that lie? I guess he must have thought if he didn't go along with the story, you would come back and finish killing him. But what was in your head when you got to think about all that that you mixed and cooked up and threw on the man? Lord, Lord, Lord, have mercy. You lucky you ain't kill him."

"He killed my baby."

"But you could have killed him or, worse, both of them."

"He was my man first. He killed my baby because of that nasty woman."

I didn't realize I was holding my breath until I felt a tightness in my chest. I blew the air out in one breath. Both Auntie Noreen and Auntie Thea looked at me. They looked sorry for me like Auntie Thea shouldn't have told that story for me to hear.

Auntie Noreen asked me, "You alright, Drea?"

I replied in a dry throaty whisper, "Yes."

Auntie Thea took a breath and continued, "When I saw Crawford, he still looked like Crawford, just older. I had my boys with me. Me and them were on our way to see my cousin Law. He was going to take us over to Breckenshaw Plantation. That's was where all of your great-great-great-great-great grandmother Milkweed's sons except her last one went back to after they walked away from Fields' plantation. I was going to see if someone knew what happened to them once they went back. Anyway, it was then that I saw Crawford.

"When he saw me, I could tell that right off he knew who I was, but he looked like he seen a ghost. My heart started to beat really hard in my chest. I was afraid. Worse than when he used to beat me. I held my breath a little and as he got right close to me, I wanted to run but I didn't. I knew that once I was in Promise Land and as he had never left, there was a chance I would see him again. This was the chance.

"He looked from me to my boys and he said, 'Thea. Is that you?' 'Fore I could answer, Bernard said, 'Yes. This is Mrs. Thea Fillmore, my mother. You got something other than hello you want to say to her?'

"The way Bernard spoke to him, I could tell that he made Crawford think and at least twice even if he wanted to say hello, but he did. He said, 'Thea, I heard that you had come back. You look good.'

"I didn't answer him. He shifted from one leg to the other then he said, not to me but to Bernard, 'Mind if I have a word in private with your mother for a minute, just over here?'

"Bernard shocked me when he said, 'Just let it be a word. If you so much as look like you fixing to raise your hand to her, my brother and I will be on you 'fore your brain can tell that hand what to do. As a matter of fact, man, any word that you want to have with my mother, you best go on and have right here. You also keep this in your mind. I am an undertaker and I will have no problem embalming you while you're still living. I'm not my mother, but I'm her son so I have at least half of her mad blood. Now, you sure that you really want to have that word in private with our mother, just even over there?'

"Crawford looked from Bernard to Willie and then back to Bernard again. I could tell that Crawford knew he couldn't fight Bernard even if he wanted to. He didn't know why Bernard was so strapping, but I did. He wasn't always like that, but from the time he started helping his father, he had developed into a strapping man. I guess a lot of that 'strap' came from having to lift so many bodies, coffins, and stuff. All that developing was now creating second thoughts for Crawford, who finally, and with more sense that I thought he had, said, 'Right here. Right here will do just fine. All I wanted to say to your mother is that I'm sorry. I'm sorry that back then, when she was living here, I treated her so badly. I deserve what I got. I know she don't need no forgiveness from me…'

"Again Bernard was talking, 'Damn right she don't. You lucky I don't just up and kick your ass right now on principal 'cause you once put your fool ass hands on my mother. I don't give a shit that it was before I was born. I just should…'

"Willie could see that his brother was getting mad. Bernard had some temper when he got mad, so Willie put his hand on his brother's shoulder as if to guide him, and he did but just a little way off. That guiding away to stop him from beating Crawford left me alone, but not quite, with Crawford for the first time.

"Bernard noticed that he and Willie had made two steps too many for him. He stopped and before they could get any further away, he walked back. I could tell that Bernard was thinking that he wouldn't go but so far 'cause he had to make sure he could get right back to me in case Crawford lost his mind. Crawford noticed that my boys had come back. He made a step away from them, but continued to talk. To my surprise, he raised his voice, no not in anger but loud enough for my grown sons to hear. I guess he didn't want to take any chances on Bernard having to guess what it was he was saying to me.

"He continued, 'It was wrong, Thea.' Bernard cleared his throat and Crawford added, "Miss Thea. Miss Thea. Don't mean you no disrespect. All of what I did to you was wrong. I destroyed a good thing. Ain't never had nobody since you.'

"I looked at him. The look I gave him reminded him that he did have someone since me and it was because of that someone that I scalded him. He looked away for a minute and when he looked back at me, he said, 'Well, after that day. That day, Miss Thea, was the worse day of my life. What you done me was bad, but that's not what makes it the worse day of my life. I sometimes wished that I had died. No, not so you would come to any trouble or anything like that, but just so I won't have to live with all that I did to you. I treated you poorly. Miss Thea, I done you some awful things and the most awful thing I done you was what happened to the baby. I think about my boy, the baby all the time.

'You know, I can get the image of how bad my skin was burned out my head. I can get my brain to forget the pain from the burns, but what I can't get it to do is forget the sight of my baby boy there on the floor. God won't let me forget. I've begged Him to make the memory of that little brown-skinned baby with his little fat hands and feet; he was going to be a big baby, taking after you, out of my head but He won't. I robbed you of the joy of touching his little hands and feet. I robbed you out of all his smiles before and after teeth. I did the worse thing that any man can do, and for what?'

"Crawford bowed his head and it looked like his head could just freely swing side to side but it wasn't swinging on its own. He was making it. Then, with his head still hung low and looking heavy and burdensome, he said, 'He would be near thirty by now and I'd probably be a grandfather. But I ruined it all, and for what, Thea? I mean Miss Thea. I'm sorry. Do you think you could find it in your heart to forgive me? I mean that with everything inside me. I know you don't think there's anything good inside of me and you have all right to think and feel that way, but know, Miss Thea, I've been begging the Lord to keep me alive and let me set eyes on you again so I could beg you myself to forgive me.'

"He went on, 'I would…' And here his head got lower to his chest but realizing that he couldn't ask for forgiveness with a head hung low, he raised it and then his eyes and he, with eyes that looked watery, said to me, "Miss Thea, I would like to ask your forgiveness for what I did to you and worse yet, to you as a woman and the mother of my child. Can you find it in your heart to forgive me for hurting you, and for what I done to the little innocent baby, our son?'

"I looked at the old man before me with the gray hair, the lines, and more than just aged ones on his face. The troubled, sloping, lazy, and watery eyes, and I wanted to say that I couldn't and wouldn't ever forgive him, but I was on a journey to set things right and he was part of it. I looked at my sons and then back at him. Finally, I said, 'A place deep in my soul can't ever forgive you for what you done to me. That's the part of me that couldn't wait to be a mother to that little boy. The part where he rolled and felt safe; the same place where I poured all my love to him and was ready to lay down my life to keep him safe. You stole that from me and made me a bad mother; unable to keep her baby safe from hurt and harm. But funny enough, it's that same part of me that allowed me to become a mother again; mother to these two before you; and she, the mother, goin' forgive you.

"'I know, and I ain't goin' tell you no lie, I'm not able to forgive you everything, but I'll work it out with the Lord; the part that I can't forgive you for. Now, me and my boys got to be on our way.'

"I don't know if he answered or not. I just turned and walk away. In my heart, I was thanking God that it went the way it had. I was grateful for Bernard and Willie being with me. I stepped between my two sons and they each wrapped an arm around my waist and, without ever looking back, we walked away. It was only when I was back in the car that I started to cry. I'm not sure why I started to cry, but I guess it was the burden of never knowing what had happened to him. Of wondering if I'd killed them, always wondering if someday he was going come and find me and kill me, and now it was finally all over, I was relieved. I guess the tears were of relief and joy that I would never have to see him again. I think too that I was finally able to say goodbye to my baby. I'd never given him a name, but there and then in the car, I named him and let him go. I said a quiet prayer to the Lord and asked him to keep my baby safe."

Auntie Noreen asked quietly, "What did you name the baby? I mean after all this time, what does a mother call a baby whose father done kill him?'"

"I called him Josiah."

"That's a beautiful name. It takes away some of the sadness that passed 'tween you two. I guess for you to get to where you could boil up some lye, grits, oil, and water and throw it on somebody, you must have had a lot of hate for him and so your hurt was beyond words. But you know that for you to get to that point, it shows how much you loved him."

A high-pitched voice cried out, "Love?" It wasn't 'till my lips blew out the air to finish saying the word that I realized I'd even spoken.

Auntie Noreen answered, "Yes. Love. The only way you can have that much hate for somebody is that you have to have a lot of love for them at one time. Strange, but it's love that would make you kill the very person you love so much. For some people, it's the idea of not having that person loving them back that drives them mad, and for some the same way they loved the person is how deeply they hate them…Drea, love is a very funny thing. Very, very funny thing."

Auntie Noreen stopped from talking to me and looking at Auntie Thea with eyes that had the most troubled look in them, she spoke in a voice that sounded like it was choking. "My God, Miss Thea, thinking 'bout it, what you threw on that man and woman and then locking them in that bedroom sounds to me like you was planning on killing them. You wasn't plan on killing them, was you?"

Auntie Thea looked Auntie Noreen dead in her face as she answered, "Yes."

Auntie Noreen clasped all her fingers together real tight like she was getting ready to pray and placing them on her mouth, she closed her eyes tightly and shook her head slowly from side to side. Finally, she took her still-clasped hands from her mouth. "My God, Miss Thea, that was a sad, sad story. You ever asked the Lord to forgive you for that?"

Looking just as sad as Auntie Noreen, Auntie Thea answered, "Some of it; just some of it."

Auntie Noreen said, "Just some? Why not all? You just said that you meant to kill them. Killing is goin' against the Lord's Commandments."

"I know that killing is breaking the Commandments but, even knowing that, if I were to ask God to forgive me, it would mean to me, and that's just to me, that I was sorry for all of what I did to him."

"You weren't sorry?"

"No. How could I be sorry for all of it? He killed my child and the Bible says, 'An eye for an eye and a tooth for a tooth.' So the way I look at it, one of them should have died in that room that day and since neither of them died, then I don't have to ask the Lord for forgiveness for all of it so that's why I say some."

"So which part you asking the Lord to forgive you for?"

"The part where I didn't kill him; that part. I didn't quite get the eye for an eye part right, so for failing to do exactly as it say in the Bible, I'm asking Him to forgive me. That's it, Miss Noreen. I've asked the Lord to forgive me for messing up; for not killing the son-of-a-bitch. Sorry to cuss in your house, and I don't mean you no disrespect but for all those years even when I lived in fear, I had hoped that I'd killed him.

"Knowing that I didn't meant that I failed to get revenge for my baby. Now, don't go and tell me that the Lord says revenge is His. I know that part too, but He also said, 'An eye for an eye and a tooth for a tooth that's the part and only part I concerned myself with. But it's done and now he can answer to the Lord. At least I know that he will never get to put a baby in anybody else. That knowledge gives me a little satisfaction.

"But anyway, Miss Noreen, I'm done with discussing Crawford. He's not part of the reason I came here. I just told you 'bout that part so you would get a better understanding on how I come to be living with Aunt Bess. Besides, I've asked the Lord for all the forgiveness I feel I need to ask for. When I see Him, it's up to Him to tell me that I should have asked for more. I'll tell you this much though, Miss Noreen, the way I feel 'bout Crawford if on that day of judgment asking for more forgiveness is goin' be the difference between me getting into heaven or hell, I goin' choose hell. I can tell you this too, once I in hell and I see Crawford – he has to be there, he can't be anywhere else – I'm goin' to spend eternity trying to get that eye and tooth from him."

Laughing a strange laugh that didn't invite you to join in, Auntie Thea continued, "Yup that's goin be my job in hell. The devil goin' beg the Lord to look past my not asking for more forgiveness and to take me into heaven so he can get a chance to torture Crawford."

Auntie Noreen stared at Auntie Thea, who said nothing. Auntie Noreen's face was very serious. It was clear that the conversation on Crawford was over. I knew that the subject of Crawford would never come up in this house again, at least not by Auntie Thea.

None of us realized it but it was almost time to start dinner and we were still in the drawing room talking. I guessed Auntie Thea felt that it didn't make sense starting on something new so she asked Auntie Noreen to call Philip Junior so she could go home and see about Philip.

Since it was just around the corner, Philip was there quickly. That set the pace for how Auntie Thea visited us. If time permitted and Uncle Philip was doing well, she came in the mornings. If he wasn't doing well, not remembering her, or needed her, she came in the evenings. Auntie Thea never came if Uncle Philip was having a totally lucid day; he got those on occasion and then it was, according to Auntie Thea, as if they had never left the house on Macdonough Street. No one ever reminded Uncle Philip that so many years had gone by.

He was happy in his present reality and so it became everyone's reality. Auntie Thea was always really happy after Uncle Philip had remembered her. She said it felt like she had her old Philip back and she worried that if she went before him, he might stay like that for a while and that would break her heart knowing that he was remembering her, wanting her, and she couldn't be there for him.

The afternoon Auntie Thea said that, she'd started to cry. She'd cried before but this time it was one of those cries where we all cried. I didn't cry as hard as they did because there was no one I loved like that, but I think Auntie Noreen was thinking of a day when either she or Uncle Neal would have to face life without the other. That thought made me sad because I couldn't imagine that a day would come and we wouldn't be in each other's life.

We were all deep in our own thoughts and there was no need for words. None of us wanted to imagine facing life without the person that made our world light up. For Auntie Thea, it was Uncle Philip. For Auntie Noreen, it was Uncle Neal, and for me, well it was all of them.

Chapter 13

Remuneration! Repatriation! Recompense or Restitution! Give Us What Is Ours!

Uncle Neal wasn't home. He'd gone to his friend Boysie Cox' house as usual. Boysie and Uncle Neal's has been friends, according to both Uncle Neal and Auntie Noreen, from the day they set foot off the boat at Ellis Island. Boysie Cox was there to get some other people from Barbados who had travelled, or were supposed to have travelled on *The Raphael* that day but, for whatever reason, they weren't there. Boysie, after hearing them speak recognized them as Barbadians and after discovering that they didn't have anyone or place to go, he said, "I came here to collect my family. Dem ain't here and the two of you and me from the same place, Barbados, so I ain't goin' leave wunna here. Come, I dun mek make space for my family so I goin' let wunna use it 'till I find out what happened to them and after I find out and dem come I gine set up some place else for the two of wunna. Come."

Auntie Noreen said she was so glad that the Lord had sent him because she and Uncle Neal had figured out the getting to America part, but they hadn't figured out the living in America part. Now, after all these years, he and Uncle Neal were still friends. Uncle Boysie, as I called him, was getting on in age and so he now needed looking after as he didn't have any family. Uncle Neal went to see him every day. There, they talked politics as Uncle Boysie ate the food Auntie Noreen sent for him daily. Uncle Neal had other friends, but none of them mattered as much to him as Uncle Boysie. I guess Uncle Boysie must be like a father to Uncle Neal. I think if the day ever came that Uncle Neal had to do without something so Uncle Boysie wouldn't have to, Uncle Neal would make the sacrifice, but he never had to. Uncle Boysie was, as Uncle Neal always said, "Well fortified." That meant he was able to take care of himself financially.

So every afternoon he went to Uncle Boysie's house where they sat and talked politics. The subject for the most part was always the same. Remuneration! Repatriation! Recompense! or Restitution! Give to the Negro, your ex-slave, child of Africa, what is rightfully theirs! That was what drove them. They went everywhere they could hear someone talk about fixing things or making conditions better for Negroes, Uncle Neal more so these days than Uncle Boysie. Those talks kept Uncle Neal going 'till he was ready to come back home. I smiled. Uncle Neal was so predictable.

"He never changed his routine and now that all the talk was about Civil Rights and the difference it was going to make for Negroes, you couldn't get him to talk about anything else. Uncle Neal didn't talk much, if really at all, but if you wanted to hear his mouth, all you had to say was, 'Steve Biko, Malcolm X, Bussa, Adam Clayton Powel, Willie Ricks, or Marcus Garvey. Now, if you wanted to light a real big fire under him, all you had to say was, 'Strom Thurmond.' That was one white man that the very mention of his name really got Uncle Neal fired up.

One day, when Uncle Neal came home, even more boiling mad than I could remember, he said to no one in particular, "I tell you this. Any white man you see with so much hate for Negroes must got a secret 'bout some Negro he wants to keep hid. Deep in his racist heart, and you know how deep and racist their hearts can be, he must be longing for a Negro woman or already had one. You know how white men be. This wanting Negro women ain't new, it been going on through the ages. You mark my words. I may be long dead and gone, but one of these days you all going see what I say come to pass and you goin' remember that I said it first.

"The way that Strom Thurmond or whatever his name is carrying on and on takes me right back to Hamlet, and you all know I know my Shakespeare. Right here, if I were up there in Washington where they trying to pass that Civil Rights Bill and he holding things up with all his quarreling 'bout what's good for Negroes and what isn't, I would say to him, 'Surely, Mr. Senator Strom Thurmond, the gentleman doth protest too much; me thinks.' Then I would hit him with some real Bajan and I would say, 'Man what you really vex 'bout? You got a Negro woman or

Negro child hide 'bout somewhere?'"

Uncle Neal let out a big blow of air like he was blowing off steam and then he added, "Nor Nor, you know that every time I go by Boysie and he and the fellows talking politics, it does boil me up; take me back to Barbados, and all the hardships we done pass through. Coming here to America ain't no different. I think it worse here. A Negro ain't worth nothing here. Every time you turn around, somebody white doing something bad to somebody and that somebody, who is a Negro, ain't got nowhere to turn for help.

"That's why I feel proud 'bout them fellows who trying to do something right for Negroes. I old now, but if when them had started all of this and I had the mindset I do right now, I would've been right out there wid them. I know how to fight now, how to get what is right for me and mine. But I wasn't thinking right back then, Nor Nor. I was just worried about keeping a job and a part of me, that part that was sleeping, was seeing this thing as a American thing. That was wrong. This kind of wrongness don't know that I'm from Barbados.

"It's wrong, Nor Nor. A Negro got less rights here in big America than a dog. Them kinda things them doing we ain't right. Did I tell you 'bout this young man that Boysie and them down at the Lodge talking 'bout?"

Both Auntie Noreen and I stayed still. It was goin' to be a few minutes and then Uncle Neal would answer his own question. That was Uncle Neal's way. The few minutes came and went and Uncle Neal answered his own question. He said, "This one calling himself "X" and he ain't full Christian, but don't hold that against him. He talking and he talking for everybody that got African in them. That mean me, you, Drea, people here in America, England, and every place where the Negro is. He ain't standing quiet. A lot of these young Negroes talking and taking a stand; them following in some good footsteps.

"Them following the teaching from that fellow who was from Jamaica, what was his name again? Yeah, yeah I remember…Marcus Garvey; he dead a long time now, but a lot of what he said then made good sense so people still talking 'bout him. Them also talking 'bout my own Prince Hall; I done talked 'bout him forever so you all know that he's the one they want to say didn't come from Barbados, but I holding onto the fact that he from Barbados and besides, he was a mason like me.

"Yes, what was I saying 'fore I get to the one who was a mason? Yes, yes, I remember now. I was goin' to mention Mr. Edward Wilmot Blyden. He from St. Thomas but his people, who were slaves when he was born, was true, true African. I don't know for sure but Boysie and them say his people was Igbo; you know, where most of the slaves them bring to Barbados was from so you know I claiming him too."

Uncle Neal's voice trailed off in my head as Auntie Noreen and Auntie Thea's voices became louder and clearer, and whatever had made me take that trip down memory lane now left my head. I was now wondering how much Auntie Thea being here was going to throw Uncle Neal off. We would never know because he'd never say anything and he would just go on doing what he does and at his own pace. It would only be if she got in his way that we, or Auntie Noreen at least, would hear anything. If she didn't, life would go on for him, uninterrupted. I walked back into the drawing room and Auntie Noreen was asking Auntie Thea if she wanted another cup of tea.

I watched as Auntie Thea just smiled and said, "Yes, I would like that very much. That would be so nice and, Noreen, can I have a piece of that cake I saw on the table? I like sweets."

"Sure. Drea, what 'bout you? You want something?"

"No. I'll just sit here with Auntie Thea 'till you come back."

Reaching the door, Auntie Noreen told me, "Don't wait for me. This is your family she's come to tell you about. You can fill me in with what I miss later."

As Auntie Noreen walked out the drawing room, Auntie Thea tilted her head and looking as if she was looking at the chandelier, she muttered, "Now where was I? Yes. I was talking 'bout Crawford but I'm done with the telling of that. Time to move on to my real reason for coming. Is the baby OK."

"Yes she is. Thanks for asking."

"Are you ready to hear about your great-great-great-great-great-grandmother Milkweed?"

"Yes, Auntie Thea. I'm very curious to hear the story that Nana was saving for when I got older." As I spoke, Auntie Noreen returned to us with the tea and cake.

"Older? Child, if your Aunt Bess was alive when your nana said that, she would have set a fire under her. She would have said, 'Older, why you got to wait 'till she's older? Start telling her now and by the time she's older, it will be well seasoned in her bones.' Older? That's what's wrong with us as a people; we like waiting too much and then by the time we get 'round to telling, it too late. We either dead or them we were going to tell it to gone.

"Well, you are older and since your nana isn't here to tell you, I'm here and I'm going to make sure that when I walk out this house, you have all the pieces and then it's my wish that you tell it to that little girl of yours up there. Don't do like your nana and wait until she's older 'cause that day may never come. You start telling her; even before she can understand what you are saying and perhaps she'll be the one that breaks this dreaded curse off us."

I looked at Auntie Noreen as if I'd never heard the word before but I had. If nothing else, Nana had gotten in the part about the curse. From the way Auntie Thea looked at me, I could tell she thought I didn't know, but before I could get to tell her that I knew at least that part, she said, "Yes…curse. It took me the best part of the last twenty-something years to get some questions answered; even questions I had that I was hoping one day to ask Aunt Bess about, but you know that we never got the chance."

Chapter 14

Everything Has a Beginning

"No one really knew who it was that told about the school for little nigger pickney that the white mistress Henrietta was running. Well, no one until I went back and started searching for someone, anyone that might have heard something from some kin that was old or knew kin that was back on the plantation."

"Did you find anyone?

"I'm here, ain't I, child? Once those stones started to turn, I started digging and turning. I wasn't leaving one stone unturned. I had to know. The first stone came from Rebeccah, Milkweed's daughter. She was still living and right there on Fields Plantation. Her body was weak and frail, but I guess something in her told her that someone was coming for the story she had in her heart so she held onto the hope."

"Is that the truth?"

"Noreen, did this little sprig of a girl just ask me if what I'm saying is the truth? Do you think I would come this far and away from my husband for a fancy tale?"

"I'm sorry, Auntie Thea. It's just that when I think of slavery times, it all seems so far away."

"The truth is if we really think about it, slavery wasn't that long ago. We in 1963 and that means it ain't but a hundred years since President Abraham Lincoln said that slaves could go free and since this family got some real long livers in it, I was able to find plenty of folk that knew one piece or the other of what happened to Fields, Milkweed, and all those children they had together."

"I still can't believe it, but I guess you're right, Auntie Thea, it really wasn't that long ago. What was it like when you saw Rebeccah, knowing she was Milkweed's daughter? "What did she look like?"

"I mind you to have manners. She isn't or wouldn't ever be Rebeccah to you. She wasn't to me and I'm way older than you. She was your great-grand-aunt four or five times removed so you give her her right respect when you speak of her. You can call her great-grand-aunt, grand-aunt, or even Nana Rebeccah but, not taking anything from you, Miss Noreen, it just doesn't sound right hearing you say Rebeccah."

"You not taking anything from me; right is right, and Drea knows right and better. Don't you, Drea?"

"I'm sorry, Auntie Thea. Auntie Noreen is right. I know better and right. What did Great-grand-Aunt Rebeccah look like?"

Auntie Thea smiled at me and answered, "She was tall; even taller than me. She was very tall for an old woman. Also, depending on how you looked at her, she had Indian features and white features, yet she still looked like a Negro. She was dark like an Indian and even though she was so old, she was beautiful. Her hair was long, I mean real, real long. It was also silver-gray then; must have been something to see when she was young. It was like a few yards of fine white cotton on her head. Her eyes were like an old woman's eyes; a little cloudy, a little teary-looking, and yet at times, they seemed young, bright, and mischievous. Her eyes were mostly young when she was talking about her dada; if you can imagine: Fields, a white plantation owner that used to have slaves – her momma amongst them – had a Negro woman calling him dada.

"She said she was the only one of his children ever called him that; but I'm jumping ahead of myself. You just asked what she looked like and here I am just running off at the mouth so anxious am I to tell you this amazing story. Let me just say that I could see some of her in Bessie, a bit in your nana, and I guess I would say even a bit in you as I look at you now; that Fields' blood strong; real strong.

"At first, I didn't want to believe it myself. She was just as Aunt Bess had described. She looked like a rich white woman. By that, I mean there she was in that great big plantation house like she was the lord of the manor, like if she belonged there."

"The plantation house? Well, did she belong? Was the house and plantation hers? Did he leave it for them?"

Laughing a small laugh, Auntie Thea cautioned me, "Gina Pearl, Gina Pearl, slow down! Oh my goodness, if you aren't your grandmother, I don't know who is. I didn't say the house or plantation was hers. What I said was that she looked like a rich white woman."

"Did you talk to her?"

"I talked to her and I talked to her and her grand-nieces. One was her real grand-niece; Neala. She was a quiet kind of spirit. I say spirit 'cause you could just feel the good coming from her. The way she looked at and cared about Rebeccah you could tell that she had a real deep love for her. She, like the other niece who wasn't a real niece but the great-granddaughter of the last overseer who lived there seem to take turns in caring for Rebeccah. The other niece, the one who wasn't full kin; the overseer; his name was O'Brien; an Irishman who, according to Beccah, believed the sun rose on his woman Anakey and then it set with Fields. Would you believe that that overseer, his Negro woman Anakey, and their child stayed right on there, living and for a long, long time right along with Fields and Milkweed?

"This niece, their great-granddaughter was the one who, from time to time, stopped in to help Neala look after Beccah; not that she really needed anyone looking after. She was able to do for herself. Not like when she was very young, but she was able to do what she needed done, within reason. Would you believe that?"

"Only because you say it happened."

"Miss Noreen, where did this chip of a girl get all this talk? I should just take myself out of here and leave you with all your wondering."

I looked at Auntie Thea to see if she was serious, but she wasn't. There was a smile on her face so I pleaded with her, "Please, Auntie Thea, tell me what happened. The excitement and anticipation is killing me."

"Don't let it 'cause I would hate to think I did all that travelling and talking only to get here and at the first few words out my mouth, you drop down dead."

I didn't know to laugh or not so I didn't. I think it was a good thing too as Auntie Thea then quickly added, "The first thing Rebeccah wanted to know was which side of the family I belonged to, and why was I now showing up. Those old-time people don't just accept anybody coming 'round and saying they are family. I took my time and told her who I was and which side of the family I belonged to. I made sure I mentioned Bessie as Bessie was, believe it or not, Rebeccah's grand-niece. That would make you her great-great-great-great-grand-niece.

"Can you imagine that? All that age and history sitting in front of me and with a look of expectancy. My heart became so full. I didn't know what to say to her. I took my time and told her what I'd heard and I told her why I was there. Satisfied that I was really kin, she started to talk to me. She, of course, had never heard any more about the family since your great-grandmother, your nana's mother had long ago stopped going by. It was as if that side of the family didn't exist anymore after she went after her Happy-Ever-After husband."

"Her what, Auntie Thea?"

"Happy-Ever-After husband. Back in 1929, your great-grandmother Etta Pearl put your grandmother, Gina Pearl, on a bus headed for New York City to your great-aunt Bess and never, not one day, looked back. Your grandmother used to think about her a lot and when Aunt Bess wasn't around, she would cry to me 'bout missing her, but soon your mother was born and discussions of your great-grandmother never came up again.

"Truth is, I didn't set out to find out what happened to her because I felt that if a woman could throw away her daughter over a man, then she wasn't worth the trouble of finding or finding out what happened to. But I knew deep in my heart I couldn't come here to tell you what happened to the family and not have an answer just in case you were like your grandmother and had a million and one questions."

Smiling, she added, "And what do you know? I was right. You are just like your grandmother. So before I start going back and back into the family history, let me start first with her. I didn't get this part of the story from Rebeccah. I got it from kin that knew her after she moved into that house with her Happy-Ever-After husband and all his children.

"Your great-grandmother put down her peaceful poor life with her one daughter to take up what she thought was going to be a rich sweet life with a man who had a big house, land, and a truck. Somehow, she didn't seem to remember or think about all those children he'd bred off Wisdom, his last wife. If she'd thought about it, she would have traded places with Wisdom and died. But sometimes greed can cloud your vision. Hers was really cloudy 'cause on the day she skipped away from her own pregnant daughter, your nana, she wasn't thinking about nothing more than it looked like she was finally going to get the life she'd always wanted, craved, and may even have felt she deserved.

"Don't think that people didn't talk about her. When news got out that she'd sent that pregnant girl away, the few friends she had fell away. The one person that really cared for her just stopped. That woman was

Berry Willow, Milton Willow's mother. Gina Peal was going to have Milton's baby. Milton had died and the only thing Mrs. Willow had to look forward to was the baby, and now Gina Pearl was gone; sent away with the baby and Mrs. Willow's hope of being a doting grandmother in her belly. People said that Milton's mother just stopped speaking to Etta Pearl. It was like she didn't exist. If Berry saw her in town, she just crossed the street or looked the other way. That was a sad, sad thing 'cause the two of them had been friends since they were little girls.

"It was said that Berry said, 'That's just like Etta Pearl. She always got her eyes on what somebody else got. She seen that old fool and all she can think 'bout is getting her greasy greedy paws on what he got. She can just stay there for all I care. She sent 'way all that I had to remind me of my Milton. I don't want to see her ever again. Don't call me when you all find her all bent up, 'cause wicked people don't just lie down and die straight. Their sins bend them up; wait and see. She's goin' be bent up like some old tree branch and when you all do remember what I said, don't call me. I won't be coming.' "That was it. Berry never talked to or about her again.

"Those that were willing to talk about Etta Pearl said that her paws were greasy all right. If it wasn't butter, she had her hands in baking cakes, pies, or whatever those children wanted. Then it was lard; frying up all that chicken, pork chops, and God knows whatever else could be fried. Yes and that land where she saw herself sitting on his porch and watching the rabbits jump and play…well, she was the rabbit that was jumping but none of what she had to do could be called playing as he had her going from one vegetable patch to another. Ernest Threadwell wasn't a man that had time for pampering. He had land to work, children to feed, and a house to keep. That's what he expected from her and that's what she did. You see, he was just like all men, and some women, for that matter. He'd painted her such a beautiful picture that it was enough for her to give away her pregnant grieving child, without really thinking about it.

"He did give her what he promised; some Happy but it wasn't Ever-After. Her Happy had a time limit, which she realized when he surprised her with an unreal and almost unbelievable demand. He wanted more children and if she couldn't give him what he wanted, her Happy-Ever-After wouldn't be coming."

Even without thinking, I asked, "More children. Wasn't she old?"

"Not as old as you think. But it was him. He was old and yet he wanted more children?"

"More children?"

"Yes, my dear, he wanted more children. It wasn't like the house wasn't full enough already. Something in that old fool wanted to see if he could squeeze at least one more child out of his old, and I'm sure, hanging-low-and-crusty man sack."

Auntie Noreen laughed out loud. "I ain't never heard nothing like that before. A hanging-low-and-crusty man sack?"

Smiling, Auntie Thea answered, "Miss Noreen, don't act like you don't know what I'm talking about. Drea here may not know, but you know that after a while, nothing stands up on them. They ain't like we. Things on us slide and slowly make their way to the floor, but things on them just drop; sudden like, straight to the floor never more to rise up again."

Still laughing, Auntie Noreen said, "Miss Thea, stop. Stop. I didn't know you was funny like that."

Auntie Thea smiled at me and Auntie Noreen and she continued, "Go on and let Drea believe what you want her to believe that you don't know 'bout how them look when they get old, but I know that you know better. So while the two of you thinking about all that old crusty skin hanging where it be hanging, I'm going on with my story 'cause I don't have all day or night to be talking. I got to eat, rest, talk, and then get back to my family. So where was I?"

Smiling, I answered, "You were getting ready to tell us 'bout him wanting more babies."

"Ok. Yes. Folk around there believed she tried, but the stork that was delivering babies didn't have the address to where she and that old crusty-hanging-down wicked man lived and so, after about two or three years of waiting on her to bring a new baby into his house, things started to change real fast. Her Happy-Ever-After became her Sad-As-Hell-Right-Now.

"She never came right out and told anyone that she was sad, but people have a way of knowing when other people are happy. They could see it in her face when they saw her, or if someone stopped by the house they could see that happy had long left her. The small children from Wisdom weren't listening to her and the big ones from his other wife didn't like her. When his oldest children came to visit, they acted like she wasn't there. They took what they wanted from the house and she couldn't say a word.

"It was here that Ernest Threadwell had a soft spot. His children could do no wrong for him, so it didn't make sense for her to complain to him. He wouldn't have listened anyway. His two biggest girls knew that and so she had a double misery on her hands when they visited. It was, people said, as if they made the small or last set of children behave worse. Then to make things even more miserable, they brought their own children along and…well you can imagine what inside that house must have been like for her."

With a look of concern on her face, Auntie Noreen said, "So why didn't she just leave? She knew where her daughter and sister was. She did know, didn't she?"

"Of course she did. It's my guess that she wanted to leave. They said that if she could have found a way to swallow her pride, she would have gotten on a bus and come to New York and asked both Gina Pearl and Bessie to forgive her. But she knew what Bessie would have told her.

"They said that after a few years where she started to look old and tired, she made her way back to Fields' plantation and was trying to find a way to beg Rebeccah to let her stay on, but that old girl wouldn't have it. She tried to get Rebeccah to change her mind and let her stay on in Milkweed's house, but even though Rebeccah was old, she wasn't forgiving of anyone that had upset her momma Pearl or her dada.

Without really thinking about not interrupting, I asked, "She'd upset them both when she was younger?"

"You really are like your grandmother. It didn't matter how many times Aunt Bess said not to interrupt, she always had a question and now here you are and you doing just like her."But yes. After Charlotte moved away from the plantation, she stayed away, but her daughter, Neala, would come by when she got older, so when Etta Pearl was born, Beccah was happy that Neala was coming by and bringing her. People said it was clear, even when she was a little thing that a longing was in her that nobody could figure out what it was, or where it came from. She wanted more. She couldn't tell anybody what the more was that she wanted, but it drove her to where she found herself chasing after one of Talbert's great-grandsons who had, like most white men in the South, a deep-hidden thing for Negro women and that mystery at the top of their thighs.

"Knowing that and the fact that she'd seen the life that Fields had given Milkweed and her grandmother, she hoped she would end up if not in the plantation house, then in a situation like Milkweed. She willingly became his deep-hidden Negro thing but they said that all she got out of it was Gina Pearl. No one ever knew for sure if your nana was really a Talbert or not 'cause neither one of them would say. Your great-nana Etta Pearl called your nana Gina Pearl Fields and so she was a Fields, but if you ever see a Talbert, it would be clear that you got some of that blood. But none of that matters to this part that I'm telling.

"Beccah wasn't bending. The story of what she'd done to her own child had reached Beccah and so she had no time for her and told her that outright. She'd made up her old Southern mind and she told her she couldn't stay.

"Here your great-nana's selfishness cost her. I guess Beccah was tired. She chased her off the place, but she didn't send her empty-handed; she went back to Ernest Threadwell with a few dollars in her pocket. If she'd had any sense, she would have taken it, gotten on an old raggedy falling apart tin can passing itself off as a bus, and headed to New York to look for her sister, her child, and grandchild, but she didn't. She did like a lot of foolish women desperate to get or keep a man. She put everything at his feet, including herself, and he, because he was a selfish cold old fool, took the money but not her. He didn't take it 'cause it would help mend them closer. He took it 'cause he couldn't have cared less if she'd come back or not. He'd found himself a sixteen-year-old girl; truth is he didn't find a sixteen-year-old girl. That poor child was a repayment of a debt."

Auntie Noreen asked, "Did you say repayment of a debt?"

I said repayment of a debt. Talk, and you know how much that is worth, had it that her momma owed Ernest Threadwell some money. He wanted his money but she didn't have it. So he, because he was nasty, told the mother that he would take her young sweet sixteen year old girl child off her hands."

Auntie Noreen asked, "Take off her hands?"

"Yes. I said take off her hands. That nasty man, with children the same age as that girl and some older, said he would take the girl as repayment. That woman gave him her innocent girl child in exchange for the money she owed him 'cause she was just like Etta Pearl."

Auntie Noreen asked, "How?"

"That fool woman was chasing a Happy-Ever-After too, and somewhere in her brain, her child, Shadow, was in her way. You would be surprised how many stupid or foolish women there are like that."

"I can't imagine women would do such a thing. I ain't never birth no child, but I know that if I had a daughter, there would be nothing that no man had that would get me to walk 'way from my child," Auntie Noreen declared.

"Ain't that the truth? Shadow's mother went 'bout her business leaving that poor girl under his roof and with all those bad behaved children. Shadow would become the talk of Greenwood, but before I get to talking 'bout Shadow, I can tell you that your great-grandmother couldn't take the shame.

"Shadow? What kind of name is that?"

"That wasn't her name but 'cause she was more blue than black her momma called her Shadow."

"How a momma gine do that to she own child?"

"Not right sure or why but she did. Anyway your great grandmother gathered what little she could, or he would let her take, and what pride she could find deep inside of her and she left."

I let out a loud gasp as I asked, "He did her the same way that Crawford did you?"

Auntie Noreen, understanding what I meant, answered, "No. Her shame was different. He had the young girl there like she was a maid or something, but Etta Pearl could see how he was looking at the girl. She'd seen that look before."

Auntie Noreen interrupted her. "Before. What you talking 'bout, Miss Thea? You mean he was in the habit of looking at little girls?"

"Some people had speculated that was the reason she'd sent Gina Pearl away, but even if that was the case, she didn't have to have him. She could have kept her girl child and they could have figured it out together once the baby came. So even if she'd seen the look before, that didn't change things for her. She was there. Shadow was there and he was there. She'd been replaced. She accepted that.

"She didn't have her little house to go back to 'cause once she'd gotten your nana on that bus headed to New York, that fool woman sold her house, would you believe it, to Ernest Threadwell. Not directly, but to someone who then turned around and sold it to Ernest Threadwell and that fool woman, the minute she had the few dollars from the sale of her house in her hand, she let him take it from her too. She was stupid and in love so I think it was more like she gave it to him. After all, he was her Happy-Ever-After so what would she need money for? He was going to take care of her 'till it was time to shut her up in a little box and put her in the dirt.

"Sad to say, but after she left his house, she knocked from pillow to post and when she reached the point where that same bus station where she'd put her daughter on a tin can passing for a bus was going be her home, one of the old women from the local church took pity on her and took her in. Shame and not wanting to see Ernest Threadwell, his children, or the young woman who was now his woman kept her mostly inside the little room she had. Nobody knows for sure what killed her, but they said that over time, she ventured about less and less. It got so that people stopped seeing her so no one remembered or thought about her. She became just one of those people that used to live around there, even though she still lived. She simply ceased to exist for people; life can be funny like that. You go to the Land Of The Forgotten once no one sees or cares about you no more.

"Ernest Threadwell got one child, or so he figured, in Shadow, but that would be the last one. What happened to him is not of major importance to this story, but since I know that you'll be curious, I can say that he got his own. It didn't happen right away, but by the time Shadow gave birth to that child, it was a good thing he was gone or he would have died anyway. That blue-black girl pushed out a nearly white baby with eyes so blue, they looked like God had reached right out into the sky and sliced little pieces of heaven and put them in that little boy's face for his eyes.

"One look is all it would have taken to know who the father of that boy was. Nope, not Ernest Threadwell. Somehow, when Ernest Threadwell, with his old, hanging-low-and-crusty man sack, was looking to have his last hurrah, someone else had slipped in and, from what people said, showed Shadow the most love she'd ever seen. By the time he was done, he'd left Ernest Threadwell walking around with his chest up in the air bragging 'bout how he could still churn them out.

No he didn't even think that somebody else would look at Shadow, so that's why he was so proud of her rising belly. The mystery man was too; he knew the truth and as he told Crawford, they were friends, he felt it in his bones each time Shadow was near him that the child in her belly was his. It turned out that his bones were right. That's all I'm willing to say 'bout Ernest Threadwell, Shadow, her mystery man, and their baby: Ruddy Blue.

"Back to your great-grandmother. One morning, the widow Mrs. Bee just started screaming and screaming. People came rushing to see what she was screaming about. When they got her to quiet down enough to say what was wrong; it was Etta Pearl. She was dead.

"People had, of course, seen dead people before but it was how she looked that made people wonder if she had, perhaps, drunk poison. She was in the little bed she used in the tiny room Mrs. Bee had fixed up for her. She was on her back yet she was all bent, arched, and twisted to where, depending on how you looked at her, she was on her stomach, or at least the bottom half appeared to be on her stomach and yet her top half appeared to be on her back at the same time.

"Her fingers were gripping the sheet, clumps and patches of her hair was missing, and a few of her fingernails were on the bed. They said it looked like she'd ripped them out with her teeth. Before you ask why they thought that let me tell you; it was because her mouth had dried blood on it. Her head was bent almost all the way so her face was touching the bed, and all her toes were curled. It was a sad sight. She hadn't found her Happy-Ever-After and if what folks were thinking was true, they would be no Pearly Gates for her to push open.

"She wouldn't get to stand before God and tell him why she'd sent away her only daughter. There would be no white flowing robe, wings, halo: golden or otherwise, to float over her head everywhere she went, nor would there be big white fluffy clouds for her to sit and peacefully play her harp on.

"Killing yourself was an unpardonable sin and from the way they said she looked, only the devil in hell could be waiting for her. No one claimed her. They told Mrs. Willow but she reminded them that she'd said not to call her and as Mrs. Bee had only taken her in and wasn't really family to her she was buried at the far side of the cemetery; the part where unclaimed people are buried."

For reasons that I didn't know or understand, I felt really sad and started crying. I said through my tears, "They were wrong. They could have gotten word to Nana. She would have gone to see 'bout her momma. Aunt Bess would have gone…she would have. They were wrong."

The sadness I was feeling was deep. I was now crying loudly at the idea that no one had claimed her. I tried to imagine how sad and lonely she must have felt to make her decide that being dead was better than alive and lonely. It was so sad to think that there was no one there to pick up her pieces. When I said that, something hit me; that's why Momma was able to just lie down and die. It was in her. Her grandmother had done it and she, without knowing it, had done just like her: given up on living as well. I slowed my tears and made a fresh promise that whatever I may endure with Leela, I would never just give up on living. The tears slowed and soon stopped.

I could feel their eyes on me and when I raised my head it was as I'd thought: both Auntie Noreen and Auntie Thea were looking at me. It was Auntie Noreen who spoke first. "I'm sorry, Drea, that you had to find out about your great-grandmother this way. I think that your Auntie Thea was right in going and finding out that part of your history for you. I know it hurting you real bad now, but at least you know."

I nodded. Auntie Thea asked me, "Do you want me to go on or have you had enough for now?"

I wanted to tell her to go on but that would've been a lie. I'd never heard of my great-grandmother and now I was hearing about her and she was dead. I needed time to get to know and to let go of a woman I'd never known about 'till now. I looked at Auntie Thea and I told her, "The truth, Auntie Thea, I don't know why this is making me feel so bad right now, but if it's alright with you, I would like a chance to think about this. I would also like to let Nana and Mommy know what happened to her. They may already know, but I would like to sit quietly and tell them."

Auntie Thea answered, "Believe it or not, I understand. I felt that same way when I thought about Crawford. I needed to accept what had happened to him and then let it go at the same time, so you go on. Take your time and when you're ready, you come back to me."

I managed a little smile. I got up, figuring I'd go upstairs to sit with Leela a bit. As I made my way up the stairs, I could heart Auntie Thea and Auntie Noreen talking. A part of me wanted to go back and join them but a part of me, the part that was grieving, decided to keep going.

Chapter 15

Picking up, Picking Up the Pieces

I went upstairs and stayed for a little while. I couldn't really figure out why I was feeling bad for a woman that had treated Nana so badly. It wasn't even like I knew her or had any idea what she even looked like, yet it bothered me. The picture of her dying like that and in so much pain that she pulled out her hair and nails was so disturbing to my spirit, I couldn't help but feel badly for her.

A fresh set of tears came. I cried 'till I was cried out. Thank God Leela didn't bother to open her eyes and need me. I was able to get a good cry in and out. While I was crying, I cried for Nana and Mommy. She was, after all, Mommy's grandmother but by sending Nana away, she'd robbed Mommy of having a grandmother. So much loss and for what?

I stayed upstairs 'till Leela woke. Then I changed and fed her and, wrapping her in a blanket, I took her with me. Auntie Thea had said she didn't have forever to tell me the story so I knew I didn't have forever to sit around and feel bad for someone who didn't have much feel bad in them. Once I got back downstairs, it was as if neither of them had moved, but I could tell they had because there was evidence of sandwiches, cake, and tea. Knowing Auntie Noreen, there would be a sandwich waiting for me in the kitchen. I went there to get it. It was one of Auntie Noreen's cheese sandwiches. Sliced cheese, lettuce, tomato, mayonnaise, mustard, and a few dabs of hot sauce; always hot sauce she made herself – her bit of Barbados always had to be in the house. I held Leela in one hand and with the other ate my sandwich. When I was done, I walked back into the drawing room.

Book Three

Rebeccah Pearl Fields

A Time to Speak

Chapter 16

Someone Wuz Coming; I Tolt Dem

When I got back into the drawing room, it was as if I'd never left. Both Auntie Noreen and Auntie Thea acknowledged my return but neither offered, as I'd thought and secretly wished, to take Leela from me. I sat with her and hoped that the disappointment didn't show on my face.

Auntie Thea took a deep breath and after taking her time to let it go, she finally spoke. "I'm here because Bessie was putting all this family history together that she'd gathered over time. Now I don't know if Bessie had told all that she knew or if there was more she was going to tell, but either way fate had other plans for her. It's not to say that I know what plans fate has for me, but I got a feeling that I'm going to get the chance to tell it all. I promised her and I aim to keep that promise.

"Drea, there aren't enough words to tell you what it felt like for me to be sitting face to face with my own history. When Aunt Bess told us about Cornbread, Molasses, Milkweed, Fields, and life on that plantation your nana and I stayed with our eyes glued to her lips; our ears couldn't be open any wider, but this was different. I was seeing someone that Aunt Bess had just gotten to talking about and then it seemed like something so far away and then there she was; not a baby or some made up person, but a living, talking page right out of our history book."

"Auntie Thea, what did it feel like?"

"You are your nana's own child. I'm going have to do like Aunt Bess and ask you to hold onto your questions so that I can get the telling of this story out of the way, otherwise I'm never goin' get done. And as you know 'cause I told you, I don't have as long as Aunt Bess to get this telling done."

"I'm sorry, Auntie Thea, it's just that I'm anxious and excited all at the same time."

"I understand. It was the same for Cousin Rebeccah. Yes; Rebeccah, because of her sister Charlotte, who was a distant kin to me, I was then a cousin to her. I don't know how many times removed. We were just glad to be seeing one another.

"That old woman just sat there looking at me and then she got all sad-looking. That made me feel really bad 'cause I didn't want to upset her none, but I understood why she looked so sad when, with tears in her eye, she said, 'I dun tolt dem over and over dat sumbody be coming. I not know'ds quite how I know'ds but I know'ds and I dun tolt dem. I suh I be holdin' on. I hab to 'cause wen dem show'd up, I hab to be ready to suh wat been pressing on muh heart all dese year and now, now look, here yuh be; kin come to know'ds wat it be dat I know'ds 'bout Momma Pearl and Dada.'

"My God when she said, "I not know'ds how I know'ds but I know'ds,' my blood ran cold. I was back there; back with Aunt Bess telling 'bout all those things that happen on Beauford, Litchfield, and even Fields' plantation. It was just as I'd heard. I was so surprised that after all that time she still spoke the same as they did before her mother was born. I wanted so badly to tell her what just being in her presence was doing to me. There she was, our last thread to what was our living history, and she was telling me that she held on because something told her that someone was coming for what she was holding onto.

"I didn't cry; don't know how I didn't, but I said to her, 'Cousin Beccah, I'm glad you waited. I'm so sorry that we made you wait so long, but I promise you I will stay until you tell me what you've been waiting to tell, and I promise you I won't keep it nor will I make anyone wait forever for whatever you are fixing to tell me.'

"That old lady smiled the most beautiful toothless smile that wasn't a baby's I'd ever seen, and then what she did next told me where Aunt Bess got her ways from. She said, 'Come. We goin' get sumthin to eat and I goin' do whatev'r I be able to do to git dis memory to empty out and tolt you all of wat dun happen frum de day dat it jis't be Dada, Momma Pearl, meh, Lavina, Eve, Poole, Charlotte, Pearl Etta Mae, and Benjamin Harold, dem last two be de pickney dat muh big sister Sarah, she not be Dada's pickney, birf, den dead, and left fer Momma Pearl to raise up.

"'It jis't be we dat left 'round Momma Pearl and Dada as muh brudders walk 'way frum 'round Momma Pearl. I tinks dat 'fore I be born, but I nots so sure right now. Dat dem leavin' near, real near, bruk she heart yuh know'd. If it not be fer Anakey, she be dead.

"'Anakey, she be de nigger that be wench to O'Brien. Him be Overseer wen nigger be slave but frum de time dat President Abraham Lincoln suh dat nigger have right to be free, all dem walk 'way or be led way by the soldiers from all de plantations, him nots be Overseer ov'r nobody. Ain't nobody fer him to do him overseering wid.'

"I followed Cousin Rebeccah to two chairs that were on the porch. She said, 'Sit, sit. I not know'ds 'bout yuh, but muh bones dem not tek too much standing dese days. I be old and I tire mite quick now so if it be fine wid yuh, we gine sit in dese chair fer a spell and den we gine gets sumting to eat. Wat? I nots be so sure, but it be good watev'r it be.'

"We sat in the two chairs and she said, "Dis morning wen I woke, I be feel a mite 'cular stirring in muh bones dat I not be feel fer sum time and I know'ds dat today be a special day. I be dat way, yuh know'd, since I be but a tiny pickney. Dada, him like that I be know'd 'bout tings 'fore dem happen but not Momma Pearl.

"'Momma Pearl, she nots wants to know'd. She suh dat it not fer man to know'ds what gine happen 'fore it happen but Dada, him suh dat what I be hab be special gift. Him suh dat I be dat way 'cause I hab blood of pure Seminole and a Mandinka African. Him not know'd dat outright. It be Momma Pearl dat tolt him. De Seminole, Lil' Mae, be grandmuddah to Momma Pearl and de Mandinka, him be Momma Pearl's Poppa Molasses. I be de one dat get de most of dem blood so I be able to know'd tings 'fore dem happen. Dat's how I be know'd to wait. Muh spirit or de spirit of de Mandinka African and de Seminole suh fer meh to wait; so I wait and now here yuh be. I be so ready to unburden muh soul, jis't as Dada unburden him own to meh 'fore him dead.

"'Him not tolt Momma Pearl 'cause him suh dat Momma Pearl dun suffer more dan any one woman, nigger or white, ought to suffer and so him wait and over time when him be old, him tolt meh wat it be like 'fore I be born and den him mek meh know'd ev'ryting him be do. Him suh dat him be mekking peace wid him God.'

"Still smiling that beautiful toothless smile she went on, "I be him favorite pickney. Him had love fer all him pickney, but wen Isham, Zack, Tuck, Willie, and Juba be walk 'way frum him place, him suh dat Momma Pearl bruk she heart and it pain him mightily to know'd dat him nots be able to jis't fix dat ting fer she. I be see Momma Pearl, and how sad she be, so I mek in muh heart dat I not be add more to she pain so I fix to stay right here 'till de Lawd call Dada and Momma Pearl and den I be stay right on here too 'till him call fer meh.'"

I knew that Auntie Thea had said for me not to interrupt but before I could keep the question inside of me, it just came out, "She's dead?"

"Yes. As I said, Rebeccah was just holding on 'till someone came so she could give them the story."

"But she had other family around her; why didn't she tell them?"

"I guess she couldn't bring herself to tell that much truth to her own."

"So why did she tell you?"

"I told her my truth. I told her I was trying to find the pieces so I could find my way to the Pearly Gates in peace. Since she was trying to make peace with the same God and her journey was the same as mine, over a seven-week period, she told me the bits and pieces of the story that I didn't know.

"Those seven weeks were something else. It's not like we sat down on that porch and didn't get up 'till seven weeks had passed. Over the seven weeks, I got to know as much of that plantation as Beccah's legs would let her take me. We sometimes talked in the old slave cabin that was Milkweed's, or we talked in the cabin that Milkweed shared with Harold Joe and her children, or in Eve and Lavina's houses, or Sara's house, Anakey and O'Brien's house, or the house that Fields built for Milkwed a little distance from the main plantation house.

"You should have seen that house. It was so beautiful, even where it was. It was as if Fields had some slaves to go into the middle of his land and cut down some trees, but not all. He left enough so that when he built the house, it would be surrounded by tall and beautiful trees. There was a tree, I'm not sure what it is but it stood off to the side as if it were standing guard over the house and even the other trees. It wasn't tall and majestic. This tree was small but the way it stood alone it was as if by just being where it was it was saying it understood loneliness. Beccah, pointing at the little giant tree said, "That thar tree be mighty special to meh. Wen I be lil' pickney it be way I come by muh lonesome to watch de sunset. Thar be oth'r places 'round here to watch de sunset but thar be no place like dis place. Here the sunset tek ov'r de whole field and sky. Mek it look like de whole place be on fire.

"'It be to dis tree dat I come wen I be happy and it be thar dat I come too wen muh heart be heavy. Thar be a next special tree here but I be tolt yuh 'bout dat later."

The house had three levels. It was painted white just like Field's house, and wherever there was roofing showing, it was red. It looked like slates but I'm not sure. It was early fall when I got there so you should have seen the colors surrounding that house. The bright reds, oranges, gold, yellow with hints of green still clinging to the leaves and shrubs. The ground was covered with the same spectrum of color; my God, it was something to see.

"The smell of wood burning somewhere on the plantation only added to the beauty and feel of the place. It didn't hurt either that a chimney was sending puffs and streams of smoke into the air. It had a beautiful closed-in front porch; it wasn't, according to Beccah always closed in. It became closed in as Milkweed got older. The first evening I was there Beccah and I went to her tree to watch the sunset. She was right. It was the most amazing reddish gold and that whole place looked like if not one bad thing could ever have happened there. It was beautiful, peaceful and serene.

"I wanted to stay on that place forever, but it wasn't meant for me to live out my days there. I was there to get what I had to, come and tell you, and then move on. I accepted that, though it was hard knowing I would eventually have to move on. I can tell you this though; that for the almost two months I was there, I made it my business to look, see, touch, feel, and absorb as much of that place as possible. I walked away with Fields plantation and Rebeccah and her sweet-touch-your heart-to-the core-toothless-smile etched so very deeply in my soul I don't know if there's room for another sweet spirit like hers. I will never forget her or there. I had a chance to go to a place that, if not for Aunt Bess' interest in the family, would never have existed for me. Now I tell you, that is something to hold onto. How many of us ever get a chance to be present in our history. I know that sounds a bit mixed-up, but that's what it felt like to me. My past was in my present, telling me things that would help pave a smoother road for our future.

"I hope someday, Drea, that you and if not you, then somebody else in this family get a chance to walk the grounds of that immense place. I think it was, no not was, is about a thousand acres or something like that. Can you imagine one man owning all that land?"

"You think that it will still be there, Auntie Thea?"

Auntie Thea looked at me with an amused look on her face and asked me, "There? Where you think a thousand acres of land, with seven strongly built houses: a main house, a smaller version of the main house, and then with five more houses and not to mention that more than a few of the slave cabins and other structures still on it is going?"

"I don't know. I guess in my mind I couldn't see them still around."

"They will be around, trust me. They will be around."

"How can you be sure, Auntie Thea?"

"You are just going to have to trust me, but that's not the first part of what I'm here to tell you. I'm here because Aunt Bess died and I never got to know what happened to Milkweed's sons after they went back to Brekenshaw's plantation. I didn't know what happened to Sara's twins, and whether or not Milkweed inherited that massive plantation.

"However, unlike Cousin Rebeccah, I don't have seven weeks to tell you this whole thing. I have to get back to my Phillip since both our clocks are slowing down and I don't know whose is going to stop first. I would hate to be here righting this wrong with you and have his clock stop and I'm not there to hold his hand, or beg the hands of time to move a little slower to give me just a little bit more time, so I can tell him how much I love and have loved him. I would want to be there to thank him one more time for coming into my life and changing it. I would want him to know, yet again, that my life started the day I met him, and I've never regretted one second of knowing him. Yes, even after all these years, I love him like the first day we met and I can't imagine what my life is going to be like without him in it. So, you see, I don't have all the time in the world to sit here and just talk and talk and talk.

"Phillip has been my best friend and the person I've turned to with every twist of life. I owe it to Phillip, if he's called first, to be there when God says it's time for him come through the Pearly Gates. So, as best as you can, I'm going to beg you not to interrupt too much. If, however, I don't get to finish the story I have in my heart to tell you, then find Bernard. I've told him the whole thing and I'd made him promise to find you and tell you if anything happened to me before I got here. He gave his word; my Bernard keeps his word so I know if I don't get to finish, he will. He, more than any of my children, needed to know. Ok. So if I don't get to finish, find Bernard. You promise, Drea?"

"I promise."

"Good."

As it was getting near to lunch time, Auntie Noreen excused herself to fix Uncle Neal's lunch. As soon as Auntie Noreen left the room, Leela started to cry. I wanted to pretend that I didn't hear her but it would've been impossible to do since she was in my arms. Auntie Thea told me, "You go on and give that baby her milk and I'll keep right on talking. You don't need your hands to hear me."

I didn't say anything and Auntie Thea continued, "Beccah, as she wanted me to call her, not cousin, kin, or nothing like that. Said that was what her father, Fields, called her even up to the day he died. I'm jumping ahead of myself. Beccah started her story telling just like Aunt Bess. This time, I didn't have to imagine the slave voice. I was hearing it for myself. Even though she wasn't a slave, it was the way she'd learned to speak and it was the way she stayed speaking even though she spent all those years taking care of and caring for Fields. This is our story, as Rebeccah Fields, Beccah, told it to me.

Chapter 17

The Bitter Breeze That Blew

Rebeccah

Dada, yes I be call him Dada. I know'ds dat Isham, Zack, Juba, Tuck, and Willie not ev'r seen him as dem faddah, but I be sees him as muh faddah and I be love him much as any pickney, nigger or white, be able to love dem faddah. Muh time wid him be different to de times and ways muh bruddahs know'ds him. Dem know'd him as Massa Fields, but frum de time I be born, I be know'ds dat him be muh faddah and well, she, Pearl Fields, who be him slave 'fore nigger people be set free by President Abraham Lincoln, be muh muddah. I call she Muddah or Momma, but most times I be call she Momma Pearl, as Dada be call she Pearl.

Anakey, when she be still here, she be call Momma Pearl 'Milkweed', but it be only Anakey and O'Brien dat be call she Milkweed. She be answer to all dem names, but it be only wen Dada call she Pearl dat she be smile.

Way yuh find meh be de onlyest place I be live. I born here on Fields plantation and soon I be dead here. Dis house dat I in be de house dat Dada build fer Momma Pearl, and it be way she birf Charlotte. She be Muddah's last pickney. All de rest of Momma Pearl's pickney she birf when she be him slave. All of dem: Isham, Zack, Juba, Tuck, Willie, Eve, Lavina, Poole, and Lilly be fer Dada. Sara, or Haroldetta, her not be Dada's pickney. I not know'ds fer a while who be she faddah, but since she be all nigger, it be clear dat she faddah be nigger mans. None of dat be matter now since she be dead. She dead mekking pickney. Momma and Anakey raise up she pickney. Dem be Pearl Etta Mae and Benjamin Harold. Dem not be here. Benjamin, him be in Canada and Pearl Etta

Mae, she and she Eli, him be she husband, dem be up north; Philadelphia I tinks but 'fore I can tolt yuh dat part and how dem get to be thar, I best be start wid Dada and Momma Pearl."

Drea

Here, Auntie Thea stopped and said, "I'd heard most of this from Aunt Bess, but I'd already told Beccah to tell me the whole thing. I didn't want to interrupt, and perhaps getting a second-hand account would give me some pieces that we missed, having gotten it filtered through the ages."

Rebeccah

"Her name not be Pearl wen him furst seen she, but it be him over time dat give she de name Pearl, and I tell yuh, Miss Thea, she like dat name a might bit better dan de name Milkweed. It be so dat soon thar not be a soul 'round here 'cept'n Anakey and O'Brien dat 'member wen Momma Pearl be Milkweed. So I tinks it be best dat I wuk muh way back frum him. Ev'n fer yuh and meh to be way we be, here on him plantation and him be dead be a right big marvel fer some, and I 'pect'n fer yuh as well.

"Yuh see, it be a might unusual ev'n frum dat part. Wat I means by dat is thar not be one soul dat can mek meh leave dis place. Dis place be called Promise Land now, but it not always be dat but it be dat now 'cause it be land promised to Momma Pearl and to meh by Dada. I hab all rights to be here 'till I dead. Dat be de promise dat Dada mek, but I be gettin' ahead of muhself. Let meh tek yuh bak to dat day dat brung meh and yuh to be sitting here now."

Chapter 18

A Fortune Dat Be a Misfortune

"If it not be fer a nigger who name be Fortune, Momma Pearl and Dada be nev'r meet. But Fortune be one of dem niggers dat hab plenty hate in him heart fer other niggers, and so him tek all dat him be learn't frum other nigger and him give de white mans a listen. I not know'd 'bout none of dis 'till it be time fer Dada to meet him maker. Him be sick and him suh to meh one day, 'Beccah, you have truly been all that a man, white or nigger, could expect a daughter to be. You have blessed these old eyes each time, day or night, that I look up and see you. My days, as you can well reckon, are but few and so there are some things I want you to know. Some will be very difficult and almost impossibly difficult for you to listen to, but you must promise me that you'll listen and not try to interrupt.'

"Dem days be hard fer meh 'cause I know'd deep in muh heart dat when him dun tolt meh wat be on him heart, dat him gine dead and I not wants him to dead. To all de nigger peoples in dese parts, him be jis't a white mans and fer plenty of dem, him be a wicked white mans, but fer meh him be muh faddah and him raise meh up wid plenty love. It not be jis't niggers dat know'd how to love dem pickney. Dada be show meh nuffin' but love since I be a lil' pickney. Dada him be love Momma Pearl furst and den him be love all of de pickney him mek wid Muddah.

"Momma Pearl mek him plenty pickney. Thar be meh, Isham, Zack, Juba, Tuck, Willie, Lilly, Eve, Lavina: dem be twins, Poole, Charlotte, Rose; she be dead same day Momma Pearl birf she. Muddah had one more pickney. She be de one I tolt yuh be call Sara, de pickney Momma Pearl mek wid a nigger. I nots know'd 'bout dis nigger mans 'till de day dat Dada fix to tolt meh 'bout seeing Momma Pearl fer de furst time. De nigger mans name be Harold Joe. Momma Pearl, when she tolt meh she part, nots know'd how to suh wat she 've to suh at furst, but den she look meh in de eye and she suh, 'Beccah, thar nots be a nigger nor white mans fer dat matter, know'ds how to love like Harold Joe. Harold Joe, him love meh wid him whole heart. 'member dat de preacher mans suh dat thar be a part in de bible way dem suh dat Jesus suh dat thar be no greater gift a mans can give him friend dan to lay down him life fer him? Dat be Harold Joe. Him be willing to lay down him life fer meh and muh pickney, ev'n though dem not be him own.'

"Momma Pearl den stop frum talking fer a while. Her eyes dem full up wid tears and den she suh, 'Love, Beccah, it nots care 'bout yuh. Love be a funny ting. I tinks love be a selfish ting 'cause it want de mans or womans dat it wants and it not mek room fer yuh to figgar if dat mans or womans be de best one fer yuh.

'Love be wants it and so yuh not hab choice but to follow love. Dat be wat love be. It be a ting all by itself and it mek yuh follow it. Love not follow yuh. Yuh follow love. First time it mek meh follow it, it tek meh to Harold Joe and wen Harold Joe be gone, it den mek me follow Fields. I nots want to follow him, no way less dat place be him grave, but love, it hab different plans and widout tinking wat I be wants or wat I tinks be best fer meh, it tek meh to him.'

"But, Miss Thea, if I be start wid Momma Pearl, I nots be gets to Dada and I tinks it best dat I be tell yuh 'bout Dada and frum de part way him come 'pon Momma Pearl. She be a lil' gal pickney wen dat happen.

"If in I fix to tell yuh sum'ting and yuh done knowd's already, jis't stop meh and suh, 'Beccah, I dun know'ds dat part a ready. I be stop and dis way I not be tek up precious time wid sumting dat yuh dun know'ds already.'

"Beccah, I think it would be best if you told me the whole think and this way I'll know I have it all. So if it's not too much bother, please go on. When you are tired and wants to rest, we can stop and when you are ready again, we'll start back."

"Dat be mighty kind of yuh, but I dun been waiting so long fer sumbody to come, I be wants to tell it and get dis burden frum off muh heart. It dun been sittin' thar heavy on meh since Dada tolt meh. I nots tolt dis to nar one soul 'cause it be hard to hear and I nots wants nobody to tink dem hard tings 'gainst muh Dada. When I get dun wid dis story, yuh mayhaps gine wunder how I be love him and it might be hard fer yuh to 'stand how Muddah grow'd to love him, but I jis't tolt yuh dat she suh dat it be love dat mek she follow him. I nots hab a better answer fer yuh. All I can tolt yuh is dat jis't like Momma Pearl, I be love him too.

"Fore him tolt meh, him suh to meh, 'Beccah, I know what I have to say to you is going to be most difficult for you to hear and there are parts of this narration that, because you love me, you are not going to want to believe, but you must. You must because I am telling it and I won't burden your heart with untruths.

'Please, my darling Beccah, hear your father out. Hear me out to the end and if, when I'm done, I've lost your love, then it's a chance that an old man must take. I don't want to lose your love, but I must tell you as you are the only child that has chosen to stay here with your mother and me. All of the others have gone; your brothers being the first and it pained me greatly that I wasn't able to get them to stay here and allow us all to be one big family.

'I understood their decision though. Perhaps, and I'm not sure, as I've never been anywhere near being a slave or enslaved other than by love to your mother, had I been a slave and had done to me what I did to them I, with my temper, would have killed me the very first chance I got if I could. However, I'm speculating but I don't think I'm that far off. I think they left so that the temptation to kill me wouldn't get greater and being niggers that killed a white man and a plantation owner at that, they would have been lynched. Anyhow, let me not dwell on that and sadden you as they are your brothers as much as they are my sons.

'Now, that notwithstanding, I feel compelled to unlock that dark place I call a heart and let you know the truth about your father. Time, that precious item we all crave and want more and more of, is now against me, as it will do to everyone. I've vowed that I will not take what has been sitting in my heart all of these years, near sixty I suppose, to the grave with me. None of it will do the grave any good and if what they say is true that a good man will push flowers up after he's buried, then I dare say, my precious Beccah, that there shall be no flowers on my grave, just weeds if anything at all dares to grow. I wasn't a good man.'

When Dada suh dat, I try to hush him. I suh, 'But, Dada, yuh is a good mans. Yuh been nuffin' but kind and gentle wid Muddah and meh and yuh dun seen to it dat thar not be a creature comfort dat meh and Muddah not have. Dat be mek yuh a good mans, Dada.'

Him suh, 'My dear child, you are indeed a true daughter. You want that there be no fault in me, but I must tell you that there is indeed fault and plenty. I've done, if not outright, then participated in some horrendous deeds that I know the good Lord won't let go unpunished. I go to Him prepared to take my punishment. I think even now what pains me more is that even the good Lord might not forgive me because it is written in His good book to suffer the little children to come unto him. Children are the Lord's most precious treasures and I've not treated them, slaves as well as my own, that way. I must, Beccah, and at great risk of losing your love, tell you this most terrible truth about your father.'

"I looks at him and muh heart it start to bruk 'cause I know'ds dat if him not tink him gine dead soon, him not suh nuffin' so I fix in muh heart dat I nots gine judge him; I gine pray dat wen it be Judgment Day, dat de Lawd Himself be de one to pass judgment on Dada and ev'n den if in I can ask de Lawd to have mercy on him, I gine beg de Lawd fer dat; him be muh faddah nev'r mind him be a white mans.

"By now, him be got de gout and consumption; it mighty painful fer him to get frum one part of him house to de next so I, not Muddah, be move in thar wid him. Muddah, she be in she house 'lone since Poole marry and be gone. Faddah, him build Eve and Lavina dem own house on de other side of de land way Muddah be living. Fer a while, dem live wid dem own mans jis't like meh, but jis't like meh, dem mans dead; not same time, but after time. I gine get back to dat.

"Charlotte, she be gone to Cedar Springs. Charlotte, she suh dat she not wants to be on plantation no more. She suh dat to be here mek she tink dat she be slave still and so she be gone. I not set eyes on she now these, oh, I nots be able to 'member now how many years. After a while, it be jis't Muddah, Faddah, and meh and now yuh come, it jis't be meh, no kin of mine be here wid meh steady, but I never mek dat be a bother. Thar be plenty of people dat be on dis place so it nots be like I be here alone ev'ry day.

"None of dat be 'portant to wat him be tolt meh. Dada him suh dat him want 'lease one of him pickney to know'd how him and de rest of dem, at de time de Patrollers, come to know'd 'bout wat Mistress Henrietta be do wen her Poppa be go'd to town 'bout him white mans business. Him suh, 'Beccah, what I'm about to tell is something that has haunted me for so long. I've wanted so often to tell your mother but I cannot; have never been able to get myself to say it to her as it is, I'm sure, positively sure, the worst day of her life and I was there. I helped to create this day of pain for her. I have told her I'm sorry, but sorry, even more than there's rice in all of South Carolina, can't take away that day for her.

'Until now, Beccah, no one ever knew how Henrietta Litchfield's Schoolhouse for Nigger Pickney, as she called it, came to be known to the Patrollers. None of us: yes I was a Patroller.

"Thea, when him suh dat him be Patroller, it be like muh heart stop, start, and stop, and it be feel like if it want to jis't stop fer ev'r. I choke on muh air and I feel a tightness in muh belly. Dem Patroller be de worse kind; de worse kind.

"Dada, him see de look on muh face and him suh, 'I know that your mother has never told you that. It's just like your mother. She would never have told you, none of you, the heinous things that I did, but I'm setting my soul free and I believe that you are the only one of my children with a heart big enough to hear what I have to say and not want to see me dead; to tell you the truth, I fear that, even now after all these years. I can't say though that I would hold a grudge if you did. I ask you though, Beccah, even if the thought should come to your mind, to hear me out first. Let me finish telling my story as there isn't anyone else to tell it. All those who knew are long gone, dead or killed, but either way, as far as I know, I am the only one left that knows about that day. So, as I said, if somewhere in the telling, you start wishing me dead and even devise a way to do it, let me finish. That would be the least thing I would ask. Not that you don't kill me, but that you let me finish tell the tale.

"None of us, as I said, knew what Miss Henrietta was doing. None of us would ever have imagined that she was doing such a thing. But there, right there on her father's own plantation, lived a nigger that had so much hate in him that he wanted what she was doing – teaching nigger pickney to read and write – to be known to us. He knew once he told that to our leader, a man named Ingram Beacham, that none of us would tolerate a white woman giving book learning to niggers; pickney or otherwise. All of us were bad and filled with a most deep hatred of niggers, but Ingram Beacham was the worst of us. None of us ever fully understood or really wanted to understand where his hatred stemmed since we all had our own hatred of niggers.

'Until I met Fortune, I'd never experienced a nigger with that much hate for other niggers. The hate he had in him wasn't a new hate or one that came about because another nigger had done him something that stirred anger in him. He had this hate for niggers from the time he was on Beauford Plantation. He, Fortune, was on Beauford Plantation and then brought onto Litchfield plantation before your mother was born. As you know, your mother was born on Litchfield plantation, but I understood from Litchfield many years later that her mother, was born on Beauford plantation and, like you're mine, was his child; not that he regarded her as such. I don't remember her name as I never cared to know it, but your mother can tell you what it was. Ask your mother about that part. She knows those details as they mattered to her.

'It was there that the hate in Fortune took its roots. You see, this nigger Fortune wasn't a nigger I knew, not that we really knew niggers on a personal basis; a nigger was just that, your nigger, your slave. There was no such thing as getting to know or developing a relationship with them, but Fortune was known to the Patrollers as he was the one that oftentimes whispered into the ears of any white man that wanted to hear the carrying on, hopes, and plans of the other niggers.

'The Patroller that Fortune often sought out to whisper to had more hate in him for niggers than Fortune did. His hatred was understood; he was a white man. Fortune's hatred for niggers wasn't understood. We didn't understand it nor did we care. His hatred was useful so, while we needed him, it was good that his hate was so deep it made him trust us. Can you imagine that, Beccah? A nigger hating other niggers so deeply that he was trusting of white men.

'I know, Beccah, that its mighty painful for you to sit and listen to the words of a dying man, a dying white man, and listen to him confess his many sins and wickedness and to know that the depth of his sins and wickedness has been against niggers. I must admit, as I'm telling you my truth, that before I met your mother, I never saw one, not one nigger, that I saw valued more than what I paid for him, or what I could get out of him.

'As for a wench, she had more value to me than a buck. I could breed her, increase my chattel. A good nigger buck for me was one that could work the field and only when I told him to rut and produce more pickney, he would rut as if I had a whip to his back, and just like that I'm richer. I could, in any one year, get more than a dozen nigger pickney from a buck. Many years ago, I had one such nigger. His name was Harold Joe. I don't really remember now how many pickney he added to my chattel, but he was like a prize boar. I think all Harold Joe had to do was bed a wench just once and she made a pickney. I used him a lot for that, but then he crossed me. I put him to cabin with your mother with explicit orders not to touch her and he defied me. He touched her.

'Here, Beccah, I am sadly and grievously ashamed. I'm ashamed because even then, I knew I was developing feelings for your mother and the idea of such deep feelings for a nigger wench shamed me. I couldn't understand how it was possible. Before her, I'd never so much as given a nigger wench consideration, again here; I'm ashamed; a nigger wench wasn't a woman to me. Of course, in the biological sense I knew she was female, like a female sheep is a ewe, a horse is a mare, a cow is a heifer, and so a nigger female was just that: a wench.

'You worked her, bred her, and then when she's wasn't able to breed or work, you sold her but love? No. No white man and not one of my standing would stoop so low as to love a nigger. It was inconceivable; an unheard of thing and there I was, Everett Michael Poole Fields, falling and in such dramatic fashion for a nigger wench and one that hated me. Oh, how your mother hated me. She had more than enough reason, but even then, even then I didn't give her the strength of character to have such a range of emotions.

'Beccah my dear child, I expected more emotions from Kelp, my hound. When Kelp found herself with a litter of pups, I watched her as she carefully and lovingly cared for her pups and when she'd weaned them, I found homes for them. I didn't think to give your mother the same consideration, but I digress. I'm getting ahead of myself. If I'm to tell this story truthfully and not leave anything out, I should go back to that fateful day when your mother was thrust into my path.

'However, before I go all the way back, I should tell you this piece as it weighs so heavily among so many other cruel, unkind, and unjust things that I did to your mother. I once told her that from the day we met, all I'd ever done was bring her sadness and pain. I do believe, Beccah, my dear daughter, that I've been the source of all your mother's pain and now, even now, I must wonder why am I forcing you to listen to the ramblings of a doddering old man.'

"Miss Thea, I nots be able to tek what him suhing easy. It tek sum time fer meh to git to way I can swallow dem hard feelings dat rise up in muh heart 'gainst Dada and yet I nots be able to tek him calling himself names and so I suh, 'But, Dada, yuh not be wat yuh suh yuh is. Yuh is still muh Dada and I nots seen yuh as nuh wicked mans.' I smile and him smile back a little at meh.

Den him suh, 'Beccah, where is your mother? She hasn't been in to see me since early this morning. That's not like her. Would you go over to her house and see what is keeping her? Even now, yes even now, her presence fills me with my greatest joys. I don't have many now, but of the few I have, seeing my Pearl counts at the top.

'Will you go, my dear Beccah, and see where she is? You know where to look for her. I would go myself but these days I tire so easily. Go first to your mother's old cabin and if she's not there, then go to Sara's old house. I don't know why of late she has taken to haunting these two places. It's here again, Beccah, I know that I've changed. There was a time her haunting of these places would have put me into a jealous rage. Jealousy would have driven me and for no other reason or provocation other than thinking she was trying to keep close the memories of Harold Joe and their daughter, Sara, I would have torn both the cabin and the house down, but now I understand. How long has it been now since her mother and father came and left?'

Auntie Thea looked at me as she spoke next. "I did just like Gina Pearl and you; I interrupted. I said, 'Mother and father?' Beccah turned her head and slowly looked at me. For the first time since she'd been talking, her eyes became misty. It was sad to see the pain rising in her face. Her eyes filled with tears but something in her held them back as she continued with her story. She said, 'If in I let dese here tears fall frum my eyes, den dat be de whole story. It be a story tolt by de tears acting like a runway slave down muh face; leaving but nots know'ds way dem be gine. I hab to get de whole ting out.'

"Beccah took a deep breath. She lets it out, bit the corner, well not bit since she had no teeth, but she folded her lip in and when she exhaled, she opened her mouth, freed her lip, and the air that came out made a bumpy sound as it rode out and over her freed lip. It sounded like phew with a long string of 'woos'. She then said, 'Thea, dat be a day and night like none I ev'r seen, but if I gets to tolt yuh dat part, I be git all mix up in muh telling so I hab to 'member to not lets muh mind wander or I be tolt yuh dis story in bits and pieces and den yuh nots be able to tek it 'part to mek sense. So I holds on dat part and yuh 'mind meh to git back to it. Yuh tinks yuh can git yuh mind to 'member meh to tolt yuh 'bout dat day?'

"I looked at Beccah and I wasn't sure if she meant it or if she was joking, but since I wasn't sure I said, 'Sure, Beccah, I'll remind you.' I told Beccah that I'd remind her but what I was thinking I couldn't say."

"What were you thinking, Auntie Thea, that you couldn't tell her?"

"I actually wanted to ask her what she was having the hardest time understanding or thinking about him. You see, for me, when Aunt Bess told us about those hard things he did to Milkweed, I never understood how she didn't just up and poison him. She had chance after chance and yet she let them, like all that flour she played in every day, slip through her fingers. If I were Milkweed, I would have killed him. I would never have given up trying 'till I saw him stretched out before me stiff as all hell. The last time he would have climbed between my legs was when he and that dried up wife of his took my first daughter. I would have taken my chance on running. But that was me. Milkweed; well she went and figured out how to love him."

"Not everything can be solved by killing everybody."

It was Auntie Noreen, and I could tell from the way she spoke that she was unaware that she'd spoken out loud.

Auntie Thea replied, "It may not solve everything, but killing Fields would have guaranteed her one less person to fear. I would have killed him. Yup, that's what I thought when Aunt Bess told me how badly he treated Milkweed, and I can assure you that I was absolutely certain when Beccah was telling me those things that were even worse than anything Aunt Bess had ever told us that I would have killed him. If he was alive somewhere in that house that day, I would have killed him. Yup, dead."

"Could Beccah tell that you were thinking of ways to kill Fields?"

"No, she was too in love with her dada to think that a stranger, who had never met her father, could or would hold such passionate hatred for him. I didn't let any of it show. I wanted to know what had happened, and voicing such a strong opinion would have shut her up and have her chase me from around her. I didn't want that to happen so I kept my mouth shut."

"I'd been quiet for a little while after I'd promised Beccah that I'd remind her where she was. When the silence had lingered just a little too long, she looked at me and she smiled that toothless smile again and she said, 'Good. It be in muh brain jis't a waiting to come out, but I hab to tell it in in right place. Yup in it right place.'"

Rebeccah

Now way I be? Yes. As I be do most days after I be visit wid Dada, I go and look fer Momma Pearl. Momma Pearl not be able to be 'round Dada all day, 'cause of de consumption and him suh dat him heart be bruk if she be come 'round him and him mek she sick and dead, so I be care fer Dada. I nots know'd why I nots get sick, but I nots. Momma Pearl. She be get a little sick and so dat mek Dada fear dat him gine kilt she so him beg and beg she nots to come often. Him nots know'ds how to go a whole day and not see Muddah so wen him nots be able to tek it no more, him be send meh to find she way ev'r she be.

'Go, Beccah, and find her for me. If she's not haunting her cabin or Sara's house, listen to where the blasted loud braying of that jackass grandson of hers, Benjamin, is coming from and you'll find her bending over backward to satisfy that son-of-a-bitch of an un-satisfy-able selfish nigger.

'That blasted Benjamin, if he doesn't leave off this place soon, he will send your mother to her grave and then me quicker than I really want to go, but it will make no sense for me to stay here without my Pearl. That blasted nigger worries her so. I hate to see her so burdened and his heart has no love for her. I'm sure he will, if questioned, say that he loves her. But Benjamin doesn't love himself. So therefore it goes to reckon that he doesn't know how to love his grandmother or anyone else. I, the least among them. I know he, like my sons, can't stand the very sight of me. If he could, he would kill me. But I tell you, Beccah, I will chance losing your mother because I will shoot Benjamin. I know that is hard to hear but…"

Dada stop and den him suh, 'Look how he treats that sweet sister of his. Neither Etta Pearl nor my Pearl deserve the treatment that either gets or takes from that selfish son-of-a-bitch. He should be glad that times and I have changed or he would have a much different ending. But times have changed and with the changing, it has softened me and changed me, but not to the point that if he weren't my Pearl's grandson, I won't take my pistol and shoot him. Men like Benjamin, white or nigger, are burdens to all that knows them and worse to the people who loves them. Death, and I mean this, Beccah, is sometimes the only way that people like Benjamin find what they are looking for; a cold blackness to match their hearts. Now go on, my dear, and see where on this place that blasted Benjamin is dragging, haunting, or braying at your mother.'

I leave Dada and muh heart it be heavy frum wat Dada suh and ev'n now de way him suh him be shoot Benjamin, I gets to dis part in muh tinking, and de next ting I know'ds, I be at Momma Pearl's house and it be jis't as Dada suh. I can hear Benjamin inside and him voice be loud. Him be using him big voice on Momma Pearl. Dat Benjamin, him know'd dat wen him use dat voice on Momma Pearl, dat she be give him wat him want. Today, it be de biggest ev'r so him must be wanting sumting big.

Benjamin Harold, him be come in dis world a big ole strapping pickney. Him come in dis world wid Momma Pearl's heart in one of him hands and de other hand be plate fer she.

Etta Pearl and Benjamin, grow'd like all de oth'r pickney 'bout de yard. Dem be too little to know'd dat dem be muddah-less and faddah-less pickney. Momma Pearl and Anakey, dem tek to raising Etta Pearl and Benjamin like dem be de muddah to dem. Etta Pearl, dat wat she be call, nev'r mind she muddah suh call she Pearl Etta, she be call Etta Pearl. She be a sweet, sweet lil' gal pickney.

"Way Benjamin be big frum a baby, she be small and she stay small, but she be beautiful. Her be full nigger gal. She be most like de color of dirt, but she skin, as Momma Pearl be suh, 'Got a good shine.' She not tall like how Benjamin be tall. She always be small to him. It be funny to see dem de way dem be. Her, de gal pickney, wid short, tight hair, and Benjamin him hair be a different kind of hair. It be nappy hair but it not be nappy, nappy. It be a little soft. Etta Pearl, she not mek dat she hair be nappy and hard be a bother to she. 'Fore she can fix it she self, Momma Pearl or Anakey be plait it fer she and she be jis't as happy as can be. Her eyes, dem brown 'till dem near black. Her got cheekbones dat sit high and her nose it be jis't like nose on nigger dat be frum somewhere else, but wat her got dat mek all de rest of she face light up be a smile. It be de warmest ting ev'r. I 'member wen she smile at yuh, it mek yuh fergit yer troubles.

"Benjamin, him much much different to Etta Pearl to tink 'bout it. Benjamin him be a right handsome nigger pickney, but him ways tek way him looks. Yuh nots see dat him eyes be black pools like Etta Pearl, and him hab de same nose. Him lips be fine nigger lips but him not hab de same smile. Truth? Him nev'r hab smile. Wen yuh be look at him face, it look like him tink dat ev'rybody ought to be doing fer him and jis't him alone. It be strange dat nigger pickney come in dis world wid white pickney ways. Him nots got one ting like Etta Pearl. I tinks dat be de ting dat mek him hateful. De only ting dat dem hab de same be Momma Pearl.

"Momma Pearl, she try and try to git love to grow'd in Benjamin's heart, but it nev'r tek root. No place in Benjamin got love. Anakey, she see dat thar be no love in Benjamin fer him sister so she gib de love she be fixing to gib Benjamin to Etta Pearl. Anakey, she love dat lil' pickney. She be more muddah to she dan Momma Pearl. Momma Pearl love Etta Pearl but she heart, well dat 'long to Benjamin who Momma Pearl be call Lil' Heart, but dat be if Dada not be near. If Dada be near, she call him Ben and wen him start to always want fer she to pay only him 'tention, she be call him Benjamin. Him get so dat Momma Pearl stop calling him Lil' Heart, Ben, or any sweet name yuh can call a nigger pickney. Him be jis't Benjamin so him never nuffin' fer anybody but dat; Benjamin.

"Him ways not be good. Him beat Etta Pearl if him tink dat she git something more dan him eve'n if it be a smile frum Anakey. It get to be clear dat him mekking it hard fer anybody to like him. Anakey, she pickney, what is that child's name?

"Yuh know'd, Miss Thea, good as muh brain be on 'membering sum tings, fer de life of meh I nots be able to ev'r 'member de name of Anakey and O'Brien pickney. I can see she 'fore muh eyes. Dat gal be 'bout the prettiest gal pickney yuh can set yuh eyes on. She had she muddah's tallness and she had she faddah's broadness and sumway in 'tween she mix up wid de two of dem. She not be nigger and she not be white. Wen it git cold though she be white but wen it be hot—she be nigger. She hair it be thick and it like copper on she head and…"

Beccah starts to laugh and she said, "Dat nigger gal be hab freckles like she faddah. She be more mix-up looking dan meh.

"I can 'member all dem tings 'bout dat nigger gal but I nots be able to 'member she name. Her name nots matter to dis telling, as I be telling yuh 'bout Benjamin. I tinks not even Dada be like him nor really want him near dem either. Benjamin, him not care 'bout none of dat long as him git de most, and de best; de best in him eyes be Momma Pearl. Him tinks dat Momma Pearl be jis't him own.

"Benjamin, him nots be able to get 'nuff of nuffin'. De more yuh gib him, de more him want. Muddah, she try and she try to mek Benjamin get wat she call a content heart, but it not be in him. Him ev'n want wat be fer him small sister pickney; even de love dat Momma Pearl try to gib

Etta Pearl, Benjamin him want dat. Dada him love dem but over time it be clear dat him not favor Benjamin and if not fer muddah, him be put Benjamin off him place de minute Benjamin start to look like man pickney. Truth be tolt, the more Benjamin grow'd, de harder it be to love him. Him wat yuh call it? Dif…dif, yeah, him be different; not like nobody round de place, nigger or white mans. Him jis't like him mek himself.

"Momma Pearl, she suh dat him be dat way 'cause him got hate fer himself in him heart and dat him not know'ds how to love himself. She try and try to show'd him more and more love, but him not want it. Him get so dat yuh nots be able to suh nuffin' to him; not ev'n fer him own good.

"Wen I gets to Momma Pearl's house and I hears Benjamin and him big voice, I hurry to see what it be dat him be trying to get Momma Pearl to do dis time. I gets in and I see Benjamin wid him big strapping-self standing over the chair way Momma Pearl be sitting and him hab de sweat running down the side of him face, and I can see clear dat him trying to get Momma Pearl to do sumting she not want to do.

"Benjamin, him be big to meh but I nots fear him one bit. I suh, 'Benjamin, wat it be dat yuh wants now? Wat it be dat yuh tinks Momma Pearl can pull down frum de sky and gib to yuh? Wat Benjamin? Wat it be dis time?'

"Him look at meh and him not suh nuffin' but him huffin' and him breavin' through him nose like him be horse. It be Momma Pearl who suh, 'Benjamin, I nots own nuffin' here on dis plantation. Dis house I be live in it, but I nots ev'n tink of it as muh own so I nots know'd wat yuh wants meh to do fer yuh. Yuh suh dat yuh wants to be happy, but happy be not sumting I can do fer yuh. Happy come frum inside yuh, Benjamin, so yuh gine hab to look deep inside yuh and see if yuh can find de road to yuh own happiness.'

"Wen Momma Pearl suh dat, him suh, 'But yuh mek Etta Pearl, Charlotte, Eve, Lavina, Anakey, and ev'rybody happy so yuh must hab a way to mek meh happy. Mek meh happy, Muddah.'

"I suh 'fore Momma Pearl can suh a ting, 'Momma Pearl nots mek dem happy, Benjamin, dem be happy 'fore Momma Pearl, but it be 'cause dem wid Momma Pearl dat dem be happy. So yuh hab to come wid yuh own happiness den Momma Pearl can add to yuh happiness.'

"Wen I suh dat, Benjamin suh, 'I nots want to hear yuh, Beccah.

Why yuh nots go back and tek care of him 'fore him dead while yuh down here in sumting dat nots got nuffin' to do wid yuh.'

"Wen him suh dat, I mek to go fight him and it be Momma Pearl dat suh, 'Benjamin! Why yuh hab to suh de tings dat yuh know'ds gine hurt ev'rybody feelings. Yuh nots hab to suh dem tings to Beccah 'bout she Dada.'

"Wen Momma Pearl suh, "Dada" Benjamin suh, 'Muddah, I nots want to be here. I wants to be gone frum 'round here.

"Momma Pearl, she nots suh nuffin' more to him but she git up and she suh, 'Benjamin, I gine up to de house and see 'bout Fields and I wants dat wen I be gone, dat yuh tink long and hard 'bout why yuh always hab to be mean and hurtful to dem dat love yuh.'

"Momma Pearl, she git up and she walk out and Benjamin, him sit down hard in de chair she be jis't git up frum and him suh, 'Beccah, I nots wants to be here no more. I wants to be gone off dis place. I do, Beccah, I really do.'

"I nots know'ds wat to suh to him so I jis't sit wid him 'till him tired sit and den him git up and him walk over to way de indigo field be. Him love being in de indigo. Him go'd thar wen him nots git him way. Him be do dat since him be tiny pickney.

Chapter 19

No Other Mistress fer Him House

I leave de cabin and I go'd to Momma Pearl's house 'cause I know'd dat after Benjamin be in de indigo field, den him go'd to Momma Pearl's house and him mek ev'rybody miserable if him not sort him tinking out. I wait and Momma Pearl she mek it back to she house 'fore him so I can jis't figga dat him still sorting him tinking out. Momma Pearl, she go'd out to she cook house and soon I can tell dat she mekking something special fer Dada. I smell de biscuits. It not matter if Dada be sick or well, him always want Momma Pearl to mek him biscuits.

Momma Pearl, she be show'd meh, Charlotte, Eve, Lavina and Etta Pearl, but it be only Etta Pearl who be got a good hand fer de flour so if Momma Pearl not mek de biscuits fer Dada, den it be Etta Pearl.

I mek muh way back to Dada 'cause I know'ds dat him not likes to be in him house by himself. O'Brien him be sit and drink brandy wid Dada sum de times, but most de times him be wid Anakey. It be like Anakey be O'Brien's whole world jis't like Momma Pearl be Dada's whole world.

See, Miss Thea, Dada be most 'lone now 'cause little by little, all him white mans friends, 'cepting maybe one or two, and dem be jis't like Dada and O'Brien, but jis't a little different. Dem be got nigger womans like Dada and O'Brien, but dem got white wife too. Dem white wife be in she house and she turn a blind eye to all de pickney dat round dem place dat only a nigger womans can mek. So ev'n though dem hab nigger womans, dem still got white mans friends 'cause dem got white wife.

Dada, him not 've a white wife so dem tinks dat Dada not be fit fer dem fancy house. Dem stop calling on Dada. Soon, Dada not get to go to none of dem balls and dem not come to get him to go riding, hunting, shooting, drinking, nor none of dem tings dat white mans do. Dada him cuss frum time to time and thar be times him be storming mad and him suh, 'To hell with the lot of them. Blast them all to hell, I don't need them to come here.'

Dada suh dat dem suh him be…wat dat be dat dem suh him be? It be a big word fer meh to 'member now in muh old age but I 'member 'cause it mek Dada turn red and suh him gine get him gun and go shoot dem all.

AuntieThea

"Drea, here, Cousin Rebeccah stared off out into the field before her as if she expected that word she's trying to remember to come floating across the field to her. I waited with her as she stared and stared."

Rebeccah

Recluse. Yes. Dat be wat dem suh Dada be, but Dada not be dat. It be O'Brien dat tolt him dat dem suh him be recluse. Him suh, 'O'Brien, what the hell are you saying? When the hell did I become a recluse? I'm not a recluse. Me, Everett Michael Poole Fields, a recluse? Why, O'Brien, am I a recluse? I'll tell you why, my trusted friend. It's because I want none of their young, stupid, giddy teenage daughters, their old spinster daughters or sisters, and worse, yes worst of all, I'm not trying to bed their fat, ugly wives. That's the only reason that they can have for calling me such a stupid insidious thing as a recluse.

'O'Brien, I have all of what I want. I have my Pearl. We have our children. None of their children can bring them any greater joy than any of mine. I ask you, O'Brien, would you trade your life with Anakey for any of their daughters? Would you, O'Brien?'

O'Brien, him jis't smile 'cause him and Anakey be 'gether since 'fore I be born and dem still 'gether. Dada not wait fer him to suh nuffin', him suh, 'Can any of their daughters give me daughters like: Eve, Lavina, Charlotte, or my Beccah? I'll tell you that they could not. Look at my sons.'

When Dada suh sons, him stop and I know'd dat him be tinking on him man pickney dat not want to be way him be. Poole be de only man pickney dat stay wid Dada. Him love Dada and Dada love him. Him not call him Dada like meh. Him call him Fields like Momma Pearl.

Poole, wen him be pickney, him be beautiful quiet pickney and him grow'd to be de same kind a man. Him not talk much 'cepting him tinks it 'portant. Fer him, de only two tings 'portant be Momma Pearl and Sara's pickney: Etta Pearl. She be him heart. Him love Etta Pearl like she be him own. De same way him love Etta Pearl, Dada be love him. I know'd dat Dada be love him 'cause him be de only man pickney dat Dada can set him eyes on. Dada him try to see de rest of him man pickney. Him go'd to Breckenshaw plantation aft'r dem walk 'way frum him place, but wen dem stand and seen him coming and dem know'd it be him frum a far way off 'cause dem know'd how him sit a horse, so by de time him get thar, dem be go'd sum place else.

It be cut Dada deep dat dem not want to be way him be. One day, him come back and I can see frum how him red and him hair be wild dat him be riding hard. Him come in de house and him suh, 'Beccah, they have turned, truly turned their hearts against me. They have become like Pharoah and I, the children of Israel. You know, as they, like you are free, Breckenshaw cannot make them shoe or cool my horse. I don't want them to do that. I want to get a chance to talk to them. I want to tell them how sorry I am for what I've done.'

Then him look at meh and him suh, 'Beccah, you do believe that I'm sorry? You do, don't you?'

I wants to suh to him, "Dada, I know'ds yuh sorry but dat not mek wat yuh dun to dem and Momma Pearl right. Yuh solt dem wen dem be jis't knee-high pickney and now dem be mans pickney dem nots got no love fer yuh. It be 'cause Momma Pearl not git to see she boy pickney mek mans. Sorry is wat sorry be, but it not be 'nuff to fix dem bruk heart.'

I not suh dat. I suh, 'I know'ds yuh sorry, Dada. I know'ds.' Dat be all I suh to him.

Yuh know'ds wat be strange. It be only meh and Etta Pearl dat call him Dada. Etta Pearl, she be like second skin to meh, and so way I be she be and I call him Dada and she call him Dada. Him answer she jis't de same as him answer meh and so it be dat meh and Etta Pearl calling him Dada. Etta Pearl she call him Dada 'till she left 'round here but I gettin' head of muhself.'

Momma Pearl, she know'ds dat him miss him white mans friends and she know'ds dat dem not come way him be no more 'cause him not tek no white womans as him wife. So one day soon after Dada and O'Brien be hab dem talk and Momma Pearl be sitting wid Dada, she suh, 'Fields, it be clear to meh dat yuh not hab no more friends and I tinks dat yuh not hab friends 'cause dem hates dat a nigger womans live here on yuh plantation and yuh not hab a mistress fer yuh house. Yuh tinks, Fields, dat mayhaps yuh ought to get yerself a white mistress and wen she hab fancy ball, den all yuh friends dem come and den yuh have friends to drinks yuh brandy and to go riding wid?'

Miss Thea, Dada him gets mighty upset wid Momma Pearl and him suh, 'Pearl, I will not say this to you or anyone else again. I am content. This place of contentment has taken me many years to get to. You are mistress to this house. You are my wife in my mind and heart, and although I can't convince you, I've done what needs to be done to see to it that no one does anything to change that. Trust me, Pearl, no one can move you one inch from this place while I live and even when I'm gone, they can move you; even less than half inch. So believe me, Pearl, I don't need another wife: white or nigger. If they don't want to come, let them stay away but I won't get a different mistress to this plantation to please others and displease myself. I don't want the peace of my life disrupted. Now, Pearl, make this the last time you mention such nonsense to me.'

Momma Pearl, she wants to ask Dada wat him mean 'bout her being de mistress to him place but her nots ask him. It be a long time 'fore I know'ds wat Dada be mean, but I hab time to tolt yuh dat part, but it hab to come in its right place. So, way I be in muh telling?

Yes, yes. I be suhing dat I be on muh way to sit wid Dada 'cause I know'd dat him not hab friends 'cause dem, de white mans and white womans in dese parts suh dat Dada be a recluse and dat Dada suh him not care wat dem suh.

Wen I gets to Dada's chambers, it be clear dat him doze off fer a minute and when him come back 'round and see meh sitting in de chair by him bed, him suh, 'Beccah, when your mother came here earlier, she seemed upset but she won't tell me. When you found her earlier, was she with that jackass of a grandson of hers?'

"I suh, 'Yes, Dada, she be wid Benjamin.'

'Let me guess, that Benjamin was braying loudly, wasn't he?'

'Yes, Dada, him be want Momma Pearl to find a way to mek him happy jis't de way dat we be wen we wid she.'

Dada, him look at meh and him suh, 'That poor braying ass. Didn't she tell him that true happiness can't be given?'

'Momma Pearl not be stay wid him. She let him stay way him be and she come up here to see 'bout yuh. Benjamin nots wants to be here no more. Him wants to go on up north.'

Dada suh, 'Good. Good. Let him take his braying nigger ass away from here. Perhaps then I can have my Pearl back. He has been nothing but a drain on my poor Pearl. I sometimes wonder why I let Dr. Washington save him. But I know that had we not saved him, I wouldn't have my Etta Pearl. Having my little Etta Pearl makes that day and all the efforts worth it. Anyhow, I know once your mother and Etta Pearl gets to be making biscuits, it's going to be a while before she comes back so let me get on with the telling of that awful time in my life.'

Chapter 20

A Time So bad

'This nigger, Fortune, the one I've been telling you about, was the worst kind of nigger you would ever encounter, but to look upon him you wouldn't think so at first glance. There was nothing about him that would say that he carried that kind of bitter hatred in him. His look, Beccah, was what you would call deceptive.'

'Wat yuh mean by dat, Dada?'

'Yes. Yes. I shouldn't use words that you aren't familiar with. Even here I've failed you. You should know your letters and how to read. There's no one to blame for that but me. Sad, Beccah, but it's never been anything I thought about; you know, teaching any of you your letters and numbers. Anyway, at this point it's out of my hands as time is now so sorely against me. Yes. I was saying how that nigger was so deceptive and by that I mean you would look at him and never, not for one second, see him doing any of the things he did. Even his appearance was deceptive; he looked like a white man and to look upon his face, you saw a white man but one who had spent his life in the sun. His hair, if he'd ever gone without a hat, would have been rather similar to mine and by that I mean a kind of reddish brown, not nigger hair at all but because he always wore a hat it, was a much darker brown to mine.

'He was tall and he had a good carriage. His legs were strong because he worked so hard. If his heart were not so bitter, he would be, by all standards, a handsome man but his black heart took all of that away. It was wasted, Beccah. His mouth looked as if it had never formed a smile; a frown yes, but a smile? His mouth wouldn't know how to do that. He used his mouth to eat and to bring messages. I believe there was some perverted pleasure derived from bringing the messages and then watching as punishment, cruel or otherwise, was meted out.

'To see a nigger with that much hate was unsettling. Beacham recognized that and told all of us how dangerous that was. You see, Beccah, I didn't know who Fortune was and neither did he know who we were. We never met him. Beacham knew him well and he was the primary contact so there was no reason for us to know him or him us. He was also known by niggers on both Beauford and Litchfield plantations, but no one ever suspected him. He was to them just the nigger driver that worked niggers harder, if you can imagine, than any white overseer anywhere.

'Niggers were able to get word to each other on a plantation when he went from field to field so it's not beyond reason to think that other niggers on other plantations knew of him. All the niggers feared him. If the truth be told, all of them: man, woman, and pickney feared him because of how cruel and heartless he was known to be. It wasn't till towards the end that he was, we understood, thought of by the niggers to be a Bitter Breeze.

'Beccah, that was the worst a nigger could be. If a nigger was suspected of being a Bitter Breeze, every nigger did his or her best, or the very best they could to stay far away from any place he was. That was almost impossible to do as they had no control over where they were put to work.

'In the beginning, the things he told were the kind of things that got that nigger, man or woman, a beating: some more severe than others, but it was always a beating. He was so clever at bringing news of what he heard that he was made a driver. Once he became a driver, the Overseer would put him over those that he wanted extra work out of. This driver, Fortune, would drive niggers 'till there was nothing left to get out of them. As a driver, that meant that he was afforded a little bit more freedom. With this freedom, he felt privileged. He was now able to move freely about the plantation and this way he was able to hear all of what the niggers were talking about.'

Miss Thea, dis part here dat I be git ready to tolt yuh Dada not tolt meh. Him not know'd 'bout dis as dis be nigger business. It be story dat nigger be nev'r figga and if not fer Fortune's muddah deading, thar not be one nigger ev'r know'd who it be. Yuh see, till him muddah be witness, yes dat be de word dat Dada suh she be, witness to dis bad ting dat happen on Litchfield Plantation, nigger be nev'r know'd she be him muddah. Her holler and holler, dem suh, wen it be over 'till she, like most of dem nigger womans, not able to holler no more. But she be older dan most and wen dem tek she to she cabin, it be clear dat she holler 'way she heart and she gine dead.

'Dis mek Fortune holler. Nigger not tink much on him hollering as most all niggers dat got mout be hollering. It be wen him go'd to she cabin and him holler, 'Muddah, I nots want yuh to dead.' Dat be wen nigger know'ds dat Affa be him muddah. Thar be nuffin 'bout Fortune dat suh dat a nigger like Affa be him muddah. Affa, she be like coal, but she be a sweet nigger womans. Her never let it be know'd dat him be she pickney 'cause him drive she hard like all de rest a niggers and it be a sad ting to see 'cause Affa be old. It be wen Affa holler and holler dat him see she as him muddah and him not want to lose him muddah.

Wen de nigger mans tek she to she cabin, him follow dem and him hollering. Him sit in she cabin and him holler and holler. Nigger all over Litchfield Plantation dat day be hollering, but Fortune's hollering be different 'cause him be de only nigger on Beauford dat hab a muddah and not treat she like a muddah. Dat be a sad ting; nigger mans got muddah him can set him eye on and not treat she like a muddah 'till she gine dead. De nigger, Hoodoo healing mans, suh to Fortune dat Affa not gine mek it to see sun up. Dem suh dat him holler fer all de more and him suh, 'Muddah, Muddah. It nots 'pose to be yuh, Muddah! It not 'pose to be yuh, Muddah! I sorry, Muddah. I be sorry. Muddah, suh sumting to meh. Call meh yuh pickney. I be answer yuh. Call meh! Muddah suh, "Fortune." Suh muh name, Muddah. I be sorry dat I tolt yuh not to suh dat I be yuh pickney.'

Dat night, Dorcus, de one dat de white preacher man suh be Preacher Man fer de niggers, be busy trying to tell niggers dat de Lawd hab reason fer ev'ryting Him do but it be hard fer Dorcus to git niggers to see how de Lawd can hab reason fer wat dem jis't seen. Den Preacher Man, him mek to go to see 'bout Affa 'cause him know'd dat frum de way she look wen dem tek she to she cabin, dat she be poorly. Him mek it to she cabin. Inside, Fortune be hollering harder dan de way him muddah holler. Him nots hear Preacher Man outside so Preacher Man jis't go'd in de cabin and wen him git inside, him can see why Fortune be hollering: Affa be dead.

'She mout it be open like she be try to git out one more holler, but it be not come out: it be stick way it be 'cause she dead 'fore it come out. Now Fortune be trying to holler it out she neck, but him nots able to holler it out. She dead and wid she deading, de holler dead right way it be; in she neck and it mek she neck look like she be a mans.

Preacher Man step in, him see Fortune put him hand on Affa's neck like him gine choke she, but him nots want to choke she. Him want to hear she last sound even if it be a holler, but de holler it not move frum way it be stick in she neck. It be a dead holler. Ev'n if him get it to come out, it not gine mek sound. Dead holler not mek sound. Dem go'd quiet right way dem be.

Wen Fortune see dat de dead holler nots gine come out Affa's neck, him tek him hand and him shut she mouth, den him suh, 'It not 'pose to be dis way. It not 'pose to be dis way. Lawd, Lawd, Lawd, it not 'pose to be dis way.'

Preacher Man, him try to tell Fortune dat it be de way dat de Lawd want it. Fortune suh, 'It not be de Lawd, it be meh. It be meh. I be de one dat tolt she not to call meh she pickney. I tolt she dat it be she fault dat I be…'

Preacher Man suh wen Fortune suh, "I tolt she dat it be she fault dat I be…" Preacher Man stop Fortune and him suh, "It not be Affa's fault. Affa not be able to stop de hollering.'

Fortune 'side himself wid pain and him not listenin' to Preacher Man. Him go'd to Affa and him put him head on she chest and him suh, "Muddah, I be sorry. I be sorry. It not 'pose to be dis way. Muddah, yuh hab to come back to meh so I can call yuh Muddah and yuh can call meh yuh pickney. I wants to be yuh pickney, Muddah. I nots mean fer yuh to dead. I nots mean fer nobody to dead.'

Den Preacher suh, 'It nots got nuffin' to do wid yuh, Fortune. It be white mans way. Dem suh dat dem come to teach nigger lesson. It be de white mans dat do dis awful ting to nigger.'

Fortune be hollering so hard dat Preacher Man jis't suh a prayer and him beg de Lawd to fix a place in heaven fer Affa and to fergive Fortune fer not treating Affa like him muddah. Fortune be still hollering so him go out de cabin. Him be most near him cabin wen him see dat him left him Bible.

Him nots be able to read, yuh know'ds. De white Preacher Man dat mek him de Preacher Man fer niggers gib him de Bible and tolt him dat all Preacher Man, nigger or white, must 've a Bible. Him proud to walk wid him Bible. Him ev'n open it de way him see de white Preacher Man do and him look down and him look up and him suh wat him tinks be in him Bible. Him be a sight to see when him get de Holy Ghost to come down on him. Him hold him Bible in one hand and him shake it like him 'pect de Lawd to fall out.

Dorcus, him know'ds dat wid de 'mount of hollering gine on all over de plantation, him gine need him Bible plenty so him mek him way back to Fortune's cabin since dat be de last place him be. Him be get ready to pull de door and go in wen him hear Fortune. Him not be hollering no more. Him be talking to Affa and him be beggin' she to fergive him and to suh dat him be she man pickney.

Preacher Man suh dat him mek to walk way and get de Bible in de morning but it be wat Fortune suh next dat mek him glad dat him fergit him Bible and dat it be night 'nuff dat thar be nobody stirring; too much grief on de plantation. De hollering, it quiet down but it not be quiet altogether but quiet 'nuff fer him to hear wat Fortune suhing to Affa.

'Muddah, Muddah, I be sorry dat wat yun seen dun mek yuh dead. I nots mean fer yuh, Clarissa, or none dem pickney to dead. I hab to tolt yuh wat I dun, Muddah. If I nots tolt yuh, I not know'd wat I gine do wen it be morning and dem come to put yuh in de dirt. I hab to tolt yuh, Muddah, so yuh can tek it to de grave wid yuh. Thar not be a soul I can tolt wat I dun and not hab dem want to see meh dead or kilt meh demself. I even tink dat dead be too good fer meh, but ev'n though I know'ds dat, I not wants to be dead, Muddah. I wants yuh to fergive meh fer all de wrongs tings I dun to yuh and all de other niggers. I know'ds yuh nots able to do dat, but I hab to talk to yuh 'till I feel dat yuh spirit know'ds I be real sorry. I be de most sorry I can ev'r be 'cause wat I dun mek yuh dead, Muddah, and yuh nots hear meh call yuh "Muddah" not since I be a lil' pickney.'

Chapter 21

A Deed So Dark

Preacher Man him listen and, Miss Thea, yuh know'ds dat him hear dis ting and him keep it in him heart 'till, jis't like Dada, him be fixing to dead. Preacher Man not tolt a soul not ev'n him wife. She be dead and not know'ds dat on de nite dat de devil and him henchmen let loose de worse evil dat nigger ev'r seen dat him hear wat him hear. It not be 'till him sure dat de next face him be looking in be de Lawd's dat him tolt meh. Him tolt meh and den him tek one long last breff and wen it dun; him dead. I be de only one dat know'ds wat him hurd dat nite. I nev'r tolt. Not muh husband, none of muh pickney, Momma Pearl, Dada; not a soul. Miss Thea, de only part of dis dat I not know'd be de part dat Dada be hab in it. It be only wen Dada be tolt meh wat him tolt meh dat I git de whole picture. It not be a good picture. It be a picture dat be nuffin' but hate, hate, and more hate. Oh, Lawd, thar be too much hate; too much.

Miss Thea, I be mek in muh heart to tek it to muh grave but aft'r Dada tolt him part, I tinks dat it nots be right to gib it to de dirt. Thar be jis't one problem.

"One?" Thea asked.

Jis um…who'd to tolt it to 'cause dis be a might heavy burden. I tinks and I tinks on it but I nots know'd, den muh spirit it suh, 'Leave it be. De rightest person be come 'long and yuh gine know'd. Wen yuh feel it in yuh bones dat dem be the rightest one; tolt dem.' Now yuh be here and I know'd in muh spirit dat yuh be de rightest one; same way Preacher Man know'ds dat I be rightest one fer him deepest secret.

"Dis tink ought to be know'd and mayhaps it be bring peace to dem dat be wanting answer, I jis't beg de Lawd to gib meh time to tolt yuh so I can go'd to him wid muh mind and heart clear. Dat be all I wants. I nots want fer nuffin' else. Momma Pearl gone, Dada gone, ev'rybody;

dem gone and all I be 've be muh memories and dem be scatter'd all over dis plantation. I hab memories here in muh house, in Momma Pearl's house, in she haunting cabins, in Aunt Sara's house, in Eve and Lavina's house, and I got some of muh most special memories in Dada's house. I been hab plenty years to scatter muh memories but now I wants to gather dem close so I can tolt dem to yuh.

I be suhing to yuh wat it be dat Preacher Man mek himself to hear dat night wen Fortune be pouring out him soul in him dead muddah's ears. Wid only him dead muddah as him witness, Fortune suh, 'Muddah, dis be how de whole ting start. After I be solt onto Beauford plantation and yuh be still in Low Country 'cause dem solt meh way frum yuh, I be mighty lonesome. Den I meets a nigger and him suh dat since I be look most like white mans, dat if I tolt de Overseer tings dat I seen and hears nigger do, den I be special to him and life be easy fer meh. Him suh dat him be do dat and him hab good life. Him gets extra tings and him be de most special nigger to de Massa and de Overseer.

'Muddah, him suh dat 'fore Massa Beauford buy yuh and brung yuh here. I be happy to see yuh, but I nots be able to suh dat to yuh since I dun tolt de Overseer dat I nots hab muddah, poppa, bruddah, or any kin so dats be de reason dat I tolt yuh wen yuh git here nots to suh dat I be yuh pickney. I know'ds dat yuh be mighty hurt, but yuh never one day let yuh hurt show'd. Yuh jis't be go'd on like yuh nots know'd meh. Thar be days dat I be wanting to be yuh pickney and sits wid yuh and eat sum yuh bittle, but 'cause Overseer be look to and aft'r meh to know'ds wat nigger be do, I nots be able to mek muh eyes see yuh. I be sorry, Muddah, dat ev'ry time yuh try to mek muh eyes see yourn, I be turn muh head frum way yuh be.

Preacher Man, him suh dat Fortune him stop talk and him cry soft and all de while dat Fortune be sobbing, Preacher Man mek himself jis't like de night so dat him can stay and hear wat Fortune be whispering in him dead muddah's ears and in him living ears.

When Fortune get him sobbing to stop, him start to talk back to him dead muddah, 'Muddah, I hab to tolt yuh how dis all come to be. Wen I be at Beaumont's plantation, dey be a nigger gal call Channy dat I be sweet on and Channy, she be grow'd a little sweet on meh, but not real sweet like I be sweet on she. I know'ds dat, Muddah, but I nots care. I be sweet on she and I figga dat de way I sweet on she be mek up fer de bit she not sweet on meh. Den wen I be tinking dat soon I be wid she, ev'rbody be solt off. She and she muddah be solt way frum Beaumont's plantation and I nots know'd way dem be solt off to. Dat near bruk muh heart but den, Muddah, I be solt to Beauford plantation and I nots be thar more dan a fortnight wen Channy and she muddah be solt frum de plantation way dem be in Low Country and dem come to Beauford plantation.

'Beauford, him buy plenty nigger 'cause him place be big and nigger dead plenty and often at him place 'cause him and him Overseer be some kinda cruel to nigger. I nots care 'bout why him hab to buy plenty nigger I jis't glad dat dis time him buy Channy and she muddah. I be happy to see dem but I be sad same time. Channy, she see meh and it like she nots see meh. She nots be glad to see meh like I be glad to see she. It be like de time we be 'part frum one 'nother mek de lil' sweet she had fer meh turn sour. Wen I see dat she be like dat, I wants de sweet I feel fer she to go 'way but it not go 'way. Muddah, it get sweeter ev'ry time I see she. I mek in muh heart to git she to be sweet on meh.

'Furst it be jis't Channy dat come wid she muddah, but den some time later, a bruddah come too. I nots know'd dat him be she bruddah 'cause wen dem be at Beaumont, it be jis't Channy and she muddah. Massa Brauford buy him but him not know'd dat him be Channy's bruddah. Wen Channy and she muddah see him, dem happy but dem not let on dat him be she bruddah. Dem fear dat if de Overseer be finds out, dat him be solt way one of dem so dem mek like dem not be know'd one another. I see dat Channy be happy wen she see dis nigger mans, and I fix it in muh heart, dat be 'fore I know'd him be she bruddah, to hate him. A bitter hate grow'd quick in muh heart fer him 'cause him hab Channy's eye.

'Channy, she see dat I be hab a hate in muh heart fer him so she mek like she be glad wen she see meh, but it nots be de same kind of glad. She be glad to see meh 'cause she tink dat if I be sweet on she, dat she be able to get meh to git de driver to nots be so hard on she. Dat be mistake. Muddah, I be nigger but I be not like dem since I be jis't de kind of nigger dat de white mans call a "special" nigger. I be special 'cause I let dem know'ds wat nigger suh and wat nigger do. Dat be wat I do and den white mans be know'ds dat I hate nigger jis't like him do. Dat be all nigger 'cept Channy. So I nots let muh feeling sweet on Channy mek meh fergit wat I hab to do fer Massa and de Overseer.

'Preacher Man suh wen Fortune suh dat him be tolt on niggers him jis't start a different kinda hollering. It be like it jis't come to him head how bad it be wat him do. Fortune stop frum talking to him dead muddah and him cry. Him cry and him jis't suhing, "I be sorry, Muddah. I be so sorry. Lawd, Lawd, I dun kilt all dem pickney and now I kilt muh muddah.'

Miss Thea, much as Preacher Man know'ds dat listening to Fortune telling him dark secret to him dead muddah's ears be wrong in de sight of de Lawd, him suh dat it not feel dat wrong 'cause if de good Lawd hab not mean fer him to hear, den de Lawd be not mek him fergit him Bible. It be, him suh, like de Lawd put him thar to hear Fortune so him waits fer Fortune to start back. Him stay real quiet since him be 'bout him Faddah, de Lawd's business, hearing de truth dat gine set Fortune free, so him wait. Thar hab to be more. Him not waits dat long. Fortune stops frum telling de Lawd how sorry he be and him go'd and gits him jug. Dis time, Preacher Man suh him nots hear the cork go'd back in. He know'ds now dat Fortune gine drink all him corn liquor. It not matter to him as long as Fortune suh wat it be dat him want him dead muddah and him to hear. Fortune tek a few swigs frum de bottle and him start bak.

'How I come to know'd dat Channy's bruddah be on de plantation be come frum Channy's own mout. Her nots do like meh, Muddah. Yuh be here. Yuh be muh muddah and thar nots be one soul, nigger nor white mans, know'ds yuh be muh muddah. Dat be 'cause Channy nots know'ds dat a ounce of shut mout, worth more dan a ton of 'xplainin' so she open she mout and tolt meh dat de nigger Silas not be she sweet-'pon mans, him be she bruddah. I nots tolt dat as I be glad dat him nots be she sweet-'pon mans. Muh heart it git all happy 'gin 'cause wen she suh dat, she smile sweet at meh and, Muddah, she let she hand touch muh hand.'

'Preacher Man suh when Fortune suh, "Muddah", it like it hit him head and heart dat she nots gine answer him 'cause him suh, 'Oh, Lawd, Oh, Lawd wat it be dat I dun nots letting yuh suh dat I be yuh pickney and dat yuh be meh muddah?'

Him nots holler, him jis't breave hard all de while he sound like he pulling snot back in him nose and den him start back, 'Channy, she be mek like she be sweet wid meh and wen ev'r she see meh, she be smile. I nots know'ds wat to do wid muhself. I starts to tink dat soon she gine be muh jump-de-broom-wid womans, when she come and she open she mout and suh de worse ting ev'r to meh. She suh dat she bruddah suh dat white mans ought not to mek nigger slave and him fixing on running frum here. She suh dat him be ready to git way furst chance dat him git, him gine run. Den Channy be smile big at meh but I know'ds dat de smile not come frum she heart and wid dat mock smile on she face, she suh real soft and sweet, 'Fortune, I nots gine run wid him. I gine stay here wid yuh but I wants to beg yuh to tinks how yuh can help; mayhaps get a extra ration or two and a blanket to help him to stay warm at night?'

'I nots answer she, Muddah. I look at de mock smile dat still on she face and I tinks dat Channy be nots care fer meh, but she be tink dat 'cause I sweet 'pon she, dat she can beg meh fer help and dat I gine help she. She look at meh steady and wen she nots see nuffin' in muh face like surprise, she tolt meh way to bring de tings and hide dem fer him. I nots gets de tings and I nots go'd to de place. I nots go'd, Muddah, 'cause I nots know'd if in she be tolt sumbody else dat be jis't like meh and den dem be know'd 'bout meh, so I go'd right way to de Overseer and I tolt him wat she suh.

'Wen I tolt him wat she suh, him look at meh stern like and him suh, 'Nigger, where did you hear this talk 'bout a nigger running?'

'Muh heart full wid fear and I know'd dat I nots be able to tolt him dat it be Channy so I fix muh heart to tolt him a lie. I suh, 'Massa, I be in de fields a far way off way most niggers nev'r come. I be moving muh bowels…'''

'Him suh, 'Nigger, I don't care 'bout none of that. I want to know who was talking.'

'I suh, "Massa, I nots be able to tolt yuh who dem be 'cause I nots be able to stands up and hab a look. Massa, I nots know'ds if in yuh 'member dat yuh gib meh a special treat; de skin, fat, and grease frum off yuh roast pork. I be a might happy fer dis. I be so happy to hab dis special treat frum yuh dat I be put too much of de fat and grease dripping in muh yams and it mek muh belly run a might soft. Muh belly be run so bad dat I nots be able to stand to see who it be dat be talking.'

'Him suh, 'Nigger, shut your fucking mouth with all that talk 'bout pork skin, grease, and your running guts. I don't care to hear. I want to know if you know who was talking. Do you know who the voices belong to?'

'Muddah, I tolt him next a lie and I suh dat dem nots be thar fer long. Dem jis't be thar long 'nuff to suh dat tonight be de night dat slave gine run.

'Him gets like him wants to hit meh wid him whip. I bends muh head to de ground and I suh, 'Massa, I be beg yuh nots to beat a dumb nigger. I be happy to runs and tolt yuh wat I be hear. I be sorry dat 'cause muh belly be run like water frum de pork grease dat I nots be able to get dis most 'portant ting fer yuh. I be most sorry, Massa, most sorry.

'Him look at meh wid a look like I be shit in him eyes and jis't 'fore him walk 'way frum meh him suh, 'You are a dumb fucking nigger; a dumb fucking nigger.'

'I be jis't stand way I be fer a spell and den I be walk 'way too. Thar be no reason fer meh to stand thar. De bruddah, him not know'd dat she not know'd to keep teet to tongue and dat she dun whisper in muh ears so wen it be full night and all niggers come frum field and de whole place be full sleeping; him run. Him not git far. De evening after de night dat him run, us brung him back. It be de Overseer, a mans name Beacham, plenty white mans, and meh. Dem tek meh wid dem 'cause I be de onlyest one dat can run fast as de dogs. I be hold de dogs and only turn dem loose wen dem pick up run 'way slave scent. I also know'd wat to suh to mek de dogs stop frum biting wen dem find runway nigger. It not tek de dogs long to find him 'cause I be tolt de Overseer 'fore him run so dem wait and gib him time to git just far 'nuff to gib de dogs a good run.

'Wen de dogs gits to way him be, him be trying to hide in de water, but him nots be able to stay under de water and wen him come up fer air, de dogs start biting and chomping at him. De white mans stand on de river bank and watch meh, him, and de dogs. Dem be wait on meh to call de dogs off, mek dem stop 'cause dem know'ds dat once de dogs taste blood, dem be jis't keep biting and tearing. De dogs not knowd's nigger blood frum white mans blood; blood be blood fer dogs. All dem dogs know'ds is to find wat be smell like wat be put under dem nose. I stay way I be and I not call off de dogs.

'I tinks dat if I mek de dogs stop too soon, dem gine tink dat mayhaps I hab a soft heart or feelings fer niggers and I nots be dem real special nigger. I turns muh head and I mek muh ears not hear him hollering and hollering fer mercy. I let de dogs do wat dem want wid him. I tinks dat it be him fault fer running so I nots care wat de dogs do to him. I not move to mek dem stop 'till one de white mans suh, 'Nigger! Stop the fucking dogs! Stop the fucking dogs! Don't let them eat all of him. Leave something for us to take back and teach them niggers a lesson just in case any of them got it in their fucking heads to run.'

'Ev'n though him suh dat, I nots mek to move and him shout harder dis time, 'Nigger! You fucking dumb ass nigger, I said to stop those fucking dogs now! Stop those fucking dogs now, nigger!"

'Wen I move to way de dogs be, I hears him suh, 'If they eat all of him, I'll just as easily take your ass back as the lesson. A lesson is a lesson and a nigger is a nigger.'

'I stops de dogs quick fast, Muddah, and wen I look it be clear dat dem 'most eat Silas. Wen dem white mans look at wat be left of Silas, dem look at meh and smile big. I smiles back and den I bends muh head low quick fast. I know'ds muh place, Muddah, ev'n thar I know'ds muh place. I nots let muhself fergit dat to dem I be nigger. Ev'ry nigger ought to know'ds him place. One of dem and I nots know'd who it be suh, 'You sure are a different breed of nigger. Look how you damn near let those fucking dogs tear him to fucking pieces. You sure you're a nigger? You sure white enough not to be one.'

'I nots suh nuffin' 'cause dem be hungry fer nigger blood and I nots want dem to go'd after de drop or two dat be in meh 'cause of yuh.'

Preacher Man suh it be like Fortune hab lots of tings in him heart and head 'gainst him nigger blood wen him hear him suh, "Muddah, I nots be sorry no more dat I hab yer nigger blood. I know'ds dat it nots be yuh fault dat yuh be nigger; I know'ds, Muddah, dat yuh know'ds dat it be hard to be nigger and if in yuh be able to do anyting 'bout it, yuh nots be nigger and den I nots be nigger. But yuh be nigger and so 'cause dem know'ds yuh be muh muddah dem suh dat I be nigger but, Muddah, I not feel like nigger in muh heart. Muh heart it be jis't like a white mans heart; it hate nigger. Dat nots yuh fault but it be mighty hard fer meh to 'cept dat I be yuh pickney. Nigger life be hard and I nots want hard life like yuh.'

Him tek sum more swigs frum him bottle and him suh, 'Wen I be git de dogs off him, de Overseer and dem dat help to track him down throw'd a rope to meh and suh, 'Tie that fucking piece of shit up and let's get it back to the yard. There are some niggers there who need a lesson in what happens to niggers who run.'

'I looks at wat be on de ground in front of meh and it mek muh belly feel like it gine go loose. I nots want to touch him, but I know'ds dat if I not do what dem suh to do, dat dem gine hab him and meh to drag bak to de yard so I tek de rope and I tie him foots 'gether den I tek de rope and I pass it 'round him neck and I mek a knot like a noose. Den I let it be go'd down him back and I brung de rope to him hands. Wen I pull de rope dat be 'round him hands to reach him foots so I can tie him hands and foots 'gether, Muddah, him head, 'cause I hab de rope round him neck, come all de way back and it look like him be looking at de Lawd. Him eyes dem open wide wide, but it not look like him seeing nuffin'. Wen I dun tie him up, I stand thar wid de rest of de rope in muh hand. It be wet and sticky wid him blood. I want to drop it and wipe muh hands in de dirt to git all de blood off it.

'De one dat suh I be a good nigger, him go'd to tek it frum meh but wen him seen de clots of blood, clumps of skin, and dirt on de rope, him suh, 'I don't want any fucking nigger blood and skin on my hands. You hold it. All that nigger shit is already on you. Tie him to the back of my horse.'

'I do jis't wat him suh. I tie him and I mek sure dat I tie him real tight 'cause I know'ds dat wen dem start to ride and him come loose, dem gine kilt meh. At one time, wen I pull on de rope, him eyes dem open and him head it move slow, slow to way I be and him fix him eyes on meh jis't way I be. Dem come to rest in de corner of him eye socket. I not be sure, Muddah, but him eyes look like he be crying. Him mek like him gine talk, but only him lips move a little. No sound come out. I turns muh head. I nots wants to see if him get him lips to move and beg meh fer help or mercy. I nots be able to help him no how and him gib up all chance fer mercy wen him fix to run.

'Wen I be dun, dem suh dat I ought to tek a different way bak wid de dogs and to mek sure to gib de dogs water as dem wuk hard chasing a useless nigger. I start bak wid de dogs and soon as muh back be turn, I hears dem tek off. I nots look to see if Silas' eyes ev'r left de corner of him head way dem come to rest. I jis't tink on wat to do to mek de dogs be quiet so nobody be hear dem.

'I be thar wen dem git to de yard as I know'ds a way fer meh and de dogs way no horse can ride. I gib de dogs water and jis't as I be dun gib de dogs water, dem mek all de niggers come to de yard. So dat niggers not know'd dat I be wid dem I go'ds and I stand in de yard jis't de same. It be den dat I teks a good look at wat tie to de back of de horse and it be hard to know'd dat at one time him be a big strapping buck dat be nice to lil' pickney. It be hard to tink dat jis't a short while bak, him be a nigger wid freedom in him heart and running in him foots.

'Wen dem git all de rope off him, dem drug him to one of de big trees in de yard. Dem tie him to it and dem start to beat him. Him not holler wen dem hit him de furst lash, but him puke. It not be like him pick to puke, but I tink dat dem hit him so hard dat wat be in him guts jis't come up and out him mout on it own. I tink dat him brain be not able to tolt him dat him be hit. Dem beat him, Muddah, till wen dem hit him de skin dat de dog dun rip and not tear full off jis't be fly off ev'ry time de whip hit him skin and come back.

'It be gittin' dat yuh nots know'd dat him be nigger nor mans 'cause one of de hits it land way him cocky be and it cut him cocky clean off. Dem beat him 'till de nigger come off him and him be jis't red and white. Wen dem seen dat dem beat de nigger off him and dem can see white on him, dem beat him sum more 'cause dem want de white off him. Muddah, dem beat him 'till dem beat de white off him. It be only wen dem git him to all red dat dem stop. Dem untie de falling apart nigger and dem string up wat be left of him. It be a sumting to see, Muddah, and yet it be sumting dat yuh ought nev'r to see. It be hard to look at wat be swinging frum de tree and know'd dat 'fore de dogs start to tear at him, dat him be sumbody pickney and now him swinging frum tree like rag tear up by de wind.

'Muddah, wen de white mans be doin' all dem tings to she bruddah, I be look quick at Channy and look 'way. She be stand thar in de yard wid all de rest of de niggers and she be watch. Her not blink. Her look and look like she nots be able to let she eyes 'lieve all dem tings dat dem be doin' to she bruddah. Muddah, long after him stop swinging, long after dem cut him down, long after dem throw'd him in a hole, throw'd in de lime on him, and hab niggers to full de hole back up, it be wen Channy start to holler. Aft'r dat first holler, she holler and holler and den, Muddah, she holler one long, long holler.

'It be like de holler not start no way and it be like it not gine stop. But it stop and same way it not seem to start no way, it stop same way; jist like dat, it gone and she quiet. She not look like if in she know'ds how to holler ev'r 'gain. In de same way she be quiet, she walk bak to de tree way dem beat and hang up she bruddah. I walk back wid she. I stop wen she keep gine to de tree. She go'd to way she bruddah blood be all ov'r de tree and ground and she walk right up to de tree and she tek she hand and she touch de tree. She not touch it quick and pull she hand back.

'She touch it slow and soft like it be she hurting bruddah. She let she hands stay resting on de tree. She shut she eyes and I look and de tears dem be coming frum under she shut eyes. I starts to feel sorry fer she de way she be in so much pain. It be like de tree sending back all de pain frum she bruddah to she. I 'pect she to tek she hand off de tree but she stand thar touching de tree like it nots be a tree no more but it be she bruddah, and she letting it know'd dat she sorry him dead. Den, ev'n slower, she pull she hands back frum de tree.

'I be look at she hand wen she pull it bak. It be full wid him blood. Her look at it and den she tek she hand and she touch she face. Her stand thar wid she bloody hand on she face and she still be crying. Her not mek a sound. Her eyes dem jis't cry and cry. It be like dem 'long to sumbody else. Muddah, it not be 'till she muddah come way she be and tek she next hand and start to walk 'way dat I tink on she. Channy's muddah not hollering. Her not ev'n crying. Her jis't tek Channy wid she bloody hand still on she face and dem walk to way dem cabin be. All de niggers dun drift way frum de yard. I nots be able to move. I nots know'd why I stay way I be but I jis't stand thar, Muddah. I be tinking 'bout how Channy's muddah heart must be feel; seeing she pickney drag back 'hind a horse near dead and den she hab to stay and watch dem beat him 'till him full dead. Den, Muddah, I hurd it. It be a sound dat I be still hear in muh head. I nots know'd wat de sound be or who mek it, but den it reach muh ears and I know'ds it be Channy. She be hollering and den de holler turn to a cry and she suh, 'Siiiiiiiiiiiiiilaaaaaasssssssssss!'

'De way she suh Silas! It be like it nev'r gine stop. It tek up de whole plantation. I be sorry fer she. I feel a sting in muh heart. I also feel water come to muh eyes, but I nots let it come out. I sorry fer Channy and she muddah but I nots be sorry fer Silas. Channy ought not to hab tolt meh dat him gine run and him ought not to hab run. It be she fault dat him dead and dats be de reason, Muddah, I nots let de tears come out muh eyes.

'Next morning, niggers talking soft 'bout wat happen to Silas and how Channy holler and call him name. Dem figga dat she holler like dat 'cause she be sweet on him. Dem not know'd dat him be she bruddah. De only one dat be know'd be meh and she muddah. Wen morning come, Muddah, meh, wid Overseer Ashmore get dem out to de field, Channy pick and ease, pick and ease, and wen she git to way thar nots be a next slave dat can hear, she suh, 'Fortune, how dem be know'd dat him gone? How yuh tink dem figga it? Thar nots be a soul but Muddah and meh and yuh be know'ds. I be mighty careful wen I be tolt yuh dat him fixing on running. How, Fortune, yuh tinks dem figga dat him gine run and wen?'

'Muddah, Channy, she be looking at meh wid she black eyes and in she eyes I see dat she know'ds. De more she watch meh, de more I see wat sweet feeling she have fer meh draining. I watch she face and I see hardness coming in she face. She still nigger but she face it gone hard like white womans. She not suh nuffin' else. I nots know'ds why but fear starts to come over meh and I wants to run frum she, but Channy watching meh and she watching meh den she turn and walk 'way frum meh. I can feel dem others in de field watching, but I nots want to turn and see who be watching. I call on Channy to stop but she not stop. Her keep walking 'way frum meh. I start to taste de fear. It be real fer meh. I gets a feeling in muh belly dat it nots gine be good fer meh.

'Soon aft'r, Muddah, Channy nots wants to be near meh or talk to meh. I nots know'd wat to do to mek she talk to meh. I try and try and wen she not talk to meh, I gets bitter in muh heart. Den one day, Massa Ashmore brung meh to way thar be lots of white mans and one of dem suh, 'I watched the way you handled those dogs the other nights. I can use a nigger like you. You are the kind of nigger that doesn't see other niggers as special and it's clear to me that you don't care 'bout niggers. That right there, not caring 'bout your own kind, makes you the best kind of nigger to a man like me.'

'I feel mighty proud and I be stand wid muh back like it hab stick down it. Den him suh, 'A nigger like you has the best kind of advantage. You look like a white man, but niggers know that you are a nigger so they won't and don't worry about you being near. Places where you can get, a white man will never be able to get; close enough to hear what those secretive fuckers are thinking. We need someone like you. A nigger like you moving among other niggers will be just right. They are never going to worry about you 'cause you are a nigger just like them. We, all of us here, are depending on you to bring us news. It's not for you to decide if it's important or not. You tell us and we'll decide the importance. You do this and you'll get special treatment above and beyond what you are getting now.'

'I wants to tell him dat I not need no more special treatment and dat him can trust meh to tolt him ev'ry tink I hear. Muh chest it git full and rise up high 'cause dat be never happen to meh 'fore now; a white mans suhing dat I be more trustworthy dan any other nigger on him place.

'Muddah, aft'r dat white mans suh dat, him reach in him saddle bag and hand meh a jug of good corn liquor and tolt meh, 'Nigger, if you get wind of any stirring with these fucking sneaky niggers that you feel we should know about, you let it be known to Overseer Ashmore that you need to get word to me and I'll come and hear what you have to say.'

Miss Thea, Preacher Man suh dat him know'd wen him hurd dat, him knowd it be de Lawd put him thar to know'd so him fix in him brain dat if it tek 'till sun crak de sky, him gine stay. Him suh dat him know'd dat Fortune not tinks dat thar be a soul hearing him 'cause him talking to him dead muddah and so him tek lil' breff 'cause him not want Fortune to ev'n hear him breave. Him suh dat aft'r Fortune suh dat, him walk way frum way him muddah be and him tek a few more swigs and den de cork go'd in de bottle dis time. Fortune walk back to way him dead muddah be and him start back to talk.

Him suh, 'Muddah, thar I be wid a white mans looking at meh like a white mans nev'r look at meh 'fore and him suh, 'You understand what I'm asking you, nigger?'

'De pride rush to muh chest; a white mans be come to meh and ask meh to be him ears 'round de niggers; dat feeling mek meh suh, but not too loud, 'Yas sir, Massa sir, I be 'stands right well wat it be dat yuh wants meh to do. Yuh wants meh to come let yuh know'd wat be go'd on here wid de niggers. I be mighty pleased to mek it be know'd to yuh wat I be hear. I be listen right hard and I be brung yuh all of wat dem suh.'

'Wen I suh dat, Muddah, I hear sumting fall at muh foots. I looks. It be a big piece a meat. It be pork. I wants to look and see who it be dat dun gib meh dat but I know'ds better dan to look up. I never tek muh eyes frum de ground.

'I stands way I be waiting fer dem to ride away. I wants so badly to pick up de piece of pork but all de while I be tinking, 'I hab to give 'em somethin right important for all dis extra meat dat him dun place 'fore meh.'

'It twan't 'till the sound of de horses fade 'way dat I be bend and pick up de piece a pork. It be covered in dirt but it be heavy and ev'n though it be more fat dan it be pork, it be still mean dat I be eat good fer a few days. I nots want none of de other slaves to see it so I put it under muh shirt and I head back to de sluice gate. I nots be back thar long when Overseer Ashmore be see meh and him suh, 'Now, Fortune, you are aware that you must keep what just happened here to yourself. You do understand that, don't you?'

'Widout looking at him or speaking, I nodded. Wid muh head bowed, I wait to hear wat him have to suh. Him suh, 'You go on back to your cabin and put down that meat and liquor and soon as you do that, you make your way back to that sluice gate. Now get your nigger ass to your cabin and you better be back to that sluice gate like you never left. Now run!'

"Dat day, Muddah, I be run to muh cabin like if de dogs be aft'r meh. I be bak to de de sluice gate like Massa Ashmore suh, like I be nev'r left.

Chapter 22

A Breeze So Bitter

'It be not long aft'r Channy's bruddah be dead dat niggers dem tek to looking at meh like dem tinking dat it be got something to do wid meh. I nots be able to suh nuffin' to dem 'cause I know'd dat him dead 'cause I tolt de Overseer dat him be fixing to run.

'Muddah, it be git mighty hard to wuk de sluice gate and do wat it be dat I be hab to do 'cause I hears dem as dem fix to sing song 'round meh. Dem not sing dis song hard de way dem sing other working songs. I listen to dem soft song and it hab words 'bout a Bitter Breezing nigger and I know'ds dat it be dem way of suhing dat dem know'd or feel dat it be meh dat mek it be know'd to de white mans dat de nigger Silas be fixing to run. Dis be dem song, Muddah:

A bitter breeze,
A bitter breeze be a blown'
Watch wat yuh suh,
watch wat yuh do
A bitter breeze dun blow'd in
'mongst we.

Bitter breeze it move like shadow
'cause it be de same
so yuh not see it come
and yuh not see it go
'till de wind suh to yuh
dat yuh too late

De bitter breeze dun know'd
wat yuh suh
and it on it way to blow
to any white mans
dat got ears to hear.

Hush, hush, hush yuh mout
'cause a bitter breeze dun come 'round we.
Hush yuh mout, hush yuh mout
'till de bitter breeze dun blow'd way.

Preacher Man suh wen Fortune start de song, him know'd it. Most ev'ry nigger know'd dat song. It nots be new song. Dat song be go'd frum plantation to plantation. It be a warning song dat nigger sing to tolt other nigger dat sumbody in dem midst be a Bitter Breeze.

Fortune go'd back to talking, him suh, 'I tinks on why dem calling meh Bitter Breeze and den muh brain it suh, 'It be Channy tolt on yuh.'

'Den one morning, Muddah, we be in de field and I go'd to way Channy be 'cause I not's be able to tek it dat she nots talking to meh and I smile at she and I suh, 'Channy, I gine ask Massa Ashmore if in meh and yuh can jump de broom.'

'I waits fer Channy to suh dat she gine be happy to jump de broom wid meh but her nots suh nuffin' and den I suh, 'Yuh nots gine hab to wuk in de field no more. I be ask Massa Ashmore if in yuh can wuk in de cookhouse.'

'I waits and still she nots suh nuffin' and den she look at meh and she suh, 'I not wants to jump no broom wid yuh. It be yuh. Yuh is de Bitter Breeze. Yuh be de one dat tolt on Silas.'

'She suh dat and I feel every one of she words come in meh like she put dem on de top of a stick and she poke dem wid all she force in muh belly. Channy, she walk 'way frum meh fast and I starts to walk aft'r she. She look back and seen dat I be walking to catch up wid she and, Muddah, she start to run. Wid each step she foots mek on de ground, de dust be rise up and den all I can see 'fore she get swallow up wid de dust be she back. I know'ds now dat Channy running to way she muddah be and she gine tolt she dat I be de Bitter Breeze blowing nigger dat dun tolt all of wat dem be suhing and dat I be de one dat mek Silas get kilt.

'I feel a worse kind of fear rise up in meh. Muh brain suh dat I hab to get to Channy 'fore she mek it to she muddah. I know'd dat if she mek it to she muddah, dat Odetta gine tolt de rest a niggers. I feel de fear rise higher. I hab to stop Channy. I hab to mek she be quiet 'fore she can gets to she muddah. I nots runs aft'r Channy no more, I run quick fast to way Overseer Ashmore be and I suh, 'Begging yuh pardon, Massa Ashmore, wen yuh suh fer meh to bring de gal pickney up to Massa Beauford, I be right please to bring de gal and I walks 'way frum yuh, but it be only wen I be in de yard clear dat I know'ds dat I not hears fer sure which nigger gal yuh suh fer meh to bring up to Massa Beauford. Fergive a dumb nigger, Massa. I be begging yuh pardon again' but did yuh suh to bring Channy, she be Odetta's pickney. Channy, she be de one dat long and stringy like she be a gelding. She be de one, Massa?

'I holds muh breff and I wait. I holds muh breff 'cause I know'ds full well dat it not be Channy dat Massa Beauford suh to bring. Him suh fer meh to bring Filis; she be Silve's pickney. It not tek Massa Ashmore but a blink 'fore him suh, 'Massa Beauford doesn't care which nigger wench comes up as long as he has a nigger to warm his bed tonight. I don't care which one you take to him. You can take a suckling right off its momma's tit for all I care, but when the sun goes down and that porch light goes on, there better be a nigger wench standing or crawling there when Massa Beauford opens that door. Now go and tell Odetta that Massa Beauford says to send Channy up to him tonight.'

'I stands not able to move. I nots be able to believe dat I be able to fix Channy dat quick. It be only when I hears him suh, 'Nigger, why are you still standing before me with your infernal stench? Move and go get the wench.'

'Turning, and widout a word, I runs to where I know'd Odetta be. It be jis't as I tink. Channy be wid she. I not look at dem. I suh, 'Odetta, Massa Ashmore suh dat yuh is to send Channy up to de big house tonight.' I hear Channy tek a deep breff and I look at she. I look and I watch as Channy's eyes fill wid fear and tears. She run closer to she muddah. Odetta, she not know'ds wat to do fer Channy so she suh to meh, 'Fortune, yuh be Driver. I nots want muh only pickney to go to de big house. I begs yuh, please. Please fer de love of de Lawd, beg Overseer Ashmore to tek somebody else pickney. I not wants muh Channy to go'd to Massa Beauford. Him cruel to womans dat dun tek mans and him worse yet to gal pickney dat nev'r tek mans 'fore. Channy, she nev'r tek mans, Fortune. I beg yuh to help meh. Please, Fortune. I begs yuh. Talk to Massa Ashmore fer meh. Tell him dat Channy not be a good pickney to go to Massa Beauford.'

'Watching Channy and she muddah, I start to feel a certain kind of pain filling up muh heart but I let what I be feeling go'd and I suh, 'I not be able to jis't up and talk to Massa Ashmore. I nots be no more special dan any nigger here at Beauford plantation so I hab to do like all niggers do. I got to do wat dem suh and Massa Beauford suh fer Channy to be de one to stand on de back porch tonight.' I looks at Channy full and I suh, 'Yuh is de one him suh to bring and so I hab to bring yuh to him.'

'Channy falls to to de dirt hollering and Odetta she starts hollering too. She suh, "Fortune, I dun tek mans a plenty and I dun mek plenty man pickney dat been solt way frum meh; I know'ds pain. Muh last man pickney, Silas, him be dead. Channy be de only gal pickney I ev'r mek and, 'sides, I be figgering yuh sweet on she. Beg fer she, Fortune. I be do wat ev'r dem suh fer meh to do. If dem suh fer meh to stay here in de field frum sun-up to sun-up, I be stay but please, Fortune, beg Massa Ashmore not to send muh only gal pickney up to Massa Beauford. I be go'd muhself if I nots be old and pass rutting time and I dun know'ds dat him not gine want meh.'

'I not lets muh heart feel fer dem. I suh to Odetta, 'Soon as yuh come frum de field I be at yuh cabin to tek she up. Don't tarry in de field or I be come and tek she frum de field.' I look at Channy and I suh, 'Way I tek yuh frum, Channy, not be matter none to meh. I hab to do wat dem suh and dem suh fer yuh to be standing on de back porch wen dat lantern be light dis evening.'

'Widout looking at dem, I walks 'way. The sound of dem hollering pounds at muh ears, beats at muh back, and rips at muh heart, but I nots let muhself feel. Soon as it be starting to mek evening; at de first long shadow, Scipio, Lemrich, Polidor, and meh cut through de yard. Us pass all de cabins. I not pays no mind to de small pickney as dem run 'round playing and kicking up de dust in front of de cabins, I not let de smells of sweet potato boiling, or de smells of Johnny cakes 'mind meh dat I be hungry. I nots let de sound of someone singing or dat sound dat yuh not much hear on de plantation often, laughter, full muh ears. I not's want to see, tink, feel nor want nuffin' other dan to get Channy up to de back porch. I mek muh step long. I move wid more reason and hurry dan de rest. I know'ds dat I to hab to git Channy to de porch.

'I look 'round at Odetta's cabin and I see dat thar not be no fire goin'. Thar be no bittle getting cook. It be dark and it be too quiet. I suh, 'We best be fixing to find Channy since her nots be standing where she ought be.' I go 'round de back of de cabin and Scipio, Lemrich, and Polidor dem walk way I walk. It be thar dat I seen Channy. She be fixing to piss. Widout a warning, I grabs she. De piss it stop coming out she pee hole but it not stop outright. It jis't run down she leg slow like if got fear mix in. She start to holler and beg meh not to tek she up to Massa Beauford. I nots let muh ears hear she, but I nots be able to stop she muddah frum hearing she. Odetta, she comes running out dem cabin and in she hand be a small bundle. Her not tinks to leave it in de cabin. I looks and it be clear dat Odetta be fixing on running wid Channy.

'I see a big fear come to Odetta's eyes and it be a bigger fear dan we tekking Channy up to Massa Beauford. It be de fear dat I know'ds dat she be tinking on running. She drop de bundle and she drop to she knees and she look frum Scipio to Lemrich to Polidor and den to meh she suh, "Fortune, Scipio, Lemrich, Polidor, I begs yuh'all not to suh dat yuh'all seen meh wid dis here bundle. If in yuh suh dat yuh seen meh wid it, dem gine skin meh and muh pickney. I begs all of yuh to give meh and muh pickney a chance. I promise dat I never gine tinks on dis ting 'gain.'

'Dem rest be look at meh. I turn muh eyes frum Odetta and I be look at Channy and I see dat a fresh flow of piss running down she leg. I know'ds now dat she frighten now more fer she muddah dan she frighten fer sheself. I nots tink, but dat. I nots give de piss time to mek puddle at she foots. I grab she hand tighter and I mek to walk but her not come. Her foots like dem done grow'd roots in de piss-soak dirt and dem nots moving. I pulls on she and she be heavy.

'It be Sciopio who suh, 'Plenty time dun gone. We best be dragging she 'cause she mekking like her dun fergit how to walk. It not be long 'fore dat lantern be light and no stubborn nigger gal dat Massa Beauford call fer gine get de skin whip frum muh back.'

'We drag Channy jis't how she be: de dirt frum the field on she foots, de sweat frum de heat of de day way she be pick cotton wid she muddah smelling in de air and de piss running down she leg. We drug she to de big house and we be get she thar jis't as Big Willie be hanging de lantern. Him look at we and den him look way. I nots like how Big Willie look at meh. Him be big and thar nots be a next nigger mans dat be near as big or strong like him on any plantation no way 'bout.

'I fears no nigger but I fears Big Willie. I nots know'd how it be if in

Massa Beauford suh fer meh to go get one of Big Willie's pickney. I nots hab time to tink on dat. Big Willie, him walk 'way and we gets Channy to de porch and gets she to stands on she foots and soon as she be standing, I walks way. I walks way and a part of meh suh, 'walk slow and find reason to look back. See wen him tek she in. I walks but I nots turn. I nots be mek it quite to de grass wen I hear de door to de big house open. I turns den and I see Massa Beauford. Him not wearing nuffin' but one of him white tings dem be call a night shirt. Him mek a step to way Channy be and him snatch she inside so fast it be like she nev'r be standing thar. Den I hear de door shut hard. Blam! No sooner dan de door shut, dan I hear Channy scream. It not be like no scream I ev'r hear.

'I turns to walk way and I seen Scipio, Lemrich, Polidor, and dem be grinnin' like dem get funny story. I meks muh way pass dem and I walks quick fast to muh cabin. Soon as I be inside, I gets to de small wooden box dat Massa Ashford let meh mek to hold muh extra rations. I reach in de box and I teks out de last bottle of corn liquor dat Massa Ashmore be gib meh. I teks out de cork, sit on muh mat, and I puts de bottle to muh head. Jis't as I be fix to swallow a next scream louder dan de one 'fore it burst de silence of de night wide open. I know'd who it be' it be: Channy. Dat scream be louder dan de one she mek when she call out fer Silas de night him dead. I waits fer a next scream, de one I be sure dat gine be after dat one, but no more come. De night it be stay quiet. De only sound now be de night creatures. I puts de bottle back to muh head and I drinks it like it be water. De night, it stay staying quiet and I be stay drinking muh corn liquor 'till wen de sun be come up. It come up and find de bottle in muh hand empty.

'I dun drink and tink all night. I be glad dat de sun dun come up and it be morning. In muh heart, I glad dat dis night dun pass fer Channy. I know'ds frum de way Channy dun scream she be mighty 'fraid of Massa Beauford and she be glad too dat now she nots hab to go bak to de big house no more 'cause Massa Beauford nev'r call fer de same nigger wench twice. Now dat Channy be dun wid Massa Beauford, I be beg Massa Ashmore if Channy and meh can jumps de broom. I gine talk to Odetta and mek she know'ds dat if meh and Channy be jump de broom, I nots be tolt Massa Ashmore dat she be fixing to run.

"I smile at dat. Meh and Channy gine gets to jump de broom; mayhaps ev'n 'fore de sun set den she be comes to meh cabin and I nots be 'lone no more. I gine hab meh own jump-de-room-wid womans. I fix muh head dat wants to be spinning on muh neck so dat I be able to stands. I stands and be jis't ready to step out de cabin and go'd and talk to Odetta when de door be pull open and it be Scipio, Lemrich, and Polidor.

Dem be standing strictly still. I looks at dem and I suh, 'Why yuh be opening muh door fer? It not yet be time fer meh to open de sluice gate so wat yuh wants?'

'It be Scipio who suh, 'Overseer Ashmore suh fer we to come get Channy?'

'Wat we gine gets Channy fer? Her know'ds de way to Odetta's cabin."

'Polidor him suh, 'It be true; her know'ds her way but her nev'r gine find she way back thar ever.'

'Why yuh suh dat?'

'Polidor him look at meh and him suh, 'Her be dead. Massa Beauford kilt she and if him not kilt her outright, it not matter, her be dead and Massa Ashmore suh dat she nots to get a box, cloth, or nuffin'. Him suh dat we hab to throw she in a hole same way we throw'd dog and jis't to put lime on she so she not stink nor she nigger spirit mek it way back to de big house to ride Massa Beauford.'

'Muddah, muh mout it be go dry and I mek to spit so I can get muh words out. I suh, 'Dead? Yuh jis't suh Channy be dead?'

'Dead and him want she out de big house now. Massa Ashmore suh yuh must come. Him suh dat it be we dat drag she thar and it must be we dat tek she frum de house and bury she. De hole dun dig. Come 'fore him suh to dig one fer each of we.'

'I be stands and looks at dem and I still not be able to get it in muh head dat dem suh dead. How come Channy be dead? Not one nigger womans be dead wen dem go to de big house so how come Channy be dead? Sciopo him suh, 'Come, we best not let de sun mek it any more cross de sky. I feel if we do, it not gine be good fer none of we. Come, Fortune. We hab to hurry.'

'I hurry to de big house and wen we get thar, Massa Ashford, him be on de back porch and him suh, 'What took you niggers so long? Just go in there and get that nigger bitch off Massa Beauford's floor 'fore she leaves a nigger stain on it and I have to take a whip to every last one of you 'till it comes off or out; either way I won't care once it's gone.'

'I opens de door and thar she be. It be like she not move but dem first few steps and her not mek it no way else. I nots want to look at she, but it be hard de way she be jis't thar on de floor; naked. She eyes dem wide open and dem full wid fear jis't de way Silas be. It mek de fear dat I be have in muh heart dat she be tolt dat I be de Bitter Breeze turn right thar to hate. De hate start with Scipio and Lemrich, 'cause of de way dem jis't grab she two foots like she be a slaughtered hog. Dem holding she foots wide apart so dat dem can see in she pee hole. I nots wants to look but it be wat Scipio suh dat mek meh look.

'Scipio him suh, 'Oh muh Lawd! Look! Look! Massa Beauford dun tek some ting and stuff in she pee hole. It be look like a leg frum a chair. Oh muh Lawd, not ev'n dog be hab dis dun to dem. Dis be de worse ting fer a nigger womans.'

'I mek muh heart not want to tink dat she suffer so I be look 'way. I be tinking dat she pee hole, which now be stuff wid sumting dat not haba right in pee hole of dog, horse, pig, and Lawd be know'd, nev'r, nev'r a womans and worse, worse dan anyting a womans dat 'fore, out of fear dat she suh I be Bitter Breeze, I be sweet on. I be de one drug she up to Massa Beauford. Muh heart start to squeeze at muh inside. I be tinking dat she and she pee hole be set side jis't fer meh to go'd in and later fer muh pickney to find dem way out and now Scipio and Lemrich be looking in she pee hole and laughing at de way Massa Beauford treat she worse dan animal. Him be treat muh Channy de worse him ev'r treat any nigger womans who be ev'r come up here. Him dun mek she red river to run all de way down she leg, on de floor, and now it be a true red river and frum de way it be look, her drown in her own red river.

'I be hate nigger 'fore now but de more I look at Scipio and Lemrich, de more I feel de hate grow'd in muh heart fer dem. I feel a most different hate fer Polidor. If Polidor be know'd how much hate be grow'd in muh heart fer him, him be jis't shut him mout but him not know'd so him keep on looking and looking and den him laugh real hard like sumbody give him joke and him suh, 'Wen yuh tink Massa Beauford gine know'ds dat him cocky not fer young gal pee hole? I be wish dat him know'ds 'cause in if him be know'ds, him not try to get him can't-rise-no-more-cocky in dis never-hab-no-mans pee hole. I be sorry dat Massa Beauford kilt she 'cause wen him be dun wid dem, dem not care who climb in dem pee hole and I be waiting 'till de sore frum Massa Beauford leave Channy's pee hole and den I be planning on begging she to let meh climb on she.' Laughing hard him start to move him hips like him rutting and him suh, 'I be rut she good and hard de way Massa Beauford be wishin' him can rid she.'

"I be want to suh to dem to stop. Dat dis woman 'fore dem be de woman dat I be plan in muh heart to jump de broom wid. But I not suh nuffin'. I feel de love and sweet feeling I be hab fer Channy dat be turn to fear wen I tink dat she gine tell Odetta dat I be de Bitter Breeze start to move frum muh heart. It move down in muh belly. It move down and down 'till it find de bitter bile dat be thar frum de time I see she dead on de floor. Dem meet and dem mix. A new feeling in muh belly now. It be a hate dat be hab love and fear in it. Love fer only meh now dat Channy be dead and gone, and hate fer eve'ybody dat be nigger. It grow'd to way ev'r a nigger be but it not grow'd far or deep 'nuff to reach Massa Beauford, Massa Ashmore, or any white mans I can tink 'bout. I not tinks 'bout why it not reach dem; it jis't nots.

'I nots want to touch Channy, but I know'ds dat if in I not touch she, dat dem gine drag she out 'cause Massa Ashford be outside. I pick she hand up and it not feel right. It be a different feel; it be cold like. I wants to drop she hand but I nots. I hab to be like dem. I suh, 'Way de box be fer she?'

'It be Polidor who suh, 'I dun tolt yuh. Thar be no box fer she. Massa Ashmore suh to jis't throw'd she in de hole. De hole dun dig. We hab to do wat him dem suh.'

'Wen him suh dat, I turn muh head and I be do jis't wat dem do and we get she outside. Massa Ashmore, him not be on de porch no more and it be Polidor who suh, 'Come dis way. Massa Ashmore dun hab dem to dig de hole over way dem be bury de animals.'

'I want to suh, 'Channy not be no animal,' but I know'ds better. I jis't walk 'cause thar not be one nigger on Beauford plantation now know'd way de dead animals be bury. We gits to de hole and I not hab heart to jis't throw'd she in. Lemrich and Polidor starts to swing she foots and I wants to suh dat it not be necessary to swing she like she be a hog. Let we jis't lower she in de hole. But I nots get de chance. De swing, and 'cause she dead, she weight tek she hand out muh own and jis't like dat, she falling in de hole.

'I know'd in muh heart dat it not tek but a blink fer she to go'd in de hole, but in muh head she stay a long, long time in de air ov'r de hole. Den it be like she turn she head and look at meh and like she eyes dem go'd frum full wid fear to sad, and den to hate. I wants to turn muh head but I nots hab to. It be like looking at meh mek de dead Channy sick. She head it turn frum meh. I know'd dat she head not really turn but wen I be look at Channy in de hole, she be on she side and she face it down in de dirt. I looks and I try to tink how she end up like dat in de hole; face down yet she be on she side. I know'ds now dat she mek she face look at de dirt jis't so dat if I look, I not see she face no more.

'I feel bile rise up in muh belly. I nots be able to let it come all de way to muh mout. I jis't look down in de hole. I sorry, sorry fer Channy, and I wants to holler like a womans having a baby, but I keep dat too in muh belly. Polidor and dem start to cover she wid de lime and den dem start wid de dirt. I fix it in muh heart to tek a beating if it gine come, but I nots be able to put one clump of dirt on she. I walks way. Lemrich him suh, 'Way yuh gine? It be go'd much faster if yuh help.'

'I not stop frum walking 'way. I walk a bit and wen I turn, I wants to run back to way dem be and shove all of dem in de hole, but I not hab strenf in muh foots to get back to way dem be. I turns back and walk to muh cabin. I hab to be far frum dem 'cause I hates dem wid all de hate dat be in meh. In muh cabin I tek de bottle and I puts it to muh head but nuffin' come out; it be empty. I puts de bottle down and I go'd to de field.

'I be in de field when Odetta come to meh and she eyes dem red red. It clear dat she be crying. She look at meh wid de most sorrowful look and she suh, 'Begging yuh pardon, Fortune, but Channy nots come back to de cabin yet. Ought Channy not be back frum Massa Beauford by now? Him not keeps no nigger womans frum night to morning wid him. I be mighty worried, Fortune. Yuh know'ds why him be keepin' muh Channy all dis time?'

'I tinks on how to suh wat I hab to suh to Odetta and in muh brain I nots be able to tink on wat to suh to she so I just suh, 'Channy be dead and we, meh, Polidor, Lemrich, and Scipio, jis't dun bury she over thar way we bury de dead animals. Polidor, Lemrich, and Scipio, be over thar now fillin' in de dirt ov'r she. It be Massa Ashmore dat suh to bury she thar.'

'I suh dat and I fix to walk way. I not mek muh furst step when I hear a sound. It be Odetta. She fall to de ground and she holler. Lawd, it be louder dan wen Channy holler fer Silas. Odetta, she be in de dirt and she suhing, 'Muh pickney, muh pickney! Oh Lawd, muh pickney dead!

Muh gal pickney dead! Lawd! Oh Lawd, help meh! Help meh! I nots hab no more pickney. Help meh, Lawd. Help meh. Muh belly burning meh. It burning meh, Lawd!'

'I look at Odetta and I be sorry fer she but I know'ds in muh heart dat I nots be able to go way she be and gib she no comfort. Some nigger womans dat be in de field, dem come close but I can see dat dem hab fear in dem eyes 'cause dem walk 'way frum wat dey be doin'. I nots care to mek dem go back to dem wuk. Dem see dat I nots gine mek dem go back so dem run to way Odetta be and dem fall on de ground wid she. Odetta, she crying and suh real soft like, 'Channy. Channy be dead. Fortune suh dem burying she now over thar way de animals be.

'Den Odetta she holler and de holler is sound like it come frum deep down by she pee hole and she suh, "Dem burying muh Channy and I, she muddah, nots be able to be thar to see and beg de Lawd to let she in him heaven. Lawd! Lawd! Oh Lawd hab mercy on meh and muh poor dead pickney! Muh pickney, muh pickney, muh pickney she deaddddddd!'

'Wen she suh dat, it be like she pull on de heart string of all de nigger womans. It not tek long 'fore it be lots and lots of nigger womans crying, hollering, and calling on de Lawd. Den I hear a sound dat I be never hear 'fore now. It be a tearing sound. I turns muh head and wen I look it be Odetta. She be kneeling in de dirt and she be tearing she dress. Odetta jis't be tearing and tearing she dress. Wen her not hab no more strenf to tear it, she jis't throw sheself full in de dirt, she hold she belly and she pour she hollering in de dirt. It be not a full holler now but it be still a holler. It be like she mek to holler in de dirt fer Channy to hear she.

'I walks way frum way dem be and it be only wen I be near de edge of de field I 'member dat de white preacher mans suh dat wen dem Jew people in de bible in nuff pain, dat dem rend dem garments and him know'ds dat nigger not know'ds wat rend be mean so him suh, 'Rend, niggers, mean that they tore their clothes with their bare hands They tore their clothes because their pain was deep and long-suffering.'

'I guess dat Odetta must be in nuff pain ov'r Channy deading 'cause she done rend she garment. Odetta ought not to hab dun dat. Her nots like Jew 'cause now her nots hab no more dress. Her gine hab to wuk in she rend dress.'

Chapter 23

Frum Bitter Breeze to Bitter Storm

'After I tolt Odetta dat Channy be dead, it not tek long 'fore dem find Odetta in she cabin dead. De niggers suh dat de evening 'fore dem find she dead dat she suh dat dis be she last evening on de earth. She feel, she suh, dat Silas and Channy be come fer she and she be glad to go wid dem. Dem suh dat she walk out de field in she tear up dress; de same one she tear up de morning dat I tolt she Channy be dead. She be go'd by de tree way dem beat wat life be left in Silas and string him up. She hug de tree and she smile. Wid de same smile on she face, Odetta walk to way de animals be bury and she go'd furst to way Silas be bury and she lie down on him grave and she be talk to him, den she go'd to de place way Channy be bury and she kneel down in de dirt; den she lie down on she belly and she be talk to she pickney fer a long time. Wen she git up, she be smiling.

'Dem suh dat Odetta walk to she cabin wid dat same smile on she face. Her not look sad no more. A few of de slaves suh dat all de sad dat she been since Silas be string up and Channy be dead gone frum she face. She look like she be a young gal pickney. Wen she git to she cabin door, she be stand thar in she rend dress wid she hands stretch 'fore she like she talking to sumbody, dem suh dat she suh, 'No more a dis. No more pain. No more sufferin'. No more seeing muh last man pickney beat 'till him like muh tear up dress. No more seeing muh only gal pickney gitting drug 'way frum meh to warm Massa bed and meh nev'r seeing she 'gain. No more running. No more dogs. No more Massa and him old evil rutting ways. No more. No more, no more, no more. Tank yuh, Lawd, fer tekking meh frum dis place.' Den she look at a spot dat be empty and she suh, 'Soon. Soon I be join yuh and we gine walk way frum dis place and no Overseer gine be able to mek him Bitter Breeze nigger set dogs on we, bury none of we widout box, nor stop we frum suhing a right proper goodbye.'

'Den she look at dem dat be near she and she suh, 'Come morning, meh and muh pickney walking way frum dis place and we nev'r gine come bak—nev'r.'

'Dem dat be near and hear wat Odetta suh and do suh dat dey be sure dat when Odetta step in she cabin, dat dem seen Channy and Silas outside, but wen dem blink again dem nots be thar.

'In de morning, Odetta be dead in she tear up dress. Massa Ashmore, him suh to bury Odetta jis't way we bury Silas and Channy. It be Polidor, Scipio, and Lemrich him mek do it. I be glad dat him not suh dat I hab to help. I be go'd to de field and wen I git to de place way Odetta be tear up she dress, I be sure dat I see Odetta, Silas, and Channy.

'Silas be on one side a Odetta, and Channy be on de next side. All of dem look jis't like I be see dem last. Silas, him look like him muddah's tear up dress and him still be red jis't like wen dem tek him down frum de tree. Channy be naked and a chair foot be coming out she pee hole and Odetta, she be got on she tear up dress but she smiling; a right peaceful looking smile.

'Dem be look at meh and Silas him tek wat be left of him hand and mek a fist. Him tek de fist and fix it under him neck hard like him cuff himself and den him point at meh. I full wid fear. I shuts muh eyes tight and wen I open muh eyes, dem still be thar but them nots be fully thar as I can see de field on de other side through dem. Channy, she tek she hand and she hold it out to meh and she tek she next hand and mek like she gine cut off she fingers. Den she point at meh. Odetta look at meh de longest and in muh head I hear she suh, 'Yuh. It be yuh. Yuh be a Bitter Breeze nigger. Yuh kilt all muh pickney and yuh kilt meh. Wat yuh gine git; yuh gine git. Yuh gine find deth. Deth, deth, deth coming fer yuh, Fortune, and ev'n dat gine be too good fer yuh. It be Silas and Channy deth all roll together. Yuh gine dead a right painful deth and thar nots gine be one soul dat be knowd's yuh to beg de Lawd to hab mercy on yuh. Yuh gine dead lonesome and fear gine be yuh only company and 'cause thar be no one to git de Lawd to fergib yuh fer yuh evil bitter breeze nigger ways yuh gine sup wid de devil at him table. Jis't like de white preacher mans suh him gine feed yuh fire and brimstone. Deth, deth, deth coming soon fer yuh.'

'Piss it run down muh leg. I shuts muh eyes tight tight and I wait 'fore I open dem. I know'd dat all dis be in muh head. Thar be no way dat dem can be thar. I know'd dat dem nots be thar. I open muh eyes. Dem be thar. And den I hear dem hollering and hollering. Silas, him holler like wen de dogs bite him. Channy, she holler like wen she holler fer Silas, and Odetta, she holler like wen she holler fer Channy.

'I feel a gripe and a tightness in muh belly and den 'fore I can stop it, muh belly go loose and shit com frum meh. Dem holler one more time together and dis time wen dem dun holler, more piss come frum muh. Piss and shit running down muh legs, muh legs too weak to move, and den in de next blink; dem be gone. I be 'lone in de field.

'I looks hard to mek sure dem gone and wen I be sure dem gone, I runs cross de field to muh cabin. I right scared to go'd in. I fear dat wen I git in, dat dem gine be thar. I not have choice 'bout goin' in since de shit and piss all de way down muh leg so I go'd in. Dis time, I hab muh heart in muh hand. It not be full in muh hand, but I can hear it beating hard and I feel dat it be out much chest. I shuts muh eyes when I go'd in de cabin and I nots want to open dem. I be sure dat I gine see dem, but I nots be able to git muh self clean if in I nots open muh eyes so I open dem; dem not be thar. I mek muh self clean and I go'd back to de field. It not be de same fer meh; I jumpy jumpy dat dem gine come back.

'Massa Beauford, him keep right on asking fer nigger gal to send to warm him bed. Fer a long time it be Bertha Mae; she be Big Willie's pickney. I be glad dat it never be meh dat hab to bring she to de back porch. Dat fall to Lemrich, Scipio, or Polidor. Den Bertha Mae be mekking pickney fer Massa Beauford and him suh to send de pickney Cornbread. I hab de most fear in muh heart 'cause Massa Ashmore send meh fer she. I get to cross de yard and I see Big Willie wid she, I stop and dem walk pass meh like I not be thar; I be glad.

'She be de last nigger pickney Massa Beauford ev'r ask fer. Him never open de door fer she. In de morning dem find Massa Beauford at de foot of de stairs in him house dead; him neck bruk. Him son come and suh dat if him tinks dat nigger hab one ting to do wid him Poppa dying, him string ev'ry nigger. I tinks dat mayhaps it be Big Willie kilt him, but I nots know'd how him be do dat since de house be lock frum inside. I fear fer Big Willie so I tinks dat I not suh dat to Massa Ashmore 'cause if dem checks and thar be no way fer Big Willie to hab dun dis ting, den dem gine swing meh. I keep wat I be tinking to muhself.

'It not tek young Massa Beauford a long time 'fore him start selling off him faddah's tings and de last tings him solt way be him niggers. I, wid, Scipio, Lemrich, Polidor, de nigger dem call Molasses, who be jump de broom wid Cornbread, de day 'fore dem solt we, a big nigger mans near big as Molasses, who be called Theo, and a few more niggers git solt to Litchfield's plantation. De nigger gal Cornbread, she not git solt same time but over time she come and so it be same as it be at Beauford. Den, Muddah, yuh come and I most shock. I nots tink dat I be seen yuh 'gain.

'It not tek meh long, Muddah, 'fore I let de Overseer thar, Massa Cuthbert, know'd dat I be de kind of nigger dat be let him know'd wat nigger be do. De hate in muh heart not go'd way. It be grow'd and grow'd.

'Nigger be nigger and soon nigger dat be on Beauford plantation finding nigger dat be on Litchfield plantation and dem jumping de broom. Scipio, him jump de broom wid a house nigger who be call Keziah. It not tek dem long 'fore dem hab a pickney. Dem call him Scipio like him faddah, but soon dat name nots be him name no more. Him grow'd wid a fat wide belly and him hand and foots be small. Soon ev'rybody calling him Tadpole. Dat name sure suit dat pickney. Him be here one blink and next blink; jis't like tadpole, him be jump sumwhere else.

'Lermrich, him soon do like Scipio and him jump de broom wid a house nigger call Phebe and jis't like Scipio, dem soon hab a pickney. It be a boy pickney and dem call him Chem.

Polidor, him jump de broom wid a house nigger too. She name be Clarasa and it be like dem all mekking boy pickney. Dem pickney be one strapping pickney. It be funny wen dem call de pickney Polidor and thar nots be one nigger call de boy pickney dat big name. Dem suh him too tiny fer dat big name. Dem call him Tiny ev'n though him be big pickney. Him grow'd to be big fat pickney and him still be call Tiny.

'De nigger Theo dat Massa Beauford's son solt frum him own plantation be show Overseer Cuthbert dat him be good wid de horses and carpentry. It not be long too 'fore him find a nigger womans and dem jump de broom. Her name be Rashell and soon dem mek pickney. Him pickney be call Lil' Theo. Him stay Lil' Theo. It suit him. All of dem; Scipio, Lemrich, and Polidor mek boy pickney. Molasses, him find him jump de broom wid womans frum Beauford's plantation: Cornbread. First she wuk in de field but soon she wukking in de cook house and de big house jis't like Keziah, Clarissa, Phebe, and Rashell. Soon she mekking pickney; she be de only one of dem dat wuk in de house dat mek gal pickney. Molasses, 'cause him be African Mandinka nigger, call him gal pickney Milkweed. I nots hab nuffin' to do wid Scipio, Polidor, or Lemrich, dem womans, or dem pickney as muh heart be still black 'gainst dem fer how dem laugh at Channy wen she be dead.

'I nots look fer nobody to jump de broom wid 'cause Channy be dead and I nots want nobody. I mek muh heart nots want nuffin'.

'I be do jis't like on Beauford plantation. If I hear sumting and I tinks dat Massa Cuthbert ought to know'd; I tolt it. Thar be days I nots be git muh mind to stay on de sluice gate 'cause I be tinkin' on gittin' bak to muh cabin and cooking up piece of pork and drinking muh corn liquor dat I be git fer letting dem know'd wat I be hear. Den one day, Muddah, muh mind be tinking on how I be cook de last big piece of pork dat Massa Cuthbert be gib meh wen I hurd de African nigger Molasses suh to Theo, de one dat be Rashell mans, 'It not be mek me feel good in muh bones. I wants fer Mrs. Henrietta to stop wid she school. Dis not be right fer nigger pickney. It not be sittin' right wid meh. I feels dat it not gine end right fer none of we.'

'De one dat be Rashell's mans, Theo, be suh, 'It nots be dat bad wat she do. She be only show'd dem de numbers and writing wen she faddah be gone and him not be on de plantation fer right some time.'

'Soon as Rashell mans be suh dat, him look up and him eyes meet wid mine and de fear rise up in him eyes. I lower muh eyes and I go 'bout opening dem sluice gate like I not hear wat dem suh, but I know'd dat it be 'portant what dem dun suh and furst chance I git, I mek it be know'd to Massa Cuthbert and I tink dat Massa Beacham, de white mans dat Massa Cuthbert suh dat I best be suhing wat I hear to, dat him gine geb meh a hand of wool fer sure and mayhaps some smoked beef.

'Soon as it be night, I mek muh way to way Overseer Cuthbert be drinking him evening brandy and I suh to him in a real soft voice, 'Beggin' yuh pardon, suh, I hab something mighty 'portant to suh to Massa Beacham. Massa Beacham suh dat I must let yuh know'd so dat yuh can git word to him.'

'Dat be how I git to tolt dem what I dun hear frum de big African nigger Molasses and de next African; de one dey call Theo. I not be know'd wat dem plan to do wid wat I tolt dem, but I not tinks on it. I tinks on de corn liquor, de piece of smoked beef, and de hand of wool dat be mine de next time I seen dem come.

'Muddah, I nots know'd dat dem gine do wat dem dun. I nots tinks fer a blink, Muddah, dat dem gine treat de lil' pickney worse dan hog. Muh mind nev'r figga dat dem gine string up de poor lil pickney de way dem do big nigger mans. It be Massa Beacham, Muddah, dat tek him knife and kilt de pickney dem call Tadpole and it be him dat tek him knife and him cut off de head of de lil' pickney Tiny. I know'd it be Massa Beacham 'cause I dun know'd how big and fat him be. Muddah, wen I seen wat dem be do, I wants to run frum de back and beg dem not kilt no more of de pickneys, but I not know'd how I gine mek dem stop.

'I watch de muddah of dem dat be getting kilt and I wants to suh to dem dat I be sorry. Dat I not know'd dat dem gine kilt de pickney. Den wen de muddah start to holler 'cause dem kilt she pickney and her nots be able to mek de holler stop, I be feel mighty sorry fer she. I wants to suh dat I be sorry and beg she to not mek noise 'cause I know'ds Massa Beacham like to see nigger blood. I nots hab time to figga nuffin' when I hear Massa suh, 'Shut yer fucking mouth.'

'Muddah, I know'ds dat when she nots be able to mek de holler stop, ev'n wen she put she hand over she mout to mek de holler stop and it not stop, dat Massa Beacham be do sumting. I nots tink that him be jis't step to way she be and shoot she full in she mout, Dat be wat mek meh de most sad. I watch, Muddah, how she mek to step way she pickney be deading on de ground but she not mek it. She dead right near way de pickney be. Ev'n though she be shot, deep in muh heart I be want she to mek it way she dead pickney be. I be most sorry fer she.

'I fear de worse fer de pickney Milkweed 'cause dem not know'd dat she be a gal pickney so wen dem grab she to put de rope over she head to string she up next to de one dat be already be up thar swinging, and de cap it fall frum she head and dem see dat she be a gal pickney, muh heart it beat de hardest since dem start. I nots want dem to kilt she. Ev'n though I nots hab nuffin' to do wid she faddah, she be a might sweet lil' gal pickney. Wen de one dat be grab she and him not kilt she wen him see dat she be a gal pickney, I be glad.

'I be glad dat she nots be dead, but aft'r dem kilt all de boy pickney and dem tie she to de back of one of dem horse and him drag she way wid dem, it be wen I hear yuh start to holler. I be want to suh to yuh not to holler, Muddah, but yuh nots be able to mek yuh holler stop jis't like de one dat Massa Beacham shoot in she mout. I fear dat him gine come bak and kilt yuh, but him not come back and kilt yuh, but yuh dead anyway. Muddah, I be sorry.

'Muddah, I begging yuh and de Lawd to fergive meh fer wat I be dun to yuh, Channy, Silas, Odetta, and mostly de pickney 'cause dem jis't be lil' pickney. All dem know'd is to run and play and 'cause I hab hate fer nigger mans and nigger womans, I mek dem lil' pickney get kilt like animals. I know'ds in muh heart dat I nev'r gine get wat I dun seens outs muh head. I gine stand 'fore de Lawd, jis't as de white preacher mans suh, and him gine open him big book and him gine read frum it and him gine suh, 'Fortune, yuh hab to go to hell 'cause yuh kil't all dem little nigger pickney, Clarissa, Odetta, Channy, Silas, and worse dan worse, yuh kilt yuh Muddah wid yuh hate. Yuh kilt she 'fore she dead 'cause yuh tolt she nots to call yuh she pickney. Now I dun pass judgment on yuh. Yuh hab to go to hell wid dem white mans dat kil't de pickney.'

Miss Thea, Preacher Man suh dat him nots care how Fortune be hollering and crying and begging de Lawd to fergive him, nor how much him be a preacher mans. Him suh dat him jis't be want to git up and go in Fortune's cabin and kilt him wid him bare hands. Him suh dat him know'd dat him be a preacher mans, but him sit thar and as him listen to Fortune tell him dead muddah 'bout all dem bad tings him dun, dat sumting raise up in him and him know'd dat it be de devil. On dat night, him be glad dat sum devil still be in him and him let de devil full rise up and jis't wen him suh dat him nots care wat dem do to him come morning, and him be mekking to go and kilt Fortune, him see de first streak of morning start to crack de sky.

Preacher Man suh dat him fear now dat sumbody gine seen him outside Fortune's cabin and him nots gine be able to kilt him and git way 'cause it be most quiet all 'round de plantation so him nots git up. Him crawl on him belly 'till him be out de way of seeing and dem him stands up and him move quick to him cabin 'cause him not wants de Overseer Massa Cuthbert or none of de drivers to see him moving 'bout 'fore time.

Him mek it to him cabin and soon as him mek it inside, him cry. It be de furst time since all de pickney and Clarissa be kilt dat him cry. Preacher Man suh him cry 'till him belly hurt and den him nots hab time fer no more crying. De sun dun crack de sky full open and it be time to bury all dem dat be kilt and Affa.

Preacher Man stay wid wat him hurd in him head as him mek to go and bury de dead pickney. It, wat him hurd, not tek de memory of seeing de dead pickney long after dem cut dem frum de tree and dem dat be on de ground. Wen dem git to way dem gine bury de dead, Massa Litchfield and Miss Henrietta be thar and dat surprise him. Massa Litchfield suh, 'I wants no more hollering. There shall be no singing of nigger songs. If there is to be a song and I'm more disposed there be no singing at all, but since they were my Henrietta's pets, then I will allow one song; it must be a proper Christian song. Mistress Henrietta's heart is broken. She has lost all her pets. Let it then, because of my Henrietta, be a somber song that should bring comfort to her until she can find more nigger pickney to replace these pets she's lost.'

It be a sad ting to see nigger nots be able to cry and holler fer dem dat dead. Wen de song be dun, Massa Litchfield and Mistress Henrietta dem jis't walk way. Preacher Man, him suh a few words frum him Bible; yuh 'member him nots be able to read, but it not matter none.

Wen nigger git to de field, de Overseer send dem bak to dem cabin. Him suh dat Massa Litchfield suh dat nigger not hab to be in de field right way. Thar be reason. Wat Massa Litchfield dun be jis't as bad. Soon as de pickney, Clarissa, and Affa be bury, him had wagons come and tek Molasses, Theo, Scipio, Polidor, and Lemrich off him plantation. Him suh dat since nigger mans be not stop de white mans frum tekking a whip to him pickney, den all nigger mans dat dem pickney be kilt hab to be solt off him place.

'Him be turning red as him suh, 'Such infernal niggers. You all just stood by and let my daughter be accosted. You will be off my land today." Him not suh one word 'bout all dem lil' nigger pickney, Clarissa, or ev'n poor Affa, who be dead 'cause it be too much fer she to see all dem pickney get kilt.

'Wen de wagons wid de mans on it pull way, Massa Litchfield send ev'rybody to de field dat had to go to de field and dem, all dem womans dat dem pickney dead or drug way, him send to de cookhouse; breakfast him suh, still had to be mek fer him and him pickney. Preacher Man suh dat it be one sad, sad day.

Chapter 24

Ev'n De Strongest Breeze Be Stop Blow at Sumtime

Miss Thea, as I be suh Dada not know'd wat Fortune be tolt him dead muddah Affa's ears. Him only know'ds white mans part. So him fix to tolt meh wat part him be play. It mek muh eyes open wide wen Dada suh dat him be thar wen de pickney be kilt. Not one nigger ev'r know'd who dem Patrollers be and wen Dada suh him be a Patroller, I not tolt another soul 'till now.

Dada, him wake frum him lil' nap and him suh, 'Beccah, at the rate I'm telling you the part I played in the awful day that 'caused your mother's path and mine to cross, I may never get done. I promise you this time that I will stay awake until I get it all out; the bad and the indifferent—there's no good.

'Know what I'm going to say to you comes from a different man. The man I was then isn't the man I am today. Back then, all I could think about was what I was hearing. We were hearing that some nigger bitches, with amazing gall, wanted what was meant for white children and women: book learning. He was what the niggers called a Bitter Breeze and he was blowing right in our ears. If not for him, we would never have known about this. But that Bitter Breeze who spoke all their secrets brought it to our hearing and left us no choice; Henrietta Litchfield, and all the niggers over at Litchfield had to be taught a lesson that they and all in Greenwood would talk about for generations and generations to come.'

Miss Thea, I nots hab to tolt yuh dis part dat Dada tolt meh 'cause I dun tolt yuh wat happen to dem pickney, one de pickney's muddah, and Fortune's muddah. Dis part here I nev'r know'ds so I be tolt yuh. Dada look at meh and him suh, 'Beccah, this that I have to tell you is so painful for me but I want you to know the kind of animal I was. I know you will tell me that I wasn't, but after you hear what I did to your mother, I'm sure you'll have a change of heart. Here, my daughter, is the truth of what happened after that day of carnage at Litchfield plantation.

'After, no, no, it wasn't after. It was before. Yes, yes. Before I'd tied your mother to my horse, I'd forgotten that she was human. In my mind, she was just a slave and so I rode as if the wildest wind, riding on one of the devil's hand-picked steeds, was at my back. I rode with the fury as if the heat of the devil's boiling sulfuric blood was coursing through my vein or if my horse had turned into a streak of lightning. It hadn't. The truth is that I needed to ride like that so I could put as much distance between me and my wicked deeds at Litchfield Plantation before my friend, Richmond Litchfield, returned to the carnage we'd left behind.

'Getting away was my only objective and so that's why I rode my prize-winning steed as if I'd borrowed it. I never once looked back or remembered the young girl who was being tossed; not just from side to side but sometimes, I'm sure, fully over onto her back and dragged. I never once concerned myself with the condition my newly 'acquired' slave would be in once I reached my own plantation, Fields Plantation, and stopped.

'Beccah, I never took her soft, wood-burnt brown, tender skin into consideration as I went swiftly over the rough, hoof-beaten, rock-strewn, and ragged terrain. It never occurred to me, nor would I have concerned myself if it had, that with each piece of her skin that was being gorged out by rock, rough grass, or gravel, each scrape on her belly, back, and arms; in some places, to the point where you could see the white of her flesh and even her bone, that I was killing her; a more painful death than I'd just inflicted on her friends because this death was slower.

'I never thought about her and the condition she would be in because I knew that at the other end of this hellish journey, she was going to be my slave and if there was any life left in her, Neala, my fiery-tongued – though never to me or any white person – stiff-backed favorite slave of my father's was going to be there. Neala, with her nigger roots and herbs, would keep her alive. She would heal whatever there was to heal and if there wasn't anything to heal, then that big nigger, Harold Joe, would build a box, put what was left in the box, and bury it.

'I rode on. The wind, accustomed to getting caught up in my burnt-brown reddish hair, did its best to keep up. It managed only occasionally to be steady enough for me to feel it on my face and for it to get through my long, untamed, horse-like mane of hair and lift it off my shoulders. On another day, I would have ridden with the wind and challenged it to keep up. Today, I wanted the wind behind me to propel me back to the safety of my own plantation. Trees melted into one another as I went by. It was all one green and brownish blur to me. I neither heard nor saw anything. Birds chirped but that day they chirped to themselves. Foxes, hearing the thundering of hooves, scampered out of the way and forest animals, accustomed to either being trampled by the stampeding hooves of my horse or shot at, hid in the under bush. Nothing or no one concerned me. Well, no one but Litchfield. Friend or no friend, I couldn't let him catch me and worse yet, with one of his slaves tied to my horse. I rode on.

'A guttural sound from the back of my horse made its way to my ears and for a second, and only the briefest of seconds, I got a flash of something flaying behind my horse and then I remembered her. But in the instant I remembered her, I turned and saw, in the nick of time a rock that seemed to be rising up to meet me. I swiftly and deftly got Ella, my horse, to get to the side of it just before she would have stumbled and thrown me. I heard a sickening thud and crack of what must have been the head of the slave tied to the back of Ella, as she surely had to have come in contact with the risen rock. Here, I must admit that I considered stopping Ella and untying what had to be now a dead nigger tied to my horse, but I didn't have the luxury of time; fear was riding me. I rode on. I would untie her once I reached home then Harold Joe could dig a hole and bury whatever was left. I wasn't stopping for her or anyone.

'As I rode, not slowing my pace for a second, I dismissed her from my mind but not before I thought of the lumber I would have to waste on her. It would be a waste because no slave on my plantation got a box free. Every slave that had ever been so fortunate as to be buried in a box on my plantation had earned it by sweat, adding to my chattel by breeding or by blood; those that didn't get a box had, been, in Olivia's opinion too insolent to realize that she, my wife, more than me kept a seriously steady hand on the running of Fields Plantation. I rode on wondering what I would say to Olivia if she were about when I returned and she saw a dead nigger wench tied to the back of my horse.

'Why hadn't I seen that rock before? I'd ridden that same path a thousand times and I couldn't recall ever seeing that rock and on that day of all days, it had risen up like some savior and robbed me of my anticipated pleasure. I, with the wind, playing catch-up, raced on.

'There truly was no need for me to concern myself. Then a fleeting thought crossed my mind. Niggers weren't so easily killed. The little nigger wench could very well be still be alive and, should she by some miracle manage to accomplish this, then survival, after I untied her, was up to her. The fact that she wasn't able to stay on her feet and do what I'd said, 'run' didn't make it my fault. It had all been up to her. She had her survival in her hands. It was she who couldn't keep up.

'Beccah, that was the way I, and all other slave owners saw it, survival was always up to the niggers: do as they were told and survive; do otherwise and death. None of that was really very difficult yet so many of them didn't get it and ended up dead.

'That again, as my friends and I saw it, wasn't so difficult to understand or do but every once in a while, niggers got out of hand and forced us, the Patrollers, to don our disguises and sometimes without disguises go out and teach them a lesson. That is what my friends and I had just done. We had just taught the niggers over at Litchfield plantation a lesson.

'We'd left a message of carnage and bloodshed that we knew that no one; nigger or white would ever forget. That was one message that was going to be etched in the hearts and minds of everyone in Greenwood for years to come if not forever. Beccah, that would be the easiest part to tell if I'd stopped there, but I didn't. I can't bring myself to tell you all of what I did, but I can tell you that it was several weeks before your mother could stand again. She stood. I made her. Then I made her follow me to the cook-house. There, I put her in the care of Neala.

'However, before I can get to your mother's life with me, I need to let you know what became of the one that we and all the niggers called the Bitter Breeze: Fortune.

'The day following the carnage at Litchfield, a fellow Patroller, a man, even though his real name was Ingram Beacham, we mostly behind his back called 'Bloody Blade' Beacham, said there was something that he had to do now that we'd taken care of the house niggers and their pickneys over at Litchfield.

'That something Ingram 'Bloody Blade' Beacham had to do was take care of the nigger at Litchfield; the one he called Pig Shit, and the slaves called Bitter Breeze. The one who had blown the breeze of what

Henrietta Litchfield was doing to his ears and with every word out of his mouth, proved the niggers to be right. He was indeed a bitter fucking breeze. If he were a white man, he would be dangerous. A nigger like him was the worst kind of nigger for niggers…even white men thought so. That Bitter Breeze nigger was indeed bitter and had to be taken care of right away. That kind of bitter breeze couldn't be allowed to keep on blowing. Against the wrong nigger match, it could start one hell of a fire; a revolt and the next thing you know, plantations owners would find themselves at the end of a gun with a nigger's finger on the trigger. No, this breeze had to cease from blowing.

'All of us rode over to Litchfield's plantation and watched as Ingram spoke to Cuthbert, the Overseer on Litchfield's plantation, one of our very own. He said to him, 'Send the nigger Fortune over here. Tell him that I want to have a word with him. Tell that nigger to run and don't let me have to come to that rice field and drag his nigger ass through that blasted sluice gate.'

'It was clear, Beccah, that that nigger truly felt he was going to get an additional reward for the information he'd given Beacham for that news. You could tell from the way he hurried from the field. He didn't know the reason for Beacham asking to see him, but he ran up to the horse and, dropping to his all fours, he made himself a stepping stool for Beacham to use to step off his horse.

'I watched him and as soon as he'd seen Beacham's boots on the ground, he backed away; crawled like an animal, on all fours 'till he was away from the horse and only stood when he felt he'd crawled a respectful distance, did he stand. Eyes looking at the dirt; he stood, waiting. When no sound came from Beacham, he raised his eyes for the briefest second to look; to see why it was so quiet around him. His eyes shone white in the mid-day sun and instantly I saw a nervous fear fill him. It was clear from the way his breath quickened that his heart was threatening to burst his chest wide open. In his eyes, there was a look that said he understood that today was going to be a different day. There would be no extra ration, raw wool, smoked beef, pork fat, or jug of raw liquor.

'It was clear that the nigger was becoming nervous and afraid. Hell, Beccah, I was a white man on a horse and that much quiet was making me nervous. I watched as he stole another quick look at Beacham. I too looked and what I saw in Beacham's eyes chilled me.

'Bloody Blade looked just as he did when he'd cut that little pickney's head off. The look was one of absolute scorn. Scorn, among other things, was the reason we were now on the far end of Litchfield's property. Cuthbert had told us of something he'd seen and overheard that had disturbed him. None of the niggers were talking to this one since the pickney and one of the wenches had been killed. The niggers were mumbling every time he went by. That wasn't good. They were calling him a blight and were whispering to each other saying that he had to be the Bitter Breeze among them and they were sure that he was the one who had whispered to Overseer Cuthbert about Mistress Henrietta's School For Nigger Pickney.

'As his nigger ass stood with his head bent and back hunched over, he had no idea what some of us were thinking and wondering about him. We'd often wondered about his kind. You know, Beccah, a nigger that for reasons only he knew and none of us really cared to know; was a nigger hater. He hated niggers just the way white men hated them. It was puzzling to most of the white men he whispered to, but it wasn't a big enough puzzle to stop none of us from listening. It might have come as a big surprise if only he knew how much we hated him; almost as much as he hated niggers. Had he known, he would have started right where he was and dug himself a hole and stepped in it up to his neck.

'I looked at Beacham and I knew, from the way his face was set, that Fortune had served his purpose and since Ingram didn't want to chance him talking to another white man and betraying him, he had to make sure that he silenced him.

'The nigger before us looked as if he were standing dead smack in the middle of an ants' nest and they were now starting to march up his legs, biting him with each step. It was clear that the nigger was thinking of running. The slight breeze that was blowing, and it wasn't the bitter one before us, brought his smell to them. It was a mixture of dirt, mold, sweat, and fear. His feet shifted. I could tell he wanted to back away, to run but he knew he couldn't. He had no way to run. Cuthbert had said that only this morning, when the slaves thought that he was far enough away and wouldn't hear him, they had started singing a song 'bout a 'Bitter Breeze.'

'Cuthbert had watched as Fortune had tried or pretended not to hear them. It was impossible not to, but he'd watched as Fortune had gone on with the business of opening and closing the sluice gate seemingly unperturbed. Overseer Cuthbert might have allowed it to continue for a few more days, but it was the song they were singing that told him another day couldn't be wasted. When he'd gone to the field, he was sure as he'd turn to walk away from where Fortune was at the sluice gate he'd heard them singing in a low groaning, moaning throat song that said:

A bitter breeze,
A bitter breeze be a blown'
Watch wat yuh suh,
watch wat yuh do
A bitter breeze dun blow'd in
'mongst we.
Bitter breeze it move like shadow
'cause it be de same
so yuh not see it come
and yuh not see it go
'till de wind suh to yuh
dat yuh too late
de bitter breeze dun know'd
wat yuh suh
and it on it way to blow
in any white mans
dat got ears to hear.
Hush, hush, hush yuh mout
'cause a bitter breeze dun come 'round we.
Hush yuh mout, hush yuh mout
'till de bitter breeze dun blow'd way.

'The song drifted towards Overseer Cuthbert and it was then that he'd sent word to Beacham. It was time. It didn't matter that we would never have known what Henrietta was doing if not for him. Beacham let that nigger stand there in the sun until he was sure that he was on his last nerve.

'Beccah, unable to take the quiet, Fortune said, 'Yas, sir, massa, sir, yuh wants to see meh, massa sir? I be come quick fast as I cans. Yuh wants to know'd what else I be dun hurd?'

'Those were the last words he spoke. No sooner had he said 'hurd' than Ingram Beacham swung his hand up swiftly and with a tremendous force as if he were giving him an upper cut, a big boxing punch under the chin, he had with that one movement pushed his knife through the under part of Fortune's chin. Beacham had hit him so hard under his chin that he'd picked him a few inches off the ground. In fact, the sudden move surprised me and made me jump with a start. It also, I'm sure, surprised Fortune as he was suddenly lifted up off his feet. The movement, you could tell from looking in his eyes, had confused him.

'It was clear, Beccah, that he thought that Beacham had punched him because he, with that confused look on his face, without thinking about it, reached up to rub where he thought Beacham had punched him under his chin. Instead of the sore spot that I'm sure he expected to find forming from the force of the blow, his hand suddenly found that it was wet with his blood and there was a rough piece of wood with metal on the end.

'You could see in his face that he was trying to figure out what it was in his neck. He'd expected to just find a sore spot; there wasn't supposed to be anything there. It was clear from the look in his eyes that his brain, the part that was still working, had just registered what the cold piece of metal could be. He didn't have to guess any further, he knew; a knife had been stuck under his chin.

'It was sad watching him as the realization hit him that he'd been stabbed. The knife, from the force that Beacham had used, was deeply imbedded in the underside of his chin, he couldn't lower his neck as the knife handle was resting on his chest. With his head now tilted backward and his eyes wide open, he had no choice but to look directly into the eyes of Beacham. He felt his shirt getting wet. He couldn't look but he didn't have to guess what it was. He knew. His blood was being drained from him.

'I'm sure that was something that Beacham had planned.

'Even with his head tilted in that position, a position that had nothing to do with him, it was clear that he knew he should lower his head and not stare into the eyes of a white man. I watched as he struggled, even with the knowledge that a knife was stuck deeply under his chin, to lower his head, but he couldn't. The knife handle prevented him. He tried to close his eyes. The shock and the pain from being stabbed wouldn't let him.

'I'm no surgeon, Beccah, but I'm guessing that the knife was sitting on the part of his brain that controlled his eyes, he had no choice but to keep them open. They were open and were going to remain open for the few seconds of life he had left. I'm sure he wanted to ask something, and even if he could think of something to ask, he couldn't. The knife had anchored his tongue to the roof of his mouth on its way to slicing through his brain. Without looking, not that he could because of the upward tilt of his head, I knew he knew that he truly now had the only real forked tongue on the plantation as the knife, I'm sure, had divided it in two.

'To my amazement, Beccah, I watched as he reached up in a vain attempt to pull the knife out. He'd no sooner gotten his hand to the knife handle than Ingram also reached for the knife. I thought he was going to pull it out, but he didn't. He didn't want the nigger touching his precious knife and so, before the nigger could start pulling it, Ingram gave it one final jab, thrusting the handle of the knife more than a little into the hole under Fortune's chin. I swear, Beccah, I saw the tip; just the very tip – protrude from the top of that nigger's head. Blood started to spray from the top of his head through the opening the knife had just made. Blood was now coming from his neck, mouth, and the top of his head.

'Satisfied that he'd pushed the knife as far as it could go into Fortune's head without losing it altogether, Ingram Beacham started to pull it down. As soon as some of the blade started to show, Fortune reached up. I don't know if he was going to try and remove it faster than how Beacham was pulling it, which was slow, but as soon as Fortune wrapped his hands around it, Beacham pulled down and quickly right through Fortune's blood-covered right hand, cutting all the fingers off at the second knuckle, well all except the thumb. Fortune didn't have to let go of the knife. He had nothing to hold onto it with. The four stubs started squirting blood, I didn't think he had anymore giving how badly he was bleeding from all his other cuts, but he did.

'The thumb jutted strangely in the air, it now being the longest finger on his hand. It looked like that last leaf left on a branch long after all the others had given in to the cold weather and had fallen to the ground. Fortune couldn't get his head to look down at his feet. Beccah, it was perhaps a good thing for him that he couldn't because all he would have seen were his four now bleeding fingers, like fallen leaves, scattered around his blood-spattered bare feet.

'Staggering back and buckling from the pain, he looked at the man whom he'd, only a few days ago, told of the school for Nigger Pickney that Mistress Henrietta was running when her poppa went to town, and now for all that much bitter breezing, he was sliced up just the way the children had been; like a hog.

'Then, Beccah, he turned his head slowly as if someone had called his name. I looked where he was looking and for a split-second, I thought I saw three niggers. There were there but not. By that, I mean I could see the field right through them. There was a buck, an old wench, and a gal pickney; more than a gal but less than a full wench. The buck and the gal pickney were standing each on one side of the nigger wench.

'The older wench had on a dress that appeared to be all torn. The rag dress, and that's all it was really, moved slightly in the wind. The gal pickney, even for that second there, appeared to have something coming out from down between her legs, I'm not sure but I think it looked like a chair foot, and the buck looked almost like the wench's dress; he was ripped, raw, and bleeding. Looking at Fortune, all three smiled and, raising their hands up, they pointed at him and slowly motioned for him to come. They stood as if they were waiting. I blinked to clear my head of that aberration as I was sure I was seeing things. When I opened my eyes, they were gone.

'Fortune was still looking off that way when I smelled before I saw that he'd shit as well as pissed himself. He fell to the ground looking the most white I'd ever seen a nigger, with his white-skin look. It was as if he'd seen something to add to the fear he was already experiencing. I watched as he writhed on the ground in pain and fear. The dirt, which, was cracked and dry before he fell was now a blood-soaked mud. It was sticking to him. For the first time in his life, the nigger was a strange kind of brown; just in places. Those were the places where his blood had mixed with the dirt and was now covering any exposed skin.

'As he bucked on the ground, he never noticed and even if he had there was nothing he could do, as Ingram Beacham indicated to the others to string him up. Had he not been trying to figure out how to stop his life's blood from gushing out the hole under his chin, the slice in his tongue, the hole at the top of his head, and from the stubs where his fingers used to be, he would have noticed when the rope went over his head, passed his now-closed eyes, nose, and mouth and finally settled down and around his neck just below where the hole under his chin was. He also would have noticed when his feet, for the second time that day, left the ground and had the knife not nicked the edge of his brain where he felt pain, he would have felt the sudden jerk to his neck.

'However, fortunately for him, enough of his life's blood had spouted from the holes in his body that by the time the horse bolted forward, there was nothing of him to hang. The sudden jerking of his neck was enough to send the final terrifying message to his heart to stop. It had stopped, but not before we all heard and felt a sudden gust of air that came from deep inside him. The air was mixed with his blood, the stench of fear, and the dirt his feet and the horse's had kicked up; it smelled bitter.

'As I watched him flutter and die, Beccah, I understood what a bitter breeze was. A bitter breeze had no right to blow. It's foul and putrid.

'Beccah, there was one thing I knew for absolute sure that day—; Beacham was the coldest man I knew. As I watched him wipe and clean his bloody knife on that nigger's pants, I knew he would find a reason to use his knife again. It was just the way he was. If he wasn't cutting up, down, across, or through a nigger, Ingram Beacham never felt right. A knife, he said, was the only way to teach a nigger a lesson. He obviously had plans of teaching many a nigger lessons because that knife was the biggest, longest, sharpest, and most dangerous-looking knife I'd ever seen.

'Lesson over; we rode back to our respective plantations. No one worried about the nigger swinging in the tree. He would be found, cut down, and buried or burned soon enough. No one, I'm sure, would miss him.'

Chapter 25

A Love Dat Be Mix wid Hate

Auntie Thea stopped and looked at us. It was as if she was stopping to give herself a breather and also to allow us time to let what we'd just heard sink in. Then, looking from Auntie Noreen to me, she said, "When Beccah stopped from talking, I wasn't sure what I wanted to do. I had a similar look on my face and as many questions as you have right now. The first thing running through my mind, well it wasn't the first thing because I wondered how anybody could just stand around and watch somebody kill somebody and not do anything, it doesn't matter if it's a grown man that, from the sound of things, deserved killing but he'd stood by and watched children get killed and then he'd dragged a child away himself.

"What I kept wondering was how, just how Milkweed could, knowing that he was there even if he didn't outright kill her friends, get to the place where she let love grow for him. But that wasn't the question I asked Beccah."

Auntie Noreen said, "I know what I would have asked her. I know."

I looked at Auntie Noreen and Auntie Thea and I said, "How do you stay loving him as a father? That would have been my question."

Auntie Thea told me, "I asked her that. It was as if she knew the question was coming because she didn't think on it long or hard, she simply answered me and then she continued telling me the story."

"What did she say, Auntie Thea?"

Rebeccah

He was Dada and had been Dada 'fore him tolt meh dat. I nots know'ds how to stop loving him, so I not stop. Dada be already fix it in him heart dat I be stop loving him so him suh, 'Beccah, I told you it was going to be a most difficult thing to hear and as I said before, if you decide that you can't love me, I will understand. I will, Beccah. I did some awful things in my younger days but since your mother agreed to be my wife, I've tried every day since that day to make her never regret her decision to stay with me. I love her, Beccah. I really do. I love her and all of you but I, at the risk of losing you, must tell you these awful truths about me. I look at your mother as she haunts the grounds and I feel badly that all she's ever known has been the width and breadth of this plantation. She has never been off this plantation other than that time I sold her.'

Miss Thea, when Dada suh, "sold her", I feel a coldness come in muh bones. It be like I walk in the icy water widout muh boots. I suh, 'Yuh solt Momma Pearl? Wen?'

Dada put him head in him hand and him suh, 'In a fit of jealous rage. After I sold our sons, your brothers, away I, in wanting to prove to your mother that I was the owner of this plantation, sold her. I sold her back to the very plantation I stole her from and then right after I sold her, I was miserable. I tried for four years to get her back. I was empty without her. My whole being wanted to see and hear her. I then did the unthinkable and unheard of, I confessed my love for her to Litchfield. He, shortly thereafter, and I'm not sure why, sent her to me. He never took payment for her or for the nigger pickney she brought back with her. That pickney was your sister, Sara.'

Then Dada suh to meh, 'My dear Beccah, all that talk has tired me and I'm sure it's a lot for you to take in. I'm going to rest for a while. Go to the cook house and ask your mother to make me some of her chicken and biscuits. I have a taste for it. It seems as if hours have passed since Etta Pearl brought my breakfast up and…' Here Dada smile and den him suh, 'My Pearl has been in. Even now, Beccah, I miss her when she's away from me and yet I know that she can't be around me and this damnable sickness.

'Go look for your mother. Ask her to come sit with me for a short spell. I would like that. I don't hear the usual noise so I know that the house is empty. Anakey? I haven't seen her for a while…is she well and about?'

She is, Dada, I be seen her this morning.'

Miss Thea, the next thing I know'd, Dada him be asleep. I watch him in him sleep and I be nots sure wat I be feeling fer him. A part of meh be look at him and I see de Patroller, den I look and I be see de white mans dat not hab heart 'nuff to know'ds dat if him tie and drag sumbody, nigger or white mans, mans or womans, dat dem be sure to dead. I be look at him in him peaceful slumber and I be wish dat him be dead, right thar way him be. I tinks it and I nots be shame. I nots be shame 'cause I nots be look 'pon muh Dada. I be looks on a old white mans dat be full wid hate fer niggers at a time in him life and it be him, dat white mans dat I be look at. I nots stop de hate frum rising up in meh but wen de hate suh, 'Tek de pillow dat be under him head and kilt him fer dragging yuh muddah,' it be wen I start to rise and reach fer the pillow dat I git a hold of muh sense.

I tinks dat Momma Pearl be muh muddah only 'cause him be muh faddah. I let de hate dat rise up in meh go back down. I nots look 'pon him no more 'cause I nots want de hate to rise back up. I fear if in it rise up 'gain, I nots be able to mek it go bak down and I gine tek de pillow and kilt him. I leave him sleep and I go'd to the cookhouse to look fer Momma Pearl.

Her nots be there. The cookhouse be empty. I listen fer Momma Pearl and I nots hear she so I go'd to she house and I nots be in she yard proper wen I hear Benjamin. Him be fussing wid Momma Pearl. I hurry and I go in de house and I seen jis't wat I tinks I be see. Benjamin wid him hand stretch 'fore Momma Pearl and him waiting, like him always be waiting, fer Momma Pearl to put sumting in it or to eat sumting frum it.

I look and him hand be empty so I know'ds him be waiting fer Momma Pearl to put sumting in it. I suh, 'Wat it be dat yuh wants dis time, Benjamin?

Him suh, 'I nots be talking wid yuh, Beccah. Dis nots yuh business. Yuh sick faddah be yuh business. Dis 'tween Muddah and meh. Why yuh nots go see 'bout him 'fore him dead while yuh be here gittin' in de midst of wat nots hab nuffin' to do wid yuh?'

I suh, 'Jis't so yuh 'member, Benjamin, she be muh muddah and I not like it dat yuh tinks yuh be de faddah ov'r she. Yuh nots be she faddah. Yuh be she pickney, and wen it be come to muh Dada, yuh best not let him name come out yuh mout 'fore I come and box yuh in it. Yuh may be big ov'r meh, but I nots fear yuh. I be tek him gun and shoot yuh if in I hab to!'

Benjamin, him look at and past meh and him turns to Momma Pearl and him suh, 'Gib meh wat yuh plan to gib meh; all of muh inheritance.'

Chapter 26

Gib Meh Muh Inheritance

Wen Benjamin suh dat him want him inheritance, I be jis't git mad like I be hab to piss real bad and nots got no way to piss. I be dat mad 'cause I knowd's dat Benjamin know'ds dat Momma Pearl nots be hab nuffin' dat be she own so she nots got nuffin' to gib him fer him inheritance.

Momma Pearl she be vex in she spirit and she suh, 'Benjamin, wat yuh talk 'bout 'heritance? Yuh not white mans pickney nor heir to some white mans and wat him owns. Dey be no such ting as 'heritance fer nigger mans and 'sides, way I be gets sumting frum to gib yuh. I not owns nuffin' so wat it be dat yuh tinks I hab to gib yuh fer dis 'heritance dat yuh tinks be fer yuh?'

Him keep plenty noise jis't like de braying jackass dat Dada suh him be and den him suh, 'But I be seen yuh in dem fancy white beads. Dem be sumting dat yuh own. Give meh dem and I be go'd up north way nigger be free mans and womans and I nots come back' round dis place. Freedom not be here. Freedom be up north. Give meh dem, Muddah, and I be mek muh way frum here and go'd see what freedom be like. I nots want to be nigger bound to dis place and dat old dying white mans like yuh no more. I wants muh freedom.'

As I tolt yuh, Momma Pearl not know'ds how to tolt him no and since him hab she heart in him hand, and him also know'd dat him next hand be she plate, him stretch him hand out dat be she plate and him wait fer she to put she fancy white beads dat Dada give she in it so him can go up north and see wat freedom be.

But Momma Pearl, she suh, 'Benjamin, I loves yuh wid all muh heart, but I nots be able to do dis ting dat yuh be asking meh to do. Dis ting, give yuh muh pearls, be too hard fer meh to do. Yuh not be needing muh pearls to find freedom. Freedom not come at dis cost. Freedom now be free. Yuh know'ds wat be sad 'bout yuh, Benjamin? Since yuh be boy pickney, yuh only know'ds how to tek; yuh nev'r gib. It be sad dat yuh be dis way, and it be sadder yet dat all dis time I be bend in which way yuh want meh to bend 'cause yuh not hab a muddah, but dis time I nots be able to bend no more fer yuh. I done all de bending I be ev'r gine do fer yuh.

Yuh ways not yuh muddah's ways 'cause wen she be live and if yuh be need she heart and she know'd how to give it to yuh, she be gib it to yuh. Yuh ways not yuh faddah's ways 'cause him love yuh muddah and him not able to live wid out she. Yuh ways not muh ways, nor Poppa Molasses', nor Momma Cornbread's and de good Lawd know'ds dat yuh not hab one bit of Harold Joe's blood in yuh. Not one bit 'cause yuh ways not be him ways. Yuh ways jis't like white mans ways. White mans tek and tek. Dem not care if in it be de most precious ting to yuh, dem gine tek it.

Benjamin, him get to way him gine walk 'way frum Momma Pearl and she, fer de furst time ev'r, she shout, 'Benjamin, yuh stay! Yuh stay and yuh hear meh out! Yuh gine listen to wat I hab to suh and wen I dun, yuh free to walk; but not now! Now yuh gine listen 'cause I dun listen to yuh all dese years and I feel de tired frum listening to yuh weighing heavy on muh bones and I nots be able to tek de weight no more so yuh gine listen to meh. Yuh gine hear meh out. Yuh listen and yuh listen good 'cause it not be right dat yuh be de way yuh be.'

Benjamin, him stop way him be and wen him turn and look at Momma Pearl, it be a look dat full a so much hate dat it not mek good sense dat him be able to look at Momma Pearl dat way after all dat she dun fer him, but none of dat mek a difference to him. She dun tolt him no and dat be hab him boiling, but it clear to see dat Momma Pearl be boiling too.

She suh, 'Benjamin, wen yuh come in dis world, yuh momma tek she last breff. She tek dat breff so yuh can live, but now dat I tinks on it, it not be fair dat muh pickney dead so dat yuh can live. Yuh not mek she deading be worth it.

'I know'ds dat a muddah ought not so suh such tings to she pickney, but sometimes it be de pickney dat mek de muddah suh dem tings and wat I gine tell yuh, Benjamin, be one of dem tings.'

Momma Pearl, she shut she eyes and she shake she head from side to side like she sorry and den she suh, 'Fer a man pickney dat be more nigger, well more nigger dan any of muh own pickney, yuh be de one wid de heart jis't like a white mans and yuh hab him ways. White mans not tink 'bout wat dem doin' to nigger and how it gine mek nigger feel. White mans, dem tek and tek frum nigger till nigger not hab no more to give, and ev'n den dem wants more frum yuh. It be den dat dem tek yuh life. Now it not be dat dem can do nuffin' wid yuh once dem tek life frum yuh, but it mek dem feel good 'cause now nigger not even got de breff dat de good Lawd gib dem.

'Dat be yuh, Benjamin. Dat be a sad way to be and as yuh muddah, I gine tell yuh now I feel sorry fer yuh. If in I nots know'd better, I suh dat on dat day yuh born, yuh kilt yuh muddah jis't so yuh not hab to share she wid Etta Pearl, yuh dada, meh… anybody. Benjamin, it not right dat yuh be like dis. Yuh suh yuh want to go'd see wat freedom be, but I gine suh to yuh now dat dey not be no way fer a mans wid a heart like yourn to walk and find freedom.

'If white mans got heart like yourn, him can mek him own way to walk, but nigger mans wid heart like yourn, dey not be no place fer yuh to walk. Way yuh headed, Benjamin, and wid yuh ways, not gine have happy ending fer yuh nor nobody dat be wid yuh. I sorry, sorry dat muh Sara be de one dat push yuh out. I wish dat yuh be a stranger to meh so dat I can walk way frum yuh and fergit dat I set eyes on yuh. But muh Sara, she be yuh muddah so I nots be able to treat yuh like stranger, but wat I can do is walk 'way frum yuh, Benjamin, and beg muh heart over time to fergit dat I know'd yuh.

Wen Momma Pearl suh she gine walk way frum Benjamin, him holler and him suh, 'I be sorry, Muddah. I be sorry but it be dat I jis't not wants to be here no more. I see de ways yuh be wid him.'

Momma Pearl, she turns to Benjamin and she suh, 'Dat be wat wrong wid yuh, Benjamin. Yuh nots be able to keep yuh eyes on wat be yourn. Yuh always hab to be casting yuh eyes on wat 'longs to somebody. Yuh never know'ds how to be happy wid wat yuh hab. And yuh see dat "him" dat yuh talk 'bout, it be dat same him dat mek it so yuh can live de day yuh and Etta Pearl be born. Times now hard fer nigger, but times 'fore freedom be worser yet fer slave. Yuh not know'd 'fore now, but since yuh gine be leaving frum 'round him and meh as yuh suh, it's best dat yuh know'd.

'Yuh, Muddah, she be in a sad way trying to birf yuh. Dey be no way to know'd dat Etta Pearl be in thar wid yuh so yuh muddah try to get yuh birf. Wen it not look like she can do it, dat same "him" yuh jis't suh yuh nots be able to see meh wid; well it be dat him dat get a white doctor to come and help so yuh can live and now yuh be grow'd and yuh wants to walk 'way frum here 'cause yuh not get all of ev'ryting fer yuhself. Dat be sad.

'If in yuh wants to leave off dis place, den leave. I be tinks of yuh often but I not gine bruk muh heart ov'r yuh. Muh heart it dun bruk too many times to add yuh leaving or mek yuh leaving one more time it get to feel bruk. I not know'd if yuh know'd, but some of dese times muh heart been bruk had to do wid wen I had to bury three gal pickney: muh Lilly, den muh baby Rose, de one dat not live long nuff to tek a next breff 'cause I beg she to dead 'cause I nots want she tek frum meh, and yuh muddah; muh three gal pickney. It also dun bruk when muh own man pickney walk way frum meh. Dem be jis't like yuh. Dem be full wid hate fer him too; dat same him dat be dem faddah. I had to live widout dem wen dem git solt way frum meh and I hab to learn to live widout dem wen Fields find dem after freedom and dem nots wants to be near him; jis't like yuh. So, Benjamin, yuh go look fer yuh freedom. I gine beg de Lawd to tek yuh to freedom, but yuh nots gine wid muh pearls; muh name sake.'

Momma Pearl den turn she back and starts to walk 'way frum him. When she git to be a lil' way frum him, she turn and she suh, 'I gine walk 'way frum yuh 'cause I not wants to see another man pickney walk 'way frum meh.'

Den Momma Pearl turn and walk 'way. Her not look back to see if him be stand thar or if him walk way.

Miss Thea, dat be de furst time Momma Pearl suh no to Benjamin and him not know'd wat to do as him be planning on dem pearls to tek wid him to freedom. Him not stop to tink dat thar nots be one nigger wid de money to tek dem pearls frum him, and if a white mans be see him wid dem, dat dem gine kilt him 'cause dem gine tink dat him tek dem frum a white womans. Him nev'r stop to tink 'bout none of dat but I tink dat Momma Pearl be tink all dem tings and she not want to be de one to give him de tings dat gine mek him dead. It be meh dat beg him nots to walk 'way frum Momma Pearl, but him had a mek up mind.

Him be mighty vex in him spirit 'cause Momma Pearl not gib him she pearls and none of we dat try be able to get him to stay. I stay 'way

Benjamin be fer a few minutes and den 'cause I know'ds dat Dada be wanting to see Muddah, I be start to go after Momma Pearl and jis't 'fore I can step outside, Benjamin suh, 'Go! All yuh go! I nots want to be way yuh be. Yuh tell Muddah fer meh dat it be she dat mek meh leave off dis place. Tell she dat wat ev'r happen to meh, good or bad, be she fault 'cause she want dem beads and dat white mans more dan she wants to see meh happy. Yuh tell she dat fer meh.' Den Benjamin, him come to way I be and him suh, 'Move! Move out muh way, Beccah!'

I nots move fast 'nuff fer him and him push meh out him way. I nots fall but I tinks dat if I be fall I be walk back to Dada's house and tek one of him guns and I be come back and shoot Benjamin fer all him ugly and hateful ways and wat him suh to meh and Momma Pearl 'bout Dada. But I not fall. I fix muhself and watch him mek him way 'cross de yard. I look 'head of him and I see Momma Pearl and she be way Dada's house be but she not go in. She turn and she go over to way dem old cabins be and she go in one of dem. Over time, I know'ds dat wen Momma Pearl be go in de old slave cabin, dat it be sumting so hurtful dat she not want nobody to see she weep.

I not follow she. I go quickly to Dada's house and I tek one of him guns down and den I go to way Etta Pearl be in Momma Pearl's cookhouse; she be jis't like Momma Pearl wen it come to flour. I go'd to way she be 'cause I know'ds dat wen Benjamin be like dis, him like to tek him ugliness out on she. I know'ds dat wid de way him be full wid anger, dat if him hit Etta Pearl today, dat it not gine be a easy hit. I dun fix in muh heart dat if Benjamin put him big hands on Etta Pearl today, dat I gine shoot him. I be a good shot so thar be no chance of missing him. I wait and wen him not come, I give Etta Pearl de gun and I suh, 'I know'ds dat it be hard fer yuh to tink to shoot yuh born wid bruddah, but I be tell yuh now dat yuh must not jis't stand here and let him mek yuh de place he put all him anger. Yuh is to shoot him; way yuh shoot him be up to yuh but yuh must let him know'd dat de day of yuh standing and letting him tek all him anger out on yuh be done. Tell him dat I suh dat today be yuh freedom day. Dat be freedom frum him and him ugliness.'

Etta Pearl, she not answer meh but she not gib meh back de gun nor she not suh dat she nots be able to shoot him. I mek muh way cross de yard to go back to Dada's house. I know'ds dat him be waiting and wanting to see Momma Pearl, but I nots mek it but a few steps wen I sees a wagon come to a stop by de gate. It not be a fancy wagon like white man's wagon but it not be like wagon dat be hitch to mule. It be a right nice wagon dat be most like a coach but not full coach. It be hitched to horses and dem be some fine looking horses, strong and proud.

Chapter 27

Mister and Mistress William Cartright

O'Brien, him be in de yard so him go'd to de gate to see who it be and wat dem want. Thar be a old nigger mans and a old nigger womans. The nigger mans, him be de kind of nigger mans way him skin be so nigger dat in de sun it be shine back white and if de sun not be out, him be like shadow or him jis't not thar. Him also sitting high and proud in de wagon. The way him sitting high and proud mek yuh tinks dat wen him git out de wagon, him gine be real tall. Him be dress right smart. Him hab on a brown hat dat sit high on him head and all round de side way him hair be stick out frum under him hat, it be white like cotton but it not be soft looking like cotton. It be look like yuh nots be able to git nuffin' through it.

Him be wearing a fine suit dat mek him look like white mans. De jacket it be brown wid some red and thar be gold buttons dat be shining in de sun. It had a right fine cut to it and 'hind way him be sitting yuh can see de tail of de coat. Him ev'n hab a vest on. De vest, well dat jis't be red and thar be gold buttons on dat too, and I be know'd dat him hab cravat, dat be tie, Dada be tolt meh dat, de cravat it be a most beautiful brown. I nots be able to get a good look at him britches but frum de way him be sitting, I can see de buttons on de front of it. Him look important but him be nigger and him not hold him head down or nuffin' like dat wen him look at O'Brien. I be look at him and I tinks dat I nev'r seen nigger in such fine clothes.

De nigger womans, she be old like him but she be a fine looking womans too. Her nots look like him. Her sitting proud too but she not sit up near as high as he be so it suh dat wen she git down frum de wagon, dat she not be tall like him; tall, but not like him. Her look like her be near a white womans, but yuh know'ds dat her not be white womans. Her be yellow. Her, ev'n though she be old, cut one fine features of a womans nigger or white. Her have high cheekbones and a nose dat suh it be proud, but her face not suh proud. It suh dat it be a kind face. Her hair, funny now I come to tink on it, it be gray jis't like him own but it be plenty, long and it be like mine, soft.

Her wearing a fine dress. The dress it, frum way I be, look soft and it be brown like him suit but it not be de same brown. De sleeves, dem be long and big and go all de way to she wrists. It stop thar and thar be plenty buttons as well. Dem be de same color and cloth as she dress. De collar of de dress be hab a fine looking lace. Thar be buttons on she dress too, but them nots be shining; dem be de same color and cloth as she dress. She be a fine figure of a womans so de dress it be neat to she waist, she be mighty tiny thar. She also be wearing a bonnet but it not cover all she hair dat be how I come to see dat it be long.

I stops and I walk to way O'Brien be by de wagon. Him suh, 'What brings you here?' The mans him not suh Massa. Him suh, 'Sir, my wife and I have travelled a long time and a great distance. We are looking for our daughter. Along the way, we were told that there is a nigger woman here that might be our daughter.'

'O'Brien, him jis't stand there looking and looking at dem. I looks and de more I looks at de nigger man, I be tinks dat him be look like Momma Pearl and Benjamin, but I nots suh dat. I suh, 'Wat her name be? Yuh be looking fer Anakey?'

"No. Her name isn't Anakey. I'm her father, William Cartright, and this is her mother, Jennie Mae Cartright.'

'De womans who not suh nuffin' 'till now suh in a voice dat be shaking, 'Milkweed. Milkweed be she name. Is she here? I'm her Momma Cornbread and this is her Poppa Molasses.'

'Wen de womans who be day to him night suh, "Milkweed", O'Brien him turn red-red and him step back frum dem like him be burn. Watev'r it be dat push O'Brien back push meh pass him and I suh in a voice dat be shaky, 'She be here! She be here! I be she pickney!'

'De old womans start to look like she be jump frum de wagon. Her eyes dem full wid tears and she suh in a voice dat be shaking, 'Where? Where is she?'

O'Brien, him turn frum dem and him start running to Dada's house and him shouting 'Fields! Fields!'

Miss Thea, I nots stands to hear nuffin' more. O'Brien him be shouting, 'Fields! Fields!' I start to holler too but I nots run. I hollering frum right way I be. I looks at dem and dey be looking at meh and I nots be able to tink so I starts to run to way I know'ds Momma Pearl be in de cabin and I suh, 'Momma Pearl! Momma Pearl! Yuh must come now! Dey be here! Come, Momma Pearl! Come.'

I nots wait fer Momma Pearl to ask who be here. I runs back to de yard and all de time I shouting, 'Come, Momma Pearl! Come!'

'Meh and O'Brien be shouting so hard dat not only Momma Pearl come but Anakey, she pickney, and Benjamin. Ev'ry body be running to way we be. Wen Momma Pearl get to way I be, I be point and I suh, 'Yuh momma and yuh poppa. Dem come to find yuh.'

'Momma, she not move frum way she be but she start to holler and holler. Den she put she hands to she belly and den she bend all de way over to way she be bend in half. She hollering, it hitting de ground and coming back up. It not sound de same 'cause wen it hit de ground it be spread all over de ground and it be bigger. Momma Pearl den drop to she knees. I be git mighty 'fraid dat Momma jis't gine holler she self to way she dead, so I go to way she be and I suh, 'Momma, Momma, Momma Pearl!' But her not stop. She den start to shake and she shout, 'Lawd! Lawd!'

'Dem be standing thar crying jis't looking at dem one 'another and I not see Dada 'till him be standing on him porch and den him be walking as fast as him be able to get to way we be. De womans, she looks at Dada and she eyes dem open wide wide and she be look like she see spook and she be look like she wants to run. It be clear dat Dada in a hurry to git to way Momma be, but jis't as him get to way O' Brien be, O'Brien him reach out a hand at Dada. Dat move stop Dada and him suh, 'O'Brien, what has you calling my name like this?'

I see him look and him see dat Momma Pearl be crying and dat thar be niggers him nev'r seen 'fore now so him suh, 'And what the hell is all this ruckus about and who are those niggers in the wagon near Pearl?'

O'Brien, him look at way Momma Pearl be and wid him eyes open wide, him point and him suh, 'Those people are her parents. Milkweed's momma and poppa."

Momma Pearl still be hollering and she momma mek she way down frum de wagon and to way Momma Pearl be hollering and she go'd to Momma Pearl and she tek she arms and wrap dem 'round Momma Pearl and pull she to she belly. Soon as Momma Pearl's momma touch she, she start to holler 'gin but dis time de holler it git bury in de folds of she momma's dress. Momma Pearl tek she hands and she wrap dem 'round she momma and she tek she head and she press it to she momma's dress. She momma tek one of she hands and she bring it to Momma Pearl's face and, looking down at Momma Pearl, she touch she face. Dis mek Momma Pearl bring she head frum de folds of she momma's dress and she turn she face up to she momma. She momma tek she other hand and she bring it to de other side of Momma Pearl's face and she look full in Momma Pearl's face. She be crying and Momma Pearl, she holler 'gin but dis time it not be de same kind of hollering. Dis time, Momma Pearl weeping. She weeping and she suhing, 'Momma! Momma! It be really yuh, Momma?'

She Momma, she crying too and den she poppa him mek him way to way she be and Momma Pearl jis't look at him and she holler, 'Poppa! Poppa!'

'It not jis't like Momma Pearl suhing "Poppa", it be like she nev'r gine dun suh "Poppa". It be like she not sure him be she poppa. She poppa, him reach way dem be. Him tek she hand and yuh be able to see dat him holding it tight. Him help Momma Pearl to git to she foots. Wen she be standing, him wrap she tight, tight in him arms. It be like Momma be lil' pickney all ov'r 'gain. She hab she arms wrap tight tight 'round she momma and poppa and she momma trying to hush she holler. She momma suh, 'Hush, hush it be over now. We've found you. We're not goin' ev'r let you go again. Hush, hush, stop your crying. We've come to take you from this place. Hush.'

'Wen Momma Pearl's momma suh dat she come to tek she frum dis place, Momma Pearl, she just holler like she be trying to mek a crack in de sky. Momma suh, 'No! No! Lawd, No!' Den she be like she wants to go bak on de ground but 'fore Momma Pearl mek it to de ground, she tek she hand and it be like she wants to stop she holler but she hands dem not strong 'nuff. De holler it come out and she momma tek she hand 'way frum she mout and she suh, 'No! No! Don't holler like that. No! No!'

It be like she momma be full of fear. It be like she tink dat sumting bad gine happen to Momma Pearl.

Dada him look at way Momma Pearl be wid she momma and poppa and him look like him see spook and him suh, 'Oh good Lord. Nooooooo!'

Wen him suh, no, it be like him wail and him want to run frum way Momma Pearl be wid she momma and poppa. Dada him go'd to step back to de house and it be like Momma feel him 'cause it be at dat same time she look and she see Dada. She too look like she see spook.

I nots know'ds why dem look de way dem do so I go to way Dada be. Him mek to step 'way frum meh and to go bak to him house and 'fore I be able to suh a ting, Momma Pearl she look at meh and she shake she head frum side to side and she raise she hand real slow to she mouth and she cover she mouth wid she fingers, and de thumb it be go by she nose. She be shaking she head frum side to side and I look at how sad Momma Pearl's face be awash in tears. De tears in she eyes dem big and dem look like sumbody be in de back of she eyes pouring water frum a bucket. I mek to suh, "Dada" and Momma Pearl she tek she hand frum she mouth and I not hear she but I know'ds dat she suhing, 'No, no, no.'

'I look at Momma Pearl and ev'n though she face awash wid de tears, she mek she mout suh no one more time and she eyes dem be fearful. I step 'way frum Dada. Dada him look at Momma Pearl and she still shaking she head slow frum side to side and thar be no place else on she face fer tears to go and wid she eyes lock in Dada's eyes, it be like she begging him to go'd frum way she be.

'Dada him turn him face frum Momma Pearl and den him look at meh and him eyes dem look like him fixing to cry. Him shake him head frum side to side jis't like Momma Pearl do and den him walk past O'Brien and it be only when him be a full way off frum way Momma Pearl be wid she momma and poppa dat him turn and look. Him stay jis't like dat; one foot on de first step of him house and one foot on de ground. I not hab to hear it but frum de way him shoulder dem be go'd up and den come down slow, I know'd dat him tek a deep breff. Him shake him head frum side to side and den him go'd in him house. Him not ev'n shut de door. I watch him walk down de hall 'till I nots be able to see him no more.

We stay way we be fer a short while and it be O'Brien who suh, 'Milkweed, why don't you take your people to your house. The other children will be happy to see them, I'm sure. I'll have someone see about the horse.'

Anakey and O'Brien, dem step out de way so dat Momma Pearl and she momma can pass.

Auntie Thea.

As if feeling we needed a break, Auntie Thea said, "By this time, Drea, Noreen, tears are running freely down my face. My nose is snotting. There's a tremble and a slight cramping in my belly as I picture this reunion. I can see it all now taking place. Two finely dressed old niggers come to see 'bout their daughter and all of this playing out at the gate of a massive plantation house. The owner, former slave master of the house, for lack of a better word, 'The Lord of the Manor', his overseer, the overseer's wench, their mulato daughter, and the mulato daughter of this former slave owner all standing around watching all this raw emotion unfold and the great house is the back drop. I could feel the crushing weight of emotions that must have been pressing on Milkweed's heart.

"As I cried, Beccah reached out her hand and patted my leg. She then said, 'Yuh wants fer meh to stop wid de telling?'

"I looked at her, took a deep breath, and, putting my hand on hers, said, 'No. I came prepared to listen though not absolutely sure what I was going to hear. Please, please, Beccah, continue.' She patted my leg one last time and then she put her hands back in her lap, smoothed her skirt for a few seconds, and that's when I noticed the exquisitely beautiful ring on her finger. She saw where I was looking and smiling, she said, 'Aft'r I be dun telling 'bout Momma Pearl's part, I be tolt yuh 'bout how I come to hab it but I hab to get dun wid Momma Pearl part furst.'

"I said, 'I would appreciate it but please, continue.'

Rebeccah

Momma Pearl, still crying as she walk slow slow wid she momma, and Benjamin him walk wid Momma's Poppa. I walk slow 'hind dem 'till we mek it to Momma Pearl's house. We mek it to Momma Pearl's house and it be like she momma and poppa nots be able to mek one more step. We be jis't stand in de yard and we wait. It be like we wait fer ev'r. Den Benjamin, suh, 'Ought we not to go'd in inside so yuh momma and poppa can rest dem foots fer a spell?'

Momma Pearl fix to mek a step and she poppa, him stop and him looks 'round and 'round and den, looking at Momma Pearl, him suh, "'This house; it's yours? How is it that you have such a fine house?'

'Fore Momma Pearl can fix wat to suh to she poppa, Poole, Eve, Lavina, and Charlotte be on de porch. Momma Pearl, look de same way dat she be look in de yard. She bend she head low and she start to cry. Her not holler, jis't crying soft. Momma Pearl momma stop frum walking and, turning to Momma Pearl, she suh, 'Dem be yuh pickney too?'

Momma Pearl, she mek she head go ev'n lower to she chest and and she suh, 'Yes. Momma Cornbread, dem be muh pickney too.'

Momma Pearl's momma try to mek she foots go faster but she be old so dem not go no faster dan dem be goin' 'fore so she suh to Poole, Eve, Lavina, and Charlotte, 'Come.'

Dem come like dem be one. Wen dem git to way Momma Pearl be wid she momma and Benjamin wid she poppa, Momma Pearl's momma suh, 'I am your Momma Cornbread.' And pointing to Momma Pearl's poppa, she suh, 'He is your Poppa Molasses; your grandmother and grandfather. We are your Momma Milkweed's mother and father. We've come, and from a very far place, to see about her.'

'Momma Pearl's momma look like she gine cry and opening she arms, she suh to Poole, Eve, Lavina, and Charlotte, 'Come. Come. Let me touch you.'

Turning to Momma Pearl's poppa, she suh, 'Grandchildren. We have more grandchildren. Come closer."

Benjamin, him walk closer to way Momma Pearl's momma be. It be sumting to see. Dem old peoples wanting to touch Momma Pearl's pickney.'

Dem be hugging and crying and den Momma Pearl, finding she voice, suh, 'Come, Momma and Poppa. Come inside.'

'Den it be like she poppa stop and him, looking frum Poole, to Eve, to Lavina, to Charlotte, and den to de house, him shaking him head him, suh, 'This house? Who built it for you?'

'I not tink or give Momma Pearl time to talk, I suh, 'Dada, him build it fer Momma Pearl.'

Momma Pearl's Poppa, him look at meh and him suh, 'Dada? Who, dear child, is your Dada?'

Momma Pearl's momma suh, 'Lasses, let's go in and there we can talk. It's been a long journey. Let's go in and give Milkweed time to tell us what has happened.'

Momma Pearl's poppa's voice, it get stern and him suh, 'I don't want to go in. I cannot. This is not what I travelled all the way from Canada expecting to see. This is not, is not right.'

Den Momma Pearl's poppa, him start to cry. Him not holler but de tears dem come frum him eyes and, looking at Momma Pearl, him suh, 'Daughter, I believed, and for years, until the Underground Railroad reunited your Momma Cornbread and me, that you had been killed.

Then your momma, after she joined me in Canada, says that you survived and have a daughter: Haroldetta, I believe is her name. My heart swelled to bursting and I made it my life-long desire to one day set eyes on you and her before the Lord called me home to rest, but this is not what I envisioned. You, my daughter, my only child, a wench to her former slave master. I cannot, will not set foot in that house.'

Momma Pearl, she start to holler, 'Poppa! Oh, Poppa! I be sorry. I be sorry, Poppa.'

Momma Pearl's momma, she suh, "Lasses, we cannot just stand here. We must sit. If you will not go into the house, then will you, for the sake of my tired legs, sit on the porch? Will you do that for me as I am weary from our travels?'

De two of dem jis't stand thar looking at dem one 'nother and den like him not know'd how to suh no to she, him suh, 'That I will do and only because you've asked, but I will not set foot in that den of iniquity.'

Benjamin, him help Momma Pearl's poppa mek it to de porch. Momma Pearl, she still be crying, but she not let go of she momma. All of we: Eve, Poole, Lavina, Charlotte, and Etta Pearl go'd to the porch. Her poppa, him sit and bending like sumbody be pressing on him back, him put him head in him hands. Him crying now dat yuh can hear him. It be one sad ting to see and hear. Momma Pearl crying. She poppa crying and she momma wid tears jis't dropping frum she eyes.

I nots see wen Benjamin go'd way, but him walk way and soon dem all be gone frum de porch. It be like dem not know'd wat to do fer Momma Pearl, she momma and poppa. I not go'd. I not feel it be right dat dem be so sad on de day dat dem shud be happy. Soon, Momma Pearl's poppa, him stop cry and him suh, 'This pain in muh heart, it's cutting me so deeply. Night after night, I see you hog tied…'

Him not get to suh wat him gine suh 'cause Momma she look at meh and she face, it still wet frum way she crying, and she suh, 'She not know'd 'bout dat, Poppa.'

Him stop and him look at meh. Him not suh nuffin' more. Sumting in meh suh, 'Yuh must walk 'way frum here. Dem hab to talk and dem not want to worry 'bout yuh.' I be look at dem and jis't like dat, I walk way. I tinks in muh heart dat I be go'd way Dada be. I go to way Dada be in him house.

Book Four

Milkweed "Pearl" Fields

A Time to Weep

Chapter 28

Crumbs Frum de Master's Table

Milkweed

I waits and den wen Beccah be gone, I go'ds to Poppa Molasses and I falls to him foots way him be sitting and I jis't holler. I holler and holler and it mek muh mind tink on wen muh last man pickney Willie walk 'way frum meh. I suh, "Poppa Molasses, I be mighty glad dat de Lawd mek it so dat yuh find way I be. I be tink dat I nev'r gine see yuh or Momma Cornbread ev'r again. I be spend nights and I look in de sky and I beg de Lawd to keep yuh safe way yuh be, but I dun fix it in muh heart dat yuh dun lost to meh ferev'r."

Poppa, him put him hand on muh head and wen I feel de weight of him hand on meh, I holler more. I tink how long it be since I feel him hand. I tinks dat him hand it be heavy but I nots mind dat it be heavy. Momma Cornbread, she come to way I be and she put she hand on muh shoulder and wen she touch meh, muh heart it suh, "Yuh not muddahless and faddahless pickney no more." I holler, "Momma Cornbread! Momma Cornbread!" And den muh shoulder way Momma Cornbread hand be get heavier and I know'd dat Poppa Molasses dun put him next hand on Momma Cornbread's hand. Muh head it suh, "Dem come to see 'bout meh. Dis be wat yuh wait fer since last time yuh seen yuh Poppa. Yuh wait ov'r.'

Wen muh head suh dat, I see Fields come right 'fore muh eyes and I not know'ds wat to do but I nots hab time to tinks on dat. Poppa Molasses, him suh, "You don't know how many nights I've cried for you. Since that day that he dragged you away, I've prayed that..." and him press him hand harder to muh shoulder, "...this day would come. Each time I got to a safe house, I searched the faces hoping that your face would be among those that had managed to escape. That made me all the more determined. I took the risk. I came back here to America, into the deep south, to where I'd last seen you, to every place that I heard slaves from Litchfield plantation had been sold."

Poppa, him crying loud now and him suh, "When de Lord made it so that I got your momma to Canada and she said that you were alive and had a nigger gal pickney, I thanked the Lord that you were not alone; that you had your own jump-the-broom with man and child. Then your momma said you were sold away and she didn't know where to. I cried. Milkweed, I cried till I became disoriented. In my heart, you had been dragged away from us again. I decided in my heart to find you if it cost me my life. If that was the case then, upon seeing you, it would have been worth it.

"Then freedom came. I, along with every abolitionist here in America and Canada, rejoiced. We knew then that you, with your Mandinka-Seminole blood would find a way to find us. Again, your momma and I searched the sea of faces making it to Amherstburg. This town was, you could say, our Heaven on Earth. We were welcomed there. Freedom awaited you at this, the last stop on the Underground Railroad. We found a place, not only where we escaped the cruel masters of slavery, but for those of us who needed a place to give our thanks that we'd arrived at our destination, there was the Nazrey African Methodist Episcopal Church."

I not tinks Momma be suh nuffin' but den she suh, "You never came. You never came. Was never among them. We asked and asked and no one knew what had become of yuh. It was yuh poppa who said that we must come for you. So we started our backward journey. From Canada to Albany to Philadelphia, to Delaware, to Baltimore, to Washington, DC, and all the other states in between. It was Philadelphia that we stayed for a while. Your poppa had made friends with a man that was very important when he was a conductor on the Underground Railroad. This man, William Still, had helped your poppa get me to Canada so we stopped there for a spell. It was not just for staying's sake; there we planned and did a lot of thinking."

I want to suh sumting to Momma Cornbread, but I not know'ds wat to suh so I jis't cry. Momma Cornbread suh, "Yuh Poppa Molasses have a different name now. It was William Still that helped your poppa with his new name. It was, he said, important to unshackle ourselves from slavery. He said, 'A man is not a man with just one name.' So him and yuh poppa dem spend days and nights thinking on a name that be jis't suit your poppa and it be yuh poppa who pick his own name."

I tek muh head frum Poppa's knee and I look at Poppa and ev'n though him be crying too, him smile jis't a lil' and him suh, "Cartright."

I suh, "Cartright?"

"Yes. Cartright because a cart takes things from one place to the next; I took people from slavery to freedom. I am a cart. Then, since in my heart I feel that was a right thing I do, I say to William Still, 'Since I be known as Lil' Willie 'fore I be Molasses, then I want to be known as William; just like you. So I'm going to be William Cartright. So your momma and I are William and Jennie Mae Cartright. That makes you, my daughter, Milkweed Cartright. You do not have to go by your former master's name anymore. You can call yourself what you want. Stand proud and call yourself Milkweed Cartright."

I feel de pride dat Poppa Molasses suh dat wid, but it not fill meh wid pride, it fill me wid fear. It be de next words dat Poppa Molasses suh dat tolt meh dat muh fear be right. Poppa, him stop. Him eyes dem git a look in dem den him suh, "Why, daughter, are you still here; still a slave?"

I nots sure wat to suh but I suh, "I not be slave, Poppa. President Abraham Lincoln suh dat nigger not be slave no more."

"Then why are you here looking, acting, and still speaking like one?"

I not know'ds fer sure wat to suh to Poppa so I suh, "Dis be de way dat ev'rybody be talk. Dat not mek meh slave. Thar be no more slave."

"But you are here and you still have a slave mentality. If you are not a slave, then come. Come away from this God-forsaken place with your Momma Cornbread and me. Come with us to Canada. Come and bring your children with you. Come and taste true freedom."

Wen Poppa suh dat, it brung all dat Neala and muh Sara suh to meh de day dem walk way to freedom and I know'ds in muh heart dat I nots gine. I gine stay here wid him but now it be different. Dis be muh Poppa Molasses and Momma Cornbread.

I tinks wat to suh to muh Poppa and all I get out be, "I be free…"

I nots get to suh wat I be fixing to suh. Poppa him tek him hand and him put it by muh chin and him raise muh head slow 'till muh head be raise full frum muh chest and him suh, "Open your eyes, daughter. Look at me and with your eyes open, tell me again that you are free."

I open muh eyes and I look at Poppa and I see in him eyes dat him know'd dat I nots know'd wat freedom be. Him suh, "Come and I'll show you. Come. Look at Momma Cornbread; she knows freedom: true freedom. Come with us."

I feel tug at muh heart and I be fixing to suh wat on muh heart wen him suh, "I've spent years, before and after freedom, fighting to right wrongs that white men and women have done to nigger; slave and free alike. I did all of that with one purpose always in my heart. To find you and now I've made my way here, to this God-forsaken place, a place that I said I would never come to again and what do I find. I find a daughter who is bound to a place and from the looks of your children, to a white man. A daughter who has never tasted one drop of freedom. This, Milkweed, is not what freedom is. Come and taste, just like Jesus says in the Bible. Yes, daughter, I can read. William Still, the abolitionist I told you about, taught me my letters, reading and writing. He helped me to ease my way out of the manner of speaking that said I was unlearned. Freedom lets you do those things. It says in the book of Mark in the ninth chapter, 'Come and taste that the Lord is good; blessed is the man who hopeth in him.'

"Freedom is like that. It has a taste. It's sweet. It has hope and endless possibilities. You ought to see what freedom is like."

"But, Poppa, I be free. All niggers free."

Poppa look at meh and I can see him feel sorry fer meh, him suh, "Daughter, it is true that all niggers be free but true freedom, as Sojourner Truth, my dear and close friend William Still, Harriet Tubman, Frederick Douglas, and many of my other friends who have been risking their lives for others have said, 'It's in your heart.'

"You are not free; your heart is bound to this place and a white man. When you are not bound to him, then and only then, daughter, will you be free."

Poppa him git up frum way him be sitting and him walk way frum meh. Him be off de porch. I git up and run to him. I throw'd muhself at him foots but him not stop. Him mek more steps and I fear him gine walk way frum muh so I suh, "Poppa Molasses, I begs yuh nots to walk 'way frum meh. I dun suffer and I dun lost all muh man pickney 'cause dem walk way frum meh. I begs yuh, Poppa, nots to walk way frum meh."

Poppa him stop and him turn. Him face wet. Him crying. Him suh, "Man pickney? You have other children?"

I sits way I be in de dirt and dust and I suh softly, "Yes, Poppa."

Poppa mek him way slow to way I be. I can tell dat bending like him be bending paining him, but him bend and den him sit in de dirt wid meh and him suh, "How many, daughter, how many children has he bred off you?"

I suh, "I not know'ds the number, Poppa?"

"But you can count; your Momma taught you how."

"I know'ds, Poppa. I nots member no more, but Fields, him suh dat I mek…"

Poppa's face it get fix and I can see dat him tinking and I fear dat him tinking him want to kill Fields. Him suh in a voice dat be fixing to turn knife and kill Fields, "I don't want to know what he has said. Tell me the names of the children and I'll tell you how many you've had."

I bends muh head. I feel shame and I cry. Though I be crying, I suh, "Isham, Zack, Juba, Tuck, Willie, Lilly, Rose, Eve, Lavina, Poole, Rebeccah and Charlotte."

Poppa's face it be twitch and him teet them fix in him mout like dem not want to open fer him to talk, but him talk and it mek meh tink on Neala. Him suh, "Twelve! You've birthed twelve children for a white man and not any white man, but one who murdered children, tied you to a horse, and dragged you away when you were just a pickney. He tied you to the back of his horse! How, my daughter, did you get your strong fighting Mandinka and brave Seminole blood to forget that; how?"

Chapter 29

Nots Hab Heart to Feel Fear or Love

I not know'd how to suh wat Poppa wants meh to suh so I holler. I holler like when muh Sara dead. I want to dead, but I want to live 'cause de Lawd let muh momma and poppa come see 'bout meh, but now Poppa Molasses be so fix in him anger dat I fear dat him gine mek him way to Fields' house and him gine kilt him.

I jis't suh, "Poppa! Poppa! Poppa!" I can feel ev'ry time I suh, "Poppa," dat piece of muh heart it tear and I fear dat I gine holler way muh whole heart and I nots hab heart to feel fear or love. I want to feel and I want to love. I want heart to love Fields. Wen I tink dat, I holler, "Oh Lawd, oh Lawd, help meh, Lawd, help meh!"

I not hear wen Momma Cornbread be move frum de porch but she move and now she way we be. She dun come down in de dirt and she tek meh in she arms and she suh, "Lasses, this is a lot. What yuh saying is a lot fer her. She got a mix-up head. That is clear. Help me to get her from here. We can't undo none of what has happened to her. Come, Lasses, help me."

I gets to muh foots and I not know'd way to go. I wants to go in muh house but I know'ds dat Poppa not gine come and I nots wants him to leave meh. I walk way frum muh house. Momma Cornbread and Poppa Molasses dem walk wid meh. We walk slow and I go'ds to muh cabin. Poppa Molasses him come in. I cry and wen it feel like I can cry no more, Momma Cornbread suh, "Dis place. Dis place. It be clean. Yuh live here too?"

"I nots live here but it be way I come to sort tings out. It be de furst place I be on dis place."

I listen to wat Momma Cornbread suh and I see dat Momma

Cornbread be talk like meh sometimes and sometimes she be talk like meh and Poppa mix up. I sits and Momma she sit. Poppa, him stand by de door and it be like him want to step out. I know'ds if him step out, him gine to Fields' house. I suh, "Poppa, I nots want yuh to go to him house. O'Brien nots gine let yuh git to way him be. Please, Poppa I begs yuh. Come back. I nots want dem to shoot yuh."

"If it will bring you freedom, then I will gladly step in front of their guns. But I tell you this, daughter, if and when they shoot, they ought not to miss. They should shoot to kill me 'because if they do not and I'm able to stand, I will get my gun and shoot, not only them but any white man that thinks he can stop this old soldier. I have climbed in 'most every hell hole called a plantation in this country and I have fought, though not in a war the way they see war, but I have fought a raging war against their tyranny and inhumane treatment of us. I will die and today if I have to in order to set you free from this white beast calling himself a man. So do not, my daughter, plead for my life. If you want to plead for a life, and I pray to God that you are not so mixed-up in your head as to look at me, your father—a Mandinka African, and plead for the life of a white dog. Plead for your own life, a life not yet lived despite your age. So, if you think you will plead for his life, daughter, I implore you; do not open your mouth."

I look at Momma Cornbread and I 'pect to see fear in she eyes, but it not be thar. In Momma's eyes be sumting I not know'd wat it be. Den she look at Poppa and she smile a little and she suh, "That is why I am proud of him. Even now where age be climbing all ov'r him, him not ready to sit still. It be like him want to right all dat be wrong and thar be plenty, dat white mans be do niggers. I right proud of him and I tell you, daughter, that they will have to kill me too. I know freedom and I will tek death 'fore I give it up.

"Now you have a choice to make. I know'ds yuh poppa and I know him well; better I tell you than anyone else alive. William, your poppa's friend, Mr. Still, the one he worked with on the Underground Railroad, thinks he knows your poppa and sometimes we will joke about it, but…" and smiling, Momma Cornbread suh, "…believe me, there is no one that knows him like I do. He will not spend but one night on this place."

Momma Cornbread stop 'gain and she look 'round. She suh, "This, being in a slave cabin, is a humiliation that neither your poppa or I ever thought we would experience again but for you, we will subject ourselves, this one night, but not beyond that. Your poppa and I are no fools. We know that we are not long or have much longer on this Earth. The Lord, I think, has blessed us because your poppa has helped many people to escape slavery. But all of that; the days and nights of worry, the wondering if he will ever make it back to me or will they find him along with those he was helping to escape and hang him from a tree.

"He made it back every time, but his heart was never happy. He hadn't set eyes on you and he wanted to do that before he went to meet the Lord. I believe, daughter, it's the only thing that has kept him. Now he has seen you. He is at peace. If, and though I hope not, that the Lord calls him one minute after we are off this place, he will gladly go. I do not want that for your poppa. I want him and me to be back in Canada; that is home for us. So do not, daughter, suffer us to be here longer than we have to.

"So we have to work fast. You must get your children ready to leave with us at first light. Should your poppa stay here beyond that, then you are sending him to his grave. He will, and I tell you, go over to that house and his only purpose will be to kill that white man. I know him. I must also tell you, daughter, that I will do nothing to stop him ev'n though I know that they will kill him and probably all of us after. He has been muh life, been by muh side since I be little pickney. Him be wat I know'd. Him be muh best ev'ryting. Him run frum slavery and den him run back to slavery to get other niggers to freedom.

"When freedom came for slaves, he, me, we watched as each new wave from the sea of niggers made it to the shores of Canada. Why we watched so hard? We were looking for you and your Sara's face to be somewhere there. We hoped that somehow you'd heard that your poppa and I were in Canada. We looked 'cause we were sure that in one of those waves our daughter would come ashore looking for us. The sea of niggers seeking a better life slowed to a stream, but still we looked. We looked when it was just a drip and a drop. Then it stopped…almost dried up and you weren't in that last drip.

"Your not coming saddened your poppa but he made himself busy. He worked hard helping slaves to set up housing and deal at the same time with the continued hatred from white men. Yes, daughter, there was the hate from white people to deal with there too. Freedom had come and, yes, we had a chance at a better life in Canada but hate is a hard thing to make go away; just like that.

"One morning, your poppa woke and he suh, 'Got to set eyes on my daughter. Can't go to the Lord and not know what she looks like as a woman. Got to go, Cornbread, and look for my only child.'

"And so I just started getting us ready for this trip. Didn't know how he was going do it, but he did. He asked every Conductor he'd ever worked with on the Underground Railroad. He asked every abolitionist he'd ever met. He asked ever nigger that he saw who said that he or she come up from anywhere in the Carolinas or the Low Country, and then about a week ago somebody said to him, 'Cartright, there's talk of two fine nigger women living on Fields' plantation; one of them fits the description of the woman you said you are looking for.'

"Your poppa didn't rest." Smiling Momma Cornbread continued, "We didn't rest; nobody that know'ds your poppa got rest. They, those men that worked on the Underground Railroad with your poppa, started planning and packing. They looked at the best way and fastest ways to get us here. Finding you was all he wanted to do. It was as if danger didn't exist. We all knew this would be his last trip.

"I watched him turning around as he packed the wagon. I could see that his bones ached as much as mine and the two of us, old as we are, had no right taking this trip but I wasn't going to stop him. That would have been wrong and besides, I wanted to set my eyes on you before I too went on to the Lord. I'm so glad that he has blessed these eyes to see you. All your poppa talked about as we travelled was you. He couldn't wait to bless his eyes upon you."

Momma Cornbread's eyes, dem fill wid tears and she stop frum talking fer a short spell and ev'n though thar be tears in she eyes, she suh, "You, his only child and grandchildren are the last ones, the last ones that he's going to take to freedom."

I bends muh head low and I weeps softly.

Momma Cornbread look at meh and she suh, "Daughter, since I've gotten here and saw that fine house he's built you out there where, if it had been just a little bigger it would be just like his own, and if it not for the fact that you are a nigger, you look like mistress of this plantation. Tell me, not how come he built it for you, but how you got your heart to look over and past what he done to you. And how you were able to take that house as payment for all the wrong things he did, not just to you but to so many; he was a slave owner, your own master. How, Daughter, how did you get to where you let your head forget all that I said and all that you saw? How did you stay after your sons left?"

I wants to run frum Momma Cornbread, but she nots turn meh loose. I be git ready to suh wat be hard fer meh to suh wen she stop meh and she suh, "Where is your Sara and all your man pickney? Yuh dun call all dem pickney names, but yuh not suh nothing 'bout Sara…way your Sara?"

I raise muh head a lil' and I looks at Momma Cornbread and de word dat I hab to suh to she it choke meh, but I gets it out. I suh, "Dead."

Momma Cornbread grab at she heart and she suh, "Dead? Sara and yuh man pickney, dem be dead? How? Wen?"

I suh, "Momma Cornbread it be only Sara dat be dead. She dead birfing pickney. Benjamin, de big pickney dat walk with Poppa; him be she pickney and de pretty pickney, Etta Pearl, she be she pickney. Muh Sara dead same day dem be birf."

"The others…the man pickney? Way dem be?"

"Dem walk way frum here."

"When freedom came?"

I look at Momma Cornbread and I suh, "No. Dem nots be here 'fore freedom. It be after freedom and after Sara be dead dat we nots know'ds way her mans be. Fields, him be suh dat Benjamin be a bad nigger mans fer nots being wid him pickney. It be den dat I tolt Fields dat him nots do better, him solt way him own. Fields, him be left frum round meh. Him be gone a long time. Wen him come bak, him hab all muh man pickney. I be plenty happy to see dem. Dem be plenty happy to see meh, but it not tek long 'fore dem nots want to be way Fields be.

"Dem tolt meh one day dat dem nots want to be way him be and dem be go'd back to Talbert's plantation. I be…"

I nots git to finish wat I be fixing to suh 'fore Momma Cornbread suh, "Talbert's plantation. Did you say Talbert?"

I look at Momma Cornbread and den it be hit meh…Momma Cornbread be at Talbert's Plantation same time as muh pickney. I holler and Momma Cornbread she crying and she suh, "Wat dem look like, Milkweed, wat dem look like. Lawd, Lawd. I be wid muh own grand pickney and I nots know. Lawd, dis slavery be a cruel cruel ting. Wat dem look like, Milkweed, wat?"

I look at Momma Cornbread and I suh, "De furst, Isham, him be most look like him be white mans. Him look jis't like Fields. Him hair it be like mine; long and black and him wear it like him be Indian. I tinks him wear it like dat 'cause him nots want to be like Fields. Willie and Zack, dem too be hab hair like mine and dem be wear it like Isham, like if dem be Indians but them nots be look like white mans. Dem be look like Poppa Molasses. Tuck, him be look like him be yuh pickney, and Juba, him be look like yuh and him hair it nots be like mine. Him hair it be brown and red and curly just like Fields, and him be look de most like if him be white mans."

Momma Cornbread, she suh through she crying, "I be in de cookhouse and I see plenty a pickney during the time I was there and I didn't seen one pickney that come on wagon that look like that. Yuh sure he sold them to Talbert's plantation? I nots ev'r 'till now seen dat white man over in that house until today not since him drag yuh 'way. I be know if I seen him. The hate I feel for him is real. It would have risen up and I would have poisoned him. Yes, Daughter, all of them just to get him; I would have poisoned every last one of them.

"If he'd come to Talbert's plantation, I would have seen him. I was in the big house. Are you sure, Daughter? Mayhaps you mean the other plantation. There was one quite near and the owner, a man who some called Pursival and some Breckenshaw, would visit Talbert's plantation. He seemed kinder, a different sort of white man; not all that different but not quite like all the rest. Mayhaps it be there dat him sold them and it was there that they returned."

Wen Momma Cornbread suh Breckenshaw, I see muh man pickney and den I hear him in muh head suhing, 'Muddah, wen tomorrow come, I gine mek muh way back over to Massa Breckenshaw's plantation.'

I look at Momma Cornbread and I suh, 'Yuh be right. It nots be Talbert's plantation. Dem be go'd to Breckenshaw's plantation. Dat be way dem be."

"Are they still there?"

"I nots know'ds. Dem nots come back and I nots go way dem be. I nots seen dem no more. Muh heart it bruk and I tinks on dem but dem nev'r come bak; nev'r."

Momma Cornbread, she look at meh and I can see dat she heart sad fer meh so I suh, "Momma, thar be so much dat happen to meh 'fore I see yuh and 'fore Sara be born. I nots tolt yuh 'cause I nots want yuh to know'd wat I dun seen. I be fear dat Sara, wen she be born, be white pickney and den I be hab to tolt yuh 'bout wat him dun meh, but she be nigger pickney so I tek it all to muh heart and I nots tolt yuh 'bout all de pickney I hab 'fore I birf Sara."

"But Sara be full nigger pickney; how be it that she be nigger and all yuh other pickney be white or near white?"

"She poppa, him be nigger mans."

"Way him be?"

"Him be dead. Field had dem kilt him de day dat him solt meh frum here."

"Solt yuh? If him solt yuh, den how be it dat yuh back on him place and wid all dese pickney dat be under Sara?"

I bends muh head lower and I starts to cry fresh, but I get muhself to suh, "Him solt way de lil' boy pickney furst and den, wen all dem be solt, him solt meh to Massa Litchfield."

Momma Cornbread suh, "He sold your boy pickney, sold you, and now you are here with even more children? How?"

"De day Massa Litchfield solt all of we frum him plantation, him solt meh to Fields 'cause Fields dun tolt him dat him love meh same way him love white womans."

"And because of that, his craving for your flesh, you are still here?"

I look at Momma Cornbread and I not be able to mek muh voice more dan a whisper so I do de best I can and I suh, "It not be craving fer meh flesh. Him love meh, Momma Cornbread, and I..."

Momma Cornbread be looking at meh sad like and she be fixing to cry. She tek deep breff like she wants to stop de tears frum coming frum she eyes but she nots able so she suh, "Lawd, Lawd, don't say that. Don't tell me that you love him. Don't tell me that you let what a white man be feeling fer you get yuh head all mix up. Why didn't you do what I told you? I told yuh to take freedom over everything, Milkweed, everything. Daughter, why didn't you take freedom when it came? You didn't have to do like me and yuh poppa and run and hide to find freedom. The soldiers brung freedom right to yuh cabin door. Daughter, Daughter, why, Oh Lawd, why didn't you take freedom when it came?"

Momma Cornbread not be able to go on no more, she crying and she start to rock way she be sitting, and I want to do like lil' gal pickney and put muh head in she lap and hab she touch muh head and suh dat it be all pass 'way, but I nots be able to move frum way I be. De way Momma Cornbread crying hab muh heart bruk. It feel jis't like de day

Willie walk 'way frum meh. Dis time, I nots be able to throw'd muhself in de dirt. I hab to suh to Momma Cornbread why I still be on dis place long after freedom come and gone.

I suh, "Momma Cornbread, I know'ds dat it be mighty hard fer yuh to tek wat it be dat I hab to suh, but it be hard fer meh to suh, but as de good Lawd be muh only judge, I not know'ds how I be do it. I be tink over dese years dat pass 'bout wat I dun and I know'd in muh heart dat wat I dun not gine go 'way no time soon. I feel in muh heart dat I dun yoke muh gal pickney and all dem gal pickney to something dat gine be 'round long after I be puts to rest in muh box.

"I wants to suh now dat I be sorry fer wat I dun, but de love in muh heart grow'd fer him widout meh trying. I know'd dat not mek no sense to yuh, but dat be de way dat it happen. I not plan to love him. Truth be, Momma Cornbread, 'fore de love grow'd in muh heart fer him, it be jis't hate of de worse kind. It be de kind way I want him dead every day."

I start to cry.

Momma Cornbread suh, "Wat it be dat mekking yuh cry?"

I suh, "It be wat I know'd I dun. I be dust and mayhaps thar not be a soul dat not gine tink on meh and not suh dat it be meh, dat 'cause I pick a white mans ov'r freedom, dat I bring a curse on all de gal pickney dat gine come after meh; any dat hab him blood. It nots be wat I want muh heart to do and it not be dat I be go'd out muh way to look fer it, but I know'd in muh heart dat down de road, a good spell frum now, muh name be mix wid him name and thar not gine be no forgiveness fer meh nor fer him."

Momma Cornbread suh, "It not have to be dis way. Thar need not be a curse on de gal pickney wid yuh and him blood. Yuh can get yuh pickney and leave this place with your poppa and me come first light and thar be no curse. It be dead 'fore it can born; come, it's not too late to keep dat promise yuh mek to meh."

"I know'ds wat I promise yuh, Momma Cornbread, and I know'd in muh heart dat it not be a easy promise I mek yuh, but dat be 'fore muh heart mek it mind up over him and muh head be get all mix up. I dun tolt yuh, Momma Cornbread, dat I be sorry dat I not fix it in muh heart to go see wat freedom be. I not know'ds way yuh be in Canada, but I know'ds dat de love 'tween a muddah and she pickney nev'r bruk, so I know'ds dat yuh dun feel in yuh heart dat I not go to freedom and dat yuh dun suh dat yuh fergive meh; I know'ds. I feel it. So I mek in muh heart to stay wid him.

"Freedom come fer meh, Momma Cornbread, same time it come fer ev'rybody. It come to de door of dis said cabin,, and I nots be able to tink 'pon it 'cause it be de night 'fore freedom dat I know'd dat I love him. I know'd wen I seen de soldiers and all de niggers walking way dat I not be follow dem. I know'ds de chance at freedom be come right to muh cabin door on dat January morning back in 1863, and I know'ds dat I not do wat I promised yuh, Momma Cornbread.

"I be stand thar wid freedom dancing right 'fore muh eyes, and all dat I be able to tink on be him, muh master and owner of dis plantation, Everett Fields, de faddah to all but one of muh pickney. Momma Cornbread, all muh insides git all tie up to one and all I can tink on be him and wat it be like not to see him no more."

I look at Momma Cornbread and I can see dat she sorry fer meh but I know'ds dat if I nots suh wat on muh heart now, I nev'r gine suh it so I tek a deep breff and I suh, "Momma, him be de furst mans I know'd and wen him do dat to meh de furst time and all dem times aft'r dat, hate grow'd mightily in muh heart fer him but by de time freedom and de soldiers come knocking at muh cabin door, all I be able to tink on be de way dat him mek meh and muh heart feel. It be mighty powerful."

Wen I suh dat, Poppa him step out de cabin. I fear fer him but Momma Cornbread suh, "He's not going there. I know him. He doesn't want to hear you talk about having love fer a white mans. It's not that I want to hear you say that either, but I'm your momma and if yuh must get this thing off yuh chest so yuh can go to freedom without it, then I'll listen. I know love but I only know love fer yuh poppa. I dun seen plenty of white men and I can suh to yuh frum de part of my heart that knows love that I've never seen a white man that is deserving of the love of a nigger woman.

"I wants yuh to know dat you not de only nigger woman to ever think dat she love a white man but I know and so deep in my heart that I would bet muh life on it that as far as I go, there's not a white man that I would take by choice. And fer yuh poppa, I can tell you that there isn't a white woman in all of Canada or America that yuh poppa be bed. Him be dead first. So it be hard on him to hear him only pickney suh dat she find it in she heart to let love grow for a white man to the point where she chose him over freedom.

"De preacher man suh that there be some sins dat the good Lawd not forgive but dem not mention a nigger loving a white man or white woman as one of them; that ought to be de first and biggest one. I nots even wants to know wat that be like. It mek bile rise in muh belly and this bile be de bitterest 'cause yuh muh pickney."

I starts to cry fresh and Momma Cornbread suh, "Daughter, nigger don't have time fer de 'mount of crying you do. Dat be show'd me dat yuh nots know'd wat real hardship be 'cause if yuh know'd hardship or feel dat what yuh been through be hard, then yuh would not be here. Yuh would never have set foot in that house and if your father's blood was really running through your veins, then yuh would have set fire to that house. Your foot should never have known what the inside felt like but yuh step in and mek it yuh home. That being said, yuh nots have time now fer all dis crying. So best as yuh can, tell me what happened to yuh so that I can untie you from dis place."

I look at Momma and I know'ds wat I be tinking dat I nots be able to suh to she. I see in muh head de way dat meh and Fields be rut de night 'fore freedom. It be a different kind of rutting. It not be like none of dem other times. Dat night, it be so strong and powerful dat it be wat join meh to him ferev'r. It be in dat joining, in dat one moment wen I be scream him name so dat it left meh throat raw and sore jis't as him mek meh whole body. I be scream him name so hard dat it mek meh feel dat muh bellybutton be come right out, and I feel all de hate dat I had fer him move and change. I know'd dat by de time him name mek it frum muh belly to de tip of muh tongue, dat I be dun forgive him all dem hurtful tings him dun meh.

"Momma Cornbread, I know'd jis't wen I be do it."

"Do what, Daughter?"

"I know'd wen I git to de place way de hate left meh and de love come in de place way it be. I know'd, Momma, wen I find it in muh heart to forgive him ev'ryting."

"Everything?"

"Ev'ryting, Momma Cornbread. Ev'ry hurt, ev'ry tear him mek meh cry, ev'ry day of all de years dat I be him slave. I fix it in muh heart to forgive him and den, Momma, I tie muhself to him fer life."

Momma Cornbread, she tek deep a breff and she shake she head slow from side to side and she look at meh and I see de pain deep in she eyes and she suh, "Dat kinda tying yuh talking 'bout, a nigger woman ought never to think of tying she self to a white man that way. Dat what yuh talk 'bout be de deepest kind of love. It's never, never fer a white man and not one that done what he's done to you. Yuh heart ought not to have forgotten the murders of your young friends. How did you get it to forget the hangings of Chem and Tiny, the gutting of Tadpole, and the beheading of Li'l Theo? How, Daughter, did you get it to forget him dragging you, hog-tied, behind his horse instead of killing you the way he and his friends had done your friends. How did you get your heart to forgive him for stealing you from Litchfield plantation, me, your poppa and all that was familiar?

"I learned in Canada that what they were doing to slaves in America was worse than how they treat animals in Canada. The Abolitionists said that it hung over the edge of inhumanity. How then did you get to where you accepted this kind of inhumane treatment; being treated worse than an animal? Did you forget that you were a human?"

Momma Cornbread look at meh and she know'ds dat I not know'ds what dem words be dat she be use and she suh, "Inhumane is when they treat you less than an animal or just like an animal. Daughter, he treated you that way. He tide you like a hog. He tied you to a horse and he dragged you away and then, at your young and tender age, he raped you. I know you don't know what rape is so I'll tell you. It is when a man, nigger or white though mostly white men as nigger men not have that same kind of animal ways as white men, put himself in you and rut you and it is not what yuh want. That is rape. He raped you and he raped you when you were jis't my little gal pickney."

Momma Cornbread stop and de tears be running down she face like dem got sumbody after dem. She look at meh and she suh, "Lawd, Lawd, muh poor pickney. Tell me how you get so your heart let all de hate dat should be in it fer him drain out. Milkweed, you've got to tell me in a way that makes me not want to go out in that yard and tell yuh poppa to get the shotgun that he's got hidden in the wagon and kill 'em all. I want yuh to tell me how it be dat yuh done give yuh heart and soul to a white man de way yuh give it to de Lawd or to a nigger man. Him be yuh Lawd?"

I look at Momma Cornbread and I know'ds dat thar be nuffin' I can suh to she dat gine mek she understand how ev'ryting inside of meh be live only fer de time wen him be near meh or I be near him.

Chapter 30

A Second Chance to Taste frum Freedom's Cup

Meh and Momma Cornbread be jis't look at we one 'nother and we not be talk. She jis't look at meh and it be de most sorry I ev'r see in anybody's eyes. It be hard fer meh 'cause dat be muh momma and she nots be able to get sheself to see how I be way I be all mix-up in muh head and ov'r a white man. We be quiet like dat and I mayhaps be de quiet dat draw Poppa Molasses. Him come bak to de cabin and him look frum Momma Cornbread to meh and him suh, "First light and not one crack after, I'm leaving off this hell hole."

Looking at meh him suh, "It is my deepest prayer that you will be with me. Your momma and I, we have a good life in Canada. I've travelled all this way to find you and bring you back to it. I want you and your children to come back with me. Come with us and give me this chance, before the good Lord calls either of us; me, your mother or yourself, to show you what true freedom is."

Right after Poppa suh dat, Beccah she come and she suh, "Pardon, Momma, but Dada him wants to know'd if yuh momma and poppa be come hab supper wid him, O'Brien, Anakey, dem pickney, meh, and yuh."

Poppa him look like him not 'member how to breave and wen him 'member, him suh through him teet, "Sup with him! That white devil! You go and you tell him that neither my wife nor I want to sit with him, another white man, or any nigger woman who has forgotten her people or the hell her people have been through to the point where she accepts crumbs from her master's table, or believe that this hell that we have suffered hasn't happened to the point where she can cook for and then sit to sup with her tormentors. Tell him that the only way I would sit at his table is if I could be sure that the meal he's about to partake of has been poisoned and he has called me to witness him, them, and anyone else who is happy to snatch the crumbs that fall from any white man's table, writhing in the most gut-wrenching pain that a human can suffer before dying.

"Tell him that not only is my wife nor I not coming, but if I see him so much as step one foot out that gateway to hell he calls a house, I'm going to shoot him. Tell him that my daughter might have forgotten the rich and proud blood that flows in her veins and allowed her Mandinka and Seminole fighting blood to cool, but I have not. Had she not forgotten, she would have, at the first opportunity, poisoned him and gladly watched him as he died. Tell him that it was my daughter's not mine or her mother's fighting spirit he has broken, and so before I would sit at a table and sup with him or any other white man of his low, beastly, and depraved character, I would rather have my hands chopped off and my mouth sewn shut. Also, tell him that I am of the strongest opinion that men like him should have been drowned at birth. Finally, tell him that when I leave here at first light, nothing will give me greater satisfaction than to see him and every white man near him or his place hanging from a tree."

Beccah jis't stand way she be, looking at Poppa Molasses and him suh, "Your dada, as you call him, has sent you with a message and I, although you've just met me, am your grandfather, your Momma Pearl…"

Poppa stop and him suh, "Pearl! Pearl? Why in God's good name is this child calling you Pearl? Where did you get that blasted name that has sucked away your Africanness, your heritage?"

I suh in a soft voice, "Fields. It be him dat call meh Pearl."

"Now you see why I should go get my shotgun and shoot him. He stole you, treated you as if you were a dog, a heifer, or some animal to just breed and then when he was done breeding you, he took away your name; the name that I, your poppa gave you. That, my dear daughter, if for no other reason, is why you must gather your children and come away from this place. Come with your mother and me. Come and get your sense of pride back. Freedom gives you that! It also teaches you what is good, fair, and humane treatment for a person, nigger or white.

Freedom gives you dignity."

Poppa Molasses be shouting now and it be like de anger tek way him old age. Him get to standing taller and him suh, "Pearl! Pearl! In addition to all the other things I've told you, go and tell him that when I leave here in the morning, I'm taking my child, my daughter, Milkweed, with me. She may not be a gal pickney anymore, but she's always going to be my child. She will not be called Pearl ever again. In Canada, she'll be Milkweed Cartright. Listen to the sound of that: Milkweed Cartright. Cartright; a proper name for my child. Pearl will be left right here."

I look frum Poppa Molasses to Beccah and I suh, "Please, Poppa, I beg yuh nots to let Beccah go back to him wid dat message. Please, Poppa, I nots want to see him come and shoot yuh."

Poppa stands so dat it be clear to meh dat him fergit dat him be a old man. All de age fall frum him face and him suh, "You need not fear that. I did not get to this age, fought the fights I have, and helped free the people I did by being afraid of one or two white men."

Reaching into his jacket pocket, Poppa Molasses tek out a pistol and looking at meh he suh, "If he so much as steps in this yard after your daughter delivers my message, I will believe he is coming to shoot me and I will, without a moment's hesitation, shoot him. I am a perfect shot with this thing so I will not miss. I will be shooting him with every intention of killing him and if it were possible, I would shoot him for every nigger that was stolen from our homeland and brought here and held against our will; bound for all these past hundreds of years. Fear! I do not know what it is. Let her deliver my message. Then the sooner I can get to shoot him!"

I look at Poppa Molasses wid de gun in him hand and I know'ds dat him mean wat him suh. I look at Beccah and I can see dat she got fear in she heart. She love she Dada and she not know'd muh poppa so I suh, "Beccah, yuh not hab to hab fear in yuh heart for muh poppa. Yuh go and suh to Fields dat Poppa Molasses and Momma Cornbread gine sup wid meh and dat dem gine be off in de morning at furst light. Go. Tell him dat and den yuh go and see 'bout dem at muh house. After yuh hab supper, yuh tell dem to come and get 'quainted wid muh momma and muh poppa. Go, Beccah. Go furst to him house and suh to him wat I tolt yuh. Go."

Beccah, she turn way and she walk slow frum de cabin to him house. Poppa, him breaving hard like him trying to get air back in him body to mek him rise up spirit go back down. Him sit facing de door wid him hand holding de piston in him lap. I feel fear rise up in muh heart. I look at Poppa and I nots know'd wat to suh or do. It be Momma Cornbread who suh, "Your poppa and I don't need much to eat. We have, not knowing if this day was going to be the day that would bring us to you, travelled with our own food. We have roasted sweet potato, yams, and dried fish. I know your poppa. He will eat nothing from this place. So as soon as your Beccah comes back and, I pray for their sake, without that white man, I will ask her to help me get what we need for the night from the wagon. It has been a long day and I am feeling the weight of the day upon me. I fear however, that your poppa will not rest tonight. His anger and his desire to see that white man dead will keep him awake.

"Don't be afraid for us. You go to your house and gather what you and the children will need to start your journey. It will be many days' ride to Canada but never fear. We have places and people along the way where we will be safe. We will travel the way of the Underground Railroad. Your poppa is known and liked by many of the persons who gave shelter to the runaway slaves. All of us will be safe. This is indeed the day I've prayed so long for, all of us together again."

Momma Cornbread look at meh and smiling, she suh, "You have trusted a white man to care for you all these years, now you must trust your poppa and me. Do you trust us, Milkweed, to take care of you, your children and your grandchildren?

Before I find wat to suh to Momma Cornbread, she suh, "Do not worry because we are old. Looking for you has been the thing that has kept your poppa going and now that he has found you, he will live forever. Tomorrow will be the best day for him. He will be bringing his last person, his daughter to her long-awaited freedom and he will be also making his last trip on the Underground Railroad."

Momma Cornbread stop frum talking and she smile. Den she open she arms to meh and suh, "Come. You will always be my lil' gal pickney, always."

I step in Momma Cornbread's open arms and she wrap dem 'round meh tight and she suh in muh ears, "Yuh did wat yuh had to do to live. Many many years ago, Momma Mae whispered in muh ears. She suh, 'Cornbread, thar gine be sumtings dat gine be hard fer yuh to do but if doin' dem hard tings mean dat yuh gine live; yuh do dem and yuh live.' So I understand, Daughter. You had hard choices to make. You chose to live. Now that is all behind you. Come now wid Poppa Molasses and meh and find out what it's really like to live."

I nots get chance to answer Momma Cornbread 'cause Beccah, she come back quick. It be like she nev'r be gone. Poppa, him stay way him be wid him hand on him gun. Beccah, she suh, "I tolt him dat yuh suh dat yuh momma and yuh poppa be sup wid yuh tonight."

Poppa suh, "And what else did you say to him?"

Beccah look at Poppa and I can see de fear in she eyes and she suh, "Dat I be sup wid yuh."

Poppa suh, "And?"

"Dat yuh be tekking off come first light."

"And what did he say?"

"Dat him understand. Him not suh nuffin' else and I come to see 'bout helping Momma Pear…"

Beccah, she mek to suh Pearl and it be de way dat Poppa Molasses be look at she dat mek she suh, "Milkweed. I come to see 'bout helping Momma Milkweed fix supper."

Momma Cornbread suh, "Thar be no supper to mek fer me and Poppa Molasses. It be in de wagon. Ask de one dat look like Poppa Molasses to go fetch it and bring it here. He will see the basket at the back of the wagon. It is in thar."

Beccah, she leave and I hear her suh, "Benjamin! Benjamin!" and then her voice it be go soft. I know'd that she be mek it to muh house. It not tek long 'fore dem back and Benjamin him got wid him a big, big basket. Him set de basket down and him wait. Him look at Poppa Molasses wid de gun in him hand and him smile. Poppa see de smile and him smile back. It be de furst time Poppa smile since him come and dat be de furst time in a long time I seen Benjamin smile. I be glad but I sorry same time. I know'd dat Benjamin be smile 'cause Poppa got him gun and him be looking at way Fields house be. Benjamin be know'd dat Poppa be fixing to shoot Fields and dat mek him smile.

Momma Cornbread tek de food out she basket and wen she git it all out, she suh to Beccah, "Go and bring all de rest. It will make my heart mighty pleased to sup wid muh pickney and all she pickney and grandpickney."

Beccah not wait to see if I got sumting to suh or not. She go'd right out and soon dem all come back. It be to meh like morning after freedom wen I feed muh little pickney in de cookhouse. But dis not be morning after freedom, dis be de night 'fore Poppa Molasses and Momma Cornbread tek we to freedom. It be de night dat muh poppa fixing be muh last night near Fields. I look at ev'rybody de way dem be eating and I tinks how it be dat de furst night I be spend on him plantation, I be in dis cabin and now dat muh Poppa Molasses fixing dat it be muh last night on dis plantation, I be back in dis cabin.

Dat furst night, I be cry fer Momma Cornbread and Poppa Molasses and now dem be here and I nots hab to cry fer dem but deep inside of meh, I can feel de tears filling up muh belly. Dem be tears fer Fields. I be deep in muh tinking and I nots see wen Poppa Molasses be git up frum way him be. It be only wen him suh, "Lord, I thank you for letting me live and that fate be kind to me to allow me to live long enough to set eyes on my pickney and now, thank you, Lord, I get the chance to be the one to lead her and her pickney away from this place."

I look and Poppa him be looking at meh. Him not suh nuffin' but I know'd wat him be tinking. Him be tinking dat soon night be ov'r and we be on us way to Canada. It be like him know'd wat I be tinking 'cause him suh, "Soon as you are done here, you and yours ought to get busy and gather what, if anything, that you'll be taking 'cause come first light…"

Poppa not dun suh wat him gine suh. Him not have to suh it. I know'd what him gine suh. I look at Poppa but I not suh nuffin'. Him look 'way frum meh and him look at Benjamin. It be den dat I see Benjamin sitting at de door and him hab de gun in him hand. Muh heart, it start to beat mighty hard. I know'ds now dat Benjamin have true hate fer Fields. I want first light to come ev'n more now. I close muh eyes fer a quick spell and I begs de Lawd to have mercy on all of we.

Chapter 31

No Way to Wave Goodbye

Benjamin, him be de furst to eat him food. Him eat fast and wen him tek him last swallow, him suh, "Muddah, I be go to yuh house. I hab to gather muh tings. Poppa Molasses suh dat come furst light, we be on we way to Canada."

I look at Benjamin and I not know'd wat to suh. Him not give meh time to suh nuffin', him jis't be gone. Poole, Eve, Lavina, and Charlotte dem follow him. Beccah, she go out de cabin too but I see dat she not go way dem go'd. She be go to way she faddah be. I know'ds now dat come furst light, Beccah not be on she way to Canada. I tank de Lawd in muh heart 'cause now I know'ds dat Fields be hab him special pickney wid him.

Night it tek long to come but, like all nights, it come. Poppa, him not sleep fer a long time. Him spend most de night talking to Benjamin and Poole. Beccah, nots be here. I nots hab to ask way she be. I know'ds. She be wid she dada. Eve, Lavina, Charlotte, and Etta Pearl, dem be at muh house. Only Poole and Benjamin be wid Poppa. Poppa, him talk all night 'bout Canada and de good life dat be waiting wen we git thar. I try to keep muh eyes open so I can hear him, but soon I nots hear him no more and den de sun start to chase way de moon same way moon come and chase 'way de sun. At furst light, Poppa stir frum 'way him spend de night: by de door wid de gun in him hand. Momma Cornbread stir soon as Poppa Molasses stir. It be like dem be tie to dem one 'nother. It not tek Poppa long 'fore him full wake and him suh, "This, Daughter, is the day I've waited for since I last saw you. This is a joyous day. We must be on our way so that we can make it to the first safe house before the sun makes it to the middle of the sky and bear down steadily on us, or we encounter some hateful white people. There are still plenty of them.

"Freedom might have come to the slaves and it has done a lot of good for us, but it has not taken the hatred of slave out of the hearts of the white men. And so, it is for that reason we must start to load the wagon."

Benjamin, him wake slowly. But soon him full wake jis't like Poppa Molasses and Momma Cornbread. Him have smile dat jis't be like Poppa Molasses. I can see dat fer de furst time in a long, long time, dat Benjamin be happy. Him look at Poppa Molasses and him suh, "Wat it be dat yuh wants fer meh to do, Faddah?"

Wen Benjamin suh, "Faddah," it be like him reach up in de sky and give Poppa Molasses de sun, de moon, and all de stars him hand can hold. Poppa Molasses, him smile big and wide and him suh, "Father! Father! I've never been called Father by anyone with my own blood in their veins."

Him walk over to way Benjamin be and him hug him. Benjamin hug Poppa Molasses back and den it hit muh brain dat since Benjamin be lil' pickney, thar not been nobody dat hug him like dat. Benjamin him hug Poppa Molasses back hard and den Poppa slap Benjamin on him back and him suh, "Son. You are my son."

Benjamin look at Poppa Molasses and him smile a smile dat I not ev'r see on him face. Him smile de same smile as Etta Pearl. I know'ds now in muh heart dat Benjamin be happy and mayhaps fer de furst time in him life, him love sumbody and sumbody love him back same way.

Momma Cornbread suh, "Just look at that. We came here to get a daughter and now we are leaving with a daughter, a son, grandchildren, and a great granddaughter. Oh taste and see that the Lord is good."

"One by one, de rest of muh pickney come. Dem not look happy like Benjamin. Dem look sorry and I nots know'd wat to suh to dem. Benjamin, him hurry past dem wid wat him gather and him suh, "Faddah, I gine to tek dese tings I gather to de wagon and wait fer yuh to come."

Poppa Molasses, him look at Benjamin and den him look at de oth'r pickney and him suh, "Go and bring what you all plan to have packed in the wagon and when you are done, help your mother to take what she has gathered to the wagon." Poppa Molasses him look and him suh, "Beccah. She's not here. One of you go and get her."

Wen Poppa Molasses suh dat, it be like Beccah float in on him last word. She suh, "I be here, Poppa, I be here."

Poppa smile and him suh, "Let's go to the wagon and pack it. As soon as we are done, we will be on our way. You, all of you, will love Canada."

"Eve, Lavina, and Charlotte, dem not move and Poppa him suh, "Hurry, you all must hurry."

Dem not move and it be Beccah who suh, "Momma Milkweed, we nots wants to go to Canada. We wants to stay her wid Dada."

Wen dem pickney suh dat, it be like dem root Poppa to de spot way him be. Him turn and him suh, "What did you just say? Did you say that none of you want to come?"

Beccah, she hang she head low and she suh, "We wants to stay here wid Dada."

I 'pect Poppa to git to shouting and hollering but him not. Him suh, "I'm going to the wagon. I'm going to pack it and make room for all of you. I know that the space will be tight, but we are family. We will make it to the first safe house and there we will get another wagon or as many as we need, but we must move on. When I am ready, I am leaving. I will not ask anyone and I mean anyone to get into the wagon. Who is on when I'm ready, I will leave with. Who is not…is not."

Poppa, him turn and him walk, wid Benjamin 'side him, to de wagon. Dem come back one more time and den him suh, "Momma, you start to make your way to the wagon. I am ready to go."

Momma Cornbread, she mek de first step frum de cabin and I walk wid she. I walk but I know'd in muh heart dat I nots be gine. I not suh nuffin'. Beccah, Eve, Lavina, Etta Pearl, and Poole be walk wid we to de wagon. Benjamin, him help Momma Cornbread to git in de wagon and den him help she to sit way she be comfortable. Den him, Momma Cornbread, and Poppa Molasses be look at meh. Dem be waiting fer meh to step forward and git in de wagon. I look at dem and I suh, "I sorry, Momma Cornbread and Poppa Molasses, but I nots be able to mek muhself git in de wagon and go'd way frum here."

Momma Cornbread, she starts to weep and I start to weep too, but Poppa Molasses him not weep. Him suh, "I said that when I was ready to leave, whoever was ready to leave I will be taking. It was my deepest hope, and I knew that I was hoping against hope because I could clearly see that your spirit is broken and that you are conditioned to this white man and his ways, but I'd hoped that you will be able to come with your mother and me. I'm sorry, Daughter, but not sorry that I've made the journey to find you. I'm sorry that you and your children are unable to leave here. I will think of you often and, until my dying day, I'll miss you but I am a man of and to my word so as much as it pains me to go away from here without you, I must. I am leaving."

I be crying hard and Momma Cornbread she be crying too, but I nots be crying dat hard dat I nots hear muh Poole suh, "Faddah, Faddah, wait fer meh. I be coming wid yuh."

Poppa Molasses him turn and him look at Poole and him not ask him if him sure, him suh, "Get in."

Poole him walk 'round back and him mek to git in and him stop. Wid him hand on de wagon, him look at meh, Eve, Lavina, Charlotte, and Etta Pearl and him stands right way him be; one foots on de wagon and one on de ground. It be like how I be de morning President Lincoln suh dat all niggers be free. Poppa, him suh, "You bring your other foot up, you are in the wagon on your way to true freedom: Canada. You take the foot you have on the jump down and you remain in this blissful state of ignorance that is holding you all bound to this white man and his ways. With both of your feet together; one way or the other, I'll be moving on. What are you going to do, son?"

Poole, him look at him sisters 'gin and him move him foot. Dem like mine 'gether. Poppa looks at him foots way dem be. I breave out a hard breff and I be look at him foots. Him not move de foots dat be tek him up in de wagon. Him foots be on de ground. I be glad. I starts to holler and Poppa, him suh, "It makes no sense to holler now or anymore. If you get in this wagon, all your children will follow you, but as long as you are rooted to that spot, they will remain rooted; move, my Daughter, and free yourself and your children."

Wen Poppa seen dat I nots move, him suh, "Come, let me touch you one more time; all of you."

One by one, dem go and Poppa touch dem head and dem step bak frum him. I waits till all muh pickney dun step to and frum de wagon and den I step to way Poppa Molasses and Momma Cornbread be. Poppa Molasses him suh, "This pains me deeply, Daughter, more than the day he dragged you away because then you had no choice; however, today with all the choices before you, you are choosing to tie yourself to him. I can't even begin to imagine leaving without you, but I must let you go. You are a woman. You have been too long steeped in this stew called slavery to fully understand what you are doing. You think its love that's keeping you here but, dear Daughter, it's not. You are seasoned; too well to know. I'm sorry I didn't find you before but there's nothing I can do about that now. I must let you go; leave you and miss you… I have no other choice."

I looks at Poppa Molasses and Momma Cornbread and I want to suh dat I be sorry, but I nots be able to mek de words come out.

Momma Cornbread, she be crying and she suh, "Every day, every day, Milkweed, I will think of you but now I don't have to wonder what happened to you. I know."

Den she too touch meh soft on muh cheek and she suh, "I'm glad the Lawd let me cast muh eyes on all yuh. That, despite the heartbreak leaving you is causing, just knowing that I've once again set my eyes on you will bring me an odd measure of joy on the long trip home."

Den she look at Poole and she suh, "Be the man that your mother and sisters need. Let no harm or hardship come to any of them. You are…"

Momma Cornbread she stop frum talking and she start to cry. First a sniffle, den it turn to a full cry dat yuh be able to tell coming frum she whole body. Her taking breff dat be short and quick and den she look at meh and she let out a holler dat be sound like trap animal. When Momma Cornbread start to holler, Poppa Molasses him turn to meh and him suh, "Come, come, Milkweed. Can't you see that leaving you here is breaking your mother's heart?

"Don't break your mother's heart and, for that matter mine, come. Let the love that you have for your mother and I be stronger than the one you think you have for this white man. Come, Milkweed, come with us to Canada. I don't know, Daughter, truly I don't know how to turn away from here and leave you behind. I almost want to do to you what he did, but for such different reasons. If I could, I would demand that you get in this wagon or drag you away from here but you are my daughter, not an animal. You have free will. Use it and come please, Daughter, come. All these years I've lived for this moment and it won't feel right knowing that when these wagon wheels start to turn, your momma and I will be turning our backs on you; leaving without you. Come, Daughter, Come."

I bends muh head and I nots suh nuffin. Poppa him breave out real hard. Him pull back on him nose and I hear de sound come out like it be lumps and pieces and den him suh, "Very well then, Daughter, the white man has won. I won't stand here and beseech my own child to walk away from a white man. I am taking my son and your mother and we are leaving. I love you, Milkweed, but I love your mother more. I will not stay here any longer and watch her suffer."

Afta Poppa Molasses suh dat, him turn him head and de next ting I know'd I hear Benjamin's big voice. Him suh, "Come, Muddah. Come wid Faddah, Muddah Cornbread, and meh."

Wen I not suh nuffin', him start to cry and him suh, "Poole, Poole, mek muddah come way frum here. Faddah dun beg, Muddah Cornbread dun beg, I dun beg now I be begging yuh now to beg Muddah to come and let we all go to Canada. Come, bruddah, come."

Wen none of we move, him sit harder and him suh, "I sorry, Muddah, dat yuh fix it in yuh heart not to leave dis place. I be tinks of yuh, but I nots wants to be here no more so I gine wid Muddah Cornbread and Faddah Molasses. I know'ds now dat sumbody love meh fer meh. I can feel it in muh bones."

Wen Benjamin suh, "Bones", it be like de word dat de horses be wait on' and de wagon it start to move off. I looks and I see Momma Cornbread be still looking at meh and she be crying soft now; de holler quiet down wen she see dat I nots be mekking no move to git in de wagon. De tears dem be coming down she face steady. Poppa him not turn him head. Him looking at de road ahead. I feel in muh belly dat I want to run after de wagon jis't to suh goodbye to dem 'gain but I know'ds dat Poppa Molasses him not gine stop fer no more goodbye. Him dun suh wat him hab to suh.

I start to holler but I nots move frum way I be. I know'ds dat I dun mek choice. I pick Fields ov'r Momma Cornbread, Poppa Molasses, and freedom. I know'ds in muh heart dat I dun brek dem heart and dat I nev'r gine seen dem 'gain, but I know'ds dat I nots be able to leave frum 'round him. Him be wat I know'ds and him be wat him pickney know'ds.

We stand way we be 'till de wagon be gone and it jis't be dust dat we seen. Den like him be watching, Fields him come slow to way we be and him suh, "You chose to stay. All of you. Thank you."

Den Fields do sumting him nev'r, nev'r do him, him cry. Him not mek to cover him face or turn him head or nuffin. Him stand thar and him cry like a pickney and him suh, "When I saw all of you come to the wagon, I was afraid that all of you, my family, were going to walk away from me. The knowledge that all of you could have walked away from me and left me had me feeling so alone it scared me. I knew there was nothing I could do to stop any of you from leaving but…" And turning to meh and taking muh hand, him suh, "When I saw Benjamin get into the wagon I felt my stomach sink but, Poole, when you made to get onto the wagon, I wanted to hurry out and beg you, yes, son, beg you not to leave; at least not like that. I know some day that all of you will leave, but God knows I didn't want all of you to suddenly leave me."

Fields tek him hand and wipe him eyes and den he suh, "I know I've done all of you wrong. I've allowed, yes allowed all of you, my children, to call me Fields. I don't know why I didn't stop that when you all were babies. I'm not just Beccah's Dada, I'm and should have been Dada to all of you. I'm sorry. I know old habits are hard to break, but it would be a blessing to my old ears to hear all my children call me Dada."

Him look frum Poole to Eve to Lavina and den to Charlotte, and I be able to tell dat in him eyes, he know'ds dat none of dem be ev'a call him Dada. Him be wait too long to tolt dem dat.

Dem jis't look at him like dem not sure wat to suh to him or wat dem ought to do and den it be Beccah who go to she dada and she tek him hand and she suh, "No, Dada, I not leave frum yuh. I not leave frum dis place. Dis be de only place I know'ds to be muh home."

Chapter 32

Love Dis Way Come

Rebeccah

"Momma Pearl cry and cry fer days and days wen dem left, but yuh know'd dat nigger not have time fer tears to last long and since it be Momma Pearl who be fix it in she heart to stay wid Dada, she soon stop crying. Etta Pearl, on de other hand, she cry and cry fer Benjamin. Momma Pearl and Anakey dem suh dat dem understand 'cause Benjamin be she born wid bruddah. De way Etta Pearl be cry, yuh'd tinks dat him nev'r one day treat she bad or beat she. She crying and she cling more and more to Momma Pearl. It be like she fear to be 'lone. Momma Pearl be missing she Momma, Poppa, and ev'n Benjamin so she not mind that Etta Pearl be she shadow now.

Tings go'd bak to wat dem be. I go'd bak to sitting wid Dada and I fear to leave him. I nots want him to dead while I be gone. Dada must be feeling dat I hab dat fear in muh heart 'cause him suh, "Go on, Beccah. Don't be so afraid. The good Lord will not steal me away from you, your mother, Poole, and my Etta Pearl while you are not looking. He has kept me here all this time so I know that He will give me time to say my goodbyes properly. Today is not the day. Now go, my precious, go and bring or send, your mother to me. My eyes and heart are longing to see her. Go; tell her to come to me, please."

I tinks 'bout wat Dada suh as I walk to way Momma Pearl house be. It be hard fer meh to get it in muh heart dat muh Dada be de kind of white mans dat I dun hear other niggers be talk 'bout. I not wants to tink dat him be like dat but I not be fool. I know'd as time come it be only meh, Momma Pearl, Eve, Lavina, Poole, Charlotte, Etta Pearl, Anakey, O'Brien, and dem pickney dat be de only ones dat be 'round Dada.

"Etta Pearl she left 'bout a year or two after Benjamin Harold, but her not jis't up and walk way de way him, wid him selfish heart do; she do like Momma Pearl. She find love, or I be suh dat love come right here and find she. Nigger not be slave but still nigger not be free de way white man be free, but dis nigger him have big ideas; some niggers gits to be like dat after freedom.

Him come round looking to wuk some of the far off land dat Dada be own. Him suh dat him gine wuk de land and frum dat him be able to mek money to move up North; New York City, Delaware, or Pennsylvania. Him be here and him wuk hard. While him wukking hard, him have eye only fer Pearl Etta Mae and she be all smiles wen him look at she. It be muh guess dat she smile at Eli 'cause next ting Momma Pearl know'ds is dat Etta Pearl jis't be talking, talking' bout Eli. It be Eli suh dis and Eli suh dat.

"We know'd den dat it not be long 'fore she or he be asking 'bout dem being 'gether. It be Eli who be ask Dada if Pearl Etta Mae can be him wife. Him ask Dada but it be Momma Pearl dat talk to him. She suh to him, "Muh Etta Pearl be not 've muddah nor faddah and the only close kin she had him be up in Canada, so muh Etta Pearl only hab meh to be she Muddah, Faddah, bruddah, and sister, so if in yuh wants to mek she yuh wife, I gine need to know'd dat yuh gine treat she right.

"If yuh know'ds dat yuh not be mans enough to be wid she wen it not be good days, yuh go on and leave muh Etta Pearl right way she be. But if yuh know'ds deep in yuh heart dat yuh gine mek she troubles yer troubles, dat if she have to cry dat yuh not gine see nuffin' wrong wid crying wid she. If yuh know'ds dat if yuh only hab two sips of water, yuh gine let she get one and yuh gine tek one and wat ev'r yuh hab to do yuh gine do it fer the two of yuh, den I gine suh dat she can be yuh wife."

"Eli look at Momma Pearl and suh, "I know'ds 'bout providing. Fore freedom come fer nigger, I be wuk and buy freedom. I be wat white man call a skilled nigger. I know'ds black-smithing. It be frum dis dat I wuk, save muh money, and buy muh freedom. I be a good man fer Pearl Etta Mae."

"Him nev'r call she Etta Pearl. She tolt him dat she name be Pearl Etta Mae and him be call she dat.

Him suh, "I be hire muhself out 'till I have nuff money and den I be tek she and go up North, but I be stay here fer a while so yuh can see dat I be tek de best care of she."

"Eli Sumpter, dat be him name, suh wen him buy him freedom, him call himself dat. Fore dat, him name be Cyprian Ellison but when him buy him freedom, him get new name and him now be Eli Sumpter. Him suh dat him want Pearl Etta Mae to be same name as him. All Pearl Etta Mae do is smile and dat be it. She be Pearl Etta Mae Sumpter. Dem stay here 'till him suh dat him ready to move on. Dada give Pearl Etta Mae a small pouch and him suh dat she must give it to Eli. It not be 'till years later dat Dada suh wat be in de pouch: 500 dollars be in de pouch. Dada also gib dem a horse and wagon wid plenty tings to start dem life up North.

"Momma Pearl, she cry but not like wen Isham and de rest of muh bruddahs walk way. Dis time she cry 'cause she suh ev'n though she gine miss Etta Pearl, she know'ds dat Eli be tek good care of she. Pearl Etta Mae, she cry but it be clear in she eyes dat she be happy. It be 'bout a year after dem left dat Dada get word dat dem mek it to Delaware and dat dem hab a boy pickney. Dem call de pickney Eli Harold Cartright Sumpter. Dada be feel bad dat Etta Pearl not gib she pickney nothing frum him name, but him suh dat him understand. She nots be hab none of him blood so him can see why she be honor she grandfather Harold Joe and great-grandfather William Cartright.

Chapter 33

A Girl, a Boy, and a Weeping Cherry Tree

"Miss Thea, I dun tolt yuh plenty but I not tolt yuh 'bout muhself. Yuh seen now dat yuh come dat I be here alone; well most alone. It nots always be dat way. Long time ago, wen Momma Pearl and Dada be here, I be hab wat dem hab: love. Him name be Levi. Dat not be him full name. Him full name be Leviticus. I dun tolt yuh dat him poppa be Preacher Man. Levi, him nots be born here on Dada's plantation. Him be come here wid Preacher Man and one more pickney dat Preacher Man hab. Dat pickney's name be Obadiah.

Preacher Man him nots come wid him wife, I tinks, though I nots be sure how she and dem pickney be git here, but Preacher Man suh dat him pray and de Lawd answer him prayer and brung dem. Him wife come wid de rest of dem pickney. Dem be Manessah, Isaiah, Ophir, and Gray Boy. Dem call de last one Gray Boy 'cause him eyes dem be strange eyes fer nigger to have, dem be like ash wid green here and thar.

Preacher Man's wife nots be here long 'fore she dead. I nots be sure how she be dead but she dead and Preacher Man him not tek next wife. Him tek care of him pickney by himself. Him be de only nigger mans on Dada's place wid dat many pickney and him never try to tek up wid a nigger womans to help him mind dem. Him git plenty of help frum de womans, but him not tek up wid none of dem.

"Dat not mean dat nigger womans after nigger womans not try to haul him in. Him be right handsome. Him hab wat be call proud features. By dat I mean him hab broad, strong-looking forehead, big wide eyes, not like dem gine pop out him head but dem be listening, caring eyes. Oh, dem be dark, not moody but de kind of dark dat suh it be ok to look in dem. Him eyes be change wen him laugh. It be den dat all de darkness leave dem; dem be light up. Him nose had a wideness to it; it be jis't like most nigger mans but it jis't dat it be him nose like it be want sumting to smell. Den him had a nice mout. It be wide, stopping at each corner full past him nose and stopping in de half of him eyes. It be funny to see nigger wid de kind of chin him hab; it be square and thar be a dent right in de middle of it. Him jis't be beautiful and Levi be him own spit out pickney. Thar be jis't one ting dat be different 'tween dem. Way him stop Levi's shoulders, Levi him go on head and shoulder over him.

Thea, it be funny how nigger womans widout a mans be try to get him in dem cabin, but him not go to nar one of dem. Him stick to raising him pickney and one by one, dem mek mans and womans. It be den dat meh and Levi eyes mek four.

If it not be fer de weeping cherry tree, I be nev'r set muh eyes full on Levi."

Thea

"Weeping cherry tree?" I asked Rebeccah.

"De weeping cherry tree, it be like weeping willow but it be a might beautiful sight to see in early spring. It be dat beautiful sight dat mek meh see Levi."

"How?"

"I be out 'bout muh business de way I be. It not dat I have full business or real business, but dis place it be acre after acre so I mek it muh business to go see wat be over here, thar, and ev'ry way. I jis't be goin' frum one place to de next wid no real purpose. Dis time it be early spring and so I be walking and walking and I see a tree dat I nots see 'fore. It be de most beautifulest ting I ev'r seen in muh whole life. It jis't be thar and I tinks dat wen I git to way it be, dat it not gine really be thar.

"I quicken muh step and I go to way it be and I nots look up, down, sideways, or no way oth'r dan way dat tree be. It be like cloud floating low to ground, but I know'ds dat it not be cloud 'cause it be pink."

"Pink?"

"Pink. It be de kind of pink dat look like it be white. Wen I tolt Dada, him suh dat de color be blush. Yuh can pick if yuh want de way I see; pink dat be near white, or yuh can call it blush like Dada. It not matter. Wat matter be de way it be beautiful. It be like lace dat mek by spiders and put on de tree by butterflies. It be like drape but not whole drape. It be like thin, thin strips of happiness.

"It be like a hush, or it be like sumbody dun pick all de dandelions dat dem can find and dem blow dem on de tree and dem stick. And wen I tinks dat it nots be able to be any more beautiful, de wind it blow. Not hard to mek one petal fall, but each time de wind blow, all dem thin, thin strips of happiness sway in the wind den de tree it do de most amazing ting; it bow a gently courtesy all de way to de ground, but it not look like it in a hurry to come back up. I be stand thar and watch it and I be wait fer de tree to come up frum de bow. It mek muh heart want to cry. Tears start sliding down muh face and I be tink dat I be by muhself when I hear, 'I tink dat it be de most beautifulest ting ever too.'

"I turns muh head to see who it be dat suh dat and wen I turns muh head, I seen de next most beautifulest ting I ev'r seen. It be Levi and him be looking at meh like I be de weeping cherry tree. I nots be sure wat to suh to him. But I nots hab to suh nuffin', him look at meh and him suh, "Yuh tinks it be beautiful too?"

"I looks at him and I nod a few times and by de time I be dun nodding, him be in muh heart. I nots know'd which one of dem be de most beautifulest. De tree it be tall. Levi him be tall. De tree it got long, long branches dat touch de ground. Levi, him hands and legs dem be long and him feet, dat be keeping him firm on de ground: big. De tree branches full wid new flowers. Levi, him be man, but him be young man, like new flowers. De tree it not suh words but it dun talk a whole lot jis't by it be so beautiful. Levi, him not talk much, but wen him do it sound beautiful to meh.

"I be stand thar tinking which of dem be de most beautiful wen Levi look at meh and him smile. Him win. Him be de most beautiful 'cause de tree it can mek meh smile, but it nots be able to smile bak at meh. I smile at Levi and it be thar standing in front of a weeping cherry tree dat I know'd dat him gine be muh husband. I not tolt him dat, I jis't smile back at him. I nots know'd how long I be stand thar smiling at him or even if I be walk way. I be guess dat I walk 'way 'cause ev'ry day, I be go'd thar hoping dat him be thar. Him always be thar. Him and him beautiful smile.

"Dat be how we court. Him come to de tree and wait fer meh. We talk 'bout trees, plants, birds, animals, and de plantation. Him love all tings dat be living. Him have gentle heart. Him nev'r bring man and woman business to meh. Him only want to talk 'but de land. Him tek meh to parts of Dada's plantation I nev'r seen. Him show meh plants dat him suh good fer healing, hurting, sleeping, waking up old man dat be sleeping in him man parts, and it keep young man's part wake fer a long long time; we laugh wen him suh, 'I be young man. I nots need nuffin' like dat to keep meh wake. I be stay awake all night 'till morning.'

"Dat day, Thea, we laugh and laugh and it be den dat I know'ds dat I nots be able to come meet him like dat no more."

"Why, Beccah?"

"'Cause it get so dat I nots be able to tink 'bout him and not tinks 'bout how him suh dat him can stay wake 'till morning. I wants to be wid him frum night to morning."

"So what did you do?"

"I nots hab to do a ting. It be Dada. Him seen dat I be sweet on Leviticus and him suh dat it be right fine wid him if Leviticus and I want to be married."

"Here Beccah laughed a full, full belly laugh and then she said, "Yuh nots gine believe meh, but I nots wait or stay after Dada suh dat it be fine wid him if in Levi and I be marry. I runs to way I know'ds Levi be; by de weeping cherry tree, it not be pink no more, all dem leaves dun come in and it be almost like weeping willow. Levi him still go'd I'm sure ev'r day jis't to see if I gine come. I runs to de tree and wen I see him I suh, 'Levi, Dada suh it be fine wid him if yuh and meh marry.'"

"Beccah, you asked the man to marry you?"

"No, Cousin Thea. I nots ask him to marry meh. I tolt him dat Dada suh it be fine wid him."

"So what did Levi say?"

"Smiling a shy smile she said, "It nots be what him suh but wat him do."

"Looking at her, I asked, "Are you going to tell me?"

"Giving me the biggest grin since I'd first met her, she suh, "Dat be jis't 'tween meh and Levi. Jis't know'd dat 'fore I left frum under dat tree, dat I know'ds dat him be all de tings I tink him to be and him let meh know'ds dat him be a true, true young man."

"Beccah, you didn't?"

"Yuh be right. I didn't, well not full outright didn't, but I know'ds dat him gine keep him promise."

"And what promise, pray tell, was that?"

"Dat him young and him not gine hab no problem staying wake all night 'till morning. Dat be all I gine tolt yuh 'bout dat part. Yuh nots need to know the fine, fine parts. Dem parts be fer muh Levi and meh."

"I smiled at Beccah and said, "Are you telling me that your Levi was a truly blessed man?"

"Cousin Thea, yuh be trying to mek meh gib yuh we bed secrets, but I dun tolt yuh dat dem be fer meh and Levi. Jis't know'ds dat I not's tink dat thar be one more woman on dis whole plantation dat beg night to come more dan meh. Thar be times dat de sun be high in de sky and I be sit on de porch and beg it to go way; ev'n if it go'd 'hind cloud."

"Beccah? Behind a cloud?"

"If in yuh be hab one night 'till morning wid muh Levi, yuh be full 'stand why I be beg de sun to go 'way."

"Oh Lord, Beccah, in the middle of the day you and Levi did night business?"

"It not be night business; it be we business and now, Cousin Thea, yuh hab meh 'membering more 'bout dem nights dan I be wants to 'member. Let meh keep muh mind on way I be or I gine nev'r tell yuh dis ting. Way I be now?"

"Beccah looked at me as if she half-way expected me to know but since she was the one telling the story, I had no idea where her mind was headed. So I said, "How soon after did you all get married?"

"Yes. The wedding. Dada and Momma Pearl gib we a fine wedding. Momma Pearl, she cry and I nots know'ds why at furst and den it be Levi who tolt meh dat Momma Pearl cry 'cause she happy fer meh, but she sorry fer she self 'cause muh Dada not be able to be she real husband. I feel bad fer Momma Pearl fer a little while, but den I nots feel bad fer she 'cause I know'ds dat she and Dada love dem one 'nother. It not matter dat Momma Pearl not be him real real wife.

"It nots be long after meh and Levi be marry dat all dat staying up frum night to morning showing. De pickney, it be born 'bout de time dat the weeping cherry tree be start to show de first signs of de blush. De pickney be a gal. I call she Pearl Blossom Fields. I be de only one dat try to call she Pearl Blossom. Ev'rybody else be jis't call she Blossom, and soon dat be mek short to Bloss. I tink dat it be Dada dat first call she Bloss.

"Well 'fore Bloss be walking strong, I hab a next pickney. It be a boy. I call him Levi Everett Fields. Him name git short too and dem call him jis't Vy. It be suit him. Him be a might handsome pickney. Way Bloss be tall and look like she be honey dat be stir up wid molasses, him be like a burn piece of wood. Him hab eyes like Gray Boy. Him hair it be jis't a mix up ting. It thick, thick, and curly. I guess dat be frum Dada and Momma Pearl 'cause it sure nuff not frum Levi or Preacher Man. Dem hair be jis't thar; nev'r moving, jis't tick and thar.

"I nots tolt yuh but Preacher Man him happy, happy wid de pickney and I guess him be so happy dat him nots notice wen one of dem nigger womans snatch him up and 'fore him know'ds it, him be married and in him old age. One day, Levi be tease him and tolt him dat him wait 'till him be old man to tek a new wife. Den Levi suh, 'Poppa, wat yuh dun dat fer? It not like yuh need a wife to keep yuh warm wen winter come.'

"Preacher Man, him suh, 'Yuh go on and laugh. But keep muh words in yuh head. De fire may look like it out, but dat not mean dat a strong 'nuff wind on dem coals nots start a new fire burning. I hope fer yuh sake, son, dat wen yuh fire look like it out, it only look out and dat it not be out fer real 'cause wen it be full out like that, thar be no breeze short of de one dat wake Lazarus gine help yuh get dem coals burning 'gain.'

"Oh, how we laugh at dat. I be look at de nigger womans who be him new wife and, Thea, she be smiling de way I smile after meh and Levi be spend we first night together. I look at she and I be tink dat she must be some good strong wind to wuk on Preacher Man's coals. Den I tinks in de bak of muh mind dat meh and Levi gine hab plenty of time to find out 'bout if him fire ev'r gine go'd out. Dat nots be de case."

Chapter 34

Frum Bud to Blossom to Leaf to Empty Branch

"Beccah, what happened? Something happened to Levi?"

"Vy be grow'd to be strapping pickney and Eve, de pickney I hab after Vy, be jis't finding she legs when I hear Bloss cry out. She shouting, 'Poppa! Poppa!' Den she suh, 'Momma! Come! Poppa be fall down!'

"I nots be able to run way she be 'cause muh belly it be high up wid muh next pickney. But Dada and dem dat be in de yard run to way him be. I gits to way muh Levi be and him eyes dem be turning back in him head and him trashing on de ground. I nots know'ds wat to do. Dada, him git dem to git him frum off de ground and dem tek him to we house. It be a right nice house dat Dada build fer meh, but wen I see de pain dat Levi be in, I nots able to tink 'bout de house. I jis't be tink wat it be dat hab him in de pain him in.

"I suh, 'Levi, Levi, wat it be dat wrong wid yuh?'

"Him nots suh nuffin', him grab him chest and wen him grab him chest, him stretch out him full length. Him eyes roll back and him stretch him neck. Den him body it go stiff. I holler fer him to not dead. I feel in muh bones dat him fixing to dead, and I nots want him to do dat.

"Momma Pearl, she be thar wid meh and she suh, 'Levi, yuh hab to hold on. Fields, him send fer de white doctor to come see 'bout yuh. Yuh hab to hold on. Beccah, she soon mek yuh next pickney. Yuh hab to stay here wid she so yuh can see de pickney.'

"Him mek him eyes see meh and him look full in muh eyes. I look in him eyes and I mek all de love in muh heart come to muh eyes. I want him to see dat I love him. Him look and look. Soon him body it not be stretch so full. It start to not be so stiff. Him keep him eyes in mine, and soon him breaving it not be so choppy. It most near match mine time de white doctor come.

"De doctor, him put him head on him chest and him tek him hand and him put it on Levi's wrist and it be like him waiting on sumting. Wen him hold Levi hand ferev'r, him put him head back on him chest. Him go'd in him bag and him tek a bottle out. Him open de bottle and him pour some of wat in de bottle in a cup and him mek Levi drink it.

"I wait to see if Levi be git up but him not git up. Him go'd to sleep. I fear dat him not wake up, but de doctor him suh dat Levi need to sleep. Him suh dat Levi's heart be weak and dat him hab to tek it easy and not burden him heart wid wuk.

"Levi him tek to him bed and him stay thar. Wen him able to stand, him weak. It be Gray Boy dat come and help him git round.

"Soon after dat, de pickney born. Levi suh to name de pickney Thessalonia Verette. It be a gal pickney. I suh dat Thessalonia Verette nots be a good name for a gal pickney so him suh, 'Call she Thessa Cherry Everett Fields.'

"I smile at dat 'cause I know'ds dat him be tinking dat it be a cherry tree dat mek we know'ds dat us love one another. Thessa Cherry, she be a beautiful pickney. She be jis't like de weeping cherry tree. Her skin be a brown dat look pink. She hair be black, and she eyes dem brown, but dem not full brown. Wen de sun shine in dem, den yuh see green and yellow. Her hab a nose dat look like it be ready to smell and her smile it be jis't like Levi. Him love all him pickney, but I tink dat it be Tess, dat be wat she name be short to, dat tek way him heart.

"I not hab a next pickney after dat, since I fear dat him heart not have strenf to mek pickney. Him and meh we not tink on staying up frum night to morning no more. I nots care, Thea, dat part of we married life dun. I tinks dat I tek him living ov'r wanting to mek more pickney. I mek muh mind not tinks on dat and 'fore yuh know'ds it, meh and him we find how to mek de other know'ds dat dem be special.

"I guess, Thea, dat mans and womans gine always find a way to keep a small fire burning in de coal pit. We keep dat lil' fire burning and I mek sure dat I never put a strong 'nuff breff on it to fan it to full flame. It be right nice de way we be.

"But one night, him hold meh like him nev'r hold meh. I tink dat him sorry dat him nots be able to stay up wid meh frum night to morning and mek more pickney so I tolt him, 'Levi, yuh ought not to worry yuhself 'bout dem pickney dat yuh tink we missing. We hab plenty.'

"Him suh, 'Dats nots be wat on muh mind. Wat be on muh mind is dat I hab to be leaving yuh. I nots want to leave yuh, Beccah, but I feel it in muh bones. I feel like I be mighty tired. I jis't wants to hold yuh, Beccah, 'till I nots hab no more strenf.'

"I starts to cry and I suh, 'Levi, I nots want yuh to talk like dat. Yuh nots gine no way. I nots know'd wat to do if yuh nots be here wid meh. I nots hab room in muh heart to love yuh no more. So yuh nots talk like dat. De Lawd dun let yuh be wid meh and we pickney all dis time, Him nots gine call yuh. I tinks, Levi, dat yuh ought to jis't rest and in de morning we gine git de white doctor to come and gib yuh some more medicine.'

"Him not suh nuffin' fer a short spell den him suh, 'Beccah, wen morning come, I gine be wid yuh, but I nots gine be wid yuh."

"I wants to holler but him suh, 'Beccah, jis't like yuh, I nots know'ds how to love yuh more. Ev'n though muh heart grow'd weak, it not lose one bit of love fer yuh. It be de love fer yuh dat keep it all dis time, but I know'd dat it nots be able to go no more. I wants to hold yuh tighter dan I be holding yuh now, but I nots hab strenf. Beccah, hold meh and hold meh tight. I nots know'ds wat it gine be like fer meh wen I starts to leave yuh but, Beccah, promise meh dat yuh not gine turn meh loose. Promise meh dat yuh nots gine run and call Poppa. I nots want yuh to holler and mek de pickney frighten. Can yuh promise meh, Beccah, dat yuh be muh guide and hold onto meh 'till de good Lawd tek meh frum yuh bosom to Him bosom? Can yuh do dat fer meh, Beccah? Can yuh, Beccah?"

"I nots suh nuffin' but I start to wrap muh arms 'round him. Him try to hold meh back tight but him nots able. I mek muhself go'd closer and closer to him. Him head it come to rest by muh neck and muh chest. I turn and turn slow 'till him most on top of meh and wen him be like dat, I wrap muh two arms tight, tight round him and I suh soft in him ears, 'I love yuh, Levi. I be love yuh frum de furst time yuh ask meh 'bout de weeping cherry tree. I be seen de two of yuh de same way. I be look at de tree and I try to tinks on which of yuh be de most beautifulest. Den yuh love meh and gib meh dem beautiful pickney. Yuh gib meh Blossom, Vy, Eve, and Thessa. Dem be de bestest tings I ev'r seen. Yuh hab to stay wid meh and see dem mek mans and womans.'

"Him not suh nuffin', him breaving it get slower. I feel him warm air on muh neck way him head be. I feel him nots holding meh as tight as wen him first start. I hold him tighter. Him breaving it get slower and him starting to feel heavy. I hold him tighter. I wants to holler, but him dun mek meh promise him dat I nots gine holler so I just let de tears come out. Dem coming frum muh eyes like dem be one long tear. Dem not be breking and I tinks dat dem like de weeping willow now, not de weeping cherry.

"Him breff it start to come on muh neck in short puffs. I holds him tighter. Him suh, 'Beck.'

"And him tek deep breff. I holds him wid all muh strenf. Him call muh name 'gin and I feel de air on muh neck and it not be as strong. Den it be short breffs dat coming quick. I suh, 'Levi, I be glad dat de Lawd mek meh go'd to dat part of Dada's plantation. I be glad dat him mek meh to know'd yuh and let love grow'd in muh heart fer yuh. I be nev'r stop not one day frum loving yuh. I know'ds now dat yuh gine to be wid de Lawd. Yuh go'ds on and wen yuh git thar, wait fer meh. If I not hab yuh pickney to see 'bout, I be hurry to be wid yuh, but dem pickney be too small not to hab no poppa or momma so I gine stay and see dem past de worse and den I be come and join yuh. I gine promise yuh, Levi, dat I nots gine ev'r tek a next man. Yuh be de onlyest one dat can full muh heart. Yuh dun full it and now dat all de time yuh hab be up; den go'd. Go'd and tek all muh love wid yuh. Tek it all, Levi. Tek it all wid yuh.

"Levi, him nots be holding meh now and him breff getting shorter and shorter and dem sound like dem mekking him tired to tek. In muh heart, I starts to beg de Lawd not to tek him and at de same time, I beggin' de Lawd fer more strenf. I suh, 'Lawd, I beggin' yuh to let muh Levi stay wid meh, but if in yuh gine tek him, den gib meh de strenf to hold him like him ask meh. Keep meh, Lawd, right here holding him like him ask meh.'

"De Lawd answer muh pray. Him gib meh de strenf to stay holding him. I holds Levi tight tight and I stays holding him 'till him breff not come on muh neck no more and him jis't be heavy. Wen I nots feel him heart beat 'ginst meh no more, I holds him tight tight and dem tears, oh Lawd how dem tears flood muh eyes. I nots holler; jis't as him ask meh to, but it tek ev'r ting in meh not to holler and bring ev'rybody to way we be.

"Time pass a little and wen muh tears git to way I tinks I can see, I ease him out muh arms. Wen him be full out muh arms, I be look at him and him be look peaceful. I turns him full to him back and I wrap muh arms 'round him one more time, and I stay like dat but I know'ds dat I nots gine be able to let him go'd if I nots git out de bed and get sum help.

"I cover him and I go'd to him poppa's house. I go'd and I suh, 'Poppa, Levi be need yuh to come.'

"Preacher Man him look at meh and him ask meh real sad wid him eyes fulling up wid tears, 'Him be gone?'

"I suh, 'Him be jis't gone. Jis't. Come. I not's know'ds wat to do now. I dun wat him ask meh to do, but now dat I dun it, I nots know'd wat else to do. Can yuh git Momma Pearl and muh dada?"

"I didn't have the heart to ask Beccah anything. She'd been silently crying as she spoke. I was as choked up as anyone can be. There was something so beautiful in what she said and somehow it made me think of Phillip. I was looking at her and wondering if I would have that kind of strength; to hold onto Phillip until he was home with the Lord.

"Beccah sat quietly. I stayed silently looking out into the vast open land that was Fields' plantation and waited. I wasn't sure what I was waiting on or to hear, but something in my spirit said it was best to just be still. The stillness stretched on but it seemed only fitting that Beccah be given whatever time she wanted or needed. She had done a remarkable job of telling me the story so far and if she needed time to think and sort her feelings, then I was going to sit quietly and let her take as much time as she wanted. I looked at her and wondered how she had done it; live with so many memories and not lose her mind."

Andrea

I looked at Auntie Thea and was amazed that she was dry-eyed. I don't remember at what point I started to cry but as Auntie Thea took a deep breath, I felt the need to just open my mouth and blow. I had to. I was choking on tears, emotions, and curiosity. I say curiosity because I was wondering what that kind of love must feel like and if everybody got a chance to experience it or if only a few people were selected.

As I was deep in thought, Auntie Thea told me, "As much as it pained Beccah to continue, she took a deep breath and when she exhaled, she continued with her story."

Rebeccah.

Dada and Momma Pearl come to muh house. Momma Pearl, 'cause Preacher Man dun tolt her dat Levi be dead, be crying. Seeing Momma Pearl crying be de ting dat mek muh heart finish bruk all to pieces. It be bruk 'fore she come, but thar be sumting, and I nots know'd wat it be holding it together, but Momma Pearl crying de way she be crying tek dat ting, watev'r it be, and mek it come apart.

I cry and cry. Preacher Man, Dada, and Momma Pearl, when she be dun cry, mek meh come out de room wen dem mek Levi ready to meet de Lawd. Dada, him tek some of him fancy clothes and him tolt Preacher Man to put dem on Levi.

I sit wid Momma Pearl and it be she dat mek we pickney know'd dat dem poppa gone home to be wid de Lawd. Dem cry and cry. It be Tess, de baby dat I be de most sorry fer. I be sorry fer she 'cause I know'ds dat soon her nots gine 'member him and thar be nuffin' I can do to mek she 'member him. I cry fer she 'cause she be too small to know'ds dat wen dem put she poppa in a box and put him in de hole, dat him nots gine come bak to de house. She be run and play like nuffin' be wrong. But den, she stop and she come to meh and she suh, "Momma, Poppa sleep?"

I look at muh pickney and sumting suh dat her nots gine fergit him. I suh, "Yes. Him sleep wid de Lawd."

I mek muhself be strong wen dem be ready to put muh Levi in de hole. Him poppa, Preacher Man, him talk 'bout how muh Levi be furst blessing to him and him wife, den how him be blessing to him bruddah and sistah, and den how him be blessing to meh and den him suh dat Levi be de best blessing to him pickney. Him suh dat him nev'r know'ds a man dat love him pickney like Levi. Him suh fer dat, if nuffin' else, him know'ds dat Levi be git into heaven.

Dada, him talk a little 'bout Levi but it most 'bout meh dat him talk. Him suh dat him be glad dat love find meh and Levi, and dat it be a good tink wen a man and woman find de love dat be right fer dem. Him suh dat him know'ds dat de love dat meh and Levi hab be dat kind of love. Him suh it nev'r be dead and so I can rest, rest him suh, in de knowledge, dat be de word, knowledge, dat Levi be love meh de best way a man know'ds how.

Blossom, Vy, and Eve dem cry and cry, and Tess she only cry 'cause dem rest be cry. But wen dem put de box in de hole, it be Tess she start to pull at dem dat lowering him in de hole and she holler, "No, no, no, Poppa! Tek Poppa out! Tek Poppa out! No, no, no! Poppa! Poppa! Poppa!"

Dat be all I know'ds of dat day. Hearing muh Tess holler and pull at dem to tek she poppa out de hole be more dan I can tek. I feel muh feet give way. It be feel like I be sinking and yet I be floating up. I gib in to de floating feeling and dat be it. It all go'd dark and I not hear nuffin' more.

Wen I wake, I be in Dada's house. I be in de room dat be down de hallway frum him. Momma Pearl, she be thar and all muh pickney. Muh head it still feel like I be floating but it be clear. I know'ds way I be and why. I know'ds dat if dem be all here wid meh, dat Levi be dun bury. I tinks dat thar be nuffin' more I can do fer him so I suh, "Thessa, way Thessa be?"

Momma Pearl she suh, "She wid Preacher Man and Christobell."

Christobell, she be Preacher Man's wife. I not worry. Thessa love Christobell and Christobell she love and tek fine care of Thessa. I tink dat Christobell be mek in she heart to tink dat Thessa be she pickney 'cause she never hab no pickney.

"I be stay at Dada's house fer a few days but den I want to be bak in muh house. I want to be way I be happy wid muh Levi. I go back to muh house and I live. I mek life de best dat I can mek it fer we pickney. It not be a hard life 'cause Dada him see dat we nots be ev'r want fer nuffin'.

I do jis't wat I promise muh Levi. I nev'r tek a next man. I stay in muh house wid muh memories of Levi and muh pickney. I face winters in muh house full wid hope. I suh full wid hope 'cause I know'ds dat soon as winter pass, I be mek muh daily travels to de weeping cherry tree. It be thar in dem blossoms dat Levi be live 'gain. I hear him voice. I hear all dem promises dat him mek to meh and dat be 'nuff fer meh.

Over time, it stars to be way it gitting harder and harder fer meh to mek de trip to we tree, but I know'ds dat if Levi be live, him be mek de trip wid meh. So I go'd and I walk slow. I walk slow so dat him can see meh and walk wid meh. Dat be wat keep muh heart full wid love; de weeping cherry tree.

It be like I go'd to sleep one night and muh pickney be lil' pickney and den wen I wake, dem be grow'd. Dem be mans and womans pickney. Blossom, Eve, and Vy be jis't like Levi; dem be de most beautifulest man and woman pickney I be ev'r set muh eyes on. Dat be true but none of dem be beautiful like Thessa. She be a pretty pickney but, Lawd, wen womanhood start to drape itself on dat pickney, it be like de angels in heaven mek choice on how she be look. She be meh, Dada, Preacher Man, Levi, and lots of Momma Pearl all mix together. It be hard to suh wat dat pickney be look like and not feel like yuh wants to cry.

She be tall like Levi and him poppa. But wen I suh dat, Momma Pearl suh, "Wat 'bout muh Poppa Molasses; him be full Mandinka African, it be thar way she git dat tallness."

Den Momma Pearl be jis't tek all de rest of Tess. She be suh, "See dem cheekbones; dem be Seminole. See dem eyes; dem be muh eyes, dat mout; dat be muh Momma Cornbread's mouth," and so Momma Pearl be go on. I know'ds dat Momma Pearl not mean no harm and it be a good ting to see she happy wid muh Tess. Dat Tess, she love it wen her Nana Milkweed be go'd on 'bout she be de most beautifulest gal pickney ev'r born.

"Wen all dem rest be gone, it be Tess who be still wid we. Wen it time come fer Christobell to go to de Lawd, it be Tess who be sit by she bed, give she water, wipe she forehead, and pray wid she. She not be thar wen it be Preacher Man's time. I be de only one wid him. It be den dat him tolt meh 'bout Fortune. Preacher Man, him tek him time and him tolt meh dat story slow so dat I not miss none and when him be dun, him be dead but 'fore him dead, him ask dat I be read frum Bible. I tolt him dat I not's know'd how and him suh dat him not know'd how either, so watev'r I suh, him be most happy wid dat.

"I suh to Preacher Man dat I be git Dada to come read fer him but him suh, "Wat I be do be fine fer nigger so wat yuh do be fine wid meh. I be ready to go to de Lawd. I dun live a good life. De Lawd bless meh see nigger not be slave no more, Him let meh hab de love of two fine nigger womans. Him let meh hab Levi, Manessah, Isaiah, Ophir, and Gray Boy. Him let meh see dem all grow'd and wid dem own pickney. It be a fine life and now dat Him be ready fer meh, I be ready to go. Beccah, yuh been a good wife to muh Levi. I know'ds dat yuh love him and yuh dun all yuh can to mek him happy. I be glad fer dat. I know'ds dat it be jis't yuh, yuh dada, Momma Pearl, and Thessa dat be left wen I be gone, but I gine look down frum heaven and I be see dat no hurt, harm, or danger be come to yuh way ev'r yuh be.

Dat be it. Preacher Man, him dead wid jis't meh in him house. I nots holler nor cry out. I cry; but I not holler. I go'd and get Dada. Dada be up in age now and so him call Thomas. Him be de one dat tek ov'r frum O'Brien. O'Brien be dead a few years now and it be Anakey and dem pickney dat be left. Dem be up North. Dem pickney, she be marry up wid a fine nigger man and a letter it be come mayhaps a few times a year to let Dada know'd dat dem be happy wid dem new life.

Thomas and some de other nigger man wukking on de plantation bury Preacher Man in de middle of him first and him last wife. Levi, him be next to him momma and thar be a hole waiting fer meh next to Levi. Dem all be bury way Poppa's people be 'cause Dada him suh dat him want meh to be near him and I be suh dat I want to be next to muh Levi, so dat be how come dem be thar.

Thea

"That day of talking was a long sad one for Beccah and I. It was as if she'd held back telling me about her Levi because she knew once she got to that part, it involved telling how she got to the place where she was so alone on a plantation this size. I also knew that we were approaching the end of her telling. She had only to tell me now about Milkweed and Fields and then there would be no more to tell.

I knew once I left her, I was headed to Breckenshaw's plantation and when I left there, I would have all the pieces I'd set out to get. Realizing that I was nearing the end was making me feel empty. I didn't want to hear of Fields' final days, so God knows I wasn't anywhere ready to hear about Milkweed.

It was Beccah who set the pace for the next few days when she said, "Thea, yuh dun been here fer a spell. We dun a bit of talking, laughing, sharing, and ev'n sum crying, but I be near de end of muh telling. I nots want to talk 'but dat part. Dat part be mighty hard fer meh, but I be tell it to yuh. It jis't not gine be today.

"Meh and yuh, we gine mek sum bittle and den we gine sleep. We gine gib God till' de morning and wen it be morning, we be come back and I be tolt yuh de rest; wat happen to Momma Pearl and Dada. I be tired. It be a tired dat I feel in muh bones so let we be on we way to de cookhouse."

With that, Beccah worked her way out of her rocker and, with more strength than I remember her having, we went to the cookhouse of the big house. It was time to make some bittle, as she'd called it. Time to cook, think, and plan for tomorrow. I thought to myself as we cooked, when tomorrow came it was going to be the longest tomorrow I'd ever been in. I wasn't in it yet and I was already wishing for the next tomorrow or the next few tomorrows. Yet not the one that would take me away from this amazing woman who had waited, 'cause she felt it in her bones that someone was coming to hear and take her story to those who needed to hear it. I was sad, but I did all I could not to let none of it show.

Chapter 35

A Morning Following a Night Like No Other

Andrea

We all woke the following morning different, but yet the same. I say that because there was a feel in the air. It was hard to describe the feeling but bones, young or old, could feel that a major change or shift was going to happen. I wasn't sure what I was feeling, but somehow I could feel it; whatever it was. Auntie Thea had stayed over. She'd taken to doing that over the weeks that she'd been telling us the story. On the nights she stayed over and after the story telling, we would sit around and catch up on the news of the day.

There was a lot going on in New York but mostly down south. A lot of what was going on was happening, at the moment, in Birmingham, Alabama. There was something in the news, almost every day, about what was going on down there. Every Negro, and the age really didn't matter, wanted to know as it was affecting or going to affect us. Auntie Noreen and Auntie Thea talked a lot about change and so what we didn't catch on the radio, Uncle Neal brought home from the Lodge or from either Uncle Boysie or Mr. Colroy. I didn't have to call Mr. Colroy 'uncle' because he wasn't as close a friend to Uncle Neal as Uncle Boysie was.

Leela had just turned six weeks when Uncle Neal came home from the Enoch Lodge on Nostrand Avenue, and he wasn't in the house properly when right after his customary, "Good night everybody," he said, "Noreen, Miss Thea, you all hear what happened today?"

Auntie Noreen said, "No, Neal, we spend most of the day talking, you know that Thea is trying to get done telling we the story 'bout Drea's kin and once we get to talking, we don't do nothing else."

"Well, today would have been a good day to listen to the radio."

"Why?"

"Them people in Alabama done gone and arrest Dr. Martin Luther King and they got him in jail. Them plan to keep him there for more than a week; can you imagine that? A man trying to change things for Negroes and them putting him in jail for that. New York's bad but it makes you glad, when you see the things that happening to Negroes in Alabama, that you ain't down there."

Auntie Thea didn't even seem surprised, all she said was, "Lord, I hope them don't do that man nothing. So much hate. You would think that a hundred years after Abraham Lincoln signed the Emancipation Proclamation, things would be better for a Negro in this country. But look where we be. Negroes still getting lynched, signs telling you where to sit, where to drink, where you can walk, who you can look at, go to school, and that Governor that they got down there must be the worst. I don't know if there's another governor in all of American that's filled with more hate for Negroes than that George C. Wallace.

"I think if he could get his hands on enough rope and he had forever to live, he would spend all his living time just stringing Negro after Negro 'till he done lynching every Negro in America. I wonder what was in his mother's belly when he was turning around in there. Jesus, I don't know who to feel sadder for. The Negroes in Alabama and them deep Southern states or we, the Negroes up here in the North."

Uncle Neal said, "Why, Miss Thea, would you say a thing like that? Negro is Negro. We, here in the North ain't seeing it no better than the Negro down south."

"'Cause so far, we never had to deal with people like Orval Faubus, or Ross Barnett."

Uncle Neal interrupted Auntie Thea. He was smiling slightly when he said, "You got me on those two. Can't say I ever heard of them."

"Neal, there are a lot of folk we ain't ever heard about, but trust me, you may not be familiar with their names but when I remind you, and I say remind because from what I've heard you talk about over the few weeks of my coming and going, I know you've heard 'bout these two. Take for instance, if I start to talk 'bout them nine Negro children who was trying to get into Little Rock Central High School back in '57, you would know 'bout that; true?"

"Yeah I know 'bout them but what about this Faubus fellow?"

"He was the governor who called out the National Guard to stop them from getting into the school."

Smiling again, Uncle Neal said, "It's funny, not laughing funny, but strange funny how you would remember some parts of something and miss out, don't remember, or don't hold onto another or real important part of the same thing. Now you mention them Negro children, I remember that man now; not his name but the way he tried to stop them children from getting an education and breaking down one more of them hateful barriers."

"You see, Neal, it's going to be the same thing with this fellow Barnett. His name might not have stuck in your head but if I say Medgar Evers, your brain goin' start remembering. You may remember the fellow who shot Evers; something Beckwith."

Uncle Neal interrupted Auntie Thea and said, "It was Byron De La..."

"Yes. Yes. Byron. True. Byron De La Beckwith. Well, remember and it wasn't too long ago that while they were re-trying that fellow's case, that Barnett interrupted Ever's wife, Myrlie, when she was testifying to go and shake hands with Beckwith. That's what I'm talking about. We may not remember people's names, but we remember the things they do. This same man, with his hateful ways, had them Freedom Riders arrested, stripped, searched, and didn't even let them people get beds to sleep on. I think that was back in '61. He wasn't any better 'bout a year later when this fellow...what was his name again? Ahmmm, yes; James something...I don't remember the something but it goin' come to me. But anyway, he was trying to get into the university there and what did this man do? He pulled every stop he could to prevent this Negro from going to college. So you see, it's important to remember names and things, but it don't make no sense remembering if you ain't goin' take what you know to change nothing."

"Miss Thea, I like what you just said. You sure know a lot."

"It's Bernard and Phillip. Them always talking politics and Civil Rights so I listen when them talking. Not everything sticks, but something I remember. I remembered these two governors: Faubus and Barnett, 'cause the way them do everything to keep Negroes down. You know that one Ross Barnett; yeah his first name is Ross, he once opened his mouth and blasphemed by saying that God, the same one up in heaven, was the segregationist."

Auntie Noreen, who had been quiet until now, joined in by saying, "He said that God was a what?"

"The original segregationist."

"Now what kind of foolishness is that?"

"To him it wasn't foolishness. He said that God was the original segregationist because God put the black man in Africa, made white people white, 'cause he wanted them white."

Uncle Neal was hopping mad by this time and he said, "That's pure shite. You think God got time to think 'bout white people like that. He ever stop to think that maybe white people was one of God's mistakes, that's why he put them far away from Africa. Look at all the beauty that God put in Africa. If God had really meant to make white people special, he would have put them in Africa and this where it's good and hot, and not some place where it's freezing all the blasted time. If you really loved somebody or thought they were all that special, you wouldn't put them where they goin' be cold."

Auntie Thea was the first to start laughing and after that, Auntie Noreen joined in and last was Uncle Neal. I'm sure he didn't mean to make it a joke, but I think Auntie Noreen laughed more at how vexed Uncle Neal was than she did at what he said.

"Neal, you sure can get worked up when you ready. From now on, when I think 'bout them two, I goin' remember you and the way you carried on like if them was ants in your underwear on a Sunday morning during church service."

Laughing, Uncle Neal said, "You're right, Miss Thea, 'cause with some red ants in your pants, you want to holler but reverence keeps you quiet. You want to dig and scratch, but pride got you but then you say to yourself, 'I ain't gine let no red ants bit the shite out of me; church or no church. I ain't gine stand here and let them make a full meal out of me. I gine show them who is boss. It's the same way for Negroes. Negroes reaching the point where if they have to die; then they goin' die, but a hundred years and we still fighting the same war. It like it ain't ever goin' end."

Uncle Neal was smiling broadly, so broadly in fact that Auntie Noreen asked, "Now, Neal Peters, what you smiling so broad at? I didn't hear nothing that would make me smile; you?"

"You see, Noreen, even after all these years, you ain't know me. Now you know that I know what Miss Thea just said ain't nothing to smile at, so it must be something else."

"So what is that something else?" Auntie Thea asked.

"That, Miss Thea, like a lot of women around, listening, caring, and getting involved with what happen to we. That's what I smiling 'bout, Noreen Peters, if you must know."

Auntie Noreen smiled. Then she said, "Doctor King, them really goin' keep him in prison?"

"I guess so. You know how it is when them want to show Negroes that them ain't making no sport."

The room went quiet and when it didn't seem like anyone was goin' to move or do anything, Auntie Thea said, "Noreen, by now I know how the rhythm of this house is, so I guess that we goin' sit down to some of that delicious food you spent all day cooking now that Mr. Neal is home. Can I be bold and ask what you cooked today?"

Uncle Neal didn't give Auntie Noreen time to answer. He said, "Miss Thea, you might have picked up a lot of the rhythm of this house, but you miss the beat on the food. Let me make a guess."

When Uncle Neal said, "guess", Auntie Noreen said, "Neal Peters, stop showing off. You know no guessing is involved with this. I cook the same thing for you every week. It don't change. So you know, like the back of your hand, what you goin' eat every day."

Uncle Neal smiled again. This one broader and then he said, "I was trying to trick you, Miss Thea. Today is Friday so it goin' be something light. By that, I mean that Noreen don't cook a lot on Fridays. I smell salt fish so it is probably fishcakes, boiled and then fried sweet potatoes, cocoa tea, or some good thick oat meal or cream-of-wheat."

Auntie Thea replied, "My God, I'm so glad that Phillip ain't like this. He just glad that I cook. Now I know my way round the kitchen, but I never know from one minute to the next what goin' come out so you know that poor Philip knows even less."

Everyone laughed at that. We ate in the kitchen since Auntie Thea had insisted, after she'd eaten with us a few times, that it wasn't necessary to eat in the dining room. Once dinner was over, Auntie Thea and Uncle Neal went out to the drawing room and Auntie Noreen and I stayed, and as was habit, put away the food and cleaned. As Auntie Noreen put away the food, she told me, "You realize, Drea, that your Auntie Thea is getting close to the end of her telling."

Looking sadly at Auntie Noreen, I answered, "I know. I'm going to miss her when she goes back home. You know something funny, Auntie Noreen?"

As expected Auntie Noreen, said, "I know a lot of funny things, but it's my guess you 'bout to tell me something that's not so funny."

"Auntie Noreen, you know what I mean."

"I do, Drea, but I was trying to stop you from getting so sad."

"That's the funny thing. When she leaves, I know I'm going to be sad 'cause in a funny way, but not ha ha funny, I'm going to miss great-great-great-great-Aunt Beccah as well as the rest of my family that Auntie Thea has talked about."

"But you don't have to miss them. The same way your Aunt Thea went to all the trouble to find out and tell you, then all you have to do is remember and tell Leela. Then when the Lord blesses you with a husband and, who knows, even more children, then you can tell them and in telling them, then they will come alive again. You can be like Ezekiel and the valley of dry bones."

I didn't have to ask Auntie Noreen what she was talking about, the same way I never had to ask what we were going to cook; I knew. I'd heard Auntie Noreen talk about the prophet Ezekiel enough. I understood what she meant. I would have to do like Ezekiel and make the dry bones of all of them that have gone on before me live by talking and telling what they went through. My telling the story would be just like Auntie Thea; breathing life into them. Each word would be like putting the flesh back on them and the deeper I told the story, and with real feelings for them, I would be covering the bones, and then adding the muscles before the skin. Then if we were lucky and Leela passed the story on, then that would be the breath that would keep the dry bones alive and going. I couldn't forget. I had to be obedient like Ezekiel and not allow the dry bones of my family to lay there in the wilderness unnoticed.

I was so deep in thought that I didn't hear Auntie Noreen the first time when she called my name. I heard her when she said, "Child, you out there in LaLa land or something? You ain't hear me calling your name?"

"Sorry, Auntie Noreen, I was thinking."

"You got plenty of time for that. Let's hurry up and go listen to

Thea. For all we know, she could finish her telling tonight."

"But, Auntie Thea, said she'll be in New York for seven weeks."

"And do you think that means she has to give you all seven weeks? She might be planning on doing something else, even seeing someone else, so come. Let's finish up this where we have more time to listen."

Auntie Noreen didn't leave me as usual to put away the dishes; as I washed the dishes she dried and put away and in what seemed like a blink, we were headed to the drawing room. As I entered the drawing room, Uncle Neal said, "A certain young miss was waiting on you."

I looked and he had Leela in his arm. For a split-second, I wanted to turn around and go back in the kitchen. It was going on seven weeks and I still couldn't get myself to think about her as my child and get excited at the idea. I was glad she was alive and all that, but I wasn't glad that she was mine. Each time I looked at her, she was a reminder to me of Hamilton and the hatred I felt for him.

"The sooner you take her, the sooner she'll stop hollering." It was Auntie Thea. I'd drifted off again and her voice was bringing me back to the fact that Leela was now revving up. If I didn't take her soon, she would be hollering down the whole house. I really didn't want to hear her when she got going, so I walked over to Uncle Neal and took her. As soon as I sat down, Uncle Neal got up. He wasn't going out. He walked out the drawing room. He never stayed around when I was nursing Leela. I didn't have to guess where he was going; I knew. He was headed to his room where he would sit, write, or maybe even nap until Auntie Noreen went up and then he would join her in their room, but until then he stayed in his room. That was Uncle Neal. He cherished his alone time, that was until Auntie Noreen said, "Neal, I ready to go in."

As I sat with Leela, Auntie Thea started.

"Yesterday or last night rather when I left off, Beccah was at the point when she was going to finish tell me about Fields and Milkweed. I can tell you that just like you, I wanted to hear but I didn't really want to hear because I knew once she was done, that I would be leaving her and I would probably never see her again. It's hard to explain how someone that earlier you didn't know existed could, in a few short weeks, come to matter. Beccah mattered to me, so I wasn't in a hurry to rush her.

"We'd been basically alone on that vast plantation for almost two months. Now, it's not like they weren't other people; there were, but not blood relation to her. All the people there were either hired hands or people who were share cropping. Can you imagine that; Negro people sharecropping from another Negro?"

"Did my great-great-great-great-great-grand-father give Aunt Beccah the place so she could sharecrop it?"

"You jumping ahead of the gun. Until I get to that part, I'll let you go on and jump the gun and I'll even let you think what you want."

Smiling, I said, "Auntie Thea, you're not being fair."

"What does fair have to do with my storytelling? I'm the one telling and you the one listening, so listen."

Chapter 36

A Cotton Picking Kind of Pain

"The morning after Beccah had said she couldn't go on anymore after telling me about her Levi, I was afraid for her to start back. I wanted to hear the rest of the story, but I was concerned about the emotional toll that the telling of the story must be taking on her. In a few words, right after, 'Morning to yuh, Thea,' Beccah showed me the stuff that had kept her going all those years.

"She made her way to her rocking chair and she said, 'Chile, yuh nots hab to hab dat sad face and be looking at meh. True, it be hard fer meh to talk 'bout dem, but none of wat I be tolt yuh, be new. I dun live wid it all dese years so a few more days to tolt it to yuh nots gine mek dat much difference.

"'I dun tolt yuh 'bout muh Levi so I nots hab to go ov'r dat. I dun tolt yuh dat Dada be doing poorly and dat 'fore Momma Pearl's Poppa and Momma be show up, I fear dat Dada not mek it. Him mek it fer a long time past dat time. I nurse him past the consumption and soon him be de happiest man ev'r 'cause Momma Pearl be able to stay wid him again, and I nots hab to stay in him house. I be right happy to go bak to muh house.

"'I nots know'd how old Dada nor Momma Pearl be, but I know'ds jis't by looking at Dada dat him hab more age on him dan Momma Pearl. Momma Pearl, oh she was still some kind of pretty and she still be sweet on Dada. It be clear dat Momma Pearl still hab plenty of love in she heart fer Dada, and him fer Momma Pearl ev'n though dem be old.

"'Wen it git dat it be jis't us dat left, Dada him suh to meh, 'Beccah, there are more than a few strong and handsome men on this plantation, you are a young and beautiful woman, have you given any further thought to a new husband? Your Levi has been gone now all these years. I'm sure he wouldn't want you to be as alone as you are.'

"'I look at Dada and I suh, 'Dada it be de same fer meh as it be fer yuh. Yuh only wants Momma Pearl and I be sure if de good Lawd be call she home to rest tomorrow, dat yuh nev'r gine tek a next woman. So I feel dat way 'bout muh Levi, I nots want a next mans. I be right happy jis't de way I be.'

"Dada him nev'r ask meh again.'

"I looked at the way Beccah's face was set; so determining, and I asked her, 'Beccah, how did you do it; get up every day knowing that you won't set eyes on the man you love ever again?'

"'It not be easy. De furst morning be hard, but dat not be de furst hard part. De furst hard part be walking way and leaving him in dat hole. No, dat not be furst hard ting. De furst hard ting be gitting yuh head to suh dat him dead and den getting yuh heart, wid all de love in it fer him, to 'cept dat him gone. Wen yuh git dem parts dun, den yuh hab to get to de part way dem gine put him in a box. So yuh git past dat. If yuh still hab yuh mind, den yuh hab to git to de part way dem gine put de box wid de man dat yuh love in a hole, cover him wid dirt, and den tolt yuh to walk way frum de hole and nots dig him up. If yuh nots git to yuh knees, and try to git de dirt out wid jis't yuh hands and yuh can walk way, yuh dun mighty so far. But thar nots be a soul in yuh bed dat night. Now, dat be de true test. If yuh heart, head, soul, and spirit mek it through de night, den mekking it through de morning be like picking cotton.'

"As she spoke, a lot of questions and moments to interrupt her was going through my mind but then she would get to another part and I would think, 'Here; you have to stop her here and ask the question.' But then she would go on, slow, not in a hurry at all and then she said, "Cotton." She compared making it through the morning without your loved one to cotton picking and I, knowing from everyone in my family who've ever picked cotton how hard that work is, so I finally found the place I could interrupt her and so I asked, "Cotton picking, Beccah? How is it like picking cotton?"

"She said, 'Cotton, it be soft and pretty but yuh hab to be out thar to start de gather frum be able to nots be able; I mean be able to see de sun to yuh nots able to see de sun, and if de Lawd bless de night wid a big ole bright moon, den nigger out thar to pick cotton by a sweet harvest moon. Dat nots be de half of it 'cause yuh hab to git it frum way it dun grow'd. Afta yuh dun bend to pick it all day, yuh back be sore and it dun hurt. If yuh nots bend to pick it and yuh go'd down on yuh knees; den it be yuh knees be hurt and not jis't yuh knees den yuh got to drag dat big ole cotton sack. Yuh fingers dem be sore frum de burrs, sharp branches, and anyting else dat be 'round dat pretty white cotton to stick and scratch yuh up. Den over time frum picking dat cotton, yuh hand grow'd hard skin to mek it not hurt.

'Dat be wat it be like wen yuh mans go on to be wid de Lawd and left yuh to live widout him. Aft'r time, yuh heart do like a hand dat dun pick cotton; it grow'd hard skin over it so dat ev'r soft and sweet ting yuh 'member 'bout him nots hurt as much; it gine hurt, jis't not as much.'

"I wanted to cry when Beccah was done describing living without Levi, but I didn't all. I said was, 'That's some description. I'll never forget that; never.'

"Beccah then looked at me and I could see she was ready to tell me about Fields. I didn't want to rush her. I sat quietly and then I heard her say, 'Dis be de part dat be jis't as hard fer meh as wen muh Levi go'd to be wid de Lawd. It be true dat I love muh Levi, but thar nots be a love in meh like wat I be hab fer Dada. Dada, him be de most special love I know'd. Well, it be most different kind of love 'cause Levi's love be one kind and Dada's love be next kind. Dem be de same yet dem be different dat mek de pain a different kind of pain, but de same.'"

Chapter 37

Thar Be No Easy Way to Suh Goodbye

"'Thea, it be nots hard fer meh or nots as hard fer meh if Dada be dead frum the consumption wen Benjamin be here. But as I be tolt yuh, him mend fully and him and Momma Pearl be tek back up frum way dem left off, loving dem one 'nother. Dada be in full spirits though him be old and getting a might frail by now. I be sitting wid him one evening, as I be tek to do wid ev'rybody Anakey, O'Brien, dem pickney wen dem be here.' Laughing, Beccah added, "Still nots able to 'member dat pickney name, it gine come to meh one day wen yuh be gone.'

"I laughed with Beccah and, looking at me with that look of warmth, love, and sincerity that is now etched forever on my mind and heart, she continued her story."

Rebeccah

Levi, Christobell, Preacher Man, all gone. We be sit, sumtimes wid Momma Pearl and sumtimes Momma Pearl, be do as Dada suh, haunt she old cabin, Sara, Eve, Lavina's house or she be go'd and sit wid all dem dat dead. Dada and meh, we jis't leave she be.

On de ev'ning I be tolt yuh 'bout, Dada him suh, "Beccah, tomorrow I think I'll go for a ride."

I suh, "A ride, Dada? Yuh nots sit a horse fer a long time. I tinks dat yuh ought not to do dat. It not long since yuh be down wid de consumption."

"That is all the more reason," him suh, "that I should go for a ride. I feel the need to see this place from one end to the next. For all I know, someone could be farming my land and I won't have any idea and besides, your mother ought to know."

I suh to Dada, "Wat it be dat Momma Pearl ought to know'd? Her dun know'ds dat yuh can sit a stead." Wen I suh dat, I see de color come up in Dada's face quick fast and den it drain back jis't as fast as it be rise up and I know'ds dat him 'membering dat him be drug Momma Pearl hind him horse. Him turn him head 'way frum meh and wen him turn back to look at meh, him suh, "I will spend the rest of my days begging the good Lord to forgive me for that and all the other heinous things I did to, not just to your mother, but to all the niggers I ever set my eyes on."

"Dada, we be not talk on dat now. Wat we be talk on yuh be yuh tinking dat yuh gine riding tomorrow. I tinks yuh ought not to do dat. Momma Pearl be not like it if yuh tolt her dat yuh gine ride out tomorrow."

Dada him mek like him hear wat I suh, but come de next morning, him come down in him riding clothes and suh fer dem to git him horse ready. Dis new horse be full wid spirit and as Dada be not ride him often, him not quite use to Dada. One de niggers, de one dat ride and take care of him, Pork Fat, be suh dat Streak, dat be de name of de horse, be got de devil temper. Pork Fat not be him real name, but wen him come to Dada's plantation, him be de only nigger dat got skin dat wen him sweat, it be like it mek it own grease and all de time it be look like him greasy.

It be him dat mek himself be call Pork Fat, 'cause one day sumbody and I nots 'member now, suh, "Wat be it wid yuh, Caesar, dat yuh sweat grease wen de rest a we sweat water?"

Caesar must not be tink 'cause him suh, "Dat be 'cause I eats de pork fat and wen de sun hit meh, I sweat grease." Dat be it fer him frum dat day. Him be Pork Fat. I tinks dat it not be stick to him if him not answer and fret de furst time, but him answer and fret and soon ev'rybody be call him Pork Fat, ev'n him wife.

Momma Pearl, she beg Dada not to go riding but him suh, "Pearl, it has been too long since I've seen the far side of this plantation. I sometimes forget how large it is. I want to see, and not just on paper, what it is that I'm leaving you and my children. Can I do that? Just one more time. I promise you that after this ride I will sit, as you want me to do, on the porch, in my rocker and wait for the good Lord to come and take me right into heaven."

Dada be smiling at Momma wen him suh dat, but Momma Pearl, her nots be smiling. Her beg him one more time and Dada him suh, "Pearl, let not your heart be troubled. I will not let Streak gallop. We will trot slowly. I no longer have a desire to part the wind or feel it rushing past my face as it blows my hair beside me, and besides, I don't have as much hair as before and even I know I'm an old man. You may not remember, Pearl, but I've been sitting a horse now for over seventy years and today these old bones feel like one more ride. I'll take that ride. I'll even slow it to a trot if that would please you. I'll be careful. I promise you, Pearl."

Dada be set in him ways so him had dem bring Streak and then Pork Fat help Dada to sit Streak. Dada him git Streak to go. Streak not bolt or nuffin. Him walk slow like him know'd dat Dada be old. Momma Pearl and meh, we be watch Dada 'till him be jis't a dot. Meh and Momma Pearl we sit thar past time dat Dada ought to be back. Den Momma Pearl, she cry out, "It be Streak!"

I look and it be Streak coming in de yard and Dada not be on him.

Momma Pearl, she start to cry and holler. Pork Fat him be de furst one to come in de yard. It be muh guess dat him be waiting fer Dada to come bak so him can give Streak him rub down. Him come to de porch and wen him see Streak widout Dada, him suh real quiet like, "I be git a few of dem dat tek care of de horses wid meh and we gine go'd and look fer him. We be nots come back 'till we find him." Den him suh, "Mistress." It be de furst time sumbody be call Momma Pearl, "Mistress."

I nots know'd if Momma Pearl hurd him call she Mistress but she suh, "Go, quick, look fer him and brung him home."

Momma Pearl, she be crying time Pork Fat tek off running and calling fer dem dat wuk wid him wid de horses. In no time plenty, dem be on horses. Pork Fat be at de front on Streak and him got de dogs wid dem; Dada him be keep hunting dogs. I looks at the way dem be and if it not be dat dem be all niggers on de horses it be like when white mans and dem dogs be go'd look fer run way slave. Dis time in be nigger mans on horses and dem be gine to look fer a white mans.

De sun it be most down wen dem come back. Dem be hab Dada on a pallet. It be Streak dat dragging de pallet dat Dada be on. Wen Momma Pearl see Dada tie, not like hog, but at de back of a horse no less, she holler and holler, and it be like she seen she self tie to de horse. Thar be no mekking she be quiet.

I be want to holler, but I know'd dat it not mek sense fer Momma

Pearl and meh to be hollering. Thar be nobody to suh wat to do if we be both hollering.

Pork Fat him suh, "Miss Beccah, we be look and look and we not seen him. If it not be fer de dogs, we be not find him. It be de dogs dat pick him scent and tek we to way him be. Him be in a mighty bad way. It look like him not be see a rock in him path and it mek Streak throw'd him. I nots ev'r tek Streak to dat side of de land so I tinks dat Streak nots be know'd dat de rock be thar and wen him come on it, it mek him bolt.

"I tinks Massa Field be hit him head on it. I suh dat 'cause on de way bak, I seen dis big rock in de path and it be hab blood on it. Wen Massa Fields fall off Streak, him foots be still in de stirrup and den him nots be able to git him foots loose frum the stirrup so him hit him head and I suppose dat Streak be drag him. I nots know'ds how far Streak be drag him, but frum de way him clothes and him skin be tear up, it be look like Streak be drag him far. Him head it be cut wide open, him whole face not be look like him. If in I nots know'd Massa Fields, I be jis't leave him thar but I know'ds him so I mek de pallet to pull him back on. Frum de way dat boot twist, I tinks too that him leg it bruk inside it. Miss Beccah, him be hurt mighty bad. Yuh wants meh to go git de white doctor to come?"

I look at Dada and him be de whitest I ev'r seen him. It be like all him blood dun come out. Thar be blood on wat be left of him coat, him britches be most off him, and him leg, de one dat look bruk in de boot, be look jis't like him leg and him boot be fold and bend in a way dat mek it look like it not be a leg. I know'ds dat him boot ought not to look like dat since him foot be still in thar.

Dada him moan but him not move. I be fixing to cry but I know'ds dat I nots be able to do dat and tink, so I suh to Pork Fat, "Tek Dada frum off dat pallet. Him be de Massa of dis place. Tek him to him chambers."

Pork Fat, him suh, "Beggin' yuh pardon, Miss Beccah, it be true dat him be de Massa of dis place but if we not put him on de pallet, thar be no way to git him back here and not kilt him fer all de pain him be in wen we find him. Miss Beccah, I be also tink dat it be best if yuh let we tek him up de stairs on de pallet since him nots able to walk. I nots like how him leg be look in de boot. I be let dem dat help to find him tek him to him chambers and I be go'd on Streak and git de white doctor."

I suh nuffin'. Dem untie Dada frum Streak and dem do wat I suh.

Dem tek Dada and dem put him 'tween dem and dem tek him slow and careful up de stairs. Wen dem be reach de top, dey put de pallet on de chamber floor jis't as careful. Dem untie him frum de pallet and best as dem be able to widout causing him more pain, dem git Dada on him bed. Him be a mighty poor sight. De blood it be coming frum him head, him nose, mouth, back, chest, de top of de leg dat be in de boot, and de leg dat be look fold in de next boot hab blood at de top of it too. I nots know'd wat to do.

It be Momma Pearl who suh, "Beccah, yuh hab to help meh git wat be left of him clothes off him. Wen yuh dun, yuh go'd to de cookhouse and yuh puts plenty of water on the hearf. Den yuh brung plenty brandy fer him to drink. I be need plenty of rags to wash him 'till de doctor come."

As Momma Pearl be talk, she be git strong. She look at him leg fold in de boot and she suh, "I hab to get dat boot off him leg. I tinks him foot bruk to pieces; dat nots be good. Yuh go to way dem mek de saddle and horse bridle and yuh git dem to brung wat dem be cut de leather wid. Dat be de best tink to cut de boot off him foot. It be more sharp dan cookhouse knife."

Momma Pearl den suh, "Beccah, I be needing yuh to go'd to muh cookhouse wen yuh dun all dem tings I tolt yuh. Wen yuh git to muh house, go'd in muh cookhouse; thar be a woodbox dat look like it be left out in de sun and rain fer a spell, inside be plenty dry leaves in it brung dat to meh. Den go'd in muh bed chambers and under muh bed, at the top way I sleep, thar be a box dat look same way as de box in muh cookhouse; brung dat to meh as well. Go, Beccah. We hab to help yuh Dada time de doctor come or him gine dead. Him be in plenty pain. Go, Beccah! Go!"

Thea, I nots know'd how I be do all dem tings dat Momma Pearl suh fer meh to do, but I dun dem. Time I mek it back to Dada's chambers, Momma Pearl and Pork Fat dem be trying to cut de boot frum him leg. Dada him nots be hollering. Him look like him sleep. I tinks to muhself dat it be a good ting dat him sleep or de pain be kilt him dead.

It tek dem a long time to cut de boot off him leg 'cause ev'n though him look like him sleep, dem fear causing him more pain. Dem wuk on de stitching at the bottom of de boot. De sole of de boot it come part and wen it fall to de floor, de blood it rush out like it be a red river left to flow widout a bank to stop it. Dem fear fer Dada but Momma Pearl, she suh, "Now dat yuh hab de bottom off yuh go'd on and open de side and de boot it gine come off. I wants wen yuh git it off to help meh fix him foot in dese here pieces of wood. Dat be hold him leg steady 'till de doctor come. Hurry!"

Dem wuk fast and soon dem hab de fold up boot off Dada's foot. De foot like it jis't wait to be free frum de boot. De instant the cut up boot come off the foot, it do like it bloat. Momma Pearl, she not cry nor holler. She suh, "Come, Beccah, gib meh dem leaves dat I tolt yuh to brung. De ones dat yuh dun steep in de hot water. Brung de water too." Momma Pearl she gits to washing Dada's leg wid de water and wen she dun, I look. Him leg bone clear out de side of him leg. Momma Pearl tek she hand and she puts it on de bone. Wen Momma Pearl do dat, Dada, him eyes open wide and I can see dat him full wid fear and pain. Him moan but him nots cry out. Momma Pearl suh, "I wants fer yuh to hold dat wood on him leg and I be wrap dis cloth on it. Yuh nots let de wood move."

De nigger mans dat be thar do jis't wat Momma Pearl suh to do. It not tek she long 'fore she hab him leg wrap. Momma Pearl, she wuk on Dada, washing and cleaning and wrapping him cuts 'till de white doctor come. At sum point, and I nots know'ds when, Dada him stop frum moaning.

Dada him not come to ev'n wid de white doctor try to rouse him. De white doctor, him look at how Momma Pearl be hab Dada all wash, clean, and wrap up, and him suh, "Nigger, I do declare, I think with your nigger doctoring you might have saved his life. You niggers and your primitive ways of doing things never cease to astound me."

Momma Pearl not suh nuffin'. De doctor him open Dada's wrap leg and him suh, "That's a nasty looking wound."

Momma Pearl and I know'ds not to suh nuffin' to him as we be know'ds dat him nots be talking 'pecting fer we to suh nuffin.' Him git Dada to open him mout and him gib him sumting to drink. Him gib de rest to Momma Pearl and him suh, "Nigger, whenever he starts to come to, you are to get him to drink this. Do not, and I mean this, Nigger, let him come fully awake. The pain will be too much. He's not to thrash about or turn. You and your nigger ways might have saved him 'till I got here, but your nigger ways will not keep him living. He's a white man and needs the care of a white doctor. I will stay tonight and watch him. One of you niggers have to stay here to get me what I want."

I know'ds dat Momma Pearl be not leave Dada's side so I jis't git up and I walk out. I nots want de white doctor to know'd dat I be sleep in Dada's house so I go'd to de cookhouse. I not's be thar long wen Momma Pearl come. She look like she be fixing to cry but her nots. Her suh, "Yuh Dada's leg be bleeding again plenty. I nots know'ds wat dat white doctor be do, but I feel in muh bones dat it not be good.

De doctor him suh him need plenty of hot water. I mek and fetch clean water all night."

Wen it be morning, de doctor suh dat him bleed Dada. Him set de leaches on Dada's foot. Momma Pearl, she not leave. It not matter wat dat doctor do; Momma Pearl she stay wid Dada.

Days drag on and on. De doctor him come and him go. Dada, him nots be able to be wake long. Him wake long nuff one morning to suh, "Pearl, I'm so sorry. I've worried you. I'm in such pain, Pearl, such pain."

It tek him ferev'r to suh dat. Him talk like words be new to him. Momma, she suh, "I know'd yuh sorry, Fields. I know'ds yuh jis't want to feel a horse under yuh one more time. I nots know'ds how dat be, but I know'd wat it be like to want sumting real bad. I be do wat I know'd to keep de pain frum yuh, but yuh hurt bad, Fields, real bad."

Dada suh, "I know, Pearl. I know."

One morning, 'fore 'round de time dat we be tinking dat de doctor ought to be coming to see 'bout Dada's leg, Momma Pearl she come to way I be and she suh, "Beccah, thar be sumting mighty wrong wid yuh Dada. Yuh must come. It be him leg. Thar be a foul stench coming frum him leg. I tinks dat white doctor nots do de best fer yuh Dada, since him be gone off dese few weeks now and him nots come bak. I tinks plenty time dun pass and him ought to be back to see 'bout yuh Dada. It be true dat him suh yuh Dada's leg be needing time to knit widout disturbing it but it be a long time and now thar be dis stench."

I suh, "Momma Pearl, de doctor suh dat we be do jis't wat him suh and nuffin' else."

Momma suh, "I know'ds wat him suh, but Fields be muh man and I tinks dat doctor not care fer yuh Dada like I be care fer him. I care 'cause muh heart be full of love fer him. Dat doctor nots know'ds dat. Him be do wat him feel like wen him come 'cause him want money. Boil some water and wen it be boil, brung it to yuh Dada's chambers. I be go'd and get wat I need frum muh garden."

Thea, thar be nuffin' to fix muh heart fer wat I seen wen Momma

Pearl tek all dem wrappings frum Dada's leg. De more Momma Pearl unwrap, de more it smell like thar be sumting dead in de room. Wen Momma Pearl be git to de last wrap by way de doctor still hab de wood on Dada's leg, it be move. Momma Pearl, she be stop and she look. De wrap it move 'gain and den de wood it be fall way and Momma Pearl, she holler, "Lawd, Lawd, him leg be eat way."

I look and thar be maggots. Thar nots be a place on Dada's leg dat nots hab maggots. It be like him leg be dead and dem be live thar. Momma Pearl, she mek to puke but she not puke. She put something in some hot water and she tek a cloth and she let de water drip slow to Dada's leg. She keep at dripping de water wid de leaves in it on Dada's foot 'till all de maggots dem start to fall 'way frum Dada's leg. Dem not move. Dem dead and dem like a pile of rice all round him leg. Momma Pearl tek she time and she ease de cloth wid de maggots on it frum under Dada's leg and she suh, "Beccah, yuh tek dis and yuh bury it. Tell Pork Fat to ride wid haste and go git a next white doctor. I nots want dat furst one to set foot back on dis land."

Miss Thea, Dada's leg be like sumting I nev'r seen in muh life nor want to see again in dis life. I know'd dat it be him leg 'cause it be by him knee. But it be purple, black, red, brown, a green dat near be brown. De parts dat not be none of dem colors be look like scalded pork fat but de fat not be white. It be yellow; dat be de pus and it most not be a leg. Him leg it dead, and Dada be still living. Momma Pearl she tek she time and she wash it. Many a time wen Momma Pearl be cleaning him foots; yuh know'd way she look to see if thar be more maggots or dem eggs, her mek to puke but she turn she head, tek deep breff, and she not puke.

Wen Momma Pearl be sure dat thar be no more maggots or dem eggs in him leg, she dress it wid fresh cloth. She nots let Dada come wake. She keep steady gibing him sumting to drink dat she mek and so him nots wake.

I do jis't like Momma Pearl suh and I tek de cloth wid de maggots outside. I nots bury de maggots like Momma suh. I fix a hole in de ground but I mek a fire over them and I let it burn 'till thar be nuffing but ash in de ground. I tinks dat if I put dem in de dirt dat dem be live and git back in him leg. I nots want dem to live fer wat dem dun to Dada's leg.

De new white doctor him come and him tek de cloth off Dada's leg dat Momma be put on it. Wen him look him, not mix words, him suh,

"This here is unfortunate. Whoever was looking after Master Fields has failed him. He has allowed gangrene to set it. There is no saving this foot. The sooner it is removed, the better it will be; the better chance he has of living. If I do not remove this leg, it could poison his whole body. Tomorrow when I come, I'll bring a surgeon with me and we will remove it.

When I come, I will not be needing you around."

Momma Pearl suh to him, "Begging yuh pardon, but thar be nobody else dat be here fer him. I gine stay wen yuh come tomorrow."

Him start to suh sumting to Momma Pearl, but him look at she face and it be set so him suh, "It is my suggestion, from having done many such amputations, that you not be here, but if you want to be here then, nigger woman, be here. Know this. When I start my work, I will not have time nor will I make time for any nigger that has, at the sight of blood, fainted. Nigger or not, this is nothing for anyone to see but those in the business of removing limbs."

All Momma suh be dis, "I gine be thar."

De white doctor him suh, "Very well then I do not want him alone. Stay with him and give him this." He pointed to a bottle that he'd brung wid him. "Fill the cover and make him drink it. Be merciful to him. Do not let him wake."

Momma Pearl and meh we do jis't wat him suh. I tinks him know'ds dat Momma Pearl be Dada's woman and I be him pickney so him nots be near as nasty to Momma Pearl as de other doctor.

De next morning, de new doctor him come back and him brung lots of white mans wid him. It be de most white mans I seen in Dada's house since I be but a lil' pickney. Dem go'd to Dada's chambers and Momma Pearl she git ready to go wid dem and I git a feeling in muh belly dat it not be a ting fer Momma Pearl to see so I suh, "Momma Pearl, I be stay wid Dada. Yuh come out and wait fer meh." She be crying. Muh heart it bruk fer Momma Pearl and fer meh 'cause I know'ds dat wen dem come frum Dada's bed chambers, dat dem be dun cut him leg off.

De doctor him open him surgery kit and I seen tings dat I not know'd wat dem be. Dem talk to dem one another like I be not thar. Dada, him be near wake but him not full wake 'cause Momma Pearl be gib him wat de doctor suh fer him to drink.

A mans go'ds to Dada's leg and him tek all de cloth off. Den him tie sumting high on Dada's leg; above way him foots be not black and purple. Him tie it tight and I see Dada wince. I go'd and I tek Dada's hand. Him open him eye. Him know'd dat it be meh but him not know'ds dat dem gine cut him leg off.

I look and dem come to way I be and dem gib Dada sumting to drink and de doctor him suh to one of de mans, "Mansfred, you stay by his head. When I start, you force that stick between his teeth. Gilroy, you and Palmer be prepared to hold him to the bed. This shouldn't be a difficult amputation as the maggots have made my job a little easier."

Thea, I be want to suh to dem nots to talk like Dada nots be thar, but I know'ds muh place. I stay way I be. De doctor him tek a saw out him box and him put it on de bed near Dada's leg. Him tek sum small knives out and him put dem on de bed too. Wen him git wat him be needing on de bed, him start. I be look to see wat it be dat him gine do. Him tek de small knife and him start to cut into Dada's skin jis't low way dem got de leather string tie. Dada him start to moan. Him grip muh hand. I start to cry 'cause I know'ds dat Dada can feel wat dem be do.

I turn muh head 'cause I nots want to see him cutting way Dada's skin. Wen I tinks him be dun cutting way de skin, I tek a peek to see wat him be fixing to do next. Jis't as I be turn to peek, I seen him pick up de saw. Muh heart it start to beat real fast and I be feel mighty scared. I want to run, but Dada him be holding muh hand. I not hab de heart to tek him hand frum mine.

De doctor him put de saw to Dada's leg and him start to saw. It be sound jis't like him be cutting a log. Dada him open him mouth and him scream. Him most sit up frum de pain. De man wid de stick, him come and him suh, "Mister Fields, I want you to bite down on this. Dr. Brickelshire is the very best surgeon in the area. Now, Mister Fields, muster your strength and bite down." Dada him bite down on de stick and de sawing it start back. Dada him squeeze muh hand and it be like him gine brek all muh fingers.

Doctor Brickelshire, him sawing and it be like de bone itself be stink. De room it smelling stink and I feel like I gine puke, but I know'ds if I puke, dat I gine puke on Dada and de mans dat be holding him down. Dada, him open him mouth. De stick it be fall out and Dada him scream and him scream. De doctor him suh, "Give him the laudanum. He shouldn't be this awake. His thrashing around is impeding my progress. Now get him still so I may proceed."

The man by Dada's head poured sumting in Dada's mouth and soon

Dada him not squeeze muh hand as hard. De sawing it go'd on and soon it stop. Dada's leg be cut off. De Lawd be merciful to Dada. Dada not wake up wen dem be dun cut off him foot, and ev'n wen dem be tek a needle and mend him skin, him not be wake up.

Dem wrap it and wen dem be dum dem leave and Momma Pearl, she open de door and she be come to Dada's bedchambers, thar be blood ev'ry way. Momma Pearl her not cry. Her suh, "Beccah, we hab to mek 'round yuh Dada clean. Him be want to be clean wen him wake up."

Dat be wat we do. We mek round Dada clean. Wen Momma Pearl be hab all de bloody bed tings in a pile on de floors, she suh, "Go and get Pork Fat. Suh to him dat him is to come and tek all des tings and burn dem. I nots want to see none of it ev'r."

Pork Fat him come and him gather all de tings dat Momma Pearl suh to gather and him burn dem. De smell of de smoke full de place. Wen de smoke mek it to way we be, Momma Pearl she cry and cry and she suh, "I be so sorry fer him. I tolt him nots to go riding but him nots listen. Him tinks him can still do all dem tinks him be do when him be young man, and now dem hab to cut him foot off fer him to live."

Afta Momma Pearl suh dat, she cry and cry and I nots know'ds wat to suh so I nots suh nuffin.

Thea, it not help Dada none dat dem cut off him leg. Him not gitting better 'cause dem keep suhing dat him nots to wake, but dem nots tinking dat if in him nots wake, dat him nots be eat. It be Momma Pearl dat tink 'pon dat and mek him wake. She be feed him wid broth. If Momma Pearl be listen to dem, Dada be dead long time.

Death be a funny ting dat not be a joke. It be a trickster. Dat be wat it do wid Momma Pearl, meh, and Dada. It mek Dada start to come 'round. Git jis't a little better. Him ev'n git to know'd dat him leg cut off. Him suh to Momma Pearl, "Now, Pearl, did you really have to let them do that so as to keep me off Streak?"

Momma Pearl be know'd dat Dada be jesting so she smile. It be she first smile since dem brung Dada back on de pallet. Dada him look at meh and him suh, "My darling Beccah, I've also worried you. I didn't mean to do that. You've had so much to worry about already in your life time. I'm glad that you've stayed here with your mother and me."

Then Dada him suh, "Pearl, after I'm gone, they will come and say that you are to leave here. You defy them. That means you do not listen. Don't leave. When they say that you've no right to be here, say to them that if they do not believe you, they are to go see Pursival Breckenshaw."

Momma Pearl, she suh, "Hush, Fields. Yuh gine mek yuhself tired."

Dada him suh, "Tonight, Pearl, will you come and stay with me? I know you have stayed with me, but you've not stayed here in this bed with me. Tonight, stay with me. Will you do that?"

Momma Pearl suh, "I be do dat, Fields. I be do dat."

Momma Pearl she be stay in Dada's house and I be go to muh house. It be de furst time in wat be feel like a life time dat I be in muh house in muh own bed. I sleep de hardest sleep I be sleep in a long time. I nots be de only one dat sleep a hard sleep. Dada and Momma Pearl sleep a hard sleep, but wen it be morning, it be only Momma Pearl and meh dat wake. Dada be dead in him sleep.

Momma Pearl suh dat she be dream dat she see Dada walk in a green field and him be walk wid Lilly, and in him hand be dem lil' gal pickney, Rose. She be de pickney dat be dead de same night Momma Pearl birf she. Momma Pearl suh dat she be thar in de green field wid Dada, and him suh to Lilly, "There, over there, Lilly, is your true momma. She, not Olivia, is your real mother. She loved you from the day you were born." Momma Pearl suh dat Lilly be look at she and smile and den Lilly suh, "I know, Daddy. I know. Mommy Olivia, in a fit of anger, once said that I was your nigger pup. She was sorry after and asked that I not let you know. I've always known, Poppa; always known. I loved Olivia, but I also love Mommy Pearl too."

Momma Pearl suh dat Lilly be look at she and suh, "Do not come with us, Mommy. It's not time for you to come. When it is time, we: Daddy, Rose, Sara and I will come for you; all of us Mommy, all of us together will come for you."

Momma Pearl suh when she woke the sun was already sitting high in the sky. She stir and wen her not hear Dada breaving, she be shake him and wen him not stir, she know'd dat him be gone.

Momma Pearl be cry and cry. I tinks dat she gine dead 'cause Dada be dead, but in she crying she suh, "Muh Lilly know'd dat she be muh pickney. She know'd, Beccah. It be wat Fields suh dat him be wish. Him suh when Lilly dead dat him sorry she dead and she not know'ds I be she muddah all dis time. But muh Lilly be know'ds. I 'member wen Olivia dead and muh Lilly cry fer she muddah. I tolt Neala, she be de one dat wuk in de cookhouse wid meh, Sukie, and Eme, I tolt Neala dat I gine tolt muh pickney dat I be she muddah and dat she muddah nots be dead.

"Neala, she be tolt meh dat if I be do dat, den Fields gine kilt meh and all de rest of muh pickney. I nots tolt she nuffin' and now look. She come in muh sleep when she come to tek she Poppa wid she to let meh know'd dat she know'ds and, Beccah, yuh Dada him be hab him him cut off foot back. Him be walk strong as wen him be young man. Him look mighty proud walking wid him two gal pickney.

"De pickney, Rose, she be still a lil' pickney. Her nev'r grow'd in heaven. I guess dat when yuh git to heaven and yuh be pickney, yuh stay pickney, but if in yuh be mans or womans and yuh foots cut off, yuh git it back so yuh can walk right proper into heaven.

"Dat be gib meh peace. Yuh Dada nots be 'lone. Him hab him gal pickneys wid him."

Thea

I look at Beccah and I said, "I'm so sorry. I know how much it must hurt to tell all of this again."

"I nots hab to talk it to 'member. It be in meh. I jis't hab to shut muh eyes and thar dem be."

Beccah was quiet. Just as she was with Levi. I sat in the quiet and then she said, "Dat morning be a strange morning, but dat strange morning be long 'hind meh. Dis be a different morning and I be feel to put muh hand in sum flour. How 'bout yuh? Come wid meh to de cookhouse and keep meh company. I be mek sum biscuits. Thar be sum cured bacon thar as well. I tinks it be time fer sum bacon, eggs, biscuits, grits, and some smothered pork and gravy. Yuh hungry?"

I smiled and as Beccah worked her way out her rocker, she said, "It be good to hab sumbody to do sumting fer. It be ev'n better wen dat sumbody be kin. Yup, it be right nice."

We walked slowly to the cookhouse and there, over biscuits, smothered pork and gravy, grits, bacon, and biscuits, followed with some rich coffee, Beccah told meh about Fields' funeral and all the white men who came. She said she didn't expect to see Charlotte, so she didn't feel bad when she didn't come.

"Thea, it be right odd de way dem white mans be. Dem nots know'd how to be to Momma Pearl. It be clear dat Momma Pearl be standing as de mistress of de place. She gib Dada a fine funeral. Him white mans friends dem eat and drink and den dem go'd way. A few weeks afta Dada be dead, two of dem come and dem suh dat now Dada be dead, dat

Momma Pearl and meh hab to be off de land. Dat it nots be nigger land.

Momma Pearl, she suh, "Fields suh dat yuh be come right afta him be bury. Him suh dat if in yuh hab questions, as he be sure yuh wid hab, yuh is to tek dem questions to Pursival Breckenshaw."

Wen Momma Pearl suh dat, dem left. Dem nev'r come back and dats how it be dat I still be here. Dada mek a promise to Momma Pearl and him keep him promise. Dada dun tolt meh muh whole life dat dis land be Momma Pearl's land and dat thar nots be a man, white or nigger, dat can mek meh move off dis land. Dis be Fields' land. I be a Fields. Dis be Promise Land."

"So, Beccah, this is your land, all of it, this whole plantation? Fields willed it to you?"

Beccah looked at me and she smiled. She didn't answer me at first and then she said, "Dada brung Momma Pearl to dis plantation him suh sumway round 1832 or thar 'bouts. It now be 1940 sumting. I be here frum de day I born. I tinks if dem be able to mek meh leave dis place, dem be hab dun it."

Beccah answered and not quite, my questions. Then she gave me one of those toothless grins I'd come to expect and she went quiet. I'd also become accustomed to her moments of silence. I decided to sit still and let what she'd shared sink in. I needed it to sink it so that when I told it again, I would have it right.

The silence lingered on but it wasn't an uncomfortable silence; not at all.

Chapter 38

A Promise to Keep

It was Beccah who brought what I was thinking to the front. We'd come back from one of our walks, this time from her beloved weeping cherry trees and she said to me, "Thea, dese hab ben de best few weeks dat I be hab on dis big ole' plantation since Momma Pearl be gone. Dat, Momma Pearl, goin' home to de Lawd, be de hardest of muh sep'ration I been through. I nots know'd wat I be do if it nots be fer Pork Fat, him wife, Myrta, and dem gal pickneys, Elvira, Sophia, and Lizbet.

"Momma Pearl, she try to be brave afta Dada gone, but I can see dat her not full want to try. She tek to haunting, as Dada call it, now ev'n more dan 'fore. Her nots go'd to all dem places she be go wen Dada be living, dis time her go'd frum she house to Dada's house, and frum Dada's house to way him bury. It be thar, I tinks, dat Momma Pearl pick de cold up in she woman parts. Her go'd all de time and her cry on him grave. It not matter wat de weather be: if it rain, her go, if de sun be bright and high in de sky, she go'd, snow, sleek, high wind, low wind; nuffin' be able to keep Momma Pearl frum gine. I tinks, and I nots be sure, Thea, dat it be laying down in de wet dirt on him grave dat mek Momma Pearl sick.

"It not matter who suh wat. If Momma Pearl able to be up and about, den she gine to him grave and it be thar dat she stay. Sumtimes, Thea, Momma Pearl not eat frum morning to night. It git so dat dem lil' pickney, Elvira, Sophia, and Lizbet, be tek food to she right way she be, at him grave. Dem lil' pickney be sit right thar wid she and dem be eat wid she. It be dem dat be de ones to git she to come way wen it be gitting dark.

"I be see de wasting way of Momma Pearl and I not let one morning come and I nots go'd to she house and sumtimes I jis't stay way she be. If she be in Dada's house, den I stay in Dada's house. It jis't be Momma Pearl and meh dat be kin. I near fergit to tolt yuh dat much as Thessa be plan to stay wid meh ferev'r as she suh, her nev'r plan on love coming right here and tekking she way."

"So Thessa be married and gone?"

"Well, she marry and plan to stay here but it be she husband, Grigsby, he be one right handsome man. Him nots be full nigger; dat be plain to see 'cause him hair it nots be black nor brown. It be like ash but it not be gray. It be soft and not ev'n need a comb. Him be tall, wid brown eyes, big, big lips dat wen him smile, dem look happy. Him be a right pleasant man and him be sumting dat Thessa like; him be a talker. I tinks him talk she right off dis land. But him be a good man. It be clear dat him love she plenty. I tinks she be try to do like Momma Pearl."

"What do you mean by that, Beccah?"

Rebeccah

Dat gal a mine mek pickney after pickney. It be like she nots be de one hab dem to birf or wen she birf dem she nots feel no pain. I nots know'd fer sure how many she mek, but dem be plenty. Dada gib she plenty but it be Grigsby's pride dat tek dem frum here. Him suh to meh, "Momma Beccah, if in I nots tek Thessa and de pickney and move way frum here, I be fergit dat I be a mans. She be muh wife and dem be muh pickney and it be in muh place to mek way fer meh and muh wife. Fields, him be a good mans and I know'ds him love Thessa plenty, but him tekking ov'r muh place. I be de man in muh house; truth be it nots ev'n be muh house. Him gib we dat house. I hab to tek muh wife and go mek way fer all of we so she can see how much man I be. If de way be smooth, I be right proud. If de way be rough, I be wuk hard to mek it smooth but we hab to be moving on."

It bruk Momma Pearl and Dada's heart wen dem pack up and move on. Muh heart it hurt meh, but it not bruk. She be muh pickney and it be true dat I nots want she to go 'way frum meh, but I know'ds dat Grigsby be right. Him hab right to mek life fer him and him family. Dem be settle in Philadelphia and, yuh know'd, dat gal of mine mek more pickney in Philadelphia.

Thar be other folk here dat be kin to dem one another, but none of dem be kin to Momma Pearl, and meh so I be stick close to she.

I love Dada, but thar be no way to suh how I love Momma Pearl. If muh heart beat one beat den de next beat be fer Momma Pearl. She be muh joy. So I tek dat joy dat be in muh heart and I go'd to Momma Pearl one day wen she be jis't sitting by Dada's grave and I sit by she and I suh, "Momma Pearl, yuh tinks dat Dada be want yuh to come to way him be bury and dead?"

She look at meh and she not suh nuffin' but she eyes, dem full up wid tears. I suh, "Momma Pearl, I love Dada too. It be true dat I not love him like yuh, but yuh be all de kin dat I be hab and I nots know'd wat to do widout yuh.' De tears dem start to fall frum she eyes and den Momma Pearl suh, 'I nots know'd wat else to do. I dun gib up ev'ryting fer him. I let muh Momma Cornbread and Poppa Molasses go way frum meh jis't so I can be wid him. Wen muh Sara be lil' gal pickney and President Abraham Lincoln suh dat nigger not slave no more, I let muh Sara leave frum 'round meh and I stay wid him.

"I let de last piece of muh Harold Joe, Benjamin, go'd fer him. I tek nuffin' fer muhself; nuffin'. All muh soul be want be him. I mek him, muh old massa, muh morning and muh night. Muh waking and muh sleeping. I be a nigger and I mek a white man be ev'ryting in muh life, and yuh know'd sumting, Beccah, I nev'r one day tink on deff coming and tekking him frum meh."

Momma Pearl shrug she shoulders and she keep dem high fer a long time and wen dem come down, dem jis't drop and she hands jis't be thar and she suh, "Wen yuh Dada tolt yuh 'bout all dem wrong tings him dun meh wen I be jis't more dan a lil' pickney, and yuh be come to meh wid yuh questions, I be looks at yuh and I be tink dat in muh heart, I be most frighten. I look at yuh and I know'd dat yuh hab ev'n more questions now dat yuh Dada dun unburden himself and burden yuh. I see how yuh be look at meh, and I know'd dat yuh hab a more mix up head dan wen I be furst mix up over finding out in muh heart dat I be love muh massa, de same man dat treat me worse dan animal. I looks at yuh and I know'ds dat I not hab de words to help unmix yuh head.

"Yuh, de only pickney dat fix to stay here wid meh and I tinks dat I dun yuh wrong. I not leave frum round him and so yuh nots know'd dat thar be better dan here. I starts to feel in muh bones dat yuh be tinking dat I not do de best ting by not leaving wen freedom come, but I not know'ds how to tell yuh dat I be tink on Momma Cornbread and wat she suh 'bout freedom. Ev'n den, I not know'ds how to walk way frum him so I mek in muh mind to stay and see wat it be dat I truly feel fer him.

"And so, Beccah, I stay. I stay and tie muhself to him and him place and den I birf yuh after freedom come and pass and I tie yuh here to him and now him dead. I be old and soon dead and yuh gine be here by yuhself 'cause I tie yuh here and yuh nots know'd better. I fail yuh, Beccah. I fail yuh and I come out here and I be let him know'd dat muh love fer him dun tie all muh pickney to him."

I looks at Momma Pearl and I suh, "But yuh not tie all yuh pickney to dis place. Charlotte, Isham, Zack, Juba, Willie, Tuck, dem nots be tie to him; dem left and Poole him not stay so, Momma Pearl, yuh nots tie all yuh pickney to him. Eve and Lavina dem stay here 'cause dem mans be here. Yuh nots tie meh, Momma Pearl, I be here 'cause I love yuh and Dada. I nots be want more dan dat and now dat muh Levi be here, dis be way I wants to be so, Momma Pearl, yuh can fergive yuhself."

"Come, Momma Pearl. Come inside wid meh; dis be not wat Dada be want yuh to do."

Momma Pearl she look at meh and she suh, "Beccah, I nots know'd wat to do. I be tired. Deep in muh bones, I be so tired but I not sleep. I nots want to sleep 'cause if I sleep, den I nots be able to tink on him."

"Momma Pearl, dis be not good fer yuh. Member dat Dada suh him be glad dat I be stay here wid yuh? Den him be 'pecting meh to tek care of yuh, Momma Pearl, and I nots be able to do dat if in yuh be out here in de rain, sun, and snow. Come in now, Momma Pearl. I be fix a baff fer yuh and den I mek yuh sum supper. We be talk 'bout Dada if dat be wat yuh want to do, but yuh hab to come in. It not matter which house yuh want to be in, but come inside, Momma Pearl. I be come back wid yuh wen yuh want to talk to Dada but yuh got to promise meh dat wen I suh we hab to go bak to de house, dat yuh gine come. Yuh tinks yuh can do dat, Momma Pearl?"

Dat be how I git Momma Pearl to stop gine to Dada's grave and staying out thar all day and night, but by den it be too late. Momma be start wid de coughing. Den she get de ague and it not matter wat I do, she still shake. I ask Momma Pearl wat be in she box dat can mek she better. She tell meh and I try but it be clear dat Momma Pearl's spirit not be in getting better.

De coughing it change and wid every cough, it sound like Momma Pearl's chest be crack wide open. De cough it be wet sounding and she breaving it be hard. She try and try but it clear dat now de cold in she whole body. Den one day, Momma Pearl suh to meh, "Beccah, I be more tired in muh body dan I can ev'r member. I be de most sleepy I ev'r be. I want to rest but I nots want to rest 'till I go way yuh Dada be."

I suh, "But, Momma Pearl, yuh sick. Yuh been in yuh bed near a fortnight now. De weather it be change. Outside it be cold and last night thar be a heavy rain and de ground it be soak."

"Yuh promise meh a while back dat yuh be go'd wid meh ev'ry time I want to go way yuh Dada be. Yuh nots gine keep yuh promise, Beccah?"

I nots answer Momma Pearl. I tek muh time and I dress she. I puts nuff clothes on she and I puts she boots on. I help Momma Pearl to stand. Her hardly able to stand, but she got a fix spirit. I wait 'till she be able to mek de furst step. She mek de step and I mek one wid she. We walk like dat 'till we be outside.

Outside, de wind it be raw, de ground wet, and thar be leaves on de ground. De leaves hab de ground looking orange, gold, yellow, and brown all mix together; pretty but pretty as dem leaves be, I nots want she to slip on dem. It be fall. The sky, 'cause it be early morning, be gold, orange, and red. Thar be not one cloud in de sky. We walk slow 'way frum Momma Pearl's house, dat be way she suh she wants to spend de night, to way Dada be bury. We walk dat long slow walk and muh heart it be brek at de way Momma Pearl old, sick, and tired, and ev'n though she nots able to walk strong or long, she wants to be way him be.

We be walk a little ways and I nots know'd wat mek meh look back, but sumting suh fer meh to look bak at Momma Pearl's house and wen I do, it be de strangest ting I see. Thar be a crack in de orange sky and one streak of light, like lightning, but it not be lightning shining down on Momma Pearl's house. It not fulling de whole place wid light, jis't dat one streak and it mek de house look like it be cut in half. I blinks and it be gone. De whole sky go'd back to a orange like it be on fire. It mek de trees 'round Momma Pearl's house look like shadows and de branches like dem suhing dem cold 'cause dem naked. Thar be one tree in particular dat look de most lonesome. I feel de lonesome coming frum de tree and I wish dat de tree be hab friends and it nots jis't be thar by itself. Wen I be dun tink on dis muh brain suh, 'Beccah, it be jis't a tree dat be all it be a tree it not know'd it be lonesome.' I look on de lonesome tree fer a short spell den I let it and it lonesomeness leave muh head.

De walk to way Dada be tek fer ev'r but like anyting else, de walk it come to a end; we be thar. Momma Pearl she wants to bend down in de dirt but age, cold, and sick in she bones nots let she be able to mek it. Her stands thar and her cry 'cause her nots be able to touch de dirt. Her not talk or nuffin', jis't cry. Fer de furst time I ev'r know'd, I be gits angry wid Momma Pearl but I nots suh a word. I tinks to muhself, "But, Momma Pearl, yuh not hab to mek me dress yuh, and 'pose yuh to all dis cold and wet ground jis't so yuh can come here and cry. Yuh nots hab to be here to cry. Cry be cry. Yuh can stay in yuh warm house and cry."

We be stand thar fer a short spell den Momma Pearl point to a place in the graveyard way a big ole oak tree be and she suh, "Yuh see dem, Beccah?"

I suh, "See who, Momma Pearl? Who?"

She turn to meh and suh, "Momma Cornbread, Poppa Molasses, Lilly, Rose, Neala, and Nester. Dem be overthar. Yuh nots see dem?"

I looked way she be pointing and thar be nuffin'. Momma Pearl be looking at meh and I know'ds she know'ds dat I nots see dem so I nots lie. I suh, "Momma Pearl, I nots see dem. Thar be nuffin thar.

Den she suh, "Yuh nots see dem 'cause dem nots come fer yuh. Dem come fer meh. It be muh time, Beccah. It be muh time to go'd and be wid de Lawd."

I feel a pain in muh heart like de pain I feel wen Levi ask meh to hold him 'till him go'd frum muh bosom to de Lawd's bosom. Dis pain it be cutting and I know'ds dat it be 'cause Momma Pearl gine be leaving meh. I want to holler and cry out, but I know'ds dat if I start, dat Momma Pearl be worry 'bout meh so I fix it in muh heart to be strong. I suh, "Momma Pearl, it be time dat yuh go'd back in de house. It be too cold out here fer yuh to jis't stand here."

Momma Pearl, she mek to turn way frum Dada's grave and she suh, "I nots see Harold Joe. Harold Joe not come. Beccah, why yuh tink Harold Joe not come?"

I be tinking on wat to suh to Momma Pearl and 'fore I can suh a ting, she suh, "I know'd why him not come, Beccah. Him not come 'cause I grow'd to love Fields ov'r him. Him not want to be way Fields be."

Dis time Momma Pearl start to cry. It be a soft cry. It nots be like wen she cry fer Dada. We starts to walk back and I can see dat Momma Pearl be mighty weak 'cause every few steps now, she hab to stop and tek a deep breff, wipe she eyes and nose. We be go'd a few steps wen she suh, "Yuh dada be love meh, but I nots tink like Harold Joe love meh. Harold Joe be nigger so him gib meh him all. Him heart be all him hab. Him gib dat to meh; him whole heart. Him dead and not know'd dat we mek pickney."

Momma Pearl stop walking and she look at meh and suh, "Beccah, I be sad in muh heart right now. I wants to go'd to de cabin way Harold Joe be muh tek up wid man. It be sad, Beccah, dat most times I nots tink on Harold Joe. Harold Joe him be love meh a fierce kind of love. It be pure and I tek him pure love and I puts it out muh head and heart to mek room fer Fields and I be jis't tink on yuh dada."

De walk back tek long 'cause Momma Pearl be talk and walk and dem each tekking she breff. De walk it come to a end at de old cabin. We go'd in and it be cold in thar. I suh, "Momma Pearl, I nots be able to let yuh be in here. It be too cold fer yuh and time I build a fire in de hurf, yuh gine be chill to yuh bones and hab ague. Come wid meh to yuh house, Dada's house, or muh house, but I begs yuh to nots want to linger here. It jis't be too cold fer yuh, Momma Pearl."

Momma Pearl not fuss. She jis't look 'round and 'round and den she turn. I turn wid she and we walk back to she house. I tek Momma Pearl to she chambers and I mek she to sit up as I tek all dem tings frum off she. Wen Momma Pearl be fix in she bed, I be go to she cookhouse and fix she some broth. Wen I be dun, I comes back to she chambers and I help she to sit up. I tek muh time and feed she de broth. I look at Momma Pearl and I can see dat she be tired. I nots try to mek she tek more of de broth. I mek she comfortable bak in she bed and I sit in de chair. Soon, Momma Pearl fall to sleep. A quiet come over de house. It be like sumting I never feel 'fore now.

Den de light dat I be see wen I be outside wid Momma Pearl, it come back and dis time it be like it mek it way in she chambers. I look at de light dat full she chambers. It fall cross she bed and den it spread wide and bright. I look in de light and I be see dem, Momma Cornbread, Poppa Molasses, and thar be people dat I nots know'd and den I seen him; I know'd who him be though I nev'r seen him.

Him be a big nigger buck and next to him be a young nigger woman pickney. She be look like him, but she be look like Momma Pearl too. I know'd who dem be; dem be Harold Joe and Haroldetta or Sara as most time she be call. Dem be smiling. De beautifulest smiles ev'r. Den I look way dem be looking. Dem be looking at Momma Pearl.

I look at how de light hab Momma Pearl's bed bright like morning. Momma Pearl open she eyes and she look in de light, den she turn she head to meh and she be smile bright as de light dat be covering she. I smile bak at she. Momma Pearl, she turn she head bak to de light and be raise she hand up slow, like she nots able, but she keep raising it and wen she be hab it full raise up, she reach like she be fixing to gib sumting to sumbody. I look way she be hab she raised up hand and den, Thea, I be see de most beautifulest ting ev'r. De big nigger buck him reach him hands out to Momma Pearl de way yuh do wen yuh be reach to tek a lil pickney. Him hands dem come close to Momma Pearl, but him nots be able to touch Momma Pearl.

I feel dis ting in muh belly. It be like I want him to mek it; yuh know'ds, to touch Momma Pearl. Dis time de light nots go way in a blink. It fade de way daylight do to mek way fer night. Time it be done fade, dem gone, fade jis't de way de light fade way. Momma Pearl she turn she head and she look at meh and she smile 'gin. It be a smile dat be mek me tink on muh weeping cherry tree. She stay smiling like dat and den she tek a deep breff and in a voice dat be so soft, it mek meh tink 'bout snow falling, she suh, "Harold." And she tek a next breff and she suh, "Joe." Den she tek next breff and she suh, "Him." She get dat breff out and she tek a next one and she suh, "Come." She try hard fer de next breff and wen she git it, she suh, "Him." She be do de same as she do 'fore and she suh, "Still."

I wants to tell Momma Pearl not to try, but I can see in she face dat her want to suh wat be on she mind and she try harder fer de next breff; she gits it and she use it to suh, "Love." Wen she suh dat, de smile on she face it get bigger and den she suh, "Meh."

She smile a slow smile. I suh, Thea, dat it be slow 'cause it like she be tinking on sumting pretty and wat ev'r it be it mek de smile stay on she face. It tek it time to go 'way. It mek she face look happy and she eyes, though dem open but nots look like dem seeing no more, gets de same happy look and she be fix she gaze on meh and she tek a next breff and wid dat, she suh, "Love yuh, Bec."

Wen Momma Pearl suh dat, she eyes dem full wid tears and de happy it leave she face. I nots tek muh eyes frum Momma Pearl and I suh, "I be love yuh too, Momma Pearl. I love yuh, Momma Pearl." I keep on suhing dat 'till I be jis't whispering it. It be like I nots want to stop so I nots stop. Den I nots suh I love yuh. I suh, "Momma Pearl,

Momma Pearl." Den I nots suh Momma Pearl. I suh, "Momma." Jis't Momma. I suh dat ov'r and ov'r, "Momma."

De same slow smile, it mek it way bak over she face and she fix she eyes on meh. Den, real slow like how de light be fade frum over, she tek a breff and I watch as de breff it come bak out. It not need she help. It jis't come out. It come out slow. As de breff come out, she eyes dem start to shut. I stay looking in dem 'till dem be full shut. Wen de top lid meet wid de bottom lid, de tears come slow frum 'tween dem. I watch de tears as dem roll down she face. Dem come out ev'n slower. And 'cause she head be turn to meh, de tears come over she nose and dem join to mek one tear.

I nots move. I know'd dat Momma Pearl be gone. I wants to holler. I nots. It not feel right to holler and disturb she peace. I jis't sit way I be. I look 'pon she face. It be still got de smile on it. I cry; not loud, jis't soft. I sits thar and I cry and cry. I know'ds now dat I be a muddahless pickney ev'n though I be old. It nots matter. I nots got a muddah no more. She be right 'fore muh eyes, but she be gone.

I know'd dat Momma Pearl be gone on to de Lawd. She be gone on happy 'cause she know'd dat I seen him. Him love she furst so him come fer she. I feel a might sorry fer Dada, but sumting in muh heart suh, "Momma Pearl pick him wen she live, and den it be only fair dat de nigger mans dat love she furst git to spend ferev'r wid she."

Thea

"Thea, I tinks on dat fer a minute and muh heart it suh, "Thar be no love like de love 'tween a nigger mans and a nigger womans. It be stronger dan time."

"Why do you say that, Beccah?"

"I suh dat 'cause Dada, him be try him whole life to be de one dat Momma be love de best and I know'ds dat Momma be love Dada, but in de end, Dada's love not be able to reach frum de grave to Momma Pearl. It be a nigger mans love dat do dat. Him love reach frum way him be to Momma Pearl. Him nots come fer Momma Pearl. Him come fer him Milkweed. Momma Pearl nots be Momma Pearl wen she left meh. Wen she went to Harold Joe, she be Milkweed."

I looked at Beccah and even if I wanted to, I couldn't find a word, not one that could do justice to anything I was thinking. I said nothing and, looking at me as if she fully understood, she said, "I mek muh way frum de chair and I do fer Momma Pearl wat I be do fer Preacher Man. I tek him Bible and I puts it in she hand and I call out to de Lawd fer she. I ask de Lawd to open Him Pearly Gates and let Momma Pearl in. I tolt Him dat she be a good womans. Dat she love she pickney and dat she be only know'd how to love and dat ought to be 'nuff fer Him to let she in."

Rebeccah

Wen I suh dat on Preacher Man's Bible, I feel de tears as dem pile up and pile up in muh eyes and I tek muh head and I puts it on Momma Pearl's chest and I cry and cry. I want Momma Pearl to wrap she arms 'round meh and suh to meh wat I 'pose to do now dat dem all be gone. It be wen I suh gone dat it hit muh heart dat I nots hab no kin I can set muh eyes on. I wants to holler and beg de Lawd to change Him mind and let Momma Pearl come back to meh. But I know'ds dat de Lawd nev'r send bak nobody once Him let dem come through Him Pearly Gates. I cry 'till I feel thar be no more tears. Wen de tears stop, I keep muh head on she bosom and wid muh head thar, I know'd dat 'till Him call meh home, dat I be de one left to do wat she be do all de time; haunt dis place.

I nots know'd how long it be 'fore I tek muh head off she bosom, but I do and den I know'ds that I hab to fix she proper to send she onto de Lawd. I go to muh cook house and I get water frum de pot dat be hanging over de fire. I mek de warm water and I wash she. I use de fancy soap dat Dada be brung fer she frum one of him visits to town. Den I tek muh time and I dry Momma Pearl's skin. I put on all de lace tings dat Dada brung fer she ov'r time. Den I tek de finest dress dat Momma Pearl be hab, it be one dat Dada brung fer she. I look at de dress and I 'member de day dat Dada brung Momma Pearl dis big ole box. Him smiling and him suh, "Hurry, Pearl, open it! Open it! There's a special surprise in there for you!"

Momma Pearl open de box and it be full wid such fine tings dat I nev'r seen 'fore. Thar be a dress, hoops, petticoats, gloves, bonnet, boots, and lots and lots of pretty lace tings fer womans. Momma Pearl look at all dem fine tings and she suh, "Fields, wat yuh brung all dis fer? I nev'r go'd no way. Wat I be wanting big fancy ball dress fer, wid gloves, bonnet, boots, and all dese fine lace tings fer?"

Dada him look at Momma Pearl like him nots know'ds wat to suh and him suh, "Pearl, it's not a ball gown. It's a Walking Suit. I should have been bringing you such finery every time I went to town. Today I listened to my heart. So will you please, Pearl, just for me, put them on and come to dinner in them."

Momma Pearl put dem on and I 'most not know'd who she be wen she come to Dada's house. Her nots hab headwrap or bonnet on. She hair it be out. It jis't go'd on ferev'r. It be like it nots hab end. It hab end. It end jis't way Momma Pearl be near sit on it wen she sit down. Dada him be smile wen him see Momma Pearl. It be frum dat day dat ev'ry time Dada be in town, him brung sumting special fer Momma Pearl. Him brung fer meh too but Momma Pearl be wear wat him brung. I nev'r care fer suh tings.

I look at de dress and I know'd dat it be de one I gine put on Momma Pearl. I puts de dress on she and I ev'n put all dem silk tings dat be wid de dress. I tek some time to get dem all on 'cause Momma Pearl nots be able to help meh so I hab to do all de wuk by muhself; I nots mind. Wen I be dun, I tek de boots dat be de same color, it be a green dat be most black, and I puts dem on she foots and I tek muh time and I lace dem to de top; thar be plenty a hooks on dem boots. I tek de cloth frum Momma Pearl head. Her hair; it be long, long and white. It be beautiful next to she skin. I brush it fer she, a ting dat she be let meh do sumtimes frum de time I be lil' pickney. Wen I be dun brush she hair, I puts de bonnet on. It be a green but it be a green like leaf and I tie de silk ribbon under she neck. Wen I be dun, I sits in de chair near way she be and I looks on she. She be beautiful. I see de Seminole Indian dat be she Momma Cornbread. I see de Mandinka dat be she Poppa Molasses, and den I seen Momma Pearl; she be finally free frum all she hauntings.

I tinks how it be dat she birff so many pickney and now dat it be she day to go'd to de Lawd, I be de only pickney dat know'd. I be sorry fer dat. I tinks on Benjamin, Pearl Etta, Thessa, Bloss, and all dem pickney dat she watch come in dis world and how she loved dem and den I tinks on Dada. It be wen I tink on Dada dat I feel de most tearing in muh heart. Momma Pearl be gib up ev'ry chance at freedom jis't to stay and love him, and now she free but it not be de kind of free way she can go'd no way. She jis't be free now to go'd to de Lawd. In muh heart, I tinks dat it nots be right but it be wat she want so it not fer meh to tink dat it not be right. I also tink dat I nev'r know'd wat freedom be and I fix in muh heart to not let it be a bother to meh.

I be do like Momma Pearl, love be wat mek she stay here and it be love; muh love fer she and Dada dat mek meh stay. I be at peace. Thar be comfort in muh heart. Momma Pearl might'n never know'd freedom but she know'd love. I tinks dat love, de kind dat Momma Pearl hab frum Harold Joe, Dada, meh, and all we dat know'd she be better dan freedom. Momma Pearl be truly free. Love and de truth dat she be tolt meh mek she free. I know'ds dat I nots disturb she rest no more.

I let she stay in she bed 'till morning. I nots stay and look 'pon she all night and I nots tolt nobody dat Momma Pearl be dead. I tinks dat I ought to let Dada know'd furst. I tek muh time and I go'd to way Dada be and I tolt him. I suh, "Dada, I comes to let yuh know'ds dat Momma Pearl be gone on to be wid de Lawd. I know'd dat Momma Pearl suh dat in a dream, yuh suh dat wen it be she time, dat yuh gine come and tek she to de Lawd, but it not be yuh, Dada. I know'ds 'cause I seen dem dat come. It be she momma, she poppa and…"

"Thea, wen I git to way I be hab to tolt Dada dat it be Momma Pearl tek up wid man Harold Joe dat come fer she, I nots be able to suh dat to Dada. I tinks dat it be bruk him heart ev'n though him be dead."

Looking at Thea, muh eyes dem fill wid tears. "I know'ds dat thar be dem dat hate Dada 'cause him be a white mans and dat thar be at a time in him life wen him be Patroller, slave owner, and dat him dun plenty wrong tings to niggers, but him still be muh Dada. Thea, him be a good Dada to meh so I nots be able to tolt him dat Momma Pearl smile and stretch out she hand wen she see dat it be Harold Joe dat come to tek she wid him so I suh, 'And she pickney Sara.'

"I suh dat to Dada and it be de furst time I tolt Dada a lie. It nots be outright lie, it jis't be dat I not tolt him all. Wen I be dun tolt Dada dat Momma Pearl be gone, I go'd to muh house. Thar I cry and cry. I cry fer all dem dat gone and den I cry fer muhself 'cause I know'd dat now it be morning, I hab to send Momma Pearl on to be wid de Lawd.

"I wait 'till muh tears stop to way I be able to see way I hab to go. I go'd first to dem dat build boxes and I tolt dem dat I be needing one fer Momma Pearl. I den tolt dem to fix a hole next to Dada fer she. Elvira, Sophia, and Lizbet dem cry and cry, and I feel sorry fer dem. I tolt dem to go and see wat flowers dem can find. I not tinks dat thar be any fer dem to find 'cause it be cold but dem run off busy to look and so dem nots hab time fer all de crying.

"I den go'd back to Momma Pearl house.

"I be dun wid Momma Pearl wen I be hear Pork Fat. Him come to de house and him call frum de porch; de box it be ready. I suh fer dem to come way I be; bring de box to Momma Pearl bed chambers. I know'ds dat I nots be able to watch dem put Momma Pearl in de box so I walk frum she bed chambers and I go'd to she parlor. I wait, listenin' to hear de sound of de hammer dat gine tolt meh dat dem dun hab she in de box but de sound it not come. Wen time pass dat I be sure dat I ought to hear de hammering and de sound it not come, I go'd to Momma's bed chambers and thar she be. She be in de box and Pork Fat and dem be jis't standing thar.

"Pork Fat, him suh, 'Mistress Beccah, dis be mighty hard fer meh to do. I know'ds dat I hab to fix de top on and nail it shut, but in muh heart it nots feel right dat we must gib she to de dirt. Muh heart it be hurting meh. Please, Mistress Beccah, can I let Myrta and muh pickney Elvira, Sophia, and Lizbet, come suh farewell; dem love Mistress Pearl. Can I, Mistress Beccah?'

"I look 'pon Pork Fat and dem rest dat nots be able to shut Momma Pearl up in she box and I suh, 'Brung de box jis't as it be to de porch. Go'd and tolt dem dat want to come suh farewell dat I suh it be right fine wid meh.'

"Elvira, Sophia, and Lizbet dem come and dem cry and cry; Lawd, how dem cry. It be like she be dem muddah. In muh heart, it be like dem be de family dat not be able to be here to suh dem own farewell. Soon, all de niggers dat be on de place come. One by one, ev'ry body come. It be go'd on like dat fer a long time. Nigger after nigger; mans, womans, and pickney. Soon dem be all come. Dem crying and ev'ry one in dem own way suh dem farewell to Momma Pearl.

"Wen thar be nobody left to suh farewell, Pork Fat put de cover on de box and dem start to nail it shut. Each time de hammer hit de nail, I feel it in muh heart. I tink dat it be de same way fer Mary wen she hear dem Roman soldiers hammering she son to de cross. Time I be lost in muh tinking, dem dun hammering. Momma Pearl be shut up in de box. Pork Fat and a few of dem pick de box up frum de porch and ev'rybody dat jis't suh dem goodbyes to she walk slow wid meh and we walk 'till we by de hole dem dig next to Dada. It be meh, thar nots be a Preacher Man, dat send Momma Pearl off to be wid de Lawd. Myrta, she lead we in singing and soon it be done. Momma Pearl be put to rest next to Dada, but I know'ds in muh heart dat it jis't she body dat be next to Dada, 'cause she spirit gone off wid dem dat love she.

"Wen I git back to de house, it be quiet. I wants to holler but I nots holler. I know'ds dat if I start to holler, I be nev'r stop as thar be no one to stop meh. I cry fer Momma Pearl, Dada, and Levi. Wen I dun cry, I tink on how I be keep Dada's place up. I know'ds dat it be more dan I can do on muh own so I do wat Dada suh fer meh to do."

Thea

At this part of the telling, I felt like I could finally ask a question so I did. I said, "And what was that, Beccah?"

Beccah looked at me and, smiling, she said, "Nuffin'."

"Nothing?"

"Nuffin.' I nots hab to do nuffin' 'cause soon dem white mans be hurd dat Momma Pearl be dead and dem come to tek Dada's place frum meh. So I waits and jis't as Dada suh, dem come."

"So what did you do?"

"I gib dem wat Dada be gib meh to gib dem."

Smiling, I said, "And pray tell, Beccah, what did you give a bunch of Southern white men that made them go away and leave you here on this big old place where you were born a slave?"

"Thea, it be true I be born here, but I nots be born a slave. Dat be de difference. Slave not able to own nuffin' but I nots be slave. I be born free to womans dat be slave 'fore meh, but her nots be slave wen she birf meh. President Abraham Lincoln mek she free and Dada, well, him nev'r be slave so dat mek meh full free nigger wen I be born, and dat mek meh able to hab wat Dada suh fer meh to hab."

"And he said for you to have this place?"

Beccah gave me her biggest toothless smile ever and she suh, "It be mine 'till de day I dead."

"And after that?"

"Dada's will, yes him mek will. Him mek will jis't as him tolt Momma Pearl. Him mek will on de day dat dem marry wid O'Brien and Anakey as dem witness. Him hab O'Brien to write dat him be dem witness and dat dem be marry. Den Dada him write dat all him pickney, and him list all dem, be rightful heirs to him land and all dat be him own be dem own on de day of him death. But Dada him tink and him put in wat de white mans suh be a clause. Dat be it; a clause."

"What did the clause say?"

"It suh dat wen him last surviving child, and him hab dem put muh name; dem read it to meh wid Breckenshaw kin present, I nots be able to read or write. Him suh dat dem be read right wat be on de paper. Dat wen I dead, dat de place it go to safe-holding fer eight generations after meh and Charlotte or until the year twenty thirteen."

When Beccah said twenty thirteen, I had to repeat it. I asked, "Twenty thirteen? He didn't change his will all that time."

"Auntie Thea, that's more than fifty years from now. Ain't going be nobody living by then!"

Would you believe that was pretty much what I said to Rebeccah? For me, it was more than fifty years, it was more like sixty or seventy or even more years. I couldn't add up that quick. It just seemed like forever to me. My reaction didn't surprise Beccah. Smiling dat smile that I'd come to expect and like, she said, "Sumbody be living. Fer sure it not be meh or yuh; but thar be sumbody living in twenty thirteen. I nots tink de Lawd gine 'come bak 'fore dat. If him come back, den it not be matter wat Dada hab on him paper; de land will go to de Lawd den, it be him own in de first place."

"So what happens to all the land and the money the land will make in that time?"

"It be put in de bank and wen in twenty thirteen, a pickney can come and show'd dat dem be him eight generations, dem gine get all him plantations."

"Did you say plantations? I thought he only owned this one."

"Dat be wen I be lil' pickney, but Dada him tolt meh one day dat wen Isham, Zack, Juba, Tuck, and Willie be go'd back to Breckenshaw's plantation, him nots want dem to be beholding, dat be him word, beholding to Breckenshaw so him mek Breckenshaw an offer fer him plantation. Dada be own Breckenshaw's plantation so him sons, him heirs as him suh, be on dem own plantation. Dem nev'r know'd dat dem own it."

"They owned Breckenshaw's plantation and never knew?"

"Dada fix it dat dem tink dat Breckenshaw be jis't kind to dem and let dem hab wat dem want. Dat not be true. Breckenshaw be wuk fer dem and Dada fix it dat him and him kin be stay thar 'till dem dead, but afta dem dead, Isham and any of him sons dat still be thar be de ones dat suh wat to be dun."

"That's amazing. Did you ever see them again?"

"No. Dem still not forgive Dada but Dada be know'd frum

Breckenshaw how dem be. Him be let Momma Pearl know'd."

"You do know that after I leave, here I'm going there?"

"I know'ds. I nots be sure who be thar now if any of dem, but yuh go'd. If wen yuh git thar and yuh find dem, yuh be sure and tolt dem dat Momma Pearl never fergit dem and dat de love she hab fer dem when she birf dem nev'r left she heart; not fer one day."

I don't know why I said it, but I said, "Twenty thirteen…that's a long, long, way from now. Beccah, was Breckenshaw's the only plantation he bought?"

"No."

"No?" I asked Rebeccah.

"No. Him also buy Talbert, Litchfield, and Beauford."

"He did. Oh my God. I've heard of those plantations. Why did he buy them?"

"Dada suh him buy dem 'cause dem be places dat Momma Pearl be and if Momma Pearl not be thar, den her kin be thar, and him want dat Momma Pearl's kin be able to do wid dem wat dem want."

I smiled and, looking at Beccah, I said, "So are you the richest woman in all of Greenwood, South Carolina?"

Smiling back at me, Beccah said, "Nigger womans. I nots know'ds 'bout white womans but I know'ds dat thar nots be another nigger womans in, mayhaps all of America, dat be hab she name next to dat many plantations."

"So what about your children, can they come and claim what is yours?"

"Beccah gave me the same wonderful smile and said, "In twenty thirteen, anybody dat can prove dem be kin to meh and Charlotte can claim it"

"What about Isham and all the sons, can their future generations make a claim?"

"No. But Dada's will suh dat if muh kin want to share wat dem git, dem free to do so wid anybody dem feel like; kin or no kin but…"

I finished it for her. "…in twenty thirteen."

Chapter 39

Time to Pack up the Past

Andrea

"Auntie Thea looked from Auntie Noreen to me and she said, "I'm not sure which one of us felt the worse; Beccah or I. We sat on that porch for what seemed like an eternity. We had talked and eaten, and over several weeks and meals, we'd become family. I felt the burning of separation coming into my soul. I didn't know how I was going to walk away from her, yet like now, I know that I too must walk away from you all and I don't know how I'm goin' do that either when the time comes."

Auntie Noreen said, "Well it's not like you goin' be far. You goin' be round the corner and we, all of we, even little Miss Scream-Down-The-House can come and scream down your house. You are still staying here in Brooklyn for a few more months, no?"

"All that is up to Phillip. He may get up tomorrow morning and decide that he wants to be back in Virginia. We don't argue with Phillip. Wherever he wants to be, we go."

"It doesn't matter. Wherever you are; we goin' come. So, Thea, how much longer after Beccah told you the story did you stay with her?"

"I had planned on moving on a few days after she was done, but I didn't know how to get my heart to pack up and walk away and leave her so alone on that place. You should see it. In all my life, I've never seen so much land. Not even in a picture show. The land goes on and on and there are so many houses on it. There's the main plantation house; Fields' house, Milkweed's amazingly beautiful house. I say amazingly beautiful because of the way it's set in the woods. One minute you are going about your business in these peaceful woods, then the land starts to clear. It clears a little bit more and you see that there's a track. You get curious to see where the track is going to lead you and the next thing you know…the trees fall back. There's a clearing and just like that, a house. A beautiful house with lots of detail. It's two levels but looks like one. The porch goes around the whole bottom floor, but none of that is as beautiful to me as the trees. The trees make you want to whisper. I say that because they were close together in a protective way around the house; sort of like they were keeping out the world's prying eyes.

"Then there was Eve and Lavina's houses, nice, but none could compare to Milkweed's house. Not Sara's, O'Brien's, or even Beccah's house. Beccah's house was simple on the outside, but inside it had a true warm feeling. One thing for sure, when you entered any of those houses, you felt the love. It was leaving all that love that was tugging at me.

"Beccah, God bless her heart, said to me, 'Thea, yuh tolt meh wen yuh come dat yuh time, it be measured and dat yuh come to get all de bits and pieces so dat yuh can go'd and tolt muh kin folk. If yuh be sit here, den yuh not be able to do wat yuh set out to do. So yuh hab to go 'way frum meh so yuh can go'd gets de rest. Yuh suh dat yuh wants to mek yuh way to Breckenshaw's. I nots know'd what yuh gine find wen yuh git thar but yuh ought to be mekking yuh way.

"'I glad dat de Lawd bless dese two old eyes to set 'pon yuh. Yuh dun muh heart happy to hab yuh here wid meh all dis time. It be a blessing to muh soul dat kin come 'round to see 'bout meh. I be glad to know'd dat on Charlotte's side, thar be five generations already. Thar still be plenty time to go 'fore twenty thirteen and it look like Dada be git him wish; eight generations removed frum him.

"'So, Thea, ev'n though I be glad fer yuh company, I wants yuh to go on see what yuh can learn 'bout muh bruddahs. I not bless muh eyes on dem since I be a lil' pickney, and I know'ds dat it pained Momma Pearl dat dem nots be able to brung demself to be near Dada, and so dem nots be near Momma Pearl. If yuh git thar and de Lawd mek it so dat ev'n one of dem be thar, yuh let him know'd dat Dada be love dem. I be ask yuh one ting, Thea.'

"What's that, Beccah?"

"That yuh not tolt dem dat Dada be buy Breckenshaw's plantation. Him nev'r want dem to know'd. Him suh dat him feel if dem know'd, dat dem not stay thar and den him not know'd way dem be. Knowing dat dem be thar be nuff fer Dada.'

"I looked at Beccah and she smiled. I understood the smile. In the smile she was saying she was going to miss me too. I smiled broader and said, 'I promise you, Beccah. I'll keep that to my heart. You have been very kind to me. I won't betray your trust.'

"I left later that day."

"Did you ever see her again?" Auntie Noreen asked.

"No."

"No?"

"I was gone about two months and when I returned, I was told by the person hired to keep the place that she'd died shortly after I left. I told him who I was and asked him if I could visit her grave."

"Did he let you?"

"Yes. I visited Beccah, Milkweed, Levi, Fields, Sara, Lilly, Preacher Man, Christobell, and yes, even Olivia's graves. They were all there just as Beccah had told me; all waiting for twenty thirteen when the eighth generation of Fields will come to claim the place and visit them. I smiled and wished I could be there to see that. I wondered also what the eight generations of Fields would look like. How far away from white would they be?"

Book Five

Isham Fields Breckenshaw

A Time to Gather

Chapter 40

A Father's Sin Too Unpardonable

Thea

As agreed, Bernard and Phillip Junior made their way to Cousin Law's house to meet me at the end of my almost-two months visit at Fields Plantation. I'd already said my goodbyes to Beccah with promises, of course, and I meant them, to come back soon to visit her.

It was a tearful goodbye. Something in the way Beccah said goodbye to me felt like it was the kind of goodbye that meant we wouldn't be seeing each other again. That pained me deeply. But I understood. She did not, as I thought she would, come to the car to say goodbye. She sat on the porch and it was only when the car was fully out the drive way and Law had made the turn to take us away from the house did she stand, hold onto the porch railing, and ever so slowly, raise her hand up and wave. I was waving and crying as if I'd known Beccah my whole life and, come to think about it, I'd first heard about Beccah back in '29 so in a way I had known her a long, long time.

"I had been back at Law's for about three days when they came. This time, Phillip Senior came for the ride. He had missed me, he said, and since I was taking to running away in my old age, he wanted to see where I was running off to.

I didn't go off to Breckenshaw's plantation right away. We stayed in Greenwood long enough for Law to make the connections at Breckenshaw and then it was time for me to go and get the final pieces. I felt as if I was embarking on finding the Holy Grail. It wasn't as important to some, but what it meant to me it had the same level of importance; it was the same thing: a quest to unearth the truth.

I arrived at Breckenshaw's plantation on a Friday afternoon. Summer was drawing to a close and so I felt a sense of urgency. I wanted to be done and on my way back to Virginia before Phillip felt he needed me. I don't know why but I felt that I wouldn't be there as long. A part of me felt that I would talk to whoever was here, get the few pieces that Beccah hadn't told me, and then, just like that, I would be on my way back to Virginia and Phillip and when he was settled or ready to travel, I would be on my way to Brooklyn to tell you what I'd learned. To me, it was that simple but as you know, nothing is ever really that simple.

Just like at Fields Plantation, I had to find out if there was anyone there on my list. I knew from Aunt Bess and Beccah that Isham and Willie had returned there, but she wasn't sure if they were still there, as there hadn't been any contact for years. She had said that at some point, and she's not sure when, but because Milkweed had been taking the sep'ration so hard, Fields had gone there hoping, against hope and commonsense, they would talk to him. He wanted to make them understand and to come see their mother.

They never knew what he wanted as they'd refused to be near him, far less hear what he had so say, so I was feeling around in the dark to see if they were there. If neither were there, I was willing to find anyone who might remember them. After all, it had been almost, seventy, if not more years since Fields' sons had gone back. As I thought about it, I realized that I might very well be on a chase that would end nowhere. At best, I could hope to find a great-great-grand-child, but a son of Fields alive? Impossible. They were long–lifers, it's true, but this long? I decided to go anyway. I was sure I would find someone that knew someone that knew or had heard something. I didn't have that many more missing pieces and I needed for someone to know something. I'd come too far to have a few pieces still scattered around. It was time to bring all these pieces from the past together and into the future.

As I approached, a beautiful girl of about eighteen to twenty came to me. She was smiling. In that smile, I saw Rebeccah and Gina Pearl. I was on the right path. This young lady had a streak of Fields in her.

"Good afternoon. Do you live here?"

"Yes, ma'am. You be looking fer somebody in particular?"

I smiled and said, "A few weeks ago, I would have said Isham Breckenshaw or Isham Fields, or Willie Breckenshaw or Willie Fields, but now I'm just looking for someone that might have known any of them."

The young lady smiled and said, "My name's Neala Breckenshaw."

I smiled a smile of relief. "My name is Mrs. Thea Fillmore. I'm your kin. Is there someone I can speak to; your mother or father perhaps? I'm just trying to find someone that might have known him; I'm sorry, I mean Isham Breckenshaw."

When I said that, Neala looked at me with an odd, almost quizzical look on her face and then she said, "Known him? You not come to see him?"

I stopped right where I was and I asked, "Pardon me, did you just ask me if I didn't come to see him? Is he here?"

Smiling, she answered, "Poppa be always here. He never goes anywhere."

When she said that, I became overly excited. I couldn't believe it. In a short space of less than three months, I was going to be meeting another one of Fields' and Milkweed's children and not just any one, but their first; the one Aunt Bess had talked about.

"Can I meet him, speak to him? Will that be ok; I mean talk to him."

Looking at me, she said, "That be up to Poppa. We never know from one day to the next what Poppa be feel like doing."

"I hope today he will feel like a visitor."

With the same beautiful smile, she said, "Please follow me. I will go and get my father. He's out back with the horses."

Walking down the long drive, I was amazed at how similar, yet different the two plantations were. On Fields' plantation, the trees stood tall, majestic, and almost commanding. They were near the house, but not hiding it. The only trees that were really close to any house were the trees near Milkweed's house. They seemed to almost want to shroud her house in secrecy. Here, however, the trees came close together, heads bowed and branches wrapped together, like family. It made me wonder if this is what Fields' and Milkweed's five sons found here on this plantation: family.

As we approached the house, I expected Neala to approach the front of the house since Beccah had told me that the house belonged to Fields. She didn't, she walked past the house and kept on walking a little further, but not much. She came to stop in front of a smaller, but very beautiful house and she said, "Come. I'll see if Father is here or out by the horses."

When she said that, it dawned on me that although the two plantations were no more than an hour's drive from each other, she spoke quite differently to Beccah. A part of me wanted to ask her about that and another part said, "Can you be any more insulting? You sound like one of those white people you used to work for so many years ago, who were surprised you knew a knife from a fork, a spoon from a cup and, most surprisingly, that you didn't much care for watermelon."

The house inside was beautiful. It reminded me of Milkweed's, in a way. I stopped on the porch and, like all porches it had rockers, boxes that I imagined would also be for sitting, flowering plants in buckets, a sleeping dog that upon the sound of my feet on the porch opened his eyes, and it's my guess he didn't feel like company or my company because he soon got up and walked lazily away.

As I stood there, I tried to imagine what Isham could look like. He had to be extremely old and, in my mind, too feeble to make it to where I was. A part of me prepared to follow Neala into a bedroom in some part of the house where I would see a propped-up, withering man. Lost in deep thought, I didn't hear her as she returned.

"Excuse me, ma'am, Poppa says he goin' be wid you in a few, and for you to have a sit down."

I looked and Neala was standing with a small child in her arms. My heart jumped. She was holding Beccah: a child that was a lot Seminole, a bit Mandinka, and a whole lot Fields. The child was beautiful and so fat. There were dimples everywhere.

I smiled and said, "That's ok, I can wait. I know no one was expecting me. Your baby?"

"Yes."

"Boy?"

"Yes. His name is Willie. Poppa said to call him that."

"Poppa?"

"Great-great-great-great-grandfather Isham. I call him Poppa too."

Neala and I stood there making small talk and getting acquainted then I heard footsteps. It was her father. As he stepped onto the porch, I smiled. If the man before me was Negro, then Fields was Negro. The man was at first glance as white a man as a man could be. I halfway expected him to say he was one of Breckenshaw's grand or great-grandchildren but as soon as the baby saw him, he started to babble.

Neala said, "Poppa, this here is Mrs. Philmore. She come, she said, at first to hear ‘bout Poppa. She didn’t know that Poppa was still here.”

“Hello. A pleasure to meet you. You are kin?”

“Yes. On your father’s side.”

Smiling a smile that matched Neala, he said, “He’s not my father. He’s my great-grandfather. I’m also called Isham; after him.”

Then he said something that amazed me and took my breath away. “This morning when he woke, Poppa said, ‘De lady, way she be?’ Of course, I hab to thinking that Poppa’s mind be wandering and he was off in some long-ago day. I was fixing to walk away and not say nothing when he said, ‘De lady? De one wid Beccah?’ That got me to stop ‘cause it be so long since Poppa mention his sister, Beccah. Truth be told, it be so many years that for a minute I had to get my head to ‘member who Beccah was. Then when he said, ‘Beccah, Beccah, muh sister ov’r thar way him be.’ I knew fer sure who he was talking ‘bout, but a lady? I had no idea. So I said, ‘Poppa, a lady? What lady?’ He said, ‘De one dat Momma suh be coming.’

When he said that, I near peed myself. There was so much about this family that was a mystery but that part that there with everybody seeing into the future was unnerving. Beccah had it. Milkweed had it, and now I was hearing that Isham had it and was expecting me. According to his schedule, it would appear I was a bit late. I looked at this Isham and said, “Tell him that I’m here.” Smiling, I added, “And tell him I’m sorry I’m late.”

He smiled back at me and said, “If it’s all right with you, I’ll go tell him you are here. He was expecting a lady and since you showed up; then it must be you. Wait and let me see if he wants to come out here and sit fer a spell or if he be wants you to come sit where he be.”

“He’s able to come out here?”

This Isham looked at me as if I was addled in the brain and said, “If we would let him, he would still try to shoe a horse.”

When Isham said, ‘shoe a horse’, my mind went to Fields and his broken mangled foot stuck in his boot and the way they had to cut the sole of the boot off just as if he’d been a horse that needed re-shoeing.

“Neala, give me Willie and go bring the lady something to take the dust off her throat.”

Neala handed him the baby and walked into the house. In a few minutes she was back with a jug of lemonade and some glasses on a tray. She poured me a glass of lemonade, which I took almost too quickly, not realizing how thirsty I was. As I sipped and waited, I wondered what Isham, this man I'd first heard of back in 1929, could possibly look like. My mind also went to Aunt Bess and I wondered if she hadn't been killed, would she have gotten around to telling me that he was still alive.

I didn't have long to wonder 'cause soon the door opened and young Isham came through the door. He was helping an older version of himself through the door. I had no doubt what the young Isham would look like when he aged. As the older Isham made it through the door, he smiled. Even at his age, it was disarming. I looked at him and he was nothing like I'd imagined. It's true that Aunt Bess had said that he was white, and even Beccah had mentioned that he was white, but I still wasn't prepared for how white. There was nothing Negro about him. He also looked stronger than I'd expected.

Truth is, I didn't expect him to be walking and if he were, then I imagined that he would be bent almost to the ground. He wasn't. He was holding onto the arm of his great-grandson and there wasn't a cane in sight; not my sight anyway. Slowly, on the arm of his younger self, he came towards where I was standing. When he was within arm's length of me they stopped.

He said, "Know'd yuh be coming. Yup; seen yuh mekking yuh way ov'r here. Yuh been wid Beccah. Yup. Seen dat too. Beccah, she gone on now. She be jis't wait fer yuh same way I wait fer yuh, and now yuh be here. Yuh brung peace wid yuh. Yuh is a good woman. Sit. Sit."

It was only when young Isham guided him to the chair that I realized the older Isham had difficulty seeing. He wasn't blind; just didn't see altogether well.

"Good day, Isham. A pleasure to finally meet you. My name is Thea Fillmore and I'm a distant cousin from Virginia."

His sense of humor threw me when he said, "No need fer dat formality; been dun meet 'fore now. Jis't been waiting fer yuh to show up. Glad dat yuh not mek meh wait ferev'r; not got ferev'r, yuh know'd. De Lawd, Him count muh days up and now Him counting dem down. De up be one ting and de down, it be sumting else. Thar be no joy in de down. De down it tek frum yuh all it can 'fore yuh gone." Laughing, he added, "I tinks de down nots want yuh to tek nuffin' back wid yuh to de Lawd; well nuffin' dats be wukking. Now, wat it be dat yuh come to know'd?"

I smiled inwardly and his joke; surprised at his directness. I knew then that he wasn't about to waste time telling me what he had to.

Andrea

"Auntie Thea, other than not being able to see well, what did he look like?"

"Like I said, if not for the fact that Aunt Bess and Beccah had prepared me for what he looked like, I would have passed him on the street and all I would have seen was a white man. He was tall, even at his age, and with the roundness of age sitting on his shoulders, which by the way had the hair that was down the middle of his back, yes, his hair was down his back and in the style of the Indians. It was gray now, but by looking at the younger Isham, you could tell the shade of red it used to be. His eyes, Father forgive me, and Noreen or Drea, no disrespect, but Jesus Christ, I never, in my born days seen eyes that were so beautiful. They looked like bits of sky floating around on a cloud. Age had taken away a bit of his sight but the blue, it let stay. His nose was like a nose on any white man and his lips; there was nothing Negro about them. He was, and I mean this, other than the younger Isham, the whitest Negroes I'd seen in forever."

Without really thinking about it, I said, "So even if he wanted to, he couldn't really get away from Fields 'cause each time he saw himself, he saw Fields."

Auntie Noreen said, "It's not always children that want to get away from their parents. Sometimes, its mothers that want to get away from the fathers of their children and vice versa."

When Auntie Noreen said that, I knew she was talking about me, Hamilton, and Leela. I said nothing.

Auntie Thea looked at me and then at Leela, and she said, "Sometimes the answer comes from places we don't expect. I done learn not to look for all the answers. Those deep personal answers God unfolds in His time. Remember; there's a time for everything and a purpose for everything under the heavens. This God that we are serving has His own way and His own time. I've learned to lean not to my own understanding but to lean on Him and He will lead and direct my path. Lean on Him. Learn to lean on Him and one of these days, I may long be dust or whatever we turn into when we go back to Him and you goin' remember this moment. Don't try so hard to figure it all out. Let the Lord be your guide; day by day, Drea, day by day."

I said nothing. There was nothing for me to say. A little bit of silence lingered and then Auntie Thea said, "I got the same feeling from Isham that I got from Beccah. He'd been waiting and he wanted to share."

"Was he ready?"

"He was ready. And since, as he said, he was waiting on me, I didn't have to do a whole lot of explaining who I was. I also knew that I wouldn't be with him for weeks. Something told me that for what was on his mind, I would have it before nightfall. Phillip and Bernard had said that they would come back for me in a few hours. I guess they also felt that I wouldn't be 'moving' in as they'd call it when I stayed with Beccah.

"You see, with Beccah I started out making daily trips and one day, she said, 'Tell 'em, yuh young 'uns, dat thar be plenty space here fer yuh. Dem need not be coming to fetch yuh like dis. Yuh stay and dem can come fer yuh in a fortnight.' And that's how it was. I visited for a fortnight. Went home and came back, but towards the last, I just stayed with her, moved in and was as comfortable as I'd ever been anywhere.

"Isham looked at me and he said, 'It be a hard ting. Walking 'way frum Momma dat day. It near bruk muh heart but if I nots be walk 'way frum Momma den, I be kilt him. It be plain to meh dat I be hab hate in muh heart fer him, but I be not know'ds how much it be 'till I be see him look at Momma. Wen I seen him look at Momma, I be know'ds dat him be a hateful, evil white mans; de worse kind of white mans.

"'Him solt meh, Willie, Zack, Juba, and Tuck; dat be de kind of white mans him be. Solt 'way pickney, him pickney, frum dem muddah. Dat be de worse a white mans can do to a nigger womans and dem pickney be him own and she own. I nev'r stop, yuh know'ds, frum letting de hate grow'd in muh heart fer him; ev'n now. I be sure him dead. If him not dead, and I nots know'd how him nots be, den him ought to be sum way in de land of dem dat suffer and only know'd pain.'"

"Without realizing it, I spoke up. "Wow! He was waiting all right. All that time he had Fields up in his mind?"

"Auntie Noreen said, "Hate like that takes a lot to keep it going. In order to keep it going, you have to stay remembering how you think the person has done you wrong. Look at Isham, he was just over a hundred years and his hate for Fields was still so raw in his soul, I'm sure that's what kept him living. If you don't let hate go, it will be with you like a second skin and the kind of skin that don't let other things come in."

"Again, I felt that Auntie Noreen was talking about Hamilton.

"I said nothing. I kept my eyes on Leela, who was fast asleep in my arms. She was gaining weight and filling out. I felt her as she breathed in and out and then to my surprise, she smiled in her sleep. It made me smile. I felt eyes upon me and when I looked up, Auntie Noreen was looking at me. She was also smiling.

"Auntie Thea looked from Leela to me, to Auntie Noreen, and then she said, "Yup, hate is a funny thing. It never makes you laugh though; it never gets that funny. Isham went on with his story.

Isham

"I be come back here and wuk. I not wuk like other niggers be wuk, but I wuk. I wuk hard to mek meh not tink on Momma. Wen we be able to go'd bak, we go'd den tings get worse fer niggers and dem be pick yuh off de road and yuh be prisoner. If yuh be lucky, yuh git to see dem yuh love one more time, but if yuh nots be lucky, den dem dat yuh be love nev'r see yuh 'gain. I mek in muh heart to not tink on Momma.

It not be de same fer dem: Tuck, Juba, Zack, and Willie. Dem keep wanting to go'd and it be Massa Breckenshaw dat tol't we how it be. Dem mek in dem minds dat if dem nots be able to go'd see Momma, den dem nots want to be here and jis't like we come bak, dem leave. Tuck, Zack, and Juba, dem be go'd up North. Dem tinks dat since dem be looks like white mans, den dem gine up North and be white mans.

"It be meh here fer a while by muhself and den one day, jis't like I be know'd yuh coming, I feel in muh bones dat Willie be about. I jis't stop wat I be doin' wid de horses and I start to walk to way I feel him be.

"I get to de top of de long road, de one dat brung yuh here, and I see a shape and I nots know'd wat it be but I gets a trembling in muh belly. De furst ting muh head suh be fer meh to be nots be thar wen de shape mek it to way I be. But sumting suh dat de shape hab sumting to do wid meh and dat I best be fixing muhself fer watev'r de shape bringing to meh. I wait. De waiting be hard. I wants to go to way de shape be, but I know'ds I better. I still be nigger and white mans still be hating nigger. So I fix to wait. I nots be waiting long 'till de shape come closer and I can mek out dat it be a niggers mans. It not be jis't any nigger mans; it be Willie. Now I know'ds why I gets de trembling in muh belly. If Willie be near way I be, den dat mean dat like meh, Zack, Tuck, Zuba, dat him dun fix in him heart dat him best be not way Massa Fields be.

De trembling in muh belly rise and it mek meh 'member wen I tolt

Momma 'bout de hate I feel in muh belly fer Massa Fields. I stand way I be and I see Momma 'gain jis't de way she be wen she be wanting meh to feel love in muh heart fer him. It be sumting dat I nots be able to do den and ev'n now thar be no love in muh heart fer him. Truth be tolt, I nots ev'n hab like in meh fer him; I nots hab nuffin' fer him but hate. I nots wants to talk 'but dat right now. I wants to talk 'bout wen I seen Willie. Yup; de shape it be Willie. I wants to run to way him be, but sumting inside of meh head suh, 'Wait.' I fix it in muh heart to wait. De wait it not be dat long. Willie, him fix to wave wen him seen meh and den him start to run to meh. Muh foots dem move on dem own and next ting I know'd, I be running to way him be. We mek a fine a pair. Two big nigger mans running to dem one another.

Thea

"When he said, 'two big nigger mans', I wanted to say to him, 'Isham, have you ever seen yourself? There's nothing nigger about you.' I didn't of course. Actually, I was so wrapped up in what he was saying that I was hardly breathing."

Isham

Willie him be calling muh name. Willie him be de one dat most favor Momma so wen I be running to him, I feel like I be running to Momma. I mek it to way him be and him stop. I be look at him and I be right surprise to see dat him sobbing. Muh heart it be start to race and beat all over muh chest. I suh, "Momma?"

Him suh, "Be wid him. She be way she wants to be."

"But why yuh be here now? I never fix in muh heart dat I be set muh eyes on yuh here at Massa Breckenshaw's ev'r again.

"I also fix in muh heart dat I nev'r come bak here, but Momma, she suh fer meh to come. It be Momma who suh, 'Willie, yuh go 'way frum here.'

"Momma suh fer yuh to go 'way frum she, Beccah, Poole, Eve, Lavina, and Charlotte? Momma send yuh way frum thar?"

"Yes. Momma, she come and she suh, 'Willie, I nots want yuh to go 'way frum meh, but I be see de hate yuh hab in yuh heart fer Fields and I nots want yuh to get yuhself kilt, so yuh go, yuh go way Isham, Zack, Tuck, and Juba be. Yuh go.'

Willie him stop frum talking and dat big nigger mans him bend at him waist and him put him hands on him knees. Him fix to holler and holler. Him suh through him hollering, "Momma, Momma. She be 'lone wid him. She 'lone wid him. She 'lone…"

I know'ds dat Willie's heart be bruk 'cause him be wid Momma more time 'fore we be solt off and him grow'd to man still wanting sumbody to call Momma. Becky, de nigger womans dat be muddah to we, try fer him to tink on she as him muddah but him nev'r. Him de one dat suh to she wen him be near man pickney, 'Yuh nots be muh muddah. I not's know'd way muh muddah, be but muh heart it suh she breaving sum place and wen freedom come fer nigger, I gine find she.'

Now he be here and him sobbing 'cause him find we muddah, and it be de hate dat him hab fer de white mans dat be we faddah put sep'ration 'tween we again. I puts muh hand on him back and it like muh hand heavy fer him 'cause him fall to him knees. I know'ds muh hand heavy, but it nots be heavy 'nuff to mek a big nigger mans fall to him knees. Him fall to him knees 'cause him hab a bruk heart. Bruk heart nigger mans be bruk spirit nigger mans. Wen nigger mans' spirit be bruk, a feather on him head can mek him fall to him knees and keep him thar.

All nigger mans know'ds dis so I suh, "Willie, yuh not de only one of she pickney dat hab to mek choice. I mek choice. Juba him mek choice. Zack and Tuck mek choice so yuh stands on yuh foots like yuh be de man pickney dat yuh muddah hab to face and send frum she. Yuh tinks it be hard fer jis't yuh? I be de furst one solt way so I be gone frum she de longest."

Wen I suh dat, Willie holler a strange kind of holler and him suh, "Dat not be why I be hollering. It be Momma. I feels a mighty pulling pain in muh belly. It be like if I open muh mout, I can jis't pour out muh holler in dis dirt."

Den him suh, "Help meh, Isham, help meh."

I bends and I picks him up. Him rise up like dead mans, heavy. We walks 'cross de field. I be mighty glad to see him, but muh heart it be heavy to know'd dat none of we be able to stands way Fields be. Willie, him nots talking as we walk. Ev'n though him dun wid him crying, I feels de heaviness in him spirit. Him ev'n walk heavy.

At de gate, him suh, "Juba, Zack, and Tuck, dem be well?"

"Dem be well. Juba, him Salley birf pickney soon after him jump de broom."

Willie, him stop and him suh, "Juba jump de broom wid Salley who come up frum de Low Country soon after freedom come? Wat 'bout Zack, him jump de broom too?"

I stop frum walking and I turn to him and I suh, "Him not stay. Him suh him want real freedom."

"Him be gone?"

"Him nots jis't be gone. It be him and Tuck. Dem gone up North. Dem gone up North to be white mans."

Willie, him suh, "White mans? But dem be nigger mans?"

"Dem be nigger mans here, but up North dem can be white mans."

"Dat be safe?"

"It be safe if dem wives not mek nigger pickney fer dem?"

"Way dem git money frum to go up North?"

"Massa Breckenshaw, him gib dem clothes, coach, money, and driver."

"Driver?"

I suh, "Him gib dem driver and a right fancy coach wid fine horses. Dem be look like dem be plantation owners wen dem left. I cry fer dem, but I nots want to go wid dem and be a white mans up North. I nev'r wants to be white mans. I be nigger mans and I be staying nigger mans 'till de day de good Lawd calls meh to him."

Andrea

"Thea, Drea, I'm going to stop there until tomorrow. I feel more than a mite tired so, Drea, be a sweetheart and call one of those sons of mine to come and get me."

I got up and as I'd been doing for weeks, I called Auntie Thea's house and told Cousin Bernard that Auntie Thea was ready to come home.

Chapter 41

Frum Painful Place to Peace

One day, I woke and the same feeling I had when I woke that first morning that Auntie Thea was going to start telling me our history came over me again. This time though, the feeling was just a little different. It wasn't excitement that filled me. It was sadness. I knew without counting the days or weeks that had gone by that Auntie Thea was reaching the end of her telling, and with her talking 'bout my great-great-great-great-grand Uncle Isham it was putting a heavy weight on my heart. I didn't want her to get there, but I'd also noticed that she was getting tired a lot lately.

So tired that Auntie Noreen and I would some days go and visit her and Uncle Philip over on MacDonough Street. Visiting her was good for all of us. She and Auntie Noreen were forging a friendship; you could tell from the way they were always so glad to see each other. There was a bigger garden for Uncle Neal to sit in with Leela and let the sun warm her skin as he and Cousin Philip talked politics. Uncle Neal didn't always sit outside with Leela. On the days we visited and Uncle Philip was having a good day, he, Cousin Philip, and Cousin Bernard got into some serious political discussions and having a baby in his lap would only get in the way of him truly expressing himself; that meant standing up when he got heated and slapping his hand on anything nearby. This was strange because Uncle Neal was never one for loud discussions; well that was until he became involved in *The Struggle*; as he called it.

I got showered and dressed slowly. I didn't want to go downstairs, but if Auntie Thea was to get on with the telling of her story, I'd better get myself downstairs. I washed and fed Leela and then I headed downstairs. I didn't have long to wait for Auntie Thea to come over.

As if she'd left a note on the table as to where to begin when she came in, she picked up right where she'd left off last night. With tea in hand and cake on the coffee table she started.

Thea

Isham had talked for quite some time or so it felt to me when Neala came and said, "Poppa, do you want me to bring something for you to eat?"

Isham looked at where she was but not directly at her and she said, "Yuh ought to ask muh new kin here too.' He stopped and turned his head to me and with a slight grin he said, 'Wat yuh name be again?"

I said, "Thea. It's Thea."

"Yes. Yes. Thea. Neala, dat be de right way. Yuh ask Cousin Thea here wat it be dat she want. Den I be hab watev'r Cousin Thea be hab."

I didn't right know what he could eat so I decided to play it safe. I said, "Neala, surprise me. Whatever you bring, I'm sure will be just fine for your Poppa and me."

When I said that, Isham laughed and said, "Lawd, Lawd, if yuh nots sound like one of dem white mistresses."

I laughed because I remember when Aunt Bess had said the same thing to me once. As we waited on Neala to come back, I said, "Neala, how did she get that name?"

Isham turned his head to me and as he did, the sun picked that second to fall on his hair and it shone back the light. His hair looked like fine strands of silver. He said, "I be git to dat. After freedom and Massa Fields be come here fer we and tek we to see Momma, thar be plenty nigger dat not know'ds wat to do wid freedom. Dem go here, thar, and all ov'r de place but in de end, nigger need a place to be 'till dem can figga out wat freedom be and wat to do wid it.

"Plenty nigger dat nots be here 'fore freedom mek dem way here. Massa Breckenshaw, him nots turn 'way any nigger dat suh dem wants wuk. Dem come strong, weak, walking, crawling, or how dem can git here. Dat be how de nigger womans come."

I interrupted him and asked, "What nigger woman?"

He tilted his head to the side slightly and was getting ready to answer me when I saw Beccah and Aunt Bess in that movement. I was going to say something about that too when Neala returned. She had with her two plates full of biscuits, molasses, and fried chicken. She set them on a box on the porch and she went back inside. She came back out shortly and she had lemonade for me, but a dark liquid for Isham. Before I could ask, she told me, "Its bush tea. Poppa still likes to drink bush tea. My Poppa knows the one to get and so Poppa here drinks it ev'ry afternoon; 'round this time."

When Neala was done talking, Isham added, "Keeps yuh living. Keeps yuh mind sharp. Keeps yuh a man."

When he said that, he started laughing and I remembered Beccah's joke 'bout Preacher Man and Levi keeping a wind on the coals in their fire. That kind of humor must be in their blood.

Isham stopped laughing and started to eat. I thought he'd forgotten where he was until he said, "I be telling yuh 'bout de nigger womans dat be come. She come wid two lil' gal pickney. She be in a bad way. She be hab bites dat nots be healing. Becky and a few of de nigger womans tek she to a cabin and it be Becky dat suh wat de woman suh. Becky, she be de nigger womans dat be muddah to meh, she suh dat de nigger womans name be Neala and she be frum Massa Fields plantation. I nots tink on it one way or de next 'cause by den, plenty niggers dun mek dem way frum one plantation to de next. Becky suh dat on de way to freedom, white mans set dogs on dem and dat be how she bite up so. Fer a long time, Becky and ev'ry body be tink dat de gal pickney wid she be she pickney but ov'r time, we git to know'd dat de pickney not be she own. Dem muddah, a nigger womans call Nester, be kilt by de dogs dat bite Neala up.

"Neala tolt dem dat Nester be hab plenty pickney and dem be more dan she be able to fend fer, so she be gits other nigger womans to tek dem rest, but she heart nots be able to let de almost womans gal pickney go. She fear fer dem dat mans, nigger or white, tek dem and treat dem bad so she move on wid dem. Dem be call Gotton and Beck. Dem be sum pretty pickney; near womans but not quite.

"Over time, I be jump de broom wid Gotton, and Willie, afta him git ov'r wanting to figga out how to git back to see Muddah, him fix himself back to wat him know'd: horse.

"It be like de Lawd fix it fer meh and Willie to hab Gotton and Beck. Dem be pretty nigger womans and dem be strong. I tinks dem be strong like dat 'cause Neala be dem muddah. We know'ds dat she nots be dem real muddah, but same way Becky be muh muddah den Neala be dem muddah.

"It be Becky, we muddah dat suh de Lawd send Gotton and Beck fer Willie and meh 'cause she suh dat him pick dem jis't right. Willie him jump de broom wid Beck. Dem mek pickney over pickney, over pickney. It be like dem not know'ds how not to mek pickney. Dem hab six 'cause Beck not know'ds how to mek one pickney. Eve'rytime she mek pickney, dem be two. Meh and Gotton, we not mek pickney like dat; over time meh and Gotton hab three pickney.

"Neala, she be right pleased dat Gotton and Beck be wid Willie and meh. Gotton, she be a tall gal and her be nigger man pickney so she full nigger."

And smiling here, Isham said, "Her mek fer pickney making. Her have full sit down, and pickney nev'r be hungry long as dem hab she fer dem muddah. Her mek plenty milk, and wen dem not want she milk no more, she mek biscuits. Dem be de best biscuits ev'r. Neala be show'd she and Beck how to tek nuffin' and mek it be de best sumting yuh ev'r put in yuh mouth. It be Neala dat show'd meh how to mek dis tea.

"Neala be know'd jis't 'bout ev'r leaf dat fer wat ail yuh. Wen Beck mek and mek pickney, it be Neala, Gotton tolt meh, dat fix it so Beck and Willie be know'd dem one another as man and wife, but dem not mek no more pickney.

"Gotton, her nots drink dat tea 'cause her not mek pickney like Beck. It tek Gotton long time after we hab dem three pickney to mek a next pickney. Dat pickney, it be gib Gotton lots of trouble to come out and wen it come out, it be a big big pickney. Gotton nots be de same frum dat pickney. Her not mek milk de way she mek milk wid all dem other pickney. It be Neala dat gib Gotton de right tea to drink and soon her hab milk plenty fer de pickney. It be dat pickney, Willie, dat be muh Isham's Poppa and dat be way we git dis Neala frum. If it not be fer Neala, den dat Willie, muh Willie, him nots be mek it. Cousin Thea"

Thea

"Every time Isham called me that, I wanted to cry."

"Why, Thea? Why would having someone call you cousin make you want to cry?"

"It wasn't just anyone. He was someone that, if not for Crawford and his cruel ways, I never would have heard about and fate made it so that I could meet him. Fate put Crawford in my path and then he put me on the path to Aunt Bess. The he put Phillip in my path; Aunt Bess in the path of that milk wagon, and so I had no choice but to go back if I was going to go from painful place to peace. That's why when he said, "Cousin Thea", it touched me so deeply. He was my past and he was sharing his past with me so that I could get it all and come here.

"All of this has been to set things right. I didn't want to go to my Maker with all that pain in my heart. My heart is free now, free."

"Auntie Thea, what was Uncle Isham getting ready to tell you when he called your name?"

"He'd talked as much as his mind would let him remember and then out of the blue, he said, 'Cousin Thea? Muddah? Did Beccah suh 'bout Muddah?'

"I looked at him and I could feel the sadness rising up in me when he said, 'I be know'd dat she gone on to be wid de Lawd. Wat I want to know'd be if Muddah be tink on we; she man pickney.'

"Cud dear, you see, Drea, a child, never mind how old, is always a child. A child's love for his or her mother never dies. What did you tell him, Thea?"

"I got up from my chair and I went over to where he was in his rocker and, touching his wrinkled hand, I said, 'Cousin Isham, every day. Beccah told me that she missed you all every day and before she went on to be with the Lord, she asked for forgiveness for giving up her children, for choosing him over everything else. She was sorry that she'd made that choice. If she had to do it over again, she would have followed all of you and faced life with all her pickney. She never, not one day, stopped loving or thinking about all of you. She told Beccah and Beccah told me that you, Juba, Tuck, Zack, and Willie lived in her heart and she was looking to the day when she would see you all in heaven."

Noreen said, "But, Thea, you never told us that part!"

"I know. Beccah never told me that."

"You told him a lie?"

"No, Noreen I didn't tell him a lie. I told a man that was almost a hundred, if not more, the truth that he needed to hear that would help him get from his painful past to a place of peace. What sense would it have made to have told him that his mother never left Fields and even when she had a second chance at freedom, with her momma Cornbread and her poppa Molasses and her grandson Benjamin, she chose Fields over that. You tell me, Noreen, what would you have told him."

Noreen's eyes filled with tears and they were sliding down her cheek so slowly that it looked as if the tears were trying to decide if they wanted to come out at all. Finally, Noreen spoke, "The same thing. The same thing. Cud dear, he was hoping that his mother had never forgotten him. That must have been so hard to live with all those years. Did you ask him what happened to Willie? I figured that if Willie wasn't there when you got there, that he must have died; did you ask?"

"After I told him that, he sat quietly for a while. He didn't cry as I thought he would, but he took a deep breath and then he said, 'Dat be mek muh heart full. I be wish dat Willie be here to hear wat yuh jis't said.'

"It was then that I said, 'Willie, where is he?' I was expecting him to say dead, but he surprised me in a way that I couldn't imagine."

Andrea

"Auntie Thea, what did he say?" I asked, breaking my silence.

"Oh, you still awake?"

We all laughed at that and then Auntie Thea said, "Would you believe Isham said, 'Canada!'"

Both Auntie Noreen and I said together, "Canada?".

Auntie Thea said, "Canada! I couldn't believe it! Canada! Of course, you know I asked him that."

"What did he say?"

"Guess?"

Auntie Thea, you're not being fair?"

"Neither is life. Ok, I'll tell you. Cornbread and Molasses!"

"Cornbread and Molasses! How?"

"On their way to Canada with Benjamin, they made their way to Breckenshaw's Plantation and finding Isham and Willie, they said who they were, where they were headed, and if they wanted to go."

"Just like that?"

"Just like that!"

"Didn't they ask why Milkweed wasn't with them?"

"It's my guess they didn't have to. Isham told me that Willie, Beck, and all their pickney loaded up a wagon and left. But here's the most interesting part."

"What?"

"Neala."

"Neala? What about Neala?" I asked her.

"She left. She climbed on board the second wagon that Breckenshaw provided and finally, in her old age, got the freedom she'd always wanted. Neala Fields Breckenshaw finally became the free woman she'd always wanted to be.

Auntie Noreen said, "I'm glad for her. I guess she must have been the happiest old woman in the world at that time."

"Isham said that when Poppa Molasses, yes he called him Poppa Molasses, got done talking about Canada and what freedom was like for a Negro, Neala was beyond happy but when he said that he'd given up his slave name and was now William Cartright, Neala started to cry. With tears washing her face Neala said, 'I dun wait all dese years to be a true, true free woman and den life put meh back on a plantation way freedom be but a dream. Now freedom come back to meh when muh bones be creaking wid age. I nots mind. I gine. I gine way freedom gine tek meh, but I nots gine wid dem name. I nots gine to freedom wid a slave name."

"That Neala still had some spunk left. Did she get her name changed?" Auntie Noreen asked.

"Yes. The man who started out life as a free man and became a slave, who stole his freedom back, and then helped others to steal away to freedom and was proudly taking his last two to freedom helped Neala get a name that she would be happy with. Neala Fields Breckenshaw left that plantation that day as Harriet Neala Wheelright."

"Wheelright?"

"Isham said that Neala said she chose Harriet because Molasses had told how he had worked with Harriet Tubman to free slaves, and Wheelright because she said, 'De wheels of freedom be finally turn muh way and so I be pick dat.'"

"How did Isham feel being left alone on the plantation? Did you ask him?"

"I did. He gave the best answer I think I'd heard from anyone since I started this journey to peace. He said, 'Willie him be de one dat always be wanting mothering and wen him tink dat mothering be never come fer him, it come. I be glad fer Willie dat him git to be wid de best Muddah him ev'r gine hab. De same Muddah dat birf we muddah. Him not only git Muddah, him git Faddah too so it be de best ting fer him. I dun be old and sides, muh Gotton be right happy wid meh and we pickney. When Breckenshaw dead, white mans dem come out. Dem walk 'round de land and dem suh dat Breckenshaw's son be come to see 'bout de place but him nev'r come and dem not come bak. It be like thar nots be a white man dat come 'bout de plantation so meh and dem dat be here stay and wuk it.'"

"Did you tell him that Fields was the one who owned it and was taking care of everything?"

"No. I didn't see the need."

"That's the best thing. I think that would have broken his heart 'cause he felt that he took care of his family on his own. I truly feel that it's not everything you know that you have to tell."

When Auntie Noreen said that, it was as if she'd put the period at the end of the sentence. Auntie Thea was done. She'd filled in all the missing pieces. We were now faced with the fact that she would be leaving. I started to cry.

Chapter 42

Time: Having Fun or Not, It Flies

Both Auntie Noreen and Auntie Thea looked at me but it was Auntie Thea who spoke. "Now, my dear, why are you sitting there crying? You knew when I walked in that I was going to be leaving once I'd told you what I'd learned. I'm hoping that you will take what you've heard during my weeks of being here and learn from it. Milkweed had to learn. In the end, she had to take responsibility for what she'd done and for what she'd brought into this family."

I looked at Auntie Thea and I had a thousand questions on my mind, but she didn't give me time to ask any as she looked at me and she said, "Just as you are going to have to do with that baby of yours, you are going to have to take responsibility for all your actions. Both those that turn out good and those that you wish you'd done differently. Sometimes we get a second chance to change things, but sometimes we don't. Milkweed had chance on top of chance to change things and she kept her blinders on. All she could see was him; Everett Michael Poole Fields. He became her everything and because she forgave him his many sins and wickedness at that moment when she gave herself wholeheartedly to him, she helped him to birth this curse into our family.

"I know that it may seem as if she didn't, but I feel, and this is just my gut feeling, that it came linked together like the pearl necklace he'd given her. This damnable curse-laden yoke fashioned from his many sins and wickedness. Her heart, fragmented from his physical and emotional abuse, glued itself together just so it could forgive and love him. That pearl necklace of sins, wickedness, hate, love, passion, pain, trial, loss, and ultimately her forgiveness was fashioned not for them but for us; her future.

"Each one of those beads represented his sins, and each knot that separated his sins was one of her tears. One half of the clasp was her love for him and the other was his damnable love for her; when joined, pressed together and closed they became this unimaginable, wretched, and seemingly unbreakable curse around our necks and, because no one has been able to understand her love for him we've been unable to break free of it.

"And so it hangs around the necks of all the women in her family. The love that fashioned this necklace never broke, as far as we know, and we know what Aunt Bess told me and your Nana, Gina Pearl and what Beccah told me. As I told you, it was because of Aunt Bess' dying that made me go back to Promise Land to get the whole story. Aunt Bess wasn't done but her dying changed it; not left it unfinished but changed."

"What do you mean changed, Auntie Thea?"

"It changed 'cause Aunt Bess had just reached the good part...you know, reaching to near to the modern times."

"So how did that change it?"

"Your Aunt Bess, she told the story of us like that, back and forth you know; modern, past, modern, and then past again. She was getting ready to reach back and tell what happened to all them children that your great-great-great-great-great-grand-nana Milkweed had for Fields when she died. When I told your Nana what I knew, I left all the cobwebs in place."

"Cobwebs?"

"Yeah, cobwebs. You know that thing you can see through, but it stops you from seeing fully. Just listen to you asking all those questions; sounding so grown. Making me think of your Nana and all them questions she had for Aunt Bess, but you aren't too young for all these questions. Don't fret yourself none too much 'bout these answers. I feel in my heart I have them all and, like Aunt Bess used to say, 'God's time. Ain't nothing goin' happen 'fore God's time. That's God, you know. One day when you least expect it, the very thing you were waiting on God for, that thing that it seems like he ain't never going send or let come, he answers. That's God. His time sure ain't ours.'"

I was so deep in thought that I never saw nor heard Auntie Noreen leave or come back into the drawing room until Auntie Thea said, "Drea, excuse me for a minute while I sip this tea."

As Auntie Thea sipped on her cocoa, my mind wandered over what she'd just told me about Nana Milkweed and how she loved a white man, and not just any white man but a white man that was her master. A man so mean that the whole side of the family, the Negro side, and it was probably the same for the white side if anybody ever knew any of them, couldn't find a way to be excited that the two of them picked each other.

Auntie Thea sipped the cocoa and took a bite of the cake and when her mouth was empty, she spoke as if reading my mind. "The white side of the family, I'm sure, weren't bearing the burden of the curse 'cause them don't know blight since they were the ones mostly responsible fór Negro folk (we're Negroes now) and their troubles. Nope, we can let them off the hook and put the blame right dead smack where it sadly, in my opinion belongs. It belongs at the feet of Milkweed."

For some reason, Auntie Thea stopped form talking. She looked as if she was trying to find words and it was then that I realized she saw Leela just as I saw her. Auntie Thea knew in her heart that Leela had defied the long-standing saying that all babies were beautiful. Auntie Thea knew that Leela wasn't beautiful to look at. She also knew she was; thank God, too young to know it. I wanted to tell Auntie Thea that it wasn't Leela's fault that she looked the way she did. I wanted to tell her that Leela was Hamilton Trindle's child.

"Didn't know her history."

Know her history! That's all Auntie Thea had paused so long to say. I was so sure she was looking for the right words to say, 'gorilla baby' other than the only way.

"Auntie Thea, but you just told me. You just told me who brought the curse into the family, is there more?"

"No, there's no more than you taking all that I've told you and deciding what you're going to do with it. Neala wanted freedom. She held on to that dream and one day, just when she thought all hope was gone, it came in the form of a Mandinka African man named Molasses and a woman with Seminole blood coursing through her veins, Cornbread.

"Now you have that same blood. You have the ability to think, to reason, and to decide. Don't let all the time I've spent here be wasted. You will have decisions to make during your life. Some will be hard and some won't require any real thinking, but even when it feels as if you don't have to think what to do think anyway, don't just do something 'cause it feels good, right, or easy. Sometimes, those are the things that will make you look back with the deepest regrets. Letting in my cousin, the one that was three times removed on my mother's father's side seemed easy and right enough but in the end it was the worst decision I made. It cost me my first round of deep pain. Even now, I sometimes think on her and Crawford and wonder what my life would have been like had she not showed up poor, hungry, and in my mind, in need of family.

"Anyhow, like most things that you'll spend a life time thinking on, and sometimes even regretting, you'll have to find that place where you can let them go and get on with life. I had to learn how to do that. I couldn't do that 'till I could almost forgive Crawford for what he did to me, then I tried to forgive her for being so needy that she couldn't see that Crawford was my man. Notice that I said 'tried' and 'almost'. That means that even now, I haven't fully forgiven them. I hope to though before I meet my Maker. Don't have much time so I better be working on that when I leave here."

Auntie Thea could see I wanted to say something but before I could, she said, "It's life, Drea. We meet those people that, after a while and sometimes it's not a long while, after you meet them, you don't know how you lived without them. You're like that to me. It's funny that if not for that same cousin and Crawford, I would never have come to New York and so much would have gone untold. So you see she, even with all her whoring ways, had to come into my life so I could go back and get all the other bits and pieces and bring them to you.

"So keep that in mind too. Not everybody that's going to show up in your life goin' mean you good. Sometimes while they're there you may get that questioning feeling in your gut. It may be so deep it goin' make you look at them and question everything 'bout them and your reason for letting them hang around. But we, humans, don't always trust or gut. We sometimes have to wait 'till everything 'round us is all broken to figure out that our gut was right. Drea life's goin' teach you a lot of lessons but I have no more to teach you. I've done my part.

"Now, I'm going to be here in New York for the next few weeks; some more tests to do at a hospital in Manhattan. When they are done; whatever the news is, I'm taking Phillip and we're going back to Virginia. The doors to my house goin' always be open to all of you; come whenever you are ready.

"Now come here, give me a hug, and when you are done, please call Phillip for me. I'm ready to go home."

Chapter 43

From Greenwood to Evergreen

About a month after Aunt Thea and Uncle Philip returned to Virginia, Bernard called. I got a funny feeling that something was wrong as soon as he said, "Cousin Drea?"

I said, "Yes, Bernard?"

He didn't answer but I heard him take a deep breath. If he ever let it out, I don't know but I barely heard when he said, "It's Mommy. She passed this morning. We'd been expecting it so everything has been arranged. It's all set for Saturday. You don't have to worry about coming here to Virginia. We, all of us, including Daddy, are coming to Brooklyn. Mommy wanted to be buried next to Aunt Bess, your nana and your momma."

I listened in stunned silence but I started to cry as soon as he said, "Your momma." It was more like a wail. I felt a deep searing pain, like a period pain in my belly. A part of my brain said, "You don't really, really know her." Then a part of my brain remembered her when she'd said, "It's life Drea. We meet those people that, after a while and sometimes it's not a long while, after you meet them, you don't know how you got on living without them. You're like that to me."

That part of me started to crumble. The part that had spent a little more than two months with her visiting, leaving, and sharing the story of my family's history started to hear her voice and a longing for her, Nana, and Momma rose in me. I cried because I was missing Momma and Nana, and then I cried because Auntie Thea had come into my life and changed, I felt, the very course that I was headed on.

I'm not sure when Bernard finished talking, but soon I heard Auntie Noreen. She was standing beside me and she said, "Drea, Drea? What's the matter? What's wrong?"

Looking at Auntie Noreen, I said, "It's Auntie Thea. She's…"

That was all I got out before I rushed to Auntie Noreen's arms and, burying my head on her shoulders, I let my pain pour out. Auntie Noreen wrapped her arms around me and became all that I needed.

In a few days, Bernard called again; they were in Brooklyn at the house. Auntie Noreen, Uncle Neal, and I went over to visit. I'd taken Leela to Mrs. Trindle earlier in the day so that I wouldn't have to worry about or care for her as we visited with Uncle Philip and the rest of the family. In my heart I was glad that Leela wasn't older. I could see me begging her to behave, sit still, or not touch anything. Even now with her just over three months old, I knew that she wouldn't have listened to me anyway. It always surprised me the way she glowed whenever Auntie Noreen or Uncle Neal were around her. Of course, that never really happened but the way she could go from devil to angel in a blink always amazed me. I was glad that today, I wouldn't have to watch either of her glows; devil red or angelic blue-white.

Uncle Phillip looked more than a little lost. It was clear that this was one time his mind had chosen to work. It had, over time, as Auntie Thea had told us, forgotten things and sometimes wouldn't let some things register. Auntie Thea's death wasn't one of them. It had registered and he was remembering. He didn't call for her or ask where she was; from the way he was silently crying, he knew and the knowledge was breaking his heart.

Cousin Phillip's wife, the nurse, sat with him when Philip came to sit with us. He looked over to where his father was and said, "Dad is taking this really hard. Had we known that it would have registered, stayed, and be so devastating to him, we probably wouldn't have told him."

Auntie Noreen asked, "So why did you all think that it would neither register nor stay?"

"Cause he'd been forgetting so much for so long. You see, we didn't really have to tell Dad that Mommy had died. It was Dad who woke with a clear mind and wanted to talk to Mommy. He tried to get her to wake and when he was unable to, he went to my room."

Auntie Noreen said, "Poor man. I can't imagine what that must be like. Lord have mercy. What a thing to wake up to; finding the one you love dead, gone from you while you sleep and you didn't get a chance to tell them you loved them nor nothing."

"I can't imagine that either." Bernard agreed.

"Dad did well. He knocked on the door and said, 'Phillip, I think Vida should come have a look at your ma. She's not waking up. I think she's gone, Phil.'

"Dad said that and before I could do anything, he'd turned and walked back to their room. Vida, who had gotten up when he knocked, jumped out of bed and ran down the hall. It was as we'd feared. Mommy was dead and Daddy, who having dealt with death most of his life, was sitting in the chair besides Mommy's bed, quietly sobbing. Miss Noreen, it broke my heart to see Dad like that. Do you know, I wished that his mind hadn't worked. You know what's odd?"

Auntie Noreen said, "I have a sad feeling that the odd thing is that his mind has worked perfectly ever since, right?"

Phillip smiled slightly and replied, "Crystal. He has been aware, alert, and even had energy ever since."

Bernard added, "He picked out Mommy's casket and when I said I would have another parlor take care of Mommy, Dad said, "Not my Thea. I won't have someone else touch her. If you can't do it, Bernard, I'll do it myself."

Looking at Bernard, I asked, "Did you, you know, take care of Auntie Thea?"

Phillip Junior answered, "No. Nor did Dad. There wasn't a need for an autopsy so Vida did it. She'd taken care of Mommy when she'd gotten weaker and so she was the one who dressed her, did her hair, make-up; everything. Daddy accepted that and now here we are; family brought together again and Mommy, come tomorrow, will get what she has always talked about; joining the two women who became mother and sister to her when she had no one else."

I will always remember Auntie Thea's funeral because the whole thing for me seemed to be happening behind a thin sheer screen. I was there but not. I was hurting, but not as deeply as I'd hurt for Nana or Mommy. In a way, I was glad. I'd endured and survived a lot of pain before because I wasn't sure where I would have put hers had it been as deep or overwhelming.

The hardest part of the whole funeral for me was the approach to Evergreen after we left Mount Lebanon. As we approached the entrance, the hearse ahead no longer contained a casket with Auntie Thea. It was Mommy in one flash, and in another it was Nana. I was once again going to watch Mommy and Nana being buried. It was here the pain rose in me. It felt like a slow rise; the way pain does when it's not sure where it's going to end up. The rise might have been slow, but when it hit my heart, the impact felt like an explosion.

A torrent of tears rushed from my eyes. When the cars stopped, I didn't want to get out or follow. I didn't want to sit and listen as the minister told us about the short life of a man born of a woman. I didn't want to hear nor did I want to be there. I looked though eyes that were barely seeing and read 'Lilly Thea Greenwood, beloved daughter and mother'. I didn't read Mommy's birthday nor the date of when she died because I would do what I'd done whenever my mind flashed on that day; and it did often. I would wonder what happens to a mind inside of a mother that would make it think that it was OK to leave two little children behind. To make it wish to be dead at less than thirty-five years? How do you get to the place where death, a thing that we all know is so final, is better than hanging around and figuring it out?

I felt an anger rising up in me towards Mommy so I decided to look at Nana's black granite headstone. As the preacher asked God to receive the soul of Thea Fillmore into his mighty kingdom, and somewhere between him saying, "Ashes to ashes, and dust to dust," I read: *Gina Pearl "Promise" Greenwood—April 8, 1909 – August 28, 1957.*

I heard but didn't look as they started to lower the casket into the ground. I made myself read Nana's headstone. What I didn't want was the image of another casket being lowered into the earth to register on my brain. As the first shovel of dirt echoed off the casket, I read what Daddy had inscribed under the line with Nana's birth and death date. He'd had them write: *Daughter, Mother, Grandmother: A heart so big with a love: matchless and eternal. A true daughter of Greenwood.*

The sound of more dirt. I turned and read Aunt Bess' headstone: *Bessie Field.* More dirt. Tears came to my eyes. I let them fall. I cleared my eyes and read: *A majestic oak of Greenwood.* The sound of muffled dirt; the hole was filling up. *A tree so strong with branches that reached into the past and brought it to the future. Rest in your earned peace.* I was crying now. Not just for Auntie Thea but for everyone that she'd told me about. As I stood there, the long list of Greenwood women echoed in my head. I felt the urge to kneel down. I didn't fight it.

When my knees touched the ground at the foot of Nana's grave, I started to cry out loud. I felt a squeezing in my chest as if it would burst if I didn't holler. I hollered. I wanted so badly to hear Nana and Mommy's voice. I started to feel as if my pieces were falling off. Fear along with the sadness started to fill me.

I felt a touch my shoulder. I felt a body kneeling next to me and then a hand reached and took mine. I didn't have to look. I knew the feel. I laced my fingers into his and allowed myself to be raised up. As soon as I stood to my feet, the hand unlaced from mine and the arms went around me. As he buried me into his chest, I let my tears out. I cried until I couldn't breathe. He never let me go. He stood there with me. When the crying felt like it would stop and air could return to my lungs, I inhaled a deep breath. My lungs filled up and expanded. I exhaled and looked into his face. He smiled; a slightly crooked half-smile at me. I smiled back, the same crooked half-smile. He led me away. As we walked slowly, I thanked God that he'd chosen Matthew David Hirsch to be my father.

Book Six

Leela Phoebe Hirsh Greenwood

A Time for War

Chapter 44

A Nation in Shock

Uncle Neal was slowing down and yet he wasn't. Uncle Boysie couldn't get out to the meeting and rallies anymore so Uncle Neal felt as if he had to do double duty; for him and Uncle Boysie. Whereas before it was Uncle Neal, Uncle Boysie, and Mr. Colroy, it was now just Uncle Neal and Mr. Colroy; he still hadn't become an uncle, not even for Leela. Actually, for Leela he was Roy. No one tried to get her to say anything else. She now had her Nor Nor, Gran Gran, Neal, Roy, and of course, I was still Drea. She made no effort, even with a mouth full of words to make one of them Mommy, Mom, Ma; nothing. I'd stopped caring a long time ago, but it was Auntie Noreen who kept trying. I looked at her each time she made the gallant effort and wondered when she was going to get it. I wasn't Leela's Mommy.

The air was festive as it always is coming around to Thanksgiving. Auntie Noreen was busy figuring out who she was going to have over for Thanksgiving dinner and who she could leave out. Every year, the list grew. Every year, Auntie Noreen said she was going to leave someone off and the closer it got to the holidays the harder she found it to leave anyone off; she just never could bring herself to do it. This year would be no different. However, Auntie Noreen had at least until tonight to find out who else, if anyone, Uncle Neal wanted to add. But Auntie Noreen wouldn't be thinking on that anymore; it was time for *As The World Turns* and nothing or no one, not even Leela could get her attention.

I had some clothes to hang so I asked Auntie Leela to listen out for Leela while I went down to the basement. Auntie Noreen answered, but never took her eyes from the TV. I'd only hung a few pieces when I heard Auntie Noreen cry out, "Drea! Drea! Come. Oh my God! Oh my

God!" I ran up the stairs to find Auntie Noreen pointing at the TV.

As I ran to her chair, she said, "Oh my God, Drea, them shoot the President! President Kennedy get shoot!"

I looked at the TV and I couldn't believe it. *As The World Turns* wasn't on the TV screen but a newscaster was talking. He seemed shaken and uncertain about what was going on.

"Drea, somebody done shoot President Kennedy. They say that he's in the hospital, but they don't know if he going live. The Governor get shot too."

I sat down and at the same time while Auntie Noreen and I were waiting for them to come back on, Leela woke up and started to cry. Auntie Noreen said, "Go and get she. Lord, when all this shooting goin' stop? Everybody that trying to do something good for Negroes, them shooting. Lord, I hope that them ain't dead."

I left Auntie Noreen looking at the bulletin on the TV and I went to Leela. I knew that I would have my hands full as she would want to be with Uncle Neal, who wasn't home yet. I wasn't sure how I was going to handle her and as I was trying to figure out how to quiet her, I heard Auntie Noreen cry out again. She called, "Drea! They just said he's dead. The President. Oh my God, Drea! Come, bring Leela and come."

I snatched up Leela and headed toward the stairs and for a fleeting moment my brain said, 'Throw her down the stairs, run ahead of her and meet her falling body at the bottom.' I knew had I done that, that Auntie Noreen with as much pain as she was in from hearing that the President had been killed, would have, in one movement, sent me to meet him by the time he showed up in heaven.

Leela was still crying when we got downstairs. Auntie Noreen opened her arms and took her from me. Once in Auntie Noreen's arms, Leela quieted as if there was something in her Auntie Noreen's arms that worked a particular magic. Slightly frustrated, I turned my attention to the TV where Walter Cronkite had just said that although it wasn't yet confirmed, Dan Rathers had said that the news was that President John F. Kennedy had been given the last rites and was indeed dead.

As we sat looking at the TV, the door opened. It was Uncle Neal. He looked visibly shaken and he called, "Noreen, you hear?"

"Yes. He's dead, Neal."

"Dead? I thought they said that he was just shot?"

"Walter Cronkite just said that he's dead. This ain't right, you know.

Right in front of his wife. Too many guns and too many people who ain't got respect for life."

"I tell you, Noreen, anybody trying to do a good thing for Negroes does vex people. I mean, they didn't have to kill him. It don't matter who it is, Negro or white, I don't believe that shooting anybody going solve anything. All this killing got to stop. It's making it hard for you to speak up. This is just like back in the time when people just used to lynch Negroes. They used to do that to frighten people. Now they doing the same things with guns. I'm sorry for the man. I mean that, Noreen. I sorry for him and his family 'cause when he stop being the President, he's somebody's son, brother, uncle, father, and husband. Now tonight all of them got to figure out what they going do without him."

Chapter 45

A Caisson, a Cortege, a Casket And a Little Boy's Salute

Over the next few days, the whole nation mourned. Watching Auntie Noreen was like watching someone who had lost a family member. I think if Auntie Noreen had said she wanted to go to Washington to pay her final respects to the President, Uncle Neal would have found a way. She didn't so he didn't have to figure it out how to do this thing for her. She contented herself to watch every second of the news coverage on TV. I think at that point Thanksgiving was forgotten, not just for Auntie Noreen, but for every other American or everybody in America; American or not. What was there to be thankful for?

Auntie Noreen was sad that the President's life had been taken from him in such a cruel way, but I think she was sadder, in a way, for his wife and two small children, especially the little boy. I tried to imagine what his wife must be going through knowing she was there; right there and someone just snatched him from beside you. One minute you have a husband and he's alive and talking, and the next, somebody who is angry over something that might not even be that important, has taken up a gun and taken the man that you love from you. For a second, an answer which wasn't really the answer came to me. She had to be feeling just like Mary Todd. She was there, almost a hundred years ago; ninety-eight to be exact if I remember what they taught me in school, when her husband, Abraham Lincoln, was assassinated.

Over the next few days as we watched the news coverage it was all you could think about. Everybody was sad. Outside was gray and it was like if the sky was crying for him. We, like everybody else, watched all those people as they lined up, lined the streets, and waited for a chance to personally say goodbye to the President. I think if they didn't say enough, the people would never have stopped filing in and filling that room up.

Auntie Noreen had me stand by the TV so I could switch from one channel to the next. It was as if she thought one of the channels was going to broadcast something different. After I'd stood there and turned, just as she'd said, from channel to channel, she accepted that it was all the same. I got to sit down.

If my life depended on it, I couldn't tell anyone what anyone ate in the house from the minute we heard that he'd been shot until the casket was lowered in the ground at Arlington National cemetery. What I think all of us, the whole world would remember, would be that little boy in his little suit, right after his mother had whispered in his ear, raising his hand and saluting at his father's casket.

I'd managed not to cry, although Auntie Noreen had been crying from the time the funeral had started, but once I saw his little hand go up, I couldn't help it. I felt real sorry for him. He was now going to have to grow up without a father because somebody was vexed at him.

As we watched, Uncle Neal, who had been quiet until now said, "It's what, six months since they shoot down Medgar Evers? They shooting Negroes who trying to change things; Evers, he dead 'cause he was trying to get rid of Jim Crow. Now the President 'cause he didn't like some of what going on in this America. Good people getting cut down in their prime. This got to stop. Noreen, it ain't right that 'cause you got a gun, you can feel that if you have a different opinion to somebody, you can just shoot them down. What's America coming to? The President? Lord have mercy on all of we. None of we ain't safe. None."

Chapter 46

A House Transformed

As Leela grew, the house on Bainbridge Street was transformed. There were baby things everywhere. No one scolded her. She had the run of the place. Daddy, Auntie Noreen, Uncle Neal, and even Mrs. Trindle were there to fulfill her every wish. At first, I didn't want Mrs. Trindle to have anything to do with my baby, but Daddy, Auntie Noreen, and even Uncle Neal said that it wasn't her fault and I shouldn't hold what Hamilton had done against her. And so Mrs. Trindle became a part of Leela's life. She truly loved Leela and whenever I would let her, she happily took Leela home.

Leela was always happy to be with her, Daddy, Auntie Noreen, or even Uncle Neal, but she always gave me a hard time. She fought me over everything. It would take me a lifetime to change her diaper, yet Auntie Noreen could walk in and change her in a half minute. Daddy, Auntie Noreen, Uncle Neal, or Mrs. Trindle could bathe her and have her dressed in less time than it would take me to get her ready for her bath. It was my guess that Leela knew I hated the father she'd never seen, and in her little ways, she did what she could to get even at me for not loving her the way I should.

Leela loved everyone but me. When she learned to talk, it seemed as if she was learning to say everything but mommy, momma, or mama. Leela said, "Nor Nor," and we knew she meant Auntie Noreen. She said, "Neal," plain as anything. Not uncle or anything that sounded like "Uncle", she would just look at him and say, "Neal," and it was all right with Uncle Neal.

Leela could do or say nothing wrong as far as Uncle Neal was concerned. Leela changed the rules of the house, made up new ones as she went along, invented different ways to beat the same drum, and all of us went along; I more reluctantly than any of the others. Whereas before, meal times were quiet times at the house, it was now a chat fest. It wasn't that Leela could get full sentences out, but that didn't stop her. She was at the table and that was all that mattered. She didn't have her own chair, plate, or anything like that. Auntie Noreen insisted. From the time she could eat solid food, she sat with us; better yet, she sat in Auntie Noreen's lap and was fed from her plate.

I didn't complain as I didn't have the trouble of trying to eat with one hand and hold Leela's free and fast-flying hands as they grabbed at the food on Auntie Noreen's plate; that was Auntie Noreen's job as she was the one who started feeding Leela at the table and from her plate. She actually loved the whole idea of Leela at the table and eating from her plate. I stayed out of it. No one, not Uncle Neal or Auntie Noreen tried even once to tell Leela to make less noise or that the dinner table was where we ate quietly and only if it was about the food or of earth-shattering importance that couldn't wait until we went to the drawing room, only then did it get discussed at the dinner table.

Everything was always, "She's too small, she's only a baby, you can't make a baby be quiet, that's how she's going to learn to talk." The list of all the reasons why Leela was being spoiled went on forever and so Leela took her place at the table and had her conversations with everyone; well, everyone except me. I wasn't on her prattling list. Actually, I didn't think I was on any of her lists. That suited me fine. I didn't want her on any of my lists either but I didn't have a choice. I was stuck with her. She was on my child list.

Today, Uncle Neal was teaching Leela to say, "Cou Cou." We were having Cou Cou and liver. She got that done in no time because it sounded just like coo coo. She loved saying it. Each time Uncle Neal said, "Cou Cou," Leela laughed and imitated him, saying, "Coo Coo." Uncle Neal and Auntie Noreen made a game out of it and before you knew it, Leela had eaten a hearty portion of Cou Cou.

Leela was one lucky little girl. She may not have a father, but she wasn't lacking affection or anyone to dote on her. She had Daddy, Uncle Neal, Auntie Noreen, and of course, Mrs. Trindle. Leela's emotional cup was full and running over, even if she didn't know it. I watched as Auntie Noreen and Uncle Neal fed and played with Leela. I ate in silence as I was all but forgotten. It hadn't reached the point yet where I was invisible in the house, but it was clear I had a very minor role in the play called *Leela's Baby World.* I didn't mind. I wasn't trying to audition for a bigger role. I liked my part or the tiny part she allowed me to play. Truth was I didn't even always like my role.

Today was going to be one of those days when I wasn't going to like my role. Somehow, she gave me particular hell on the nights Uncle Neal went to meetings and today was going to be doubly difficult as he was dressing and going out, but it wasn't to the Lodge and it wasn't in the evening. I had no idea how she knew, but she always seemed to know when he was going to the Lodge. I was hoping that because he was going out in the early afternoon, he would be able to trick her and just go out. I doubted it but figured I'd wait and see.

As the food disappeared off the plates, I started my countdown to hell. It was always the same. We ate. Uncle Neal would take her from Auntie Noreen and the two of them would head out to the drawing room, leaving Auntie Noreen and I in the kitchen. Auntie Noreen stayed behind to put away any extra food that was left and help me clear off the table. Once that was done, I was left alone to wash, dry, and put away the dishes, pots, and pans.

While I cleaned up, Auntie Noreen would take Leela, give her a bath, and get her ready for bed. By the time I finished cleaning the kitchen and came out, Uncle Neal would be ready to leave for his Lodge meetings. Once Leela saw him in his suit, she would start wailing. Now that she could get more than a few words out, we all understood that she didn't want him to go without her.

I made it to the living room just as Uncle Neal made it down the stairs. Leela, I guess, smelled his Old Spice aftershave; his signature 'I-am-going-out' smell. Once she got a whiff, she started squirming away from Auntie Noreen. It didn't matter to Leela that the sun was high in the sky. He had the suit on and that smell. She had to get to him; that was her only objective.

Auntie Noreen didn't let her squirm too long as she would just put her down and let her go where she wanted: to Uncle Neal. By this time, Uncle Neal was standing by the coat rack to get his hat and coat; that was if it were fall or winter and if it were summer or spring, Uncle Neal just took his fedora. It was February and it was cold outside so he would be taking his coat, scarf, his beloved fedora, and the last thing he would pick up would be his gloves. The rest of us stuffed our gloves in our coat pocket, but Uncle Neal was the extra neat one. His gloves came off at the door along with all his other outer garments. He hung everything up but his gloves, and they were stretched out, fingers to fingers, and laid flat on the storage chest attached to the coat rack. Somehow, Leela never toddled over to the coat rack and bothered the gloves. Look at them, yes. Touch them, yes. Move them…no.

We waited for her screaming to reach siren pitch. It didn't. Tonight her cry was different. It had a pitch to it that was as if she was worried, concerned even. As she cried, she clung to Uncle Neal's leg. She'd never done that before. Her clinging stopped Uncle Neal. He picked her up and was trying to give her to Auntie Noreen as he knew once Leela got a good screaming going, she wanted no part of me. As Uncle Neal bent to hand her to Auntie Noreen, who was sitting in her favorite high-backed Queen Victoria chair, Leela said, "No, Neal, no. No go X."

We all stopped and Uncle Neal said, "What did you say, Leela?"

Leela quieted her screaming and repeated, "No go X, Neal. No go."

The room went quiet or so it seemed. Uncle Neal sat down. As he sat, he kept looking at Leela in his arms. He'd never quite gotten to hand her to Auntie Noreen. Uncle Neal looked at Auntie Noreen and asked, "Did she say 'X'?"

When Uncle Neal said 'X', Leela started a fresh wailing and said again, "No go X." No go X."

There was no mistaking what she was saying. She was telling Uncle Neal not to go to his meeting this afternoon. All week, it had been all Uncle Neal had talked about. Uncle Boysie was taking Uncle Neal not only to a meeting where the Honorable Malcolm X was scheduled to speak, but Uncle Boysie had also arranged it where Uncle Neal was going to get a few minutes to speak with him after he'd given his talk.

All week, it was all we had heard and as the day drew closer, nothing came from Uncle Neal's mouth other than something to do with his meeting today. Uncle Neal had even written a special poem that he had worked on from the evening he'd come home with the news that Uncle Boysie had made the arrangement for him to meet the Honorable Malcolm X until yesterday when he was satisfied that it was perfect.

Uncle Neal had come home that evening exploding with excitement. He'd hardly closed the door before he started talking. He'd shouted from the door, "Noreen, Noreen, you never goin' believe this!"

I knew what Auntie Noreen was going to say even before she spoke. It was what she always said anytime Uncle Neal told her she wasn't going to believe something. As expected, she said, "If it's coming from you, Neal Peters, I goin' believe you. What is this thing that you think I'm not goin' to believe?"

Uncle Neal had, by then, made it into the drawing room and was settling in his chair and smiling like it was his birthday or Christmas. Once Uncle Neal was sitting in his chair, Leela walked over to where he was and as she expected, he picked her up. With Leela seated comfortably on his lap, he said, "Leela, girl, Boysie done it. Pulled it off. I'm going to get to meet a famous person. This man is going to make things better for the Negro."

Auntie Noreen looked at Uncle Neal as if he wasn't himself and she said, "Neal Peters, what foolishness you telling that child? You think she knows what you saying?"

Uncle Neal replied, "Noreen Peters, we don't give babies and their little sponge brains enough credit. How you know she ain't understanding me? Look how she looking at my mouth."

Auntie Noreen started to laugh her teasing laugh and said, "Sure, she looking at your mouth. She looking at your big teeth. She making sure you ain't goin' yam off her head."

That made Uncle Neal laugh and he said, "Say what you want, but I bet you she knows what I'm saying." Turning his full attention to Leela, he said, "Don't pay your Auntie Noreen no mind. Listen to your Uncle Neal. Auntie Noreen's jealous 'cause I'm goin' to meet Minister X and she's got to stay home."

I watched as Leela kept staring at Uncle Neal's mouth like she was looking for his next word. Then she reached up and pulled at Uncle Neal's lips. He said, "You mark my words, our Miss Leela Meela here is understanding me well enough. She knows how important it is for me to meet Minister Malcolm X." Then, turning to Leela, he said, "You don't worry, as soon as I see him, I'm goin' make sure he hears 'bout my favorite girl; my Leela Meela. Right, Leela Meela?"

That got Leela laughing. Uncle Neal put her down and went to wash up for dinner. When he returned, he said, "I'm seeing his friend, the one that used to belong to the Nation of Islam under Elijah Muhammad but now belongs with El-Hajj Malik el-Shabazz."

When Uncle Neal said that, Auntie Noreen said, "I thought you were talking about this Malcolm X fellow. Who is this El-Hajj, or what it is you said, fellow?"

"It's the same person. Malcolm X changed his name."

"So what are you trying to tell me, Neal?"

"That I'm goin' get to meet Malcolm X when he speaks at the Audubon Ballroom. Nor Nor, you have any idea how important that is? Just imagine; me, a poor, half-naked boy from Barbados goin' to get to meet an important man like Malcolm X. There are some people here in America that ain't meet him and I goin' get that chance."

By this time, Uncle Neal was grinning and had his chest all puffed out. Auntie Noreen looked at him for a while and said, "Well, can I come with you and meet this all-important Mr. X?"

Uncle Neal looked at Auntie Noreen as if she'd suddenly grown another head and a few arms and legs."

Auntie Noreen saw the look and said, "It's not like you're going to the Lodge. You goin' to hear a man give a talk. I don't see how I can't come to that."

"Noreen, this is man business. It's just going to be men. Muslims don't do things like Christians. There's a place for women and there's a place for men. This is for men."

"You sure you got this part right Neal Peters? It's a talk and won't a big important talk like this be for everybody?"

"Truth is Noreen I don't really know. I guess women and children could be there for this talk but…"

I could see that Auntie Noreen was fixing to give Uncle Neal a hard time, but just as quickly, she stopped. I guessed she looked at him and could see that he didn't want her to be vex. She looked at him, smiled, and said, "Go to your meeting and if you goin' write something for someone as important as him, you better start. I think, Neal, when you are done, you should read it to us so we can tell you if it sounds good."

That got Uncle Neal to laugh. He said, "You just being malicious. You want to find out what I got in the thing before I read it to him. I ain't doing that. I gine write it and give it to him and when I come back home, I gine read it for you."

That was it. Uncle Neal floated around for days. He kept writing and changing his mind, and now that he was satisfied and getting ready to go, Leela was telling him not to go. What was surprising to all of us is that she had listened, understood, and was now telling Uncle Neal not to go. Not only was she telling him not to go, she sounded worried; that is if a three-year-old could sound worried.

The big day had arrived for Uncle Neal. He'd written his poem, polished and shined his shoes, dusted off his suit, creased, and re-creased the pinched sides of his favorite charcoal gray fedora, and he must have ran his hand down the crease on the top a thousand times. There also was no counting the number of times he'd run his hand over the edge on the front brim. He'd flexed that a few times as well. He was ready and now Leela was telling him not to go.

Holding her, he said, "Don't worry, Leela Meela, as soon as I done talk to Minister Malcolm X tonight, and…" Touching his breast pocket where he had the envelope with the poem, he added, "…as soon as I get to give him what I wrote for him, tell him 'bout you, your momma, and your Auntie Noreen, I coming right back. Ok, Leela Meela?"

Leela started a fresh wailing. "No go. No go, Neal, X sleep."

Uncle Neal passed a crying Leela to Auntie Noreen and smiling at Leela. "Listen to her. She's telling me not to go 'cause Malcolm X is sleeping. She is something else. Just listen to her. Said like a true woman in the making; willing to say anything to get me to stay home."

As habit, Uncle Neal kissed Leela on the forehead, said goodbye to me, and only when he heard the car that was taking him and Uncle Boysie to Harlem did he gently touch Auntie Noreen's shoulder and, just as she'd always done, she reached up, touched and patted his hand. However, instead of just sitting as she usually did, she said, "Neal. Wait a minute. This little girl's too upset for you to just walk out and leave her like this. Hold her and soothe her for a minute. Boysie and them ain't gine mind. They know Leela and how she is when it comes to your leaving her behind."

Uncle Neal stopped and took Leela from Auntie Noreen. The minute she was in his arms, she threw her fat little arms around his neck. She was still crying. Uncle Neal held her a little away from him and, looking at her, he said, "Don't worry, Leela Meela, I promise you I'll come back. I'll come back and when I do, we goin' to the store for candy."

That was the magic word. Leela's fountain of tears stopped and her Everest-size mountain became an ant hill and while that transformation was taking place, there was an even greater outward sign that Uncle Neal had indeed found the magic word to her heart…she smiled. I didn't look, but I think if I had, I would have seen the sun go behind a cloud just for a second so it wouldn't be shamed by Leela's dazzling smile.

Satisfied that he had Leela's permission to go, he handed her back to Auntie Noreen. She didn't seem to mind but this time Leela didn't stay in Auntie Noreen's lap too long. As soon as Uncle Neal headed towards the door, Leela climbed down from Auntie Noreen's lap and quietly followed Uncle Neal to the door.

Past experience had taught me that once Leela had that air of independence, even at three, it meant that she didn't want anyone and particularly me stopping her. It wasn't that Leela always got her way with whatever she'd figured on having her own way with, but today we could tell that she just wanted to watch Uncle Neal leave. She'd done it before so today was no different.

Leela walked just slightly behind Uncle Neal as he headed out the drawing room to the door. As soon as Uncle Neal opened the door and stepped out, Leela softly but in a most dramatic fashion said, "Come back, Neal, OK?"

Uncle Neal turned and, smiling at her, replied, "Don't I always, Leela Meela? Don't I always?"

Leela looked at him as if she would cry again. She didn't answer. She stood in the open door watching him. Habit kept her there. She watched him go down the stairs and once he reached the last step, he stopped, turned and waved. There would also be one more wave to satisfy Leela; the one from the car as it drove away. Uncle Neal would stretch his hand through the passenger window and raise it up high enough for her to see him wave. Leela only came back inside when she couldn't see the car anymore. It was what we'd learned stopped her from losing her mind and gave us some peace. It worked for all of us, especially me as she liked taking out her little girl frustration on me. Letting her stay at the open door, stepping back in when she was ready, and watching her triumphantly closing the door was worth her weight in gold for me.

Chapter 47

A Time to Kill?

Auntie Noreen and I were in the kitchen talking and putting the finishing touches on dinner a little earlier than usual so that when Uncle Neal came back from his meeting, everything would be ready. Auntie Noreen had guessed that since the meeting was for four o'clock, Uncle Neal probably wouldn't be back home 'till sometime after seven, if not closer, as she liked to say about time, to eight. That was going to be late for us to eat, but it wouldn't have been unusual and, besides, this was a special day. Auntie Noreen wanted everything done so we could sit right down and hear how things went for Uncle Neal. We knew how excited he would be to tell us how his meeting with Malcolm X went and since he'd promised to read the poem, we couldn't wait to hear it and what Malcolm X thought of it.

I started to tell Auntie Noreen something about how his meeting with Malcolm X must be going for Uncle Neal and how important this was going to make Uncle Neal down at the Lodge when we heard keys in the door. I looked at Auntie Noreen and I could see that she too had a surprised look on her face. We knew it could only be Uncle Neal, but he shouldn't be coming back in the house yet. It wasn't time.

Whatever our individual thoughts were, we never got a chance to express them before we heard Uncle Neal shouting, "Noreen! Noreen! Noreen!"

Auntie Noreen, who had already started out the kitchen, quickened her step at the sound of Uncle Neal calling her name with such urgency in his voice. I followed quickly behind. When we got to the drawing room, an obviously deeply shaken Uncle Neal cried out, "Oh my God! Oh my God! Noreen, them shoot him! Shoot him like a animal. Them shoot him, Noreen!"

Auntie Noreen went to Uncle Neal and, touching his arm, she said, "Who Neal? Who they shoot?"

Looking at Auntie Noreen with eyes wide open, he answered, "X. They shoot Malcolm X!"

Auntie Noreen stepped back from Uncle Neal and, looking as if she would stumble and fall, sat in the nearest chair. She didn't sit. She was in a seated position but it looked as if her body just crumbled into the nearest thing to her; a chair. Softly, she asked, "He dead?"

"Dead, Noreen. Them ain't give him time to even really start to talk. It was like them was planning it. Somebody near where me, Boysie, and Colroy was sitting in the back 'cause we got there late, started to shout something 'bout a nigger with his hand in his pocket. Then Malcolm, who had only come in the room a few minutes 'fore, tried to get them to be peaceful and quiet down. He called them 'Brothers. Brothers, Noreen!' And then the next thing, a loud boom sound ring out, not like a bomb, but 'cause we was inside it sounded like a bomb. And I see him fall back, Noreen."

Uncle Neal stopped from talking. I didn't know if it was to catch his breath since he was breathing so hard like he was running, or if it was to let what he was saying sink in, but whatever the reason, he stopped talking and he started to bring his hand to his head but never seemed to be sure if that was what he wanted to do. He lowered his hands again and no sooner were they lowered than he had them back up again. He looked at Auntie Noreen with a look like he wanted to scream, cry, holler, or something, but he was too confused to decide which one so he looked away. He looked at me with the same look and as with Auntie Noreen, he looked away too.

Pacing with the same hand motions, he said, "Oh my God! Them shoot the man. You know when I hear the sound, I thought to myself, 'Them shooting at him?' I don't get the thought to finish when two more men jump up on the stage and they go to where Malcolm X is down on the ground and his people trying to figure out what to do to help him and… Oh my God, Noreen, them got guns too and…"

Uncle Neal started to cry. This time he figured out what to do with his hands. He got them to hold his head and, standing right where he was he, started to rock back and forth and it looked like his knees were going to buckle, but they didn't. He held himself in place and with tears streaming down his cheeks, he said in a voice that was now being racked with sobs, "Noreen, them shoot and shoot and shoot and shoot. Oh my God, them shoot 'till it sounds to me like them never gine stop shooting. I know them was shooting fast but, Lord, I was frozen and it seemed like time freeze up wid me 'cause I never hear nothing go on for so long."

Uncle Neal took another deep breath and it wasn't a smooth one. It sounded like it was bumping down his nose, uncertain where it was going to end up, when it made it all the way in. I watched and although I'd only heard about him what Uncle Neal had said, I started to cry. I wasn't sure if I was crying for him or if I was crying because Uncle Neal was crying. I didn't cry out loud. Tears just slid down my cheeks.

"Noreen, then pure pandemonium break out in the place. It's like them let mad men in the place. You got the sound of the guns going and going and going, people, his people hollering, people scrambling, some to get out, some to get at the man that had shot with the sawed-off shotgun, and some to see 'bout Malcolm X. Noreen, them shoot the man and his wife was right there to see the whole thing."

A sound escaped Auntie Noreen's mouth. It was the first one she'd made after she'd asked Uncle Neal if Malcolm X was dead. The sound from Auntie Noreen was almost inaudible. It was like a painful moan with a question. Uncle Neal finally made it to a chair and was sitting, suddenly he stood up and said, "Leela! Noreen, that little girl knew something was wrong. She either felt or saw it. That's why she was so upset; didn't want me to go. Remember, she said, 'Neal no go X. X sleep.' Lord have mercy. That little girl saw it all, Noreen. My God, if that little girl saw what I saw, tonight no wonder there was no calming her."

"Them kill that man in front of his wife?"

"And she belly big."

"She's pregnant too? Cud dear!"

When Auntie Noreen said, "Cud dear," I knew just what she meant. Over time I'd heard that expression enough from her, Uncle Neal, and other people from Barbados who came to the house; cud dear said they were feeling the person's pain. In this case, she was really, really sorry for Mrs. Malcolm X.

"Cud dear and she's pregnant? How them gine do a thing like that?"

"Cud dear is true. She belly big, Noreen; big, big."

"Nobody should see that. That ain't right. What them kill him for, Neal?"

“I don’t know. But it was a Negro; all of them was Negroes.”

“Negros shoot him?

“Negroes…what’s this world coming to? Negroes shooting down Negroes the same way white people shooting Negroes. This ain’t right, Noreen. It ain’t right. The man had good ideas. It’s true that not everybody cared for what he was saying but, my God, just to shoot down the man like that and to leave them children without a father and his wife alone to raise them up. Why?”

Uncle Neal couldn’t go on anymore. Auntie Noreen got up from her chair and, walking over to where Uncle Neal had sat down again, she sat on the ottoman near his chair and said, “Some things ain’t meant for us to understand. I guess it comes down to having something to hold onto ‘cause if his wife ain’t got God, she goin’ be in a lot of trouble.”

“They believe in Allah.”

“Allah? Who is Allah?”

“God. Just a different name for him.”

“So why you ain’t just say God?”

“Because, Noreen, them call him Allah so I say Allah too.”

“If you call him Spoon and I call him Fork but believe in what He says, don’t that still make him God?”

“True but none of that don’t really matter now, you know, Noreen. What happen is that he dead and he ain’t the first one. It’s like every time you turn around, somebody killing off somebody ‘cause they don’t like what this one or that one’s doing.”

“Today just don’t seem right, Neal. One minute Leela’s crying and don’t want you to go and the next, or so it seems, you back home and you saying that the man dead; that them shoot him. Before, you used to know that a Negro didn’t have no value to a white man or a woman for that matter but now Negro people shooting Negro people. Oh Lord, that’s the worst.”

“When’s it goin’ stop, Noreen? All this killing?”

“I don’t know, Neal. I don’t know. But I feel like you. I want it to stop. I don’t want to hear ‘bout nobody else getting killed. If them keep shooting everybody, then we ain’t goin’ have nobody who goin’ want to help we poor Negro people.”

Auntie Noreen’s eyes filled again with tears and they slowly slid down her face. Looking at Uncle Neal, she said, “I feel sorry for she; his wife. Pregnant and now her children don’t have no father. I guess we should thank the Lord; even their Allah, that them ain't shoot she too."

Uncle Neal came to where Auntie Noreen was crying and he reached into his pocket. He pulled out an envelope. He handed it to her. Auntie Noreen turned it in her hand, and read what was written on the front and she said, "I'm sorry, Neal. Sorry you didn't get to meet him. Did you finish your poem, Neal?"

"Yes. I wrote it 'bout Africa 'cause he was talking 'bout all Negro people and all Negro people start out in Africa. I worked on that thing for a long time, you know. I wanted it to be right. I wanted when he read it that he would know I'd been paying attention to what he'd said. I was going be so proud to give it to him."

"What you call your poem, Neal?"

"Rend."

"Rend?"

"I called it that 'cause I was thinking 'bout Africa and all people that got ties to Africa. Even if we from Barbados, Trinidad, St. Vincent or America don't matter; we all African people. I gine read it for you, but not tonight. My head too full with seeing the man gunned down like some wild animal and to think Negroes just like him do it. Negroes, Noreen, Negroes; ain't that something?

"Them take we from Africa where we had all that we wanted, knew what we wanted, and was doing it. Them bring we and scatter we all over the place and make us slaves. Now that them ain't got no more use for we, them don't want we and now Negro don't want Negro to do nothing for Negro. I got to side with you; that's the worst. Negroes turn into animals and eating them one another."

Uncle Neal sat back down. It was as if he'd gotten tired. I saw how both Auntie Noreen and Uncle Neal looked so sad. It made me sadder because Malcolm X wasn't family, but he was important to Uncle Neal and so, with Uncle Neal watching him get shot, it made it feel like we'd lost a family member.

No one spoke. We sat in silence. Dinner or the idea of dinner was slowly forgotten. I looked out the window onto Bainbridge Street and it was dark. Night had come and we hadn't noticed. I wasn't sure what to do so I sat wrapped in the blanket of silence that enveloped us. From time to time, Uncle Neal shook his head and sighed. Every time Uncle Neal sighed, Auntie Noreen would raise her head and look at him. Her eyes were filled with such sadness; I wished that I had something I could say. There was nothing to say.

As I sat there wondering how anything could replace the sadness that was in the house, a sound worked its way to my ears. It was Leela. I think we'd remembered but forgotten her at the same time. From the doorway to the drawing room I heard, "Neal. You come back. X sleep?"

Even though Leela spoke softly, what she said echoed and sounded as if she had spoken into a bull horn. Uncle Neal looked at the little girl standing in the doorway framed by the light from the hallway and it all became scary real.

Leela asked again, "Neal, X sleep?"

I expected Uncle Neal to answer. I didn't expect to hear him cry out loud. Uncle Neal buried his head in his hands. I never saw Leela move, but she must have because she was standing by Uncle Neal and as she pulled on his hands she started to cry. She said, "Neal! Neal!"

Uncle Neal took his hands from his face and wrapped his arms around her. Leela started crying harder. Uncle Neal tried to soothe here. I felt as if her crying was never going to stop, but I didn't worry too much because Uncle Neal had her. He was always able to quiet her crying; that was before tonight. Tonight I had my doubts simply because Uncle Neal and Auntie Noreen were both sad as well. I wanted to comfort Leela but deep inside of me I knew that if I got up and went to her it would make matters worse. I looked at her wrapped in the safety of Uncle Neal's arms and decided to leave. I couldn't help any of them and I had to realize that there really was a time for everything.

This thing that had brought such sadness to the house had to be a time to hate, a time to kill, a time to weep, a time to mourn, and a time to embrace all wrapped up in one. I started to walk out. No one noticed. As I got to the door, I looked back at them in their shared sadness and I realized that the person who wrote Ecclesiastes should have added in, 'A time to hang around and a time to leave.' This was a time to leave. I left and went to the kitchen. It was a time to put away the food. No one was going to be eating.

As I put the dinner away, I thought about what it must have been like for Leela to see all of that carnage and not know what it was, but to feel that it was bad for Uncle Neal. I didn't know if I should be happy or sad that she might be able to see into the future. A part of me wished it would just be a one-time thing. I didn't wonder much where it came from; she did after all have Seminole, Mandinka, Jewish, and Trindle blood. That was a lot for a little girl.

As I finished putting away the dinner and washing up the dishes, I decided to put out the tea things. Uncle Neal and Auntie Noreen may not eat dinner, but I knew for sure they wouldn't miss having their night tea. Eventually, they would make their way to the kitchen and make tea. It would all be ready for them: cups, saucer and cake, Uncle Neal had to have something sweet at night; it was his habit.

Chapter 48

What Are We Going to Do Now?

The next morning, the talk was of Malcolm X's assassination. I didn't have to go anywhere to get news. News came right to us. Uncle Boysie and Mr. Colroy, the men who had gone down to the Audubon Ballroom with Uncle Neal, came by to see Uncle Neal and to talk about what they'd all seen. Mr. Colroy was the most vocal. He was a Pan-Africanist; a student of Garveyism, as he called it and therefore was hit the hardest. He'd done all he could do to keep as he said, "My own hands free of blood. If they'd let me, I would have killed that…that…that." He stopped and blew a long breath out and then he started again, "That blasted nigger with my own hands."

Mr. Colroy stopped when he realized that Auntie Noreen and I were still in the room and he said, "Sorry, Miss Peters and young Miss Peters. Neal, I don't mean your wife or granddaughter no disrespect, but I'm just so angry, man. I just can't get my head to understand how a Negro could do that? How do you go to sleep the night before and wake up in the morning knowing that before the sun sets, you goin' murder somebody? How?

"What kind of low, depraved animal can come among decent people, look at a man; knowing that he has a wife and children and, worse yet, that the wife is pregnant and present; right in front of you, and you still raise up a gun and shoot a man. I'm so sorry they held me back. I would have gladly spilled every drop of that man's blood for my brother. The Honorable Malcolm X. Malcolm was saying something. He was about something. He had a message and now, just like that, they have silenced him."

Uncle Neal sat stone-faced and silent. He'd been so quiet since he got up. He was moving around as if he were in a fog. I felt so sad for him. It was as if he'd lost a son. I looked at Auntie Noreen and I could feel the love coming from her and going to Uncle Neal. I wished there was something I could do, but just like last night, I knew there wasn't anything I could do. I got up to leave and at the same time, Auntie Noreen said, "Boysie, Colroy, you all want me to get you anything?"

Both of them said no. Auntie Noreen said, "Alright then. I'm going to leave you all alone. Ain't nothing I can do by being here. Neal, I'm going to be in the kitchen if you need me for anything."

Auntie Noreen and I walked out the drawing room. She went to the kitchen and I went upstairs to see about Leela. She was having her afternoon nap and I knew it was soon time for her to get up. Upstairs in my room, I let my mind drift. So much had happened in the three years since Leela was born. I sometimes couldn't believe that it was three years.

The time had passed quickly because I didn't have the full responsibility for her. I don't think if I were alone it would have passed that quickly but God was kind to me. I wasn't alone and so it had passed quickly. Leela's world had many bright and wonderful spots in it, but I think that next to Uncle Neal and Auntie Noreen, whom she saw every day, her next bright spot was Daddy.

When she saw him her world lit up. It was Dada, Dada until he picked her up. Once Daddy had Leela in his arms she turned into the most giggling and talking little girl you'd ever seen. It was as if she'd saved up everything from the last time she saw him and now she was telling him everything. Sometimes she was in such a hurry that all her words got jumbled and Daddy would beg her to slow down. It never worked. I think she was afraid that if she took her time, he would be gone before she got it all out. So she hurried it out. What he understood he understood, and what he didn't had nothing to do with her. She'd told him and that was her objective. Daddy never seemed to mind. Leela was his heart and whatever she said or did was good enough for him.

The same was true with Mrs. Trindle. Leela usually couldn't wait to see her. She talked and carried on in the same happy manner, but the difference was she didn't call her anything. Auntie Noreen was Nor Nor, Uncle Neal was Neal, Daddy was Dada, I was Drea, but Mrs. Trindle didn't have a name. Leela's face just lit up when she say her. Then one day, to everyone's surprise, Mrs. Trindle brought Leela home from her weekly visit and as she prepared to leave, Leela said, "Bye bye, Gran

Gran."

Knowing that none of us had told Leela anything about Mrs. Trindle being her grandmother, we correctly suspected that it was Mrs. Trindle who had told her that and taught her how to say Gran Gran. We left it alone. It annoyed me that Leela could get out Gran Gran, but somehow she couldn't get the same tongue to say Ma, Mama, or Mommy. It didn't matter how many times we tried. She simply and most adamantly said, "Drea." It didn't matter who was trying to coax her to say Mommy, she refused to say Mommy. There wasn't anything that any of us could do to get her to call me anything other than Drea. We left it alone. I didn't care. She didn't have to call me anything, ever.

My own child called me Drea and she said it with such emphasis that you would think she knew better and was doing everything in her little power and body to defy me. Daddy said to leave her alone and someday when I least expected it, she would call me Mommy. Secretly, and deep in my heart, I didn't really care if Hamilton Trindle's daughter ever called me Mommy. I loved her, but each time I saw her, I saw Hamilton and it was as if he was using her little body to reach out from where he was and make my life miserable. Leela understood and took on her job as my personal tormentor with glee. I gave her over to the care and love of those who wanted the job. Mrs. Trindle wanted it and so, little by little, she got her precious Leela.

I never gave her over wholeheartedly but enough that Leela and Mrs. Trindle had their own bond. I didn't mind. I was glad for Leela that she had that kind of unconditional love. As for Auntie Noreen and Uncle Neal, they loved her, but I always felt that she was a reminder to them of my interrupted future. They loved her, but not in the total devoted way Mrs. Trindle did. Only Mrs. Trindle and Daddy loved Leela the way a little girl ought to be loved. I tried but I just couldn't reach the level the others had.

I remember when I'd said that to Auntie Noreen. She had said to me, "Andrea Matti Hirsh Greenwood, never let me hear you say something like that again. You should care. She's your daughter. Nobody ain't send you to get she. You made that choice. Now you are her mother whether you like it or not. So if you would look like you really have an interest in this child, perhaps she'll feel it, and then she could get her tongue to say what her heart is feeling. Start acting like her mother, Drea. As small as that little girl is, she's telling you that you haven't earned the right to be called Mommy. Earn it, Drea. Earn your daughter's love."

I, as her mother, had to earn her love but it was clear from very early on, one person who was never going to make any effort to get the smallest amount of her love was Andre. She was almost one before Andre had seen her. He'd heard that I was pregnant. He'd seen Hamilton just once and had such a dislike for him that he'd told Daddy he could wait to see Hamilton's child. Somehow, he had separated me from Leela and always saw her only as Hamilton's daughter. There was nothing that Daddy could say to persuade him to come down to see her.

Chapter 49

A Truth Too Hard To Hear

It had been the summer before Andre was to go off to college, a couple years back; he came home with Tony and Troy for a few weeks. He was staying with them at their home in Connecticut. No one knew that he had even come down 'till one day I was pushing the carriage along Fulton Street when a car pulled close beside me and someone said, "Hey, good looking, do you know where a guy can find a pretty girl around here."

I wasn't going to look, but the voice sounded so much like Andre that it made me look, and as I looked, he pulled the car closer to the curb, parked, and jumped out. I was amazed at how tall and broad he'd become. I hugged him and started to cry. I didn't know why I was crying, but I was so happy to see him.

"Now, sis, what you crying for? Did I scare my big sister or something?"

"Andre, you should have called and told us you were coming home."

"Would a phone call make me anymore welcome than I am now?"

"No, it's just that I'm so surprised to see you and you're driving. How long have you been driving?"

"Almost a year now, do you want me to give you and the baby a ride home?"

Until Andre had mentioned Leela, I'd forgotten that she was with me. She was sitting up and looking at him, but making no attempt to get his attention. It was as if she instinctively knew that she didn't matter to him. I watched Leela as she looked from me to him and then back again and as if to answer his question, she started to wail. It was such a wailing that I knew she would keep it up the few blocks 'till I got home and probably just a little longer. I started to shake the carriage a little to soothe her, but when she wouldn't cut short her wailing litany, I told him to go on home as Auntie Noreen and Uncle Neal were sitting in the front yard.

As Andre ran the few steps back to the car, it was then that I fully realized that Tony and Troy were with him. As I looked, I thought that Troy wasn't just looking at Andre and me, but that he was looking at me. His look had a certain intense curiosity and there was the making of a slight smile at the corner of his mouth. It matched the look in his eyes and it warmed me. The feeling surprised me as it traveled from my head to my heart, where a beat without any rhythm was going on. I felt the same unsynchronized bounding and erratic beating in an area of my body that had, from that horrible day with Hamilton, only had three purposes; to pee, push out Leela, and each month be the conduit for which my period followed a familiar path.

I looked at Leela and for a 'baked, just out of the oven, sweet potato in your bare hand' second, I wished that I didn't have her. The hate in my heart towards Hamilton ignited again as I watched the car drive away. They had only gone a few feet when I noticed Troy turning his head to watch me through the back windshield. That look fueled the feelings that were now dueling in my body. It was a colossal battle. For a second, I didn't care which one won, but then I realized that if the 'baked, just out of the oven, sweet potato in your bare hand' second wish that I didn't have Leela won over the hate in my heart for Hamilton, or even worse the erratic feeling in my girl parts, then Leela would lose the most. She would lose her mother's love; little as it was right now. The hate for Hamilton had to win. I wanted to keep on hating him; I didn't want that to change.

I begged my heart, just for this minute, to get more than a little warm towards her. As much as I willed it, nothing happened. I think nothing happened because Leela was still wailing. As her voice reached frenzied, it sounded to me like, "You hate my daddy, you hate my daddy, why? Why? Why? Why? Why?" I didn't have an answer so I let the feeling where I'd wished I didn't have her stay with me. It stayed with me as I started to push the carriage.

I didn't even try to hurry because it didn't seem as if it would make any difference to Leela. She had climbed on her little baby soap box and was now acting as if she would never get off. I looked at her and the feelings towards her grew stronger. As a matter of fact, and to my surprise, all the feelings remained. I wanted to walk away and leave the carriage just where it was and what happened to her would be someone else's problem.

As I looked at the sweating and wailing baby, I was sorry I'd decided I would try to change my feelings towards her. It wasn't right that I'd focused so much anger towards her; she deserved a little better. It didn't become so deep as to be a true longing. The only thing I longed for was to get her home, change her, and take her over to Mrs. Trindle. I would worry about the feelings I was or wasn't having towards her another day. Today I wanted her out of my sight and not just upstairs.

By the time I reached home with a screaming and wailing Leela, the hatred in my heart for Hamilton had won. It was now a fire raging out of control. If it had consumed me, I wouldn't have cared because I would be free of thoughts of him and his ugly, screaming, gorilla baby. The moment I had the thought; well the part about Leela, I was sorry. My hatred towards him had made me think, and seemingly out loud, an unspoken untruth. Well, not a total untruth. I did want her out my sight and I did want her, as quickly as possible, over to Mrs. Trindle's but I didn't want to be gone from her forever.

I started to hope that with her out of sight, the raging fire inside of me would subside and I would find some pre-Hamilton peace. I pushed her now with some urgency. I wanted to find that place where the pre-Hamilton peace existed. I didn't know where it was, but I started wishing to stumble into the part of the world where the invisible hole was and that it would open, suck me in, and there I would find that peace. It didn't happen so I pushed on toward the only destination I was certain of: home.

I reached the house with a child who was now screaming at a pitch that didn't even make sense. I walked past Auntie Noreen and Uncle Neal, who were hugging, kissing, and patting Andre. I walked quickly past Troy and Tony, who were standing quietly by the car, and went straight into the kitchen. Leela continued to scream as if somehow Andre, whom she'd never seen until minutes ago, had awakened some buried memory in her. Her insistent screaming sealed their relationship. Andre would never recognize Leela as his niece. She would remain, for him, Hamilton's daughter. I didn't have to ask, I knew. It was a knowledge borne out of being his big sister. He liked whom he liked, but when he disliked someone, it was easy for him to totally ignore them.

While Leela hollered and screamed, Andre never came into the house to see if I needed a hand; or asked Auntie Noreen to come into the house to see if I needed help with the screaming baby. Andre stood right outside and talked and laughed as if I, his only sibling, wasn't inside struggling and losing what was left of my sanity with a screaming, angry baby. By some mercy of the angels, I was able to get her cleaned and changed. I packed a fresh bag of things for her. I called Mrs. Trindle to let her know that Leela and I were on our way over. With the same degree of frenzied energy I'd brought the carriage into the yard, I walked back out and headed towards Mrs. Trindle's. I'd grown to appreciate that Mrs. Trindle lived on the same block.

As I pushed Leela, I knew that I was pushing her towards love, but I also knew deep in my heart that I was pushing her away from me as quickly as I could. I was pushing Hamilton's daughter into the arms of his mother and what she did with her once I walked away was her and Leela's business. This evening, the mother in me wasn't feeling very maternal. I reached the house in record time. Mrs. Trindle, who was always ecstatic to get Leela, didn't give me time to get near the bell. She was in the yard and almost taking Leela out of the carriage before I could stop. I looked at the two of them and watched in awe as my screaming, wailing, angry daughter, upon the sight of her grandmother, calmed.

She stopped her major theatrical performance. She was now cooing and smiling in her grandmother's arms as if Mrs. Trindle was her savior and I'd been her tormentor. Mrs. Trindle, with one look at me, said she believed that I'd been tormenting Leela. Ordinarily, I would've tried to explain but this particular evening, I didn't care what Mrs. Trindle thought. Without a word, she carried Leela into the house and I, still not caring, walked behind with the carriage. I left the carriage in the hallway and followed her into the kitchen with Leela's things. I didn't really have to bring anything over for her, but a part of me always felt that I should and so I did.

Leela and her grandmother became absorbed in each other with their own Trindle language, which left me out and also made me laugh inside, because I remembered Auntie Noreen asking me when she's first seen Hamilton when I'd learned to speak gorilla. I hadn't learned and so now I was left out of their conversation. I didn't have the faintest clue what Leela and her grandmother were saying to each other. For all I knew, they could have been planning to axe me the minute I turned my back. I kept my back away from them as I watched them going on with their gorilla talk as if I weren't there. I left. Neither noticed. I closed the door behind me but not before shouting, "I'll see you tomorrow, ok?" There was no reply. I'd learned a long time ago not to wait for an answer as one never came. I guess it was hard for Mrs. Trindle to switch back to English once she'd started speaking gorilla. I walked quickly back down the block, afraid to breathe lest the wind made its way towards my heart and fanned the smolders that had quieted themselves down.

When I got back home, no one was outside. I was anxious to talk to my brother but I was more anxious to talk to Troy. He had finally noticed me. I hurried into the living room to find them all talking and laughing. Uncle Neal was enjoying the attention as Daddy wouldn't be arriving for another twenty minutes. My heart started to pound. I wondered deeply if Troy would say something to me, or would he pretend that he hadn't turned his head to give me a second look. I wanted to join in the conversation, but at the same time, I didn't want to remind him that I was a mother.

At the thought of anything Trindle, the spark ignited. I reached into the ice bucket and took an ice-cube and, putting it between my teeth, I quickly cracked it and for reasons only I understood, I swallowed the pieces in their assorted jaggedness. Auntie Noreen looked at me and shook her head from side to side as if to say, "Girl, where are your manners? Where did you pick up that uncouth habit of crunching ice and swallowing them big old pieces from? I ain't ever seen you do that before. Have you forgotten your good upbringing? Or do you want your brother to think I ain't taught you nothing over these years?"

I smiled at the thoughts filling my brain. If I were bold enough, I would have said, "You see, Auntie, there are some things that you haven't seen and my ice-eating trick is one of them." It would've been a lie, but it would've been harder to explain that I was trying to put out the fire of hate that was burning deep in my heart. I'd tried ever since he'd made me pregnant, but each day that Leela became more and more like him, I had to keep working harder and harder on squelching the hatred for him before it went to his daughter. I didn't want the flame to ignite and burn her up. I sat next to Auntie Noreen. I hoped that sitting next to her, the flame would be contained. Auntie Noreen was nothing but love. No one mentioned Leela and neither did I. Well, actually I tried once and

Andre acted as if I hadn't mentioned her. So I decided to leave it alone.

Daddy was true to his word as always, and within twenty minutes he was ringing the bell. Andre practically jumped over Uncle Neal rushing to the door. As soon as the door opened, he and Daddy were hugging and kissing. As big as Andre was, he wasn't embarrassed to have Daddy kiss him on the cheek. They walked into the living room with their arms around each other. As they walked into the living room, I looked from Andre to Daddy and it was amazing how much they looked alike.

As I sat admiring Daddy and Andre, I felt a warm blush rising up in the back of my neck. I turned and I caught Troy's eyes just before he turned away. I looked down at my feet. I didn't know what else to do.

"Excuse me, Princess, what have I done that you aren't over here kissing me? Don't tell me that you're suddenly jealous of your brother."

I got up from the sofa and pretended to force my way between Daddy and Andre. Daddy started to smile and he put one arm around my waist and the other arm around Andre's and he turned to Neal and said, "Neal, did you ever imagine the day that I would have a son taller than I and a daughter who is a mother? And speaking of which, the house is quiet, Princess, is Leela asleep?"

Before I could answer, Andre said, "Hey, Dad, you haven't said hello to Troy and Tony. They came down with me so I could have some help driving back up."

"What do you mean, driving back up? Aren't you guys staying for a while, at least a few days?"

"No, Dad. Troy has landed a good job and his dad has promised to help Tony and I find some work as well."

"That's all well and good Champ, but we haven't seen you for a while. Why didn't you plan to stay here at least for a week? You know, spend some time to catch up with your sister and get to know your niece."

I realized that everyone was looking at us. We were standing almost in the middle of the living room and we were still hugging. At the mention of Leela's name, Andre stepped away from Daddy as if the mention of her name fanned a flame in his chest equal to mine. If Daddy realized he said nothing but Auntie Noreen, not one to let anything slip by her, said, "Andre, I notice each time Leela's name is mentioned, you act like somebody poured boiling oil on you, what's happening inside you? You don't like your sister's baby?"

The house went quiet and it was then that I realized that everyone had noticed, but no one wanted to say anything. Andre was on the spot but not for long. As a little boy, he'd never backed away from a challenge or the truth, and now that he was on the brink of adulthood, he still didn't. He turned and spoke his truth, not to anyone in particular, but yet to everyone.

"Auntie Noreen, you're right. I've never been able to hide anything from you or lie to you. I'm having a problem with the idea of Drea being a mother. I'm also having a problem with the idea that the father of the baby was allowed to make my sister pregnant, walk away from her and his child, and not suffer any consequences for his irresponsible behavior. It has bothered me from the day I heard that Drea was going to be a mother instead of going to college. I might have been small, but I remember Nana talking about the hopes and dreams she had for Ma. Dreams she never saw fulfilled because Ma had Drea."

At the mention of my conception, Daddy's color faded. He looked pained. Andre turned and looked at Daddy, and in a few quick steps, he was back in Daddy's space and he put an arm around our father. I was the only blood relation left out of the family circle. "Daddy, I'm not bringing this up to hurt you, but I expected more from Drea. I've waited ever since that baby was born to hear that Drea had made some effort to go back to school but, Daddy, the fact that Drea has made no effort has bothered me the most."

When I heard my brother speak the truth that I'd been unable to admit to myself, I sat down. I'd stopped doing everything but hating Hamilton. Almost a year had gone by since Leela was born and I'd done nothing but stew in my hatred of him. Time wasted that I could have used to go to night school and probably be on my way to college by now. I looked at Andre and I wanted to rush over to him and tell him how sorry I was for having disappointed him, but I didn't. I was embarrassed because everybody including Troy was there. I turned from the place where I was, and finding energy, I ran from my brother's truth and straight into my room, where my own truths greeted me; it was like running into a brick wall.

Chapter 50

Please Somebody; Anybody Come See 'bout Me

I slowed almost to a crawl and went in the direction of my bed. I wanted to scream that life wasn't fair, and I wished I were dead. The minute the thought crossed my mind, I remembered that I'd promised when Ma died that I would never wish to be dead. What I would wish for was some backbone so I could do something about the mess that was my life. I wanted answers to all the questions that had made my brother turn his back on me. I didn't want to lose anyone else in my family.

Even if I tried to pretend not to love Andre, I couldn't. I sat on the bed and faced my reflection in the mirror. I willed my reflection to give me an answer. My mirrored-self just looked at me with regret in her eyes. I looked back at her and felt sorry for her. I wanted to ask her where Daddy's princess had gone. Why did she steal my brother's sister, and why did she let herself become a mother, and to a child who, at the age of one, acted as if she wanted a different mommy? I wanted so much to ask her these questions, but I didn't. I could see in her eyes that she didn't have the answers. My eyes shifted and then it dawned on me. I was looking in the mirror that Nana had looked in so many years ago.

I started to wonder if Nana had sat in front of this same mirror and wondered as I was wondering now. I stopped seeing the hurt me and saw Nana's granddaughter. I knew that I had to find some of Nana's strength if I were ever going to become the woman my brother wished me to become. I didn't know where to start so I looked in the mirror at the sad girl who was now crying and joined her. Our thread of familiarity was my painful disappointment of becoming a mother before I'd allowed myself to become a woman. The mother looked at the girl and cried for her.

I stayed in my room for the rest of the night. I waited hoping that someone would come to see about me so I could tell them how I was hurting. I wasn't sure who would come, but one thing I knew for sure, if no one else came, Auntie Noreen would. The night wore on. I waited. No one came. Not even Auntie Noreen. That made me cry harder. The mother that was still a little girl yearned for mothering. I'd not perfected the art of mothering, so I couldn't extend it to myself. My yearning remained just that. I cried myself to sleep.

The sun and I rose the same way the next morning. We were both hotter than hell; it with heat and I with anger. While I'd slept, the yearning from the night before had turned into anger. The anger in me was being fueled by the unbelievable heat. It got me going. Ordinarily, I would care about the beauty of a sunrise, but this morning, as hot and angry as I was, I couldn't give a rat's ass if the sun had come up purple. I was pissed.

I made no attempt to fix my mood. I decided to greet the day just as it had greeted me. I shoved the covers from me and threw myself out of bed. The heat had already gotten into the thickness of my hair and was weighing it down with sweat; it felt wet and matted. I forced my hands through it and raised it off the nape of my neck, hoping to let some air through. It didn't work. I let it go and felt it flop across my shoulder like wet coils of rope. I decided to fix all that damn hair that wanted to keep me hot. It would find out in a minute.

I stood up and dragged the now wet and clinging nightgown over my head. One of the small pearl buttons found my nose, but it wasn't enough to stop me. I pulled anyway; if it ripped my nose wide open, it ripped it. It didn't and once free of it I threw it, well it was more like pelted it into a corner. It crumpled into a small pile. Free of it I stormed into the bathroom like I was on a search and destroy mission. I wasn't. I had to pee. I snatched at my damned panties and felt a certain satisfaction when the stitching at the sides gave way. I had two perfectly matching holes. Putting my fingers through the holes I ripped at the panty. When the elastic at the waist didn't pop I had no choice but to step out of them. With one leg free the panty sagged on my other foot. I kicked it off my foot. It sailed into the air and landed on the top of the shower curtain. For a split second I wonder how it had done that.

I didn't have time to figure it out. The pee was trying to ease out. I didn't want to pee on the floor so I did a quick jump spin and sat on the toilet. I didn't have long to wait once my bottom touched the toilet seat. The pee came gushing out. It felt thick. The water in the bowl started to hiss and bubble. I'd pissed out lava. Afraid to wipe myself, I stood up not caring if the drips of lava piss ran down my legs taking skin with it, dripped on the floor and burned the rug, or melted the side of the tub when I stepped over to shower.

I shoved the shower curtains until they parted, just the way I had when Hamilton forced his way into me. I turned the faucet on with such force I expected the handle to come off. It didn't. The water came gushing out. It had been off so long, the air came out in bursts and sputters sounding like surprised farts. Reaching without looking, I pulled the little lever to turn the shower on. I listened as the water hit the sides of the tub. Even the water sounded angry as it sprayed over the side of the tub. I didn't care. I threw my body into the shower. The water was cold and the minute it hit my hot angry body, it sizzled. The droplets started to bubble. Steam rose and filled the bathroom. I didn't care.

With the frenzy of a crazed woman, I scrubbed at my skin hoping somehow to rip it open and find the person I was. In my anger, I envisioned the metamorphosis. I could see the skin of resentment and frustration falling away. I scrubbed harder; had to be successful. Nothing. I tore angrily at my skin; and waited. Nothing. I gave up. I'd rubbed my skin red and raw for nothing. I looked as if it had been in a cat fight and lost.

I turned the water off. My anger quitted down a notch. Accepting the skin I was in, I dried it a little softer and rubbed some mineral oil into the welts that were forming. My skin, though it had nothing to do with what I was feeling, joined me in my war; we were now both angry. I dressed my angry skin that housed my angry spirit and I decided to go downstairs to face the world. I was ready to fight.

There would be no flight. I wouldn't run again. My angry spirit, in my red and raw angry skin was in such a hurry, it missed the top step. I was falling. I didn't care. I did nothing to stop or slow the fall. I let my angry spirit in my angry body fall all the way to the bottom. I was in a crumbled winded heap. I waited for someone to rush out to see who had fallen. No one came. Angrier than when I'd gotten up a little while earlier, I looked around at my now upside-down surroundings; everything was familiar just upside-down. I'd somehow landed ass up and head down; I struggled to get up.

I got up and stormed into the kitchen. I was going to have it out with my family for not coming to see about me last night or just now when I'd fallen down the stairs. I could have broken my neck, a rib, or something. There was no one there. This made my already angry spirit even angrier. It was beginning to dawn on me that they had gone out and left me alone. How could they? They had never done that before so why this morning? Then I remembered that this was no regular morning. This was the morning after the night that my brother had said what no one else in my family had dared to say.

My brother had spoken the truth about me wasting my life and it had cut me to the core. I understood now why no one was here. This was their way of giving me time to think. I looked around the kitchen and, seeing one of Leela's bottles, decided that I would call Mrs. Trindle to see if she would keep Leela for one more night. I would be honest with her. I would tell her that I needed time to think. Think about my future and Leela. I called but there was no answer. I decided that I would get some hot tea and while I drank it, I would get my thoughts together. I'd no idea how that processed worked, but I knew I had to start somewhere. I wanted though, more than anything else, to know where my family was.

The tea worked on my anger and it started to subside. The more it subsided, the clearer my thoughts became. I remembered where my family was. Daddy, of course, had gone back home. Tony, Troy, and Andre had probably driven back to Connecticut, and Auntie Noreen and Uncle Neal were at their church cleaning.

Family all accounted for, I started to think. There was a lot to think about. Leela would be getting big soon and then her financial responsibility would fall on my shoulders. Until now, I'd done nothing more than bring her into the world. Daddy, Mrs. Trindle, Auntie Noreen, and Uncle Neal had provided for the two of us. The idea of doing what all of them had done for us filled me with dread. I understood better why Andre was so angry. I wasn't trying to be responsible. I'd broken Nana's rule and he knew.

She'd always said, "Child, I don't ask much from you or your brother other than the two of you be responsible. If you're responsible, it will save you a whole lot of regret."

Nana's philosophy was simple: Be responsible and you won't have to regret. I'd failed to be responsible and now I had to handle my regrets. There were plenty.

Chapter 51

A Time to Mourn

After the shooting, Uncle Neal didn't want to do much of anything, go anywhere, or see anyone; he said he was just waiting 'till he could go to Harlem and pay his final respects. Uncle Boysie didn't press Uncle Neal. He understood so he and Mr. Colroy came over and they talked and planned. They were going to brave the frigid February weather and as Mr. Colroy said, "Freeze to death if I have to." Just so they could pay their final respects."

They didn't have long to wait. Two days after the assassination, a wake was scheduled to be held at Harlem Unity Funeral Home. I didn't go as everyone including Mrs. Trindle wanted to go. Auntie Noreen started to get dressed to go and in the midst of getting ready, she told Uncle Neal that she would stay home with Leela and me. A part of me was glad. I didn't really want to be alone. Uncle Neal, Mr. Colroy, Uncle Boysie, the men from the Lodge, and it seemed every Negro person in New York was going.

It took Uncle Neal much longer to get back from the wake than it took him to get home the day that Malcolm X was assassinated. He came back sad, but not like the night of the shooting. Tonight there were no surprises, he was sad; just plain sad. Uncle Neal talked about the crowds and how long it took him to get in to walk past the casket but somehow there was no energy. He came in, went to the bathroom to wash his hands as he and the rest of us did when we came in off the street. He walked slowly and softly into the kitchen and as he pulled a chair out, he said, "Noreen, I'm sorry and I'm glad that you didn't come."

"Now how you goin' be sorry and glad at the same time and over something like a funeral?"

"I don't mean it the way it sounds. What I mean is that they were so many people waiting to get in. It was like every Negro in all of Harlem, Brooklyn, Queens, and the Bronx came."

"What 'bout Staten Island? You ain't mention Staten Island."

"I ain't forget Staten Island, it's just that I don't know if Staten Island got any Negroes and besides, what would any Negro be doing out there? I think somebody, and I don't know who, said there's safety in numbers. If that's true, then any Negro with any sense would find themselves in Harlem. Now, come to think 'bout it, all them Negroes might just have been from Brooklyn and Harlem since I ain't too sure that Negroes out in Queens. You know I don't get out to those parts. Anyhow, that ain't important to today. Today we waited quietly outside that chapel and in the cold; you know how cold it was outside this morning. I was glad you weren't there 'cause you know how the cold bothers your knees."

"Don't feel sorry for my knees, Neal Peters, it's not like you got bones younger than mine. The cold didn't bother your knees?"

For the first time since the assassination, Uncle Neal smiled a little. He looked at Auntie Noreen and he said, "You know that I know 'bout cold. I think that cold had these old bones creaking loud enough that a few loud creaks could've undone those assassins' bullets, my knees would have done it; but cold or no cold, creaking or no creaking, I'm going back tomorrow."

"You think you going be able to get in, Neal?"

"I don't think so but that don't bother me none. I have to go and say a proper goodbye to him."

"But you went there today and you stand up so long waiting to get in, so why you feel like you got to go back? Why you don't stay home and watch it on TV with me and Drea?"

"Cause if he was my real life brother, I wouldn't stay home and watch it on TV. I would be right there for him. I know he ain't my brother in the true true sense of we having the same mother, but my spirit won't let me rest 'till I go. I got to go, Noreen."

Chapter 52

Saying Goodbye to a Prince

The next morning, Uncle Neal was up bright and early. He had a nervous energy about him. He wanted to be on his way. He wasn't certain if he would get in but he wanted to do the best he could so just in case he didn't, he would at least hear what they had to say. Auntie Noreen said nothing. We ate breakfast in silence. As soon as Uncle Neal was done, he excused himself and before we could get out the kitchen, he was ready to leave.

Uncle Boysie and Mr. Colroy must have done the same thing because in less than five minutes, we heard the car outside. With a hasty goodbye, Uncle Neal was out the door. Leela, who would ordinarily follow him to the door and watch the car drive away, didn't. Today she stayed right where she was; still eating her cornflakes and raising her eyes just slightly from looking at her cereal she said, "Bye, bye, Neal. You go see X sleep?" She didn't blink or seem to even be aware of what she said. By the time Auntie Noreen and Uncle Neal could exchange concerned glances, Leela was back at her cereal. She seemed quite fascinated with a few that had fallen from her spoon. Uncle Neal didn't answer or come back to Leela. He walked to and through the door. Auntie Noreen and I looked at Leela. As she was busy playing with her cornflakes, we said nothing. Leela ate and played with her cornflakes, making no effort to be done. We left her. Today it made no sense to rush her.

The day dragged on. After Leela had mentioned Malcolm X again, Auntie Noreen didn't think it was a good idea for us to watch the funeral. She felt it might upset Leela. With Leela playing on the floor, Auntie Noreen and I made busy work. We didn't really have anything to do but we just couldn't stand not doing anything.

When the day couldn't drag on any further or stretch itself any thinner, Uncle Neal came back. Both Auntie Noreen and I were glad to see him. His absence had also weighed the day and had probably contributed to the day dragging and thinning.

We didn't have to ask him anything. We could look at him and tell that it had been a trying and emotional day. His eyes were red. He'd been crying. A day that had dragged and thinned now became heavy with the weight of the emotions Uncle Neal had brought home with him; those both expressed and that were waiting for the right conduit; his eyes or his mouth, tears or a holler.

After Uncle Neal hung up his coat and hat, draped his scarf over one of the hooks, and stretched and laid his gloves on the chest, Auntie Noreen went to him and, putting her hand on his arm, she said, "Neal, I'm real sorry. Come and sit down. I'm real sorry, Neal, but you did what you could. You went and said goodbye."

Auntie Noreen led Uncle Neal to his chair. He followed as if he didn't know the house or where his chair was. When he sat down, Auntie Noreen, as she'd done so many times before, sat on the ottoman, taking Uncle Neal's hand as she spoke. "I feel real bad for everybody. I know you wish there was something you could have done to stop this whole thing but it wasn't up to you. God or Allah, as they call him, knew it was going happen. Why it happened, we may never know, but know, Neal Peters, that you can't do anymore for him."

Uncle Neal looked at Auntie Noreen with a dazed look and then he said, "I know, Noreen. I know." He was quiet for a while like he was letting that sink in and then he said, "They were a lot of people; just like yesterday. Nobody didn't mind that it was cold. You saw how many people was there?"

"We didn't watch it. Didn't think that Leela needed to see that and I'm glad now that she's sleeping so she can't see you sad like this."

Uncle Neal just nodded and then he said, "That makes sense. You know the film star Ossie Davis? He gave the eulogy. He said a lot of things, but I don't remember all of it but the part I remember goin' stay with me forever. It suited Malcolm X. It wasn't for Malcolm X, it was more for the people who didn't like him."

"What did he say?"

"He called him a Prince." Uncle Neal smiled. Not a big wide smile but one that looked like it was a secret."

"A Prince?"

"A Prince of Harlem. Then he licked them up with something like this, 'Here at this final hour you won't want me to say nothing good 'bout Malcolm X, but I have to say something good. Cause I talked to him. Did you ever talk to him? I touched him; did you ever touch him, or have him smile at you? He smiled at me. Did you ever really listen to him? You see, I listened and listened real hard to what he had to say; it was worth listening to. Did he ever do a mean thing to anyone of you?'

"Noreen, them was all real quiet. It was like what he was saying was making them think. But he wasn't done with them, you know. He, that big Negro man with that big Negro voice, went right on talking and he said, 'Other than going to prison when he was young, any of you know him to be mixed up with anything bad or disturb the public peace? The answer goin' be no. Then I would say to all of you, if you all had taken the time to get to know him, then all of you would be siding with me. You would agree that I doin' the right thing by honoring him.'

"Noreen, I thought that he was done there, but then he said something that almost knock off my hat: he called him an Afro-American Prince of Harlem. He ain't stop there, you know; he had more licks for them. He said, 'Malcolm was an Afro-American because he'd outgrown Negro….Negro was too small for him.'

"I don't know if he said more after that 'cause my heart and head was full with thinking about Malcolm X being called an Afro-American Prince of Harlem. I was feeling so bad, Noreen, 'cause the things he was saying was the kind of things that a man like Malcolm X should have heard. It make no sense to me that people live and dead and it's only when they dead that people say good things 'bout them. I think, and it's only my thinking, that Malcolm X would have been pleased to know that all them people loved him. I know that some only come out to look, but I think that the most of the people there came 'cause them loved him. I never met him, but through Colroy and Boysie, I learned to love him. I'm sorry; real sorry he's dead.'"

Auntie Noreen was now crying softly and as she cried, Uncle Neal's emotions that were waiting for the right conduit, his eyes or his mouth, tears or a holler, finally decided. They did both. Uncle Neal stopped from talking and it was like the minute he stopped from talking, his mouth needed to do something else; it cried out. "Oh God! Oh God! Oh God! Lord have mercy."

As if knowing his head would be welcomed, Uncle Neal started to lean forward and didn't stop 'till his head came to rest on Auntie Noreen's shoulder. I couldn't take it anymore. As Auntie Noreen welcomed Uncle Neal to her, I walked out. It was a time to leave.

Chapter 53

Someone To Watch Over Him

It took Uncle Neal a long time to stop mourning Malcolm X and even that wasn't quite true. He never intended to read the poem after he never got a chance to read it to Malcolm X, but one evening as we sat in the drawing room, he decided to read his poem. He just said, "Noreen, I never intended to read this thing but I want you and Drea to hear what I'd written for him." Both Auntie Noreen and I sat quietly and waited. Uncle Neal took the paper out the same envelope he'd addressed to Malcolm X. He was sad when he started. He said, "As you know, I called it Rend. So here goes:

Rend

The emotional and physical tearing apart of **Mother Africa**
by the kidnapping of her children:
men – old but filled with experience and wisdom,
young men virile and carrying the seeds
of future generations in their loins;
brave and healthy as all sons of **Mother Africa** are – **Rend.**

Women – old but filled with wisdom
needed to nourish, heal and keep
Mother Africa's children strong;
young women – fertile with the hope
of future generations
being cradled and protected in their wombs;
children – **Mother Africa's** future resplendently robed
in adornments of tomorrow's Kings and Queens…

kidnapped from their homes and lives and enslaved – **Rend.**

The immeasurable depth of pain, suffering,
confusion and anguish endured by **Mother Africa**'s
as she watches, unable to help
as her children are herded together and
away from her arms
unable to keep her children safe and protected
She cries out in despairing anguish – **Rend.**

The countless rapes, cesarean sections, and DNC performed on **Mother Africa**
as her womb is ripped opened and all her children,
regardless of their stage of gestation:
embryos, fetuses, babies, are snatched or scraped from her womb
and she's left cut open, raw, bleeding – to heal,
if and how she can – **Rend**.

The guttural screams of **Mother Africa**
as she's subjected to even further torture
as more and more of her children are needed by the enslavers and
labor is induced by the slavers and her "babies" are roughly snatched
from her sacred womb by the forceps of greed, depraved indifference,
ignorance,
and a bitter hatred called slavery
They are dragged through a dry birth canal called the
"Gate Of No Return" – Elmina's Castle
and other places to be shipped to the ends of the earth – **Rend.**

The gut-wrenching anguish experienced by **Mother Africa**
as she and her children are suddenly
and brutally forced to leave each other without a word goodbye
a goodbye that **Mother Africa** would never have said to her children
as she had no intentions – ever of sending one;
not one of her precious children away from her – **Rend.**

When Uncle Neal was done, both Auntie Noreen and I were crying. Uncle Neal however wasn't he looked angry yet disappointed. Looking at

Auntie Noreen he asked, "Do you think he would have liked it?"

Auntie Noreen didn't say anything, she just nodded. We remained like that for a long time, silence and memories our companion. It was clear by Uncle Neal reading his poem that he'd made a decision. What Uncle Neal had decided to do was not talk about Malcolm X much. He started going back to the Lodge and then again not as much as he used to. Lately, he'd been spending more and more time with Uncle Boysie. Uncle Boysie was starting to slow down, but didn't want to nor would he let Uncle Neal make a fuss about or over him. He made one anyway and so Auntie Noreen made sure each time he went to visit Boysie, he took him some good Barbadian food. Uncle Boysie was always very glad for the food, which he took and ate, but the fuss that was being made about him was, as he said, "Making me feel like a feeble old man."

Not feeling his best didn't slow Uncle Boysie down. After they saw Malcolm X gunned down, they went to even more meetings. Anytime a Negro was having anything, and it didn't matter what, they were there.

Everyone, well every Negro, not just Auntie Noreen, Uncle Neal, and I were moving to the same beat. We were not all dancing the same dance or at the same pace, but we were moving forward to music made for and sung by Negroes.

Talk of Negroes doing for Negroes, supporting Negroes, and better conditions for the Negro was pushing and driving everyone in almost every state, and Uncle Neal and Uncle Boysie were involved in everything one way or another. It was Auntie Noreen who reminded Uncle Neal that he and Uncle Boysie should slow down. They heard her but they kept up the pace. A rally, they said, needed an extra voice and so they were they. Someone needed a placard held so they were there, flyers handed out, count them in. It didn't matter what it was, they wanted to be a part of it if it meant liberation of the race.

I think Auntie Noreen was starting to worry about Uncle Neal because one evening, when he came home a bit more worked up than usual over something the police had done, she said, "Neal Peters, what happening to you? Why you busy, busy now? You didn't used to be like this? Negroes being treated bad ain't nothing new but what I don't understand is why you feel you got to be in everything now? You ain't just come to America. You in America almost fifty years and you wait 'till the dew settling on you to try and do what you should've done when it was raining hard. I ain't 'gainst you caring and helping, but I think at the rate you and Boysie goin', one of you goin' push too hard."

Uncle Neal didn't interrupt Auntie Noreen. He waited 'till she was finished and then he said, "I told you before, Noreen, the last time you ask me 'bout this, that my awakening; my consciousness as Colroy calls it, came late. When it was raining, as you call it, and I was young and full with energy, I was too busy driving them white people where they had to. I was doing everything I could think of to do what them rest back home expected from we that get a chance to come to America. I don't have to tell you, Noreen, you know how hard I done work in this man's country. I work hard and save 'till I had passage money so we could get home and see the place again. America's problems was America's business, but and this ain't new to you either, it was meeting up with Colroy and some of them other boys from the Lodge that got me playing catch up.

"I want to make a difference. I may not make a big difference, but I want to use what time I have, a little or a lot, to help make a change. You know what it would feel like for me if in my time, we could get America and England to admit that what them do to we, all Negro people, making we work so hard for no wages, beating we, killing we, selling we, and even now the only thing them ain't doing is making we work for free. If them would say that was wrong, I could shut my eyes in peace.

"So you see, Noreen, it might not make much sense to you that now in my old age, I running all over the place trying to fix things for Negroes, but if we don't do it, who goin' do it? White people?"

Uncle Neal stopped talking and just looked at Auntie Noreen. I could tell that she was done. She wouldn't be asking him about his running and ripping anymore. She would be doing what she could to support him, Boysie, Colroy, and all the men down at the Lodge. We sat in silence for a few more minutes and Uncle Neal seeing the resolute yet sad face on Auntie Noreen walked over to her and, hugging her, he said, "There are some things that we sometimes get too old for, but there are some things that it don't matter how old you are, you can still help. This is one of them. I'm glad you worrying 'bout me and stuff, but I got to do this. Now that I know, I can't pretend that I don't. I don't want it to kill me but, Noreen, if this is what goin' kill me, then I'll be deading for a good cause."

Chapter 54

Neal Boy, Fight!

The fire for correcting all the wrong things which had been done to Negroes had been lit in Uncle Neal and was now on high. He seemed even more driven and with Uncle Boysie making fewer and fewer rallies, Lodge meetings, and demonstrations, Auntie Noreen tried again to get Uncle Neal to slow down. He didn't. He reminded her that they'd already had that conversation and there was no sense in bringing it back up.

Auntie Noreen tried her best not to be as vocal, but to still let Uncle Neal know or feel that he and Boysie should slow down. He listened, but not nearly as much as she wanted. She did her best to keep Uncle Neal from getting too worked up, as she called it. Uncle Neal heard but didn't hear Auntie Noreen and so when he went out and needed her to listen, she listened and for as long as he needed her ears. Most times, that's all he needed, but if he needed her opinion, he waited for it. She always gave him what he wanted; the truth unfiltered as he knew she would. That didn't stop her from worrying. She still worried, but she told him less often how much she worried. She didn't tell him but she told me. Then the day that Auntie Noreen feared came.

Uncle Neal, Colroy, and Uncle Boysie, were attending a protest rally. Uncle Boysie had started to feel, as Uncle Neal put it, "Strong again or strong enough to get back in the jungle." In the midst of it all, Uncle Boysie's heart, with all the passion and love for Negro people, just couldn't go on any more. It started to flutter, falter, and come close to failing. Uncle Neal, always concerned for Auntie Noreen, didn't want to alarm her so he called Daddy from the hospital where they'd rushed Uncle Boysie. He didn't want to be alone as he waited. The wait wasn't long, though it felt it.

Later, when Uncle Neal came home, he said that as things started to look bad for Uncle Boysie, he went to the gurney where they had him in the emergency room, and he took Boysie's hand. Uncle Neal said he took his hand 'cause Uncle Boysie was struggling to breathe and with each struggled breath he took, Uncle Boysie looked more and more afraid. Uncle Neal felt sorry for him. He wanted so badly to change things so Uncle Boysie wouldn't be so afraid but he didn't know how so he held his hand. As he took Uncle Boysie's hand, he started to cry and said, "Neal, I ain't gine mek it, you know. I ain't winning this fight. Neal Boy, I ain't gine win this time. Muh time up. Deading is hard, Neal. It hard."

Uncle Neal said that Uncle Boysie looked harder at him and looked into his face, crying, and said, "Neal, I glad that you here. You is a real friend. When I gone, Neal, and it ain't gine be long, Neal Boy, fight."

Those were his last words. He died but not alone. His life-long friend had held his hand and helped him cross over. By the time Daddy got there, they were getting ready to take Uncle Boysie out of the room. They let Daddy and Uncle Neal have a few more minutes with him.

Uncle Boysie's dying took a lot out of Uncle Neal. The funeral had to be planned, but tried as he might, he couldn't bring himself to make arrangements. Auntie Noreen, who was still in touch with Bernard called him; he came and took care of everything.

Uncle Boysie didn't really belong to a church, but as Auntie Noreen and I went to church at St. Leonard's where most Bajans went, they said it could be held there. People from the Lodge, the neighborhood, and people who knew how much Uncle Boysie meant to Uncle Neal came. Daddy, Auntie Noreen, Mr. Colroy, and I sat along with Uncle Neal on the front pew, which was for the family; Uncle Boysie didn't really have any.

He'd been married but he and his wife never had children and after she'd died, he'd stayed by himself. And as will happen with people who don't really have family around, they usually are alone or very lonely or both, and when they die they don't have anyone to sit in the pews reserved for family. Then the seats remain empty during the funeral and have that lonely feeling. This wasn't the case with Uncle Boysie; we were his family so we sat there.

The Lodge men and all the men who attended the meetings and rallies with Uncle Boysie had kept Lonely from ever moving into his house and now that Death had come, not because Uncle Boysie wished it, but because Uncle Boysie's time in Death's book was up, they were there again.

Along with Death came Alone; it was something that Death almost always insisted on. Now, alone in death, Uncle Boysie looked at peace. He had done his best to hold onto life, but Death and Alone wanted his company. They'd come and so we'd gathered to say goodbye so they could take him with them.

Uncle Neal got up at the appropriate time to speak. He said a lot of good things about Uncle Boysie, but the thing that stayed with me was when he said, "Sometimes there's a different person inside of you. You know it but you can't find the door to let that person out. Then out of the blue somebody shows up and says the right thing and, just like that, the door opens and the person inside you, the real you, steps out.

"That was me. I had a person inside of me. He had opinions, thoughts, ideas, a big heart, and love for justice, but I didn't know how to get him out. Boysie Cox, that man in the box over there, not only told me he was there, but he helped me get him out. He encouraged me, even at my old age, to join the struggle for liberation for the Negro people. I didn't think I could be much use but he told me I have a voice and I should use it for the good of the Negro race.

"Now I don't know how much more fight I have in me, but I gine do like Boysie asked me to do. His last words on this Earth were, 'Neal Boy, fight.' So I gine do that. I gine fight. I gine make the almost fifty years of friendship that Boysie Cox shared with me matter. And when it's my time, say that I, like Boysie here, fought a good fight."

Without another word, Uncle Neal started to walk away; well he made a few steps and then he turned back. He went to the casket and he said, "Boysie, a man couldn't have asked for a better friend or teacher. I was lucky to have both in you. Wherever the place called Peace is, find it and rest. You deserve it. I gine miss you, man." When Uncle Neal said this, he started to cry. He shook his head slowly from side to side and with tears slowly sliding down his cheek, he touched the casket and repeated, "I gine miss yah. You was my true, true friend."

Uncle Neal walked back to his seat. As he sat down, Auntie Noreen took his hand. They held hands and said nothing; there was nothing else to say.

Soon the funeral was over and we left for the cemetery. Uncle Neal was even sadder at the grave site. He cried openly and loudly. I felt really sad for him, but I knew because I remembered when it was Nana and Mommy that he would have to work through his sadness on his own. I also knew that it would take a long time. There would be days when it would hurt really bad and then days when it would just hurt, but you could still do what you had to do.

The repast was held at the Lodge so when we left Cypress Hills, we went back to the Lodge on Nostrand Avenue. We hadn't been there very long when Uncle Neal told Mr. Colroy that he'd had enough and could he please drop us off at home. Without any protest, Mr. Colroy walked us to where his car was parked on Halsely Street and he drove us home.

Uncle Neal went up to his space. We, knowing how sad he was, left him alone. Even Leela, once Mrs. Trindle brought her home, was quiet and didn't go through the house shouting, "Neal! Neal! Where are you?" Today, she was quiet and didn't make the slightest hint or effort to climb the stairs to find him.

Uncle Neal stayed in that slump for a few days then one morning he came down and said, "Boysie wouldn't want me moping around like this so today I goin' over by his house and let some air go through the place." He asked Auntie Noreen if she wanted to go with him, but she told him to go on but if while he was over there, he really felt like he needed her, he was to call and she would come.

No call came but a very official letter addressed to Uncle Neal came by special delivery. When Uncle Neal came home, he opened it. It was from a lawyer; Uncle Boysie's lawyer. Inside was a letter explaining the official letter. Uncle Boysie had written the letter a long time ago and had given it to his lawyer. It was to be delivered to Uncle Neal after his death. The letter wasn't long. Uncle Boysie simply thanked Uncle Neal for his years of true friendship and gave him all that he owned. His house on Hancock Street, his house in Barbados, and the three house spots in Bayfield in St. Philip. He'd included his bank books, insurance policies, and all the documents that would make claiming what he used to own easier.

Uncle Neal read the letter and cried. He turned to Auntie Noreen and said, "Noreen, what I gine do with all this property at my old age?"

"He didn't say you had to keep it, Neal. You and Boysie was fighting for the liberation of the Negro people, why don't you find a way to use what he left you to continue that fight. I don't think Boysie would mind.

I think he would be glad if you did something like that."

Uncle Neal did just that. He went to Uncle Boysie's lawyer and made arrangements to rent out the house on Hancock Street. The rent money was to go to the Lodge, some to Malcolm X's children, and some to the NAACP. Uncle Neal also set up *The Boysie Cox Feet First Foundation* with the money from the insurance policies. This foundation was to always keep the first floor apartment, Uncle Boysie's apartment, in the house on Hancock Street furnished and available to anybody coming from Barbados who had no place or family to go to when they got here. It was to help them with food, clothing, and help them find work; get on their feet just the way Uncle Boysie had done for him and Auntie Noreen when they'd gotten off the boat at Ellis Island. Once that person or family got on their feet, they had to help somebody else get on their feet. Over time, the place became known as Feet First, but most times it was affectionately called Boysie's House.

Chapter 55

If You Haven't Broken the Mold Yet; Please, God, Do So Now

I can't recall an easy day with Leela and despite the fact that everyone was chipping in to take care of her, my life with her was as close to a day in hell was going to be. It's not that Leela never had an easy day; it's just that I can't remember one that had she and I in it together. Other people told me about Leela, the good child. The Leela who could sing so pretty, it would make you want to cry. The Leela who gave hugs, kisses, and smiles. I always listened intently to these stories because I'd never seen that child, never heard the voice that so many raved about, never got the hugs, or the smiles, and God knows, never the kisses. I saw a Leela that, like her father, held me responsible.

It's true that there were some things I was responsible for, but I had to place either credit or blame where it belonged; in this case it belonged at God's feet, right beside Jesus. He was the one, not me, who had decided who Leela's father would be. He knew with those gorilla genes what Leela would look like. He also knew the kind of temperament she would have; the fire in her spirit and the razor sharpness of her tongue. Leela was too small to grasp a concept of God or to figure out that He was responsible for the way she turned out, but since I was the once closest to her, the one that was supposed to give her that unconditional loving and I wasn't, she kept the good that was in her from me. To me, Leela's good was some kind of fairytale.

Leela always spoke quickly as if she had a lot to get off her chest and couldn't wait until later because later might be too late. Whenever she opened her little mouth, she spoke her mind. Her tongue had an edge that could cut the frost off morning. dry dew off grass and God knows and icicle was in for a quick melting. You would've believed that I'd put a sharpener, not a nice soft rubber nipples on her bottles. She also had a strange way of being. She never really wanted me or needed me, but I was hers and she made sure everyone knew I was her ma. She'd finally gotten around to calling me ma. She did it grudgingly. As if I should feel honored. I felt something, but it wasn't honor.

In those moments when Leela cried after me, and acted as if her entire world depended on me, it warmed me. Her needing me kept the smoldering embers of my hatred for her father as close to being out as they could ever get. Then, just as I would make myself wholly available to her, she would abandon me sometimes for something as silly as a piece of paper on the floor. She would then look at me as if she were saying, "I know you didn't really believe that I needed you." I would become angry and that would fan the flames of resentment for her father into a raging fire that threatened to consume me.

It didn't take me long to start a little prayer that became my mantra. I would look up to the heavens each time she pulled this little stunt and say, "Please, God, if you haven't already broken her mold, please, I'm begging you, do so now." I couldn't imagine another woman being mother to another child like Leela. One Leela in this world was more than enough. I often hoped that He had heard me and Leela's mold was somewhere up in heaven in a pile of dust with a sign over it that said, "**Son, Peter, Gabriel and all others with miracle and restoration powers, "Work no miracles on this mold. DO NOT, DO NOT and this is no joke, put this together again! Thank you."**

God had to have broken it. There was no spite in God. He couldn't ever let that mold be used again. Even I could tell Him that the results would be the same. That mold, I'm sure, had been used once before to make Hamilton, and those results were disastrous and now that it had molded a girl Hamilton, it was beginning to look as if history was about to repeat itself. I prayed so often that I was sure that He heard me and broken it. Well, if not God Himself, then one of the angels.

Auntie Noreen always told me to go, have some fun, but if Leela cried and made a fuss for me, I gave up and gave in. I was approaching my twenty-third birthday and was the mother of an almost five-year-old. I'd never really made love, never dated, and only one male private part had ever been near mine. I was growing tired. I was coming into my womanhood and all that made a woman a woman was still hooded to me: a mystery. I wanted a change. My body had had an opportunity, with pregnancy, to change but the person inside still needed love.

Although I didn't fully understand what love was, I was sure that I would recognize it if I ever saw it. If it looked even remotely like what Auntie Noreen and Uncle Neal had, then I would know that I'd found it. I waited, but it never came. Nothing came. Not school, evening classes, training, or anything, not even friends. I stayed by myself.

Andre and Tony were attending the same college in Boston and were rooming together. He would call on occasion, but Andre never came back. Seasons changed and Andre was in his last year of school when Daddy arranged for him to go to Europe. This sending away of Andre to Europe felt like he'd fallen out of my life. It wasn't like he was dead or anything like that, but he felt really far away; gone and I didn't know how to reach out and find him. I couldn't explain that to anyone so I kept it to myself. Leela turned six, still not needing me and that same year, Andre and Tony graduated from college and, to everyone's surprise, decided to move to Barbados. They purchased a house in St. James and found jobs in Bridgetown. Knowing how he felt about Leela and about me not making any attempt at getting my life back on track, I resigned myself to the fact that Andre had tasted a slice of the good life and since it didn't seem to him like I wanted any, he was moving on and away from me, and going about seeing what other parts of the pie called life tasted like.

I missed Andre with a pain that was almost like childbirth. Leela was the wedge that had come between the two of us. I withdrew painfully from his world and tried to make Leela my world, but she didn't want me. I withdrew from her and left her rearing to Daddy, Auntie Noreen, Uncle Neal, and Mrs. Trindle. All of them acted as if they believed the sun wouldn't rise in the morning unless Princess Leela gave it permission. I watched in amazement as she ruled Queen Supreme in her little world. She gave orders and everyone bowed, obeyed, and obliged; if they didn't, she hollered. They obeyed and she rewarded them with smiles, hugs, kisses, and snippets of songs. I was happy to be the only casualty from Leela's war. Never having received any of her special treats, I didn't miss them, though I did yearn for hugs, kisses, and smiles that were meant just for me. All my yearnings got answered rather unexpectedly.

One evening, about a year after Andre and Tony had been living in Barbados, Daddy dropped by unexpectedly. It was his birthday and we'd never celebrated any of them with him. He had always come the day before and we celebrated then. When Momma was alive, she never acted as if it mattered that she never got a birthday with him. She took the day before and made it special. The fact that Daddy was here today filled my heart with an enormous joy. Right after I'd let him in, he said, "My princess, I want you, Noreen, Neal, and Leela to get all dressed up. I want to take my family out to celebrate my birthday."

I didn't question him or anything, I just hugged him around his neck and ran right up the stairs calling out to Auntie Noreen at each step, "Auntie Noreen, Auntie Noreen, guess what, guess what?"

Auntie Noreen, who had been in her room resting, heard me and came out to the landing, "Lord, child, you screaming as if the house on fire. So unless the house on fire, quiet down."

I reached Auntie Noreen and before she could say anything else, I told her, "Auntie Noreen, its Daddy's birthday and he wants us all to get dressed up. He's going to take us out to dinner."

"I know that it's his birthday. Now what is this you saying about him taking us out to dinner? Us who?"

I was about to answer when Daddy shouted from the bottom of the stairs. "All of you, Noreen, all of you. Today, I'm fifty-five years old and I want to spend it with the people that I love the most in the world."

Looking at Daddy I couldn't help but speak what was in my heart so I said, "Daddy, I wish that Andre was here. Did you hear from him today? I heard from him on Sunday and reminded him that today was going to be your birthday. Did he call you, Daddy?

"Princess, you haven't changed. Still firing off a thousand questions before the first one is answered. To answer your litany of questions; I too wish that your brother was here. Yes, I heard from him and very early today. As a matter of fact, I told him what I'd planned for us later and he said that he knew we would have a great time and, yes, he wished me happy birthday. Now would you please go and get yourself and little Miss Leela dressed so that I can go and show off my three ladies."

"You got it, Daddy, we'll be ready in a flash."

Daddy smiled and walked away and I rushed into Auntie Noreen's room, almost spinning her around as I rushed over to where Leela was playing and just picked her up. Nothing upset the Supreme Queen more than having anything she was doing interrupted. She started to scream as if I'd threatened to bite her head off. Auntie Noreen started in on me. "Now, Andrea, you would think by now that you would understand that child of yours. You're no closer to understanding her than you are to understanding why the sky is blue. Now why did you go and just snatch her up from what she was doing?"

"But Daddy said to hurry."

"Fine, he said to hurry, but who's going to quiet her down now so that the rest of us can get organized?"

I looked at Auntie Noreen and admitted defeat. She knew that the person wouldn't be me. I'd never been able to get anything from Leela and, worse, if she suspected that it was something that would make me happy. She knew now that her being quiet would make not just me, but everyone in the house happy, so she gave a performance worthy of a grand prize. Auntie Noreen sat on the bed with her and suggested that I go to my room, get myself together, and she would see about herself, Uncle Neal, and Leela. She didn't have to ask me twice I walked out of her room, crossed the hall, and entered the sanctuary that was totally mine. Leela's room adjoined Auntie Noreen and Uncle Neal's. We were all happy.

It took Auntie Noreen the same amount of time to get the three of them together as it took me to get myself together. I hadn't gone anywhere special for such a long time that I'd practically emptied my closet looking for something to wear. Satisfied with a small black dress and the set of silver earrings and chain that Daddy had given me for Christmas, I slipped on a pair of black sling-back two-inch heels with a small silver tassel on the top. I looked at my reflection. I hardly recognized myself. My hair had stayed in those two braids so long, I'd almost forgotten how long, soft, and coppery it was. I didn't like to wear make-up so I put just a touch of lipstick on; enough to give my face a little color.

Daddy smiled at us when we came down. Auntie Noreen had picked out a pretty pink party dress for Leela, combed her hair and put it in two thick cornbraids, with little pinks bows on the end. She had her favorite black patent leather shoes on. Leela looked like an angel but I knew that this angel was waiting for any moment to explode and spoil my fun. I looked at her and silently pleaded with her not to pretend to want me. I didn't want her to want me this evening. I wanted to have a good time and her wanting me would spoil it.

Auntie Noreen, sensing my anxiety, said, "Neal, let's take Leela with us in our car. Let Andrea go with her father." Without a word I thanked her and Auntie Noreen smiled, and before Leela could figure out what was going on, we were out the house and on our way. I breathed a sigh of relief but quickly took it back and held it. I knew Leela. She was going to pick a moment to perform. So I waited.

We arrived at the restaurant and just as we were about to be seated, we heard a familiar voice say, "Now, you didn't really think I would let my old man turn fifty-five and not be here, did you, Daddy?"

Daddy froze. The look of surprise on his face was absolute. It was one of joy, happiness, and pleasure rolled together. It was the best look I'd ever seen. Not only was Andre walking towards our table, but so was Tony and Troy. Daddy, still frozen, struggled for words. Andre closed the distance between them and with his customary hug, made the words unnecessary. He and Daddy hugged and exchanged kisses as if Andre were five or six years old. Time became an unnecessary intrusion between father and son. The fact that everyone in the restaurant was watching mattered not to either of them. They loved each and that was the only thing that was important.

"Andre, you could have given me a heart attack. Why didn't you tell me this morning that you were in town?"

Troy spoke before Andre could say anything, "Because it would have ruined the surprise." As he spoke, his eyes were on me. I felt a blush creep all over me. I was happy to see Andre, but even happier to see Troy. Auntie Noreen brought some sense and order to our just standing around.

"Can we sit down or should I tell these people to come and serve us all standing up?"

Everyone laughed. We sat down. There were enough chairs and place settings for everyone. Andre had called ahead and added three people to Daddy's list. Andre sat to Daddy's right, I to his left; Troy sat next to Andre, Auntie Noreen sat next to Troy with Leela between her and Uncle Neal, and Tony sat between Uncle Neal and me. From across the table, Troy was looking at me. I started getting goose bumps. Every now and again, I would feel a strange chill come all over my body and settle right in my neck, and I would try to steal a quick look at Troy to see if he was watching me and causing my skin to dance all over my body. Each time I looked, he was watching me and each time, he caught me. I noticed the same kind of stealing glancing action with Tony, but it wasn't me he was looking at, he was stealing to look at Andre. At one point, Tony caught me looking at him. He looked away quickly, but not before I noticed that Troy had noticed; Troy looked annoyed, even a bit angry as if he would get up and punch Tony in the face. I wondered, for about a split-second, why Troy looked so annoyed.

Dinner was served and so I didn't think about that or anyone as I ate. We were talking, laughing, and when no one was looking, stealing looks at each other. I understood Troy and I, but I didn't understand what was going on with Tony and Andre.

I was trying to figure out what was with the looks between Tony and Andre when the band leader asked that everyone be quiet as he had a special announcement to make. The entire room quieted. The band leader said, "Ladies and gentlemen, it gives me great pleasure to acknowledge Mr. Matthew Hirsh. Today, we here at Lilly's, Brooklyn's finest restaurant, are proud to wish Matthew Hirsh, the owner of this fine establishment, a happy fiftieth birthday." Daddy put his hand to his forehead and smiling, and shook his head from side to side. Everybody started clapping and singing.

It was the first time I learned that Daddy owned something other than his law practice. While everyone was singing, the waiters brought out the biggest cake I'd ever seen. When Daddy looked at it, he looked as if he would faint. The cake was in the shape of a pond and in the middle of the pond was a giant lily, surrounded by seven small lilies were the words: 'Happy Birthday – you've made our pond beautiful.' Tears filled Daddy's eyes and slid down his cheeks. It was over for the rest of us.

The room erupted; the applause was almost deafening. Daddy was the first to regain his composure and, looking around; he looked directly at the headwaiter and said, "I should have known you wouldn't let me get away with a quiet dinner. Thanks, man, you're the greatest." The waiter smiled and said, "Not me this time. It was your son who called and ordered this cake."

Daddy looked at Andre and all Andre did was smile. Looking at Andre Daddy said, "Thanks son. It's a perfect birthday cake."

Then Daddy said, "If these lovely ladies would join me, I would like to cut this incredible cake." Leela, Auntie Noreen, Daddy and I cut the cake. After we were done, they wheeled it away.

Then the bandleader said, "I believe that at this time, our birthday boy gets to dance with one of his pretty ladies."

Leela, who loved music and dancing, took Daddy's hand and pulled him to dance. The four of us, Daddy, Auntie Noreen, Leela, and I, held hands and danced. Then Uncle Neal joined us. He took Auntie Noreen's hand and then, to my surprise, Troy came and stood beside us and said, "Mr. Hirsh, would you mind if I were to dance with Drea?"

Daddy looked at him and laughingly said, "Now why would you want to steal my daughter from me and on my birthday at that?"

"I don't want to steal her sir; just a dance?"

"OK. One dance. She's all yours."

I looked to Andre for help, but he was oblivious to all of us dancing on the floor. He was looking at Tony as if Tony had turned into the birthday cake. Tony caught my eyes and turned his head away from Andre's glance. As he turned his head, Andre noticed me watching him. He got up and walked over to the dance floor where Troy and I had only made a few steps and said, "Now do you really think I would let you steal my big sister away?"

"No, I didn't think you would, but please, Andre, go and cut in on Uncle Neal. He looks as if he could use the help."

Andre patted Troy on the back and walked over to Uncle Neal and Auntie Noreen and stole Auntie Noreen right from under Uncle Neal's nose. Uncle Neal walked back to the table looking very tired. Although I was the happiest that I'd ever been, it also dawned on me that Uncle Neal had been looking very tired lately. As soon as the song was over, the room erupted in even louder applause. We walked back to our table with the sound of the applause bouncing off our happiness and adding to it. The applause ended just as the cake made its re-appearance, this time on many plates. The waiter brought Daddy an opened box and inside the box was the giant Lilly – untouched. Daddy smiled again, a smile filled with memories of a Lilly he'd loved so deeply.

When the waiter brought our cake, Leela was the first to reach for hers. She just took her hands and picked it up off the plate. As if she was setting some new trend, Daddy followed her and picked his up, and then everyone at our table, except Andre and Tony, had their cake in their hands. We were all laughing at the mess we were making, but it was making Daddy happy and that was all that mattered. The band started to play, *Earth Angel*, and with all the cake and icing sticking to our hands and fingers, Troy looked at me and asked me to dance. As if on automatic, a waiter was standing right beside me with a hot towel saving me from figuring out what to do with all the cake stuck to my fingers. I wanted to be in Troy's arms again so I quickly wiped my hands. Just as Troy touched my hand, Leela noticed and started crying. She broke into a litany of, "Mommy! Mommy! I want my mommy."

I was preparing to turn around and give her the attention that I knew she didn't want when Andre, who had ignored her all evening, said, "Leela, your mommy's going to dance. If you want, you can dance with her, but only if you stop crying."

Leela looked at him with something in her eyes that, had she been older, I would have called hatred. Rolling her eyes slowly away from him, she took her crying up a notch. Andre ignored her eye-rolling and even though he was a stranger to her he didn't back down.

"Fine, if you insist on crying, then." To my surprise Andre touched his niece for the first time. He picked her up and with a little bit more force than even I thought necessary, he plunked her down in a nearby chair and with a stern face said, "Sit your little ahh." I knew he was getting ready to say ass but realizing she was a little girl, he said, "Behind here and cry!"

I'm not sure if it was the fact that she couldn't get to me, or the fact that he'd had the nerve to touch her that made her holler but Leela started crying so loudly, people were staring. I was ready to forfeit the dance and stay just to quiet her. Andre would have none of it. Leela started to get down and come towards me. Andre, quick as a leopard, was on her. He had her in his arms and back in the chair so quickly, it was as if she'd never moved. Leela went into emergency alarm wailing. Andre looked at me as if he dared me not to dance and said, "Andrea, go; enjoy yourself."

Leela hit a new octave. I expected glasses and mirrors to start shattering. Andre gave me another look. I walked away as quickly as I could. I don't know what Andre had said or done, but just as she'd started, she'd stopped. I, like Lot's wife, looked back; it was Leela, not me, who had turned into a pillar of salt. I guessed he'd become the fire and brimstone she hadn't expected. She also never joined us on the dance floor. I'm not sure, but I'm guessing it was hard for a pillar of salt to move, far less dance.

I settled into my happy moment. Troy was a wonderful dancer. Not being much of a dancer, I managed to keep up and not make us fall. Other people joined in on the dance floor. Troy and I stayed right on dancing. I think we would have stayed dancing if Andre hadn't come for us. He was smiling when he said, "I see, Troy, that you really are planning on stealing my big sister. Now that I know, I'm going to keep an extra eye on you."

Troy smiled, but said nothing. I blushed until I matched the color of my hair. Daddy's birthday celebration was over and it was time to go. The whole restaurant stood up and applauded Daddy as we left. Daddy smiled. He looked very happy, but sad at the same time. I guessed that he was thinking about the Lilly that made his pond beautiful.

Outside, we had more cars than people. I'd come to the restaurant with Daddy, but he wasn't coming back to Bainbridge Street with us. He was going to Brooklyn Heights. Auntie Noreen and Uncle Neal put Leela in the back seat of their car. Tony and Troy had rented a small two-seater and Andre had his car. Then as if the thought had just occurred to him, Daddy turned to Troy and said, "I trust that you can get my daughter home safely."

My heart stopped. Troy looked as if he'd won the biggest prize of the night. Auntie Noreen, anticipating Leela's hollering, started to drive away and as she reached where we were standing, she said, "Now, Troy, you drive carefully with my princess, ok?"

"I will, Mrs. Peters."

"Now what's with this 'Mrs. Peters' business? You go back to calling me Auntie Noreen and just make sure that you bring Drea home safely, that's all." Auntie Noreen drove off before he could answer. I think it was more to get Leela away than anything else. I got into Troy's car but instead of getting in, he walked over to where Daddy and Andre were and the three of them talked for a few minutes. Troy walked back to the car and waving at Tony, he got in. He said, "I've asked your father and brother if I could take you for a little drive. They said it would be fine. Would you like to see some more of Brooklyn?"

I smiled and nodded. Daddy drove out the parking lot first, followed by Tony and Andre, and then Troy and I followed behind. Daddy went left as that was the direction that would take him towards the bridge and home; Tony and Andre went right as that direction would take them towards Greenwich Village where they were staying. Troy and I went left as well since we also needed to get to Brooklyn. Troy wanted to go to

Coney Island. I'd never seen Coney Island at night. The thought of seeing it with Troy made my knees tremble. It was clear to me that Troy wasn't sure why he'd asked me to come to Coney Island because once we arrived, he seemed lost, even a bit confused. Never having been to Coney Island at night time, I sat there waiting. For what, I wasn't sure, but I waited; after all it was Troy's idea.

"Andrea, would you like to go for a walk?"

"Sure."

And that's how our first night together started; a walk. Nothing earth-shattering or moving. A walk along a stretch of sand with a man I didn't know who had lost the reason why he'd asked me to come with him. We walked down once, not really talking, and when he felt that we had gone far enough, he turned around. Since this was his plan, I turned around too. He headed in the direction of the car and I followed. It didn't make any sense not to follow; after all I didn't have another way of getting home. We reached the car and it felt as if we'd never really left. I was sure that if I'd touched the hood, it would still have been warm. Troy opened my side of the car and I got in. He walked around to his side, opened the door and got in, but didn't start the car as I'd expected him.

"Andrea."

Yes, Troy."

"Never mind."

"Never mind what?"

"Nothing."

"OK."

"OK what?"

"Troy, you were the one who called my name as if you wanted to say something and now you have me all confused. Look, if you're sorry that you brought me here, don't fret yourself, just turn the car on and drive me home. I'm sure there are hundreds of other girls you would rather be with."

"Why do you say that?"

"Because."

"See, now you're doing it."

"Doing what?"

"Starting to say something and then changing your mind in the middle of the sentence."

"See, I can't please you," I told him.

"I didn't know you were trying. Why are you trying to please me?"

"Because."

"Let me guess. You don't really have an answer."

"That's where you're wrong."

"I'm wrong?" I asked.

"Yes, you are."

"So why were you trying to please me?"

"It's not important."

"Tell me and let me decide on the importance of it."

"Ok, fine."

"Jesus Christ, Drea you're wearing me out."

"Wearing you out? You're the one who brought me out here and dragged me up and down the beach as if I was on some speed tour. Just so you know, Troy, I have feelings and don't ever do this foolishness to me again. I'm not a child. I'm a woman."

"I can't help remembering you as a little girl."

"But I'm not a little girl, Troy. I'm a mother and a woman."

Troy's voice and eyes softened; leaning close to me, he said, "You sure are, Drea."

Leaning closer and to my surprise, he kissed me. My first real kiss. Troy's lips were soft and moist. His tongue wasn't hurried. It entered my mouth as if it were a diamond being placed in a velvet sachet. I touched it apprehensively with mine. Troy responded by pulling me closer to him. I have no idea how long the kiss lasted, but one thing I knew for sure; when Troy released me I lost my balance and fell deeper in love with him. I didn't brace my fall. However the landing turned out, I would accept; for now though, the fall was perfect.

Troy and I stayed there and made out as if we'd invented it. I was in my glory. I had no recollection of leaving, the drive home, or any memory of what time he actually brought me home but what I did know was that I couldn't wait to see him again. I had a blissful week; not even Leela got to me. I'd been a good mother; sacrificed what felt to me like a lifetime, and now I was being rewarded.

Troy was coming to get me. Where he was taking me, I'd no idea nor did I care. The doorbell rang and as the sound echoed throughout the house, I jumped right out of my skin. Excitement left me no choice. By the time the echo had died down, I returned to my skin. My skin felt a little tight. I guess that was from the hurried way I'd exited it and re-entered it. I guessed that I was in sideways. I couldn't worry about that now. Troy was waiting. I bolted to the door to let him in. He was standing at the door looking like an early Christmas gift. Santa Claus sure had a good sense of humor.

In one quick glance, I'd made a mental image of Troy. He looked so handsome standing there in his chocolate-colored corduroy pants, double-knit shirt, and sports jacket with the tan-colored patch on the sleeve that I wanted to pretend that he was a candy wrapper and I was his favorite candy – how I wanted to be wrapped in him. Looking at him made me want to jump, cry, faint, or just… God I wasn't sure what I wanted to do, but it was something. One of those un-nameable things that women do when there are no words to describe happiness. I was there. Swooning would have been perfect but it was just so, ahhh, Victorian. Anyway, I didn't. I just smiled at him and prepared to follow my heart.

Ordinarily, if I were going anywhere Auntie Noreen would have been downstairs to watch me leave. She wasn't this evening as Uncle Neal wasn't feeling very well. She was sitting upstairs with him. Not to disturb either of them, I just shouted up to them from the bottom of the stairs that I was leaving. I caught the tail-end of her goodbye as I was closing the door behind me. I'm sure the rest of her goodbye slammed into the door as I closed it. I didn't worry too much about Auntie Noreen's goodbye slamming against the door and splintering into a million pieces or anything like that since Auntie Noreen always spoke softly and especially when she talked to me. I walked away with little guilt. Her sentence, whatever it was, would land softly.

Troy reached for my hand as soon as I closed the door and it was then that I worried if my heart had made it out the door. I felt a sudden tightness in my chest and I knew that my heart had made it out. Troy was handsome and, without his knowing, he was killing me. I loved every second of this killing. With Troy still holding my hand, I breathed a sigh of relief because if he wasn't, I would've floated right up into the sky and perhaps gotten caught between the naked branches of the trees.

He headed onto the express way. I knew enough to know we were headed to Long Island although I'd never been there before. I sat in awed silence as the stretched-out highway got sucked up by the car and before I could get used to the way the car was just cutting through the darkness, we were stopping. I'd no idea where Troy had brought me and neither did I care. I was with him; that was all that mattered.

"Troy, where are we?"

"It's a surprise"

"I don't need a surprise, Troy; it isn't my birthday or anything."

"Well, I thought you needed one because I do."

"Why do you need a surprise Troy?"

"Because this has been the hardest week I've ever had."

"Of course you know I'm going to ask you why, Troy."

"'Cause I couldn't get you off my mind for one single second. I have no idea what I did this week. It's amazing that your father didn't fire me. I think the only reason he didn't fire me was because he might have guessed I was thinking about you."

This, almost confession of love from Troy, threw me into a tailspin. I looked at him and I could tell he was feeling what I was feeling. He leaned over and kissed me. We held hands as we walked toward the house. He opened the door and my eyes immediately went to a big sign that said, "Welcome, Andrea Hirsh Greenwood. Welcome to your future!"

Troy started to kiss me passionately the second my foot crossed the threshold. I kissed him back with the same passion. He used his foot to close the door. The minute it was closed, he bent down and swooped me up into his arms and started walking. He could have been taking me to a waiting barbeque pit and it wouldn't have made any difference to me. I closed my eyes and wrapped my arms around his neck. After a few steps, he put me down. I never opened my eyes. I didn't want to for fear that I would be dreaming.

He kissed me again. I still didn't open my eyes. When he reached to take my clothes off, I let him. When he laid me down on what must have been a bed, I let him. When he started touching my naked body, I let him. When he climbed over and onto me, I let him. I allowed Troy do whatever he wanted because whatever Troy wanted, I wanted. When he parted my legs and I felt him try to make his way into my entered-and-exited-only-once private parts, I struggled and pushed against him, not to push him away, but to help him make his way into me. When he succeeded, I didn't cry out or let him know that it felt just like the first time all over again. It was only when he cried out that I joined him. We were joined in body, spirit, and a cry that I was sure had pierced the heavens. I cried. This time I was happy.

We made love all that night. It was very late when he drove me back home. I was hungry and tired and only then did it dawn on me that I never found out what the surprise was or what the sign meant. I dismissed it all. I was happy. I gave up the idea of trying to find something to eat as I wanted nothing to delay me from reliving the evening I'd waited a lifetime for. However, the replay wasn't to be. The minute my head hit the pillow, I was asleep. I dreamed of Troy all night. I woke in the morning to the first frost of the season. If I weren't so dizzy in love with Troy, I would've taken that as sign, an omen that something chilling was about to happen but I was in love and therefore I failed to pay attention to the major sign that Mother Nature had sent my way. I didn't have long to wait before its true meaning was revealed.

Chapter 56

Head in the Sand

Andre and Tony stayed a week before they returned to London. On the day they were returning, Andre came to see Auntie Noreen and Uncle Neal. He looked happy. Whatever was in London was now in Andre, and he had become a part of it. I would let him go and miss him. If London held the key to his happiness, then who was I to stand in his way? I would continue to love him from afar.

Uncle Neal hugged both Tony and Andre, but he hugged Andre the longest and hardest. It was the way that Uncle Neal hugged Andre that finally broke my heart. For different reasons, it looked as if Uncle Neal was saying a different kind of goodbye to Andre. Auntie Noreen looked on as Uncle Neal said goodbye and she cried. She cried loudly as if her heart were breaking. She kept looking at Andre in a funny way; the way she did when we were little and she knew that there was something we weren't telling her. Auntie Noreen knew or felt that Andre had a secret; one that was tearing him apart. She hugged him hard and cried like she was never going to see him again. I couldn't watch anymore. I walked away.

It wasn't the first time Andre was going to London, but somehow this time felt different. They were returning to London and not Barbados because Andre had landed a very important job in London and Tony didn't want to stay in Barbados without him so he packed up, shipped their things from Barbados when they'd come for Daddy's birthday and now they were headed back to the place that was familiar. Even now Tony looked a little nervous and lost. He looked as if he were watching the saddest goodbyes he'd ever witnessed and somehow none of these goodbyes would be happening if it weren't for him. Tony looked as if he felt that he was stealing Andre away from us; to me that was silly because we had come to accept that it was always Andre and Tony, or Tony and Andre since high school. I couldn't remember a time when I'd seen them apart. They were together so long that one day Auntie Noreen had said, "Neal you think Tony would know his right hand if Andre wasn't around to point it out to him?" Uncle Neal had looked at Auntie Noreen and without missing a beat had said, "Do you think that boy, I mean Andre, would know his right hand if Tony wasn't there to point it out to him. Them boys so foolish that if one was headed over a cliff the other couldn't him to come back."

Both Auntie Noreen and Uncle Neal had laughed really hard at their own joke but now even as I remembered it I couldn't laugh. I hugged, and kissed them both and cried. Tony had replaced me in my brother's life.

My crying days didn't last very long. Troy and I were inseparable all summer and into the fall. Somehow, he made me forget, at least for a little while, that his brother had replaced me in my brother's life. I guess in a strange way, Troy and I had exchanged. Our brothers had replaced us with the other's brother and we were left alone to fend for ourselves. We accepted our roles and became the other's replacement. Actually, it wasn't a bad deal. I believed I'd gotten the better half of the bargain. We had our brothers to thank for leaving us so alone we had no choice but to find solace in each other.

We accepted our stand-in roles by sometimes going out to eat, seeing a show, or most times just driving out to Troy's house on Long Island. We spoke of love, happy things and even hinted once of spending 'till forever together. I wanted forever with Troy. I wanted what Auntie Noreen and Uncle Neal had. I wanted Troy to be the one I turned to when all that was left was gray hair and grace. I started to believe that everyone was hoping right along with me. I could tell that Auntie Noreen was really wishing that I would get my chance at a Happy-Ever-After; not like the one that Nana's momma got, but the one that had a happy ending.

Auntie Noreen's smile welcomed me back after each date and seemed to say, "Soon, soon you'll have your chance."

Daddy accepted my dating Troy with open arms. I guessed he believed that Leela and I would be safe with him. Andre and Tony, along with everyone else, gave us their unofficial blessing. I accepted everyone's well wishes and stayed in my perpetual state of blissfulness; well, that was until the week before Christmas.

I'd been seeing Troy for almost five months and in my blissful ignorance, hadn't paid any attention to the fact that I'd not seen a period for almost three of those five months. The absence of my period finally dawned on me when, during my yearly exam, the nurse asked, "When was your last period?"

I started thinking back and the harder I thought back, the more I panicked. Seeing the fear that was consuming me, the nurse suggested that I take a pregnancy test. I did so reluctantly. The rabbit died and I cried.

Later Daddy, Auntie Noreen, Uncle Neal all cried and I imagined Andre and Tony when the news reached them. They didn't cry because the rabbit died. They cried because they had high expectations of Troy. They expected him to do the right thing. Marry me and make an honest woman out of me. He didn't.

For reasons that no one understood, he went home to his parents in Connecticut, told them that he'd made his boss' daughter pregnant, and they fixed it for him. They offered him a way out and he took it. Troy left. He left his job, his friends, his house, and he left me. Without so much as a word to me, Troy Adams, the man I believed loved me, left me with his child growing in me. He left taking my love and my hopes of a Happy-Ever-after with him.

Book Seven

Troi-Anna Hirsh Greenwood

A Time to Plant

Chapter 57

Dandelion Tears and a Hungry Fire

My heart broke. I cried. The tears were hot. They scorched a permanent path down my cheeks. My face looked like it had the beaten paths to hell tattooed on it. Not even with those scorched tattoos on my face did I stop crying. The pain was still there and it needed an out and because crying had become a habit, I continued to cry. It was to me, like after you'd vomited and there was nothing left to bring up, but your body still wanted to vomit so it went through the motion, well, that's what my eyes did. They went through the motion of crying.

I cried, or better yet, pushed the shape of tears from my eyes. It was strange to see the dry transparent shapes fall from my eyes and, just like dandelions blown into the wind, they just floated away. They were light and that was odd because the pain that had created them was so heavy that those tear shells should have bounced right off my tear-scorched face and hit the ground, shattering on impact. The sight of all those empty tear shells floating away so light and carefree made me cry harder. I cried 'till my eyes became so dry that blinking felt like the inside of my lid was coated with sandpaper yet I still tried, and hard, to cry.

I wanted to cry, had to cry, didn't know what else to do, but I'd run out of tears. That didn't stop me. I pushed my body, forced it to search for a reserve. I had to have a reserve. I was, after all, a daughter of Greenwood; we'd perfected crying. We'd cried off and on for more than a hundred years. Pain and passion had kept us readily supplied with tears. Where were those tears now I needed them? I asked God to let me tap into the River Greenwood that was created from all the tears the daughters of Greenwood had cried, but nothing, and then one day fresh tears came.

I couldn't figure out where my body had finally found this new source of water until the baby Troy and I had made in love moved. My heart missed a beat. Shit. I'd tapped into the water that was surrounding the baby. My crying came to an abrupt halt. I couldn't cry that out. The baby needed it. I'd heard of the horrors of a dry birth; I didn't want to go through that. I adjusted to Troy's abandonment of me and his baby and went about the business of nourishing my baby without another tear.

Everyone, including Leela cooperated. She was excited about the baby and so, for the first time since I'd been her mother, she was nice to me or as nice as she could let herself. I accepted it. My pregnancy was uneventful and at the end of my term, almost nine months to the day after I'd walked into Troy's house on Long Island for the first time, I gave birth to his daughter.

She came into this world as quietly as she was conceived. She looked around at her surroundings as if to say, "I didn't ask to be here," and then closed her eyes. She opened them again and looked at me and somewhere in those hazel green eyes, I saw a fire. It was a different kind of fire. Not like the one that burned in Leela, it was a hungry fire. She was going to be a quiet smoldering volcano until pushed; a fire that would seek to be fed often. Passion was going to be the fuel propelling this baby. Passion had created her and passion would feed her.

I looked at my baby and loved her with almost the same kind of all-consuming love I'd had for her father. No one had to tell me, I knew that nothing or no one was going to take his place in my heart, life, or home as long as his child was in it. No one was going to take the love I had for this baby or her father. The love I felt for Troy was going to be as fierce as the fire of hatred that burned inside my heart for Hamilton. The only difference was the fuel. One was fed by love; the other hatred. I called her Troi-Anna Hirsh Greenwood.

Everyone came to the hospital to see her. She was everything that Leela wasn't. Troi-Anna had taken the best of everything that Troy and I had. She had the kind of completion that if you looked at her quickly, you would think she was white. She had my hair, my hazel green eyes, and my nose. She was an absolutely beautiful baby, but she was a strange combination of sadness and haste. She was in a hurry.

Everyone doted on her, even Leela. Daddy was very good with his granddaughters. He always included Troi-Anna in everything he did with Leela. By the time Troi-Anna was a little less than two weeks old, she'd become T'Anna. No one wanted to call her Troi-Anna. It reminded them that Troy had abandoned us. Auntie Noreen, being Auntie Noreen, had asked me the day I named the baby, "Child, why you got to go and name a baby after a man that done left you and her? Ain't it going be hard enough looking at her every day and seeing him since she took so much from him? Why, child, you gone and done something like this to this baby."

My answer was simple, "I'm keeping her, ain't I, Auntie Noreen? So what difference does it makes what her name is? It ain't like I'm ever going to look at her and forget who her father is." That was the end of that discussion. My Troi-Anna became T'Anna.

I thought of Troy often, but I never let on or allowed anyone to know that I missed him. I had two daughters to contend with, and two flames burning in my heart. One flame was for Hamilton, who after all these years I'd still never been able to forgive. The other was for Troy Adams, who I'd forgiven and continued to love despite the fact that he'd done the same as Hamilton. I often wished that the doorbell would ring and Troy would be on the other side. It never happened. He never came back. We all continued.

T'Anna always seemed as if she was waiting for something special and the next minute without thinking or planning, she was rushing as if going to get this special something that only she knew existed.

Chapter 58

A Change Is Gonna Come

Two Fridays before Easter, I asked Mrs. Trindle to watch the girls for about an hour; two at the most, so that Auntie Noreen could head downtown Fulton Street to May's Department Store to pick up Easter clothes for them. I knew we weren't going to be long because I was nursing. Troi-Anna was just about to turn two months and although Auntie Noreen could have picked up the dresses, I wanted to be there. It was going to be Troi-Anna's first Easter.

I tried to get them matching dresses but Auntie Noreen said, "Now you know that Leela is already jealous of T'Anna, why would you put her in the same dress? T'Anna may not know she's wearing the same dress as her big sister, but you know Leela is going to know and there'll be no peace in church when she tries to take that poor baby out her dress. You know Leela is going to see it as hers."

I started to feel as if I would cry and I didn't realize how close I was to crying until Auntie Noreen said, "It's not worth crying about. Leela won't give us a moment's peace and God knows I want to hear what Reverend Harcourt has to say, and besides I don't want all those dignified Bajan church folk thinking that my Miss Leela ain't got no manners. So I tell you what; you go and pick out what you want for T'Anna and I'll pick out for Leela. This way we don't have to regret T'Anna's first Easter."

Before I could blink twice, we were done and on our way back home with enough time to start cooking. I left Auntie Noreen to start frying the fishcakes and told her that I would be back to make the oatmeal. She said she would put the sweet potatoes on to boil so that by the time I got back and had the oatmeal done, Uncle Neal would be home.

These days, Uncle Neal wasn't staying at the Lodge as late as he used to. A lot of 'fire' as Auntie Noreen called it had gone out of Uncle Neal since Uncle Boysie died. Sometimes I would look at Uncle Neal when he came back from a meeting or a rally and he always seemed so tired. A lot of times, he looked as if everything was taking too much from him, yet he wouldn't quit.

We had just finished eating and Auntie Noreen and I were fixing T'Anna's bottles as I wasn't making as much milk as with Leela so we'd gotten in the habit of fixing her bottles right after dinner was done and the dishes were put away.

Leela, who was taking her role as big sister seriously, was outside with Uncle Neal and if T'Anna made even a whimper, Leela came and got me. Tonight she was quiet and that allowed Auntie Noreen and I to get what we had to do done. I'd put the last bottle in the fridge and was heading out with a bottle in my hand to feed Troi-Anna when I heard, "Oh, God No! No! No! not a-blasted-gain!"

Auntie Noreen and I ran out the kitchen to find Uncle Neal standing holding his head and he looked like he was a second from screaming or crying. Auntie Noreen said, "What's wrong, Neal? What happened?"

Uncle Neal could barely speak. He pointed to the TV. Auntie Noreen and I looked at the TV in time to hear Walter Cronkite say, *"…they rushed the thirty-nine year-old Negro leader to the hospital where he died of a bullet wound to the neck…"*

Auntie Noreen sat down at the edge of the settee and started to cry. I wanted to go to her, to comfort her, but I didn't know how to comfort her as I was crying myself. No one went to anyone. This time we cried alone. Uncle Neal didn't come to comfort her nor did he try to comfort me. He was trying to figure out for himself what to do. He was pacing and crying. Leela started to cry. Auntie Noreen opened her arms so that Leela could have a place to put the sadness she didn't understand. She was crying because we were.

The news played on. I don't think any of us heard it. We were crying loudly. Uncle Neal was the first to slow, not stop, his tears. He sat down and turned up the volume of the TV. Perhaps in doing so, he hoped that he would hear something different. Walter Cronkite would probably say that what we and all of America, Negro and white alike, had heard was a mistake. He didn't. If anything, he went on to describe how.

That was enough for Uncle Neal. To my surprise, he turned off the

TV. He got back up from his chair and started pacing and then he said, "Not too long ago, a few years or so, and I don't know if you remember but me, Boysie, Colroy, and a few of the men from the Lodge were getting ready to join Dr. King, Bayard Rustin, A. Philip Randolph, and all them rest who was planning that march on Washington for jobs and freedom and what did they do? They kill Medgar Evers.

"That would have been enough to stop some other people but we was on a mission. Nothing was goin' stop we 'cause we already had to figure out how to live with what they done to us from the time we were slaves to now. How many of we went to Washington to march on their behinds? How many, Noreen? We don't know and them don't know, but we went. If it had wheels, was moving and headed in the direction of the Washington Monument, we took it.

"Anybody worth anything was there. You should have seen the crowd. I was never so proud to see so many Negroes. We was standing up for something. We had a cause, a purpose. Speaker after speaker get up and, man, they made your chest swell out when they talked and the woman? The pretty one that sings and dances? The one that live over in England or something?"

"She ain't live in England if you mean Josephine Baker."

"Yes. She. She talked 'bout how this struggle was important. Noreen, we got to keep doing this thing; fighting 'till some blasted body, sorry 'bout cursing in front you and Drea Noreen, but somebody got to stand up to them or them gine mek we frighten again.

"My God. Dr. King. What they shoot the man for? He talking 'bout non-violence and what them do; shoot de man? How you gine shoot down somebody who talking non-violence. He ain't doing nobody nothing but trying to get better conditions for Negroes.

"In this war, and yes, it's a war; we got to do like a real army and raise up new people to fight and maybe even do like them; kill when the old ones like me, Boysie, Colroy, and the rest of we dead off."

When Uncle Neal said, "Kill," Auntie Noreen said, "Don't say that, Neal. That's not something you want Leela to hear you say."

Uncle Neal pointed to the TV and said, "All over America tonight, everybody hearing that another Negro, and not any Negro, Dr. King shot down like some wild animal. So she gine hear. She might as well hear it from me 'cause some day somebody not gine care 'bout she and they gine say worse for she to hear.

"This foolish wickedness goin' on long enough. Look at the shite them was doing down in Alabama back in '55 on the buses. Negro people, tired as shite from working for next skin to nothing, trying to get home like anybody else and 'cause them say so, Negroes had to stand up in front of empty kiss-me-ass bus seats. You can imagine that. Them got to stand up and leave them seats empty; pure shite, empty just in case some blasted white person, who ain't work near as hard or as long as a Negro get on the bus and want to sit. You tell me that ain't shite.

"All that kinda shite goin' on 'till Negro folk get tired and say they had enough. Negroes walked to work rather than take the bus. Why? I know you ain't ask why but you just got to ask the question though; imagine people, suffer themselves to walk, beg for a ride, anything rather than get back on them buses 'till them could sit down. That's what you got to do. Get them son-a-bitches where them gine feel. In them pockets. It ain't easy for a Negro nowhere in this blasted world. Not even in Africa. Ask Patrice Lumumba."

"Patrice who? Loo Mum Who?"

"Lumumba."

"Neal, where you getting all this stuff? And what's it got to do with Dr. King getting shot?'

"What's it got to do with Dr. King getting shot? Plenty. If them can shoot down King, you think them going have a problem shooting down any one of we?"

"In ain't saying that they ain't gine got a problem but, Neal, you didn't use to be like this. Who are all these people you now talking 'bout?"

"I know, Noreen, that you use to me not really saying much, but it hard to just sit by and say nothing when all over the place people living and some dying just so things can get better for Negroes. Patrice Lumumba was a Prime Minister in Africa, the Congo I think, but they didn't even let him be that for too long before them had him standing in front of a firing squad and shoot him dead.

"He ain't the only one, everywhere you look them going after all the people who want better conditions for Negroes. It don't matter where the Negro is: here, Barbados, Jamaica, down South. It don't matter. So I got to listen and I got to talk up. Drea got Leela and that baby there and I want when I'm dead and gone that them little girls can walk where they feel like, sit where they feel like, eat where they feel like, and not have to look up and see if them in the right spot. That the sign over them head saying Colored and that somebody done take Jim Crow and do to him what they do to all crows…pelt a rock at he and kill him dead. Jim Crow and all his laws got to stop."

"You think that day ever going come, Neal?"

"I got to believe that it's coming. Didn't Miss Thea, when she was here, tell you and Drea all 'bout what life was like for Drea's people? Them come from slave to where Drea is so I got to believe that more changes can happen. That's why I was following Boysie to all those meetings and things. Somebody got to care."

Uncle Neal sat down. It was like he'd become tired. Auntie Noreen got up and turned the TV back on. Senator Robert Kennedy was talking. It was about Dr. Martin Luther King.

Uncle Neal looked up and said, "Hmmmmh, everybody got something to say." Pointing to the TV he said, "Ordinarily right now, the way I feeling, I won't want to listen to no white man but see him, I would listen to him 'cause he knows what it's like when hate snatch somebody from you. But this thing, hatred getting harder and harder to kill.

"It ain't even that they just killing the people in the struggle. Negro people ain't got no value in this country. How long is it now since that woman shoot Sam Cooke and said that he come after she? Come after she for what? I bet you she do like the rest. Let him in and when she think that somebody white see a Negro smelling round, she pull out a gun and defended she self from somebody that she invite to come and smell. I tell you, Noreen, when Negro men gine learn 'cause it look good don't mean it is good. How long that is now? What, a little over a year after Kennedy.

"These people ain't got no conscience. What was he doing? Singing? I mean…he was singing for Christ's sake. He was singing 'bout change coming and for that; Lord have mercy, he dead. Now they shoot down King 'cause he want change. It's hard not be vexed over this shite, Noreen, it's hard."

Uncle Neal didn't have to stay in his anguish alone. Auntie Noreen, with Leela in tow, got up from where she was on the settee and went to him. She stood beside his chair and Uncle Neal leaned his head towards her hip. Leela sat on the floor next to me, to my surprise, and put her head by my shoulder. I let her. I knew she won't be there long. As soon as she figured out how to fit in with Uncle Neal and Auntie Noreen, she was going to get up and take up that space. She hadn't yet so she stayed close to me. For the few seconds or minute she felt she needed me, I would be here for her. I wrapped my arm around her and she, again to my surprise, let it stay.

Auntie Noreen took her arm, draped it around Uncle Neal's shoulder, and started a gentle swaying. Uncle Neal allowed the rhythm of her swaying to take him with her. Then Auntie Noreen said, "You know something, Neal. It's funny how here in big America, change can't happen without somebody killing somebody. But we in little Barbados make change happen and nobody ain't get assassinated. Dead yes, but not assassinated. We West Indians fighting for what we want from time of slavery. Killing a white slave master back then wasn't an assassination that was different. Them came and find we there so we had to fight 'gainst what them was doing; keeping everything for themselves and working we to death. That's why Bussa and them rise up.

"Drea, that rising up ain't like what them doing here in America; killing 'cause them can kill. Back then, it was 'cause we wanted freedom. After Bussa rebellion in 1816, you had one in Demerara in Guyana. That was but seven years or so later in 1823 and then the Jamaicans followed in 1831. If not for all them rebellions, we might still be slaves. I know that's different to what happened here today, but it's not really that different, you know.

"One set a people can't keep on oppressing the rest. I hate to say this, but there ain't nothing you can say and end the sentence with, 'and then the white man came' that ain't goin' be something bad. By that I mean, here in America you had the Indians living free doing what they wanted to do and…then the white man came. We know how that end up. Over in Africa, people goin' bout their business living, inventing things…and then the white man came; again we know how that end up. It don't matter what you think about if you add…'and then the white man came', it ending bad."

The gently swaying continued. Uncle Neal said nothing. Auntie Noreen continued, "Seventeen months ago, Barbados became independent. True, it ain't make no big big news over here and you know why it ain't make no news?"

Auntie Noreen didn't wait for Uncle Neal to answer; she continued, "'Cause people acted civilized. Errol Walton Barrow fought for our independence. I ain't trying to make it sound like it was a one, two, three thing, 'cause it wasn't. A lot of hard work went into making we a free nation but what I'm saying is that nobody ain't get a gun and assassinate nobody.

"One minute, the Union Jack; that was England's flag, flying over Barbados and the next, after them dim the lights and bring them up again, we own flag flying. We thank people in Barbados. We thanked Grantley Prescod for designing we beloved flag and we don't make sport when it come to the pledge. We take that serious. It don't matter where we are. I wasn't in Barbados when we got independence but we celebrated. Independence didn't just come for Bajans in Barbados, it come for every Bajan everywhere.

"We was proud, proud that night. You remember, Neal, we ain't sleep that night. We didn't worry 'bout anybody killing Barrow. I don't even think anybody at all think 'bout that. We were excited, happy, proud. Independence had come while we was living to see it.

"I made it my business to know the National Anthem and to learn the pledge. We know the pledge. There ain't no blood on the pledge."

I didn't expect Uncle Neal to say anything, but in a soft voice, just more than a whisper, he said, "*I pledge allegiance to my country Barbados and to my flag. To uphold and defend their honor, and by my living, to do credit to my nation, wherever I go.*"

When he was done, Auntie Noreen said, "See, Drea, we got all of that and nobody ain't assassinated. When is America gine stop killing people who trying to do or get better for people that everybody walking on?"

Chapter 59

No Room to Wallow

The assassination of Martin Luther King took a toll on Uncle Neal's spirit. It was as if he felt The Cause, as he called it was losing ground. He started to believe again that things couldn't happen when President Lyndon B. Johnson, with one stroke of his pen, put one more layer on the cake called Freedom. Uncle Neal celebrated. I remembered Colroy coming by. He was excited. He said to Uncle Neal, "Look where we are. All that rallying is paying off. Man, we've come a long way from when Abraham Lincoln signed the Emancipation Proclamation Act back in 1863; that was the first layer of this cake called Freedom.

"Now, man, after almost a hundred years, thousands of Negroes dying at the hands of white people, some losing their lives 'cause they were thirsty and the only fountain they could see said, "Whites", and they took a chance to get that life-saving and in their case it became life-losing sip of water. Some died because they had steel down their backs; pride, and refused when a white person felt that they should have to bow their head, that nod or refusal to step onto the streets so a white person could go by was enough reason why that head bowed later, with a rope as its support."

Some foolish men, Colroy said, "Died 'cause they didn't learn that they didn't have to find out what it was that a white woman had between and at the top of her legs. They didn't have to be that curious. In their cases, curiosity didn't kill the cat, it was the "white cat" that killed the Negro called Curiosity. Curiosity didn't know how to run 'way fast from the fast white woman who wanted her lust, yearning, and curiosity for and about them satisfied.

"She, the same fast white woman, was like a cat when she couldn't get the taste for Negro Lions out of her loins or mouth. She crawled to and under the Negro foolish enough to believe what she said to him 'bout him being the biggest and best dick she ever had or wanted. And, after she'd satisfied her yearning had, in cat-like fashion, and all attempts to lick her white cat clean of the smell of the Negro Lion called Curiosity had failed. She, again, in the same cat-like fashion figured out how to land on her feet. She went home and rubbed against her white man's leg, purred, and said to him, the one called Bigotry and Prejudice whom she knew was filled with hatred for the Negro Lion called Curiosity, 'He, the big, black, nasty, Negro Man "raped" me with his big nigger 'thing'.'

"Then the next thing you know, Neal the stupid, ignorant Negro Lion that should have been protecting not only his pride but should have used some when he saw the wicked white witch coming; is dead and loin-less caused he'd used it to "deflower" a wild-bush that never would have flowered in the first place."

Colroy was almost jumping up and down when he said, "Man, Neal, Old Jim and all his laws goin' have to crow somewhere else. Ain't it something...little Negroes goin' now get to find out what's in Jane's book, a tired Negro woman coming home from scrubbing their floors goin' now get a chance to sit on a bus and rest her tired feet, and we ain't goin' have to step off the sidewalk when them coming towards us. Ain't that goin' be some shit."

Colroy was excited. Uncle Neal joined in the celebration, though not as excitedly. He was glad that the Civil Rights Bill, though it was only four years old, was having an impact. He'd talked about it often over breakfast. When The Voting Rights Bill got passed, he talked about that over dinner and so he told Leela and Troi-Ann, though neither knew what he was talking about. "Children, it look like America moving forward in the right direction. All those things I'd struggled and worked so hard to see come to pass have come to pass. This is going to be a better America for you all."

Then another shot rang out. This one took down Bobby Kennedy. Uncle Neal listened to the news like it was old hat. Martin Luther King had only been dead about six months and here the nation was, again thrust into another collective hurt and mourning. I think the shooting made Uncle Neal feel even more tired and frustrated.

He talked about it but not like with Malcolm X. None of the killings that happened after Malcolm X affected Uncle Neal as much. He was wearing down. He still went to meetings and he still had a rallying cry, but now he didn't shout as loudly. He marched, but not as often.

He even found a moment to laugh and tease Auntie Noreen. One night, Josephine Baker was on TV and Auntie Noreen said, "Neal, ain't that your secret girlfriend?"

Uncle Neal said, "What you talking 'bout, Noreen? You know my heart belongs only to you."

Auntie Noreen, laughing, said, "Neal Peters, don't think I don't know how all you men wish that the rest of we looked like she."

That made Uncle Neal laugh and he said, "Only a foolish man would pine behind she. A man like me got sense. Josephine Baker never gine stir a pot of Cou Cou for me, or make me some bakes and lemonade. I ain't foolish, Noreen. I know where my rice boils down. So don't try to trick me talking 'bout some pretty, pretty, coke-bottle shaped, long-legged, light skinned woman."

Auntie Noreen laughed and threw a piece of paper at Uncle Neal. He caught it and, laughing, said, "So you can still get jealous? That's good to know. We can fix your jealousy later."

When Uncle Neal said that, Auntie Noreen smiling shyly, said, "Neal Peters, behave yourself. We ain't got nothing to fix later or no other time and try and remember that you old as dust. Dust don't fix nobody."

Uncle Neal wasn't about to let Auntie Noreen off the hook so easily. "Keep it up, Noreen, keep it up. I know you showing off 'cause Drea's here. Say that when Drea ain't here and I gine show you dust. I ain't done wid you."

Auntie Noreen started to get a little vex and she said, "Neal Peters, stop with all that foolish talk and respect yourself or I gine get up and go set up de pot if you don't stop."

"You ain't got to get vex. I was just making some mock sport. I done. I was just making a little sport with you. You ain't got to worry 'bout goin' sleep tonight. I gine keep my dusty self to myself. You ain't bound to let my dust fall on you."

Auntie Noreen wanted to be vex at Uncle Neal but when he said that, she started to laugh and then she said, "Bring your dusty self near me tonight and I gine get the vacuum for you."

Laughing Uncle Neal said, "Now you talking my speed. A Hoover in the bedroom…vroom, vroom."

We laughed and laughed about that for the rest of the night. Then

Uncle Neal said, "Noreen, your old bag of dust is ready to go up. You want to get the vacuum and come."

"Neal Peters, I done tell you to behave yourself. When you ready, go up. I coming as soon as I help Drea wash up and put the girls to bed."

Getting up, Uncle Neal said, "Don't be long. I serious, Noreen. I feel real tired and somehow I don't feel like goin' up without you. I'll sit here and wait for you. Let we walk upstairs together like when we were young. I would like that. So; go on. I gine wait for you."

Somehow, Auntie Noreen didn't tease Uncle Neal. Smiling, she said, "Alright. I gine hurry. Wait for me. I ain't gine be long. You right. That would be nice; yeah, real nice."

As I took Troi-Anna up, Leela took Auntie Noreen's hand and we headed to the bathroom. For some reason, the girls didn't fuss, carry on, or beg to stay in the tub longer. In a few minutes, we had them dressed and when Auntie Noreen kissed them and said, "Goodnight, see you all in the morning, no one cried or tried to follow. I was tired so as soon as they were asleep, I slipped into the shower, bathed, and was in bed and asleep as soon as my head hit the pillow.

Chapter 60

'till I Can't Hold You Any Longer

When I woke in the morning, the first thing that struck me as odd was how quiet it was; not just outside but inside. Inside was the quietest. It was the kind of quiet that comes after everyone in the house has fallen asleep. The kind of quiet that makes you whisper, even to the person who is right next to you. I listened for the sound of Auntie Noreen moving around in the kitchen; no noise came. She wasn't in the kitchen.

Because it was that quiet, I listened for the sound of Uncle Neal's cup touching the saucer as he read the morning paper; not even that noise came. He wasn't sitting at the kitchen table reading his paper and keeping Auntie Noreen's company; as they called it. Keeping someone's company was important to all of us, keeping company said, "I care about you and what you are doing. I'll spend time with you until you are done, this way you aren't alone."

I came out my room and my first thought was to head to their room, to knock, wait for one of them to say, "Come in," before I pushed the door and went in. In this house, we always knocked before going into anyone's bedroom. I was just about to knock to make sure they were alright when I remembered that Uncle Neal had teased Auntie Noreen about bringing the vacuum to their room. I smiled as I remembered that he'd also waited for her so they could go upstairs together. Thinking of them walking up the stairs hand in hand the way they used to do when I was a little girl made me smile even wider. I let the idea of interrupting them go.

It was still early and the girls were sleeping so I decided to go back to my room and enjoy a few more minutes of peace before they woke and dragged everything, including fussing and fighting, with them out their beds and down the stairs. I wasn't in my room five minutes when Auntie Noreen knocked softly and, after I said, "Come in," she came into my room.

Looking at the girls, who were still asleep, she said, "Drea, come in the kitchen with me a minute."

My heart started to race, but Auntie Noreen was calm so my heart settled down. I started to think that she probably wanted me to reach something that she wanted from one of the top shelves in the cupboard and as usual, I did the climbing.

I got up and followed Auntie Noreen. When we got downstairs, I started to head to the kitchen but Auntie Noreen put her hand softly on my arm and said, "Come in here for a minute. I have to tell you something."

Despite Auntie Noreen's calm exterior my heart started the wild beating again. Inside the drawing room, Auntie Noreen guided me to the settee. I don't know what made me sit but I sat. Auntie Noreen sat next to me and, taking my hand, she said, "Drea, my morning came differently today."

I looked at Auntie Noreen and wondered what she was talking about. I didn't have to ask I could tell from looking at her face that another sentence was waiting so I did like the sentence. I waited my turn, there would be time. In the silence of her pause, I noticed that dust continued to dance on a sunray that was using the stained glass over the drawing room window to come in. In the beauty of that dance, I waited for Auntie Noreen to speak. She was ready. I could tell. She'd taken a deep breath and then very calmly, she said, "The Lord has called your Uncle Neal home to rest. He's dead."

I felt all the air getting sucked out of me. I started to scream and holler. I did everything that people do when they receive news that someone they love has died. Auntie Noreen took me into her arms and shushed me. She quieted my fears, calmed my spirit. Even when I tried to run; don't know where I wanted to run to, she held me. Kept me next to her and when the initial shock left me, she welcomed me back. Returned, I listened as she told me to call Mrs. Trindle, to wake and dress the girls, and to take them over to her. She didn't want Leela or Troi-Anna to see their Uncle Neal like that. Calmed by her love and reassuring voice, I did just as she said. I don't know how I did it, but I called Mrs.

Trindle, who said that I could bring them. I don't remember anything after that. I do remember that by the time I was getting ready with the girls, the doorbell rung and it was Mrs. Trindle. She'd decided that she would come and get the girls. She didn't think that Auntie Noreen should be alone; not even for that short amount of time. She was West Indian so she understood 'bout keeping company. I stayed to keep Auntie Noreen's company.

When Mrs. Trindle left, I had no idea. I just knew that soon Auntie Noreen and I were alone. Auntie Noreen very calmly said to me, "Drea, will you please call your daddy. Tell him what has happened. Tell him I need him to come. Tell him, Drea, that it's just me and you now and we need him to come."

As Auntie Noreen talked, tears rolled down my face. I'm not sure how I moved or if I moved but I know that I called Daddy. When he answered the phone, I wasn't as calm as Auntie Noreen. I started to cry and said, "Daddy, its Uncle Neal. He's dead."

When I said that, I had the same feeling of the air being sucked out of me. He said, "Who's with you?"

Crying, I said, "Auntie Noreen." If Daddy said goodbye, I had no idea. I remember still holding the phone when the sound that it was off the hook snapped me back to my present reality.

I was sitting with Auntie Noreen on the settee when Daddy, followed by the police as well as two emergency ambulance men came in. Auntie Noreen's friend Mrs. Braithwaite came into the house last. I guess that Daddy had called her. She closed the door and when Auntie Noreen saw her, she said, "Lou; Neal's gone."

That was it. Mrs. Braithwaite comforted Auntie Noreen and talked to her when they took Uncle Neal's body out of the house. She was right there to hold Auntie Noreen when she finally broke down. Daddy didn't know quite what to say to Auntie Noreen so he just sat quiet. I'd already screamed myself quiet so I sat next to him. I didn't know what a person did after they'd screamed themselves quiet so I just sat and watched as Auntie Noreen slowly went to pieces. Mrs. Braithwaite, who knew what Auntie Noreen's pieces looked like, picked them up.

Sometime later that seemed like an eternity to me, Auntie Noreen said, "Lou, last night Neal didn't want to go up by himself. He said he wanted to wait and walk up the stairs with me. I ain't think nothing 'bout it, you know. When I was done helping Drea with the children, he come to me and taking my hand, he said, 'I can't think of a better person in the whole world to climb Jacob's ladder with.' I ain't pay that no mind. On another night, I might have paid that some mind, but I don't know why it didn't register. I just let my fingers feel comfortable in his hand and we walked up; just like when we was young."

Mrs. Braithwaite said, "Noreen, you ain't got to talk, you know. Not if it gine upset you."

Tears were slowly streaming down Auntie Noreen's face and, looking at her friend, she said, "I was real tired so soon after me and Neal went up and I put my head down, Neal brought foolishness to me. I push him 'way. Not rough, but I push him 'way nonetheless, but he ain't pay me no mind, Lou. That foolish old man said to me, 'Don't push me way, Nor Nor.' You know how long Neal Peters ain't call me Nor Nor? Anyway, he start back with his foolishness and he say, 'I bet ya I gine surprise you.'"

Auntie Noreen started to laugh, not hard it was like a shoulder shrug laugh and touching her friend's leg softly, she said, "He surprised me. Would you believe it? Neal Peters managed, in his old age, to surprise me. Then when I think he done he say to me, "Remember down stairs I said I wasn't done with you…well I mean that Nor Nor…I ain't done with you." Smiling a shy smile Auntie Noreen added, 'When he was finally done with me Lou I fall asleep like I ain't fall asleep in years. I don't know when Neal went to sleep 'cause his surprise take 'way all my energy. I remember though him hugging me and holding me like when we first started out.

"At some time, I wake up from my sound sleep and I thought Neal was sleeping to, but when I went to tease him 'bout surprising me and what a good surprise it was, is when I find out that Neal's sleep was sounder than mine. While I was in my deep surprise sleep, death had sneak in we bedroom and steal Neal from right next to me.

"Lou, I didn't scream, holler, or anything. You know that ain't me and not even Death was going to change that in me. I did what I always did with those I love. I welcomed my Neal back to the same arms I'd wrapped him in so tight when he was surprising me. Last night, he'd held me close close to him, but this morning, Lou, he didn't hold me back. It didn't matter that I was holding him close to me. But he ain't resist me either; Death hadn't claimed him that long, – there was still warmth in his body.

"I claimed the warmth that was left in his body as mine. I held him gently to my two old bubbies and just as I'd done for more than sixty years, I spoke softly to my Neal. This was the first time, Lou, that I knew he wouldn't answer me, but I talked to he anyway.

"As the sun started to come up, I talked to Neal 'bout we life together. I told him everything, Lou. Things he knew and things he didn't. I went down the long list of those things that had made being his wife my greatest joy.

"When I talked to Neal, all them tears that had mustered up in my eyes, you know, sat on my eye lids began to fall. I wanted to hold onto the tears but it was at that time, and for the first time ever I realized that there are no edges, ridges, rims, or ledges to tears. Tears are smooth and soft and even if you want to hold onto them, they don't let you.

"Tears are tears. They are wet; they don't dissolve and they have only two purposes. To purge your pain or to express your joy. The tears on my face early this morning were purging or attempting to purge the pain of losing my man, the only man who had ever really taken up space in my heart. I cry real bad for Neal and then I cried for me 'cause I was wondering what would happen to my heart when the only person it has ever loved was no longer here to give it reason to beat.

"In my whole life with Neal, there was only one regret and, Lou, you know what that is. It always bothered me that I couldn't do that; give him a child. He always wanted children, but God and life didn't deal we that hand and now he was on his way back to his maker, never knowing what it was like to be loved like a father."

As the tears tumbled down Auntie Noreen's face and dripped onto her robe, I cried. I didn't cry out loud as she wasn't, but I couldn't stop my tears. I was missing Uncle Neal. Again, Lou tried to get Auntie Noreen to stop from talking, but I think if Auntie Noreen didn't talk, she was going to go mad so she just looked real sad at Lou and then she said, "As I'd told him a million times in life, I told him once again, as the shroud of death thickened, taking him further and further away from me. I said, 'Neal, my sweetheart husband, I'm so sorry that I couldn't make you a father.'

As he'd done in life every time I'd told him I was sorry, Neal didn't answer me. You know when Neal was living, every time I would bring up the subject 'bout not making any children for him, he always said to me, 'Noreen Peters, the love I got for you will always outweigh any disappointment I may feel 'bout not having children.' I knew that this time he didn't answer me because the weight of death had sealed his lips and was keeping his tongue to the floor of his mouth.

"That didn't stop me. I spoke to my Neal 'till the warmth left his body and then I kissed his cool lips and worked him out of my embrace. I straightened up the bedclothes 'round him, then I folded those beautiful strong arms that would never hold me again. I folded them across his chest. Satisfied that he looked dignified, I looked at my Neal and then I said, 'Neal Peters, for all the tea in China, the diamonds in Africa, flying fish and sugar cane in Barbados, I wouldn't have traded one day of knowing and loving you for none of it. You taught me what it means to stand by your word, to believe in something, and even now in death, you still teaching me. I don't like this lesson, Neal Peters. You didn't have to teach me this one. I really didn't have to find out what it feels like to know what 'till death us do part feels like. I can tell you now, Neal Peters. It's the worst pain in the world.' Once I told him that, I kissed him again, put my head on his chest, and told him I was going to tell Drea.

"It was then that I really started to cry. I started to cry 'cause I knew I had to turn 'way and leave him. When I couldn't bring myself to walk way and leave him, I climbed back in the bed. I put my head on his chest and, Lou, I started to beg his heart to beat again. With my eyes shut, I begged him to unfold his arms, to hold me, and to hug me up just as he'd done a few hours earlier. His heart didn't start back nor did his arms move, unfold, nor hold me. It mattered, but there was nothing I could do about none of that. I stayed there and when the wishing felt like it was just going to come and do like one of them duppie parasols and cover me up, I got off the bed.

"Lou, I always thought I was going dead before Neal, but you know what's funny? I glad in a way that I didn't dead instead of Neal."

All of us looked at Auntie Noreen when she said that and without even giving our looks a second thought, she said, "Me and Neal had a 'till death us do part for real marriage and love. So I couldn't imagine Neal the way I am now. He would be dead already if it was me that they had just taken out of here instead of him. Neal Peters taught me one last lesson in his dying."

Mrs. Braithwaite asked softly, "And what's that, Noreen?"

Auntie Noreen said, "What it feels like to get to the day when you realize that the only thing that ever could've come between me, Neal, and our marriage was death. Death done come between we and it's the worst feeling in the world. Right now, I wish I was dead and on my way to the morgue next to Neal. I ain't lying. If I could just go upstairs and know that when I lay down, Death gine walk in and take me too, I would get up from here and go lie down. That's the truth from my heart. I can't begin to tell none of you what's goin' on inside of me. My heart's drying out. I don't know what to do now."

Turning to Daddy, she started a fresh and different kind of crying, then she said, "Matthew, what am I supposed to do now? I don't know what to do without Neal. Matthew, he was all I had. I ain't got nobody else in this world. What to do, Matthew? What to do?"

Daddy went and sat next to Auntie Noreen. Soon as he sat down, he took her in his arms and Auntie Noreen started to scream and scream and scream. It seemed as if the screaming would never end. Then at one point, it looked like Auntie Noreen wanted to run. She started shaking and shaking. Daddy held her and then he said, "Noreen, you aren't alone. I'm here. I'm here."

Chapter 61

Sing a Song for Me In the Land Where I Was Born

The next few days were very busy. Auntie Noreen said that Uncle Neal had always said that when the day came and he died, he wanted to be buried in Barbados and so she would take him home to be buried. Daddy took care of everything. I left Leela and T'Anna with Mrs. Trindle the night before we left for Barbados. It was the first of many things for me. My first time leaving my girls alone, leaving America, and my first trip on a plane, and so in an odd way, I was excited yet sad at the circumstances that had me on a Pan American Airlines headed to a place I'd heard so much about. I couldn't wait to see it and yet I could. Uncle Neal's funeral was the reason I found myself sitting on the plane staring out the window watching with a mixture of excitement and a searing sadness as his beloved Barbados came into view.

When we were finally able to leave the plane, I was still surprised to see that it was a bright sunny day. Even though it was sunny when the plane started it descent and even when it landed, I somehow expected it to be raining when I stepped outside the plane. It should have been raining. It was hard to believe that Barbados wasn't crying. I guess it didn't know that one of its children had died. I guess Uncle Neal had been gone so long that Barbados had grown accustomed to him not being there and now that he had returned from the foreign land where he'd died, she wasn't mourning. I had a hard time accepting the fact that Barbados wasn't crying or mourning her dead son. It didn't matter how long he was gone; a son was still a son; ask the father of the prodigal son.

We got through immigration and customs effortlessly. Auntie

Noreen wanted to wait until the hearse, which was going to take Uncle Neal's body to the funeral home, left. We waited quietly with here. Auntie Noreen went with her friend, Mrs. Braithwaite, to the home that she and Uncle Neal had built for their retirement. Daddy, since he was taking care of the funeral arrangements, wasn't with us. He'd decided to go directly to the funeral home to finalize payments and arrangements. With the business of the funeral arrangements taken care of, Daddy returned to the hotel.

He and I were sitting around reminiscing about Uncle Neal and just when we were about to take the trip down memory lane that had tears on one side and heartbreak on the other, there was a knock on the door. Daddy went to see who it was and from the expression on his face, my heart started to beat wildly. Then I heard an unmistakable voice, "Now, Daddy, are you going to let us in or are you just going to stand there staring." I would know that voice anywhere despite the now heavy British accent that was wrapped around every word he spoke.

Without saying a word, Daddy stepped back from the door and in walked Andre with Tony slightly behind in tow. It had been almost two years since we'd seen them and now here there were. Tony closed the door as Andre rushed to Daddy, almost knocking him over; he was hugging him so hard. Daddy hugged him back as if his life depended on it. I waited my turn for Andre but Tony, who was never one to not act like family, hugged me. He was used to Daddy and Andre. He interrupted my anticipation and eagerness for my brother's hug by filling the wait with his. He hugged me with love, tenderness, and apology. I understood. He was apologizing for his brother. I whispered in his ear, "It's ok, Tony. I would've loved him anyway. We made a very beautiful girl together. It's really ok." Tony didn't reply. He just hugged me harder.

Freeing himself from the hug he and Daddy were sharing, Andre stepped over to where Tony and I were and, jokingly pushing him aside, said, "Hey you turn my sister loose. I haven't seen her for a long time either."

In his next step, he was hugging me. Through the corner of my eye, I could see Tony hugging Daddy. It seemed just like old times. Only Troy was missing, yet he was present. None of us mentioned him.

His name never came up or any subject concerning him, not even when we all went out to dinner and Daddy and I talked about T'Anna. We all acted as if I'd made T'Anna all by myself. Later, Andre and Tony drove us back to our hotel and then headed back to where they were staying in St. James, which was near to Auntie Noreen's house, but far enough not to intrude on her. We agreed to meet back at our hotel in the morning so that we could go over to Auntie Noreen's house to help her with the information for the program.

Although St. Barnabas Anglican Church wasn't Auntie Noreen's or Uncle Neal's church in the true sense of the word because they'd been gone too long, it was, however, where Uncle Neal wanted to be buried. To ensure that he wouldn't be forgotten, he had for the last fifty-two years seen to it that his and Auntie Noreen's offering were sent each month. At each Harvest time, Christmas, his birthday, his mother's, and Auntie Noreen's, he'd sent a little extra. He didn't want them to forget about him. He had always felt that as long as he was diligent about sending his offering, they would remember that he truly wanted that place near his mother to rest and wait, if he had to, for his beloved Noreen. He and Auntie Noreen would, he'd said, share the same grave; just as they had the same bed. He'd always joked that he didn't want his hands resting crossed on his stomach. He wanted them at his side so that if he got his wish, Auntie Noreen would be buried on her stomach with her head turned slightly to the side; this way he could raise his arms up and hug her and they would rest in eternity just as they'd rested each night: he on his back and she on her stomach with her head resting on his chest.

Now here he was ready to take up that long-earned and awaited residency, and it was beginning to look like it might not happen. Mrs. Braithwaite was on the phone with someone at St. Barnabas church and that someone was saying something about the graveyard and or the uses of the graves was only for regular attending church members. Whatever the woman on the phone had said to Mrs. Braithwaite got her to say in a very angry and annoyed voice, "I know you at a church and all, but don't tell me no shite 'bout you ain't got nah record of them being no church member and that you can't find de last time them been to church. Miss, what's your name? Greenidge? Ok. Miss Greenidge, let me tell you now I don't want to hear that foolish shite you talking, but he must not be nah regular church member. Miss? Miss? Why you don't stop talking for a minute. Stop and listen to me. If you would stop and listen, you would hear that I done told you, and at least a thousand times now…he didn't live here.

"He and his wife.

"No, she ain't dead! Jesus Christ, woman, what's wrong with you? You this stupid for real or you pretending? Didn't I start out talking to you by saying I calling on behalf of his wife. You think I would be calling you on behalf of a dead woman?

"I don't want to hear 'bout you sorry. I just trying to get this business sorted out. Like I was saying just before you ask me shite 'bout if his wife dead or not, he and his wife, the living one I making this call for, been living in America for almost a hundred years.

"No, miss, not a real, real hundred years. She would be dead to. Tell me, miss, that you working there for free. I would hate to believe that them paying you. Anyway as I was saying, Mr. Peters and only Mr. Peters dead and now that he dead, he wants to bury here in Barbados.

"No he didn't tell me that. His wife told me that and before you ask, no he didn't tell her that after he died. Did you say your name was Greenidge? You could fool me. I would swear that right about now I talking to Ossie Moore. Miss, when Mr. Peters told his wife where he wanted to be buried, he was living. Anyway, you wasting my good time with these stupid questions. What you need to know is this: he told her he wanted to be buried in Barbados and at St. Barnabas church; that's all you got to concern yourself with.

"What you mean, no record?

"Miss, stop going on with this foolishness 'bout you ain't got no record of him; dig fer it and let me tell you where to dig since I don't think you could dig your way out of a bowl of ice cream even if they gave you a heated spoon and a map.

"Go and dig in the drawer where you all does keep the money that comes from people in America, England, Canada, and wherever else Bajans are. In there, you should find over fifty years of envelopes from him for him and Mrs. Peters. I gine hang up and wait for you to call me back when you find that drawer. When you find it, don't be too surprise that it stop you from calling me back 'cause I gine be waiting. Don't tek forever."

Mrs. Braithwaite slammed down the phone and before the echo of the phone rattling in the cradle could quiet down, she was cussing. "Noreen, I ain't willing to hear no foolishness and especially from a woman that I don't think can even put she panties on right. I bet you that all like now the crotch of she panty on she hip 'cause she done put both legs through one leg hole and she trying to figure out why her cat is out its cage and getting a fresh breeze every time she step. She also trying to figure out where the big hole on she other hip come from.

"I ain't mekking no sport, that woman stupid as shite and yet she has the nerve to talk 'bout the fact, and she called it a fact, that Neal has been gone too long. I ain't listening to that 'cause nothing she said is goin' to stop me from turning over every stone in Barbados to try and get done what Neal Peters can't do for himself."

When it seemed that she might not be able to do this one thing for her friend; have him buried next to his mother, she became both frustrated and angry. She said to Auntie Noreen, "Noreen, that kiss-me-ass woman down at St. Barnabas church getting on my last nerves. All day I on the phone with she 'till my mouth turning white and she keep telling me shite. I would bet you anything, Noreen that she, and a whole lot of them that fretting me, must be done help count up Neal's money all these years. I don't have time for this long rigmarole story. Can you imagine some blasted jackass gine tell me 'bout call back tomorrow. I tell them I don't got tomorrow put down. I ain't calling back. Neal Peters done particularly buy that whole church with all the money he send back from America so I ain't want to hear no foolishness.

"Noreen, if them don't call me in the morning with the news I expecting to hear, I gine down there for truth, not to argue with them, 'cause I ain't got time for that shite. I gine through that graveyard like I gone mad and I skinning out every rass-hole duppie if I have to so Neal Peters can rest where he say he want to rest."

Mrs. Braithwaite made Auntie Noreen smile; her first since Uncle Neal died. Seeing that Auntie Noreen had smiled, Mrs. Braithwaite said, "I ain't mekking no sport, Noreen. If them don't let Neal Peters get his rest in there, nobody, duppie nor man, ain't resting. You know I ain't mekking no sport. I'll skin out every last one of them. You watch me. Noreen, you know me and them down at St. Barnabas think they know me, but them ain't really know me. Them hear I mad as shite but them ain't see mad yet. I bet you, come tomorrow, them gine be ready for me; them better be. Them got all night to get ready. To make sure I ready for this next world war, I would stay awake if need be so I already done beat them to it. When them planning on getting up early to beat me to it, I done up 'fore them 'cause I ain't sleeping. Neal is my friend and you is my friend so them ain't coming between me and my friends; not for shite."

As Mrs. Braithwaite worked herself up, Auntie Noreen looked at her friend and with tears threatening to fall, she said, "Lou, if them say no, I ain't goin' argue and I don't want you to argue or skin out anybody. Neal is my husband and my concern and I want him to rest in peace. I don't want any fighting to go on over where he is to rest. I'll find someplace else."

Daddy, who had been out most of the day, came into the house with Tony and Andre at that moment and seeing how close to tears Auntie Noreen was, he said, "Find someplace else for what, Noreen?"

Auntie Noreen tried to hold the tears back but she couldn't and with her face getting a fresh washing, she said, "To bury Neal if St. Barnabas says no."

"Noreen, don't worry yourself; I told you I was going to take care of it and that's what I worked on today. We, the Funeral Director and I, were able to work things out. It's all taken care of. It's just as Neal wanted it. He's next to his mother and you, when the time comes; in about a hundred years or so if I get my prayers answered, will be with him."

Auntie Noreen smiled and her tears were now falling almost in summersault fashion down her cheek to her chin and onto her dress. Mrs. Braithwaite reached out her hand and patted Auntie Noreen's. That made her, even with all the tears rushing down her face, smile. As Auntie Noreen smiled and cried, and Mrs. Braithwaite said, "Dem lucky as shite that Matthew here took his sophisticated talk to them 'cause I was goin' down there tomorrow and it wasn't going to be no sophisticated nuffin', every last soul; living or dead was getting skin out."

Reaching and touching her friend's leg, Auntie Noreen said, "I'm glad, Lou, that you don't have to go down there tomorrow. I'm glad."

Chapter 62

The Day Thou Gives, Lord, Has Ended

Uncle Neal's funeral was beautiful if you could say that about a funeral. His boyhood friends came, those still able to get around and those that had to be brought. Neighbors young and old came. Family, both his and Auntie Noreen's came. Some crying, some trying not to cry, some stone-faced and some, because they either didn't want anyone to see them crying or didn't know how they would get through the afternoon had stopped at a rum shop on their way to coming to say goodbye.

These few men, with a woman or two amongst them, infused, slightly inebriated but not totally, swayed, stumbled, and even tottered a little but like true rum drinkers, they weren't yet drunkards by Bajan and only Bajan standards; they stayed standing even if it were Pisa-type standing. They and everyone else filed pass the highly polished mahogany casket at the main entrance of the small church. There were two other entrances but if you wanted to pay your last respects, get your last look or touch in, you came to this entrance. The procession was long, somber, and sad. Some people cried unabashedly; I was among those that did.

As I looked at Uncle Neal dressed so elegantly, I thought he looked as if he were going to a wedding or some formal function. Daddy had selected a black tuxedo, a white dress shirt, black bowtie with a white satin kerchief in his pocket and a small Barbados flag on his left lapel. His hair was freshly cut. He wasn't wearing gloves. His hands were just as he wanted them; at his side and bent ever so slightly at the wrist. They had already taken his wedding ring off and Auntie Noreen was now wearing it on a chain. Uncle Neal didn't seem to mind that he didn't have his wedding ring on as he had a very slight smile on his face. He looked as if he were waiting on Uncle Boysie to come and get him so they could go to the Lodge. Uncle Boysie might be coming to meet him, but it wouldn't be to take him to the Lodge. Daddy, Andre, Tony, Mrs. Braithwaite, and I stood with Auntie Noreen near the head of the casket. Despite the urging of the ushers and a few of their friends, Auntie Noreen refused to sit or be taken away from Uncle Neal. We all understood, especially Daddy. He'd had to say goodbye to Mommy so he understood that feeling of not wanting to be away; not even for a second.

Soon, everyone had filed past and it was time to bring the casket into the church. Auntie Noreen allowed herself to be seated then, but only after she'd walked ever so slowly behind the casket. Daddy and Tony walked on either side of her. Mrs. Braithwaite and I walked together. That wasn't how it was usually done but since it was clear that Auntie Noreen wasn't going to have it any other way, they left her.

As we walked up, I looked around. The church was full; both sides and the center of the church. There wasn't room for anyone else. Women's perfumes, men's cologne, the scent of moth balls, and the smell of hundreds of flowers on wreathes, sprays, and assorted floral arrangements permeated the air. In the dry heat, it was a good thing the windows of the church were open. The music played softly. The choir sat at the front on the left and right behind the pulpit. The funeral went according to the printed program. Auntie Noreen was quietly sobbing as she sat between Daddy and Andre. Soon it was time for the obituary. Auntie Noreen had asked Daddy to read it. At the right time, Daddy stood up and read it and when he was done, he started to walk away but just as he reached the casket, he stopped. He looked down and then he started to speak again. He didn't speak to the people present. He spoke to the closed casket. As first, he was whispering and so only the people close by could hear. Eventually, his voice rose louder and I think because of the hushed quietness a funeral brings upon a place, Daddy's voice echoed through all the arched halls that led to the different parts of the church. I imagined his voice climbing the stairs to the balcony, wrapping itself around the pulpit, and eventually coming to rest at the near-naked figure of a perfectly fit and toned Jesus hanging on the cross at the front of the church.

I listened enraptured as he spoke. He poured from his heart truths that perhaps he himself didn't know were buried so deeply within him. He spoke more like a man whose father, not his servant, had died.

He said, "Neal Peters, I'm so sorry. I'm sorry for many things. First of all, I should have come and seen your beloved Barbados when you could have shown me this island you loved so much. I listened to you all those years and yet not one day did I think to come with you when you and Noreen came. I'm sorry about that. I'm also sorry that I never spoke to you of the feelings that were deep in my heart. I should have told you when I first realized how very much you meant to me.

"You were there when I was a little baby. You helped me to stand and then celebrated with me when I walked. You listened to me, I'm sure, as I attempted to talk and when I finally mastered talking, you talked back to me. When I made it from little boy to teenager, you were there. When I got in trouble, or when I was afraid, you chased those fears away and those you couldn't chase away you taught me how to confront; never, you said, let them get you in a corner. It's harder fighting your way out of the corner. But, you said, if you ever end up in the corner, come out with a vengeance. Never worry 'bout the next guy. Always remember that he's aiming to take you down or out so you've got to have the same aim as he, so think fast how to take him out or down first.

"When everyone, because there was always more money to be made, left me with you and Noreen, you never seemed to mind. You found ways to make me feel as if I mattered to you. Those days when Hebrew school was hard for me, you told me that it was part of my heritage and as such I should give it more than a half-hearted try. You told me to give it my best; my heritage deserved that. I did and I made it through. When I didn't understand why, on the days when Noreen took me to the park, she couldn't drink from the same fountain as I; you took the time and explained Jim Crow and all his laws to me. When my mother, in her usual hateful and prejudice ways, said those God-awful things to you and Noreen, you humbled your fighting spirit. You told me you took what she said because you had a dream of you and Noreen returning, in your golden years, to Barbados and no one; not even my mother and her hatred was going to stand in the way of that dream. I understood.

"When no one noticed when I experienced my first heartbreak, you noticed and encouraged me through it. You, even though in the beginning you didn't talk much, talked to me a lot and often about love. You promised me that someday, the right girl for me was going to come along. You said I would know her. You were right. She came along and just as you promised, I knew her. When death stole her from me and I didn't know what to do, I turned to you. I called, said I needed you, and that was enough for you. Nothing stood in your way. Nothing stopped you from coming to me. I called, you came. You didn't come because I was going to pay you; as a matter of fact, I don't know the last time I paid you. You've raised my daughter and now my grandchildren and never have you stretched your hands out to me for payment. You loved her and her children so it didn't feel right, you said, to take money from me to raise them. You changed me, Neal Peters. You were like a father to me."

All along as Daddy talked, he struggled with tears. I watched as he choked, forced tears back, wiped at his eyes, took deep breaths, and even stopped intermittently, but it was clear nothing was going to stop Daddy from talking, not even tears. He started to cry and this time it was clear he couldn't hold this deluge back. He didn't try. He continued talking through his tears and sobs.

"No, Neal Peters, that's a lie. You weren't like a father to me. You loved me just as you would a son. I know that you did and I loved you as a father, but I never told you. You were the only true father I've known. I'm so sorry that I never told you that you had transformed me from an unloved little boy to a son. I knew what it felt like to be loved simply because and for no other reason than you wanted to love me."

I looked at Daddy and knew he was speaking the truth. In his dying, Neal Peters had been transformed from a servant to a daddy and a grandfather. Daddy had lost his dad; Andre and I, our grandfather; and Leela and T'Anna, a great-grandfather. Uncle Neal no longer existed. It was granddaddy who was in the box. I felt sorry for all of us, but especially Daddy and my new grandfather Neal, because neither had had an opportunity to bask in the expressed love of father and son. I looked at my brokenhearted father and wished that he'd told Uncle Neal.

The look on Daddy's face said that he'd wished he'd told him too. Daddy looked at all the people in the church. There was so much pain in his eyes and it had nothing to do with the fact that he'd told them things he'd never told anyone before. He struggled to continue through his pain. He said, "Do not look upon me and wonder how or why I didn't tell him, or look at me and feel sorry. Also, don't wonder about me being white and him being black or him being anything other than the most amazing man I've ever known. Don't wonder anything. Know this; this man here, Neal Peters, was a gentle and loving man. He worked hard for everything he wanted. When his back was against the wall, he did just what he told me to do. He came out swinging and fought until he found a way to get his back off the wall. He encouraged others to do the same. He stood up for what he believed was right. He fought hard for change. He wanted things to be better, not just for his people, but for all people. I always knew I loved Neal, but I never knew until the phone call came saying I would never hear his voice again, never be there to discover when he finally got a joke that had been told a week, a month, a year, and sometimes so long no one remembered it but out of the clear blue, Neal would get it and he would laugh. We all laughed with him and then at him. He didn't mind. To understand Neal Peters meant you had no choice but to love him. I understood him. I loved him. He was my father."

When Daddy said that, he stopped. He looked exhausted. He rocked a little unsteadily and for a moment he looked as if he would fall but he didn't. He straightened himself and, touching the casket gently, he started to walk towards his seat. Auntie Noreen, who had cried from the time Daddy had begun talking until he stopped, was looking at him with such love, it tore at my heart. Through her tears and pain, her joy was showing. She had finally given her beloved Neal what he'd always wanted; a son. Daddy stopped and, lowering his head, he kissed the casket, said, "Rest in that place of peace, Daddy. I love you." Then he did something I'd never heard him do before, well, not in public anyway. Daddy started to sing. He sung the same song that Auntie Noreen and Uncle Neal had sung at Mommy's funeral.

Halfway through, a voice from the pew joined his. It was Auntie Noreen. She'd stood up and was singing as if her life depended on it. The tears were streaming down her face but she sung. When she said, "I've had some good days, and I've had some bad days…" Daddy was crying so uncontrollably that he couldn't continue. Auntie Noreen came out of her seat and, still singing, she went and got Daddy from the place that only she could bring him back from. Daddy hugged Auntie Noreen and clung to her as he cried; he held her like a son would his mother. If Auntie Noreen finished singing the song, I don't know. I, as well as the whole church, was crying unashamedly. The only dry eyes in the place must have been Grandfather Neal, and even that I couldn't be sure of.

The rest of the funeral service was a blur to me. I know the

Reverend spoke. I know the choir sung, but what was spoken and what was sung, I have no idea. I remember walking out behind the recessional being supported by Mrs. Braithwaite and my new grandmother, Nana Noreen, as the whole church made its way to the gravesite. At the gravesite, it took Daddy and Tony to hold and support Nana Noreen. My insides hurt just as with Mommy. After the funeral all of us, except Nana Noreen and Mrs. Braithwaite, left Barbados.

Daddy and I returned to New York and Andre and Tony went back to London. Daddy went with me to Bainbridge Street. I entered the house. Gloom hung everywhere. It was like moss on river rocks. I felt alone. I'd been in the house without Auntie Noreen and Uncle Neal before, but they were always on their way back. Even when they went home to Barbados, I did what I had to do because they were just going to be gone for a little while. Today was different. Grandfather Neal would never be returning because he'd died and I had a sinking feeling in my heart that Nana Noreen didn't want to come back to America 'cause Grandfather Neal wasn't here anymore. The girls and I wouldn't be enough to keep her here.

I felt as empty as the day we'd returned to Lexington Avenue after Ma's funeral. I started to cry and Daddy, always being Daddy, hugged me. As I hugged him, I remembered the promise I'd made so many years ago: not to love him openly like this just in case God was paying attention and decided to take him away from me. I reminded myself again, but also decided that I would pretend not to love Daddy another day, another night, or another time; just not tonight. I would have to take my chances tonight with God.

"Daddy, I love you so much."

"And I love you too, Princess."

After all these years, Daddy still called me Princess. I was glad that he'd never stopped. I needed so much to be someone's princess. I'd hoped to transfer my royal kingdom to Troy, but he hadn't stayed around long enough for me to bestow it on him. I guess I would continue to be glad that Daddy loved me enough to see me as the princess I wasn't. I made a mental note to thank God again for choosing Matthew David Hirsh to be my father.

Chapter 63

Meet Philip Rancor

About three months after the funeral, Nana Noreen returned to New York. As soon as I saw her, I could tell that something had gone out of her. She'd changed. She looked sad, broken, and older. Looking at her made me miss Grandfather Neal more than I'd been missing him all these months. She didn't have to say anything. I could feel it; I knew she wouldn't be staying. I also understood that. I'd seen that look before in Ma. Nana Noreen's eyes weren't as vacant as Ma's but her eyes said her mind was weighed down with whatever she was thinking about. Ma had been weighed down with trying to figure out how to join Nana. Nana Noreen's weight was different. I didn't have to guess; I knew. She was missing Grandfather Neal. She didn't need any more; that was more than enough. He had been, after all, her all and all.

As she'd always done when she had important decisions to make, she called Daddy. He came over and they talked. She told Daddy that as soon as she could settle things here, she would return to Barbados as she could no longer stand to be in America without her Neal. Daddy said he understood and would do whatever she wanted.

For the first time since I'd known Auntie Noreen, she called Daddy by his first name. She said, "Matthew, you do what you feel is the best thing. I've known you before you were born. I raised you, your children, and turned around to help raise your granddaughters. I'll accept whatever you do. If you choose to sell the house and keep all the money, I'll accept it. If you send me a few dollars each month to keep me until the Lord calls me to be with my Neal, I'll accept it 'cause right now, nothing is important to me anymore. I don't have Neal and without Neal, none of this, the house or the money means nothing to me. Other than you, your children, and grandchildren, I don't have nobody else in America or anywhere else for that matter, so it's you that I have to put my trust in."

All Daddy said was, "Now, Noreen, you know I won't keep your money. I have more than enough of my own and as good as you and Neal have been to me, how could I even entertain keeping your money? We are family. Family doesn't do that to family. Now you go on back home and I'll take care of everything. "

Auntie Noreen returned to Barbados one month to the day she'd returned to New York. She packed, shipped, or arranged to have shipped what she wanted. The girls and I stayed in the house. Daddy said that we could stay until he made a decision about the house and where the girls and I should go. He said that he realized that the girls were all Mrs. Trindle had and it was up to me how far I wanted to move away from her. If Daddy had said that when Leela was first born, I might have said to the other side of the moon, but over the years, Mrs. Trindle had been very good to me and the girls. Leela was almost ten and T'Anna almost five. I wasn't quite ready to be alone with them. I decided to stay close to Mrs. Trindle. She was getting older and needed my help as much as I needed her and hers. I couldn't abandon her now. I was all that she had. Hamilton had never, not one solitary day, come back to see about her. If he was alive and Mrs. Trindle knew, she'd never mentioned it.

True to his word, Daddy took care of everything. He decided to sell the house but not before I found an apartment. I looked everywhere for one and when I couldn't find one, Daddy gave me the phone number of someone he knew. A real estate agent named Philip Rancor. The name Rancor rang a bell, but I couldn't remember when or where I'd heard it before. I called the number and spoke to him for a few minutes. I told him what I was looking for and he said that he had a few places he could show me. I agreed to meet him at the first address on MacDonough and Marcy Avenues.

When the car pulled up, I was expecting to see an old man. Philip Rancor's name didn't suit him. I'd imagined some old wrinkled man in high-waist pants that had once fitted him but now, because of age and perhaps frugality, would be swinging freely around his hips, hoola-hoop fashion if not for the suspenders. I was so wrong. Philip Rancor turned out to be all of thirty-one years old and the only thing wrinkled on him were his white linen pants. He was tall, but not as tall as Daddy. His hair was light; if it were any lighter, it would've been the color of the sand.

Actually, Philip looked like a beach. His hair shone in spots when the sun hit it, just like the specks of glass in sand. His eyes were sea-blue and then in the sun, like his hair, they became lighter; even sky blue. You couldn't stop from looking at them and wanting to dive in. His cheeks jutted out from under his eyes the way the rocks did at the beach in that very Mother-Nature-crafted, jagged angular fashion.

The lines that led to his full and beautiful mouth looked traveled but not worn; he was a smiler. His lips were like a blush and each time he spoke or smiled, they made me think of a sunset pink or the soft-tipped fringe of a pink hibiscus. His lips had a natural pout that, had he not been so masculine, would've looked odd on him because they were so sexy. To top it off, Philip was very muscular. From under his lightweight yellow cotton shirt, you could see his tight and taut muscles; they flexed and relaxed with each of his movements. Philip was just plain old beautiful and I found myself looking forward to every opportunity to spending time in his company. Philip, without his knowing it, became my escape.

As a realtor, Philip was persistent about finding me a place. He took me out often to look at apartments. Many of the places weren't willing to rent to me because I had the girls, but Philip didn't give up. Sometimes he would come for me early in the morning and even when he had nothing to show me, he would still turn up. It wasn't often he didn't have something to show but if nothing suited me and he had nothing else on his list to show me, he would take me to get something to eat. Soon he started coming back to Bainbridge Street with me. At first we talked; soon Philip and I found ourselves in a growing friendship. I started looking forward to his visits almost to the point of forgetting that he was supposed to be helping me find an apartment so Daddy could move on with the business of selling Nana Noreen's house.

I would want to tell anyone, if I were pressed, that I didn't know for sure how, when, where, or why Philip Rancor's place in my life changed. I would say I don't know how he went from being the person who had found me the perfect apartment with a front garden, two bedrooms with one and a half baths, and the prettiest little patch of dirt called a backyard and funny enough right on Stuyvesant and Putnam Avenues, to the person who was occupying my every waking moment, and when I could steal away from the girls, my bed. I would like to say I really didn't know, but the truth was I knew; I saw it all happening and welcomed it. Philip

Rancor became that person to me because I was lonely and I trusted him.

Within three months of finding the apartment, I found myself pregnant. I didn't know who to turn to since Nana Noreen was in Barbados and so, just like when I found myself pregnant with Leela, I turned to Mrs. Trindle. She, who had never interfered in any of my business before, asked, "Andrea, what are you doing to yourself, child? You hardly even know this Mr. Rancor man and now you're pregnant by him. How are you going explain a third child to your father? Have you figured out what you're going say to him?"

I didn't have an answer for her. I wanted to tell her that she was only voicing an opinion now because Philip was white, but I knew that was wrong, stupid, and a lie. For about a month after I told her, I said nothing to Daddy and then when I couldn't hold it back any longer, I told him I was pregnant. He didn't bother to ask me who the father was; he knew. He also did what I never thought he would do. He lost his mind. He became angry and he called Philip over. I didn't expect Philip to come, but he did. He came, looking like a lamb being led to the slaughter.

When Daddy started talking to Philip, I thought he was going to have a heart attack, he was so angry. He spoke to Philip in short crisp sentences. When he was done, he turned to me and spoke in even shorter and crisper sentences. They were so crisp, I expected each sentence to snap and scatter vowels, consonants, ellipses, and his lightning-bolt-shaped exclamations points all over the floor as soon as each word left his mouth. They didn't; well not on the floor. They exploded in my head. It was clear that Daddy's anger was beyond containment. For the first time in my life, Daddy said that he wasn't going to support me. He looked at Philip and said, "I'm not sure what either of you were thinking, but I'm going to say this and only once: Philip, if you fashioned yourself to be man enough to make a child with Andrea, then fashion yourself to be man enough to support, not just her, but the other two fatherless children she already has."

I sat there expecting Philip to become my knight in shining armor and tell Daddy that the girls and I would be fine. That he had a plan to take care of us. That he would fill in the void left in Leela and T'Anna's lives by Hamilton and Troy. He didn't. Instead, he sat there with a wide-eyed yet vacant stare. Then he started shifting that strange stare all over the apartment from one place to the next. He looked intently as if he was secretly searching for the sacrificial table so he could climb upon it, put the knife in Daddy's hand, and let Daddy take him out of my misery. Unable to find the table, Philip never had the chance for Daddy to sacrifice him. Realizing that Daddy didn't see him as a worthy enough sacrifice, Philip did just like Hamilton and Troy; he sacrificed me and his unborn baby instead. He stayed behind until Daddy left and the moment the sound of Daddy's car faded away, without looking at me, he slithered across the floor and out the door. I sat there staring at the door that he should have opened yet hadn't. Was my mind playing tricks on me? Did I miss it when he opened it or was it as I was thinking? He simply didn't open it. He'd just slithered right under. Either way, I was still halfway expecting him to come slithering back and claim me and the girls, but he didn't.

I started to cry. I'm not sure if I cried because he was gone or at the thought of Daddy being so upset with me that he'd walked away in anger and disgust. I wanted to stop crying, but I couldn't get my tears to stop. The more I thought about how he, like the rest, had just left me, the more the tears tumbled out. I cried until the baby in my belly started to go rigid; my belly started to feel like one big knot. I became afraid over what I was doing to my poor baby, and then out of the blue, I started to feel despondent. Then to my astonishment, my brain, and it was just for a split-second, started to understand why or how people could kill themselves.

Soon as the thought entered my mind, I panicked. I didn't want to think like that. The baby in my belly, T'Anna, or Leela didn't deserve a mother who, and even though it was a fleeting thought, could understand such a weakness as suicide. I'd lived the aftermath of such weakness. Ma had weakened and that weakening caused Andre and I to have to live without her. It's true that Ma didn't put a gun to her head, jump from a bridge, or anything dramatic like that, but she'd simply gone to bed and willed herself dead. Dead was dead. I wasn't going to do that. My girls and this baby in my belly deserved better. I didn't want them to ever suffer any of the pain I'd suffered 'cause Ma wasn't there.

In the midst of my despair, I heard Nana's voice. She was saying to me, "Drea, when you have a problem that's too big for you, just go to bed and give it to God; you got to give God 'till morning."

I did just that. I went to bed, told God all about my problems; as if he didn't already know, and went to sleep…well I tried. I must have drifted off at some point because just as the sun was starting to stretch her arms across the heavens, my eyes opened. I came wide awake. There was excitement in me. I started thinking that if I were awake, the sun was stretching her arms across the heavens, then it had to be morning. I'd done it. I'd given God 'till morning.

I had an exuberant feeling. Inside of me felt that with God having a whole night to work more than one miracle in my now-shattered life, all my problems were now irrevocably solved. Before getting out of bed, I thanked Him. I thanked him for all He had done for me while I slept. Feeling that He fully understood that I was grateful from the bottom of my heart, I bounded out of bed; after all it was a new day. It was one without any problems in it, at least for me. What was there for me to worry about? The Lord had spent a whole night mulling over and sorting out my problems. I didn't have any outward signs that things were changed, but this was God. I didn't need an outward sign. The God I believed in didn't always do dramatic.

The minute I said that, my mind said, 'Don't do dramatic? What about the time He looked into the dark void and said, "Let there be!" and seeing it was good, He kept at it for seven days and nights 'till there was a heaven and an Earth, birds, and beast, and fish and fowl. Don't do dramatic? What about the time he did the burning bush thing so he could get Moses' attention? That was dramatic. What was Noah's ark with all those two-by-two lined up animals, cats walking peacefully infront dogs, elephants infront mice, lions behind lambs? Don't do dramatic? You've got to be kidding yourself, Drea. You don't call what happened to Lot's wife turning to a pillar of salt dramatic? Then let's see that thing with Sampson crumbling that whole building on himself, or tiny David killing Goliath with a rock and a sling shot, or how 'bout the one where dried up Sarah produced a healthy baby for an old-as-dust, almost sperm-less Abraham? Don't do dramatic?

By the time my mind got done listing all the dramatic and not so dramatic ways God had let His people know that He wasn't a God that fooled around, my feeling that all was well with me started to weaken. I started to feel as if I needed a sign. I quieted myself and waited. I didn't need an earth-shattering sign, writing in the sky, or even an angel to appear in my room; just something that would give me a hint that He'd spent the night giving me and my dilemma some consideration. I waited. Got even stiller and when no sign came, I decided that the resolution of my problems would be without fanfare. There would be no sign.

I anxiously waited until I was sure that Daddy would be in his office and called. I wanted to hear his voice, tell him how very sorry I was that I'd disappointed him, and I also desperately wanted to hear him call me Princess. He never hung up the phone without saying he loved me or calling me Princess.

The ringing went on forever. Finally, it was picked up. I waited excitedly for his hello but it never came. Daddy didn't answer his private line. It was his secretary, Mrs. Northup She didn't do like the secretary in Philip's office would do and say that Daddy was out. She said, "Andrea, your father said that he suspected you would call early. He's not taking your calls. He has asked me to deliver a message to you."

"A message? Daddy gave you a message for me? What?"

As I listened, she told me all of what Daddy had told her to tell me. She delivered it in short crisp sentences that matched Daddy's voice from the night before. That surprised me because I'd known Theresa Northup my whole life and she'd never, not one solitary day, been unkind to me and now she was being short and more than a little crispy with me. When she was done, I said, "Mrs. Northup it's me…Andrea. Why are you talking to me like this?"

She said, "Your father has said that I'm not to have any long, drawn-out conversation with you. I was to deliver his message and just as he gave it."

"Daddy really told you to tell me that I'm not to contact him unless I have a life-or-death situation, or if something happens to any of the children; including the one I'm having, but other than those extreme situations, I'm not to contact him?"

"Yes."

"Daddy really said that and just like that?"

"Yes. He also said to tell you that he loves you."

"He said that?"

"Yes. He loves you, Andrea. He just doesn't like what you are doing with your life."

"Daddy said that?"

"No. That's me. I'm letting you know how deeply hurt and disappointed your father is. Hurry up and change your life so your father and you can get back to that good place called family."

"He said that?"

"No, child. It's me talking to you. Now this is turning into the long, drawn-out conversation he said it shouldn't be. You go on and take care of yourself, those beautiful daughters of yours, and I wish you a safe delivery with this new baby. You take care now. I have to go."

"Thank you, Mrs. Northup, for your kind words. I'll turn it around, you'll see."

"It's not for me to see. You must show your father. This separation is breaking his heart and, before you ask, yes, he said that."

I hung up the phone and cried. I think I cried harder than when Ma died. A part of me felt as if Daddy had died. That scared me. I couldn't even begin to imagine being on the outside of Daddy's love. I'd never been there, didn't even know there was such a place, and now thanks to a man I felt was so beautiful, I was in this ugly place. I needed someone to assure me that everything would be alright. I called Philip. I was told by his secretary, Trudie, that he wasn't in yet; it was early. But as the day wore on and each time I called she told me I'd just missed him, I started to feel that she wasn't telling me the truth.

Over the next few days, a lot of truths became apparent. Philip had stopped caring too. Not that he'd started supporting me or anything like that, but Philip found a different way to stop. I think it started the minute Daddy told him that I was his responsibility. He stopped being available. He stopped finding his way to my house, me, and my bed. For Philip, I stopped existing. Even though I'd come to the realization that Trudie was covering for him, I left message after message. Philip never returned any of my calls. Eventually, I stopped trying to reach him and since there was no more room in my heart to light another angry hateful fire, I stored the angry and hateful thoughts of him in my mind, where they sat alone and unattended.

Daddy's absence in my life had such a profound impact on me and the girls that thoughts of Philip only managed to annoy me. Daddy kept his word and he stopped. His stopping was different to Philip's. Philip aborted the hopes I had in him. Daddy stopped everything that I'd become accustomed to. For me, it was like I was running at top speed and out of nowhere, a brick wall loomed up and, unable to stop myself, I careened into it. He stopped calling, coming by, sending surprise gifts for me and the girls, and then he did the unthinkable, well for me; he stopped supporting me. He'd always supported me. I was sure, even though Daddy had said he would stop, that he either didn't mean it or that he wouldn't go through with it. I was, after all, his Princess. I was his only daughter and first-born with his only grandchildren. I knew deep in my heart that Daddy wouldn't do that to me; he was just kidding. There was no way he wasn't going to support me and spoil the girls; no way.

I was so very wrong. With the dawning of how wrong I was came the realization of how much I'd taken Daddy for granted. All of it hit home like a tornado-wrapped earthquake spewing lava when the bill box started filling up and spilling over. I had gotten so used to life just going on that I'd never thought about how things happened. The basic things I'd taken for granted. The lights came on when I flipped the switch. The stove burned when I put a match to the gas. Food was always in the fridge, and the girls and I always had more than enough of everything.

After Daddy stopped taking care of me, fear set in the evening I came home with the girls from our weekly visit to Mrs. Trindle and I flipped the light switch when we entered the apartment and nothing. The lights didn't come on. I'd seen the notices, but as always, I didn't pay them any attention other than to put them in the bill box. Daddy always came by and collected everything that was in the bill box. All I had to do was put whatever mail came to me in a bill box in the kitchen and each time he took whatever was in the box. I'd never really thought about the how of that box. I knew it wasn't magic that paid my bills, but all I ever had to do was put them in the box and life continued uninterrupted for me and the girls. Now the box was overflowing and the lights didn't come on. The bill box had lost its magic.

I'd taken Daddy and his love for granted and now I was in the dark and the girls were afraid. They'd never been in the dark before, as a matter of fact, neither had I and a different kind of fear was settling in. I was afraid to be in the dark with the girls so I tried once again to reach Philip to see if he would at least help me get the lights back on. As before, I'd just managed to miss him. I was too ashamed to call Mrs. Trindle so I made a game out of it. I told the girls that we had to huddle close together because the baby, being in the dark, wanted us to experience the same darkness. They believed me and huddled with me in my bed. Soon, they were asleep. I cried all night. I never slept. In the morning, I didn't even bother to make them breakfast. I had them wash up and I took them over to Mrs. Trindle. I asked her if they could stay with her for a few days. I didn't explain and she neither asked nor refused. I returned to the apartment. I looked around. It felt foreign;

even a little strange, and that was only because I knew that the lights were turned off. As the hours passed, I accepted that soon night would come and I would be alone in the darkness I'd created.

I started to get hungry so I walked into the kitchen to make myself something to eat. As I got to the doorway, my heart sank. There was water all over the kitchen floor; the fridge was defrosting. Had I made the girls something to eat or had I come into the kitchen earlier, I would have noticed. The reality that what little I had in the freezer and perhaps even the fridge was spoiling made me cry. I got the bucket and mop and started to clean up the water. As I mopped, I wished there was some way I could mop all my troubles up and away. There wasn't a mop that could do that, so I opened the fridge and started taking out the few items that could last outside the fridge for a few days. There wasn't much but I knew the few apples, pears, and oranges would last. The other stuff I just bagged up and threw out; it didn't make sense holding onto it.

Exhausted from all that unexpected work, I filled the kettle with water to make some tea. I set the kettle down and, reaching for the matches, I turned the gas on and struck the match…nothing. Shit. The gas had been turned off as well. I stood there with the match in my hand and cried. My belly growled. The baby moved. We were hungry. The lit match made it to my fingers. I dropped it in the sink. Taking two of the apples off the counter, I turned the water on, thank God that worked, and washed them. I made my way to the table. There I pulled the chair out to make room for my burgeoning belly. I sat and ate the apples. The baby quieted.

I had to figure something out. The girls couldn't stay at Mrs. Trindle's forever. They would want to come back home to their things eventually. I started to wonder if there would be a home for them to come back to as I'd already started having to find one excuse after another for the landlord as to why I didn't have the rent. The rent was approaching three months past due. I tried desperately once again to reach Philip and this time, I kept my pride out of it and told Trudie to tell Philip his baby and I were hungry, the gas and electricity were turned off, I was three months behind on the rent, and the landlord was threatening to evict me and my other two children.

Trudie listened and this time, she said, "Miss Hirsh, I can't give Mr. Rancor that message."

I said, "Please, Trudie. I don't know what else to do. Tell him that

I'm willing to beg if I have to. I just need some help. Tell him I don't want it forever. I just need some help until I can figure out what to do. Can you please tell him that I'm in the dark and could he please, please, I'm begging you to ask him if he would turn the gas and the electric back on for me? Can you do that for me, please Trudie? Can you? I'm afraid of the dark."

"I'll tell him, Miss Hirsh. I'll tell him when he comes back. He just isn't here now. When he comes back, I'll tell him everything you said."

I hung up and waited. When I felt that enough time had passed where the lights would be back on, I flipped the switch; nothing changed. The electricity was still off. Hour after hour, I tested the lights and when it was near time that if I didn't get some help soon I would miss my opportunity as the light company would close, I called Philip's office again. This time, it wasn't Trudie who answered. I didn't know this person's voice. I asked who it was and she answered, "This is Miss MacIntosh. I'm the temp."

I said, "Temp? Where's Trudie?"

"She no longer works here. May I help you, Miss…?"

"Hirsch. Miss Hirsh. I would like to speak with Mr. Rancor, please."

She didn't even miss a beat when she said, "Sorry, Miss Hirsh, but Mr. Rancor has stepped out of the office and I do believe he's gone for the day. Please call back tomorrow."

Before I could say a word, she hung up. As the sound of her dismissal echoed in my ears, I started to cry again. Night wasn't far off. As a matter of fact, it was too close. I accepted that to call back would be an exercise in futility, but fear of being out on the streets with my girls made me take desperate enough to hope. With hope sitting on the tip of my heart I dialed his number again without looking. Each time the phone rang, I hoped against hope that this new girl would answer and say that he was coming. I was wrong. The minute she answered and I said, "This is Miss Hirsch," she interrupted me.

"Miss Hirsch, Mr. Rancor would appreciate it if you didn't call this office again. Have a good day."

The phone went dead. I finally accepted that he didn't want anything to do with me. I thought to call Tony but I was ashamed and I didn't want him to tell Andre I was pregnant again. I couldn't take Andre's disappointment as well as Daddy's. When it started to look as if I would face another night in the dark and hungry, as well as face the possibility that come morning, the girls, my things, and me with my burgeoning belly, could get kicked to the curb, I swallowed my pride and called Daddy. Doing all I could not to cry, I told him that I was in the dark, the electricity had been turned off, I had no food, and the girls were at Mrs. Trindle's because I didn't want them in a dark apartment. I asked him to help me. It didn't make sense to say it was only until I found a smaller place as I couldn't afford any place; small or big.

Chapter 64

A Changing of the Guards

Daddy still sounded annoyed at me but when I said I was in the dark, alone, and hungry, I heard a shift in his voice. I could tell he was still anything but pleased, but it said he was my daddy and I was his princess; he would take care of everything.

"Andrea, this is no way for you to be. You are pregnant. Give me the account number; as a matter of fact, don't do that. I think it may be too late to get that bill paid now. I'm not sure what time the company closes, but I have a feeling that it's already closed. It will have to be paid first thing in the morning. Why didn't you call me before?"

"Daddy, I'm sorry. I was too embarrassed and I didn't know what to do."

"I tell you what; go to Mrs. Trindle's. She will let you spend the night. In the morning, come back to your apartment and I'll meet you there. I'll bring you up-to-date with your rent, all the bills that are overdue, and I will do as I did before you became pregnant. After the baby is born, I'll see about everything for three months and after that, you'll be on your own. For ten whole years, I've been waiting on you to want something, but all you've done is make children for men that don't want them or you."

I wanted to be angry but he was right. I'd wasted a lot of good time and hadn't made good choices in choosing men or fathers for my children and now, here I was in the dark; hungry, and having to beg my father to come and rescue me.

With a watershed of tears, I thanked Daddy. His voice softened as he said, "I don't like that you are in this situation, Drea, but you haven't left me with much of a choice. I expected you to make better choices than the ones you are making. I really did, Princess."

"I'm sorry, Daddy. I really am. I'll fix it. I mean that."

"I want you to. Remember, you are the example that your daughters are seeing every day. I'll send Theresa over in the morning to collect the bills. Take care of yourself, Drea. Take care of yourself."

Daddy hung up before I could say anything else. I don't know how long I stayed where I was, but soon it was pitch black outside and just as the fear started to settle in, the kitchen light flickered and came on and the fridge started to hum. I smiled. It was the sweetest sight and sound I'd ever heard. I didn't know how he did it, but Daddy had fixed it for me. Shortly after the lights came on, the doorbell rang. I went to the door. It was Mrs. Northup and her son. They had groceries. Daddy had sent her shopping. It looked as if they'd bought everything they could imagine a pregnant woman and two growing young girls could eat. I thanked them both. Mrs. Northup didn't say much after she said, "Your father sent this stuff."

I didn't bring the girls home that night. I needed time to think. This time I was giving it all to God but come morning, I was going to give Him a helping hand. After I got the girls, I searched the phone book and I found an evening school where I could take some typing and shorthand lessons. Mrs. Trindle said she was so happy that I was finally going to do something positive for me and the girls that she would pay for the evening classes. I smiled and accepted. I did in the next few months what I hadn't done in ten years. I went to typing and shorthand classes. I never missed a class and was surprised how quickly I caught on. I worked hard at learning because I knew soon my belly would be too big and it would be hard for me to get to class. At the end of three months of classes, and at the beginning of my seventh month, the school sent me to what they called a training program for the disadvantaged. I suspected that Daddy might have had something to do with it. The man said that he liked how I was working and after I had the baby and if I wanted to come back, he would see about taking me on a few days a week. There I was, almost twenty-eight, almost seven months pregnant, almost about to get my first job, and almost standing on the edge of being my own independent woman. I cried.

Mrs. Trindle, not Daddy, brought me a second-hand typewriting machine so I could practice. For the next couple of months, I went to my training job two days a week and to my classes the other three. When

I was at home, Mrs. Trindle would help Leela with her homework and watch T'Anna so that I could practice my typing. One morning, I woke up and knew that I wouldn't be going to class that day. For the third time, and if I could help it, the last time in my life, I was about to become a mother.

Mrs. Trindle kept the girls and I went to the hospital alone. Fourteen hours after I'd left home, Lillian Noreen Hirsh Greenwood was born. My heart used my eyes to look at her, it just ignited and anything that wasn't made of pure love got caught up in the fire she'd started. I fell in life and love with my daughter and knew that what I hadn't done for the others, I would do for her. There was a fire in this baby, but she wasn't angry like Leela or in a hurry like T'Anna. Her eyes were filled with curiosity. She looked as if she wanted to know everything. I looked at my baby and knew without really knowing that she was going to be the fulfillment of every dream, mine and everyone else's. There was a fire under her feet. It was going to propel her to great heights.

No one came to the hospital. Mrs. Trindle had to keep the girls, Andre and Tony never knew I was pregnant so I had no expectation of them returning to America. Philip, as he had been since I became pregnant, was unavailable; I didn't leave a message. Nana Noreen, who was still in Barbados, probably would have come, but I hadn't the heart to tell her I was pregnant again so she, like Tony and Andre, didn't know. Daddy, who was still pretending not to love me, didn't come but acknowledged her birth by sending over tons of stuff to the hospital.

I cried every day I was in the hospital and accepted that it was my own actions that had caused me to be here a third time. I cried for Ma, and Nana. I remember what both of them had gone through with their own daughters and like them, I hadn't planned and so here I was; a daughter of Promise Land, Greenwood, struck down by the curse that had befallen all the Greenwood women before me. I wished I could undo it. I couldn't. The girls were here and I, like Ma and Nana, had no choice. I would do what all daughters of Promise Land, Greenwood did; I would survive. I had no choice.

I never tried to reach Philip again, nor did he try to find or reach me. I took the thoughts I'd had about Philip and tried to start a fresh fire in my heart for him, but for whatever reason, it never caught. I had three girls to see about and couldn't keep on wasting energy on men who were gone and not worrying about me or their children. I decided to use my energy on my girls. They needed me. Lillian, who I'd decided to call Lillie after Ma, left the hospital with me on a very important day in American history. No, it wasn't important because she was born, but while I was in labor with her, all of America and the rest of the world were glued to their television sets watching, listening and waiting. No, they weren't listening for news of my baby's birth. It was bigger than that. It was Watergate and President Richard Nixon was in the thick of it.

The House Judiciary Committee had charged him in the bill of impeachment with high crimes and misdemeanors. When I'd heard that, I wished there was some way I could get them to charge Philip with the same thing. What he'd done to me was a high crime; they could have left off the misdemeanor part. But this was the House Judiciary Committee and a man having sex with a woman, making her pregnant, and leaving her was not important to them. The break-in at Watergate was important. It involved the thirty-seventh President Richard Milhous Nixon and everything was pointing to him making history; there was talk of his resignation.

Had everyone at the hospital not been talking about it, I wouldn't have noticed because all my thoughts were of the baby that had been placed on my chest and the two that were with Mrs. Trindle. So on that August morning when I walked out, I really didn't care that in a few hours there was going to be a new President because Richard M. Nixon, the first ever sitting President in America's history had resigned the night before, and in a few hours Gerald Ford was to be sworn in.

People will always ask you where you were when something happened, and until that morning I didn't have anything I could add but now I had my own story. I could say that on the morning I walked out of the hospital with my third fatherless child, America had watched one President resign and another sworn in. It was August 10, 1974; one month and six days after I had, for the first time in my almost twenty-eight years of living, finally understood the word independent. I'd gone into the hospital a dependent woman with Richard M. Nixon as my President, and had walked out; still an independent woman but there had been a changing of the guard at the White House; Gerald R. Ford was now my President. I didn't really care because I was afraid of what my life was going to be like with three girls. With my new-found independence, I knew I would never again depend on anyone for anything, even if it meant that my three girls and I were going to have some rough times. I accepted full and independent responsibility for them and for myself just the way Richard M. Nixon had accepted his; well kinda.

True to his word, when Lillie was three months old, Daddy stopped supporting me. He didn't do it in a way that would surprise me. He had Mrs. Northup call me the month before to remind me that the upcoming month would be the last where he was picking up my slack. I asked her to thank him for me. I also asked her to tell him I loved him since he didn't or won't to come to the phone.

It was almost three months now since Daddy had kept his word about supporting me. In not supporting me, Daddy also did something that was so painful, it tore at and almost broke my heart; he continued staying away. He didn't come to see me and the girls. Lillie was almost six months and hadn't been held by her grandfather. I couldn't believe that Daddy had turned his back on us. I cried a lot, but I cried often for Lillie because she had never gotten a chance to experience the warmth and love of her grandfather the way Leela and T'Anna had. It was sad that the granddaughter that looked the most like him was the one furthest away from his heart. I was sure that if Daddy ever saw Lillie, he would love her.

I told her about him even when she didn't understand what I was saying. As she grew to understand, I told her again. I told all of them. I told them about their grandfather and their uncle Andre who lived in Europe. I didn't want them not to know or love them. What I never did and asked Mrs. Trindle not do was mention their fathers. Although Leela and all the girls called Mrs. Trindle 'Gran', neither Mrs. Trindle nor I explained that she wasn't T'Anna's or Lillie's Gran. We left it alone.

The job at the small law office wasn't paying me enough to keep the small apartment I'd found and feed and clothe three girls and myself so, not knowing what else to do or where to turn, I turned to Mrs. Trindle. She was all that I had now and she opened her home to me. Mrs. Trindle, Hamilton's mother, not only took in her granddaughter, but she took in her mother and sisters as well. Mrs. Trindle, who I couldn't bring myself to call anything other than Mrs. Trindle, put T'Anna, Lillie and me in the basement. It was finished with two bedrooms, a bath, small kitchen, and an area that doubled as a living room and dining room.

As for Leela, she gave her Hamilton's old room. I didn't argue or care. I needed someplace for me and my girls. The basement apartment wasn't bad. She said she wasn't going to be charging me anything, but the first week after we moved in, I offered her something. She refused at first but I kept on insisting. Realizing that I wanted to be independent, she finally agreed to take fifteen dollars from me each week.

I accepted that. In a way, I was glad she didn't want anymore. That left me with fifty dollars a week to take care of me, T'Anna, and Lillie. I didn't have to do for Leela. Mrs. Trindle saw to it that whatever Leela wanted, she got. She was, after all, the only one of us who had any blood connection to her. Now it wasn't that Mrs. Trindle didn't give T'Anna and Lillie anything; she did. She just gave Leela more but never in front of the other girls so they would feel badly.

I provided for all my girls and insisted that Leela eat some of her meals with us even if we were having hot dogs with or without ketchup or bread and Mrs. Trindle had made steak. Leela never fussed; she understood because there was always Sunday. On Sundays, we ate with Mrs. Trindle. The Sundays we didn't eat with Mrs. Trindle, neither T'Anna nor Lillie fussed. The only times they fussed or were upset was when Leela was around and was in one of her bad moods. Leela was so 'sometimeish' with them. Sometimes she acted as if she loved them and sometimes she acted as if they were stopping her from getting something.

She was hardest on Lillie because whenever she got mad at her, she would say, "It's all your fault that Granddaddy don't come and see me or T'Anna."

Lillie would cry and say it wasn't her fault. That would be all Leela needed before she'd fight her. Leela kept me busy, especially when she wanted to play momma to her sisters. She was the big sister and she reminded them all the time.

Lillie, because she was so much younger than Leela, would let her be the big sister, even if Leela was just being plain old mean to her, but not T'Anna. T'Anna fought her back even if she lost the fight. Yes, that was Miss T'Anna Hirsh Greenwood; she might lose the fight but she always won the war. She and Leela knew exactly what buttons to press on each other to get a fight, a quarrel, or a good ole drag-down, knock-out brawl going. Those two fought and sometimes like strangers. Where the almost ten years between Leela and Lillie kept Lillie pretty much out of the fight, and Leela knew it, the six years between Leela and T'Anna seemed to be exactly what T'Anna needed to even the score. Those two kept me busy and I tried not to imagine what it would be like as they got older.

Chapter 65

Goodbye Keeps Getting Harder and Harder

When I started thinking of Leela and T'Anna getting older, I knew that it was time that Daddy and I found our way back to where the only thing between us was love. I'd gone on missing him as much as I could. I'd tried hard to do what Daddy wanted; to be independent and stand on my own feet, but if not standing on my own two feet meant not having him in my life, then I was willing to cut the feet off. I'd gone on missing Daddy as much and as long as I could take it so one day I picked up the phone, called, told him I'd missed him asked him if he would please come by and see us. He said he would after work that evening. The wait was unmerciful.

Just before eight, the bell rung. I ran to the door, forgetting that I was now full grown. The girls were watching me, but I didn't care. I wanted to feel Daddy's arms around me. I opened the door and there he was. He had come as he said he would. I started to cry. I didn't give him time to step in; the longing to see him, to be his little girl again was overwhelming. Daddy hugged me back as if he'd just rescued me from the jaws of death and didn't want to chance me slipping away again. I clung to him and his reality.

"My God, Princess, what have I done?"

"You haven't done anything, Daddy, it was me and I'm so sorry."

"Princess, I've missed you so much, thought about you; wondered how you were making out with the children and…."

Daddy couldn't go on. We were crying like babies and probably would've continued crying in the half-open door had Leela not come to see who was at the door.

"Granddaddy!" I saw her coming and stepped aside.

With one shriek, she was off her feet and jumping into his arms. She'd forgotten that she'd grown up and her grandfather had grown older. The force almost knocked Daddy to the ground. He stood there with his very big-boned granddaughter in his arms. I understood completely the emotions that were washing over Leela. She'd missed her grandfather as much as I had missed my Daddy. Daddy looked at me and then past me. I looked where he was looking and I saw them. T'Anna and Lillie were standing together, holding hands, and looking at all of us. T'Anna knew her grandfather but she was very protective of Lillie, and since Lillie didn't know him, she was keeping her distance.

"T'Anna, come and say hello to your grandfather."

"Can Lillie come too?"

Daddy didn't answer; he freed himself from Leela and quickly crossed the floor to where they were standing. T'Anna hugged and kissed him. She also clung to him. It amazed me that I'd failed to notice how starved we were for his love and affection. We were clinging to Daddy as if he could save us from our deprivation. The girls were too little to know that they were deprived, but I watched them, watched myself, and knew. All of us had gone without the love of someone other than ourselves for too long. I made a mental note to be mindful to add more love to my girls' lives so they wouldn't feel so needy.

Lillie stayed where she was. She watched and waited. She didn't have long to wait, as soon as Daddy was done hugging T'Anna and she had untangled herself from him, he bent to his knees. He didn't make any attempt to either pick Lillie up or to hold her. I knew Daddy well; he wanted Lillie to know that it was ok and that he would wait until she was comfortable. Daddy was like that; he would wait and give you time and by the time you decided to love him back, you were hooked and his. You never wanted to be out of the reach of his love. I'd experienced what it felt like to be out of the reach of his love and I was praying, even now, that I would never again experience that kind of void or hurt again. I watched Lillie and knew that once she'd decided to trust her grandfather, there would be no separating the two of them.

"Lillie, what a beautiful girl you are."

"Thank you."

"You can say grandfather."

"Grandfather?"

"Yes, grandfather. I'm Leela and T'Anna's grandfather, and I'm also yours."

"You are?"

"Yes, my little princess, I am."

I looked at Lillie and I could see her little heart melting. I looked at Daddy and wondered how much longer he could hold out waiting on her to throw her arms around her neck. Leela and T'Anna were watching. T'Anna had a look as if she were holding her breath, which made me smile, however, the look on Leela's face puzzled me. She looked as if Lillian was about to either get or take something that was hers.

Both Leela and Lillie moved at the same time. Lillie to step into her grandfather's outstretched arms and Leela to reclaim her grandfather. Lillie's stepping into her grandfather's arms at that precise moment foiled Leela's plans. Leela returned to her side the arm that was getting ready to pull her grandfather to his feet. She stopped and looked at Lillie in her grandfather's arms and if I didn't know better, I would swear that Leela looked angry. Neither Lillie nor Daddy noticed.

Lillie had fallen under her grandfather's spell and it would be a spell that would never be broken. I felt whole again. With everyone welcomed back into the fold and love filling the air, the girls brought their grandfather up to date as I sat and listened. I forgot Mrs. Trindle. She who had given us shelter, food, and love went unthought-of as the girls and I filled Daddy in. Had it not been for Leela who said, "Granddaddy, Gran Gran will soon be coming in from church; will you wait until she comes? I think she would be really glad to see that we are one big happy family again."

It was at that point I realized I'd not given a second thought to her. I looked as Daddy told Leela that he couldn't stay that evening, but if she would let him know which evening Mrs. Trindle didn't have service, he would visit on that day. Leela smiled very wide and promised to call him in the office. By the time Daddy was ready to leave, we were back in love again. It was the happiest I'd been in almost a year and a half. I prayed to God that I would never again do anything to make Daddy feel as if he had to go away from me again.

As he hugged me goodnight, he said, "Princess, I want you to know that the past year and few months have been, next to your mother's dying, the hardest thing I've ever had to do. I didn't want to do it, but you needed to grow up."

With my head resting on his chest, I said, "It was hard on me too, and I never want to be away and apart from you. I love you so much."

"I love you too, Princess. Take care."

I stood by the door until Daddy's car was out of sight and when I turned around, I saw three of the happiest girls I can remember seeing; ever. I smiled and walked towards them. It was good to be a family again.

Chapter 66

Be Careful of the Company You Keep

I'm not sure what I felt the most guilt or guilty about, but I was guilty. Guilt got up in the mornings with me, sometimes exactly at the same time and sometimes before I did. When it woke before me, it sat on the edge of the bed and waited for me to rise. I might, on occasion, over sleep but guilt never once did. It was everywhere and in everything. When I ate, and if I didn't eat a mother lode of it, it sat next to me at the table. When I dressed and I didn't put it on, and wear it out, it followed me out. It was everywhere.

The day Mrs. Trindle died was the day I had the most guilt. I was guilty because she'd died and never one day since I'd known her had I said 'I love you' to her. I'd never, never spoken those words to her despite the number of times and ways she said it, not just to Leela, her natural granddaughter, but to all my girls. The girls had said it back to her, but I, Andrea Matti Hirsh Greenwood, had never one day opened my mouth and said it, not even the way people in her church said it. I'd never allowed my brain to think it, my heart to feel it, or my mouth to utter it because and despite how much she'd done for me and mine, I still held her responsible for what her son had done to me. He'd started me on my journey up the rough side of the baby-making mountain and because of him and that, I'd held her in my heart.

If Mrs. Trindle had been waiting for anything, it wasn't my love. I was sure of it because she'd never acted as if she were sitting around waiting for anything from me. She was waiting, but it was for Hamilton to make his way back to her. She had waited until the day she died and he'd never come. Mrs. Trindle didn't have any long, drawn-out illness. It was kinda sudden. One day she didn't feel well. The next day, I stayed home from work to keep the girls because she was going to take herself to the emergency room up at St. Mary's. The day after they'd admitted her because her blood pressure and sugar was sky-high, Mrs. Trindle went into diabetic shock, had a heart attack, went into a coma, and died. No fuss or anything; just like that. She died and I was all alone with my three girls.

I didn't know what to do because I wasn't her family or anything, nor did I know of any other family that she had, so I called her Pastor. I didn't have a lot of money to pay for the funeral so the church's Helping Hand Funds helped me pay the funeral home. We waited over a week before we had her funeral because her Pastor said that we should wait just in case word or the Spirit got to Hamilton and he made his way home. When it appeared as if neither word nor Spirit had made its way to him, we went on and set the date for the funeral.

Mrs. Trindle was very active in her church so the church planned a nice home-going service for her. She'd served on the Usher Board so all of the members were there. The choir sung her favorite songs and then Leela, who was the most heartbroken of all my girls because after all it was her grandmother, got up and sung for her. Leela, who had denied me hearing her voice all these years, sung and hit notes as if she would, could, or intended to part heaven with them just so she could be sure her Gran Gran would get in.

I listened to my daughter sing that day and when she was done, I was sure that Mrs. Trindle had used every one of those notes and formed her own Jacob's Ladder and climbed her way right into heaven. The church was on fire when Leela was done. Mrs. Trindle's church was Pentecostal therefore they didn't think for one second of squelching the Holy Ghost Fire that was going from heart to heart all over that church. They let the Holy Ghost have its way, funeral or no funeral, and since it seemed to me that it had also dawned on Pastor that Mrs. Trindle had already made her way into heaven thanks to Leela, he just let the rest of the people go on and have their anointed and blessed moment.

We waited. Pastor waited for what seemed like a year and a day before he could continue Mrs. Trindle's home-going service. Since he knew that a funeral was never for the dead, he just let the people get their mixed up grief and joy out. The shouting, praising, and singing might have gone on forever if an Usher hadn't walked a man quietly and quickly down the main aisle. I was sure that most of the church didn't know him, but I recognized him instantly because of the sudden heat in my chest. I looked down at the front of my dress expecting it to be burning, but it wasn't. The fire for Hamilton was now burning out of control but it was contained. Until that moment, I didn't know that my chest was fireproof.

I watched as he walked up to his mother's casket. He was trembling so badly that two men from the Male Usher Board went and stood beside him. They expected his legs to fail him. I'm sure they wouldn't mind him falling, but they didn't want him grabbing onto the sides of Mrs. Trindle's casket causing her to be thrown to the floor. Sure, this was a fire-breathing, baptized-believing, and Holy Ghost tongue-speaking church, but if Mrs. Trindle had been thrown from her casket, it would be a fire-breathing, baptized-believing, and Holy Ghost tongue-speaking empty church. All them saved, sanctified, filled with the Holy Ghost Christians would be breaking their necks to be the first one outside. The Ushers didn't want that kind of pandemonium going on. It was easier to stand beside the man and catch him if he should start to fall. They were trained for moments such as this; they were good at catching folk who the Holy Ghost had 'caught' hold of.

The church quieted down, the Holy Ghost momentarily forgotten. That could happen sometimes if human nature got in the way of a worship experience. Curiosity was now bigger than the Holy Ghost. The momentarily forgotten Holy Ghost watched from the rafters as Curiosity took over the whole church. Curiosity was used to this. It always amazed him how soon people forgot what they were doing the minute he showed up. There was no anger or jealousy on the part of the Holy Ghost because he understood human nature. He would wait. There would be time enough for Him. After all, He knew that Curiosity didn't stand a chance against Him if He decided He wanted the service back.

The Usher, who had walked the man down to the front of the church, went to the Pastor's Aide and whispered something in his ear. The Pastor's Aide went to the Pastor and whispered something in his ear. The man at the casket stood there with one hand behind his back, holding a folded felt hat and the other hand covering his sobbing face. The Pastor, putting his hand to his Aide's ear, whispered something in his hand, which made its way to his Aide's ear. The Aide walked over to the undertaker and, putting his hand to his ear, whispered something into the undertaker's ear.

The church wished so badly to know what all the hand-to-ear hush-hush whispering was all about. They soon found out. The undertaker, who had already closed the casket just before the choir had started to sing, opened it up again. The man, who by now the church had figured out was Mrs. Trindle's long-gone-from-his mother son, hollered and slowly slid to his knees besides the casket. A hush quieter than the cloak of death that was shrouding Mrs. Trindle fell on the church. The only sound that could be heard was Hamilton as he labored to bring forth the seventeen-year fetus that had started growing inside of him the day he'd walked away from his mother and never looked back.

Hamilton's labor was hard. It looked as hard as the labor I had to bring his daughter into the world. It was hard, but not as hard as Mrs. Trindle's had been. In the end, she'd given up. Although many of the people who were in the church had accepted the doctor's diagnosis of a heart attack induced by a diabetic shock, those of us who knew her knew that it was a broken heart. Mrs. Trindle had waited almost seventeen years for him to return and now that he had, she couldn't see, feel, or touch him.

I watched Hamilton as he struggled to birth all those woes, regrets, frustrations, and suppressed love for his mother and felt nothing but pity for him. The instant I felt pity for him, the fire that had been burning in my heart for so many years and had started to rage out of control when he'd first walked into the church fizzled and went out. There was no need to keep it burning. The satisfaction of knowing that an unquenchable hellfire was raging inside of his heart allowed me to stop hating him. It was indeed true that funerals were for the living. I found my life back at Mrs. Trindle's funeral.

I sat there and, like the rest of the church, waited on Hamilton. The organist started to play softly and with Hamilton kneeling and crying at the side of the casket containing his mother's body, the Pastor got up and started the service. The male Ushers never moved from standing beside Hamilton. They stood there like guards. Hamilton stayed on his knees and cried. He had stopped hollering and was now whimpering. His body shook with sobs. I guessed that for the first time in his life, he was taking responsibility for something. This he couldn't undo or blame on anyone else.

He had to say the longest and hardest goodbye anybody can say to anyone. Pastor finished his sermon and opened the doors of the church.

Hamilton stood up for the first time since he'd walked into the church and saw his mother in the casket. He stood up, shouting, and started begging God, the church, the Pastor and most of all, his mother for forgiveness. He pleaded with her, begged her to forgive him, to understand that he was a broken man and without her forgiveness, he couldn't live. A part of me wanted to let him just go on begging Mrs. Trindle to forgive him, but the part of me that had received years and years of kindness and gratitude from Mrs. Trindle got up. I walked to the altar and accepted the call of fellowship. I opened my heart to a better relationship with God, and it was only as I felt the peace of God; the kind that passes all understanding, that I could go to him. Hamilton hadn't seen me in as many years, as he hadn't seen his mother, but just as I'd recognized him, he recognized me. He started to ask me for forgiveness, but I quieted him. I knew deep in my heart that only God could get me to forgive him. I wasn't about to rush God. I could wait.

After the doors of the church were opened and 'closed', the funeral for Mrs. Trindle was over. It was time to take her to her place of rest. The processional started. It now had one more person than it did earlier. The Hamilton that walked behind his mother's casket was different to the Hamilton who had walked into the church a little while ago. This Hamilton, for the first time in his life, had before God and the whole congregation, accepted responsibility. A few minutes after he'd accepted Christ into his life, he'd asked for a moment to speak. The Pastor, seeing how burdened he was, allowed him.

Hardly able to stand, breathe, and speak at the same time, he said, "For years, I've been running away from myself. Wherever I went, I took me along and yet I couldn't bring myself to come back to the person who loved me the most in the whole world. I couldn't because almost seventeen years ago, I'd taken someone's trust and betrayed them. I inflicted great pain; both physical and mental. I caused that person to suffer. My mother, the woman in this box, had come to me and said, 'Son, what you done is wrong. Take responsibility for what you done. Go; admit to them that you've wronged them and ask forgiveness.'

"I refused. I cursed my mother and told her that unless she admitted that I'd done nothing wrong, I would never set eyes on her again. My mother told me that she was a God-fearing woman and she couldn't stand there and tell me that my wrong-doings were right-doings. My mother stood her ground. I walked out her house and away from her. I never looked back. I left her all alone, or so I thought. I look around here in this church and I see that the only person who was alone was me. I was the one who had gone without the benefit of her love. I…" Hamilton started to cry again. He couldn't continue. He just slid to the floor and sat at the foot of Mrs. Trindle's casket.

Pastor finished the service. The undertaker readied the casket to be taken out to the hearse for its ride to the cemetery. Hamilton was helped to his feet by the Ushers and because he'd come by a taxi and had no way of getting to the cemetery, Pastor made room in one of the cars for him. At the cemetery, Hamilton cried the loudest and it was clear by the sounds that Hamilton made when Mrs. Trindle's casket was lowered into the ground that he'd finally given birth to his almost seventeen-year fetus. Hamilton fainted from the pain and pressure of his labor. He had said goodbye to her before, but this goodbye was his hardest goodbye ever. This time he, not she, would be the one crying. She'd cried her heart dry and now Hamilton was drowning in her sea of regrets.

Chapter 67

Too Far To Turn Back Now

After the gathering at the church, I returned to the house with the girls. People from the neighborhood were coming by to pay their respects. The house was almost full when Hamilton showed up. He stood at the door looking at me. I guess he was wondering if I was going to let him in. I couldn't refuse to let him in. It was more his house than mine. Actually, it wasn't mine at all. I was there at the mercy of Mrs. Trindle. If he wanted to, he could make me and my children leave.

He came in and sheepishly accepted the condolences as though he didn't have a right to them. People came to him anyway because he was her son. It made no difference that some had never seen him or that many hadn't seen him since he was a very young man; they expressed their sadness for his loss. By the time the last person left, Hamilton looked as though he'd aged another seventeen years.

The girls had gotten tired and as Leela was older and feeling lost and hurt without her Gran Gran, she'd gone downstairs to the basement with T'Anna and Lillie.

"Andrea, can I talk to you for a minute?"

"Talk, Hamilton, but you're going to have to talk to me while I clean up. Your mother wouldn't want her place less than neat."

"I know and if you want, I can help you, but I need you to hear me out."

I put down the tray that I was getting ready to take into the kitchen and looked at him. I looked at him and the only thing that moved inside of me was pity. Hamilton took my stopping still as his cue to speak.

"Andrea, there ain't really a lot that I can say, but I want to tell you that I am sorry. I am sorry that I put you in the position that I did and then didn't do as Ma said and go to your family. Ma had said I should face up to my responsibility and go and speak to Mr. Hirsh and your uncle and auntie. But I couldn't do that. I couldn't do that 'cause I was small-minded. I'd always looked at your daddy and hated him."

When Hamilton said, "Mr. Hirsh," my heart stopped. I hadn't called Daddy to let him know that Mrs. Trindle had died. He would have come. I started to feel very sad. How could I have forgotten to let Daddy know? He would have been there for Leela. The hatred that I thought had gone out flickered again. I could feel it igniting. Hamilton saw the look cross my face and I'm sure he thought it was as a result of what he was saying because he said, "I know I shouldn't be saying now that I hated your daddy but since I'm telling my truths, I have to say that even though it's wrong. I didn't hate him because he was your daddy. I hated him because he was a white man. I did you wrong because your daddy was a white man and in my small limited mind, I was getting back at him and his kind for all that had gone wrong with me and my life. I was wrong."

I looked at Hamilton and wanted to slap him. I wanted to slap him not because he'd tried to hurt me but because he'd wanted to hurt Daddy. Hamilton looked at me and, undaunted by my chilly stare, continued. "Andrea, I ain't going stay around here. I looked at those children of yours and I figured out which one was mine. Not that it would take a rocket scientist. I also know that your two youngest girls don't know who I am, but the big girl, she knows that I'm her father, right?"

"I'm figuring that she knows since she called your mother Gran Gran, but if she knows, Hamilton, believe me it's not because I told her. I never intended to but I couldn't explain how much she looked like your mother. There would have been no logical way to explain your mother away. Your mother loved her and that "big girl", as you called her, loved her back. Hamilton, your mother was a good woman. She was kind to me, but the one thing you should have seen, even if it was just for one day, was the way your mother and Leela were with each other. The love between them was real. It was so real, Hamilton, you could almost touch it. Anytime you were in their presence, you felt it. It was contagious."

"Leela? That's her name?"

"Yes, Hamilton, your daughter's name is Leela Phoebe Hirsh Greenwood. Yes, Hirsh; that same white man's last name. She is as much a Hirsh as I am."

"Andrea, do you think I could talk to her, perhaps explain a little?"

"Explain what, Hamilton?"

"You know, 'bout my being gone and stuff like that."

"And what do you think that would accomplish, or are you looking to blame her for your tired ass not being able to stand up and face reality and responsibility like a man?"

"Andrea, I don't want to fight with you and I understand if you're angry with me, but she's my daughter too."

"You see, that's the kind of shit that pisses me off. Here you are, gone from before she was born, and now you're standing here saying some shit ass nonsense about if I'm angry and she's your daughter. Well, for starters it's not a matter of "if" I am angry. Let's clear that up one time now and forever. Angry wasn't a word I could have used to describe what I was feeling for you. I'm not even sure if there's a word for what I was feeling towards you. But whatever the word was, I realized today when I saw your weak sorry ass that you weren't worthy of the energy it took to keep that kind of shit going. So I let it go. As for the 'she's my daughter' nonsense you just opened your mouth and let spew out, I'll tell you one thing: she's more man that you will ever be. Now, if you want to talk to her, that's going to be her decision. I'll go down and I'll ask her. If she wants to talk to you, she'll follow me up these stairs, but if you see me come back up alone, that will be your answer."

I turned away before Hamilton could say anything else and I went down to the basement. I found Leela sitting in her sisters' bedroom. The TV was on but no one was watching it. I looked at the three of them and it was hard to tell who was consoling whom.

"Leela, come with me to my room for a minute."

"Sure, Ma."

Leela got up from between her sisters, but not before doing a very un-Leela-like thing; she promised them that she would be back in a minute. She said it as if she meant that she would be back to save and protect them.

I looked at my daughters and said, "She'll be back quick. It won't take long; promise."

T'Anna and Lillie looked at me as if they were afraid. They'd never experienced death before and I could tell that they were afraid. Hamilton wouldn't keep me from being a mother to my girls. Not if I could help it. Leela walked with me to my room. Her stride matched the intensity I was feeling. Somehow, I felt that Leela knew what I was getting ready to ask her and as soon as we reached my room, she spoke.

"Ma, don't ask me to do it. Don't make me go upstairs and act all nice to him."

"I'm not going to make you do anything, Leela. This is your choice. You're fifteen, almost sixteen years old. You're old enough and smart enough to decide. I've long suspected that you have known all along that Hamilton was your father. I also guessed that you took your questions to Mrs. Trindle and she answered them the best that she could."

Leela looked at me with a confused look on her face. Then her resolve softened. Some of the crispness in her voice came off and when she spoke, I knew that she was going for me. Or so she thought.

"Ma, I'm going to go, but I want to say what's on my mind. I have a lot on my mind."

"I'm not going to stop you, Leela. You have a right."

Hamilton didn't have to guess if Leela wanted to talk to him or not. She walked ahead of me up the stairs and almost bounded into the room so the first person he saw was her.

"Hi, Leela."

"Ma said you wanted to talk to me."

"Don't I get a hello?"

"What do you have to say? Or should I ask the questions and you come up with the answers."

"I guess that means I don't get a hello."

"Either you start talking or I'm going back downstairs to my sisters. They need me. They need someone to tell them not to be afraid because Gran Gran has died. So if you have something to say, start talking or in a few seconds, it will be the back of my black ass you'll be seeing."

Hamilton looked at me as if he was expecting me to tell Leela not to talk to him like that. I turned my head and looked at Leela. I'd given her my word that she could say her piece. I wasn't going to take it back from her now.

"Are you going to talk?"

Leela waited all of what might have been five seconds before she started. "Fine. Since you're not going to start, then I'll be the man and start this talk. First of all, where do you get off not coming back here even one day to see my Gran Gran? Do you know that every day, Gran Gran would sit and look for you? She believed that someday, some magical day, you were going to do like Houdini and appear. She then got me to start believing that once you came, you would have a good explanation and fix everything.

"You see, "Daddy", unlike Gran Gran, after a few years I stopped waiting. I stopped believing you would ever come. That was right around the time I stopped believing in fairies, ghost, goblins, Santa Claus, the Easter Bunny, Christmas, magic, and all that other pagan idol bullshit. And just so you would know, I hate magic. 'Cause it's not like I could say abracadabra and you would be gone. I know that I would be abracadabraing for a month of Sundays and you would still be here when I'm done. I hate magic.

"""Daddy", what you've missed is that you don't have a right to be here anymore and especially today. You don't have a right to any part of today anyway. Your self-imposed exile took away that right. Today was our day, but you had to show up and spoil it. You couldn't just have let us have our day because something told you that being a son gives you some bragging rights. Fine, you may have bragging rights over Ma, T'Anna, and Lillian, but you don't have none over me. But the way I figured it out, you have just about three years of bragging rights over me and…"

Leela stopped to take a breath and I looked at Hamilton. He was standing stiff as a dead with his mouth wide open and his eyes bulging. It was as if each word she'd spoken was acting like embalming fluid and was causing rigor mortis to set in. I'd promised her she could say what she wanted to and I wasn't about to stop her now. She'd earned the right. Almost sixteen years of it. Hamilton opened his mouth to say something and all he did was give Leela an opening so she climbed right down inside of him and started to rip him to smaller shreds, Leela style, from the inside.

Leela thought that Hamilton had opened his mouth to say something and in a flash, she was on him again. "Don't go saying anything to me. I ain't done."

Hamilton closed his mouth. He was too late. Leela was already inside. It was clear where the completion of his annihilation would commence. I could almost see his guts in her hand. I knew Leela well. She would leave the destruction of his heart for the last.

Watching Leela's face, I knew that she had, without his noticing it, put on her war paint. I was sure if I'd look at her feet, I would have seen combat boots. Hamilton, in his innocent ignorance, had asked me to go and bring the young, angry, hungry Tasmanian she-devil out of the basement so she could have dinner. I wonder how he knew she was hungry and had the taste for Trindle meat. There was no time to ask him anything. From inside him, she spoke.

"Yeah, and save that look for someone who gives a shit. I don't. I've heard about you every day from the time I could understand and even before that. Gran Gran loved you. She loved you so much she never one day realized that it was your ugly-ass genes that were responsible for me being this odd composite of mismatched human features and limbs.

"None of what I look like had anything to do with Ma, my other grandmother, my grandfather, or anyone on my mother's side of the family. It was you and your genes. I'm all Trindle. I got everything from you but your inability to take responsibility. But today, you're going take some responsibility for me being almost too ugly to love.

"You see, now that Gran Gran is gone, I'm not sure who else is going to love. Ma goin' love me because that's what mothers do, and if she wasn't my ma, I don't think she would take the time for all that I've put her through. You want to talk to me! Talk to me about what!"

For another split-second, it looked like Hamilton was going to be brave enough to respond to what his daughter was saying. Leela again, didn't give him the slightest edge to get a word in.

"That's right. Pull your own set of ugly mismatched human features together and talk to me. Tell me that Ma deliberately chose you to be my father? Try to tell me that bull and I'll call you a damn liar. You know why I would call you a damn liar, "Daddy"? Because I've had to live with my sisters my whole life. They are beautiful. You had to have been a hateful or spiteful accident 'cause you're ugly inside and out."

The almost immobile Hamilton flinched and Leela noticed. She wasn't missing anything with him. Not today. Today, this moment, was hers.

"Why you looking at me like you wondering what I'm talking about? I'll explain it to you. Ma chose their fathers from high up on the evolution chain because they had already evolved and she wanted beautiful daughters. And why did she do this, you're wondering? Because she's been forced to look at me from birth and realizing she'd missed seeing all this ugly shit in you, she wasn't about to do a repeat."

Hamilton, who still hadn't learned Leela's annihilation method, opened his mouth again. Leela, fearing he might try to regurgitate and get her out, dug her claws deeper. The pain registered on Hamilton's face, but he couldn't speak. She was shredding the bottom of his heart. She was no way near done. He still had more to endure. Leela, with his heart fragments in her claws, continued.

"Ma took one look at me and knew that there had to have been some latent gorilla-swinging-ape-man-ass-missing-link type gene trapped in your ugly mutated recessive sperm. When she saw what your sperm had created, she didn't want to take any more chances on having another baby that looked like me so she chose carefully. Now if that's not what you wanted to talk to me about, then tell me what you want to talk to me about?"

I flinched and Hamilton looked as if he was going to faint. Because Leela was focused on him, she hadn't noticed my flinching. I was glad for her because if she had, she might not have been able to empty all the stuff that had been building in her all these years. Leela's voice started to get tighter.

"If you could tell me something other than that and get me to believe it, then you could go on and tell me about how much you loved my Gran Gran, and how much you missed and worried about her. When you're done telling me about all that, then tell me about this earth-shattering love you had for Ma, and then my dear sweet, never-here-for-me-one-day-in-my-whole-life-daddy, tell me about your love for me, Leela Phoebe Hirsh Greenwood. I'm a Hirsh Greenwood, "Daddy"; a Greenwood! You didn't even have enough decency to make me a Trindle."

Hamilton turned his head.

When Leela said, "Trindle" she started to cry. When Hamilton turned his back, a crying, now almost-hysterical Leela screamed at him, "Don't you turn your ugly hateful head away from me, Hamilton Trindle! Look at me! Look at what your evil ugly ass made! Look at me! Look at me and tell me that you just up and left because you were afraid of my grandfather or some bullshit like that. Look at me and tell me that you were young and didn't think you could take care of us. Tell me that nonsense and I'll tell you that you are weak and full of shit. I know because my granddaddy wasn't sitting around and waiting for your two wooden nickels to support me or Ma. Granddaddy never needed a penny from you to help take care of us. Ma needed you. Not for money or some dumb shit like that. She needed you to be here and to be a father to me."

I couldn't take it anymore. I rushed over to where Leela was screaming at him and took her in my arms. She, for the first time that I could really recall, wrapped her arms around me. She wrapped her arms around me as if she hoped in doing so, she could press her hurt into me and I would help her bear it. I opened my heart to receive her pain. The intensity of her anguish broke my heart. She had suffered under the weight of looking like her father; a father she had no choice in choosing and had never seen. Leela hated him for making her, as she saw it, ugly.

Hamilton didn't speak for what seemed like an eternity and when he did, all he said, as he looked at her with tears streaming down his face was, "I'm sorry."

"Sorry, sorry!" Leela sobbed. "That's all you can say. Almost seventeen years of your being gone, years me and Gran Gran waited and wished for you to come and love us, and now, today, the day she is placed in the ground, you look at me, the only grandchild she ever knew, and say you're sorry. You're right though. You're sorry. You are one sorry ass excuse for a son, a man, and a father. If I live to be one hundred years and a day, I hope never to see your sorry ass again. Consider me dead. Dead! You hear me, Hamilton Trindle? I, Leela Phoebe Hirsh Greenwood, am as dead to you as your mother is."

Leela pushed her way out of my embrace and headed in the direction of her room. I realized she didn't want her sisters to see her like she was. She didn't want to explain her pain. Until today, I'd never seen her hurt; she'd managed to keep it deep inside. She was showing that unlike what I'd started to believe, her skin wasn't coated with a thin sheet of granite. She was as human as anybody else.

"Hamilton if you're waiting for me to apologize for what my daughter has said to you, stop waiting. It's not going to happen."

"Andrea, she's right. I had no right to expect her to talk to me any differently. I should've prepared something to say to her, but I didn't know I was coming back; didn't have any plans really on coming back, but it was hearing about Ma that made me come back like this. You know, sudden. It was only yesterday that I found out about Ma. It was by accident, you know. A man I work with back in Chicago was talking 'bout one of his mom's old friends back in New York who had died suddenly, and how her old church had been holding a prayer vigil 'cause her only son didn't know she was dead, and they didn't want him showing up years later only to find out his mother was dead and buried. I wasn't paying much attention to what he was saying 'till he said his mother's friend was a West Indian woman from St. Vincent. Drea, I got this funny feeling in my gut. I knew without really knowing that it was Ma he was talking 'bout. I was the son that was delaying her funeral. I blurted out her name. He wasn't certain 'bout the name, but he said that Trindle sounded like it could be the name.

"Drea, I started to holler at the top of my lungs. I knew in my whole body that Ma had died and she had died waiting for me to come see her and even now in death, she was still waiting. I'd kept Ma waiting in life and once again, I was keeping her waiting. I couldn't do it to her any longer."

"Why didn't you call somebody?"

"I was too scared and besides, I didn't know who to call anymore. I just got on the first plane that could get me here as quickly as possible. When you saw me, I'd come straight from the airport."

I wanted to feel sorry for him, but I couldn't. He'd made some bad choices and we, not him, had been forced to live with them. Now he would have to learn to live with them just the way we had. Hamilton was openly crying. I'm sure it was more than what Leela had said to him. He had almost seventeen years of stuff to cry for. I walked away from him. I had to see about my children. He'd taken care of himself all these years, he could manage now. I said nothing to him. I simply walked away. I went to see about Leela. He and his misery would have to do without my company.

Leela was in her room sitting on her bed with a picture of her Gran Gran in her lap. Tears were dripping onto the glass of the frame. As soon as I walked through the door, she asked, "What did he come back for? Did he come back to sell Gran Gran's house and put us out? Is that why he came back now? Is it, Ma?"

I didn't have answers to Leela questions so I just sat beside her. She looked at me with the most sorrow and hurt I'd ever seen. Something in her eyes reminded me of Ma the day she'd come home from Nana's funeral, and I became afraid. I was afraid that my own child would do like her grandmother and will herself to death. Silently as I looked at her, I asked God not to let her do that. I asked him not to take anyone else away from me.

"Ma, is he gone?"

"No, Leela, I left him outside; pretty much where you saw him last."

"I wish he would just go back to wherever he was living and leave us alone. We don't need him, Ma. Tell him we don't need him and to go and leave us alone."

Leela's tears started anew. I looked at my child and I didn't know what to do. I started to get up, but Leela got up first. She looked at me and she said, "Ma, T'Anna and Lillian are alone downstairs in the basement. They are afraid. I don't want my sisters to be alone any longer. I'm going back down there. If he stays, he stays. If he leaves, he leaves; but tell him that whatever he does, he's not to go near my room. Gran Gran said that that will always be my room; always."

I walked out of the room with Leela. Hamilton was still standing where I'd left him. He watched Leela as she came out, but she didn't so much as glance at him. She headed towards the basement door and disappeared into the bowels of the basement as if it were a giant beast that had swallowed her.

"Andrea, I need to talk to you."

"And tell me what, Hamilton? Don't you think Leela told you enough? What, you want to hear it from me too? If that's what you're waiting on, it isn't going to happen. I'm too tired and I have three upset girls that I must see about."

With a voice almost as burdened as when he gave birth to his grief, Hamilton said, "Andrea, I don't have any place to stay."

"Hamilton, this is your house, you can do whatever you want in it." I stopped from talking and went back to cleaning up the house. Hamilton started to help, but then he stopped.

"Andrea, I'd like to stay here tonight."

I stopped from cleaning up and looked at Hamilton. I wanted to see what a man looked like who'd just lost his ever-loving mind. After what Leela had said to him, how could he ask such a thing? Hamilton saw the way I was looking at him and raised his hand as if to stop me from saying what was on my mind. I waited for him to speak.

"Just for tonight, Andrea; just for tonight and could you let Leela know that I'll be staying?"

"Man, you must be out your fuckin' mind. Me tell Leela? You want me to go downstairs and tell my daughter that you want to stay here tonight? You got to be stupid. If you want Leela to know, you go and tell her yourself. I'm not taking any responsibility for anything else that concerns you. I don't owe you nothing, and besides it's not like I even know you. I don't know you. I don't know nothing 'bout you and what I remember 'bout, I would love to forget. I remember you were a hateful, irresponsible boy who deliberately stole my virginity, made me pregnant, interrupted my dreams, poked holes in my peace, and clouded my father's hopes for me. That's what I remember 'bout you, and trust me, I don't want to know anything else. Oh and, Hamilton, besides telling you to tell Leela yourself, there's one thing I'll ask you not to do in this house and especially tonight."

Looking as if what I'd said to him surprised him, Hamilton spoke in a voice a little more than a whisper. "What, Andrea, what is it you'd like to ask me not to do in this house tonight? Like I'm goin' try to do something other than try to get a little rest."

"Die, Hamilton, die."

Almost as if in disbelief, Hamilton said, "Die? Did you say die?"

"Yes, Hamilton Trindle, I said die. Whatever you do in this house tonight, don't die. My girls and I don't deserve that. So if you feel that when you lie down, that there's even the remotest possibilities of your ass dying, please let me know so that I can find somewhere to take my girls so we won't have to witness it or feel inclined to help you."

Hamilton sat down on the couch as if I'd shot him. I didn't care.

Shaking his head from side to side, Hamilton said, "Whew. I see now where she got that spit fire tongue from."

"No, Hamilton, she didn't get it from me. You're just meeting Leela for the first time, but I've had to live with her for fifteen, almost sixteen years. Leela's style is different to mine. She has a preference for disembowelment. I'm selective. I only go after those persons who have either hurt me or my family and you, Hamilton, qualify on both levels."

I walked out of the living room and as I reached the kitchen, I heard Hamilton's feet moving. I didn't look back. Then I heard the door. I went back out to the living room. It was empty. Hamilton had left. He never came back that night, but came back a week later. He said that he'd gone to the bank to see about the mortgage and stuff like that. He said that after he left the bank, he went to see the man who had taken care of his ma's business. His ma, he said, had taken care of everything. There was a will and it was all done right. He told me that his ma had arranged for me and the girls to stay in the house for one year after her death and after that, the lawyer's office was to handle it from there. I accepted what Hamilton said. We'd come too far to turn back now.

Chapter 68

More Flies with Honey

The year following Mrs. Trindle's death was hard. I felt like it was me and my girls against the whole world. I was working full-time at the law office doing some typing, filing, and whatever they told me to do, but I was also going to school at night. Leela was in tenth grade and T'Anna and Lillie were attending public school. I was still having problems adjusting to all the changes that I'd been through. My life was so empty. I missed my old life. I missed the life when it was me, Momma, Nana, and Andre. It was hard to believe that I was alone. That it was nearly a year after Mrs. Trindle died and just before we had to move.

Leela was almost back to her old self. She had been quietly returning to her old self since her grandmother died, and with the anniversary of her death fast approaching, Leela had almost made it all the way back to being the Leela that took no nonsense or prisoners. I braced myself for life with my daughter. I strapped myself in because I knew that there were going to be many bumps and mountains to climb before it was all over.

Daddy would visit and chase some of my loneliness away. When he visited, the girls couldn't wait to fill him in what they felt he'd missed. After they went to bed. he and I talked for hours. I'd missed him so much. He was my family and with him angry at me, I'd felt incomplete. I now felt complete and whole enough to do what I hadn't done for years. I asked Daddy about Troy and then about Philip. Daddy looked at me as if he were wondering why now. I answered his unasked question.

"Daddy, the girls don't know anything about their fathers, but every now and again, I wonder why neither Troy nor Philip could come and see them; even ask somebody about them."

"Princess, they do ask."

I looked at Daddy shocked. He spoke before I could formulate a question.

"A few years ago, Troy returned to the states. He knew from Tony that you had a girl. He also knew from Tony how she was growing. However, Tony was having difficulty keeping his brother informed after your brother found out and almost lost his mind with anger. Tony pointed Troy in my direction."

"But, Daddy, why didn't you tell me?"

"Tell you what, Princess? Tell you that although Troy had been gone all these years, he'd not built up enough nerve to come see you or to take responsibility for what he'd done. What was there to tell you? Sure, I could have told you that he came by the office; sure, I could have told you that I showed him the pictures of all your girls, but what else could I tell you? I couldn't tell you that I waited for Troy to ask for you and that although he made a million small hints towards that subject, he never did. How do I tell you that, Princess? You see, Princess, Philip might have been one of those things, a moment, a passing fantasy, but I know love and I know you. Princess, I would go to my grave believing that you had a genuine love for Troy and Troy for you. I'm just sorry that Troy was too weak to realize he was old enough to make his own decision."

"Daddy, I would have listened to anything. Every time I look at T'Anna, I miss him. I missed him when he left, the day she was born, and I missed him when she got old enough to ask me about her daddy. I didn't have an answer for her, Daddy. I didn't have an answer then and I still don't. Now I have two daughters I don't have answers for. I feel badly when Lillie asks about her daddy. There's nothing I can tell her. Nothing because I don't know anything about Philip Rancor other than the fact that he gave me a very beautiful and intelligent daughter."

"Well, at least Leela knows about Hamilton. Whatever happened to him after she saw him last year?"

"All I know is that he said that the girls and I could stay here for one year and after that, we would have to move. Daddy, I'm getting tired of moving. I've moved so much since Momma died. I want a place to go to where I know that I won't be moving again. My girls need stability and I'm trying hard, Daddy, but it's going to be a while before I can give it to them on my own."

"I know, Princess, that's one of the reasons I came."

"One?"

"Yes, one."

"Well, what's the other?"

"Remember I told you that I saw Philip."

"Yes, what about him?"

"It seems that after all these years, Philip's conscience has started to bother him. He wants to see Lillie."

"What? It sounded to me, Daddy, as if you said that Philip wants to see Lillie. That is what you said, right?"

"Philip's father has gotten wind that he and I share a grandchild."

"So why should that matter after all this time? Lillie is almost four."

"It matters, Princess, because Philip's father is very ill and there isn't much time left."

"So what does that have to do with Lillie?"

"Philip is an only child and Lillie is Philip's only child. His father would like to see her before he dies."

"Daddy, since when did Lillie become his only grandchild, or did he decide on his deathbed that he will now acknowledge her? Did either of them think about me or Lillie before death took up residence at the foot of his bed? What am I supposed to do? Take Lillie over to them, introduce her to a father and grandfather she's never seen; one that will die before she can get a clear image of him in her brain, and the other who will be gone the minute her little heart makes room for him. Tell me, Daddy, do they really expect me to do that to my daughter?"

"Princess, you don't have to do anything. I'd never told Charles that Lillie was our granddaughter. He took it awfully hard when he found out that his son's daughter was also my grandchild and that I'd known all along and hadn't told him."

"How did he find out, Daddy, if you didn't tell him?"

"Believe it or not, Philip told his father. He told him after he found out Charles was dying and one of Charles' deepest regrets wasn't living long enough to see Philip have children."

"So why did Philip tell him?"

"He told him because the guilt, deceit, and lies were too much for him."

"That's all fine and good that Philip has developed a conscience at this late date, but you still haven't told me why I should subject my daughter to them."

"Do it for me please, and for my friend Charles; two old men that have made many mistakes."

"But what about Lillie? Daddy, she has been the only one of my daughters that has gone without your presence, your love, affection, and attention for no other reason than she existed. Daddy, that wasn't fair. She never asked to be here and now you're asking me to do for people who have never done anything for her other than to ignore her existence. Think about how unfair that is to Lillie. How can I trust you to protect her, considering that you know her just as much as Philip and his father?"

"I'll protect her because, if for no other reason, she's your daughter and I love you."

"How will you protect her?"

"I'll handle it. I know that I've done Lillie wrong as well, and if in any way I can start to correct the wrong I've done her, I'd like to start now. Give me a chance, Princess. Give me a chance and I promise you that no harm whatsoever will come to her. I'll make sure that Charles doesn't tell her that he's her grandfather or Philip that he's her father. I'll stake my life on it."

"You don't have to do that, Daddy. If you say that you'll take care of Lillie, then I'll trust you to take care of her. Arrange it and let me know the day and you can come and get her."

"You've got it, Princess. Leave everything to me."

Chapter 69

Invisible Daddy

Just like that, Philip Rancor and his father were in Lillie's life and then again they weren't. I'd no real feelings for Philip or his father and so I made them all promise that they would remain in the shadows of her life. I didn't trust Philip. I had a feeling that he had an ulterior motive for "finding" his daughter, dusting her off, and presenting her as daughter beloved. We had managed, before his conscience got bleached, to get along well enough without anyone and we were going to manage long after they were gone. Lillie, God bless her, spent a few days a month in her father's and grandfather's company and never knew who they were. Daddy said that on one of their visits, Lillie had called him Grandfather and Charles had said, "Matthew, how lucky you are. You have such a sweet little girl to call you grandfather and I don't."

Daddy said that before he could say anything, Lillie asked, "Mr. Charles, you don't have nobody to call you Granddaddy?"

Charles replied, "No, Lillie, I'm not as lucky as your grandfather here. I've never heard anyone call me Grandfather."

Lillie had taken the bait. She looked at Mr. Rancor laying on his deathbed and said, "Granddaddy, can I call Mr. Charles Granddaddy Charles? Can I, Granddaddy?"

Daddy said he looked at his friend and realized that he didn't really have that much longer to live and knowing how much it meant to him, he said, "If that's what you would like, Lillie."

"Thank you, Granddaddy; now I have two granddaddies. I have Granddaddy Matthew and Granddaddy Charles."

Charles Rancor smiled. Someone had called him Granddaddy before he died. His wish had come true. I allowed Daddy to take Lillie to see

Mr. Rancor. She was becoming very fond of him and it worried me. I knew that he would soon be gone and I didn't want it to hurt her. Ultimately, I was more worried for Lillie than necessary. After she and Daddy had been going to see Philip's father for about six months, Lillie came home one day and said to me, "Mommy, today Granddaddy Charles went to heaven. Me and Granddaddy won't be going to his house to see him anymore. I liked him, Mommy, and I'll miss him. Do you think, Mommy, that Granddaddy Charles was happy that I'd made him my pretend Granddaddy?"

"He was, Lillie, and you don't have to ever think of him as your pretend granddaddy. He loved you and your visits very much."

"I liked him a lot too, Mommy, he was very nice. I'm going to miss him, Mommy."

I looked at my little girl and realized that she was going to be ok. I was happy in my heart that she'd gotten to spend some time with him, even if it was just for a few months. Lillie went off to play and Daddy and I talked for a little while.

"Princess, I want to thank you for allowing Lillie to visit with Charles. It meant a great deal to him. I think her visits helped him to accept his dying. Of course, it became harder for him to accept that he would have to let her go, but he was just happy that he'd gotten to see her. He wanted me to make sure and thank you for him. He also wanted me to let you know that he was sorry that Philip was such a coward."

"Daddy, Charles didn't have me to thank. He had you. If you hadn't asked me, I wouldn't have allowed her to go. Now that he's gone, our life will go back to normal. I don't want Philip around us. He's weak and I don't want his weakness to rub off on her. Lillie is different, Daddy. She's smart and caring and I can tell that she's going to be different to her sisters. All of my girls are very smart, but there's something extra about Lillie. I'm not sure what it is, but there's something there, Daddy. You'll see."

"You don't have to tell me, Princess I can see for myself. It was amazing the way she made room in her little heart for Charles. I think she knew without really knowing that it was important to him, that her calling him Granddaddy Charles made him happy, so without any prompting from anyone, she just did. She's one very special little girl. There's something to be said for her being called Lillie."

Life with my girls continued and before I knew it, the year was up.

The notice came for us to move. Hamilton never came to see about his mother's things so I let Leela take what she wanted. She took her time and packed up what she wanted; the rest, Daddy arranged to have stored. Leela never mentioned Hamilton's name after the day she'd walked out of that house. I understood about the pain of leaving someplace you loved. I'd left Lexington Avenue.

We moved from Bainbridge Street back to Lexington Avenue. Daddy had never sold the house and now that I needed someplace for me and my girls, he gave me the keys to it. We moved from Bainbridge Street but no one moved in. The house remained closed for a long time. I kept waiting for a For Sale sign to show up on the front yard. It never did. It bothered Leela that her father had made us move out of the house and yet no one moved in. Hamilton had killed all possibilities of any kind of relationship with Leela when he made her leave her grandmother's house.

Things on Lexington Avenue had changed but even with all the changes and the years that I'd been gone, they had remained the same. Some people had aged and died, some had grown up and moved away, but some people were just where I'd left them. Mrs. Lewis, who I'd thought was old when I was little, had finally grown into a real old woman. She was still busy watching everybody's business. She'd seen me grow up, go away, and now she was watching me and my girls come back. I spoke to her out of respect. She didn't know it, but if there was no such thing as respect, she wouldn't have received my hellos, my good mornings, or my good evenings. I would've had nothing to say to Mrs. Lewis because I still remembered her calling me and Andre half-white nigger children. Anyway, that was then and this was now.

Time moved quickly once we settled back on Lexington. One minute the girls were growing and the next minute they were grown. Leela was going into the twelfth grade. T'Anna was in ninth and Lillie wasn't that far behind. She was so smart, the school kept on wanting to skip her over grades. I didn't let them because I didn't want her to skip right over T'Anna and somehow get out of high school before her big sister. I was proud of all my girls.

Daddy had started to help us out again and with him turning the deed of Momma's house over to me, he'd lifted a tremendous burden off my shoulders. For the first time ever, I felt as if I could make it. My girls and I were going to be fine. T'Anna was becoming grown and loving her new body. It was as if she'd suddenly discovered that she was a girl. She was beautiful, but something in her spirit was haunting and hungry. She was the opposite of both her sisters. Leela needed no one and made sure that everyone knew and understood that. Lillie needed no one but her books, the library, and anyplace where she could learn something. T'Anna, though, was always searching. There was a hunger in her that couldn't be satisfied. It didn't matter what she got, where she went, or what she did when she got there, it was never enough. My daughter was going to move into the land of "Need More" and it was going to be her own destruction. I could feel it.

T'Anna was my only daughter that was affected by being a fatherless child. She wanted a daddy. More specifically, she wanted her daddy. She wanted her daddy even if he were invisible. She questioned me constantly about her father. No answer I could give satisfied her. So she wrote. She used her writing to fill the void in her life and heart. She wrote of romance, love, and family. She wrote the kind of life she wished for. She created wonderful stories with daddies that stayed around and loved their children. There were no invisible daddies in any of her stories. I wanted to tell her about Troy, but it made no sense to tell her about someone who had abandoned not just her, but the very idea of her. Why should I tell her that this father she hungered so much for never had fatherhood in his plans? I'd loved Troy Adams since the first day I saw him and even now, almost fifteen years after I'd first seen him, and despite the fact that he'd abandoned me and his daughter, I still loved him.

Personally, it didn't matter to me if I never saw Hamilton or Philip Rancor again in this life, but Troy; I always wished to see him. If he had ever brought himself to my door, I would've forgiven him because I still loved him. My heart had never opened to anyone else again, nor had I made myself available. Many men had tried to date me, but I was content to be a mother to my girls, take care of my home, and on a very rare occasion, accept an invite to a picture show or get a bite to eat, but a relationship? There was never room in my life or heart for any. I kept my heart open just in case Troy ever made his way back to me. I understood T'Anna. She'd never known Troy, yet her heart was still waiting for his love.

After all these years, he still occupied my heart, most of my day, and night dreams. There were times I missed him. Times when I would cry for him, but never once, never once did I let on to anyone. I confided only in God. I trusted God that He was watching over all of us and He was keeping Troy safe. I believed that when the time was right, God would send him back to me, but until that time I was fully devoted and committed to God. He was the only Master that I served. I also saw to it that all my girls served Him faithfully with me.

Lillie was passionate about her worship experience. T'Anna came because she had no choice, and Leela; well, Leela came because she had questions for Him. I understood my daughters' relationship with God. It wasn't my place to question them. My only job was to love them and that I did; unconditionally, even Leela, who sometimes still pushed away from me. The more she pushed, the harder I pulled. I couldn't let Leela break away from my love or there would be no bringing her back. I made sure that love flowed between me and my girls and from them to one another.

Lillie and T'Anna were able to get their love relationship going. There were times that Lillie and Leela had a marginal relationship, and that was because Leela bullied Lillie all the time. She took what she wanted from Lillie even if it were something that Lillie really wanted; it never mattered to Leela, if she wanted it more, she bullied Lillie until she got it.

Leela and T'Anna; that was another story. Those two were a constant test of my faith and motherhood. I didn't do it often, but when the two of them started up, it would be the only time I would wish for a visible daddy for them. Daddy was getting on in age and he could no longer stop those two so when they fought, I took care of it the best way I could. God knows it was never easy. Sometimes, Leela acted as if she'd invented hell and had some kind of ownership to it. She was always sending someone there. She never cared how you got to hell; she just wanted you there and quickly.

Chapter 70

Something Better to Sing

It's amazing how swiftly time can go by and you don't always have to be having a good time for it to happen. I know because I wasn't having all that much fun and it was still flying by. I'd been working very hard. I'd even grown used to the wars between Leela and T'Anna. They still had their respective fires burning and sometimes they collided. Their fires were burning big and bright and somehow, they thrived off one another's. There was no putting those two fires out once they got started. I often tried to stop them from colliding but somehow, they always found a way to get around me to fight. I gave up trying after I got burnt in the process. I learned my lesson; anytime those two wanted to go at it, I just got out of the way.

By the time T'Anna made it to eleventh grade, Leela had been out of school just a few years ahead of her. Leela should have been out of high school before T'Anna made it in, but somehow Leela got stuck. She repeated almost each grade in high school. She did ninth grade twice, got through tenth, repeated eleventh, and by the time she was repeating the twelfth, T'Anna left the world of Junior High and entered Leela's high school world. To Leela, T'Anna, the very source of her discomfort, had made it to the same high school. Life became a bigger hell for Leela. For a while, they didn't even let on that they were sisters.

It was easy for them to do because they looked so different. T'Anna, with her lighter than light skin and very beautiful face, had no telltale signs that she was related to Leela, with her burnt brick to deep dark chocolate coloring; thick hair that appeared to challenge combs or combing, and features, though they had been mix-matched and disproportioned on her as a child, had somehow straightened out.

Leela's nose, which had been the source of her greatest discomfort, had by puberty lost a lot of its flair. It was now just prominent. She had what my Nana would've called, "Them good African cheekbones." They sat high and proud with a hint of disdain. Somehow that didn't look bad on her; the disdain. Her mouth was different. The lips were full but they suited her. I couldn't imagine her with any other kind of mouth.

It didn't matter what anyone said, when Leela looked at herself, she saw an ugly girl; I looked at Leela and finally saw what Daddy and Mrs. Trindle had seen when she was first born. My first-born had features all her own; they suited her, and she was a very good-looking, dark-skinned, young woman. None of that mattered to Leela. When word got out that she was "that light-skinned" girl's sister, Leela wanted nothing more than to be out of high school and everyone's questions and questioning looks.

She wanted to be out and didn't want to hear a word from anybody 'bout anybody's college. She made no effort whatsoever to get into college. She'd accepted that she wasn't learning and couldn't get out of school fast enough. Leela wanted to be out so bad that she just left.

I sometimes think that Leela left when she did because everybody else was younger than she. She figured it out, faced reality, and left. Leela's favorite expression became, "There's got to be something better than this."

She always had an argument and one that none of us could win. She would remind us that my Nana cleaned houses, Ma never worked a day in her life, her Gran Gran never worked, and as for me; she reminded me that I'd never set foot in college either and I was doing ok. She said that ok was good enough for her. We left her alone. Leela had won. She went off to work.

As much as Leela had dreaded high school, T'Anna was loving it. She was popular because she was pretty, and when she put her mind to it, she was very smart. All we could hear from T'Anna was how she was going change things. She was going to go to college, become a writer, and fulfill as she called it, "The Daughters of Greenwood's Dream." She made it seem like it was a part in a school play she was auditioning for.

Each time she mentioned Greenwood, I would remember Nana and her Greenwood dreams and hold my breath. So far, I'd done alright. Leela might not have gone to college, but she also had no babies either. Actually, Leela had never brought a boy around the house. I wasn't sure if it was because she didn't have anyone, or if it was because she didn't want us to see. We all knew that the man that undertook Leela had to be a special kind of man. Daddy and I waited for Leela to tell us about someone or to show interest in somebody somewhere, but she never did. She contented herself by working. Daddy had one year to retire and he tried again to talk Leela into taking some typing classes or something that she liked. She refused. Daddy left her alone again. She was getting ready to turn twenty-one and, as Daddy said, a full woman.

As much as Leela was refusing all of Daddy's offers to help; Lillie was keeping him busy. She was in her last year of Junior High and already knew which college she wanted to go to. She had Daddy busy getting literature for her on colleges. Daddy was the happiest I'd seen him in years. It reminded me of when he was preparing to send Andre away to college. I smiled each time Lillie talked about college. I could feel it in my heart: my Lillie was going. A daughter of Greenwood, South Carolina, a Greenwood woman was going to make it after all.

I hadn't counted T'Anna out but it was clear that her mind wasn't as focused on college as it had been before. Each time somebody else brought up the subject of college, she was eager to join the discussion, but she never brought the subject up; what came up with her were boys, boys, boys, and dating. All T'Anna was concerned about was boys. For some reason, each time she would mention a boy at school, it would ignite something in Leela and the two of them would be fussing and fighting like two stray alley cats. It was hard to accept but there was something growing between Leela and T'Anna that had nothing to do with them having different fathers. It was almost like Leela blamed her for being.

I accepted T'Anna's fixation with boys and the attention that they paid her. I also accepted that she and Leela had to get at least one good fight in every day, but what I had the most difficulty with was the way Leela treated her sisters. Sure, she fought with T'Anna every chance she got, and if Lillie ever raised her head out of her books and looked at Leela, she was ready to pounce on her too. Lillie didn't fight with Leela. She kept her nose in her books and the rest of her body out of Leela's way. She and T'Anna were close because T'Anna fought Leela for her every time. They fought Monday to Saturday, and somehow just as if they re-enacted creation, come Sunday they rested. They rested their arms, fighting, fussing, and cussing so that we could go to church. Sundays and the day that Daddy visited us was the only peaceful day in the house.

A lot had happened in Daddy's life since the day Momma had died. He'd lost his daddy two years after Momma, but again, that only mattered to us because for a short while, Daddy was sad but nowhere near as sad as he'd been after Uncle Neal had died.

Daddy came to us with his sadness and we did all that we could to cheer him up. Daddy's wife had also died. He'd told us just so we would know. He also told us that they had had no children. Me and Andre were Daddy's only children, and Leela, T'Anna, and Lillie were his only grandchildren. With everyone in Daddy's life gone, he became more available to us. We now had more of Daddy than when I was little. With his momma in the nursing home, he was almost all mine. Daddy came and went when and how often he pleased. He'd said, however, that he was considering moving to Florida because he was getting tired of the cold. I looked at him and found it hard to accept that Daddy had grown old. I began to prepare myself for whatever decision he'd made. I grew to accept that changes in my life were inevitable.

We were approaching the homestretch of T'Anna getting out of high school and Lillie wasn't far behind. T'Anna hadn't decided which college she wanted to go to, but Lillie had settled her heart on Spellman and Daddy was doing more than pulling a few strings to get her in. Three more years and all my girls would be out of high school. The thought made me smile; it seemed like only yesterday I was bringing them home from the hospital and now here I was with one grown daughter, one daughter almost out of high school, and one daughter with just three years to go.

Oh, how I was praising God. I now had time to attend midweek service and even a few revivals when the church had them. T'Anna was no longer fighting with Leela and peace seemed to have taken up residence in my house. A nagging doubt about the truce between T'Anna and Leela started to make its way into my head, but I refused to let Satan steal my joy. I put my hands on all my blessings and claimed them. I wouldn't let him come now and take anything from me. I'd worked hard and changed my life around. I'd made sacrifices and now the Lord was rewarding me. I dressed myself for the battle that was ahead. I was, however, a little too late. I hadn't gotten up early enough to defeat him. He'd found the weak link in my family and had, unbeknownst to me, been using her.

T'Anna, with her hunger and fire, was ripe for the picking and he, accustomed to knowing, picking, and offering good fruit to anyone willing to take and bite, had reached my family tree and had his evil hands wrapped around the fruit that I'd borne. I blinked to take a tiny speck out of my eye, and he plucked her right off the branch and offered her up.

Chapter 71

Same Song Just a Different Singer

T'Anna

Ma always said that it was me who brought the curse back into the house, but whether she wanted to believe it or not, the curse had never left. It had just changed faces and it was Ma herself who'd brought it in. Ma was the one who had brought Leela among us. We had all missed it. Everyone had missed the fact that Leela had some evil seed growing in her. None of us had ever really noticed, but saying none of us noticed is a lie. I'd noticed. Every time Leela was near me and I took a deep breath I swear, I smelled sulfur. Ma claimed that she never smelled it, but there's no way she couldn't have. It was strong. It was there; everywhere Leela went, that smell was there. It was like cat piss; you couldn't see it, but you knew that it was around somewhere.

Sometimes I could understand some of the stupid things that we fussed and cussed about, but I swear to God, sometimes there was no good reason for Leela to be the way she was other than the fact she had something real wicked growing in her. Lillie and Ma were too busy with church to really ever notice that Leela was some kind of she-devil. The demon rose full out of Leela the night I took in to have Mazilli. Nothing prepared me for Leela's reaction. I still can't believe all the evil dramatics that she unleashed. When my belly started to hurt, I woke Leela.

"Leela, Leela?"

"What you waking me up for?"

"Leela, I think the baby is ready to come out. Can you take me to the hospital?"

Leela woke fully up when I said baby, but still she looked at me as if she hadn't heard me right.

"T'Anna, go back to sleep. You're having a bad dream."

"Leela, I ain't dreaming. I'm having a baby."

"What you say?"

"My bed's all wet."

"That don't mean you having a baby. You just pissed the bed."

"Lee, for real, I'm going have a baby. Go and get Ma."

Leela sat up and looked at me. "Get Ma? You must be out of your fucking mind, I ain't going in there and wake up Ma and tell her no shit 'bout you having no baby."

"Help me, Lee. Go and get Ma."

"You the one that knocked up; you go and get her."

"Lee, it's hurting. Help me please; I think it goin' come out now."

Leela jumped out of bed and ran to Ma's room screaming, "Ma, T'Anna is having a baby."

I heard Ma ask, "A baby? Somebody having a baby? Who's having a baby?"

"It's T'Anna. She's having a baby in my room!"

"A baby?"

"Yes, Ma, you gotta come and help."

Andrea

I jumped out of the bed and started to run down the hall. I was outside Leela's room, the door was wide open and there on the floor was my second child in obvious labor. I looked at T'Anna and wonder where all that belly had come from. I'd seen T'Anna last night and I hadn't noticed anything different about her. Now she was in labor. What the hell? When was this curse going to be broken? For a split-second I wanted to curse Milkweed and Fields and the shit their love had done to all of us. Me with three, and now one of my three was sitting on a bedroom floor hollering 'bout having a baby.

I looked at T'Anna with her protruding belly and all I could say was, "Leela, go get Miss Mitchell. Tell her your sister is having a baby and it looks like the baby is coming out now!!"

T'Anna

"Ma, my business is hurting me real bad."

Leela didn't give Ma a chance to say anything, she screamed, "Your hot ass should've been thinking 'bout that before."

"Leela!"

"Ma, she tricked us. She knew she was knocked up. She can't fool me she didn't know she was having a blasted baby. This ain't right, Ma."

"Leela, stop all this talk, there ain't nothing we can do about it now; this minute."

"That's why she in the shape she's in. You always got to be so forgiving. I don't see why you don't slap her stupid ass and knock the baby right outta her."

"Leela!"

"Sorry, Ma."

From the door Lillie called, "I'm dressed, Ma, what you want me to do?"

"Nothing."

"I'm sorry, Ma, I really am."

Leela came back in the room and when I said I was sorry, she turned on me. "Sorry my ass. Now don't tell me that you didn't' know that your ass was pregnant."

"I didn't. I swear to God, Leela. I didn't know."

"Leela, stop this now."

"Ma, she's a stinking liar and I ain't sorry for her. I hope that baby tears her up. That will teach her hot ass a lesson."

"Leela, watch your language. Where's Miss Mitchell?"

"She coming. But, Ma, she's a liar and a sneak and now all her sneaking around goin' bring another mouth in this house for me and you to feed. Feel sorry for her? I ain't feeling sorry for her one bit."

"Leela, I swear.....oh, my God, oh my God, Ma! Ma! It's coming out. Help me. Please."

Andrea

Lillie ran down to the hall at the same time the doorbell rang. It was Miss Mitchell. T'Anna started screaming at the top of her lungs. The screams filled the house and threw me back a thousand years to a time when I too was screaming and pushing for hours trying to get Leela out. I found myself wondering when this vicious family curse was going to be lifted off the Greenwood women.

I'd started to believe that the curse had been broken. My daughters were going to break the pattern that had plagued me, Mommy, and

Nana. All of us had had children before the age of twenty and none of us had a man around for their children to call Daddy, well, except Mommy. Even then, Daddy wasn't a full-time daddy. He'd been a daddy at a distance until lately. But it had taken the death of his best friend, Charles Rancor, his wife, and having to put his mother in a nursing home before he could become a full-time daddy. Tried as he might, being full-time fathering, which wasn't really needed now since we'd grown up while we waited, came with some limitations. I was sharing him with his momma, since he visited her regularly. Now the evidence that I'd taken my guard down too quickly was before me. The curse was still alive and well.

I was snatched back to my present reality by my she-devil screaming, "Ma, make her tell you who she's having that baby for. Make her tell you, Ma! "

"Leela, if she tells me now or after, it isn't going to change anything."

"See, Ma, that's just like you. She goin' do just what you did. She ain't going tell you 'cause you ain't never told her or Lillie who they father is, and I know that you know, Ma. You know and you keep keeping it a secret. I bet you, Ma, when she have this baby and you ask her who it belongs to, she going do like you and keep it a secret."

T'Anna

As Miss Mitchell and Ma helped me get in my bed, I decided that I would do just like Ma. I would keep the father of my baby a secret too. I would say I didn't know and since Ma never did tell me who my father was, she wouldn't going press me. If she pressed me, then I'd press her back.

I closed my eyes and listened to what Miss Mitchell was saying. The baby didn't need any help from me, Ma, or Miss Mitchell. The minute they got me on the bed, the baby slipped out. I might not have broken the curse, but I changed what the curse had always produced. Up until now, all the Greenwood women had given birth to girls. I had a boy. For me, this meant that I would never have to worry about my child reaching the age of sixteen, seventeen, or eighteen, and getting pregnant. At least with having this boy, that part of the curse was over, or so I believed.

Mrs. Mitchell had the baby in her hands and I held my breath. I was sure that he would look just like his father and everybody would be able to tell, but when she put him in my hands, my heart skipped a beat. The baby didn't look like who I thought it would look like. The baby looked like M'iyahtu Issam, the new boy that had moved to Halsey Street with his family about a year or so ago. They were from some place in Africa called Lagos. His mother had joined the church and she made him join the choir, because he could sing and play the piano. He was the last person I expected my baby to look like. Now it ain't like I wasn't with him, but I was sure that my baby was for Reginald Ward.

Reginald was the best-looking boy at my school. He was going in the Air Force after high school and said that when he was flying all over the world, I could come and stay on the base with him; be his girl all the time. Now Mrs. Mitchell had put a baby in my arms and he wasn't what I'd expected. I sat there looking at that baby trying to figure out why he wasn't looking like Reggie as me and M'iyahtu ain't done it but one time and he didn't even finish 'cause we thought we heard somebody coming, and now my baby was looking like him. I started to panic. I'd already told Reggie that I was pregnant. When I told him, all that talk about me being his girl and coming on every air force base with him went out the window. He'd cussed me and said that the baby wasn't his. Crying at his anger and rejection, I'd sworn up and down that I wasn't with nobody else. I knew when I said it that it was a lie, but since I was so sure that since M'iyahtu hadn't finished, I was also sure that my baby was for Reginald and would look like him. I never thought, God knows, not for one second that any of M'iyahtu's stuff had come out and now Reginald was goin' know I was lying.

Chapter 72

Mazilli Matthew Greenwood

Before the baby was born, I wanted to name it after Reggie although I knew I couldn't come right out and name it Reggie. I was going to name the baby some "R" name to match Reggie, but now all that "R" naming stuff went out the window. I couldn't look at him and tell him that this baby was his. I looked at the baby and decided. I just ain't going to say nothing to nobody. I just going to say that the baby is mine and that's what I'm going name him. I'm going give him a name starting with M, not because of M'iyahtu, but 'cause it's always going say to me that this baby belongs to me and only me. I named my son Mazilli Matthew Greenwood. Mazilli meant sent by God. That name would suit him because I had no real or other explanation for him.

Inside of me, I was really hurting because deep in my heart, I liked Reginald Ward. It wasn't supposed to be like that. As I watched Ma looking at the baby, she didn't look angry, to my surprise. She looked at him as if he was a missing puzzle piece to her dream. Leela didn't look. She didn't want anything to do with him. She felt as if she was going be the one who was going have to support him and me. All I'd done was wake her up. I didn't ask her to help any more than that. I knew that Granddaddy was going be mad at me, but I also knew that he and Ma would help me out. Ma and Mrs. Mitchell took me and the baby to St. John's Hospital.

I brought him back home a few days later and I could tell that Ma was still figuring on how and when she was going ask me who the father was. While Ma was figuring, I was figuring too. I was figuring that I was going to have to come up with something that somebody in my family was going to believe. Granddaddy came by and he looked at the baby with an even more puzzled look than Ma. Then he did what Ma hadn't. He called me to him and said, "T' Anna, all of us were here with you. We gave you what you wanted, when you wanted it, and for the most part, as much as you wanted. What I want to know from you are a few basic things. To begin with, who is the father of this baby?"

I looked at my grandfather and lied. I lied because if I'd told the truth, he would have been disappointed. I said, "I don't know, Granddaddy."

"Ok, if that's what you want me to believe, then I have to ask you how you plan to support this baby. This baby that, according to you, doesn't have a father other than the explanation of the name you've given him; God sent him."

Again, I looked at my grandfather and said, "I don't know right now, Granddaddy, but I'm planning on getting a job."

"And where do you plan on getting this job?"

Granddaddy just looked at me and he could tell that I was lying again because he knew that I'd hoped that he and Ma would take care of the baby for me; but his voice was sounding like I was goin' be the one who was going to take care of the baby.

"Then I guess if you don't have an answer for that, then you might not have an answer for this either. Where are you planning on living with this baby, who doesn't have a father or a way for you to support?"

This time when I answered, it was the same answer as before, but this time it was the truth. "I don't know, Granddaddy."

"You see, T'Anna, this is what happens when you don't plan. It's one thing not to plan and be in a position to take care of mistakes if one should happen. You didn't plan and now you don't have a plan for you and this baby that you conceived all by yourself. You have no job, and no place to take the baby, so tell me, what are you going to do?"

I looked at Ma and I started to cry. My crying didn't stop Granddaddy. He went on, "T'Anna, I didn't think you would have a plan and so I have one you. You will get only one chance though. I'll arrange to have this baby cared for, but you must go back to school. Find a college and register. When you start, I'll see that the baby is taken care of while you're away at school. If you agree to my plan, there's only one condition."

"What's that, Granddaddy?"

"You must agree to the plan before you hear the condition."

"But, Granddaddy, that ain't fair. What if I can't do the condition?"

"Then that would be your choice. You will forfeit the plan and you will be on your own with this baby. The way I see it, you don't have much of a choice. Now, do you accept the plan?"

I was afraid to be alone with Mazilli so I said, "Yes, Granddaddy."

"Good, now do you want to hear the condition?"

"Yes, Granddaddy."

"The condition is this: if you become pregnant again before you finish college, you're on your own. It's that simple. You go to school; I'll take care of you and the baby. You get pregnant again; you're on your own. Now, I can't tell your mother not to help you, but what I'm saying is that I won't. The choice is yours, Troi-Anna Hirsh Greenwood."

Granddaddy had called me by my whole name. He wasn't kidding. I don't think I'd ever heard Granddaddy call me Troi-Anna before. That was it. I had all summer to get myself ready for twelfth grade, find a college, and show Granddaddy that I was ready. I could do that; I knew I could.

I'd really meant to do it too, but somehow, something inside of me was hungry. I would see a boy and I would want to know what his thing looked like, or how it would feel. That was how I'd gotten in trouble in the first place. Reginald, who came to my church, had asked me one night after the young people service if I wanted to see his thing, and I'd said yes, and the next thing I knew, we were trying to get it in me. We kept on trying until we finally got it in. It felt good and right. From that point on, I wanted the feeling. I felt empty if I wasn't feeling somebody's thing so I looked and found plenty to feel.

It was easy for me to get plenty to feel. I would smile. Act all girly, and before I knew it, I would have one in my hand and then it would be between my legs. It didn't matter to me who the thing belonged to; I wanted the feeling. It was the feeling that cost me the agreement with Granddaddy. I'd been good for a while; all through May, June, and July, but something about summer and men and boys wearing sleeveless tee shirts, open-chest shirts, and sometimes no shirt…stuff like that.

I couldn't help myself. I went to the store at the end of the block one day and Manuel, the store owner, started talking to me nice and stuff. At first, I didn't pay him no mind but as summer went on, I wanted to see his thing. I think he knew too 'cause one day when I was at the store and they weren't a lot of people around, he asked me to come to the room in the back of the store; said he had something to show me. I didn't ask him what or anything; I just went. I kinda knew anyway. I was right.

He didn't really talk to me a lot or nothing. He touched my arm a little, hugged me a little, and kissed me on my cheek, and then he showed it to me and just like that, I let him. It was the best feeling ever. He was older and I guess he'd figured out how to do it really good. We just kept doing it. I couldn't stay away from him. Every chance I got, I went to the store. If the store was busy, he would let me know when to come back. There wasn't one time I went that he didn't put it in me. He'd keep it in 'till I couldn't take the good feeling no more. Well, at least for that day.

I was sneaking in that store so often that it got so he asked me if he could be my man. He wanted to be my man, he said, because he kept telling himself that each time he went to the back room with me would be the last time because I was young and he didn't want to get in no trouble because of me.

Each time he would ask me to be his girl, I would say no and he would say, "You wait. You wait. You will make up your mind and I'm going be your man. You wait." He was right. One day in the back of the store in the little room, he touched all the right places and gave me the best feeling I ever had, and just like that, he became my man.

Everything was fine for a while. He was giving me things for me and Mazilli, and he even said that he wanted to come to my house and tell Ma that he was liking me and stuff. I couldn't let him do that because he would mess things up with me and Granddaddy. I hadn't told him about my promise to Granddaddy. Manuel was getting more and more serious. He was making plans for a life together. I didn't know how to tell him that we couldn't have a life together. Then I figured it out. I would tell him that Ma wanted me to go away to college and that I would be leaving soon.

One day in the back room, I told him and then 'cause he looked really sad and wouldn't put his thing in me, I acted like I didn't want to be away from him but I didn't have a choice. I was acting like I believed it and so he believed it too. I was just acting; the last thing on my mind was college, well, at that moment. Standing there with him and thinking about how he felt in me and how he moved—so rough yet smooth was driving me nuts. I wanted that feeling again. As I always did when we were back there, I started to rub the front of his pants and I could feel him growing. The more he grew, the more he groaned. I knew then that I could do anything I wanted to with him. I reached for his zipper and as soon as I had the zipper down, I put my hand in his pants and had his thing out.

He'd showed me what to do to make him feel better, so I lowered myself to my knee and as I slid down his leg, he put his hand in my hair. I wasn't down there but a few minutes when he raised me up and, bending me over some boxes that was in the room, it didn't take him but a minute 'fore he had it in me and was moving just the way I liked to feel him move. That day, it was the sweetest 'cause he was thinking that soon he was going be losing me. I pushed back to him and moved just like he was moving. At one time, my foot knocked down a box but I didn't care that somebody outside might hear us. I wanted him to be all the way in me and moving like he'd told me once, "I moved like that, chica, 'cause I be do a samba in my head when I be in you."

That day, he must have been doing the best samba ever 'cause when he was done, he grabbed me real hard and when he cried out, I started to figure how I was goin' walk out the store and not have everybody in the store look at me. There was no way that they couldn't tell what we was doing. When we was done, I just pulled my clothes down and stood there trying to get my nerves up just to walk out the store. Manuel didn't say anything to me. I knew he knew that this time, I didn't know how to walk out. It was a Friday at the end of the month and a lot of people was in the store.

He said, "I be go out first and when you be ready, you come out the door. Walk the back of the store to the coolers and when you gets to the cooler, just walk up the aisle by the beans and stuff and you can walk out that way; it be easier for you." I did just as he said but when I stepped outside there was no way I could just walk out. It looked like everybody in the whole neighborhood was buying something. I held my head up like I didn't care who was looking as I headed toward the door. None of their looks could take away my sweet feeling. Once I was outside the store, I headed home. I wanted to lay down and remember how sweet that feeling was. That sweet feeling lasted for all of maybe two days. After that, I found his back room even more often and learned more in there than I ever would in anybody's college. I no longer wanted Ma or Granddaddy's dreams. I wanted my own. I wasn't quite sure what those dreams were, but if leaving Manuel and his sweet-feeling thing behind was part of it, then college wasn't part of my dreams.

As it got closer and closer to when he felt I should be graduating and going to college, Manuel started acting like he was interested in me and school. He kept on asking me about which college I was going to. I was running out of lies to tell him. When it got to the point where he knew I should know and I didn't, he stopped asking. Soon he was asking me again about us being a family. I didn't say no and so he started acting strange; like I was his woman and worse, like he owned me or something.

I didn't like feeling as if anybody owned me and I told him so then I stopped from going in his store and being with him. I decided I would see whoever I felt like. When I stopped seeing him and started walking in his store with other boys, he lost his ever-loving, Spanish-speaking mind. He said, "T'Anna, why you behaving like this? You be a pretty girl. Why you got to be acting all loose and shit like them girls from the streets? You a good girl. Stop acting like that and let people see the good girl in you."

I didn't pay him no mind. I kept right on doing what I wanted. I'm not even sure where I picked up the habit but in addition to just being with any boy, I picked up being loud. Anytime I was around him, I was louder. One day when I was in the store by myself, he tried to get me to go to the back room. I didn't and when I told him no, I was real loud. He said, "You see that. That shit you picked up from them street girls makes no sense. Why you got to be loud like that? You acting like you want people to hear you. Like if you ain't loud, people not goin' see nor notice you."

I didn't answer him. Then he said, "T'Anna, as pretty as you be, there ain't no way people not goin' see you. Stop this. Come back to me."He smiled at me and said, "Come, let we do some samba. I miss you. I really mean that. I not messing around or nothing. I just want you. Come, Chica."

As I stood there listening to him, I could feel him moving all inside me. I wanted so bad to just be in that room with him, but something said to me that if I went in there, I was coming out his woman. I walked out the store. I had to think.

Granddaddy was sending the money and stuff but taking care of Mazilli was real hard 'cause the thing inside of me wasn't hungry to take care of no baby. I wanted Ma to help with Mazilli and she would, but after she'd watched him for a while, she would give him back to me. She said he was my responsibility. I couldn't turn to Lillie for any help. She always had her head buried in a book or she was headed somewhere looking for a book. As for Leela, she couldn't stand him; didn't want him near her. She disliked him ever more whenever Granddaddy gave him anything. She acted like he was taking something from her.

Chapter 73

Scream at Me, But Not My Kid

I put up with Leela and her hateful ways towards my baby for as long as I could stand it and then one day, she cussed at Mazilli. I might not have been the best at mothering or anything, but he was having the colic or something and he was crying; he just wouldn't stop. She came storming out of her room screaming at the top of her lungs at me, "Why don't you stop that second-generation, fatherless piece of shit from crying in this house and keeping all that noise in my ears?"

I swear to God before she could get her mouth shut, I had my whole fist in it. I didn't worry about cutting my hand on her teeth, but I cared that she had cussed at my baby. This time she'd gone too far. I wanted to kill her. We were on the floor going at it like bitter enemies when Ma came through the door. For a second, I could see Ma's face as if she were in shock and then I heard her. She was loud enough to make us stop. "Leela, T'Anna, stop! What are the two of you doing? Is this what my good Christian home has come to? The two of you trying to kill each other, and over what? Over what this time? One of you better tell me and quickly or there will be three of us rolling around on the floor."

I took my hand from around Leela's neck, but kept an eye on her, "Ma she called my baby a second-generation piece of shit. Leela ain't had no right to call nobody names and that's why I punched her in her ugly mouth."

"Leela, why did you talk about your sister's baby like that? He's an innocent baby."

Leela was boiling mad and couldn't hold her tongue back. "Innocent my ass, Ma, she's around here screwing everybody on the block and all over the place and coming back in here and acting innocent. She's acting innocent so that she can get Granddaddy's money. Innocent? She couldn't tell you who his father was because she didn't know. Ask her, Ma, ask her how many boys, men, young and old alike, that she's already had. Ask her, Ma. And when you done asking her that, ask her how many of them pays her to do her. Ask her, Ma! Ask her!"

Leela stopped talking and looked at me. The expression on her face said, "Go ahead and call me a liar and I'll prove that the only liar is you."

"See, Ma, she can't say anything now. She can't try to fight me on that and it's not because you standing there. Ma, she's screwing everybody that got a thing. They talking 'bout her all over the place, Ma. Go ahead and ask her if they don't talk about her and if they don't pay her to do her."

I wanted to call Leela a liar, but she wasn't lying. I'd taken money from the ones I didn't like and then even from those I liked. I saw Ma watching my face. I guess she was looking for something on my face that would say Leela was lying. I looked away and Ma stumbled toward her chair. She dropped in the chair; from her sudden weight the air got forced through the plastic. I thought the plastic had bubbled and busted. Ma was breathing heavy; I'd burdened her again.

Ma spoke. Her voice was almost too soft to hear. "T'Anna, tell me that your sister isn't telling the truth. Tell me that's she's just angry and speaking out of her head. Tell me, Tee Tee, that it's not true. Tell me that you do know who the father of this baby is, and that you just don't want to say. Tell me, Tee Tee."

I got away from Leela and stood up. I knew she wouldn't hit me anymore. She didn't have to. She'd delivered the punch I hadn't expected. All the dislike I'd had for Leela over the years bubbled to the top. I looked at her and hated her. There was no turning back. I would hate her for the rest of my life. Ma took my silence as my way of saying that what Leela was saying was true. She said to me, "Why? Why, T'Anna? Why would you do that to yourself? Why?"

I didn't have an answer. I couldn't even look at her so I picked Mazilli up and went to my room in the basement. I wanted to cry, but there was something inside of me that just wouldn't let me. I stayed downstairs for the rest of the evening and only came up when I had to get milk for him. It was hard to look at Ma. I kept wondering what she was thinking. I wanted to know but I didn't have the courage to ask or hear it. I also didn't have an answer for her if she'd asked me why I did it.

Beside telling her that I just liked being around men and how they made me feel I wouldn't know what to say to her. There was no way I could look at her and say, "Ma I like it when they talk to me, touch me, hold me, or when I have their thing in me; it makes me feel good."

Good wasn't even the best way to describe what it felt like. I guess full was the best way to describe it. It was as if I had a deep hunger and being with them filled it. When I wasn't with a man, I was empty. I couldn't explain that to Ma. She'd chosen a long time ago not to have anybody. I couldn't recall ever seeing a man around my ma. It was always Ma, her church people, or her work. No man. I couldn't do that. I was hungry for men and the full feeling they gave me.

I tried to be good after Leela had told Ma. I stopped seeing everybody, but the bigger Mazilli got, the greater the hunger became. I gave up trying to be good and went back to Manuel. I'd tried to just be with only Manuel, but even that was hard. I would see someone I hadn't had or felt and I would wonder about them and their feel so badly. I would make conversation with the guy 'till we were talking like that and then he would ask me 'bout touching his thing. I didn't have to feel it inside of me. Sometimes, just touching it with my hand was enough because if I wanted more, I went to Manuel. For a while, Manuel didn't know that I was touching other men's things but, 'cause some of the guys were stupid, they talked, told other people. It got back to Manuel and he got real mad. At first I cared, but after a while I stopped giving a shit. Manuel got over being mad and he stayed with me. He liked being my man.

Chapter 74

Still Without a Plan

Summer had passed and fall was almost over. Still I'd made no plans to go back to school. Granddaddy gave me 'till spring. I was going to go. Then I wasn't. I couldn't. I'd messed up. I was pregnant again. I knew then that I wouldn't be going to any college, ever. This time my baby wouldn't be a surprise to me. I knew who it belonged to. It was Manuel's. I'd only been giving myself to him. I told Manuel I was pregnant before I told anybody else. He'd never had a woman pregnant for him before. You would've thought that I was the only woman who'd ever gotten pregnant. Manuel lost his mind. I became delicate.

While I was still delicate, I told Ma. I wasn't going waste time by trying to hide it. I asked her to tell Granddaddy. She did. Granddaddy stopped the money. I didn't mind so much because Manuel kept his word. He was taking care of me and Mazilli. I didn't tell Leela nothing 'cause she and I'd long stopped speaking, ever since the day she'd told Ma 'bout what I was doing. She just stayed out of my way. For reasons that only Leela knew, she had also stopped talking to Lillie; like Lillie had done her something. Leela was like that. If she was mad at one person, then the whole house suffered.

It bothered Lillie and she started tipping and whispering whenever Leela was around. That was Lillie. But me, I didn't give a shit. If I had something to say, I said it. I was waiting for her to forget herself and say something to me about my belly or my baby and then I was kicking her ass. I also planned to cuss her ass out if she so much as looked at me wrong, belly or no belly; baby or no baby, I would kick her ass.

Ma acted like Leela. She didn't say much of nothing to me either. I understood Ma. I wasn't mad at her or nothing. I'd disappointed her.

That was real. She would look at me and I could see she wanted to ask me what I was doing with my life, but she never asked. I started to feel that she was afraid to hear my answer.

I guessed she was also guessing who the father of the baby was, but Ma was being Ma. She didn't ask. Manuel answered her unasked question. He just came by the house one day and simply told her that he was the father. He told her he would like to take me and Mazilli to live with him over at his house on Bushwick Avenue. He wanted us to be like a family. Ma didn't say I couldn't go. So I went. The more the baby grew, the nicer he was to me. I was beginning to like being delicate. Life was good for me and Mazilli. He liked Mazilli and Mazilli really liked him.

Ma never came to Bushwick Avenue. It was as if she had given up on me for good. Again I didn't get mad. I'd given up on me first. Now I didn't know how to find the me that used to want stuff. I wasn't even nineteen and I was about to have a second child.

Granddaddy moved to Florida. I knew it had nothing to do with me being pregnant but I would often think that he'd just gotten tired of watching one pregnant belly after another. I asked Ma about him, but I could tell from the way she answered that he wasn't asking about me. I started to feel like Mazilli and I were alone.

I went into labor at Manuel's house. I was alone. I called the ambulance and even before they could get through the door, the baby was half-way out. They took me and my almost-out baby to the hospital. I called Manuel and Ma. They both came to the hospital. It was the first time that Ma had seen Manuel since I moved in with him. I knew that Manuel was mad that she hadn't ever once come to the house to see where or how I was living. He didn't show none of that at the hospital though; he was polite to her. She was the grandmother of his first child.

When Ma saw my baby boy, she looked as if she would cry. The baby was beautiful. If not for Manuel's dark hair, the baby looked just like me. Well, except for his nose. His nose was straight on top and wide on the bottom. It wasn't my nose, Ma's, Granddaddy's, or Manuel's. I figured that the nose belonged to somebody else in the family. Maybe one of Great-Nana's people back home in Greenwood, South Carolina. Ma looked at my baby's nose and for a second, she looked as if she saw a ghost but she said nothing.

Ma convinced Manuel to let me and the baby come home with her for a little while; 'till I got my strength again. At first, Manuel didn't want to do it, but then he gave in. The baby and I went to Lexington Avenue. Manuel brought Mazilli by later. Leela was mad. She never looked at the baby. She avoided me even more. Mazilli, having learned not to go near her or her things, clung to me.

It was sad the way she just shouted at him, hurt his feelings, and often made him cry. Each time she made him cry, she and I would go at it. I didn't care if we had to cuss every day, but I was going to defend my child. I started to get tired of fighting Leela. Manuel was trying to manage with me and the children over at Lexington Avenue, but it was hard for him. He'd manage until now not to have any children and now that he had one, he wanted his child in his house. After about two weeks, he'd kept asking me to come home. I took the boys and we went back. He started talking to me and treating me like he was my husband. He kept treating me like I was still delicate. I liked it.

I settled into my life on Bushwick and before I knew it, he did it to me again. I went over to Lexington Avenue to tell Ma. I was afraid. How was I going to manage with three babies? I wanted to come back home again. Ma didn't even want to hear me. She said that when she had her children, she had to climb her mountain and make her way. She said that since I didn't seem to want to do anything but make babies, I would have to figure out a way to climb the mountain with them. She also said that I shouldn't always depend or expect Manuel to be there. I looked at her and wondered if she knew something about Manuel that I didn't. I was her daughter so I didn't ask. I left it alone.

Ma didn't take me back. I wasn't sure what hurt the most. The fact that she didn't even seem to be hurting when she refused to take me and the children back in, or the fact that she didn't even seem to be worried about how I was going manage to take care of her grandchildren alone on Bushwick Avenue.

I returned to Bushwick Avenue and did all that I had to do to keep a roof over my head and my children's. I accepted my situation. I was, after all, a daughter of Greenwood. I did what I had to do. I managed…I had no choice.

Chapter 75

Finding My Place

The pregnancy was hard. I was bigger than I'd ever been. Mazilli was almost three and with Lil' Manuel just walking and getting into everything; life was rough. Manuel was proud of his sons and was even prouder when he got home and found food and no fuss. I didn't have the energy to fuss with him and besides, I needed him.

It's funny how something that you swear you would never do, you end up doing. The one thing that I'd sworn I'd never do was anything that would endanger my baby, but I came so close to losing my baby that I didn't even think about it 'till after the whole thing was over. Maybe it was the baby or maybe I just wanted to be home for a little while, but either way, I started to miss Ma so I took the boys and went over to Lexington Avenue. I still had my keys so I let myself in. Just as I stepped into the hallway, Leela was there. She looked as if she'd decided to come out and stop me from coming in. Without a hello or a hey or anything, it was, "What you doin' here?"

"Leela, do you think you could start with a hello. Why you got to be like that all the time?"

"It keeps shit from happening if you get to it first."

"Why you always got to be coming at everybody like the bells done rung and you trying to defend your title or something?"

"Cause I am. Now back to the first question. What you doin' here?"

"Yes, back to the beginning, hello, Leela. How are you?"

"Don't ask me shit, what do you want?"

"I don't want nothing, Leela."

"Then if you don't want nothing, take your swollen ass and get outta here. Don't forget to take your little puppies with you 'cause I was trying to get something to eat and would like to get back to it before the sight of you pregnant once again turn my mind and stomach from my food."

"What, what, you mad cause you..."

"Don't start with me today, T'Anna. It ain't like you accomplish anything."

"I ain't come over here for none of your shit today, Leela."

"Now you done said you didn't come for nothing, so could you take your 'aint come for nothing' ass and get to stepping. I wouldn't want your presence in this house to remind you that I was right when I told Ma not to believe you or none of them fantasies you was telling her 'bout you going be some writer someday. I'm glad as hell that Ma ain't waste none of her real energy by believing in you and your shit."

"Leela, there are times and days that I hate you so much, I could wish your fat black, thick lip, thick hip, nappy hair ass dead and not half-way dead either. I mean glue your evil ass eyes and lips shut; mortician-type dead. Actually, you know something, Leela, today is one of them days. Who the fuck you think died and gave you fucking authority over me, my dreams, my children, or how Ma thinks or feels about me?"

"T'Anna, you shut up in this house. Who you think you talking to like that? Don't think for one more minute that I'm goin' put up with your shit. I ain't got no problem kicking your ass. 'Cause if truth be told, I don't care that you 'bout ready to drop that next load of garbage. I don't give a shit 'bout you, your hairy-ass Puerto Rican, or that refried-beans baby you let him drop in your 'always ready to receive any kinda man with a dick' ass."

"Screw you, Leela!"

"No, it's screw you, T'Anna. From what I hear, anybody with a dick, a nickel, dime, or quarter can swing your hinges open and screw you."

I looked at her and started to feel weary. Weary from always having to battle with her. I'd been battling with Leela my whole life. I could feel the tears in my eyes. I started to walk away. I was trying to make it to the door before they could escape and slide down my cheek. I wasn't fast enough. Leela saw the result of her handiwork and started coming in for the kill.

"Don't start that shit with me, don't even start to fix your face like you hurt or something, 'cause I know your baby-breeding-pop-one-in-pop-one-out slutting ass can't know nothing 'bout hurt. You can't know nothing 'bout hurt or you would've stopped all this whoring and breeding long before you reach this point. How many you going make before you stop, T'Anna, eight, nine, ten? How many? How many little multi-national little johns you going get before you stop whoring."

Hearing Leela refer to my sons as johns stopped the flow of tears and, like a mother lion defending her cubs, I was on Leela. Leela never saw it coming because she never expected a very pregnant me to jump her ass. Never in all her born days did she think she would ever go too far and have someone kick her ass and now here she was in that place called "Gone Too Far." I, her own sister, a few weeks short of delivering my baby, was sitting on her belly with a demented look of absolute hatred melting from my face and dripping onto hers. Wherever sisterly love was that day, there was one thing for absolute certain; it wasn't in that room at that moment. I hated Leela with all that was in me.

Momentarily stunned, Leela didn't move. I could tell her first instinct was to push me off her and kick the living daylights out of me, but something stopped her. The baby moved. The baby moved and Leela, because I was sitting right on her, felt a baby move on her belly. That stretching and probing movement of the baby stopped us both. I realized that Leela was quiet and so I stopped the hand that was about to come down and smash into her face. I rested my hands on the floor and worked my mountain of a belly off Leela. I sat on the floor and cried.

Leela, not one to admit or show defeat, started in again, "T'Anna, get outta this house before I kill you, that lump of recycled puke in your stomach, and those two other little lumps of shit you brought into this house. But before you leave, let me set the record straight for your yellow ass. I haven't given a shit about you since you decided that you were going to become the neighborhood slut. That's right, T'Anna, there was a time I loved your yellow ass. You was goin' be somebody. Yeah, that's right, you, my little sister, was goin' be a writer. You was goin' to mount up to something and get your ass out of this dumping ground called a neighborhood."

At first, I was just going to gather my frightened boys and go back home, but Leela, unable to stop once she'd gotten started, had pushed me over the edge. "Who you talking about that was going mount up to something. You forgetting that you had the same chance as everybody else. You forgetting that you was smart. Ok, it's true that you weren't smarter than me or Lillie, but you could have made something out of yourself if you had made a different choice. You forget that it was you that stopped you from being somebody. Ok, fine, you didn't screw some man and get pregnant like me, but you got screwed just the same way, Leela. At least I got two children to show for all of mine, but what you got Leela? What you got for all you gave away? N-O-T-H-I-N-G! You got nothing, Leela, 'cause your womb's dry. It dried up from all your hateful ways."

"Get out!"

"Yeah, Leela, I'm goin' but you keep this in mind. Just because shit didn't ever seem to work out for you, it ain't nobody's fault and neither does it give you a license to be the kind of cold-ass devil you are. You're cold, mean, and hateful even when you don't have no reason to be. Even Ma, with all her praying and faith, can't understand why you're so hateful. One day you goin' wake up with your womb and bones all dried up and you going wish you'd been different and it going to be too late for you."

"T'Anna I've told you to take your yellow ass and get outta here. Don't make me wish that I didn't kick that pile of garbage out of you. Now get out of this house and don't come back. Ever!"

My hand was already on the door, but I was thinking of turning right back and starting with her again but the baby had moved down and around so much that it was now hurting me. I took my frightened boys and went back to Manuel's. It wouldn't have made any sense for me to stay there when I couldn't promise I wouldn't kill her. I left hating Leela so much, I was wishing her dead.

When Manuel came home, he could tell that something had happened but I didn't tell him. None of it would've made sense to him. He and his whole family loved and adored each other. He didn't understand why my sister and I were the way we were. I couldn't explain it to him. I left it alone. I never told Ma what happened and since she never asked, I guessed that Leela never told her either. I went back to Lexington Avenue only when Ma was home. If she wasn't home, I didn't go. I knew that if Leela had started with me even the day I went into labor, I would've kicked her ass even if it meant giving birth to my baby when I raised my leg to kick her. I really missed being able to go over by Lexington Avenue whenever I felt like.

I didn't have much time to worry about missing Lexington Avenue though because my baby was ready. Getting it out was all I thought about; I was tired of being pregnant. This birth wasn't as easy as the other two. When I finally got him out, I called him Malakai. I didn't spell it the same way as in the Bible, but to me it meant the same. In the book of Malachi, it said to bring your tithe into the store house of the Lord. That to me seemed a fitting name. Malakai was perfect for my son. The labor had been so hard, I felt as if I'd given up more than a tenth of my life trying to push him out.

Everything was sore and hurting so badly, I promised myself that I would give me and my body a break from making babies. I needed time to heal and to clear up the muddle that my life was becoming. I liked Manuel, but not enough to keep on making babies for him and not getting anywhere in the process. I had to find a way to get back on the path that Ma and Granddaddy had laid out for me. I kept thinking that if Ma found her way back after getting sidetracked with all of us, then so could I. I went to the clinic and got some pills to block all those other babies that was lining up to find their way in and out my womb. I never told Manuel. He wouldn't have been happy 'cause he was talking 'bout me having more babies; to hell with that shit.

Chapter 76

One More Day of Being Tired

I stayed with Manuel 'till Malakai was about two then I couldn't do it anymore. Life with Manuel wasn't changing but I was. We started to fight. We fought about two things only: marriage and our sons. He wanted to be married and I didn't. I didn't love Manuel. I wasn't too sure what the hell love was, but whatever it was, I wasn't feeling it for him. I didn't tell him that though; I just told him I didn't want to get married. That pissed him off and soon after that, he started telling me 'bout giving him his boys and leaving his house. I would look at Manuel and think that he was some kind of idiot to think I would just walk away from my children. I was a lot of things. Ma once said I acted like an ostrich when it came to the boys, which was sad but true, but despite that, I loved my sons.

I got tired of Manuel. Every day it was the same song. "T'Anna, give me my boys. T'Anna, leave my house."

At first I didn't know what to do 'cause I didn't have no job or nothing, but one day he said to leave his house in such a way that I knew if I didn't' leave, I was goin' be carried out. I didn't feel like leaving this world no time soon so I knew I had to figure something out. I went to Ma and told her that me and Manuel was fighting all the time. I told her he was telling me to leave his house almost every day, then I asked her if I could come back with the boys.

Ma, who had refused to let me come back three years earlier, agreed and offered me the one-bedroom apartment upstairs. She didn't offer me it for free. She said that I would have to figure out a way to pay some kind of rent; how I got it was up to me. Soon as we were done talking, I took my yellow ass down to the welfare people and begged them for some help. They gave it to me. I went over to Bushwick Avenue and packed. When I'd had as much as I wanted out of Manuel's house, I took my boys and left. I didn't slip off like a thief in the night though. I left him a note saying: *Me and the boys are at Ma's and I we ain't coming back.*

That was it for me and Manuel.

I returned home with three boys and an even bigger longing in my heart. At first, I was trying to live the plan I'd told Ma about. I was sure I was going do it, but the plan started getting away from me. The further away it got, the more I changed. I became even more changed than when I'd left. I started to become someone that I disliked. I became loud and neglectful. Sometimes I think that I was that way because I had more problems than solutions.

I was trying but it wasn't easy. Ma would help me with the boys but mostly I was on my own with them, and the more I struggled to make changes the more things stayed the same. The only real change that I could see was in my boys. They were getting bigger and wanting more and more of my attention. Attention that was being divided in too many ways to describe or explain. I was hungry. I kept searching for the thing that would satisfy my hunger. Nothing did. At first I was thinking that some good sex would do it, but remembering where it had gotten me before, I fought the urge. I fought like I was fighting for my life. All that fighting made me think I would die. I lost the fight. Having lost, I started looking for someone that could get deep enough to where I was empty and fill me up. I went after getting filled up with a vengeance. I acted like somehow it had changed while I lived with Manuel. I wanted as much as I could get, but I didn't want no more children. I went down to the clinic and got them to give me some more baby blockers. I think knowing that I couldn't get pregnant made it worse. If I weren't so empty, I would've taken the time to be ashamed of how sluttish I was acting, but I didn't.

Manuel stopped talking to me. I guess he heard how I was acting. I became angry at him. I was so angry that I no longer took the boys to see him. When he saw me and asked to see them, I made him wait weeks and weeks before I would take them by the store. It's not like I hated him or anything, I just hated the fact that he kept on asking me over and over for his sons like I wasn't good enough to raise his children.

Ma also started nagging me about taking the boys to see their father. I'd tried to tell her how he was always on me about giving him his children. None of that mattered. She kept on with the same tune: "Take the boys to see their father."

This surprised the shit outta me 'cause it wasn't like Ma was that crazy 'bout Manuel. Manny could have been a goat for all she cared, but goat or no goat, he was the father and somehow, in her mind, that goat had some inalienable right to my children. I disagreed, but there was no arguing with her.

Ma was unrelenting. I got tired of hearing her mouth; hearing what she thought. When she wasn't saying, "T'Anna, you ain't doing right," she was saying, "you don't have no right denying them boys their father."

The way Ma was nagging, I started to think that maybe somehow she was thinking that I didn't have a right to them. I wanted to interrupt her "Let The Boys See Their Father" sermon and say to her, "Ma, those are my boys. If I don't want that fool to see them, then I don't have to and if you don't like it, you can kiss my ass."

That was what I thinking but I wasn't stupid enough to ever open my mouth and say that to her. She would be like a mad woman and kill me on the spot. Manny wasn't worth it.

It wasn't so much her nagging that did it, but I could see that the boys were missing him. I couldn't take her nagging or their pitiful begging looks anymore, so I decided to take them to see him. The way I figured it, they would tell her the minute we got back home and this would get her off my ass.

The minute we got to the store, the boys started to run toward the door that would let them behind the counter. The shelves stocked with cans of grandules, gabanzo beans, stacks of rice, bottles of salsa, syrup, ketchup, and other assorted items went unnoticed. As they propelled their bodies forward; getting to him was their only concern. I'm not sure if he noticed or said hello to the boys, but the minute he saw me, he started in. "Give me my boys. Why you don't let me have my sons?" Why are you playing these stupid games, keeping my boys from me?"

The boys stopped dead in their tracks; frozen right where his ambush on me found them. Their excited screams of "Hi, Daddy" coagulated and froze in the air. They could neither get up or down. My frozen boys, with their coagulated "Hi Daddy," hanging over their heads like captions in a comic book, pulled at the heart of the mother in me. I didn't know what to do. His unprovoked attack on me had them riveted them to the spot. They were afraid. It showed in their eyes. Their eyes darted from me to their father and back to me. Finally, their eyes locked onto me. Their frightened eyes pleaded with me to provide a place of safety for them. I looked at them and got really sad and pissed all at the same time. I was sad because they were witnessing the final meltdown of their parents' relationship and pissed at myself for bringing them here; listening to Ma and her bullshit about keeping children and their father together. I stopped being an ostrich for a moment.

I reassured them with my eyes. I would do something. Find them that place of safety. Reassured, they unfroze. The three of them eased into each other like mercury and became one. Moving as one, they stepped back from the door where only seconds ago they were getting ready to burst through. Manuel, still ranting, hadn't noticed that it was he who had scared them. Somehow, seeing his sons all bunched together made him madder. Pointing at the boys, he said, "See what you've done, T'Anna. Look, Look! You keep my boys away from me so long now my own children don't know me. They bunching up together like I's some kinda monster or something. T'Anna, that's your doing!"

"It ain't me, Manuel. It's you. You acting like an asshole, Manuel, and scaring them."

"I ain't scaring them. It's you that got them not knowing me."

I looked at my frightened boys and figured this shit wasn't worth it. Just when I was goin' get my boys and leave, he opened his mouth and went where no man should.

"That's right, T'Anna, play like you is some kinda good mother. One day you running the street like a hot-ass whore, and the next you want to play saint. Life ain't like that, T'Anna. You can't be whore one day and saint the next."

I let that shit roll off my back. I wasn't going to answer him. I didn't want to upset my boys no more. I looked at him, rolled my eyes, and turned to walk out the store but before I could make a step, he shouted after me.

"That's right, bitch. Take your whoring ass out my store. I was a fool to make children with you. I should've just given you a few bucks and fucked you like everybody else, but I was stupid. I thought I could stop you from whoring and make you into somebody worth keeping. I was wrong. Now give me my boys and your whoring ass will be free to go and screw the half of Brooklyn you missed when I stopped you to try and make something outta your hot ass. You could go and be as much whore as you want to be. Deme mis niños, puta. ¡No quiero que te ven con tu cadena de hombres!"

"What the fuck did I tell you about talking to me in that goobly gook shit? If you goin' cuss me, cuss me in a language I can understand, you fucking idiot."

"I ain't the idiot. I can speak more than just Spanish. But so your whoring ass can know what I'm saying, I said, 'Give me my children, whore. I don't want them calling your string of men pappi.'"

I couldn't help it. Right there in front of my boys and all the people in the store who were watching us like they was expecting a fight, I said, "Only you, Manuel Luis Ruiz Santiago Ortega, or whatever the fuck your dumb Puerto Rican ass name is, would open your dumb-ass mouth and say some shit like that to me in front of my boys. Who you think going have they children calling you or anybody else pappi? I know you ain't thinking that I going be doing that. If I ain't got them calling your plantain-eating, Spanish-goobly-gook-speaking, mother-fucker ass pappi, who else you think I going have my sons calling pappi. My boys ain't ever going to see your crazy ass again so get that in your Puerto Rican, Bacardi-drinking pipe and smoke it."

"You see, that's why I want my boys from 'round you. You disrespectful. You don't know how to be anything good. You don't even know how to be a mother. I want my boys from you 'fore you have 'em on the streets turning tricks for you."

In the few seconds it took for that last thought to make it from his lips to my ears, something in me snapped. Without thinking or blinking, I snatched a large bottle of mayonnaise from the display in front of me and threw it straight at his mother-fucking head. My eyes wanted to follow the bottle to see if it connected to his hateful face, but the part of me that was beyond caring about him blindly grabbed at my boys. I gathered their small hands in mine and stormed out the store. I never looked back. If the bottle made its target, I neither knew nor cared. I wouldn't have cared if it had split his whole head to fuck wide open. Where did he get off saying shit like that to me and in front of my boys? When was he goin' get it? Those were my children and nobody, especially him, was going get them from me.

Long after I was home and days, perhaps even months, had passed, I kept on thinking about what he'd said. The more I thought about it, the more determined I became. I would show him. I didn't need his ass for nothing; not one stinking-ass thing. I would show him.

Chapter 77

Revenge Is a Witch With Tits of Steel

The next time I went by the store, I didn't want nothing more than to piss Manuel off for trying to show me up the last time I was there. I had a new man. Well, he wasn't really my new man, but I was hoping that he would be able to do two things for me; first, reach my deep itch and second, scratch that part of Manuel's that got raw and bleeding every time he saw me.

Just as I'd hoped, Manuel saw us the minute we got off the bus. I could tell that seeing me was doing just what I'd hoped; causing the sore in Manny called T'Anna Hirsh Greenwood to open, ooze, and plain old flake the scab raw. Manny's face, at the sight of me, filled with so much hate and rage, he looked like a water balloon being filled at Coney Island. He was about to burst and there wasn't a prize for me to get. When he exploded, the hate was going be like a mad man's shit on a blanket. Something should have told me that I'd gone too far, but I was hell-bent on revenge so I wouldn't have listened even if the flashing lights going around Manuel's Bodega flashed "**STOP! T'ANNA, WHAT YOU'RE DOING IS SHIT**!" I wouldn't have paid it no mind. I would've still pressed on. I pressed on.

I'd no idea what the hell Manny was thinking. How was I supposed to know anyway? So because I didn't know and was pretending that I didn't have any idea what that look on his face said, I took Kamarra's hand and boldly stepped in the store like we was in love or some shit like that. Being ignorant is never bliss; it's stupidity; plain ole' stupidity, nothing else. If I'd had the slightest inkling of what was really on Manny's mind, I might've toned down the way I was acting in front of his face. That was the problem. I didn't figure on him figuring on doing anything.

The only thing I knew for sure was that I wanted him to see me. I wanted him to be pissed and get the picture; leave me and my boys alone. Manny watched me with all that hate and anger dripping off his face the way butter does the side of some hot biscuits and he didn't say shit to me. That should have said something right away. You know; sent up a red flag. 'Cause if you didn't know that me and Manny had children together, you would've thought I was a stranger to him. I looked at his ass pretending like he didn't know me and that pissed me off and pushed me harder into the wall of ignorance where bliss was supposed to exist.

For no reason other than I didn't have any good sense, I looked Manny dead in his eyes and, acting like I invented love or some shit, I put one hand on Kamarra's shoulder and then tip-toed and kissed him all soft and sweet-like on his cheek. Manny didn't flinch. Manny stayed like a frozen Puerto Rican ice pop or something 'till Kamarra got to the counter and asked Manny to give him a box of rubbers. Manny's face turned fourteen or fifteen different shades of red. Then, unfreezing, he chose one of the shades of red. He chose "red as all hell" and then, with eyes that matched, he looked at me. His eyes narrowed. He focused on my forehead and it was like he was picturing a bullet hole smack in the middle. I got scared and faked a smile. That fake smile was the move that was my undoing. Manny sent more hateful looks my way. Kamarra, not knowing anything about me and Manny, said, "Hold on, don't ring me up yet. Let me get grab something cold."

I let go of Kamarra's hand and said, real soft-like, "Hurry up, baby. You know I don't like waiting."

Manny looked at me as if he could just stretch his hand right over the counter and cut my throat with a fingernail. His eyes said, "Swoosh, one swipe and your head goin' be rolling on the fucking floor."

I looked away. I looked at Kamarra, who was still trying to decide on one beer. Something made me sneak a peek back at Manny and I noticed that he was also taking a long time. I knew that he couldn't be deciding on what brand of rubbers to give Kamarra because everybody knew he only sold one kind: Rubbers; so what was taking him that long to get one box from under the counter? For a split-second, I became worried, but I dismissed it and laughing a loud and unnecessary laugh, I got Manny's attention and while he tried to pin me to the wall with his hateful stare, I pulled my eyes away from his and, swishing my ass at him one more time, I went outside to wait for Kamarra. I'd proven my point.

When Kamarra finally joined me outside, I took his hand. I was hoping that Manny was still watching us. I walked home satisfied that I'd done the first part of what I'd set out to do. I'd gotten to the part of Manny called T'Anna and had picked years of scab off. He was bleeding. With any luck, he would bleed out and be dead by the time I made it home. All that was left was getting Kamarra to start digging at my itch. I couldn't wait. Ma and the boys were out and they wouldn't be back for a few hours. I didn't have to worry about Leela 'cause I think the witches were having a convention somewhere and with her being the head witch, she had to be there. She would be gone just as long as Ma and the boys.

As soon as we were in the house, I turned him loose to do his scratching. His scratcher was the biggest I'd seen in a long time. Shit, come to think of it, I think it was the biggest I'd ever seen. As he approached my itch, I closed my eyes. I wanted him to reach it and scratch it just as deeply as I'd scratched at Manny. He was near, but not quite. I decided to help him. I started grinding my hips harder into him. The grinding didn't have the effect I'd hoped for. It threw his thrusts out of control. He was now thrusting so hard, he almost sent me to the floor. I wrapped my legs around his hip and grabbed onto his back with both my arms. If I was going, he was coming with me. We both going hit our asses on the floor.

All my wrapping and grabbing sent the wrong message to that dumb ass. A sound almost like an animal's burst outta his throat and I knew that any second now it was going be mission accomplished. In a desperate attempt to help him get deeper and reach my itch so I could get mine before he got his, I arched my back 'till my forehead was almost touching the headboard. He didn't reach, but he was in as deep as he could go.

Arched the way I was, he used me as a launching pad. I braced myself as the rocket named Kamarra shuddered and ground himself deeper into the dark void called T'Anna. He was grinding so hard that I was sure the friction was going cause a rubber meltdown and his stuff was going to leak out and get me pregnant. I smiled at the thought of a meltdown and dismissed it. This was a new kinda rubber. It was made for this kinda grinding. I raised myself up to his brutal animal thrusting. He shuddered and missed. My itch went unscratched. I unwrapped my legs from around him as disappointment wrapped itself around me like a large wet spot.

Some six weeks later, I realized that the rubber had melted down. There was going to be yet another mouth for the state to feed. There was nothing about the whole incident I wanted to accept. I didn't want to accept that the rubber had melted down, nor did I want to accept that I was pregnant. Nothing had anything to do with what I wanted to accept.

My mind kept playing the whole scene over and over in my mind. I couldn't be pregnant. I just couldn't. I'd seen it, the rubber, whole in Kamarra's big hairy ass ape hand. I'd seen it. Watched him take it off. My watching had nothing to do with me. It wasn't like I'd a choice. Shit, he pulled that thing outta me so hard, it had made the strangest sound I'd ever heard. It sounded like somebody was pulling a suction cup off a wall – a kinda reverse woosh sound.

Still between my spread legs, he'd stayed on his knees as if he was going to pray, pay homage to my cat, or do some weird religious ritual, or some shit like that. But no, it was none of that. Instead, he'd methodically unsheathed that monster of a scratcher and then with the scratcher in his left hand, he held the rubber in his right hand. I looked at him, not noticing that he was dripping his extra shit all over my thigh as he raised the used rubber up to his face like he was raising a frigging trophy or something. He took his eyes off it for a brief moment to look at me. He had a proud puffed up look on his face. He smiled.

I'd half-way expected him to beat his chest. He didn't. Instead, he looked at the stupid rubber in his hand and said, "Girl, I was full. That was a full load. You see that shit, baby. I almost full this shit up. Ain't one drop got 'way."

I waited for him to put it to his lips and kiss it for working so well. He didn't, instead he'd tied a knot at the top and dropped it in the garbage can next to the bed. He really was stupid. Did he forget that I had children? Did he want them to see it?

I swung my leg in front of him and got up. Standing over the garbage can, I looked back at him still kneeling with his scratcher now in both hands and wondered why I hadn't kicked his stupid ass in the head and knocked him out while I was swinging my leg around him. I smiled at the picture of him falling off the bed had I kicked him. He looked at me and smiled back. I wrapped the tied up rubber it in a paper towel; relieved that none of his shit had escaped. Nothing having escaped reduced the risk or worry of a pregnancy. I closed my eyes against the image of what a child of his would be like. I reached for the rubber and wrapped another piece of paper towel around it. Didn't want to chance none of it getting on my hand and slipping into my stuff when I went to wash up.

So how come I was pregnant? It took some thinking on my part but I finally figured it out. It was Manny. While Kamarra had gone to get the beer, Manny had to have pushed a pin through the box of condoms. I was right when I'd wondered what was taking him so long under the counter when Kamarra had bought the rubbers from him. I should have followed my instincts, but that wasn't my real mistake. My mistake was going into Manuel's store to buy rubbers in the first place. That was the move Manny hoped would be my undoing. He was wrong.

He'd figured that once I found myself with yet another child, that I would let him have his sons the next time he asked. He was so wrong, it was amazing. He would have his sons, but over my dead body. Those were my boys and I was keeping them. I was never going to say, "Manny, go ahead, take the little shits if you and your Tia want them so bad." No, never. Not in a million years.

Manny was counting on many things, but what he didn't count on was me changing. The pregnancy he had planned for me changed me. I became more determined to keep my children: all of them. I didn't know a lot of things and so I set out to make it my business to learn what I didn't. The first thing I learned and it was from TV was how to stop my destructive ways. I watched a whoring drug addict mother on TV turn her life around so she could keep her kids. I know it was TV, but I took it as a sign. First, I admitted that my ways were whoring ways. Second, men were my drugs, and third, the boys were my life. Those were all the lessons I needed to know. Then I set my mind on learning what determination and perseverance was. It took me a long time. While I worked on keeping men off and outta me, I took myself off the streets. I took a page from Ma's book and learned to mother my boys. It wasn't easy.

The street called; my body wanted to answer. I did the best I could to teach my body a new response when the street called. I taught my hands to quiet the purring that came from my cat. That place that no one had reached still yearned to be scratched. It yearned for the man or the men that could reach it. I focused on my boys and the life growing in my belly. The calls from the street came fewer and fewer; the yearnings also came fewer as I stopped giving in to them, even with my hand. I decided that it and I could and would wait.

Life quieted down in Ma's house. Everybody was on some kind of waiting list. I was waiting for Leela to make the mistake that was going to let me nail her ass to the floor. Leela was waiting for one of my boys to do something wrong so she could cuss at them; that was going be her mistake. Lillie, she was waiting for the day she would walk outta Ma's house and into her precious Spellman. Ma, she was waiting for that day too because then she would know that the curse had finally been lifted. All of us were waiting and Ma, feeling secure and confident in her wait, took her eyes off Lillie and the minute she did, life blindsided the both of them.

I pulled up a chair; not that I really wanted to but having been here before, I knew what an emotional toll it was going to take on Ma, Lillie, and the rest of us; yes even Leela. I wanted a front-row seat because I knew Ma wasn't going to take life blindsiding her again easily. Ma had learned to fight her way out of any corner and as much as this corner was deep and dark, I had my money on Ma. She wasn't going to lose again.

This time, she wasn't the understudy; she had the lead. Leela was best supporting actress. Lillie was the understudy this time around. Her character was the dutiful, brilliant, doted-on daughter and granddaughter. She was the one Greenwood daughter with potential and promise. She was studying her lines, doing everything that was required of her. I think if she was in the Garden of Eden, she would have refused the apple, got a few stomps in on the snake, and later, even though Adam wouldn't know what to do with them, she would've presented him with the first pair of snake-skin shoes and there would be a stew; snake and apple with a pinch of Tree Of Life leaves.

She would never tell Adam what he was eating, but one thing for sure, sin and all its ugliness would never have gotten a chance to debut. However, she wasn't the one chosen to be in the garden. She was chosen for a garden, well it wasn't really a garden. It was like a garden, but people in New York called it Central Park.

Lillie, because she looked just like those people that found it exciting doing nothing in the park, had taken up this past-time and was now deeply entrenched in the ways of white folk. A snake was slithering her way and she, because she didn't have snake-stomping instincts, looked at it and smiled when she saw the apple in its mouth and now Ma was preparing to figure out what to do with the spinning top called her life.

Chapter 78

When No One Was Watching

Lillie

I was counting down the months and couldn't wait 'till it got to where I was counting days. I had one full year left and I would be gone. It's not that I hated Bed-Stuy but I hated all the things that Bed-Stuy stood for and meant to other people who heard about it. I hated the foolishness of the disease called "Not Wanting Nothing", which seemed to plague many people who took up space in and around Bed-Stuy. I wanted something. I was going after what I wanted and when I finally got it, everyone would have to say Doctor Lillian Greenwood. I wasn't going to settle for anything less. Spellman was going to be my ticket out. Granddaddy made me the same offer he'd made Leela and T'Anna; get into college and he would pay for it.

On Lexington Avenue, T'Anna and Leela had found new ways to cuss and abuse each other. Mazilli, Malakai, and Lil' Manuel were either tearing the place up, their usual routine, or getting in Leela's way, making her cuss them and ultimately bring T'Anna out of her corner. I wasn't feeling like all of that so once it got started, I did something I'd never done; I put my coat on and left the house. All I needed was some place to get some peace and quiet.

At first, I was going to walk up to Robert Fulton park and sit for a while, or at least 'till I felt that Leela and T'Anna had worn themselves out or killed each other, but the more I thought about sitting in the park, I knew it wasn't going to be any better. Indian summer had been hanging around for a few days and although it wasn't quite summer, folks were acting like it. That meant there would be women there like T'Anna or

Leela: loud, foul-mouthed, cussing, and ready to fight anybody.

I decided instead to walk over to Tompkins Avenue and take the bus to the Botanical Garden. My feet, as if they had a mind of their own, took me to Kingston and Throop train station. I bought a token and when the train came, I got on. With no real destination in mind, I decided I would to do like the homeless people; I would ride 'till I was tired or 'till my mind said, "Get off here."

At 59th Street, it said just that. I got off the train and came out the subway. I couldn't believe what my eyes saw. I felt as if I'd taken a ride to a movie set. My feet took me across the street and into the park. Not only had I never been to Central Park, I didn't even know that it was so close to home. I was amazed. There I was, seventeen, almost eighteen, getting ready to go to Georgia to get away from the madness that was Lexington Avenue and Bed-Stuy and by going to a nearby park and right up the street, in a matter of speaking, was a haven. I walked, looked around, and allowed the park to absorb me.

I'd found it; that place where quiet, peace, solitude, and anonymity existed. It was peaceful in a busy kinda way but not enough to change my mind from getting the hell away from Bed-Stuy. But for the time I had left, it would provide me with some much-needed quiet. I walked 'till I was tired and then I went home. I wanted to go back the next day but I knew I couldn't pick up and go whenever or wherever I felt like so I came up with a plan that would give me a chance to go and not make Ma suspicious. I told her that I would be doing some extra studying at the library. That was a lie but not really since there was only one thing different between the two – walls. I studied as I said I would. I didn't have a table or chair, but I had a lake, a bench, and weather that wasn't in much of a hurry to turn to winter.

Finally, winter arrived and it didn't make any good sense to continue going so I stopped. With winter in full swing, I sought refuge at the library. Although I missed the quiet beauty of the lake, I did have my quiet space. I couldn't wait for the winter weather to break because as soon as it looked like spring, I was going right back to my bench. Winter dragged on forever.

Finally, there was no more snow on the ground and somewhere spring was nearby. I got through class and as soon as it was over, I got on the train and was on my way. I got there and was surprised to find that not many other people had felt the way I did about getting there.

The park was almost empty, but I didn't care. I'd waited too long. I found my bench and as if the sun had been waiting for me, it draped itself all over me and my bench. It was warm but not toasty; it was the kind of warmth you feel after you've warmed your spot and you don't want to move 'cause you know the minute you do, it's goin' be cold again.

I sat on my sun-drenched bench, got my book out, and started to read. Well I wasn't really reading; I kinda had the book open because the occasional small gust of wind was making it harder and harder for me to concentrate since each gust flirted with the pages of my book. As if that wasn't bad enough, I also had to fight to keep the wind from finding the tiny opening in my clothes. It darted in and out of every tiny opening, chilling me even as I sat in the warmth of the sun. Each time the wind found a way through some different opening in my clothes or fluttered the pages of my book, it made me think that perhaps my coming wasn't such a good idea. I looked around to see who else had ventured out; no one else apparently had the same idea as me. The sun went behind a cloud briefly and while it was gone, I had to face reality; it was still too cold to be sitting outside by a lake.

Spring might have received the baton from winter, but it was nowhere near the finish line and everything in the park but me knew this. The park was still caught in a winter frame of mind. The trees were still naked, the birds, if they were in the trees, weren't chirping, and only an occasional squirrel darted along the ground or, finding no competition for the branches, jumped from branch to branch.

Smiling, I wondered why I was still sitting there. I'd nothing to prove, so why didn't I take my behind out of the people's park and get back to where I belonged? It was that thought that reminded me why I'd come. I'd chosen the park over home because here I had peace and quiet. At home, where this brisk April chill would be shut out, there would be no peace because Leela, T'Anna, and her children were there. This always meant screaming and hollering. It was either Leela shouting at T'Anna or Leela shouting at T'Anna's boys, which invariable meant T'Anna shouting at Leela for shouting at her boys. Nothing made T'Anna louder or got her to cuss worse than Leela cussing at her boys.

Remembering all of the reasons I'd come to the park, I pulled my coat a little closer to me, tied my scarf a little tighter around my neck, and pulled my hat down a little lower on my head. I was about to put away the book and reach for my gloves when a shadow came over my book. At first I thought the sun had gone behind a cloud again but when I looked and saw that there was sunshine by my feet, the hairs at the back of my neck stood up. I decided to look and see who or what was blocking the sun. I could tell when I looked that it was a man but I couldn't really see his face because his head was slightly bent and there was so much hair. I could see enough to know that he was white. I wondered what this white man wanted with me, as my heart started beating very fast. Before I could clear my thoughts or still my heart, I heard, "Excuse me, do you mind if I sit down?"

I never looked up to see the face but I could tell that the voice was young. I said, "It's a public place. Sit where you feel like."

"I know it's a public place, but I would like to sit here and I would like to feel invited."

"Nobody has to invite you to sit on a park bench. If you want to sit; sit. The bench ain't mine."

"Would it make a difference to you if I introduced myself?"

"Look, I don't want to know your name. I ain't trying to get to know you."

"My name is Elliot. Can I sit down now?"

I was starting to feel really annoyed. "Look, I don't care 'bout you, your name, or if you sit down or not."

"I won't sit unless you tell me your name."

"I don't have to tell you nothing or invite you nowhere. You can stand there for all I care."

"Why are you acting annoyed at me?"

"Cause you're annoying me. If you were sitting here reading your book, I wouldn't come and stand over you and stop you from reading, or keep on bugging you to let me sit by you."

"That's the difference between you and me. I want to sit next to you and would like to do so because you've invited me. You see, this way I won't feel as if I've intruded."

"You are intruding. So would you please go away and leave me alone?"

"No."

I ignored him and went back to my book. I didn't have much time left to sit here and I wasn't going to waste it on an idiot. He didn't say anything else for a while but I could feel him standing there. I pretended not to notice but it was clear that I wasn't reading anymore.

"You see, not only are you rude, but you're also being selfish," he told me.

At the words rude and selfish, a part of me started to feel a bit of Leela coming over me and God knows I'd never acted like Leela. "You got some nerve talking about selfish. You come into the place where I'm sitting minding my own business, and you stand over me annoying me about not sitting on a hard public bench unless you're invited, and you call me rude and selfish. You're the one that's rude and selfish. Why don't you take your white, long-haired ass and go jump in a lake or something."

I started to breathe a sigh of relief when he turned away and didn't say one word. I didn't look to see where he went, but the next thing I knew, I hear a big splash and a whole big commotion. The fool had jumped in the almost-frozen lake and suddenly, people, who I hadn't seen or heard since I sat down, were shouting at him to get out. I put the book up to my face as I started to laugh. I peeked over the top of my book and saw he was being fished out the lake by a few white men who had waded in to help him. The men's pants were wet only to their knees but he, because he had jumped in, was totally wet. His clothes were clinking to him and his long hair was dripping soft ice onto his shoulders. People were asking him if he was ok and stuff like that and as if they weren't saying or asking him anything at all, he turned to me and said, "Now may I sit down? This is the only place in the park with some sun and if I don't dry out soon, I'm going to catch a cold."

The men who had helped him out and all the other white people who had suddenly appeared because a white person was in the lake looked at him as if they wanted to throw him back in the water and hold him down 'till they were sure he was dead, and then giving me a look that also said that the same fate awaited me, started to walk away. It was obvious to them that they had wasted time in saving this one.

I looked at him standing there, obviously chilled to the bone, and probably half-frozen and because the white people who had come out of nowhere to rescue him weren't gone, I laughed out loud and said, "It's a free park and the sun belongs to everyone. I can't tell you what to do with God's sun."

He sat down. As soon as he sat down, I put my book in my bag and stood up.

I could hear his teeth knocking as he said, "Hey, where you going?"

Laughing, I said, "Home."

With the color draining from his face, he told me, "You can't leave me here like this."

I finished putting my book in my bag. "Yes, I can. You ain't my problem. You were the one stupid enough to jump in a lake; what if I'd said go and play in the middle of the street, would you have done that?"

"If that's what I thought you wanted."

I started to walk away and I'd only gone a few steps when he ran up to me and said, "I've gone to a lot of trouble to get to talk to you. The least you can do is tell me your name. This way, if I catch a cold and die, I would at least know the name of the woman I'd died for."

I looked at him and continued walking. He didn't give up. "Come on, I'm all wet. Doesn't it matter that I did this for you?"

I stopped and looked at the wet, white fool dripping soft ice on the ground and said, "Elliot? That's your name, right? Well, you and your wet things are your problem, and I ain't telling some crazy fool my name."

"Fine, then I'm going to follow you out this park and keep annoying you until you tell me your name or something."

"The only thing I'm telling you is this; 'If you keep on following me, I'm going to tell that policeman over there that you're annoying me.'"

"And which one of us do you think the police would listen to first. You doubt me, watch this."

Then before I could say a word, he ran up to the policeman and spoke. "Officer, Officer…" I froze. I didn't know what to think or do. A white man was telling a white policeman that I'd done him something. That fool was probably telling the police I pushed him in the lake or worse. I wanted to run but my feet wouldn't move. I couldn't hear what he was saying to the policeman but his lips were moving and the next thing I know, his lips aren't moving anymore but the policeman was – in my direction. As the policeman neared, I turned my head and started walking towards them. I had no choice. They stood between me and the gate—my escape. I was figuring to walk past and ignore both of them, but Elliot said, "I'm going to have this policeman arrest you for pushing me in the lake."

I looked at the policeman and my heart almost stopped.

To my surprise, the policeman smiled and said, "Elliot, I don't think we should do this. Look how scared the poor girl is. Let her go home."

I almost fainted. My heart started to beat again. Then to make matters worse, he turned to the policeman and said, "You're right, Officer Frank, but can you keep an eye on her for me? If you don't, she's going to leave. I'll be back in a few minutes. Thanks, Frank." Turning to me, he said, "Hey, stay here with Officer Frank for a few minutes. I'm going to change my clothes and I'll be right back. Don't leave, ok. I'll be right back."

I looked from him to the policeman and as soon as he turned his back, I walked away. I was so angry that I wanted to shout to his retreating back, "Kiss my ass, you long-haired white idiot."

But I wasn't Leela or T'Anna so I stormed out the park and headed to the subway. I'd just bought my token and gone through the turnstile when I heard his voice again. I looked and there he was, buying a token. He'd changed his clothes and he was wearing a hat, I guessed his hair must have been still wet. I turned my head and stiffened my shoulders. I was so angry I felt as if T'Anna and Leela had both climbed inside of me. I was hoping that he would leave me alone 'cause if he didn't, I might cuss him.

He had no intention of leaving me alone. He came and stood beside me. I started to smolder; the heat coming off me must have told him that this wasn't the best time to talk to me as he just stood there. When the train came, I got on and so did he. I sat down; he sat next to me. I moved over, he moved to close the space between us. I stood up. He didn't stand up, but continued to sit across from me. From 59th Street to 14th Street he said nothing but as the train approached West 4th Street, he said, "I'm sorry. That stunt with Officer Frank wasn't as funny as I thought it would be. Would you please accept my apology?"

I turned my back to him. At West 4th Street, a pregnant white woman got on; he got up to give her his seat and stood beside me. He held the pole and allowed his hand to slide down and touch mine. I moved my hand. He leaned in, not touching my hand or me, as he said, "Look, I'm really sorry. I made a mistake. Say something."

As the train left West 4th Street, I said something. I looked him full in the face and with a look that should have melted him to a puddle of human fluid, I said through clenched teeth, "Leave me alone."

As the train pulled into the Chambers Street station he did. He got off but not before he said, "I'm really sorry, really. I just wanted to get to know you."

I didn't answer. The train started pulling out; I took a deep breath. I looked to make sure he was still on the platform and as I did, my eyes caught his. He smiled and mouthed, "I'm sorry." I looked away.

Chapter 79

When Worlds Collide

I stayed out of the park 'till it was truly spring. I'd been going there for about a month before I saw him again. Instantly I was chilled. I got up and started to leave. He spoke, "Miss, please don't leave. I don't want you to leave the park whenever you see me. I won't bother you again, but please let me say I'm sorry for the way I acted the last time I saw you."

I said nothing but I left. I was mad at myself for leaving because the park wasn't his and I shouldn't let anyone make me leave. I promised myself that no one was ever going to chase me away from any place ever again. The following week, I went back. This time I was looking for him. I was prepared for him. One word out of him and I was going let him have it and then I was going to stay and enjoy my space. I saw him, but he didn't come near me. I was glad. That went on for about a month. I would get to the park and he would be there but he would never say anything. He read or played his violin, but he never came near me.

One evening he wasn't there. I was disappointed. I'd gotten used to him sitting and playing. I read, but to my surprise I didn't stay as long as I would have. I got my things together and went to the train station. I looked to see if he was there. He wasn't. I boarded the train feeling disappointed. All the way to Brooklyn, I wondered why I was feeling so stupid. He had obviously gotten the message that I didn't want to be bothered and had gone off to bother someone else. For about three weeks, I didn't see him. I looked for him but I never saw him; the park didn't feel the same. Without realizing it, I'd grown accustomed to his presence and his playing. For no apparent reason, I became angry at him for not being there; unable to concentrate, I packed my bag and as I was about to leave I saw him coming towards me. I don't know where it came from but a smile lit my face up. He smiled back and hurried towards me. I was glad. I sat back down. He came and as he had done the first time I saw him, he said, "Excuse me, do you mind if I sit down?"

This time, because I'd actually missed him, I said, "No, I don't mind." He sat down.

He extended his hand and said, "Hi, I'm Mark Elliot Anderson, everyone calls me Elliot though."

I took his hand and said, "I'm Lillian, everyone calls me Lillie." We both smiled. Neither of us spoke. Silence seemed the best thing. No sooner was I was getting comfortable in the silence, he said, "Mind if I play?"

I looked at him all the while trying to get my thoughts together. He took my silence as a no and said, "I wouldn't if it would bother you."

Smiling, I said, "No, it won't bother me." And before I could get the rest of my thoughts together, I heard my mouth say, "I like hearing you play."

He smiled and started playing. He sounded so beautiful. The sounds had my mind drifting all over the place. If not for the sun shifting, I would've forgotten that I had to get home. As soon as he was done, I told him I had to go. I could see that he was disappointed but he didn't try to follow me. He sat where he was and asked, "Can I see you here tomorrow?"

I smiled and said nothing, but I knew he knew I would be there.

Elliot and I met every day after that. If it wasn't by the lake then it was by Belvedere's Castle. We would either sit and talk or explore places in and around the park. If it rained, we'd find a place where they didn't stare too hard and we would talk for a while; if we couldn't find a place, I went back home. Elliot would ride the train with me; but not really. We didn't let on like if we really knew each other. He would mostly sit across from me. That was my idea because I was nervous. He also never rode the train any further than High Street or if he felt bold sometimes, then he would come as far as Jay Street Borough Hall. After that, he went back up town. I understood.

As time passed and I got to know him better, he would offer to buy me things but I didn't take them as I couldn't take them home. I took little things I could sneak into the house. I would look at them when I was alone. My favorite thing was a small, two-inch framed picture of us we'd taken at Woolworth's. He had one and I had one – our secret.

Elliot and his world were different to me and the people and things in mine. In some ways, it was like if Bed-Stuy and Manhattan were on two different planets. I didn't care. All I knew was I couldn't walk away from him. It was getting harder and harder keeping my thoughts focused on going back to school in September. There was something at the back of my head that said, "Walk away from him now," but Elliot, with his sweet gentle ways, made it very difficult and eventually he wore me down. It wasn't a bad kind of wearing down but one that came with a lifestyle I'd never seen nor never imagined being a part of. I started to become comfortable in Elliot's world.

One afternoon towards the end of summer, Elliot and I met at our bench by Belvedere's Castle. We had planned to see a movie when he said, "Lillie, my parents have gone to Europe to look at the house that we'll be moving into next month. Would you like to see where I live?"

I'd never been to Elliot's home before because the same way I hadn't told anyone at home about him; he hadn't told his parents about me. We existed only for each other.

"I can't. I have to go home and if I'm late, my sister Leela will start so much hell that Ma would eventually join in."

"We don't have to stay long. I promise you. Tell you what, Lillie; you don't even have to come in. I want you to see where I stay awake at nights thinking about you. Please, Lillie; let me show you my house."

"Where's your house anyway?"

"61st Street."

"61st Street?"

"Why do you say it like it's a curse or a dirty word or something? Lillie, you know that I live across from the park, so what's the big deal about the street?"

"I didn't mean anything by it. It's just that I don't know anyone who lives over there."

"You aren't coming to see the people over there, you're coming to see my house and you know me. So forget about where my house is. Just come and see it."

Elliot and I walked the short distance in quiet. I would have been ashamed to tell him that as many times as I'd been to the park, I'd often wondered about the people who lived around it. We walked to Broadway and 60th Street and by the small cinema, Elliot turned in. I wondered where he was going. I didn't see a house. It looked like the entrance to a another kind of park. I followed and then I saw them; white people everywhere sitting around a man-made oasis. I wanted to sit and join them. Pretend that this was a part of my world; that I belonged, that I had a right to sit and stare into the water just the way they were.

He was looking at my face and then he said in a voice a little more than a whisper, "We'll come back on a day when it's not so crowded and you can sit, ok."

I looked around at the grand buildings. They spoke the language of money – in every language and at any exchange rate. I wanted to take in all this junction where wealth, prestige, and power met and was right at home. As we stood looking, Elliot slipped his hand into mine. I wanted to pull my hand out of his and run. After we stood there for a few minutes, Elliot said, "Come on, Lillie, my house is over there." Elliot pointed to one of the grand buildings and started to walk. Outside I stood with my mouth a little open. The doorman, upon seeing Elliot, walked to the door and opened it.

"Do you want to come inside, Lillie?"

I didn't answer. Elliot took my hand. I followed.

Elliot's apartment looked as if I'd tripped and fallen into *Town and Country*. The apartment was so huge it could have been a whole catalog. Everything was perfect, picturesque, properly placed, and pricey. I could feel Elliot watching me. He was pleased that I'd come.

"Let me show you the house quickly." I followed Elliot from one page to another. The last page was his bedroom. Outside the door, Elliot said, "This is my bedroom. Would you like to see inside? If you don't want to see it, it's ok."

I would like to say I didn't know what I was doing when I put my hand on the doorknob, but I would be lying. I wanted to see and be inside. I'd made up my mind to accept what happened once I stepped in. The part of me that felt once he and his family went to Europe, I would never see him again wanted to be with him. The part of me that was waiting on the acceptance letter from Spellman turned my back and looked the other way. Ma had said a person was only responsible if they'd witnessed something and did nothing. I wasn't witnessing anything. Elliot put his hand on mine and opened the door. We walked in and became an "us". I walked out of that room knowing that I would love Elliot for the rest of my life. Elliot and his family left for Europe a week later.

Thoughts of Elliot slowly but eventually replaced all thoughts of school. It wasn't like I gave up the notion of going, it was just that now my thoughts were divided. One half said Elliot, the other said Spellman, and like the Egyptian people crossing the Red Sea, I was caught in the middle. With Elliot away in Europe, all I had to do was keep my eyes focused on the distant shore and I would make it across and into the new land called Spellman. I was almost there and then it happened. My red sea of emotions closed over my head and so too did the mouth of my womb. My red sea stopped flowing. I didn't need forty days to figure out what had stopped my red sea; it was a staff, just not one as big or mighty as Moses'.

I sat right there on the shore of disappointment and watched as my dreams of Spellman got swallowed up. I was pregnant and alone. For days, I stayed in my room waiting on a Moses to climb to the top of my mountain of troubles and come back down with an answer chiseled on a stone. I didn't need ten like those other folks. One would have been enough. When he didn't show up, I accepted the fact that I was on my own. I tried really hard to come up with a solution to my dilemma and when I couldn't, I told Leela that I was pregnant. That would turn out to be the second biggest mistake I would make in my life.

Chapter 80

Parallel Collision

I wasn't sure what I was expecting when I told Leela I was pregnant for Elliot. I guess I was expecting her to act the big sister part and help me figure out a way to break the news to Ma. I watched Leela as she absorbed the news. I waited. She was quiet, so I figured she was thinking. I started to relax. She was going to help me figure this thing out. Leela was thinking alright but none of it had anything to do with helping me figure out a way to break the news to Ma. When Leela opened her mouth, the first few words were soft, caring. "Lillie, how could you let something like this happen? What about your promises? What about college?"

"Leela, I didn't mean for it to happen. I'm sorry."

Leela didn't respond to what I said. It was as if I said nothing. The soft caring sister left and in her place was something without an edge. Evil ugly words start to flow from her. The words coming out of Leela's mouth were like a million double-edged razor blades being shot out of a cannon and I was the intended target. I closed my eyes so that I wouldn't see them coming but I was unable to close my ears. I heard my sister's venom-laced words as she lashed out at me. I tried as hard as I could to pull myself out of the way so the slicing wouldn't be so deep. No luck. Her aim was dead on. I was unable to lift myself above the range of her hatred. I cowered to the far corner of my mind and watched. My heart ached as Leela, acting like a woman possessed, forgot I was her sister. She moved as if to destroy me.

Fear settled over me as she pushed the door to my soul, opened it, and barged right in, stomping and stepping all over the trust I'd placed in her. Deeply wounded, I fell to my knees. Neither T'Anna nor Ma was home to help me. Bleeding emotionally, I began to pray. No sound came. She'd cut the vocal chords to my soul. Leela didn't care that I was praying. She had something against everybody. God, for reasons known only to Leela, was at the top of her list. I was afraid but not enough to let her stop me from asking God to be my bridge over these troubled waters that she was stirring up and getting ready to throw me into. I didn't mean to be pregnant nor to bring another child into the house for Leela and Ma to feed, but none of that gave Leela the right to forget that we shared the same mother. It didn't give her the right, but she took it anyway.

She was transformed and I was transfixed. I stole a look at her face. It was granite, chipped, cracked, and jagged. I was wondering what was changing her like this. It had to be more than my being pregnant that had turned her into this black granite mamba. As I cowered in the corner, I could almost see the venom coursing through her veins. There was enough there to kill a man twice her size, yet it didn't kill or paralyze her 'cause she was the carrier. Leela fixed her gaze on me and slithered over to where I was. She unleashed her poison. "You might as well get up from there and stop acting like you so pious. Get your ass up and face your reality."

She waits for all of a hot second. I take too long to stand and, running out of patience, she screams, "See where all that Cinderella, Sleeping Beauty, and Snow White shit has gotten you. Look at you, knocked up because you thought you were white like him. Your ass went and got caught up in all that fairytale bullshit."

Leela stopped, took a breath, and in that instant, she knew that she was about to go over the top and she didn't care. It didn't matter that I confided in her because I expected her to help me. It was the idea of my being pregnant that was pushing Leela over the brink of her sanity. She started in on Elliot. She stepped all up in my sexual privacy.

"Did you ever think of the word succumbed? Doesn't it sound like suc-cum and bed put together? I would bet that it was somebody in your man's family back in slave times who came up with that word. White men; they nasty like that. How else would white men get the taste for black women if somebody in their family didn't teach them?"

Leela spewed her venom-laced words at me as if she was making a bridal veil for Akasha, queen of the dead. "Did you ever think about it, Lillie? Or were you too busy thinking that your white prince had come to rescue you and that's why it didn't matter when he said, "Bed, cum, suc."

I wanted to tell her to stop but she was beyond stopping. She leaned in closer to me as I was crying hysterically and continued. "I imagine that you never thought of biting off that maggot-infected piece of dead meat, now did you? I bet you loved it. You see, he did that sick shit 'cause he knew that you was thinking that he loved your skinny beige ass."

With tears pouring down my cheeks, I pleaded with her, "Leela, you got to listen to me. It wasn't like that; not at all. Elliot and I love each other. It wasn't like what you trying to make it out to be."

Leela ignored my pleas. It was as if she had forgotten that it was me. She continued taking me apart as if she was dismantling a complex puzzle, but it wasn't a puzzle she was taking apart; it was our bond of sisterhood, one venomous word at a time.

"Lillie, if it was me, and it wouldn't ever have been me 'cause I ain't like you and the rest like you that like white men. He would've had to force me to touch that shriveled up, maggot-filled nasty thing. Anyway, while he was grinding and slapping his old dried up balls in my face, I would be planning. The minute he'd drifted off to sleep, I would stab his ass. I would stab him hard, fast and a lot. Then my spiteful ass would cut the little shriveled up maggot's nest off, and I would ram it down his dead, stinking throat and let the maggot eat his ass."

I sucked at the air. I was having a difficult time breathing. Leela heard me sucking at the air but she didn't stop. "Yeah, I hate white people. Well, all white people except Granddaddy. White people remind me of stewed pork. That's why I don't eat pork."

I make another feeble attempt to stop her. "Leela, you're supposed to help me."

My cry fell on deaf ears. I gave up trying to reach the part of Leela that was supposed to care about me. I rose, not to attack Leela, but to look for a place in the room where her angry and bitter biting words wouldn't reach me. I found myself wishing that Ma was in the room. I would climb right back into her and stay there until Leela was done. Leela, unable to control her unleashed anger, screamed at me, "Now you ain't ever going to that uppity college. You goin' be just like T'Anna; popping one man's baby in and then squeezing it out to make room for another. This is what you get for thinking you so special that you went to Manhattan to look for a man. I ain't got no problem with you going to Manhattan to look for a man, but you didn't even go to Harlem, you went to the West Side. Whoever heard of a black woman looking for a man on the West Side?

"Now look at you. College? You going spell it like T'Anna: W-E-L-F-A-R-E. That's your college. I ain't sorry for you. That white boy ain't going think your black ass so fine once he finds out you pregnant. Did you really think that you were more than a piece of black ass to him? If you did, then you dumber than I thought. Go ahead and tell me that shit again about how he loves you so that I can really laugh at your knocked up black ass!"

Somehow, with Leela in my face and screaming at me, I heard Ma come in. Something in me snapped. All I could think about was getting Ma to come to my room and save me from Leela's vitriolic assault. I started to scream. Nothing. No words. No sounds. My mind said try again. Scream louder. Ma would hear and come and see about me. I tried again. This time I got out, "Ma!"

It came out loud and wrapped around everything. I watched my scream wrap around Leela. It bound her. It stopped her for a split-second. Leela's face told me she was wondering if perhaps she had gone too far. In the longest splitting of a second that I'd ever experienced, Leela, the one who is splitting the second, recovers and looking at my screaming shell, she said, "Oh, shut to hell up! What you think all that screaming goin' do for you? Who you think in this house can do me anything?"

I didn't answer. I continued screaming. Suddenly, the door burst open. It was Ma. My screams had gotten me the results I'd hoped for. I looked from Leela to Ma. All I had to do was make it to Ma and I'd be safe from Leela. I rushed to Ma. I made it to her arms. She opened them and I rushed in. She looked at me and I could feel her concern. I also felt something else.

"Lillie, what's going on in here?"

I wanted to answer her but all that came out were more screams. Ma hugged me closer to her and I could feel her heart; it was beating faster as she talked to Leela. "Leela, what is wrong with your sister? Why is she screaming like this?"

I watched as Leela, ignoring my screams, shouted over them and said to Ma, "Cause she's pregnant and it ain't for nobody round here. She's pregnant for a white man from uptown."

As Leela was telling on me, all I could think about was grabbing onto Ma. I hugged her harder. I clung to her as best as I could as the undertow called Leela tried even harder to drag me under. I held on for dear life. I was drowning and Ma was my straw. I couldn't let go or Leela would drown me in her sea of bitter betrayal. I didn't want to drown. I clutched at desperately at Ma.

Unsure of what I'd been through, Ma took a look at me and guessed. She didn't respond to the news that had shattered her. She hugged me back hard. In the safety of her love, my legs gave out. I was unable to stand. I slid back to the floor.

Leela looked at me and then back to Ma and said, "Ma, don't let all that falling down to the floor and shit fool you. She's just acting. She doesn't want you to kick her ass out."

"Leela, stop! What have you done to your sister?" Ma sat down on the edge of the bed; she cradled my head on her lap. Without letting go of me, she stood up. I didn't. I stayed on the floor and hugged her legs. I wasn't sure why she stood but I was guessing it was to talk to Leela eye-to-eye.

Ma looked from Leela to me. She looked like she was thinking of slapping Leela but she realized that slapping Leela wouldn't change anything. Leela realized what Ma was thinking but when Ma hesitated, it gives Leela the room she was looking for to continue her attack. "Look at your sorry ass now. Where you think them tears and all that hollering going get you?"

Leela looked at Ma but anger and hatred had clouded her vision and she didn't see that she and Ma weren't connecting.

"Ma, tell her. Tell her that you've seen the same fake tears from T'Anna each time she came in here knocked up. Tell her those tears don't mean shit!"

Ma looked from me to Leela and something snapped in her brain. She shouted at Leela. "Leela, shut up! Stop cussing and talking all that nasty talk before I forget my good Christian training. Which part of your brain has told you that you can disrespect me in my own home? Why you treating your sister like this, and in front of me to boot?"

Leela looked at Ma and I could tell she didn't believe her ears. She opened her mouth to say something to Ma, but Ma started to talk before Leela could get a word out.

"Leela, have you forgotten that you're supposed to have respect for me and charity towards your sisters? Help me understand why, in your sister's hour of need, the devil has to climb all over you? Why you have to show all your ugly, hateful ways at once? Help me to understand how you could forget that I'm a God-fearing, Bible-believing, saved, sanctified, filled with the Holy Ghost Christian woman. In the name of Jesus, Leela Phoebe Greenwood, help me to understand where the Christian in you went."

Leela was still in a state of shock. She wanted to believe that her ears were deceiving her. Was she really hearing Ma attack her? Did Ma not hear her when she said I was knocked up? What part of her brain was playing tricks on her? She was sure that Ma didn't just ask her some dumb shit about the Christian in her. Before she could unscramble all what Ma was saying, her mouth opened and she, in what could only be considered a disrespectful tone, said, "Went, Ma? Went? It didn't go nowhere. It didn't or couldn't go nowhere 'cause I ain't phony like you and your little princess here. True, I followed you to church each Sunday and it's true that I tried, but that Christian shit never got me nowhere. I can look at the way you standing there, all sanctified and holy-like and know that even now with that half-white piece of garbage fermenting in her, you're going forgive her.

"You see, Lillie, you don't even have to say one word and already, like Jesus forgiving the fornicating woman, and yes, Ma, I was in church and listening the Sunday pastor preached on that. Yeah, what was the topic? I got it. Don't help me. It was, if I remember correctly, '***Blemished, But Not Broken***. And at this point, you should be getting ready to tell her to go and sin no more."

"Leela, don't say another word. Get out!"

Leela stepped forward; closer to me. I wasn't sure what she was thinking but Ma was one step ahead of her.

"Don't move any closer to your sister! Don't touch her. Don't speak. Don't do anything! Don't say anything! How could you, Leela! Get out of my sight!"

"But, Ma."

"Don't you 'but Ma' me. You've disrespected me in my own house. You took your right to call me Ma and threw it right out the window. And, yes, in case you forgot with all that hatred that you were spewing, I'm still the Ma here and I'm always going to be the Ma." Leela took a deep breath as if she wanted to say something else. Ma, seeing Leela's chest expand, stopped her. "Don't you go trying to look as if you can bring up any more hatred and venom from where that first set came from. I would want to believe that you have run out. God help us if there's still more in you. So take your hateful ugly ways out of my sight. Get out of this room, Leela!"

Leela looked at Ma and could see that Ma was the angriest she'd ever seen her. She thought for a minute to stop but she couldn't help herself; she had to get the last piece out. "Lillie, you can kiss my ass and, Ma, I'm going out before the sight of your knocked up princess makes me puke." Leela could see that Ma was getting ready to scream at her again, but before she could open her mouth, she said, "Never mind, I know, Ma, you going tell me 'bout disrespecting you and all the while, little Miss Pretending Pure over there cries her heart out at your feet. Yes, Ma, let me leave before watching you in your starring role as Jesus makes me wish I'd never heard of forgiveness!"

Without so much as a glance in the direction of either me or Ma, Leela walked over to the door. As I watched Leela, I wasn't even sure I saw the door open. If I didn't know better, I would have sworn that Leela had just walked right through it.

Chapter 81

Where Did I Go Wrong

Andrea

There were no words to describe what was happening to me, my girls, my home, or my world right before my eyes. It was imploding, exploding, and collapsing all at the same time, but yet there was a rhythm; a frenzied fanatical rhythm. Buried things were surfacing and all that was being unearthed was ugly, hateful, and heavy.

I looked around Lillie's room and wondered how my whole life could once again be dangling on the end of some marionette's strings. I'd done this all before. I'd paid my dues. I'd paid it with sweat, regrets, self-sacrifice, humility, and blood. I'd done the impossible. I'd bled through my eyes when I'd run out of tears. Bled through my pores when there was no more sweat and now here I was, bleeding again. This time my heart was bleeding and that was the worst.

Leela's hatred was echoing throughout the house. I looked at Lillie, who still had the wide-eyed look as if she was waiting for the train to hit her. She had braced herself so much for the impact that she hadn't noticed that the train named Leela had left. I didn't know what to do for her. A part of me wanted to bend down and pick her up, take her in my arms, and comfort her. The part of me that was the disappointed mother wanted to ask her how she could let something like this happen. Then the part of me that had made the same mistake as every woman in my family reached out to her. I reached out because to date, every woman in this family had done the same thing. We'd all stepped into the dance circle and put our hands into the outstretched hooves of the devil himself. We were told, knew better, and yet…and yet.

Even now if I'd admitted all my truths, part of my confession would be admitting that I still carried love for the devil that had given me T'Anna. I also understood that there were things in this life that don't make sense and trying to figure them out made less. I wrapped her in my arms. I was sorry for this child of mine who, although she'd seen what dancing with the devil had done to her sister, still stepped in when he said, 'Care to dance, Lillie?" She had smiled her innocent smile and stepped into his brimstone-lit arena.

Her whole body was trembling and it wasn't from being cold. The sister she had hoped would hold and support her had turned on her and had sucked all the warmth out of her. No one, and I mean no one, had ever been unkind to Lillie. Even Leela, until this moment, had spared her from enduring the same kind of treatment she unleashed on T'Anna. At the thought of T'Anna, I was glad that she wasn't here to hear this. Had she been here, it wouldn't be Lillie and I standing here alone in a bedroom filled with shock and unshed tears. We would be knee-deep in assorted Leela and T'Anna body parts.

As my daughter made her way into the folds of my love, I was wishing for her that she found that place of comfort and peace that she was seeking. I was also wondering what to do with Leela. However, at this moment, I couldn't think about her. My brain, mind, body, spirit, and soul were still reeling from her onslaught. How could I help one daughter to heal from another's wounding? I'd watched dazed as she had grown larger and uglier with each hate-drenched word. I had no idea how deep her river of anger, resentment, and bitterness had run.

The part of my brain that wasn't completely frozen with horror didn't want to really see her anymore. I was sure that I would see tentacles coming from her and reconnect her to hell for more of this hateful sludge. I could have seen that Leela wasn't going to stop until she'd started spinning and created some third-dimensional vortex that would destroy all of us. It was in her face. We'd stopped being her mother and sister. All she wanted to do was to see us sucked into the vortex of her anger.

I could feel the life-blood draining from me but it wasn't because of something I'd done or failed to do but because my youngest daughter's heart had gone the way of all Greenwood women's hearts. It had followed love. Why couldn't love and common sense ever work this stuff out? Why did one always disappear when the other appeared? I stood in my daughter's room where her sister's venom had been spewed and realized that I'd witnessed a strange kind of Armageddon. I'd always imagined what that day would look like, but would never imagine that it would have started in my own home.

In my mind, it would involve God, Gabriel, Michael, and all the other good guys, but this time they would be angry because they would be tired from all the nonsense humans had been doing. There would be fire, brimstone, and all hell to pay. Things would be exploding, imploding, fragmenting, and crumbling. People would be panicking, crying, and cowering from fear and fright. Armageddon was supposed to happen someplace else; not in my house on Lexington Avenue with my oldest daughter being the chief administrators. It wasn't supposed to have anything to do with Satan. Well that's how I'd always figured it. I'd figured it wrong.

Chapter 82

Trouble Sure Can Seem to Last Forever

T'Anna

All over the house there was trouble. At first I didn't know there was trouble but my boys had gotten into the habit of drinking their milk at night with Ma and so each night they got themselves together and went downstairs to their Nana Drea. Nothing made Ma happier than pouring those three glasses of milk. She acted as if her life depended on it. So as usual, I went downstairs with the boys but the house had an unusual quiet. It felt like somebody died or something. So I started calling out to see if anybody was home. Leela didn't come out and tell me to shut my loud-ass yellow-self so I figured she wasn't home. I didn't hear Ma or Lillie and I got to thinking that it was odd because tonight wasn't a church night. I started to worry.

Nobody answered so I called out again. Then the boys started calling, "Nana Drea, you home? You home, Nana Drea?" No answer came back. I was getting even more worried. I was getting ready to push Lillie's bedroom door when Ma came out of it and she looked bad. I could tell that she'd been crying. Panic rose up all over me. I wasn't sure what to do. I didn't have to ask anything. She stated in a matter-of-fact voice, "Lillie is going to have a baby. The baby will be born next May."

I looked at Ma and the disappointment hung off her like an oversized dress. She looked as if she was tired of trying to fulfill her nana's dream of getting a daughter of Greenwood into college before she had a child. Then she said, "Lillie is still going to go to college though. Daddy has worked too hard to get her in there. She's going. I don't quite have all the answers right now, but during the next few months, I'll figure something out. No, I won't be telling Daddy or your uncle. I don't want to hear from your uncle again about his disappointments. I don't."

Ma sat down and the boys, sensing that something was wrong, sat down too. They were quiet, which surprised me because I didn't know they knew how to do that. I sat with Ma and I wished there was some way I could lift the weight that was pressing her into the ground. But there was nothing I could say or do. I was the first to bring a baby into her house and now here I was; twenty-two and with three children. I would be the last one to say anything. I sat with her. The silence enveloped us all and the pain of yet another unwed, pregnant Greenwood's daughter glued us to our seats.

I was sad but a part of me was also glad. None of my being glad had anything to do with Lillie, but it sure had to do with being pregnant again. I had been. And I was so glad now that things had worked out the way they had. Ma would've known that it wasn't for Manny because Manny and I hadn't been seeing each other for almost a year now. I looked at Ma and wondered if it would make any sense to bring that up now. I wanted to tell her how I'd sat on my bed with a towel wrapped around me trying to figure out how I was pregnant again and then it started.

It felt like I was peeing myself. Not the kind of pee like you giving birth, but a pee that was a period. A period that a few minutes earlier was a baby, and now it had gone lumpy, clumpy, and loose. It was as simple as that. One minute I was almost three months pregnant, and the next; I'd lost it. I was sorry at first but as time went by and I realized how stupid Kamarra really was, I'd actually thanked God he'd reached His almighty hand into my very fertile womb and uprooted Kamarra's seed. It was a good thing too because Kamarra had gotten his ass locked up soon after for some petty shit. Anyway, that was about six months ago and I was changing. I started wanting a different outlook; a different place from which to view my life. From where I was looking, shit was bleak.

I sat there looking at Ma and I knew in a way that knowledge was a little bit of good news but given what Ma was going through, my little bit of good news would have made her more upset. What was Ma going do with this trouble that had come and knocked the wind out of her? To my surprise, Ma got up and then she called my boys. "Hey, which of my boys wants to run get the milk out of the fridge for me?"

All three of them shouted, "Me! Me! Me!"

Ma and the boys walked into the kitchen and I got up and went to Lillie's room. I figured she might need a big sister to talk to.

I knocked softly and I went in. Lillie was sitting on the edge of her bed with her head down. She looked worse than Ma. My heart hurt for her because I knew how much she wanted to go to that fancy college she'd been talking about since eighth grade. It was all she'd ever talked about and she'd worked so hard to get in. I couldn't see her not going and then it dawned on me. There was no reason why Lillie shouldn't go off to her fancy college. Ma could leave the baby right here at the house and all of us, except Leela, could help mind it. I started to tell Lillie that and she started to cry and all she could say was, "Leela."

"Why you calling Leela for? Leela don't care nothing for no babies."

"T'Anna, Leela cursed me and Ma."

When I heard that, I forgot 'bout raising Lillie's baby. "What you mean, Leela curse you and Ma?"

"She cursed us with lots of bad words and stuff. She said lots of nasty things to me about Elliot and putting his thing in my mouth and . . ."

Lillie couldn't continue and I didn't want her to. All I was thinking about was finding Leela and punching her right in her mouth. "Lillie, where is Leela? Where is she? Cause when I find her, I'm going to punch her right in her hateful mouth. She may curse me all she wants, but she can't curse at you or Ma. I'm going to kick her right in her face. Where is she?"

"I don't know; she left after she got done cursing me and Ma."

I forgot all about Lillie needing a big sister and all I could think about was finding Leela. I got up and was halfway across the floor when Lillie started this strange wailing like if I was getting ready to kill her.

"T'Anna, don't go and start nothing with her, please. I don't want to see the two of you fighting. Please, T'Anna, don't fight with her."

I looked at Lillie and could see that she looked as if she would run and only God knew where so I sat down. I sat down to give myself a moment to figure out how and when I was going find Leela by herself and kick the living shit out of her. I could let it go for today, but I was going to get my chance and if it was the last thing I did, I was going to beat her for cursing at Ma.

Ma came into Lillie's room and she had a cup of milk and a

sandwich for her. I looked at Ma with her milk and sandwich and knew that she had come to some decision. She was going to help Lillie as she had helped me and Granddaddy had helped her. I knew Ma and she was probably thinking, "Trouble sure can seem to last always."

I knew Ma. I could see that resolute look on her face. Even if Lillie didn't know it, Ma knew it. Lillie was going off to college. The curse that had hung over our heads forever was finally going to be broken; it was written all over Ma's face.

I started to run several scenarios over in my head and however I turned them over, one and only one kept coming to my head, but that in itself just made no sense. It made no sense to me but it had popped into my head from somewhere. I looked at Ma again and almost wished that I didn't have that second-sense that we Greenwood women had. I'd gotten the idea from Ma. I'd somehow gotten into her head and I wanted out and badly. What I was seeing was just dumb and desperate. Ma needed to rethink that thought; it was just plain wrong and unrealistic.

What would make sense would be Ma taking a realistic look at the price she was getting ready to ask Lillie to pay for her mistake. We, well all except Leela, had made the same mistake and no one had exacted from us the kind of punishing price Ma was preparing to exact from Lille. I looked deeper at Ma and wondered why, when she had the chance to leave Leela on a rock somewhere, she didn't. Talk about unleashing a curse on somebody; look at the shit Ma did to us by dragging Leela into all our lives.

I know I'd said that I'd take a front-row seat and just watch the fiasco unfold but I couldn't. I loved my sister too much and what I felt for Lillie was almost maternal. It would be wrong to sit back and watch Ma unleash Leela on Lillie. Why? Since I can remember meeting Leela, and I always like to think of it as a meeting as opposed to becoming her sister, Id wanted to kick her ass. I hadn't done it yet and so there was that part of me, deep in my soul that was dissatisfied. I had to satisfy my soul. It wasn't going to be in the next few months but if what Ma was thinking came to fruition, I knew my day was coming sooner than I'd hoped. That thought brought a smile to my face at a time while I was thinking there would be no joy coming from this dismal day.

Chapter 83

Not Happening to Ma Again

You had to have understood Ma to understand the next few months in her house. Ma did and didn't forgive Leela. In a way it was Leela, who had to keep remembering her hateful ways each time she saw Ma. She tried not to see me and Lillie, but it was hard. None of us changed, nor did we try to include Leela in anything that was going on with Lillie.

Lillie joined the clinic and either Ma or I went with her. Leela tried to act as if she didn't see Lillie's growing belly. It grew, and bigger than mine at any of my pregnancies. Lillie never complained. She did what she had to do. If Ma said jump, she was halfway up to the sky before she would ask Ma if it was high enough.

Everybody was waiting. Soon the wait was over. Into Ma's house came another boy. All my sons were handsome boys, but this little boy…he was beautiful. He looked exactly like Lillie. Each time Ma looked at him, it was as if she was reliving someday that none of us knew about. Lillie called him Frederick Elliot Anderson-Greenwood and with that, she also broke a tradition. He was the first baby born into the family in almost forty years that wasn't named Hirsh-Greenwood.

At first, Ma minded but then she said that it was Lillie's baby and Lillie could do whatever she wanted. Well, that was until Ma got to calling him something other than Frederick, Freddie, or Fred. She changed his name. He didn't become a Greenwood, but he never became a Frederick either. Ma had taken one look at him the day he was born and said, "Look at my grandson, Lillian, he's the spitting image of you. Lillian, he's your image."

Just like that it stuck. Sure, Lillie tried to call him Frederick Elliot after his father, but Image stuck, and he was Image from that day on.

Lillie tried to convince herself that she could really do what she wanted with Image, but we all knew that wasn't really true. Lillie would do what Ma wanted her to do because if things were left up to Lillie, she would really want to mother her son, but Ma wouldn't let her. Ma said she was going to college in a few months and didn't want her becoming too attached. Whether she really wanted to or not, Lillie did what Ma wanted. She left the mothering and most of his care to the rest of us. She focused on her books just the way Ma told her.

Again, Ma said jump and Lillie took off to the sky; this time her sky-hopping had a destination: Spellman College. She took off leaving her precious Image behind and while she was in the sky; on the ground Image became our baby just as Ma had planned. The day Lillie left for Spellman, Ma cried. She didn't cry because there was a little motherless and fatherless boy left behind. She cried because it had finally happened: a daughter of Greenwood had finally made it to college. Our great-great-great-great-great-great-great-great grandmother Cornbread's dream had finally come true.

None of them: Cornbread, Milkweed, Charlotte, Neala, Etta Pearl, Gina Pearl, or Lilly were here to see it but Ma was. Ma beamed and then she beamed some more. Granddaddy, who didn't even know that Lillie was pregnant, felt relieved. The part of the dream that had become deferred because of him was now fulfilled. A daughter of Greenwood was in college. She was in, but at what cost?

I looked at my family: Ma, Leela, and Lillie, and wondered how they could do that; all that pretending. It made no sense to me. Was Ma really willing to turn Image into a modern day Isaac and put him on the sacrificial table just so she could break the curse? Was it fair to Image to strap him with a pretend mother like Leela? Where was all this madness headed? It couldn't be headed anywhere good. Leela was as close to a wild wicked bitch as anybody could be and there was nothing maternal in her. I was making mistakes left and right with my boys, but I was making them raising my boys. It was true but at the end of the day, my boys would know who I was. This wasn't going to be the same for Image. How was Lillie going to feel watching her son call that bitch Leela Mommy? That would drive a hole in my heart and I would have to snatch Ma right off her "I'm Doing The Right Thing Mommy Pedestal." This shit wasn't right and it was going to end ugly. I didn't know when, but the end was going to be unreal. It was going to be like some "B"-

rated movie.

I could cast this one myself. Playing the part of the doting psychotic mother: Leela Phoebe Hirsh Greenwood. In the role of the heartbroken real mother: Lillie Hirsh Greenwood, and in the role that he was never supposed to play but thanks to his slightly deranged grandmother Andrea Matti Hirsch Greenwood and her desire to get a Daughter of Greenwood into college, he could now perform without the benefit of a script.

Ladies and Gentleman, making his world debut in *The Daughters of Greenwood* as the neglected boy turned serial killer thanks to his psycho, pretend mom; a woman that should never have been in his life…Image Hirsh Greenwood. The curtains rises and Image steps forward.

www.ingramcontent.com/pod-product-compliance
Lightning Source LLC
Chambersburg PA
CBHW020602310726
48979CB00008B/1315/J